PHARMACEUTICAL ORGANIC CHEMISTRY

for

B. Pharm Students

As per New Revised Syllabus

Dr. Meenakshi N. Deodhar
M. Pharm., Ph.D.
Professor in Pharmaceutical Chemistry,
PDEA's Seth Govind Raghunath Sable
College of Pharmacy, Saswad, PUNE

Mrs. Jayashri R. Jagtap
M. Pharm.
Assistant Professor in Pharmaceutical Chemistry,
PDEA's Seth Govind Raghunath Sable
College of Pharmacy, Saswad, PUNE

Dr. Ashok Bhosale
M. Pharm., Ph.D.
Principal and Professor in Pharmaceutics
PDEA's Seth Govind Raghunath Sable
College of Pharmacy, Saswad, PUNE

N1618

PHARMACEUTICAL ORGANIC CHEMISTRY   **ISBN 978-93-86084-63-7**

Second Edition : **February 2017**

© : **Authors**

Published By :

NIRALI PRAKASHAN

Abhyudaya Pragati, 1312, Shivaji Nagar,
Off J.M. Road, Pune – 411005
Tel - (020) 25512336/37/39, Fax - (020) 25511379
Email : niralipune@pragationline.com

☞ **DISTRIBUTION CENTRES**

PUNE

Nirali Prakashan : 119, Budhwar Peth, Jogeshwari Mandir Lane, Pune 411002, Maharashtra
Tel : (020) 2445 2044, 66022708, Fax : (020) 2445 1538
Email : bookorder@pragationline.com, niralilocal@pragationline.com

Nirali Prakashan : S. No. 28/27, Dhyari, Near Pari Company, Pune 411041
Tel : (020) 24690204 Fax : (020) 24690316
Email : dhyari@pragationline.com, bookorder@pragationline.com

MUMBAI

Nirali Prakashan : 385, S.V.P. Road, Rasdhara Co-op. Hsg. Society Ltd.,
Girgaum, Mumbai 400004, Maharashtra
Tel : (022) 2385 6339 / 2386 9976, Fax : (022) 2386 9976
Email : niralimumbai@pragationline.com

☞ **DISTRIBUTION BRANCHES**

JALGAON

Nirali Prakashan : 34, V. V. Golani Market, Navi Peth, Jalgaon 425001,
Maharashtra, Tel : (0257) 222 0395, Mob : 94234 91860

KOLHAPUR

Nirali Prakashan : New Mahadvar Road, Kedar Plaza, 1st Floor Opp. IDBI Bank
Kolhapur 416 012, Maharashtra. Mob : 9850046155

NAGPUR

Pratibha Book Distributors: Above Maratha Mandir, Shop No. 3, First Floor,
Rani Jhanshi Square, Sitabuldi, Nagpur 440012, Maharashtra
Tel : (0712) 254 7129

DELHI

Nirali Prakashan : 4593/21, Basement, Aggarwal Lane 15, Ansari Road, Daryaganj
Near Times of India Building, New Delhi 110002. Mob : 08505972553

BENGALURU

Pragati Book House : House No. 1, Sanjeevappa Lane, Avenue Road Cross,
Opp. Rice Church, Bengaluru – 560002.
Tel : (080) 64513344, 64513355,Mob : 9880582331, 9845021552
Email:bharatsavla@yahoo.com

CHENNAI

Pragati Books : 9/1, Montieth Road, Behind Taas Mahal, Egmore,
Chennai 600008 Tamil Nadu, Tel : (044) 6518 3535,
Mob : 94440 01782 / 98450 21552 / 98805 82331,
Email : bharatsavla@yahoo.com

niralipune@pragationline.com | www.pragationline.com
Also find us on ▣ www.facebook.com/niralibooks

Preface

We are glad to present a book on **"Pharmaceutical Organic Chemistry"** to you. The contents of this book are based on the syllabi of **F. Y. B. Pharm.** of major universities across India. The book has been written especially keeping in mind the understanding level of F. Y. B. Pharm. students. However there has been no compromise on the content of each topic so that the book can be used by a post graduate student also if desired.

The first couple of chapters of the book provide an introduction to the general concepts of organic chemistry while the rest pertain to the important classes of organic chemistry. Each chapter also provides the students with practice questions. Solving the questions by the students will ensure that the learning objectives of the chapter have been met.

The authors would like to thank the office bearers of Pune District Education Association and Principal Dr. Ashok Bhosale for extending all the facilities required for the completion of the book. We are grateful to Shri. S. B. Gokhale, Shri. Dineshbhai Furia and Shri Jignesh Furia of Nirali Prakashan for their motivation. We also appreciate the efforts of editorial staff of Nirali Prakashan especially Mrs. Prachi Sawant and Mr. Kiran Velankar for their efforts in compiling of the book.

We hope that not only the students will find the book useful but the teachers will also find it a useful teaching tool. We look forward to suggestions from the readers regarding the content as well a presentation.

Authors

Pune

Contents

Chapter 1

BASIC PRINCIPLES AND CONCEPTS OF ORGANIC CHEMISTRY

1.1 INTRODUCTION

The mode of arrangement of the constituent atoms in a molecule regardless of their orientation in space gives its molecular constitution. When this is projected on the plane of paper we get the gross structural formula for the molecule.

To understand the meaning of structure of a molecule we need to study the structural theory. This deals with:

(i)   The forces that hold the atoms together in a molecule.

(ii) The shape and size of the molecule.

(iii) The distribution of electrons over the molecule.

(iv) The intermolecular forces.

Before we understand the molecular structure, let us first have a look at the structure of an atom.

1.1.1 The Electronic Structure of Atom

According to Rutherford-Bohr theory, the atom is made of a central positively charged nucleus containing positively charged particles called protons and neutral particles called neutrons both having unit mass. The nucleus is surrounded by negatively charged particles called electrons which carry one unit negative charge and negligible weight.

According to the modern concept the electrons in an atom are arranged in shells of different energy levels around the nucleus. While the electrons move in such a level, it neither emits nor absorbs energy. The shells of different energy levels are indicated by 1, 2, 3, 4, 5, 6 and 7 or by the letters K, L, M, N, O, P and Q starting from the nucleus. The energy of the shells increases in the order 1, 2, 3 ...... Each shell can accommodate a definite number of electrons which is twice the square of the shell number. The maximum number of electrons that a shell can accommodate is obtained by the expression $2n^2$.

n = Ordinal number of the shell

For example,

$$K = 2n^2 \quad (n = 1) \qquad\qquad L = 2n^2 \quad (n = 2)$$
$$= 2 \times (1)^2 = 2 \qquad\qquad\quad = 2 \times (2)^2 = 8$$
$$M = 2n^2 \quad (n = 3) \qquad\qquad K = 2n^2 \quad (n = 4)$$
$$= 2 \times (3)^2 = 18 \qquad\qquad\quad = 2 \times (4)^2 = 32$$

Within each shell there are subshells. These are designated as *s, p, d* and *f*. The maximum numbers of electrons which these subshells can accommodate are 2, 6, 10 and 14 respectively. The subshells which differ amongst themselves in energy they contain are composed of orbitals.

An orbital is a three-dimensional space within an atom in which an electron is most likely to be found. It may contain one or two electrons or may remain empty also. The number of orbitals that a shell can have is given by the expression n^2, where n = ordinal number of shells. The orbitals in a subshell do not differ in their energy content. Subshells *s, p, d* and *f* have 1, 3, 5 and 7 orbitals respectively. The lone orbital of *s* subshell is designated by the same letter '*s*'. The three *p* orbitals are represented as p_x, p_y and p_z.

Table 1.1: Subshells and orbitals of K, L, M and N shells

1.	Shell	K	L	M	N
2.	Ordinal number (n)	1	2	3	4
3.	Max. no. of electrons $2n^2$	2	8	18	32
4.	Subshells	1s	2s, 2p	3s, 3p, 3d	4s, 4p, 4d, 4f
5.	Max. no. of electrons per subshell	s = 2	s = 2, p = 6	s = 2, p = 6, d = 10	s = 2, p = 6, d = 10, f = 14
6.	No. of orbitals / shell, n^2	1	4	9	16
7.	No. of orbitals/subshell	s-1	s-1, p-3	s-1, p-3, d-5	s-1, p-3, d-5, f-7

According to Pauli principle, any one orbital can accommodate upto a maximum of two electrons with paired spin (↑↓). On the other hand, two electrons with parallel spins cannot form a pair. Downward (↓) or upward (↑), represents an electron with its spin, and ↑↓ is the symbol of paired electrons in an orbital.

Orbitals are filled up by electrons in an order of increasing energy (Fig. 1.1). The increasing order of energy levels of orbitals in atoms is *1s, 2s, 2p, 3s, 3p, 4s, 3d, 4p, 5s......*

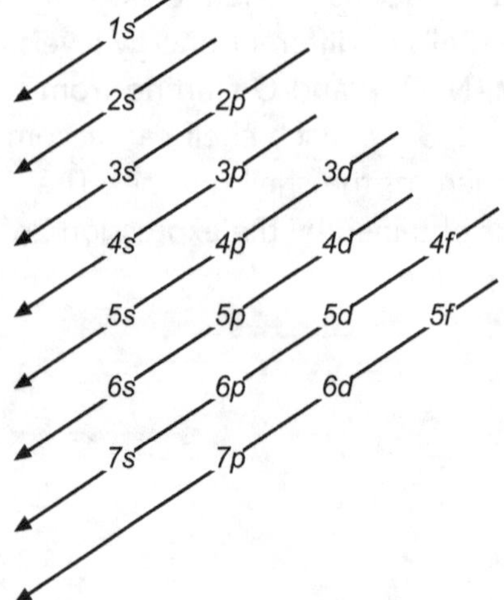

Fig. 1.1: Order of energy levels of orbitals

1.2 SHAPE AND SIZE OF ATOMIC ORBITALS

An orbital represents a well defined region in space in which electrons can be found. They have definite three-dimensional shapes. In organic chemistry we are mainly concerned with *s* and *p* orbitals.

1.2.1 Shape of *s*-orbitals

The *s*-orbitals (*1s, 2s, 3s* etc.) are spherical in shape symmetrical about the nucleus (Fig. 1.2 (a)). Naturally the *2s* orbital is bigger than the *1s* orbital, the electrons in the *2s* orbital are farther away from the nucleus and have greater energy (Fig. 1.2 (b)). Between the *1s* and *2s* orbitals there is a zone called nodal zone where the probability of finding the electrons is zero.

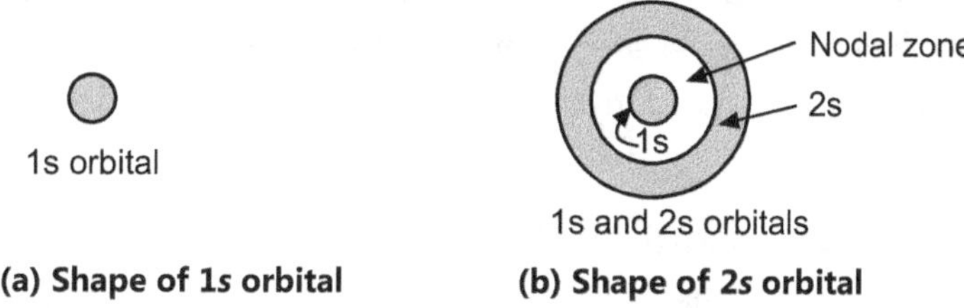

(a) Shape of 1*s* orbital   **(b) Shape of 2*s* orbital**

Fig. 1.2

1.2.2 Shape of *p*-orbitals

A *p*-orbital is dumb-bell shaped. There are two lobes associated with this orbital. There are three *p* orbitals each of the same shape and same energy and oriented mutually perpendicular along x, y and z axes, with the point of intersection at the nucleus of the atom. They are designated as p_x, p_y and p_z to indicate their directions along the coordinate axes. A *p* orbital being non-spherical, its electrons are more loosely bound to the nucleus than the 's' orbital electrons. In such an orbital, there is no chance of finding an electron at the nucleus. The nucleus, therefore is called the nodal point. These orbitals also possess nodal planes, in which the probability of finding the electron of p_x orbital along the yz plane passing through the nucleus is zero. This plane is called the nodal plane. For electrons of p_y and p_z the nodal planes are xz and xy respectively (Fig. 1.3). It is therefore for this reason that the three *p* orbitals extend slightly beyond the radius of 2s orbital.

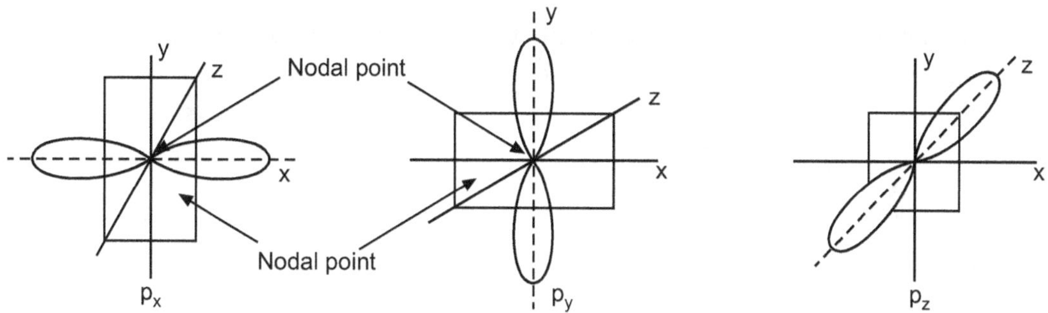

Fig. 1.3 : Shape and orientation of *p*-orbitals

1.3 HYBRIDIZATION

The number of covalent bonds formed by an atom is equal to the number of electrons in its outermost shell. The strength of covalent bond arises from the exchange of electrons between two atoms and magnitude of this exchange energy is proportional to the amount of the overlap of the atomic orbitals (AOs) forming the bond. Maximum overlap of AOs will result in the strongest bond. Pure AOs very often, are not suitably oriented to ensure the maximum overlap with the orbital of the approaching atom. Therefore, AOs must undergo modification in a direction so as to provide a favorable orientation to have the maximum overlap. This modification involves a linear combination of pure AOs of the same atom to form an equal number of modified orbitals. This process is called hybridization. The mixing and recasting of AOs with different energies in an isolated atom to form new equivalent orbitals of equal energy in an excited state of the atom is known as hybridization and the newly formed orbitals are called hybrid atomic orbitals. The hybrid atomic orbitals then combine with other orbitals (hybrid or unhybrid) to form molecular orbitals.

1.3.1 Features of Hybridization

(1) In hybridization, orbitals of the same atom are used and these orbitals should have comparable energies.

(2) The number of hybrid orbitals formed is equal to the number of atomic orbitals used for hybridization.

(3) The shapes of hybrid orbitals are different from those of pure atomic orbitals which produce hybrid orbitals.

(4) Each hybridised orbital is more concentrated on one side of the nucleus.

(5) The advantage of hybridization is that the hybrid orbital becomes concentrated in one particular direction so that greater overlapping is achieved resulting in the formation of stronger bond.

(6) Due to repulsive forces between electrons, hybrid orbitals containing electrons try to keep themselves as far away from one another as possible. Hence, hybrid orbitals are oriented in space and the orientation depends upon the number of hybrid orbitals formed on the atom.

(7) The shape of the molecule and the bond angles are suggested by the type of hybridization and orientation of orbitals.

Hybridization	Character		Angle between orbitals
	s	p	
sp (diagonal)	1/2	1/2	180°
sp^2 (trigonal)	1/3	2/3	120°
sp^3 (tetrahedral)	1/4	3/4	109° 28'

1.3.2 Hybridization of Carbon Atom

Atomic number of carbon = 6. Let us consider the electronic configuration of carbon in ground state (G.S.),

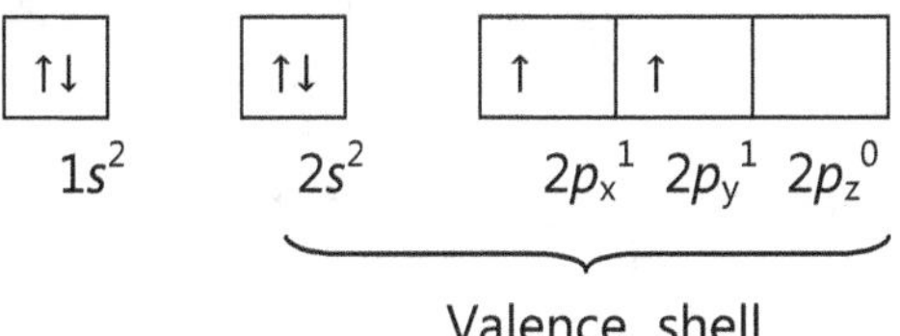

Since there are only two unpaired electrons, it might be expected that carbon can form only two single covalent bonds. In the ground state of carbon, a molecule CH_2 will result which is highly reactive. But from chemical analysis we know that simple stable compound that carbon forms with hydrogen is methane (CH_4) and this compound contains four identical C–H bonds. In saturated hydrocarbons there are sp^3 hybridized carbons, whereas ethene possess sp^2 hybridized carbon and acetylene have sp hybridized carbon.

Thus there are three types of hybridization of carbon.

    (1) sp^3 (tetrahedral) hybridization of carbon.

    (2) sp^2 (trigonal) hybridization of carbon.

    (3) sp (diagonal) hybridization of carbon.

(1) Tetrahedral hybridization (sp^3)

In sp^3 hybridization one s-orbital and three p-orbitals mix together and form four equivalent hybrid orbitals. Each of these has 25% s and 75% p character. Due to mutual repulsion of electrons in these four hybrid orbitals, sp^3 hybrid orbitals try to keep themselves as far away from one another as possible like regular tetrahedron. Hence four sp^3 hybrid orbitals are directed towards the corners of a regular tetrahedron making an angle of $109^{\circ}28'$ with one another. Each hybrid orbital is more concentrated on one side of the nucleus (Fig. 1.4).

sp^3- hybridization of carbon

The electronic configuration of carbon in its ground state and excited state is as shown below.

Ground state electronic configuration   Excited state electronic configuration

Carbon in the excited state has four unpaired electrons and therefore sp^3 hybridization occurs.

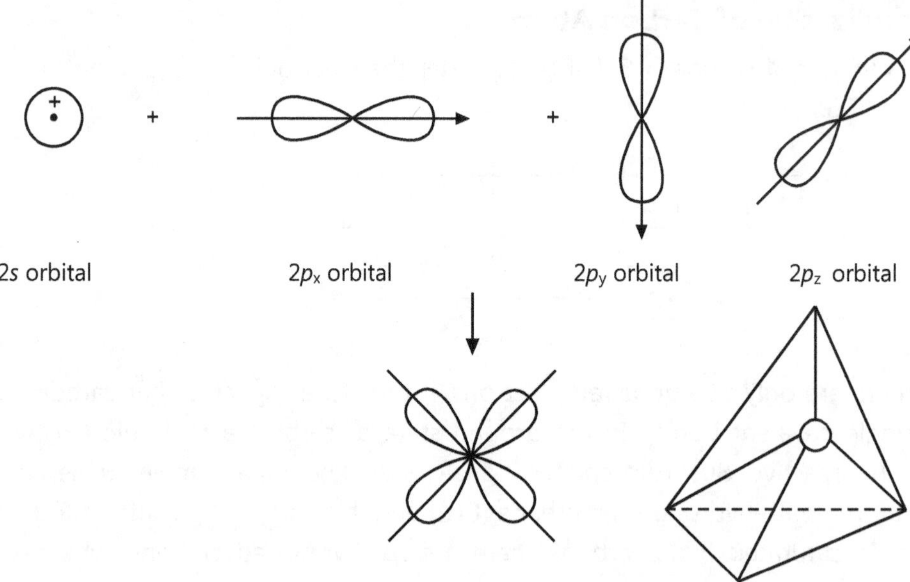

2s orbital $2p_x$ orbital $2p_y$ orbital $2p_z$ orbital

Tetrahedral sp^3 hybridized orbitals of carbon

Fig. 1.4 : sp^3 hybrid orbitals

Whenever carbon is bonded to four other atoms or groups, it uses sp^3 hybrid orbitals.

For example: Bonding in methane (Fig. 1.5)

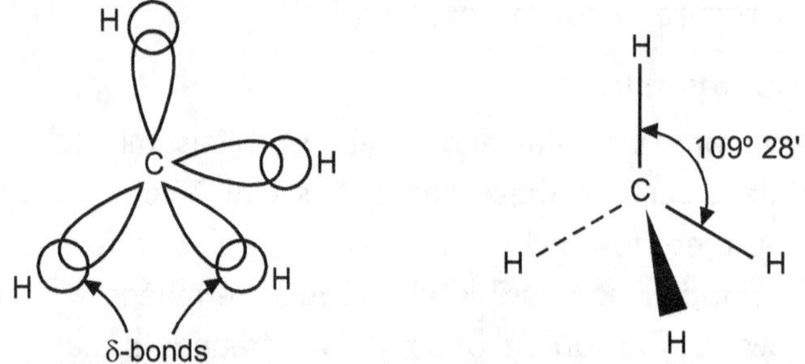

sp^3 hybrid orbitals of methane   **Shape of methane molecule**

Fig. 1.5 : Bonding in methane

(2) Trigonal hybridization (sp^2)

In sp^2 hybridization, one s-orbital and two p-orbitals mix and form three equivalent hybrid orbitals. Each of these has 33% s character and 67% p character. The shape of sp^2 hybrid orbital is also different from that of s-orbital and p-orbital. Due to the mutual repulsion of electrons in these hybrid orbitals, the three sp^2 hybrid orbitals will try to go as away from one another as possible and will lie in one plane making an angle of 120° with one another.

Thus, these sp^2 hybrid orbitals are directed to the corners of a regular triangle and hence the hybridization is known as trigonal hybridization (Fig. 1.6). Each hybrid orbital is more concentrated on one side of the nucleus. The unused electron occupies the *2p* orbital oriented along the axis perpendicular to the hybridization plane.

sp^2-hybridization of carbon

If in an excited electronic state of carbon atom, sp^2 hybridization occurs, one *p* orbital remains perpendicular to the plane of three hybrid atomic orbitals and hence it is at right angle to each of the three hybrid sp^2 atomic orbitals.

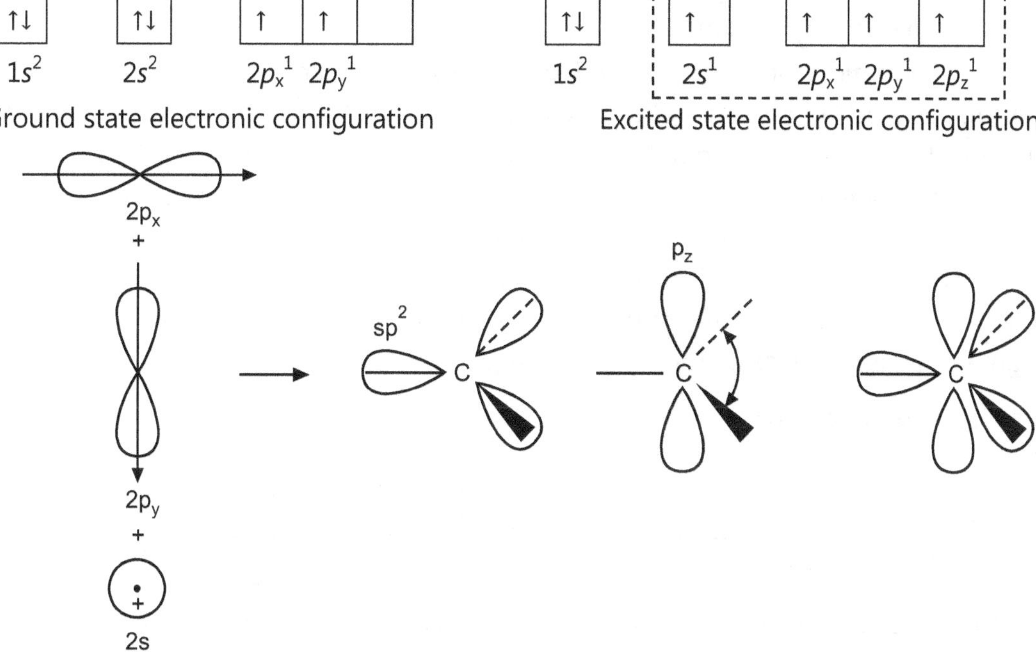

Fig. 1.6 : sp^2 hybrid orbitals

For example- Bonding in ethylene (Fig. 1.7 and Fig. 1.8).

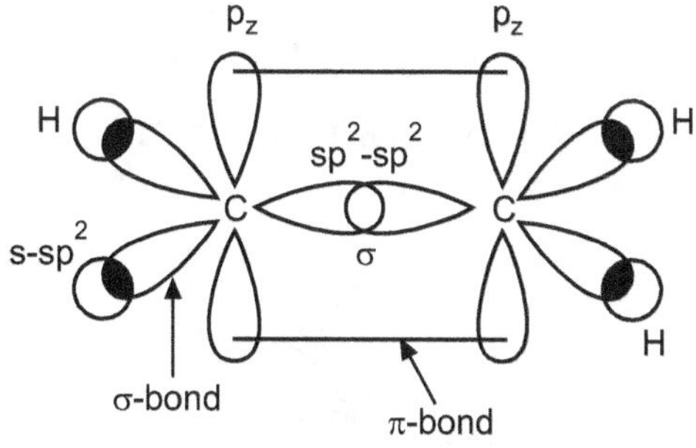

Fig. 1.7 : Molecular orbitals in ethylene

Although the C–C double bond in ethylene is represented by two equivalent lines, one line represents a σ-bond and the other a π bond.

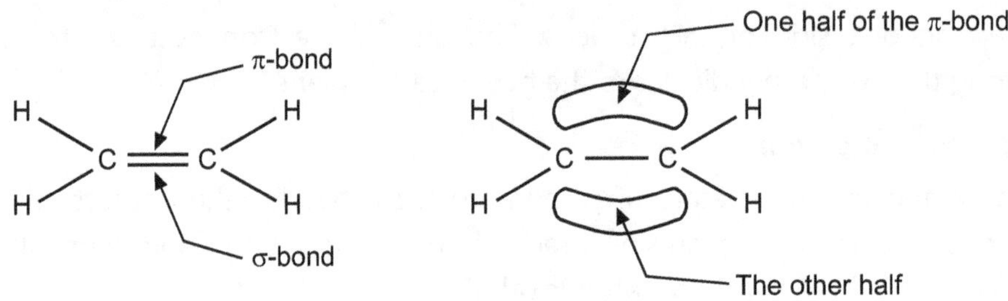

Fig. 1.8 : Bonding in ethylene

(3) Diagonal hybridization (*sp*)

In *sp*-hybridization, one s-orbital and one *p*-orbital mix and form two equivalent *sp* hybrid orbitals. Each of these has 50% *s* character and 50% *p* character. The shape of *sp* hybrid orbital is also different from that of *s*-orbital and *p*-orbital as shown in Fig. 1.9. Due to the mutual repulsion of electrons in these hybrid orbitals, the two *sp* hybrid orbitals will try to go as far away from each other as possible and hence will lie along a straight line making an angle of 180° with each other. Each hybrid orbital is more concentrated on one side of the nucleus. The two remaining *p* orbitals are capable of forming two π orbitals with the analogous orbitals of adjacent atoms (Fig. 1.10 and Fig. 1.11).

sp-hybridization of carbon

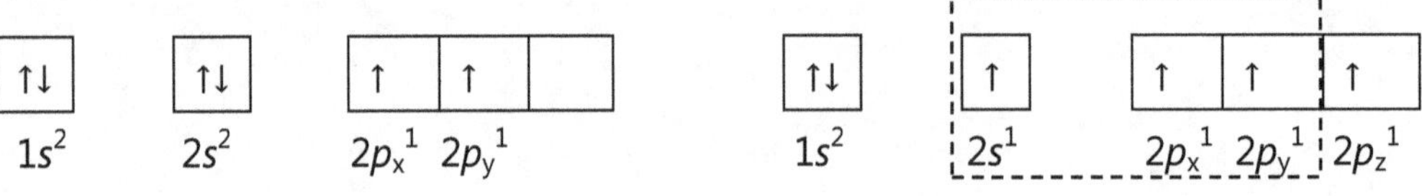

$1s^2$ $2s^2$ $2p_x^1$ $2p_y^1$

Ground state electronic configuration

$1s^2$ $2s^1$ $2p_x^1$ $2p_y^1$ $2p_z^1$

Excited state electronic configuration

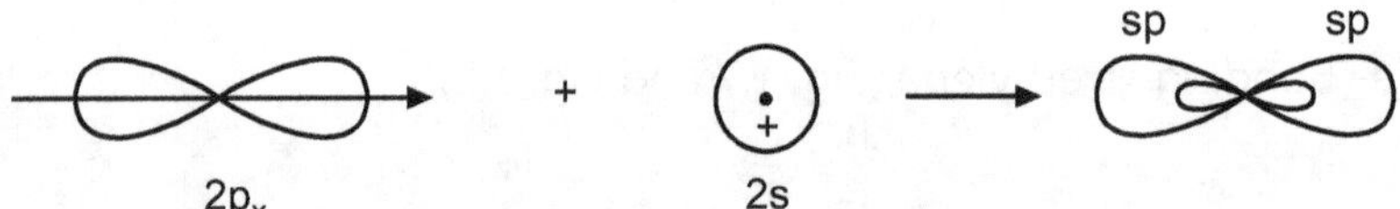

Fig. 1.9 : *sp* hybrid orbitals

Fig. 1.10 : Orientation of p$_y$ and p$_z$ orbitals of an sp hybridized carbon atom

For example – Bonding in acetylene (Fig. 1.11).

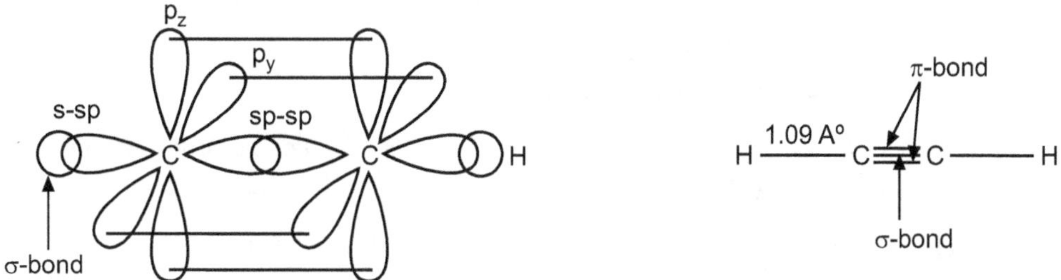

Fig. 1.11 : Bonding in acetylene

Although the C–C triple bond is represented by three equivalent lines, the one line represents a σ bond and the other two π bonds.

1.3.3 Hybridization of Nitrogen

Like carbon, nitrogen atom also undergoes sp^3, sp^2 and sp hybridizations.

Nitrogen in NH_3 is sp^3 hybridized, in imines sp^2 hybridized and in cyanide sp hybridized.

(1) sp^3 hybridization of Nitrogen :

Atomic number of nitrogen = 7. Let us consider the electronic configuration of nitrogen in ground state (G.S.).

Electronic configuration (G.S.) =

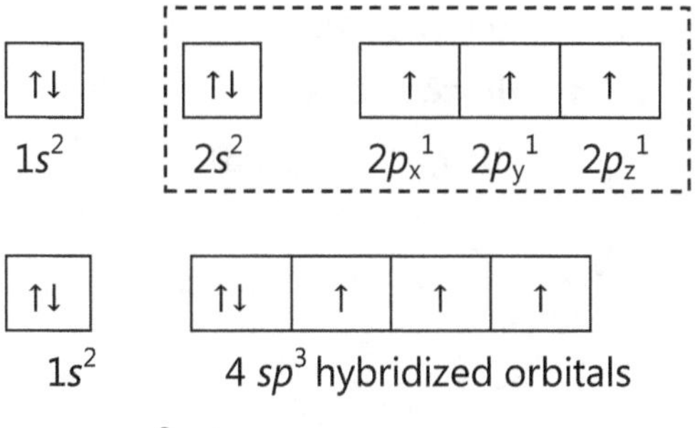

sp^3 hybridized state

In sp^3 hybridization of nitrogen, one s-orbital and three p-orbitals mix together and form four equivalent hybrid orbitals. The four sp^3 hybridized orbitals of nitrogen are directed towards the corners of regular tetrahedron same like sp^3 orbitals of carbon. Nitrogen has one more electron than carbon. As a result one of the sp^3 hybrid orbitals of nitrogen is completely filled and cannot take part in bond formation. Whenever nitrogen is attached to three other atoms or groups, it always uses sp^3 hybrid orbitals to form its bonds.

For example : Bonding in ammonia

The three N-H bonds in ammonia are sigma (σ) bonds. Each of these bonds are formed by the overlap of an sp^3 orbital of nitrogen with s orbital of hydrogen. The H-N-H bond angle is 107.5°. This angle is slightly less than the normal tetrahedral angle of 109° 28'. This is because the sp^3 orbital containing unshared pair of electrons somewhat larger than those containing bonding pairs. Thus, the angles between the σ-bonds on the other side of the molecule are compressed slightly (Fig. 1.12).

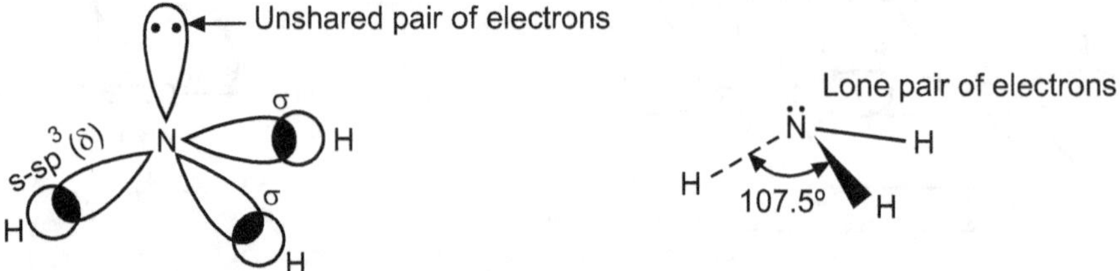

Fig. 1.12 : Bonding in Ammonia

(2) sp^2 hybridization of Nitrogen:

Nitrogen can form compounds using sp^2 hybrid orbitals (Fig. 1.13). Whenever nitrogen is bonded to two other atoms or groups, it uses two sp^2 hybrid orbitals and the unhybridized p_z orbitals to form its bonds (Fig. 1.13).

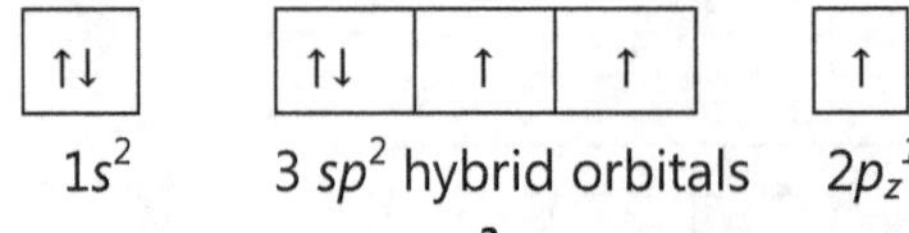

Ground state Electronic Configuration of Nitrogen

sp^2 hybridized state

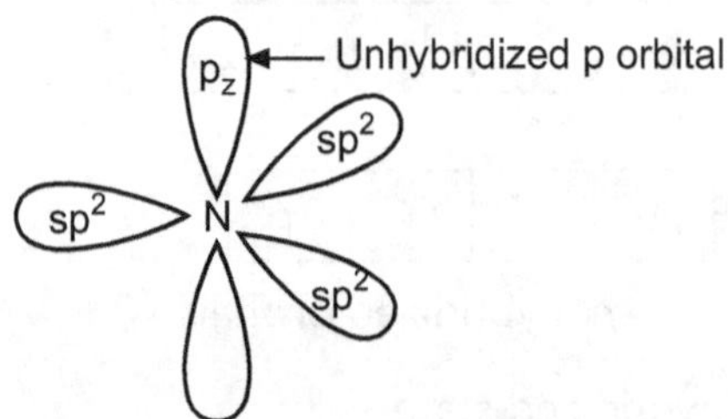

sp^2- Nitrogen (trigonal)

Fig. 1.13 : Shape of sp^2 hybridized Nitrogen

For example : Bonding in $CH_2 = N\text{-}H$ (Fig. 1.14).

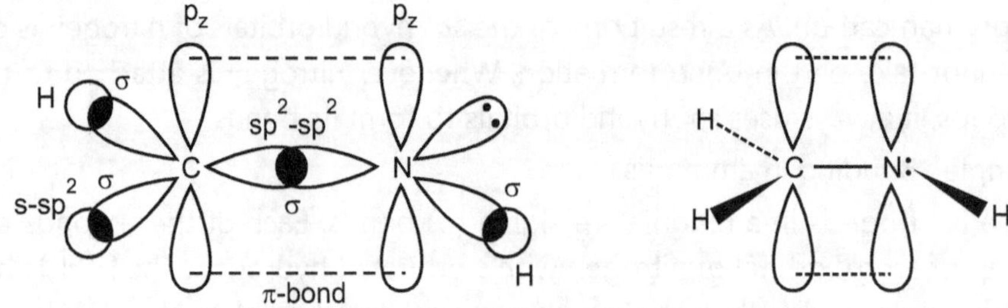

Fig. 1.14 : Bonding in $CH_2 = N – H$

In $CH_2 = N - H$ both carbon and nitrogen are sp^2-hybridized (Fig. 1.15).

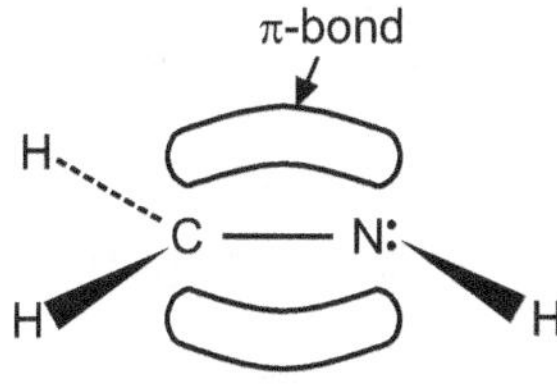

Fig. 1.15

(3) *sp* hybridization of Nitrogen :

Whenever nitrogen is bonded to only one other atom or group it uses an *sp* hybrid orbital and the two unhybridized orbitals (p_y and p_z) to form its bonds. (Fig. 1.16, 1.17 and 1.18).

$1s^2$ $2sp$ hybrid orbitals p_y^1 p_z^1

sp hybridized state of Nitrogen

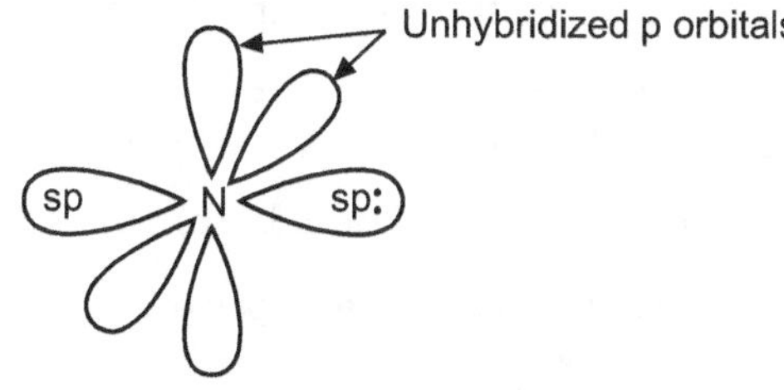

Fig. 1.16 : Shape of *sp* hybridized Nitrogen (Diagonal)

For example : Bonding in $H - C \equiv N$ (Hydrogen cyanide)

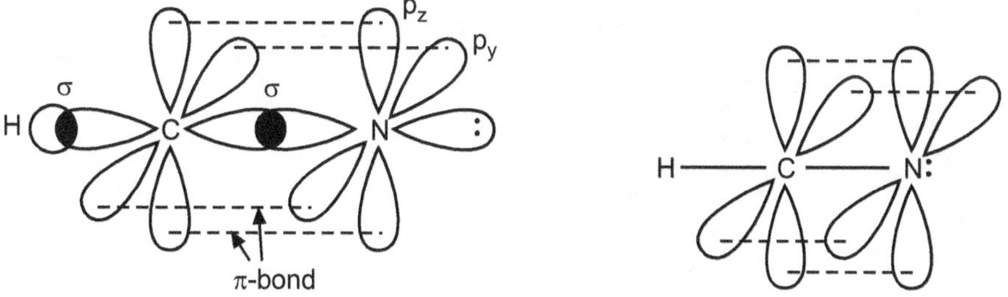

Fig. 1.17 : $H - C \equiv N$ contains one σ bond and two π bonds   **Fig. 1.18 :** Bonding in $H - C \equiv N$

1.3.4 Hybridization of Oxygen

Oxygen atom in alcohol is sp^3 hybridized and in carbonyl group it is in sp^2 hybridized state.

Atomic number of oxygen = 8. Let us consider electronic configuration of oxygen.

$$1s^2 \qquad 2s^2 \qquad 2p_x^1 \; 2p_y^1 \; 2p_z^1$$

Ground state electronic configuration of oxygen

It has six electrons in the valence shell (outermost shell). Like carbon or nitrogen, the oxygen atom undergoes only sp^3 and sp^2 hybridization.

(1) sp^3 hybrid orbitals of oxygen:

The following figure illustrates the formation of sp^3 hybrid orbitals of oxygen.

$$1s^2 \qquad 2s^2 \qquad 2p_x^2 \; 2p_y^1 \; 2p_z^1 \qquad\qquad 1s^2 \qquad 4sp^3 \text{ hybrid orbitals}$$

Ground state electronic configuration sp^3 hybridized state of oxygen

The $4sp^3$ hybrid orbitals of oxygen are directed towards the corners of a regular tetrahedron same like sp^3 hybrid orbitals of carbon or nitrogen. Oxygen has one more electron than nitrogen. As a result two of the sp^3 orbitals of oxygen are completely filled and cannot take part in bond formation. Whenever oxygen is bonded to two other atoms or groups (as in water, ether and alcohol) it always uses sp^3 hybrid orbitals to form its bonds.

For example : Bonding in water molecule (Fig. 1.19 (a), (b) and (c)).

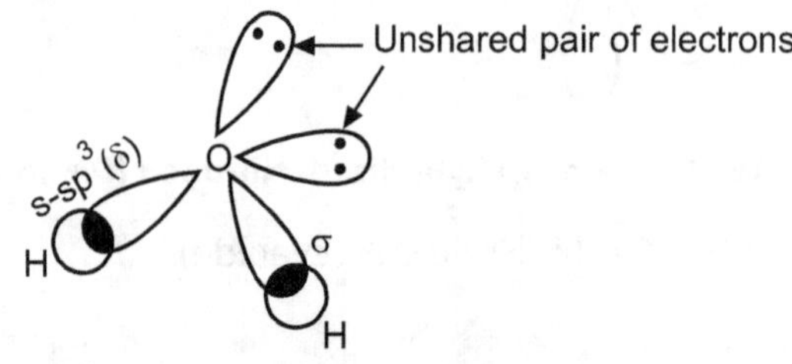

(a) Molecular orbitals of water

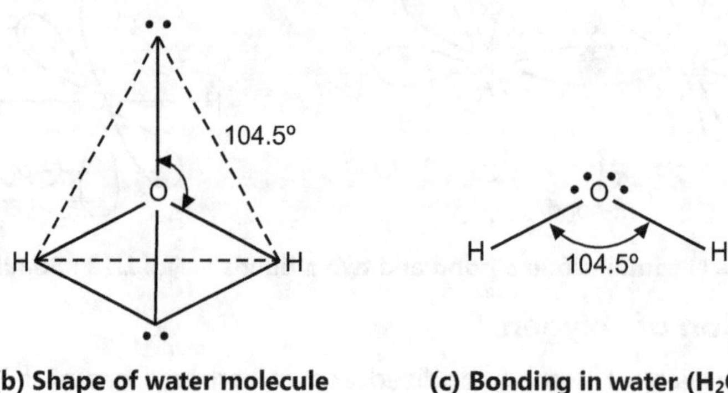

(b) Shape of water molecule   **(c) Bonding in water (H₂O)**

Fig. 1.19

H_2O contains two sigma bonds formed by overlapping of $2sp^3$ hybrid orbitals of oxygen and $1s$ orbital of hydrogen and it possesses two lone pair of electrons in $2sp^3$ orbitals of oxygen. Refer Fig. 1.19 (c).

(2) sp^2 hybrid orbitals of oxygen:

Oxygen can also form compounds using sp^2 hybrid orbitals. Whenever oxygen is bonded to one other atom or group, it uses sp^2 orbitals and the unhybridized p_z orbital to form its bonds.

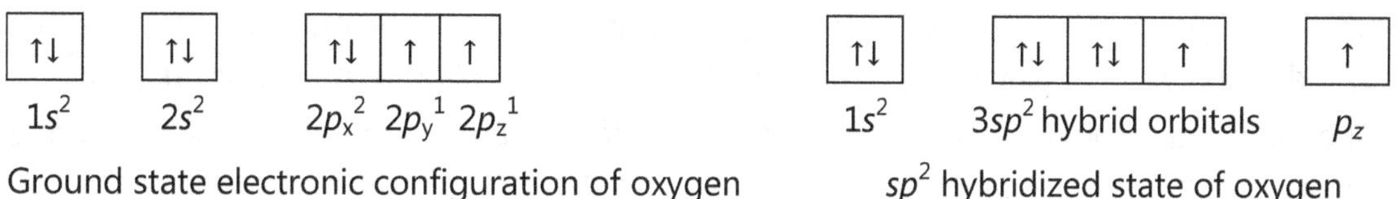

Ground state electronic configuration of oxygen sp^2 hybridized state of oxygen

For example : Bonding in $H_2C=O$ (Formaldehyde) (Fig. 1.20).

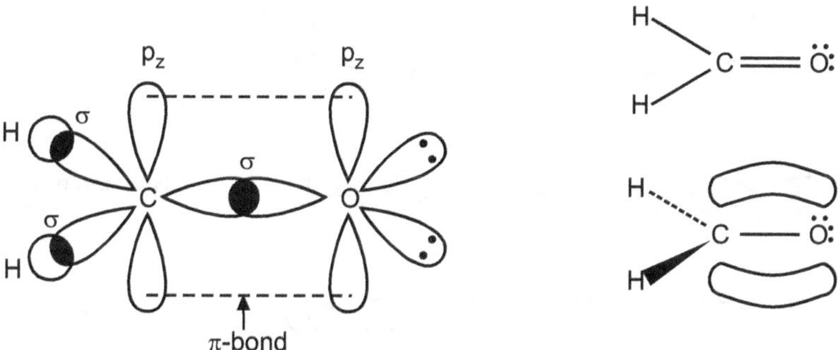

Fig. 1.20 : Bonding in formaldehyde

Oxygen does not undergo sp hybridization.

1.4 MOLECULAR ORBITALS

An orbital is the property of the entire molecule rather than of an individual atom. The overlap of two atomic orbitals results in the formation of two new orbitals called molecular orbitals (MOs). Like an atomic orbital, a molecular orbital can accommodate only two electrons. Mathematically it has been shown that the addition of two atomic orbitals generate a bonding molecular orbital and subtraction of one atomic orbital from the other generates an antibonding molecular orbital. This method of ovelap of atomic orbitals is called a linear combination of atomic orbitals (LCAO).

Types of molecular orbitals

(1) Bonding molecular orbitals:

In a simple diatomic molecule, molecular orbitals can be viewed as overlap between the atomic orbitals on each atom. For overlap to occur, the atomic orbitals must be of similar energy, and must have the proper symmetry. If the overlap is constructive (in-phase), electron density will increase in the region between the two nuclei, resulting in a bonding orbital. In the bonding molecular orbital both electrons reside mostly between the two nuclei in the ground state and hence aid to the binding of the two nuclei. The bonding molecular orbital has lower energy than the atomic orbitals that combine to produce them.

Atomic orbitals can overlap in a variety of ways as shown below.

(i) Sigma (σ) molecular orbital:

σ-molecular orbitals (means σ bonds) are formed by the head-on overlap of the atomic orbitals. This type of overlap is possible between two neighbouring s orbitals, between an s orbital and a p_z orbital, or between two neighbouring p_z orbitals. The molecular orbitals that are cylindrically symmetrical about the internuclear axis are called σ-molecular orbitals.

The molecular orbitals for the combination of different atomic orbitals on neighbouring atoms are drawn below. The bonding orbital is given the designation σ and will be lower in energy. The antibonding orbital, which will be higher in energy, is given the designation σ*.

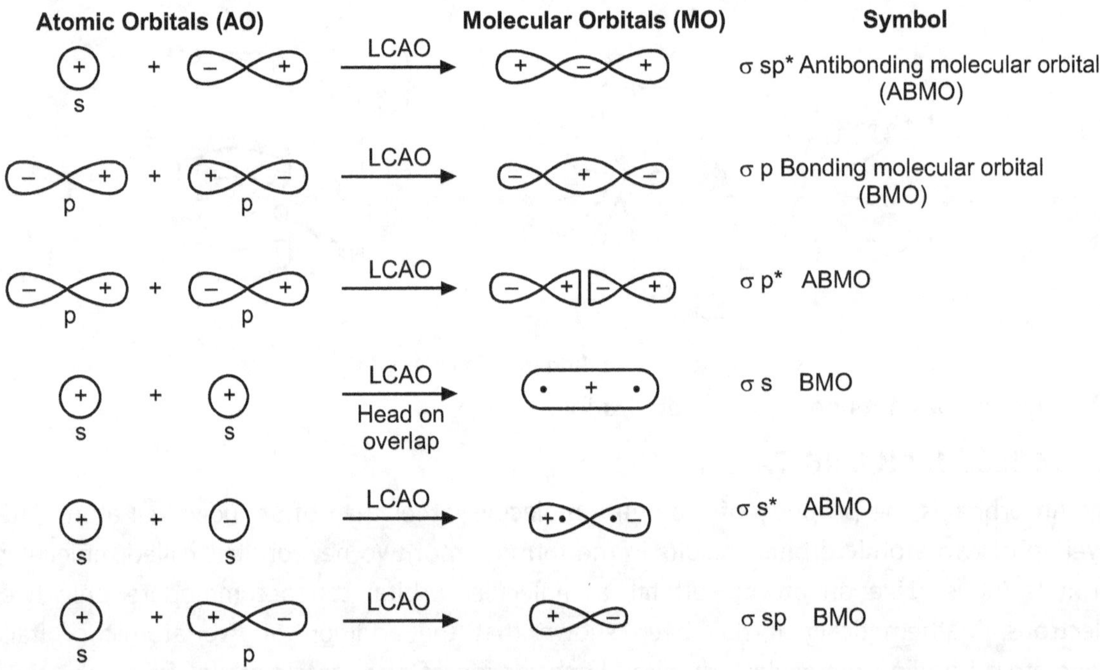

Fig. 1.21 : σ-molecular orbital (means σ bond)

(ii) Pi (π) molecular orbitals:

π-molecular orbitals are formed by sideways overlap of adjacent atomic orbitals. This type of constructive overlap results in electron density above and below the internuclear axis, and is called a π bond. Neighboring p_y or neighboring p_z orbitals can overlap in this way. If the internuclear axis lies in a nodal plane, the molecular orbital is called a π-molecular orbital.

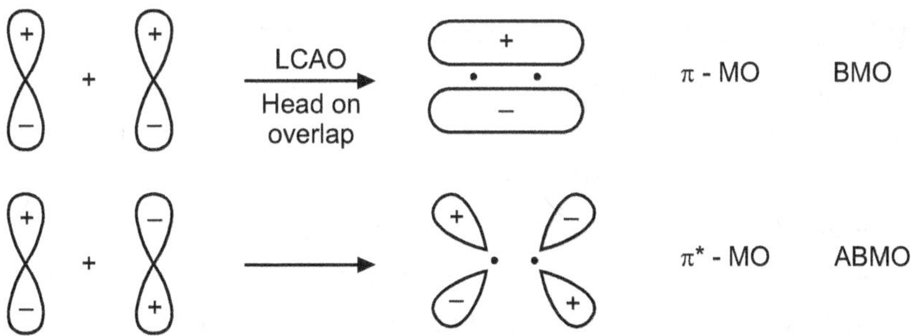

Fig. 1.22 : π-molecular orbital (means π bond)

Since σ-molecular orbitals are formed by the head-on overlap of the atomic orbitals and π-molecular orbitals are formed by sideways overlap of atomic orbitals. A σ-bond is more stable than a π-bond. A σ bond being symmetrical about the internuclear axis, one of the bonded atoms can rotate around the bond axis keeping the other atom fixed. This rotation does not destroy the charge symmetry of the σ bond orbital and the bond remains intact. But the strength of a π-bond is function of parallelism of the two p-atomic orbitals. Any rotation around the bond axis will destroy this parallelism and hence the π-bond. This needs energy. Therefore, free rotation around the bond axis of a π-bonded molecule is not possible under ordinary conditions.

(2) Antibonding molecular orbitals (ABMOs):

If the interaction of the two atomic orbitals is destructive, nodal planes result between the nuclei, resulting in a destabilizing or *antibonding* orbital. In the antibonding molecular orbital the electrons are at a greater distance from either of the nuclei than individual atomic orbitals. Hence the antibonding orbital does not results to the binding of the two nuclei and is of higher energy than the atomic orbital. Antibonding σ-molecular orbitals are denoted by σ* and antibonding π molecular orbitals are denoted by π* (Figs. 1.21 and 1.22). ABMOs possess an additional nodal plane than the corresponding bonding molecular orbitals.

1.5 COVALENT BOND

Covalent bond is a type of chemical bond. The compounds formed by sharing of electrons between atoms are called covalent compounds and the bond uniting these atoms by shared pair of electrons is called a covalent bond.

According to molecular orbital theory, a bond is formed between two atomic orbitals when they overlap each other. We have already seen above that when two atomic orbitals approach each other they share the same region in space and new orbital called a molecular orbital (MO) is formed. This molecular orbital is a covalent bond. Molecular orbital can accommodate only two electrons, same as atomic orbitals. A covalent bond is formed only if:

(1) The two overlapping orbitals are half filled i.e. must have unpaired electrons.

(2) The bonding orbitals of two atoms approach each other in proper alignment needed for an effective overlap.

(3) The overlapping orbitals have opposite spin (antispin) electrons.

1.5.1 Energy Changes During Covalent Bond Formation

It should be noted that the formation of a chemical bond is possible only if the approach of atoms is accompanied by decrease of energy. There are forces of attraction and repulsion between two approaching atoms. Attractive forces are between nucleus of one atom and electrons of other atom and vice versa. Repulsive forces between two nuclei (as they both are positively charged) and between the electrons of two atoms (as they both are negatively charged). If the attraction is the net result of these two types of forces, then energy decreases and bonding takes place. On the other hand if repulsion is the net result, then energy increases and bonding does not take place.

1.5.2 Types of Covalent Bonds

Overlapping of atomic orbital leads to the formation of two types of covalent bonds or molecular orbitals:

(1) Sigma (σ) bonds

(2) Pi (π) bonds

(1) Sigma (σ) bonds :

σ-bond is formed when two atomic orbitals, pure or hybrid, overlap around their axes i.e. head to head. In other words, linear overlapping of atomic orbitals occur.

An axis is the imaginary line which joins the two nuclei and is known as bond axis. Sigma bond orbital is bigger in size than that of the overlapping of atomic orbitals. It has cylindrical charge density around the bond axis and hence symmetrical in nature. The charge density is maximum between the nuclei (Fig. 1.23, 1.24 and 1.25). Single bonds are σ-bonds. Sigma bond orbitals may be formed by linear overlaps of following orbitals.

(a) Two s-orbitals :

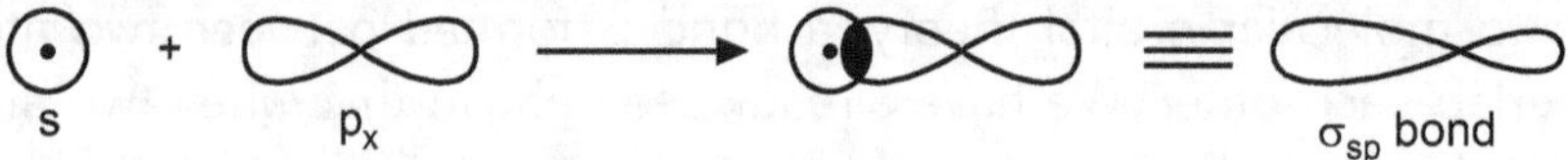

Fig. 1.23 : Linear overlap of two s-orbitals

(b) One p_x and an s-orbital :

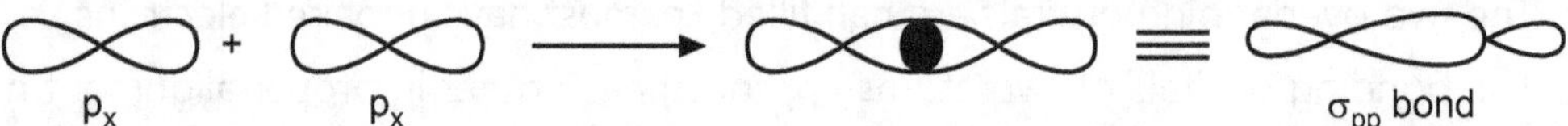

Fig. 1.24 : Linear overlap of p_x and an s-orbital

(c) Two p-orbitals :

Fig. 1.25 : Linear overlap of p_x and p_x orbitals

It may also be formed by the overlap of several types of atomic orbitals like s-sp, s-sp^2, sp^2-sp^2 etc.

In sigma bond, the electron cloud is more dense along the internuclear axis and hence binds the two nuclei firmly. Hence a σ-bond is a very strong bond. The electrons that occupy a sigma bond are called σ-electrons. A sigma bond has no nodal point or plane between the two nuclei. A σ bond being symmetrical in so far as its charge is concerned, one of the bonded atoms can rotate around the bond axis keeping the other atom fixed. This rotation does not destroy the charge symmetry of the σ bond orbital and the bond remains intact.

Rotation around bonds gives rise to certain important phenomenon like conformational isomerism and diastereomerism.

(2) Pi (π) bond :

A Pi (π) bond is formed by parallel or side to side overlap of unhybridized p-orbitals. A double bond is considered to consist of one sigma and one π-bond, triple bond considered to consist of one sigma and two π-bonds. Pi (π) bonds are formed by p_y-p_y or p_z-p_z overlap (Fig. 1.26).

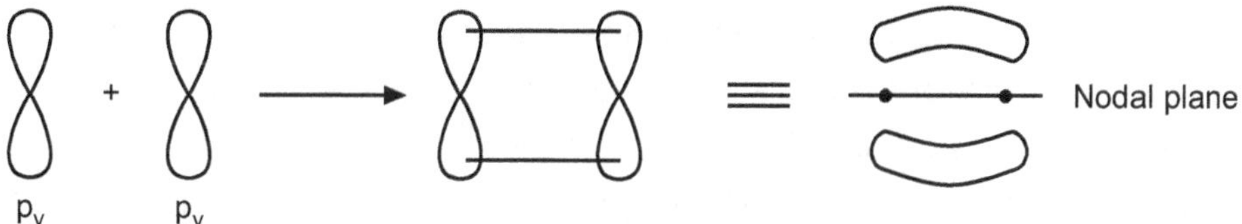

Fig. 1.26 : Side to side overlap of p_y and p_y overlap

Like p-orbitals from which it is obtained, a π-bond has two lobes. One half of the π-bond lies above the plane containing two nuclei and other half lies below. The plane perpendicular to Pi bond orbital has no π-charge density and is called a nodal plane. The line which joins the two nuclei is called bond axis and it lies in the nodal plane. π-bonds are weak and easy to break because they have a node. The electrons that occupy π-bond are known as Pi (π) electrons. Pi-electrons are loosely held than a pair of electrons in a σ-bond. As a result π-bonds are more easily broken and are more reactive than σ-bonds.

Rotation of atoms is not possible around a π-bond. If any attempt is made to do so, the lobes of p-orbitals will no longer be coplanar and will not overlap to form the π-bond. Due to this there is a restriction of rotation around a π-bond. This phenomenon is responsible for *cis and trans* isomerism in alkenes.

1.5.3 Polar and Non-Polar Covalent Bonds

The covalent compounds unlike ionic compounds are uncharged. However, when the bond is between two dissimilar elements (elements having different electronegativity), the shared pair shifts slightly towards the more electronegative element of the two elements.

One end of such a bond is relatively negative and the other end is relatively positive. It is indicated by δ- and δ+ signs respectively (Fig. 1.27). The molecule is thus unsymmetrical. Though they are electrically neutral, such molecules are polar molecules and the covalent bond between the atoms is known as polar covalent bond. For example, the N-H and O-H bonds are called polar covalent bonds.

N — H bond is a polar bond   O — H bond is a polar bond

Fig. 1.27

When the covalent bond is between two similar atoms (having same electronegativity) the shared pair occurs at the mid-point between the two nuclei. The molecule is symmetrical and electrically neutral. Such a molecule is non-polar and the covalent bond thus formed is known as non-polar covalent bond. For example, H_2, F_2, Cl_2, N_2, I_2, etc.

1.6 ELECTRONEGATIVITY

Electronegativity of an atom is defined as the tendency of an atom in a covalent bond to attract the bonding electrons to itself in a compound. For example, in a homonuclear diatomic molecule such as H_2 and Cl_2, the shared electron pair is attracted equally by both the bonding atoms and so there is no net polarity in the molecule. This is because the electronegativity of both the atoms is the same.

However, in heteronuclear molecule such as HCl, the shared electron pair is not equally attracted by the bonding atoms i.e. H and Cl. The electron pair is shifted more towards the chlorine than hydrogen and the molecule acquires the polarity ($H^{\delta+} \rightarrow Cl^{\delta-}$). These charges are of equal magnitude but of opposite sign and the overall charge is zero. Arrow implies that chlorine is more electronegative than hydrogen.

Electronegativity values have been calculated from different theoretical assumptions by Pauling, Mulliken, Huggins and Sanderson. But the values given by Pauling are widely used. If the combining atoms have a large difference in electronegativity, the bond between them is ionic. Thus greater the difference in the electronegativity of the combining atoms, greater is the ionic character of the bond.

Electronegativity depends upon the distance between the valence electron and nucleus. Shorter this distance i.e. smaller the atom, greater will be the electronegativity.

1.6.1 Trends in Electronegativity

It has been observed that:

(1) In a periodic arrangement the electronegativity decreases from top to bottom. In this case the size of an atom increases from top to bottom. It means electronegativity

decreases with increasing size of atoms. Thus, electronegativity decreases from fluorine to iodine.

$$F \quad < \quad Cl \quad < \quad Br \quad < \quad I$$
$$(4.0) \qquad (3.0) \qquad (2.8) \qquad (2.5)$$

(2) In a periodic table, electronegativity increases from left to right. In this case atomic size decreases and nuclear charge increases from left to right. It means electronegativity increases with increasing nuclear charge.

$$B \quad < \quad C < \quad N \quad < \quad O < \quad F$$
$$(2.1) \qquad (2.5) \quad (3.0) \quad (3.5) \quad (4.0)$$

Hydrogen was arbitrarily given electronegative value as 2.1 by Pauling.

Electronegativity values of common elements deduced by Pauling are as follows:

F = 4.0	P = 2.1
O = 3.5	B = 2.1
N = 3.0	Si =1.8
Cl = 3.0	Be = 1.6
Br = 2.8	Al = 1.5
I = 2.5	Mg = 1.2
S = 2.5	Li = 1.0
C = 2.5	Na = 0.9
H = 2.1	K = 0.8

1.7 BOND FISSION

A covalent bond between two atoms in a molecule, A-B contains a shared pair of electrons and may be represented as A:B. Every reaction of organic compounds involves the fission (breaking) of at least one bond and making of another bond. The energy has to be supplied to break a covalent bond. A covalent bond can undergo fission in two ways.

(1) Homolytic fission or Homolytic cleavage.

(2) Heterolytic fission or Heterolytic cleavage.

1.7.1 Homolytic Fission

The breaking of covalent bond in a manner so that each of the two species formed retains one electron of the shared pair is called a homolytic fission.

$$A - B \text{ or } A:B \xrightarrow[h\upsilon]{\text{Homolytic fission}} A^{\bullet} + B^{\bullet}$$

The resulting $A^{\bullet}$ and $B^{\bullet}$ are uncharged species with unpaired electron and are known as free radicals which are highly reactive neutral species containing unpaired electrons. The reactions which proceed through homolytic cleavage i.e. through the formation of intermediate free radicals are known as free radical reactions. These reactions are initiated by light, heat and organic peroxides. Homolytic fission is the most common mode of fission in the vapour phase.

For example,

$$H \overset{\frown}{-} Br \xrightarrow{\text{Per acid}} H^\bullet + Br^\bullet$$

$$Cl \overset{\frown}{-} Cl \xrightarrow{\text{Light}} Cl^\bullet + Cl^\bullet$$

1.7.2 Heterolytic Fission

The breaking of covalent bond in a manner so that one of the atoms acquires both of the bonding electrons is called a heterolytic fission.

When B is more electronegative than A

$$A \overset{\frown}{-} B \xrightarrow{\text{Heterolytic fission}} A^\oplus + :B^\ominus$$

When A is more electronegative than B

$$A \overset{\frown}{-} B \xrightarrow{\text{Heterolytic fission}} :A^\ominus + B^\oplus$$

For example,

$$CH_3 - Br \xrightarrow{Ag^+} \overset{\oplus}{C}H_3 + AgBr$$

The reaction intermediates of heterolytic fission are two ions i.e. cation (+ve) and anion (–ve). Heterolytic fission occurs most readily with polar compounds in polar solvents. The reactions which proceed through heterolytic fission of at least one covalent bond are called polar or ionic reactions.

1.8 HYDROGEN BONDING

Hydrogen bonding is a strong kind of dipole-dipole attraction. Hydrogen bond may be defined as an intermolecular or intramolecular weak electrostatic chemical bond which is found to act between one covalently bonded H-atom to a electronegative element of a species and a highly electronegative atom like F, O, N, Cl, S of another species in the same molecule or in some other molecule.

When a hydrogen atom is covalently linked to a strong electronegative element, the molecule formed is a dipole. Thus H–F is a dipole. In H–F dipole-dipole interactions take place when they come very close to each other (Fig. 1.28). Hydrogen bonding is indicated in formulas by a broken line.

$$\overset{\delta+}{H} - \overset{\delta-}{F} \quad \overset{\delta+}{H} - \overset{\delta-}{F} \longrightarrow \overset{\delta+}{H} - \overset{\delta-}{F} - - - \overset{\delta+}{H} - \overset{\delta-}{F}$$

H-bond

Fig 1.28 : Hydrogn bonding in hydrogen fluoride

1.8.1 Types of Hydrogen Bond

Hydrogen bonds are of two types:

(1) Intermolecular H-bond

(2) Intramolecular or internal H-bond

(1) Intermolecular H-bond: When H-bond occurs between two or more molecules, it is known as intermolecular H-bond. For example, hydrogen bonding in water molecules (Fig. 1.29) and in methanol (Fig. 1.30).

Fig. 1.29 : Association of water molecule   **Fig. 1.30 : Association of methanol molecule**

(2) Intramolecular H-bond: When H-bond is formed between two atoms within a molecule, it is called an internal or intramolecular H-bond. For example hydrogen bonding in salicylaldehyde (Fig. 1.31) and in *o*- nitrophenol (Fig. 1.32).

Fig. 1.31 : Salicylaldehyde   **Fig. 1.32 : o-nitrophenol**

1.8.2 The Effect of H-bonding Force

(1) Effect on M.P. and B.P.:

Due to the association of identical molecules by intermolecular H-bond, the intermolecular forces amongst the molecules increase to a relatively greater extent. An extra amount of heat energy is required to break the H-bond. Hence compounds with intermolecular H-bond have greater melting point (M.P.) and boiling point (B.P.) than those of compounds without intermolecular H-bonds, provided they have comparable molecular weights.

CH_4, HF and H_2O molecules have comparable molecular weight. CH_4 cannot form H-bond, because carbon atom has low electronegativity. HF can utilize its lone H atom to form H-bond but a water molecule forms H-bond with both the H-atoms.

M.P. order H_2O (0°C) > HF (–110°C) > CH_4 (– 190°)

B.P. order H_2O (100°C) > HF (19.5°C) > CH_4 (– 161.5°C)

On the other hand, intramolecular H-bonding in a compound prevents intermolecular H-bonding and thus prevents association which would raise melting point (M.P.) and boiling point (B.P.). Therefore two compounds of comparable molecular weights, one with intermolecular H-bond and the other with intramolecular H-bond, should have different melting and boiling points. The former compound will possess higher melting point and boiling point than those of the latter compounds. This difference in boiling point often helps in the separation of two compounds from their mixture by steam distillation. The compound possessing intramolecular H-bonding being of lower boiling point, distils out with steam when subjected to steam distillation but the other remains in the distilling flask. For example, separation of *o*- nitrophenol and *p*- nitrophenol by steam distillation.

(2) Effect on solubility :

H-bonding in a compound makes it soluble in water and in other solvents possessing H-bonding. The H-bond in solvent molecules and that in solute molecules break on dissolution. New H-bonding occurs between the solvent and the solute molecules. For example, alcohols are soluble in water but alkanes are insoluble in water. This is because an alcohol molecule capable of hydrogen bonding can accommodate into the hydrogen bonded sequence in water (Fig. 1.33). It can replace the hydrogen bonds that must be broken to allow it in water whereas a nonpolar alkane molecule cannot break hydrogen-bonded sequence in water (Fig. 1.34). It cannot replace the hydrogen bonds that would have to be broken to allow it in water.

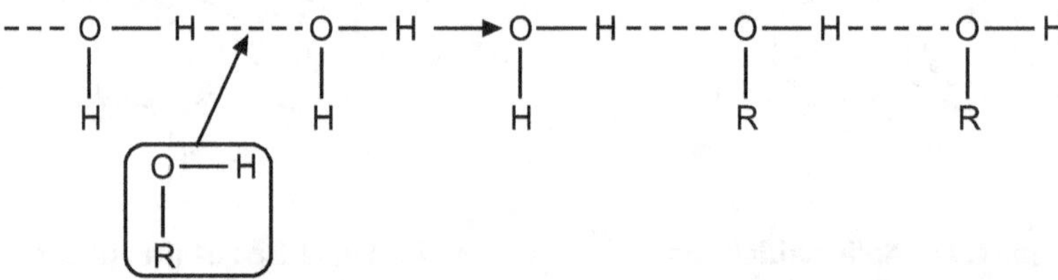

Fig. 1.33 : Polar alcohol molecule forms H-bonding with water

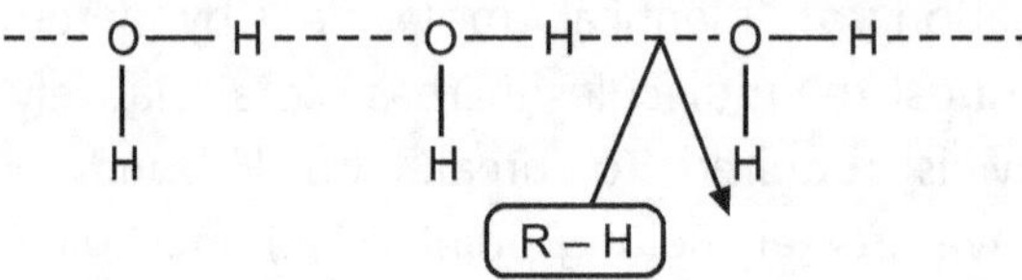

Fig. 1.34 : Nonpolar alkane molecules cannot form H-bonding with water

(3) Effect on stability of molecules :

Intramolecular H-bonding brings stability to a compound. For example, acetylacetone molecule in liquid state remains in two tautomeric forms, keto and enol. Due to the intramolecular H-bonding (Fig. 1.35) and conjugation in the enol form, it is more stable than keto form in the liquid acetylacetone and in an n-hexane solution and their percentage is

80% and 20% respectively. In the aqueous medium, however enol form is 16% and keto form 84%.

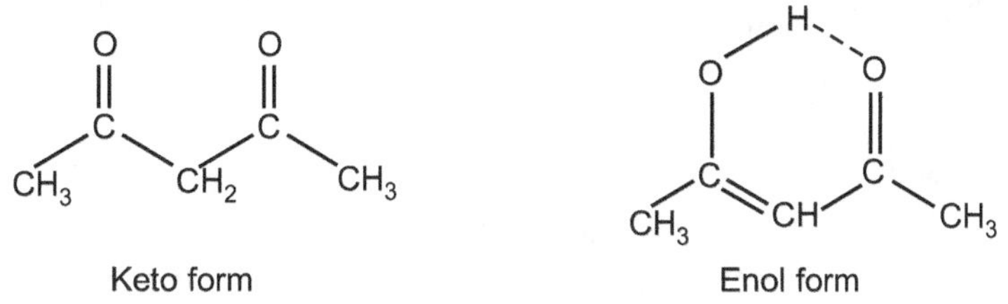

Keto form   Enol form

Fig. 1.35 : Tautomeric forms of acetylacetone

(4) Effect on acidity and basicity :

If a conjugate base is more stable than the parent acid, the base will be relatively weaker than the acid. The relation between stability and strength of a base and its conjugate acid follows the same principle. For example, dimethylamine is a stronger base than trimethylamine in aqueous medium as the conjugate acid of the former base is more stable than that of the latter compound. The stability is because of the greater hydration effect on dimethylammonium [Fig. 1.36 (a)] ion than that on trimethylammonium ion [Fig. 1.36 (b)].

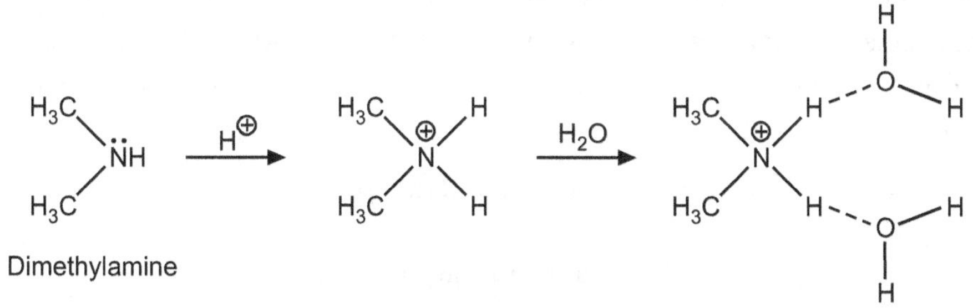

Dimethylamine

Fig. 1.36 : (a) Hydration of dimethylamine

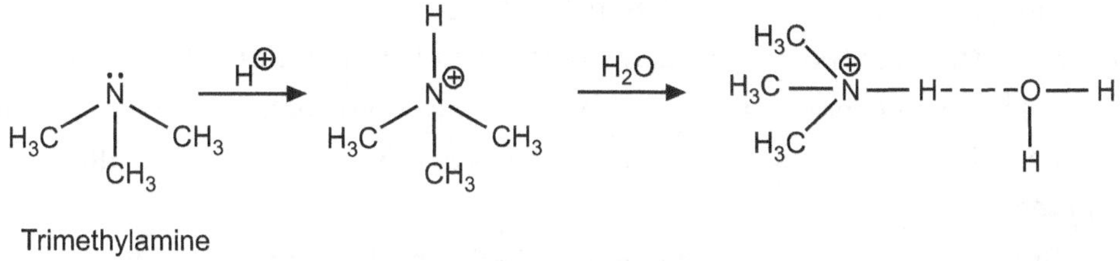

Trimethylamine

Fig. 1.36 : (b) Hydration of trimethylamine

Similarly, the conjugate base of salicylic acid gets stabilized by the intraionic H-bonding [Fig. 1.37 (a)], but *p*-hydroxybenzoate ion, the conjugate base of the *p*-hydroxybenzoic acid, is not stabilized by such a hydrogen bonding [Fig. 1.37 (b)]. Thus, salicylate ion is a weaker base than *p*-hydroxyl benzoate ion. This means salicylic acid is a stronger acid than *p*-hydroxybenzoic acid.

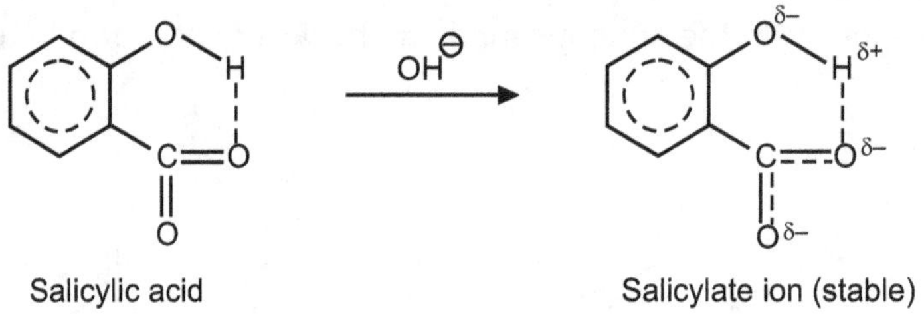

Salicylic acid   Salicylate ion (stable)

Fig. 1.37 (a)

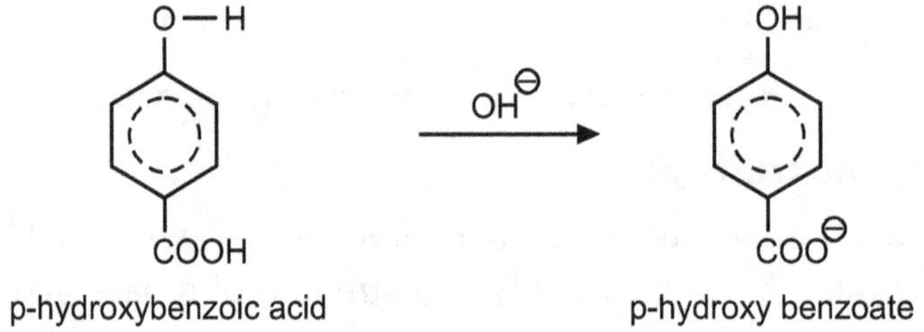

p-hydroxybenzoic acid   p-hydroxy benzoate

Fig. 1.37 (b)

(5) Effect on biological system :

Intermolecular and intramolecular H-bonding is found to play important role in a biological system. The long helical structure of protein molecule and double helical structure of DNA molecules is stabilized by the existence of H-bonding. For example, a protein molecule contains a large number of heteronuclear groups and H-bonding occurs between these two groups (Fig. 1.38).

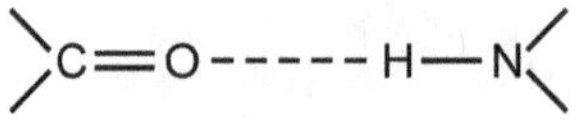

Fig. 1.38 : H-bonding in protein

1.9 BOND LENGTH

The equilibrium distance between the nuclei of the two bonded atoms is called the bond length or bond distance. Bond lengths are very small and are measured in angstrom unit.

(1 A° = 10^{-8} cm), in nanometer (1 nm = 10^{-7} cm) or in picometer (1 pm = 10^{-10} cm). The single bond lengths between two particular atoms A and B are found to be almost constant in their different types of compounds.

Single bond length > Double bond length > Triple bond length

1.9.1 Factors Affecting Bond Length

Bond lengths are affected by the following factors:

(a) Nature of overlapping orbitals : s orbitals being symmetrical in nature, greater the 's' character in an overlapping atomic orbital, the shorter is the bond length. For example,

$$-C–H = 0.109, -C–C = 0.154, C = C = 0.133, C \equiv C = 0.120.$$

(b) Resonance: Ionic structures involved in the resonance hybrid of a molecule make the ions come close to each other and hence bond distance decreases.

1.10 BOND ENERGY

During chemical reactions some bonds may be broken and some new bonds may be formed. When a chemical bond is formed between two atoms, some energy is released. This energy is called bond formation energy. Hence, bond formation energy is defined as the amount of energy released when a chemical bond is formed between two atoms. On the other hand, to break the chemical bond between two atoms, energy should be supplied. The energy that is to be supplied for breaking a chemical bond is called as bond dissociation energy (D). Bond dissociation energy is defined as the amount of energy required to break the chemical bond in a molecule producing free atoms or radicals. The average bond dissociation energy is called bond energy.

The bond energy is expressed in terms of bond dissociation rather than bond formation.

1.10.1 Factors Affecting Bond Energy

Factors affecting bond energy are :

   (a) Size of an atom.

   (b) Multiplicity of bonds.

(a) Size of an atom :

The bond length increases with increase in size of atoms.

   For example, HI > HBr > HCl > HF

     ($\because$ size of I > Br > Cl > F)

Shorter the bond length, greater is the bond dissociation energy. As the size of the atom increases, bond length also increases and bond dissociation energy decreases.

   For example,

$$H\text{-}F \quad > \quad H\text{-}Cl \quad > \quad H\text{-}Br \quad > \quad H\text{-}I$$

High bond dissociation energy   Less bond dissociation energy

(b) Multiplicity of bonds :

Since the bond length decreases with multiplicity of bonds, greater the multiplicity of bonds, greater is the bond dissociation energy. Greater the *s*-character, shorter is the bond length.

   For example,

$$C \equiv C \quad , \quad C = C \quad , \quad C\text{-}C$$

$\longleftarrow$ Bond dissociation energy

Bond	Energy (kcal/mole)
H – H	104
O – H	110
C – H	99
C – C	83
C = C	145
C ≡ C	198
Cl – Cl	58
O = O	118

The unit of bond energy is kcal/mole.

1.11 REACTION MECHANISM

An organic reaction is a process of breaking and making of bonds. In a reaction, the molecules undergoing a change are called reactants and the new molecules formed are called products.

In any organic reaction the steps depicting the breaking and making of new bonds of carbon atoms in the reactant called substrate leading to the formation of final products through the transitory intermediates is known as reaction mechanism.

$$C + A - B \longrightarrow C --- A --- B \longrightarrow C - A + B$$

Substrate   Intermediate   Products
                             (Transitory)

Theories of Reaction Mechanism: There are two general theories to explain the mechanism of reactions.

(1) Collision theory

(2) Transition State theory

1.11.1 Collision Theory

According to this theory,

(a) For chemical reactions to occur collision amongst the reacting species is a necessary condition.

(b) The higher the collision frequency i.e. collisions per unit time, the higher is the rate of the reaction. The collision frequency depends on:

(i) The concentration or pressure of the reactant – higher the concentration, higher will be the collision frequency.

(ii) Size of the species – the larger the size of reacting units, the greater is the collision frequency.

(iii) Temperature of the reacting species - the higher the temperature of the colliding particles, the greater is the collision frequency due to their higher speed.

(c) All such collisions do not give rise to a chemical change, only fraction of them is effective. A chemical change occurs through those collisions which take place between the reactants containing certain critical amount of energy above the average value. This critical amount of energy which is necessary for a mole of reactant to undergo a chemical change is called energy of activation and the species carrying the energy of activation is known as activated species (complex). Therefore, only the activated species undergo chemical change and hence the rate of reaction depends on the energy of activation of reactants (E_{act}). The energy of activation is defined as the energy required for the creation of the transition state from the reactants.

(d) Orientation of activated units : The chemical reaction takes place only if the orientation of activated species is proper. For example, AB molecule will decompose to A_2 and B_2 only if the orientation of activated AB species colliding with each other is as given below.

$$\begin{array}{ccc} A\text{-----}A \\ | \qquad\quad | \\ B\text{-----}B \end{array} \longrightarrow A_2 \;+\; B_2$$

If the orientation is as given below then decomposition products will be AB.

$$\begin{array}{ccc} A\text{-----}B \\ | \qquad\quad | \\ B\text{-----}A \end{array} \longrightarrow A-B \;+\; AB$$

This factor may be called orientation factor.

The rate of reaction may thus be represented by the following equation.

The rate of reaction = Collision frequency $\times$ Energy factor $\times$ Orientation factor

1.11.2 Transition State Theory

A chemical reaction may be considered as a gradual change from substrates to products through a very unstable state called a transition state (T.S.).

$$A-B + X-Y \longrightarrow A-X + B-Y$$

To obtain AX and BY from AB and XY it needs to break $A - B$ and $X - Y$ bonds. For bond breaking it requires absorption of energy. Therefore, the reaction proceeds so that the energy for the cleavage of bonds is partly compensated by the energy liberated during the formation of new bonds (A-X and B-Y). Pictorially it may be shown as follows:

$$A-B + X-Y \longrightarrow \left[\begin{array}{ccc} A\text{-----}X \\ | \qquad\quad | \\ B\text{-----}Y \end{array}\right]^{\#} \longrightarrow A-X + B-Y$$

$$\text{Substrate} \qquad\qquad\qquad \text{T.S.} \qquad\qquad\qquad \text{Products}$$

Where $\neq$ = T.S.

Transition state is not at all a separate molecular species. It is highly unstable and transient and has both partial and complete bonds, some bonds may be forming and some bonds may be breaking in this state. Transition state is of very high energy. According to Hammond, in an endothermic reaction, the transition state resembles the products in so far as geometry, charge distribution and energy content (Fig. 1.39), while the transition state resembles the reactants in all those in an exothermic reaction (Fig. 1.40).

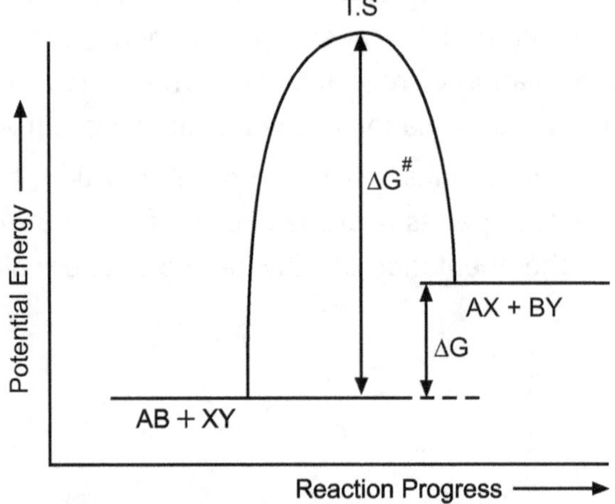

Fig. 1.39 : Energy profile for one step endothermic reaction

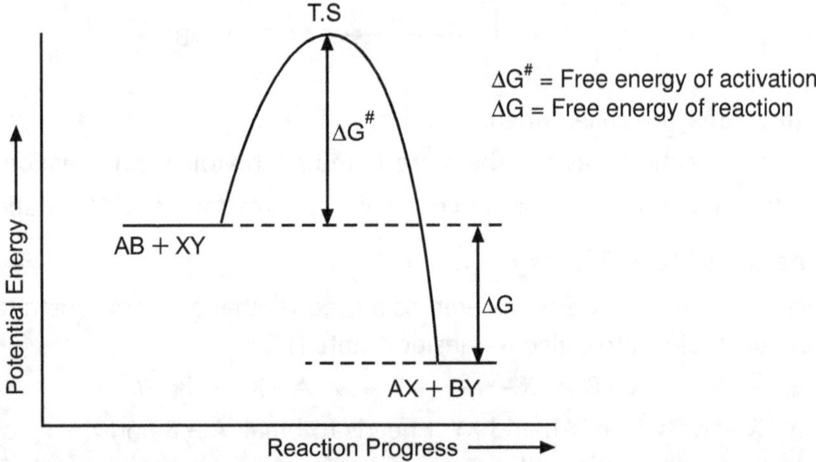

Fig. 1.40 : Energy profile for one step exothermic reaction

1.11.2.1 Characteristics of Transition State Theory

(1) The reacting species must be forced to come very close to each other when each of the species loses its own identity and assumes the most unstable state called as a transition state.

(2) The transition state is an activated complex in the collision theory. Only those reacting units that acquire the E_{act} can reach the transition state. All the transition states are converted to the product at the same rate.

(3) Higher the number of chemical units that reach the peak, the higher is the rate of the reaction.

(4) The number of chemical entities involved in the transition state of the rate determining (R.D.) step is called the molecularity of the reaction. For example, unimolecular, bimolecular and trimolecular reactions involve only one, two and three chemical entities respectively in the transition state of rate determining step.

1.12 FACTORS AFFECTING ELECTRON AVAILABILITY

The reactivity at a particular bond or atom is influenced by the electron density in a particular bond or a particular atom towards a particular reagent. A species with high electron availability will be easily attacked by electron deficient reagents, electrophiles like NO_2^+, Br^+, BF_3, $AlCl_3$, H^+ etc. Similarly, a position of low electron availability will be attacked more easily by electron rich reagents, nucleophiles like OH^-, OR^-, SH, H_2O etc.

Electron availability depends upon following factors:

(1) Inductive effect

(2) Resonance effect or mesomeric effect

(3) Electromeric effect

(4) Hyperconjugation

(5) Steric effect

(6) Tautomerism

1.12.1 Inductive Effect

The polarization of one bond caused by the polarization of an adjacent bond is called the inductive effect. For example, consider the covalent bond between homoatomic molecules (H_2, Br_2).

$$H - H \quad \text{and} \quad Br - Br$$

In these molecules, the bonding electron pair is equally shared and is expected to be held at the centre of the two atomic nuclei. Such molecules are said to be non-polar molecules. However if we consider the covalent bond between two different atoms such as HCl and HBr, the bonding electron pair is not equally shared because the electronegativities of the two atoms are not same.

$$\overset{+\delta}{H} - \overset{-\delta}{Cl} \qquad\qquad H \rightarrow\!\!- Cl$$

$$\overset{+\delta}{H} - \overset{-\delta}{Br} \qquad\qquad H \rightarrow\!\!- Br$$

$$\overset{+\delta}{CH_3} - \overset{-\delta}{Cl} \qquad\qquad CH_3 \rightarrow\!\!- Cl$$

In HCl, chlorine is more electronegative than hydrogen. Therefore, the electron pair is pulled slightly towards the chlorine atom. As a result, the electron density around hydrogen decreases giving partial positive charge ($\delta+$) on it and the electron density around chlorine increases giving partial negative charge ($\delta-$) on it. Thus, the H – Cl molecule is said to be polarized.

The inductive effect is a permanent effect and is supposed to operate through single bonds. If the carbon atom bonded to chlorine is itself attached to further carbon atoms, the effect can be transmitted further.

$$\overset{\delta\delta\delta+}{\underset{3}{CH_3}} \longrightarrow \overset{\delta\delta+}{\underset{2}{CH_2}} \longrightarrow \overset{\delta+}{\underset{1}{CH_2}} \longrightarrow \overset{\delta-}{Cl}$$

The C_1 – Cl bond in the chain C_3 – C_2 – C_1 – Cl is a permanent dipole because of the greater electronegativity of Cl atom than that of C. This dipole induces permanent dipole in C_2 – C_1 bond and C_2 becomes slightly positively charged, the magnitude of which is smaller than that on C_1 and represented by symbol $\delta\delta+$ where $\delta+ > \delta\delta+$. In this way the induction of positive charge may transmit down the chain; but the effect decreases with the increasing distance from the starting dipole.

1.12.1.1 Features of Inductive Effect

(1) The inductive effect is the permanent polarization in the ground state of the molecule and is developed due to the polarity of an atom or group of atoms.

(2) The magnitude of inductive effect is very small.

(3) It is associated with σ-bond connecting two dissimilar atoms or groups.

(4) It goes on decreasing with increasing distance from the polar group or atom in the molecule.

1.12.1.2 Types of Inductive Effect

The inductive effect is of two types:

(1) Electron donating inductive effect (+I effect)

(2) Electron withdrawing inductive effect (–I effect)

(1) Electron donating inductive effect (+I effect) : If the atom or group of atoms attached to a carbon atom pushes the shared pair of electrons away from it, it is said to exert electron donating inductive effect or +I effect.

(2) Electron withdrawing inductive effect (–I effect) : If the atom or group of atoms attached to a carbon atom attracts the shared pair of electrons towards itself it, it is said to exert electron withdrawing inductive effect or –I effect.

For example, in case of $CH_3 - Cl$, chlorine pulls electrons towards it. Therefore chlorine is said to have –I effect, on the other hand, the CH_3 group donates electron density and said to have + I effect.

Electron donating group (+I effect)	Electron withdrawing group (–I effect)
$-\overset{\ominus}{O}\ > -\overset{\ominus}{COO}\ > -CR_3\ > -CHR_2\ >$ $-CH_2R\ > -CH_3$	$-\overset{\oplus}{N}R_3 > -\overset{\oplus}{N}H_3 > -NO_2 > -SO_2R > -F >$ $-Cl\ > -Br > -I > -C \equiv C-R\ > CH = CR_2$
Decreases acid strength	Increases acid strength
Increases base strength	Decreases base strength

1.12.2 Resonance

If two or more structures are written for the true structures of a molecule or ion but no single structure can be said to be represent it uniquely, the phenomenon is called resonance or mesomerism. The true structure of the molecule is said to be a resonance hybrid of various possible alternative structures which are called resonating or canonical or contributing structures. The resonance hybrid of an entity is a more stable structure than any one of the resonating structures contributing to it. The resonance energy is a measure of the extra stability of the resonance hybrid. Resonance energy is defined as the difference in energy between the actual structure of the entity and the most stable structure of the hypothetical structures.

For example, benzene is ordinarily represented as

or

1   2

These two structures differ only in the position of electrons. Neither (1) nor (2) is a correct representation of benzene. The actual structure of benzene lies somewhere between these two structures (Structure 3)

1   2   3
Resonance structures   Resonance hybrid

Vinyl chloride is a resonance hybrid of the following contributing structures.

Vinyl chloride

Resonating structures differ in the position of electrons only and position of atoms remain same.

1.12.2.1 Conditions for Resonance

One of the most basic conditions for resonance phenomena to exist is that the system must be conjugated.

The second condition is that the atoms involved in resonance must be coplanar or capable of adopting coplanar conformation.

1.12.2.2 Rules of Writing Resonance Structure

(1)   The resonance structures are represented by double headed arrow ($\leftarrow \rightarrow$)

(2)   All the resonance forms must confirm to Lewis structure. For example, carbon cannot be pentavalent in any of the resonance forms.

(3)   The location of all the atoms in all resonance structures must be the same.

(4)   Resonating structures with more covalent bonds are normally more contributing than those with a fewer number of covalent bonds. Thus the structure (I) of CO_2 has major contribution in its resonance hybrid and the structures (II) and (III) have minor contributions.

$$:\ddot{O}=C=\ddot{O}: \quad\longleftrightarrow\quad :\overset{\ominus}{\ddot{O}}-\overset{\oplus}{C}=O: \quad\longleftrightarrow\quad :O=\overset{\oplus}{C}-\overset{\ominus}{\ddot{O}}:$$

$$\text{(I)} \qquad\qquad \text{(II)} \qquad\qquad \text{(III)}$$

(5)   If the different resonating structures have the same number of covalent bonds, then uncharged structures have major contribution in its resonance hybrid. Thus structure (I) has much greater contribution than structures (II) and (III) of CO_2 in its resonance hybrid.

$$:O=C=O: \quad\longleftrightarrow\quad :\overset{\ominus}{\ddot{O}}-C\equiv\overset{\oplus}{O}: \quad\longleftrightarrow\quad :\overset{\oplus}{\ddot{O}}\equiv C-\overset{\ominus}{\ddot{O}}:$$

$$\text{(I)} \qquad\qquad \text{(II)} \qquad\qquad \text{(III)}$$

(6)   Structures with negative charge on the most electronegative atom and a positive charge on the least electronegative atom have significant contribution. Structures with opposite charge distribution are less contributing. Thus structures I and II of CO_2 are more contributing than structures III and IV.

$$:\overset{\ominus}{\ddot{O}}-\overset{\oplus}{C}=O: \;\longleftrightarrow\; :O=\overset{\oplus}{C}-\overset{\ominus}{\ddot{O}}: \;\longleftrightarrow\; :\overset{\oplus}{\ddot{O}}-\overset{\ominus}{C}=O: \;\longleftrightarrow\; :O=\overset{\ominus}{C}-\overset{\oplus}{\ddot{O}}:$$

$$\text{(I)} \qquad\quad \text{(II)} \qquad\quad \text{(III)} \qquad\quad \text{(IV)}$$

(7)   Resonance forms exist only on paper i.e. they have no real existence.

(8)   All atoms taking part in resonance must lie in the same plane. Thus, any change in structures that prevents planarity will diminish / inhibit resonance. This phenomenon is known as steric inhibition of resonance.

(9)   In writing resonance forms, we can move only electrons. The relative position of atoms must remain same in all the resonance forms.

$$CH_3 - \overset{\oplus}{CH} - CH = CH_2 \longleftrightarrow CH_3 - CH = CH - \overset{\oplus}{CH_2}$$

(10) More the number of equivalent resonance structures, more is the stability of the resonance hybrid.

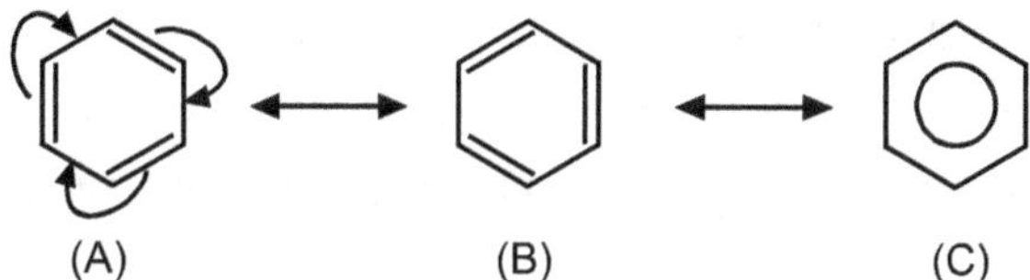

(A)   (B)   (C)

Structures A and B are equivalent and therefore their contribution to the resonance hybrid (C) is more than any other resonance structure.

(11) Structures which involve charge separation make less contribution to the resonance hybrid than those structures which do not involve charge separation.

$$CH_2 = CH - CH = CH_2 \longleftrightarrow \overset{\oplus}{CH_2} - CH = CH - \overset{\ominus}{CH_2} \longleftrightarrow \overset{\ominus}{CH_2} - CH = CH - \overset{\oplus}{CH_2}$$

(A)   (B)   (C)

$$\longleftrightarrow \overset{\oplus}{CH_2} - \overset{\ominus}{CH} - C = CH_2 \longleftrightarrow \text{etc.}$$

(D)

Structures B, C and D are less stable due to separation of charges. The structure (A) is a more stable structure as it does not involve any charge separation.

1.12.2.3 Types of Resonance

There are two types of resonance:

(1) Isovalent resonance: If each contributing structure of resonance hybrid contains the same number of bonds, it is known as isovalent resonance. For example, carboxylate ion exhibits an isovalent resonance.

(2) Heterovalent resonance: If a resonance hybrid has contributing structures which contain different number of bonds, it is known as heterovalent resonance. For example, resonance in vinyl nitrile. In this resonance, bonding electrons are delocalized.

$$CH_2 = CH - C \equiv N\!: \longleftrightarrow CH_2 = CH - \overset{\oplus}{C} = \overset{\ominus}{N}\!: \longleftrightarrow \overset{\oplus}{CH_2} - CH = C = \overset{\ominus}{N}\!:$$

1.12.2.4 Mesomeric Effect (M) or Resonance Effect (R)

It takes place in unsaturated and especially in conjugated systems via their π-electrons. It causes permanent polarization. The permanent polarization of a group conjugated with a π-bond or a set of π-bonds is transmitted through π-electrons of the system resulting in a different distribution of electrons in the unsaturated chain. This kind of electron redistribution is called mesomeric effect. Thus, the mesomeric effect refers to the polarity produced in a molecule as a result of interaction between two π-bonds or a π-bond and lone pair of electrons. The effect is transmitted along a chain in a similar way as are inductive effect. Mesomeric effect or resonance effect is denoted by M or R respectively.

Consider the example of carbonyl ($\diagdown$C=O) group. We know that carbonyl group is a resonance hybrid.

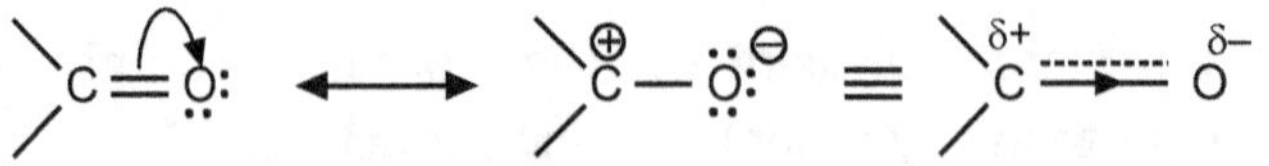

The mesomeric effect or resonance effect is shown by double headed arrow ($\leftrightarrow$).

If the carbonyl group is conjugated with a C=C, the above polarization will be transmitted via the π-electrons of the carbon chain.

Types of mesomeric effect or resonance effect : There are two types of mesomeric or resonance effect.

(1) Positive mesomeric (or resonance) effect (+M or +R effect): In the +M or +R effect the direction of electron displacement is away from the group. A group or atom is said to have +M or +R effect if the direction of electron displacement is away from it. This effect is shown by groups having lone pair of electrons.

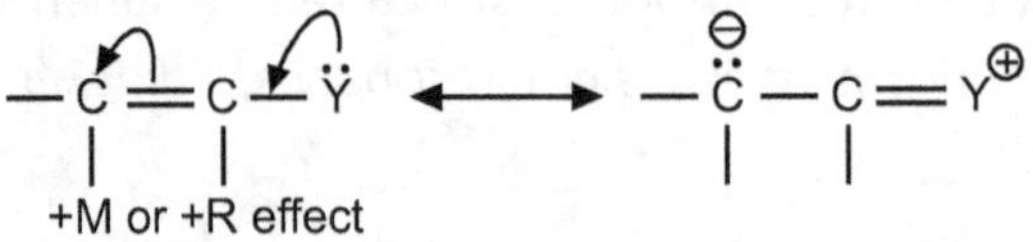

This effect extends the degree of delocalization and imparts stability to the molecule.

+ M or +R effect groups :

Halogens (F, Cl, Br, I), NH_2, $-OH$, $-OCH_3$, NR_2 and $-SR$.

The NH_2 group conjugated with C=C brings about electron displacement as shown below:

+M or +R effect activates benzene nucleus for electrophilic substitution (S_E) reaction at *o*- and *p*- positions, hence +M or +R effect groups are *o*- and *p*- directing. The +M or +R effect of chlorine atom is shown below.

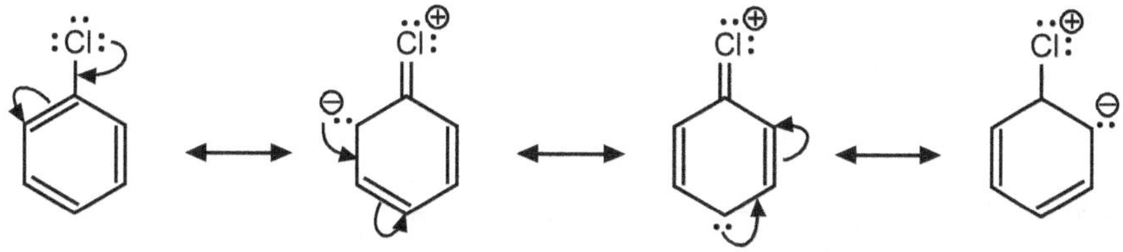

(2) Negative mesomeric (or resonance) effect (–M or –R effect): In the –M effect, π-electron displacement takes place towards the electron withdrawing group (but away from conjugated system). A group or atom is said to have –M effect if the direction of electron displacement is towards it. –M or –R effect is pictorially represented as follows :

–M or –R effect groups :

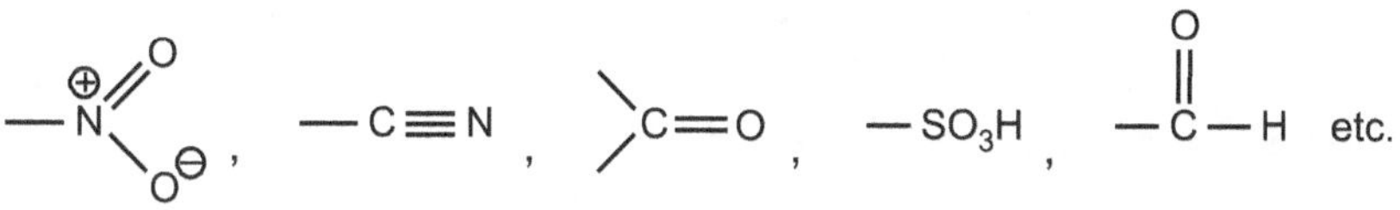

–M or –R effect deactivates benzene ring for electrophilic substitution but activates for nucleophilic substitution reaction. –M or –R effect groups are *m*-directing. –M or –R effect of nitro group is shown below.

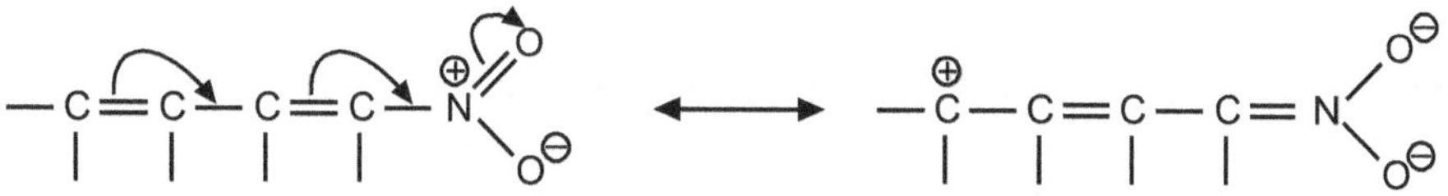

Mesomeric effect does not depend upon the presence of a reagent.

The inductive effect and mesomeric effect indicate the charge distribution in a molecule. Thus, they provide an effective way of determining the point of attack of electrophile and nucleophiles on the molecule.

1.12.3 Electromeric Effect

When a double or a triple bond is exposed to an attack by an electrophilic reagent, the two π-electrons which form the π bond are completely transferred to one atom or the other. The electromeric effect is represented as:

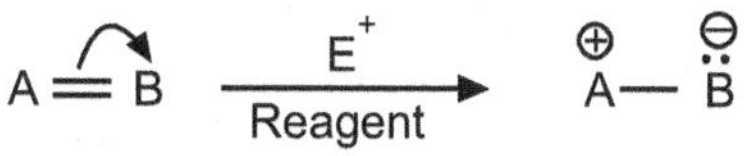

The curved arrow shows the displacement of the electron pair. The atom A has lost its share in the electron pair and B has gained this share. As a result, A acquires a positive charge and B a negative charge.

For example,

$$H - C = C - H \xrightarrow{\quad E^+ \quad} H - \overset{\oplus}{C} - \overset{\ominus}{C} - H$$

If an electrophile is removed, charge disappears and substrate attains its original form. Thus, this effect is reversible and temporary. The electromeric effect is denoted by E.

1.12.3.1 Types of Electromeric Effect

There are two types of electromeric effect depending upon the nature of the group or atom attached to the π bonded carbon atom.

(i) Positive Electromeric Effect (+_E_ effect): When the displacement of π-electrons is towards the attacking reagent, it is known as +_E_ effect.

For example,

$$C = C \quad + \quad H^{\oplus} \longrightarrow \overset{\oplus}{C} - C$$

(ii) Negative Electromeric Effect (–_E_ effect): When the displacement of π-electrons is away from the attacking reagent, it is known as -_E_ effect.

For example,

$$C = O \quad + \quad CN^{\ominus} \longrightarrow C - O^{\ominus}$$

Consider an example of nucleophilic attack by chloride ion on vinyl cyanide.

It is –E effect of cyano group which is directing the orientation of attack of chloride ion as shown above. Other such groups which cause –E effect are $-NO_2$, –NO, CHO, –COOH etc.

1.12.4 Hyperconjugation

If the alkyl groups having at least one hydrogen atom on the α-carbon are attached to an unsaturated carbon atom (C = C) or a vacant _p_-atomic orbital (A.O.), then they release electrons by a mechanism which is similar to that of the electromeric effect. This mechanism of release of electrons due to the presence of the system H – C – C = C or H – C – C$^+$ is known as hyperconjugation. Hyperconjugation involves delocalization of C – H sigma electrons into an adjacent _pi_ system or into a vacant p-atomic orbital. Hyperconjugative effect increases the electron density at C = C bond or in the empty _p_-atomic orbital.

A hyperconjugation, therefore is a special type of resonance effect where a C – H α-bond snaps and the σ-electron pair is delocalized on to a C = C bond or a vacant p- AO. Since, in the resonating forms no bond exists between the C and H atoms this phenomenon is also termed as no bond resonance. The concept of hyperconjugation was developed by Baker and Nathan and is also known as Baker and Nathan effect.

This effect plays an important role on the rate and regioselectivity of the electrophilic substitutions of the alkyl benzene and also on the stability of alkenes and reaction intermediates.

For example.

The hyperconjugation effect in toluene increases electron density on o- and p- positions.

1.12.4.1 Applications of Hyperconjugation

(a) Heat of hydrogenation: Greater the number of α-hydrogen, greater is the stability and thus lower heat of hydrogenation. For example,

$$CH_2 = CH_2 < CH_3 - CH = CH_2 < CH_3 - \underset{\underset{CH_3}{|}}{C} = CH_2 < CH_3 - \underset{\underset{CH_3}{|}}{C} = CH - CH_3 < CH_3 - \underset{\underset{CH_3}{|}}{C} = \overset{\overset{CH_3}{|}}{C} - CH_3$$

(b) Stability of carbocations: Greater the number of α-hydrogens, greater is the stability of carbocation. For example,

(i)

$$\overset{\oplus}{CH_3} < CH_3 - \overset{\oplus}{CH_2} < CH_3 - \underset{\underset{CH_3}{|}}{\overset{\oplus}{CH}} < CH_3 - \underset{\underset{CH_3}{|}}{\overset{\oplus}{C}} - CH_3$$

No. of ⟶ 0   3   6   9
hyperconjugative
structures

(ii)

$$CH_3 - \overset{\oplus}{CH_2} < CH_3 - CH_2 - \overset{\oplus}{CH_2} < \underset{H_3C}{\overset{H_3C}{>}}CH - \overset{\oplus}{CH_2} > \underset{H_3C}{\overset{H_3C}{>}}H_3C - CH - \overset{\oplus}{CH_2}$$

No. of ⟶ 3   2   1   0
hyperconjugative
structures

(c) Dipole moment: Hyperconjugation causes the development of charge. Hence, it also affects the dipole moment of the molecule. For example,

$$CH_2 = CH_2 < CH_3 - CH = CH_2$$

1.12.5 Steric Effect

The volume of atoms or groups on the reacting part of an organic species has varied types of effect on the stability and reactivity of the species and those effects may be called steric effect.

1.12.5.1 Types of Steric Effect

There are four types of steric effects.

(i)   Steric strain (ii) Steric acceleration (iii) Steric retardation (iv) Electron-availability.

(i) Steric strain: If the constituent atoms and groups of a chemical species require more space than what is available for them, due to their bulky nature, the mechanical interference amongst the groups and atoms takes place and the species is said to be under steric strain. Consequently, distortion of normal bond angle occurs, which in turn brings instability to it. For example, owing to the great bulk of the tert-butyl group and small available space for it, 1, 2, 3-tri-tert-butylbenzene is under strain and very difficult to prepare.

Even small groups may cause steric strain due to the overlap of their van der Waals radii known as van der Waals strain. This strain develops repulsion between two such non-bonded atoms or groups which is called steric repulsion.

(ii) Steric acceleration: Strained chemical species try to avoid the steric strain and thus react readily to produce less strained species. When a steric strain speeds up a reaction, it is said to be steric acceleration and as the steric strain has assisted the reaction to occur, it is called steric assistance. For example, tertiary alkyl halides on hydrolysis form tertiary carbenium ions readily, this is because of their tendency to get free from the steric strain.

(iii) Steric retardation: A complete physical blockage due to the greater bulk of the groups and atoms on the reactive part of the substrate hinders some reactions to occur or slows down the rate and the phenomenon is called steric retardation or steric inhibition or steric hindrance. For example, it is very difficult to esterify 2, 6-disubstituted benzoic acid. This is because of the steric hindrance, due to the crowding of bulky –COOH group and two ortho substituents which physically block to attack C atom of the -COOH group.

(iv) Steric effect and Electron availability: Sometimes steric hindrance increases the electron availability on a particular atom or group in a chemical entity. For example, in N, N-dimethyl-o-toluidine, three methyl groups are very closely spaced. This creates steric strain in the molecule. To avoid steric strain, –N(Me)$_2$ group with its lone pair of electrons rotates about the C-N bond axis, and as a result the filled sp^3 orbital of the nitrogen atom is no longer parallel to the six p orbitals of the sp^2 carbon atoms constituting the benzene ring.

Thus, delocalization of the lone pair of electrons of the nitrogen atom cannot occur. This increases electron availability on the N atom; whereas in aniline those electrons are less available. As there is no steric strain, the electron pair on nitrogen atom in aniline completely delocalises. Thus, electron availability on nitrogen atom in aniline is low.

1.12.6 Tautomerism

When two interconvertible structural isomers co-exist in equilibrium with each other, the phenomenon is called as tautomerism and the isomers as tautomers. Tautomers are constitutional isomers. Tautomerism is symbolized by double headed arrow. Tautomers have real existence and they are isolable. The positions of the atomic nuclei are not the same in tautomers.

1.12.6.1 Classification of Tautomerism

All the compounds exhibiting tautomerism are classified under three headings.

(i)　Open-system of tautomerism or Ionotropy.

(ii)　Ring-chain tautomerism.

(iii)　Valence tautomerism.

(i) Open-system of tautomerism or Ionotropy: In this type of tautomerism, both tautomers are open chain substances. This can be further divided into two groups:

(a) Cationotropy: Tautomerism is called cationotropy when atoms or groups of atoms shift as cations. A great majority of cationotropy, however, is prototropy in which protons are involved. For example, keto- enol tautomerism.

Ethyl acetoacetate (EAA) exists in two forms, the keto and enol form.

Keto (93%)　　　　　　　　　　　　　　　Enol (7%)

Ethyl acetoacetate shows properties of ketonic group as well as that of enolic group (the –OH group attached to double bond). This indicates that both these molecules are in equilibrium with each other. These two differ from each other in (i) electron distribution and (ii) position of a relatively small atom such as hydrogen. The phenomenon is therefore said to as prototropy. Such interactions are catalyzed by both acids and bases. Following are some examples of prototropy.

$$R - \underset{\underset{H}{|}}{CH} - \overset{\oplus}{N} = O \quad \rightleftharpoons \quad R - CH = \overset{\oplus}{N} - OH$$

Nitro form   Acid nitro form

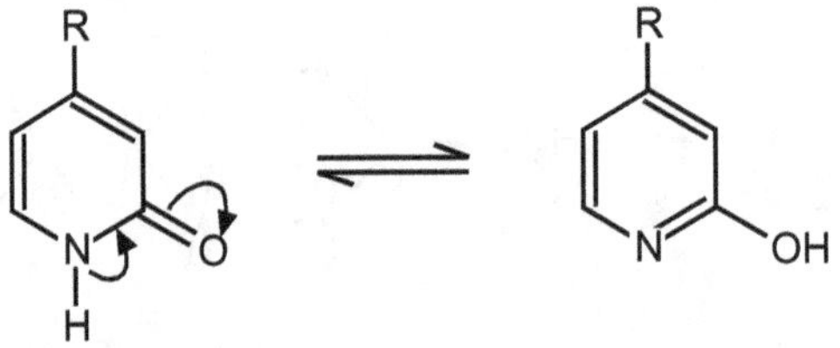

Amide form   Imidol form

(b) Anionotropy: Tautomerism is called anionotropy when atoms or groups of atoms shift as anions. For example,

$$CH_3 - CH = CH - CH_2Cl \quad \rightleftharpoons \quad CH_3 - CHCl - CH = CH_2$$

Crotyl chloride   Methylvinylcarbinyl chloride

$$C_6H_5 - CH(OH) - CH = CH_2 \quad \rightleftharpoons \quad C_6H_5 - CH = CH - CH_2(OH)$$

α-Phenyl allyl alcohol   Cinnamyl alcohol

(ii) Ring-chain tautomerism: In this type of tautomerism, one form is cyclic and other is acyclic (open-chain). The two forms of this type differ in the position of either a proton or anionic atom or group. For example, tautomerism in carbohydrate.

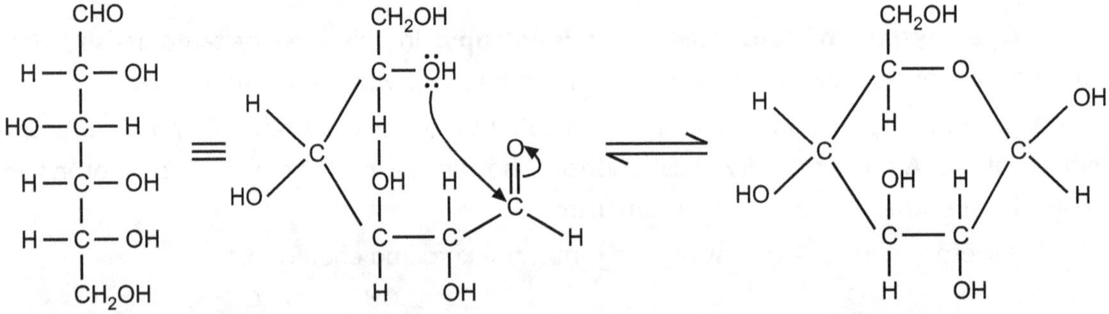

D-glucose   D-glucose   β-D-glucose
                              (Coiled structure)

(iii) Valence tautomerism: In this type of tautomerism, the two tautomers differ only in the redistribution of valencies.

QUESTIONS

Q.1   What is hybridization? Explain the types with suitable example.

Q.2   Distinguish between sigma and pi bonds.

Q.3   Write a note on sigma and pi bonds.

Q.4   Write a short note on hybridization.

Q.5   Define :

(1) Covalent bond

(2) Hybridization

Q.6   Write a note on

(i) Electronegativity.

(ii) Atomic orbitals.

(iii) Molecular orbitals.

(iv) Inductive effect

(v) Bond energy

Q.7   Write a note on: (i) sp^3 hybridization (ii) sp^2 hybridization (iii) sp hybridization.

Q.8   Discuss orbital structure of ethane, ethylene and acetylene

Q.9   Define or explain the following terms with example.

(i) Covalent bond

(ii) Ionic bond

(iii) Sigma bond

(iv) pi bond

(v) Hybridization

(vi) Bond fission

(vii) Tautomerism

(viii) Hyperconjugation

(ix) Mesomeric effect

(x) Steric effect

Q.10   Define and illustrate resonance.

Q.11   What is inductive effect? Explain it with suitable example.

Q.12   Write in short about tautomerism.

Q.13   Draw as much resonance structures as you can for following:

(a) Benzaldehyde

(b) Phenol

(c) Aniline

(d) Acetophenone

(e) Acetanilide

(f) Acetic acid

(g) Formic acid

(h) Nitrobenzene

(i) *p*-Nitrophenol

Q.14   What is hyperconjugation? Explain with suitable example.

Q.15   Write a note on hyperconjugation.

Q.16   Explain in brief about factors affecting electron availability with suitable examples.

Q.17   What is resonance ? Explain the rules of resonance with suitable example.

Q.18   Differentiate between resonance and tautomerism.

Q.19   What is resonance? State the conditions necessary for resonance and discuss its applications.

Q.20   Arrange the following in decreasing order of the base strength and give reason:

Ammonia, aniline, m-nitroaniline, and p-nitroaniline

Q.21   Draw as many resonance structures as you can for the following species.

(a)   OH

(b) $CH = CH - \overset{\overset{\displaystyle OH}{|}}{C} = O$

Q.22   Give reason : Chloroform is polar whereas carbon tetrachloride is non polar.

Q.23   Comment briefly on various factors affecting the availability of electrons at individual atoms and bonds.

Q.24   Give reason : N, N, 2, 6-tetramethyl aniline is six times more basic than N,N-dimethyl aniline.

Q.25   Compare the stability of following pairs of ions.

i) $CH_3 - CH_2 - O^-$, $CH_2 = CH - O^-$

Q.26   Arrange the following compounds in the increasing acidity order (less acidic first):

i)   Phenol

ii) Cyclohexanol

iii) p-bromophenol

Q. 27   Distinguish between inductive and electromeric effects with suitable examples.

Chapter 2

NOMENCLATURE OF ORGANIC COMPOUNDS

2.1 INTRODUCTION

The term nomenclature means the system of naming of organic compounds. The name of the organic compound should be such that it can represent its structural features and hence can provide information on the properties of the compound.

Organic compounds are classified into two main groups depending on the nature of carbon chains they possess:

(1) Open chain: Organic compounds possessing open chains are called open chain or acyclic compounds or aliphatic compounds. e.g.

Neopentane   n-Butane

(2) Cyclic compounds: The compounds in which the terminal carbon atoms join with each other to form ring like structure are known as cyclic compounds.

These are of two main types:

(i) **Carbocyclic compounds:** A large number of organic compounds possess rings consisting of carbon atoms only; these are called **carbocyclic compounds.**

(a) Some of the carbocyclic compounds behave like aliphatic compounds and these are known as **alicyclic compounds.**

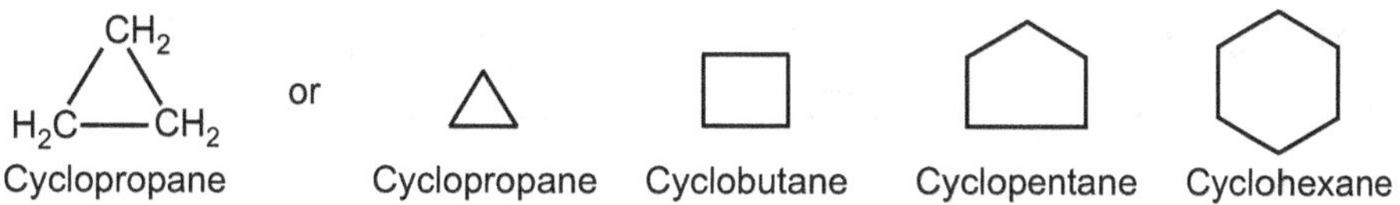

Cyclopropane   Cyclopropane   Cyclobutane   Cyclopentane   Cyclohexane

(b) There are other carbocyclic compounds having benzene ring and these are said to be **benzenoid aromatic compounds** as they possess characteristic smell.

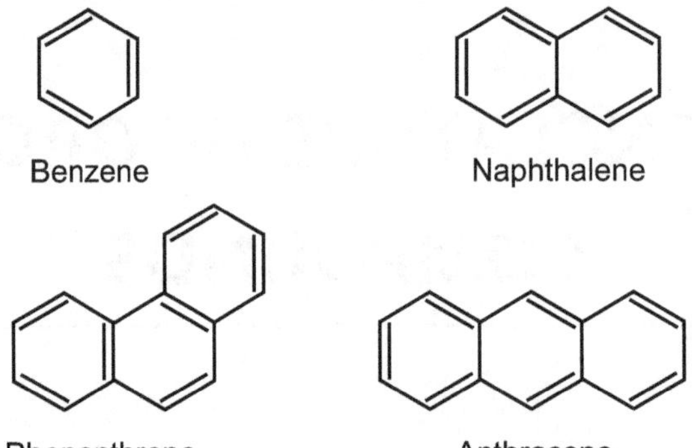

Benzene   Naphthalene

Phenanthrene   Anthracene

(ii) Heterocyclic compounds: The cyclic compounds which contain at least one atom other than carbon like O, N, S, etc. are termed as **heterocyclic compounds.**

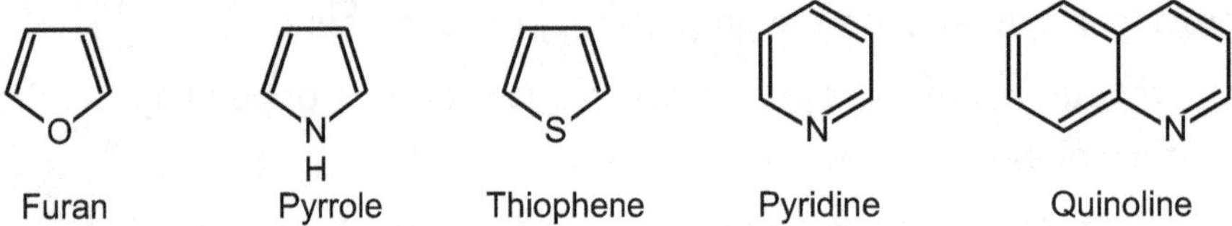

Furan   Pyrrole   Thiophene   Pyridine   Quinoline

2.2 FUNCTIONAL GROUPS

A group or a group of atoms which determines the properties or function of a compound is termed as functional group.

e.g., $R - NH_2$ ... Amines (Basic compounds)

$R - CONH_2$ ... Amides (Neutral compounds)

Most of the functional groups we shall come across are included in Table 2.1 which also contains details for their nomenclature.

Table 2.1 : Common functional groups in organic chemistry
(arranged in order of decreasing priority) and IUPAC nomenclature

Priority	Functional group	Formula	Prefix	Suffix
1	Cations		ammonio-	-ammonium
	e.g. Ammonium	$- NH_4^+$		
	Sulphonium	R_3S^+	Sulfonio-	-sulphonium
2	Carboxylic acids	$- COOH$	carboxy-	-oic acid
	Thiocarboxylic acids	$- COSH$	thiocarboxy-	-thioic acid
	Selenocarboxylic acids	$- COSeH$	selenocarboxy-	-selenoic acid
	Sulfonic acids	$- SO_3H$	sulfo-	-sulfonic acid
	Sulfinic acids	$- SO_2H$	sulfino-	-sulfinic acid
	Sulfenic acids	$- SOH$	sulfeno-	-sulfenic acid

Contd...

3	Carboxylic acid derivatives e.g.			
	Esters	– COOR	R-oxycarbonyl-	Alkyl alkanoate
	Acyl chlorides	– COCl	chlorocarbonyl-	-oylchloride
	Amides	– CONH$_2$	carbamoyl-	-amide
	Imides	– CON = C<	-imido-	-imide
	Amidines	– C(=NH) NH$_2$	amidino-	-amidine
4	Nitriles	– CN	cyano-	-nitrile
	Isocyanides	– NC	isocyano-	isocyanide
5	Aldehydes	– CHO	formyl-	-al
	Thioaldehydes	– CHS	thioformyl-	-thial
6	Ketones	>CO	oxo-	-one
	Thioketones	>CS	thiono-	-thione
7	Alcohols	– OH	hydroxy-	-ol
	Thiols	– SH	sulfanyl-	-thiol
	Selenols	– SeH	selanyl-	-selenol
8	Hydroperoxides	– OOH	hydroperoxy-	-hydroperoxide
9	Amines	– NH$_2$	amino-	-amine
	Imines	= NH	imino-	-imine
	Hydrazines	– NHNH$_2$	hydrazino-	-hydrazine
10	Ethers	– O –	-oxa-	ether
	Thioethers	– S –	-thio-	sulfide
11	Alkene	>C=C<	alkenyl-	-ene
12	Alkyne	—C≡C—	alkynyl-	-yne
13	Halides	– X	halo-	halide
14	Nitro	– NO$_2$	nitro-	---
15	Alkanes	—C—C—	alkyl-	-ane

2.3 HOMOLOGUS SERIES

A series of similar compounds which have same functional group, same general formula, similar chemical properties and one member different from other by – CH$_2$ – group is called as homologus series and members are called as homologues.

Structural Formula	Names
CH_3NH_2	Methyl amine
$CH_3CH_2NH_2$	Ethyl amine
$CH_3CH_2CH_2NH_2$	Propyl amine
$CH_3CH_2CH_2CH_2NH_2$	Butyl amine

This is a homologus series. This series have same functional group – NH_2, same general formula C_nH_{2n+1}. NH_2 show similar chemical properties and differ from one another by – CH_2 – group.

2.4 CLASSIFICATION OF C AND H ATOMS OF AN ORGANIC COMPOUND

2.4.1 Depending on the Modes of Arrangement of C Atoms in a Chain

There are four types of C atoms and three types of H atoms :

(a) **Primary or 1°C and H atoms :** The carbon atom which is not attached with other carbon or attached with one carbon is known as primary carbon and the hydrogens bonded to it are known as primary hydrogen atoms.

(b) **Secondary or 2°C and H atoms :** The carbon atom which is simultaneously linked with two other carbon atoms is known as secondary carbon atom and the hydrogens bonded to it are known as secondary hydrogen atoms.

(c) **Tertiary or 3°C and H atoms :** The carbon atom which is simultaneously bonded with three other carbon atoms is known as tertiary carbon atom and the hydrogen bonded to it is known as tertiary hydrogen atom.

(d) **Quaternary or 4°C atoms:** The carbon atom which is simultaneously bonded with four other carbon atoms is known as quaternary carbon atom.

e.g.,

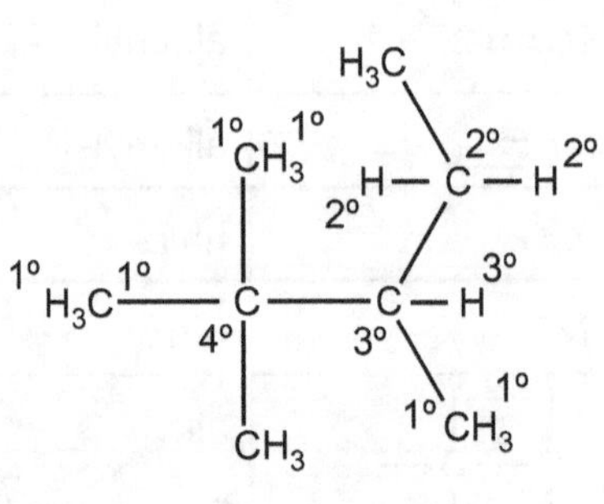

2.4.2 Depending on the Functional Group

In this method the relative positions of different C atoms in a molecule are designated with respect to the functional group it contains. These designations are done by small letters of Greek alphabet. The C atom directly attached to the functional group is designated as **α C atom**; the C atom next to it is indicated as **β C atom** and that next to β C is **γ C atom** and so on. Each of the H atoms is given the similar α, β, γ or δ designation as the C atom to which it is attached.

e.g.,

$$H_3C - C(CH_3)(CH_3) - CHO \quad \text{Functional group}$$

2.5 SYSTEMS OF NOMENCLATURE

There are two systems of nomenclature.

(1) Common name system (or Traditional or Trivial system).

(2) IUPAC system of nomenclature.

2.5.1 Common Name System

According to this system of nomenclature, the names are given to compounds according to their origins e.g. formic acid is derived from Greek word *'Formicus'* which means red ant. The sting of red ant contains formic acid. Similarly, the name acetic acid was derived from acetum (Latin: acetum means vinegar). Some other examples are given below.

(A) Alkanes:

Structural formula	Common name
CH_4	Methane
$H_3C - CH_3$	Ethane
H_3C $-CH_2-$ CH_3	Propane
$H_3C-CH_2-CH_2-CH_3$	n-Butane
$(CH_3)_2CH-CH_3$	Isobutane
$H_3C-CH_2-CH_2-CH_2-CH_3$	n-Pentane

Contd...

Structure	Name
(branched structure) CH_3 on CH, H_3C and CH_3 on C/H_2	Isopentane
(branched structure) $H_3C-C(CH_3)(CH_3)-CH_3$	Neopentane
(chain structure) $H_3C-CH_2-CH_2-CH_2-CH_3$ with CH_3	n-Hexane
(branched structure) CH_3, CH, H_3C, CH_2, C/H_2, CH_3	Isohexane
(branched structure) H_3C, C/H_2, C, CH_3, H_3C, CH_3	Neohexane

(B) Alkenes :

Structural formula	Common name
$H_2C=CH_2$	Ethylene
$H_3C-CH=CH_2$	Propylene
$H_2C=CH-CH_2-CH_3$	α-Butylene
$H_3C-CH=CH-CH_3$	β-Butylene
$H_3C-C(CH_3)=CH_2$	Isobutylene
$H_2C=CH-CH_2-CH_3$	α-Pentylene

(C) Alkynes :

Structural formula	Common name
$HC \equiv CH$	Acetylene
$H_3C - C \equiv CH$	Methylacetylene
$HC \equiv C - CH_2 - CH_3$	Ethylacetylene
$H_3C - C \equiv C - CH_3$	Dimethylacetylene

(D) Alcohols:

Structural formula	Common name
$H_3C - OH$	Methyl alcohol
$HO - CH_2 - CH_3$	Ethyl alcohol
$HO - CH_2 - CH_2 - CH_3$	n-Propyl alcohol
$HO - CH_2 - CH_2 - CH_2 - CH_3$	n-Butyl alcohol
$HO - CH_2 - CH_2 - CH_2 - CH_2 - CH_3$	n-amyl alcohol or n-pentyl alcohol
$HO - CH_2 - CH(CH_3) - CH_3$	Isobutyl alcohol
$HO - CH = CH_2$	Vinyl alcohol
$HO - CH_2 - CH = CH_2$	Allyl alcohol

(E) Alkyl halides :

Structural formula	Common name
H_3C—Cl	Methyl chloride
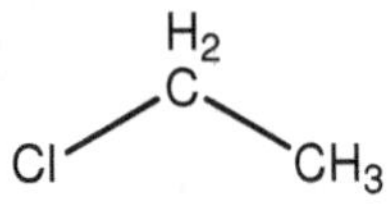 (ethyl chloride structure)	Ethyl chloride
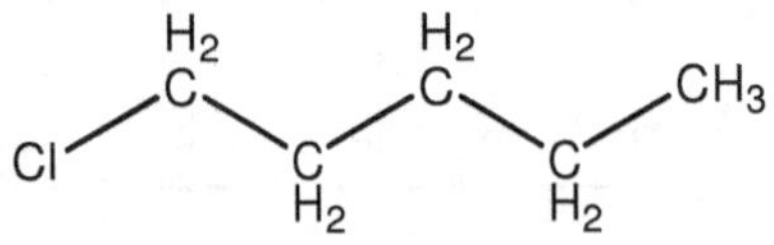 (pentyl chloride structure)	Pentyl chloride
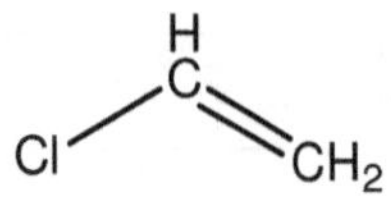 (vinyl chloride structure)	Vinyl chloride
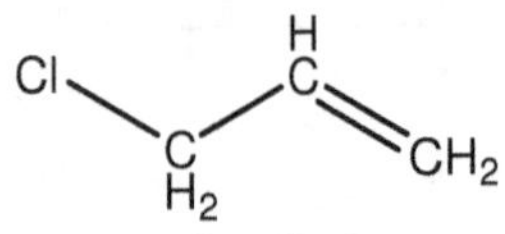 (allyl chloride structure)	Allyl chloride

(F) Carboxylic acids :

Structural formula	Common name
HCOOH	Formic acid
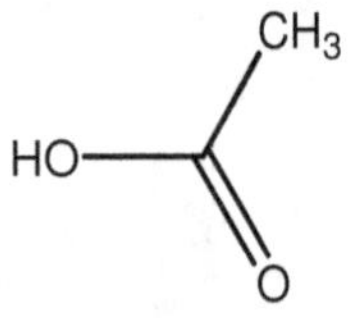 (acetic acid structure)	Acetic acid
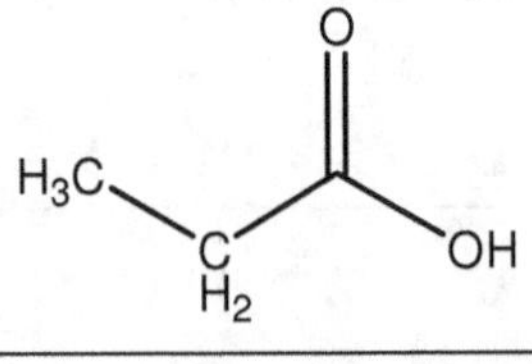 (propionic acid structure)	Propionic acid
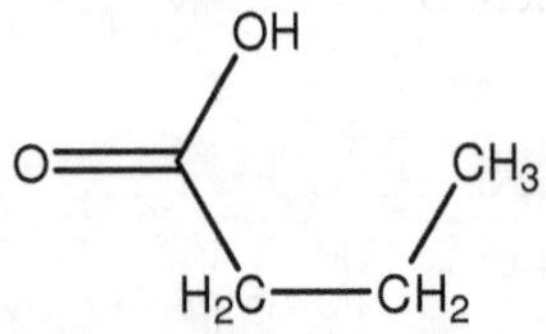 (n-butyric acid structure)	n-Butyric acid
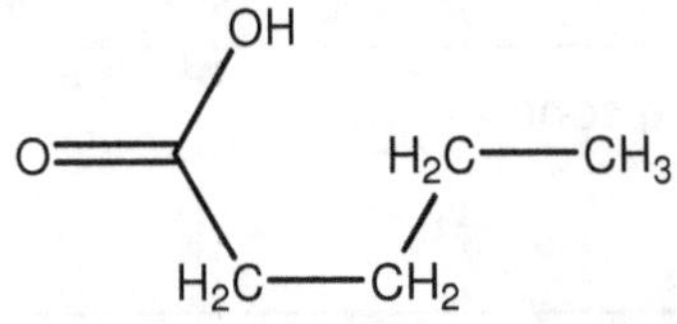 (n-valeric acid structure)	n-Valeric acid

(G) Aldehydes :

Structural formula	Common name
HCHO	Formaldehyde
CH_3CHO (structure shown)	Acetaldehyde
CH_3CH_2CHO (structure shown)	Propionaldehyde
$CH_3CH_2CH_2CHO$ (structure shown)	n–Butyraldehyde
$CH_3CH_2CH_2CH_2CHO$ (structure shown)	n–Valeraldehyde

(H) Acid halides :

Structural formula	Common name
HCOCl	Formyl chloride
CH_3COCl (structure shown)	Acetyl chloride
CH_3CH_2COCl (structure shown)	Propionyl chloride

(I) Esters :

Structural formula	Common name
$HCOOCH_3$	Methyl formate
$H_3CO-CO-CH_3$	Methyl acetate
$H_3C-CH_2-CO-OCH_3$	Methyl propionate

(J) Amides :

Structural formula	Common name
$HCONH_2$	Formamide
$H_3C-CO-NH_2$	Acetamide
$(H_3C)(CH_3)N-CHO$	N,N-Dimethyl formamide (DMF)

(K) Acid anhydrides :

Structural formula	Common name
$H_3C-CO-O-CO-CH_3$	Acetic anhydride
$H_3C-CH_2-CO-O-CO-CH_2-CH_3$	Propionic anhydride

(L) Ethers:

Structural formula	Common name
$H_3C-O-CH_3$	Dimethyl ether
$H_3C-CH_2-O-CH_2-CH_3$	Diethyl ether
$H_3C-O-CH_2-CH_3$	Ethyl methyl ether

(M) Ketones:

Structural formula	Common name
$H_3C-CO-CH_3$	Acetone or Dimethyl ketone
$CH_3-CH_2-CO-CH_2-CH_3$	Diethyl ketone
$H_3C-CH_2-CO-CH_3$	Ethyl methyl ketone

(N) Primary amines:

Structural formula	Common name
$H_2N - CH_3$	Methyl amine
$H_3C-CH_2-NH_2$	Ethyl amine
$H_2N-C_5H_9$ (cyclopentyl)	Cyclopentyl amine

(O) Secondary amines:

Structural formula	Common name
$H_3C-NH-CH_3$	Dimethyl amine
$H_3C-CH_2-NH-CH_2-CH_2-CH_3$	Ethyl propyl amine

(P) Tertiary amines:

Structural formula	Common name
$(CH_3)_3N$	Trimethyl amine
$H_3C-CH_2-N(CH_3)-CH_2-CH_3$	Diethyl methyl amine

(Q) Cyanides:

Structural formula	Common name
$N\equiv C-CH_3$	Acetonitrile
$N\equiv C-CH_2-CH_3$	Propionitrile

(R) Isocyanides :

Structural formula	Common name
$C\equiv N^+-CH_3$	Methyl isocyanide
$H_3C-CH_2-N^+\equiv C^-$	Ethyl isocyanide

2.5.2 IUPAC System of Nomenclature

(International Union of Pure and Applied Chemistry)

In the nineteenth century the number of organic compounds known was so large that it became difficult to remember individual names of organic compounds. In order to rationalize the system of nomenclature, an international congress of chemists was held in Geneva in 1892. It led to the development of Geneva system. Further improvement in Geneva system in 1931 led to the development of International Union of Chemists i.e. IUC system.

The IUC system has been further revised by the International Union of Pure and Applied chemistry due to practical difficulties. This revised system of nomenclature has been accepted all over the world and is abbreviated as IUPAC system of nomenclature.

According to this system of nomenclature, the name of organic compounds consist of three parts,

(a) Root word

(b) Suffix

(c) Prefix

(a) Root word: It tells us about the number of carbon atoms present in the compound.

Number of carbon atoms	Name of Alkane	Root word
01	Methane	Meth
02	Ethane	Eth
03	Propane	Prop
04	Butane	But
05	Pentane	Pent
06	Hexane	Hex
07	Heptane	Hept
08	Octane	Oct
09	Nonane	Non
10	Decane	Dec
11	Undecane	Undec
12	Dodecane	Dodec

(b) Suffix : It tells us about the nature of the carbon chain (i.e. whether saturated or unsaturated) and the functional group present in the compound. Suffix is added at the end of root word.

Functional group	Suffix	Functional group	Suffix
$-\overset{\mid}{\underset{\mid}{C}}-\overset{\mid}{\underset{\mid}{C}}-$	-ane	$-C=O$, NH_2	-amide
$-\overset{\mid}{C}=\overset{\mid}{C}-$	-ene	$-C=O$, OR	-oate
$-C\equiv C-$	-yne	$-C=O$, X	-oyl halide
$-OH$	-ol	$-\overset{\parallel}{\underset{O}{C}}-O-\overset{\parallel}{\underset{O}{C}}-$	-anhydride
$-O-$	ether	$-C\equiv N$	-nitrile
$H-C=O$, R	-al	$-\overset{+}{N}\equiv\bar{C}{:}$	Isonitrile or carbylamine
$R-C=O$, R	-one	$-\overset{\mid}{N}-$	-amine
$C=O$, OH	-oic acid	$-SO_2$, OH	-sulphonic acid

(c) Prefix: There are certain groups which are treated as substituents. These are added before root word.

Substituent group	Prefix	Substituent group	Prefix
–F	Fluoro	N=N	Diazo
–Cl	Chloro	$-OCH_3$	Methoxy
–Br	Bromo	–OR	Alkoxy
–I	Iodo	$-CH_3$	Methyl
$-NO_2$	Nitro	–R	Alkyl

Therefore the main constituents in the IUPAC name of organic compounds are:

Prefix + Root word + Suffix.

2.6 ALKYL

Alkane with one hydrogen atom less is called alkyl.

$$\text{Alkane} \longrightarrow \text{Alkyl} + H^+$$

$$C_nH_{2n+2} \xrightarrow{\;-H^+\;} C_nH_{2n+1}$$

Table 2.2 : Some alkyls along with their prefixes

Alkyl group	Name of alkyl group (Prefix)	Abbreviations	Corresponding alkane
— CH_3	Methyl	Me	Methane
— CH_2 — CH_3	Ethyl	Et	Ethane
— CH_2 — CH_2 — CH_3	n-propyl	Pr	Propane
— CH_3 — CH — CH_3 |	Isopropyl	i-Pr	Isopropane
— CH_2 — CH_2 — CH_2 — CH_3	n-butyl	n-Bu	Butane
CH_3 — CH — CH_2 — CH_3 |	Sec. butyl	Sec-Bu	Butane
— CH_2 — CH — CH_3 | CH_3	Isobutyl	i-Bu	Isobutane
— CH_2 — CH_2 — CH_2 — CH_2 — CH_3	n-pentyl	n-Pent	Pentane
— CH_2 — CH_2 — CH CH_3 | CH_3	Isopentyl	i-Pent	Isopentane
CH_3 | CH_3 — C — CH_2 — | CH_3	Neopentyl		Neopentane

2.7 BASIC PRINCIPLES

In IUPAC nomenclature, a number of prefixes and suffixes are used to describe the type and position of functional groups in the compound.

The steps for naming an organic compound are:

1. Identify the parent hydrocarbon chain (the longest continuous chain of carbon atoms).

2. Identify the functional group, if any (if more than one, identify principal functional group i.e. use one with highest priority):

   (i) Identify the position of the functional group.

   (ii) Number the carbon atoms in the parent chain. The functional group should have the lower number. The number is written before the name of the functional group suffix (such as -ol, -one, -al, etc.). If the functional group is at the end of a chain-only, (such as the carboxylic acid and aldehyde groups), it need not be numbered.

NOTE: If there are no functional groups, number in both directions, find the numbers of side-chains (the carbon chains that are not in the parent chain) in both directions. The end numbering should be such that the placements of side chains have a lower number, for example, 2,2,5-trimethylhexane is preferred over 2,5,5-trimethylhexane.

$$H_3\overset{6}{C} - \overset{CH_3}{\underset{H}{\overset{5}{C}}} - \overset{H}{\underset{H}{\overset{4}{C}}} - \overset{H}{\underset{H}{\overset{3}{C}}} - \overset{CH_3}{\underset{CH_3}{\overset{2}{C}}} - \overset{1}{CH_3}$$

2, 2, 5-Trimethylhexane

3. Identify the side-chains and number them.

    (i) If there are more than one of the same type of side-chain, add the prefix (di, tri, etc.) before it. The numbers for that type of side-chain will be given in ascending order and written before the name of the side-chain. If there are two side-chains on the same carbon atom, then the number will be written twice.

    (ii) Different side-chains will be grouped in alphabetical order (The prefixes di-, tri-, etc. are not taken into consideration for grouping alphabetically. For example, ethyl comes before dimethyl, as the "e" in "ethyl" is alphabetically precedent to the "m" in "methyl". The "di" is not considered).

4. Identify the remaining functional groups, if any, and group their numbers and ion names (such as hydroxy for –OH, oxy for =O, oxyalkane for –O–R, etc.) alphabetically with carbon chains using the same method.

5. Identify double/triple bonds. Number them with the number of carbon atoms before them. For example, a double bond between carbon atoms 3 and 4 is numbered as 3-ene. Many double bonds are named with a prefix (di-, tri-, etc.).

6. Arrange everything like this: Group of side chains and secondary functional groups + prefix of parent hydrocarbon chain (eth, meth) + double/triple bonds + primary functional group.

7. Add punctuation:

    (i) Write commas between numbers (2 5 5 becomes 2, 5, 5).

    (ii) Write hyphens between numbers and letters (2 5 5 trimethylhexane becomes 2, 5, 5-trimethylhexane).

    (iii) Successive words are merged into one word (trimethyl hexane becomes trimethylhexane).

2.8 VARIOUS RULES FOR WRITING IUPAC NOMENCLATURE

2.8.1 Nomenclature of Hydrocarbons

General Rules:

Rule 1: Select the longest continuous chain of carbon atoms as the parent chain. If some carbon-carbon multiple bond is present, the parent chain must contain the carbon atoms involved in it. Longest chain may be straight or branched. The number of carbon atoms present in the parent chain determines the word root. The carbon atoms which are not part of parent chain are considered as alkyl substituents and determine the prefixes.

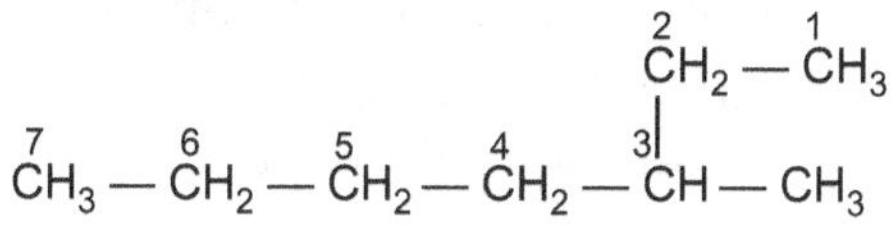

Prefix: methyl, Word root: heptane 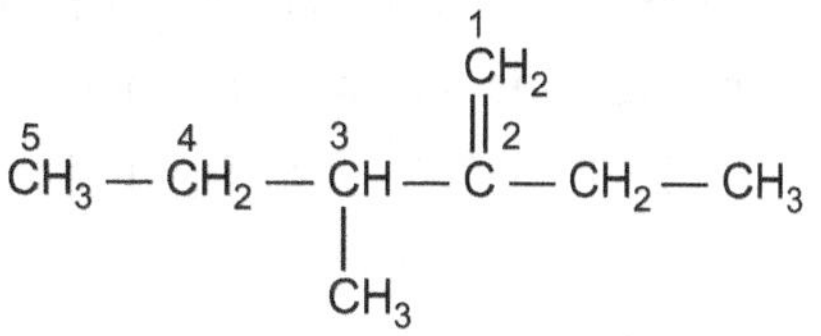   Prefixes: ethyl, methyl, Word root: Pentene

If two long chains are possible, the chain with maximum number of side chains is selected as the parent chain.

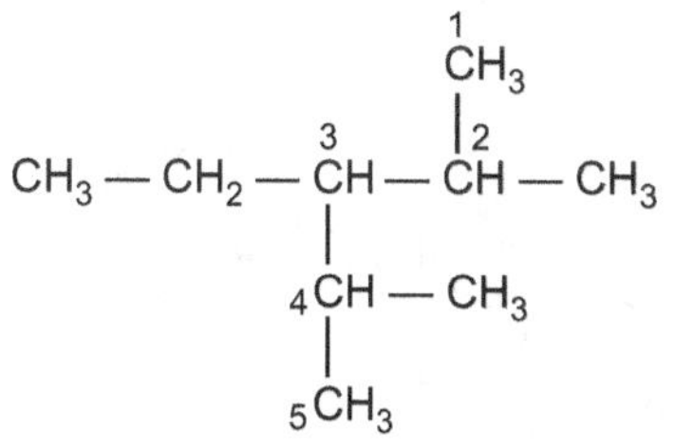

Prefixex: ethyl, dimethyl, Word root: pentane

The IUPAC name of compound consists of a base name with or without a prefix; such a prefix may be called a prefix to the base name.

Rule 2 : Lowest number rule:

Number the selected parent chain as 1, 2, 3 ... etc. starting from the end which gives smaller number to the carbon atoms carrying the substituent. The positions of the alkyl groups are indicated by the number of carbon atoms to which the alkyl group is attached.

e.g.

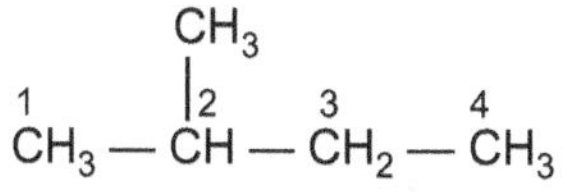

2-Methylbutane 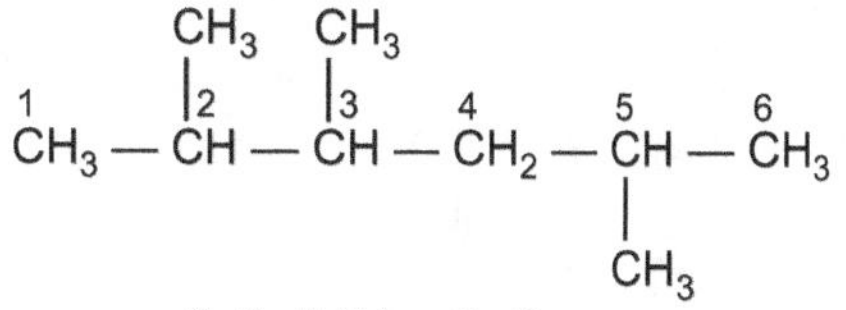   2, 3, 5-Trimethylhexane

In case of unsaturated hydrocarbons, the carbon atoms involved in the multiple bond should get the lowest possible number. Some examples are as given below.

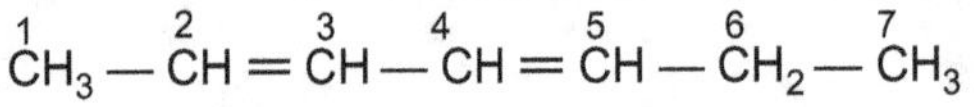

$$\overset{1}{C}H_3 - \overset{2}{C}H = \overset{3}{C}H - \overset{4}{C}H = \overset{5}{C}H - \overset{6}{C}H_2 - \overset{7}{C}H_3$$

2, 4-Heptadiene

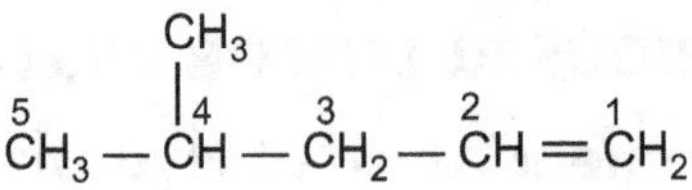

$$\overset{5}{C}H_3 - \overset{4}{C}H(\overset{}{C}H_3) - \overset{3}{C}H_2 - \overset{2}{C}H = \overset{1}{C}H_2$$

4-Methyl-1-pentene

$$\overset{4}{C}H_3 - \overset{3}{C}H(\overset{}{C}H_3) - \overset{2}{C} \equiv \overset{1}{C}H$$

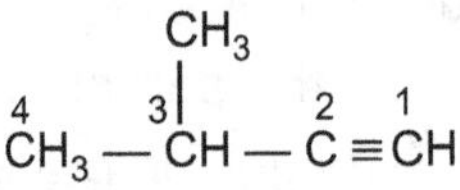

3-Methyl-1-butene

Numbering on alicyclic ring and benzene ring :

Alicyclic compounds consisting of one ring and also for benzene derivatives, the numbering of carbons starts from that carbon which carries the principal functional group and to that direction which gives the lowest number to the other substituents.

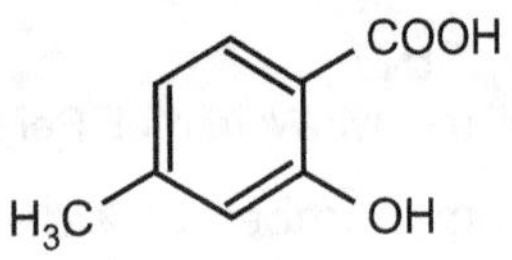

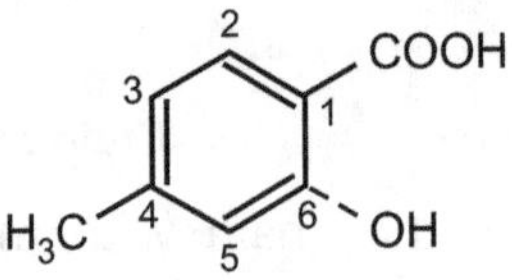

Wrong numbering 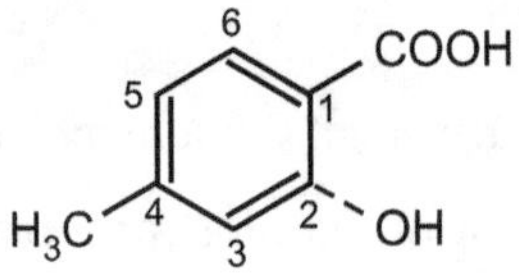   Correct numbering

e.g.

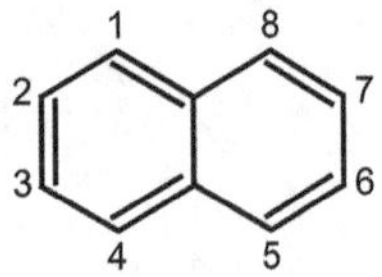

A 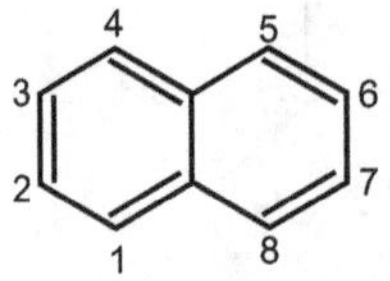   B 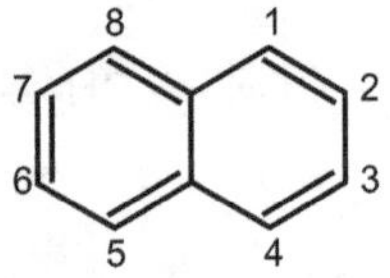   C 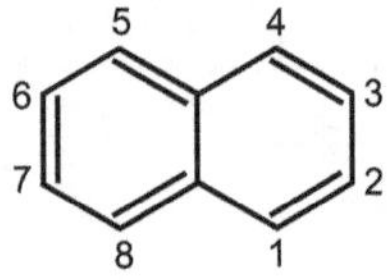   D

Numbering on carbons of anthracene being done as follows :

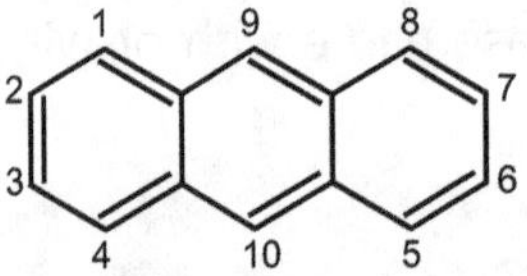

a 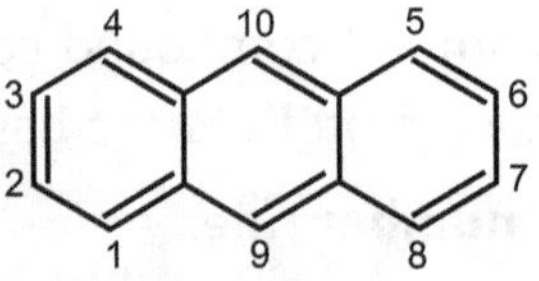   b

To number the naphthalene we must remember the following points :

a) The numbering will start from that position which will give the smallest number to the highest priority group as illustrated below:

e.g.

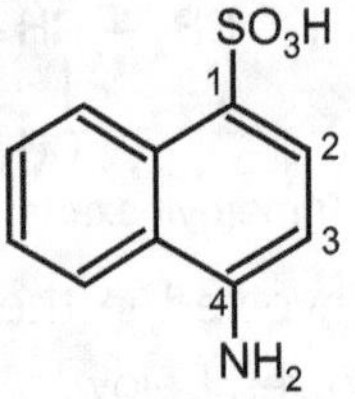

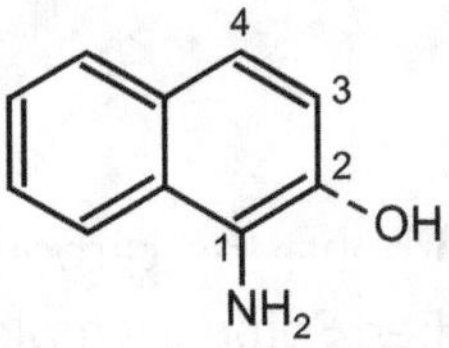

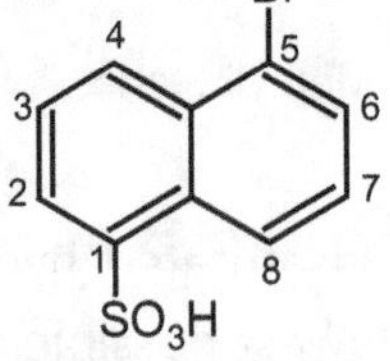

Numbering to heterocyclic compounds starts from hetero atom in compounds consisting of one hetero atom.

e.g.

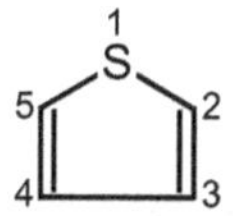

Thiophene 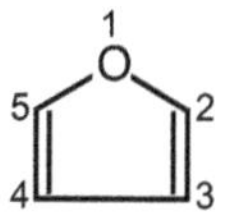 Furan 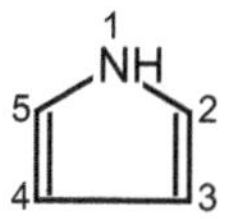 Pyrrole 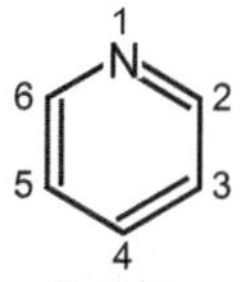 Pyridine 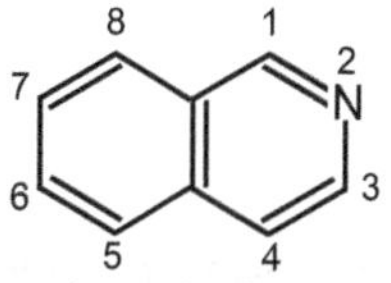 Isoquinoline

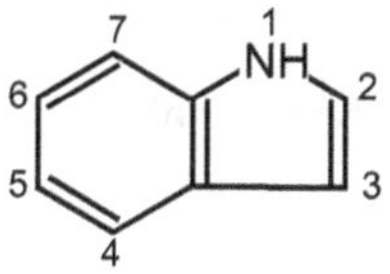

Indole 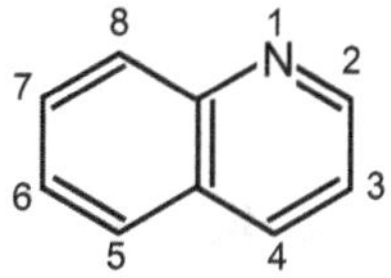 Quinoline

Rule 3: Use of prefixes Di, Tri, Tetra etc.

If the compound contains more than one similar alkyl groups, their positions are indicated separately and appropriate numerical prefixes: di = two, tri = three, tetra = four, penta = five, hexa = six, etc. are added to the name of the substituent. The positions of the substituents are separated by commas. For example,

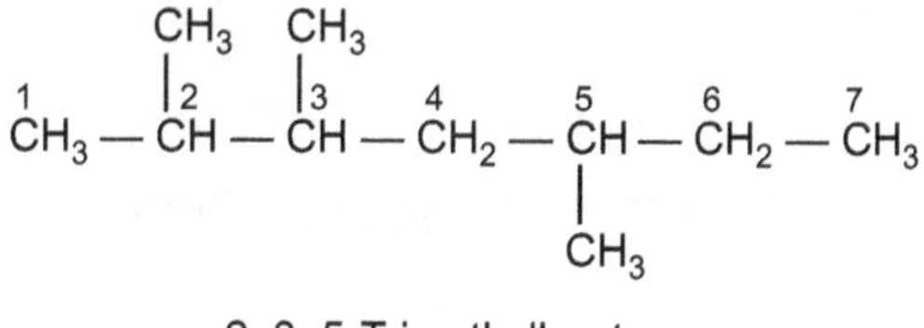

2, 3, 5-Trimethylheptane

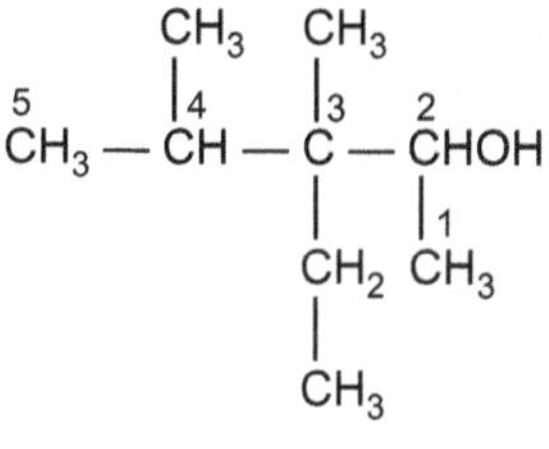

is 3-ethyl-3, 4-dimethyl-2-pentanol

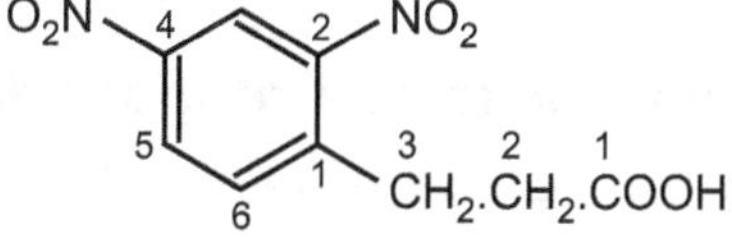

3-(2,4-Dinitrophenyl) propanoic acid

Rule 4: Alphabetical arrangement of prefixes:

If two or more substituents are present on the parent chain, then they are named in the alphabetical order. However, the numerical prefixes such as di, tri, tetra, etc., are not considered for alphabetical order.

For example,

$$\overset{9}{C}H_3 - \overset{8}{C}H_2 - \overset{7}{C}H_2 - \overset{6}{C}H - \overset{5}{C}H_2 - \overset{4}{C}H - \overset{3}{C}H_2 - \overset{2}{C}H - \overset{1}{C}H_3$$

with substituents CH_2-CH_3 at position 6, CH_3 at position 4, and CH_3 at position 2.

6-Ethyl-2,4-dimethyl nonane

If two different alkyl substituents are at equal distance from the two ends of parent chain, then they are numbered in alphabetical order. For example,

$$\overset{1}{C}H_3 - \overset{2}{C}H_2 - \overset{3}{C}H - \overset{4}{C}H_2 - \overset{5}{C}H - \overset{6}{C}H_2 - \overset{7}{C}H_3$$

with substituents C_2H_5 at position 3 and CH_3 at position 5.

3-Ethyl-5-methylheptane

Rule 5: Naming the complex alkyl substituents:

When the same complex alkyl groups occur more than once, it is indicated by numerical prefixes bis, tris, tetrakis, etc.

e.g.

1,3,5-tris-(1-ethylpropyl) cyclohexane

$$\overset{7}{C}H_3 - \overset{6}{C}H_2 - \overset{5}{C}H_2 - \overset{4}{C} - \overset{3}{C}H_2 - \overset{2}{C}H - \overset{1}{C}H_3$$

2-Methyl-4,4-bis(1-methylethyl)heptane

2.8.2 Nomenclature of Monofunctional Compounds

The various rules which are followed while writing the name of compounds containing one functional group are as described below.

Rule 1: Longest chain rule:

Select the longest continuous chain containing the carbon atom having functional groups like –CHO, –COOH, –CN, –CONH$_2$, etc. The number of carbon atoms in parent chain decides the word root.

Rule 2 : Lowest number rule:

The numbering of atoms in the parent chain is done in such a way that the carbon atom bearing the functional group gets the lowest number. In case the functional group does not have the carbon atom then the carbon atom of the parent chain attached to the functional group should get the least possible number.

Rules 3, 4 and 5 are used in similar way as described in case of hydrocarbons earlier.

For example,

$$CH_3 \overset{\underset{\displaystyle |}{CH_3}}{\underset{\underset{\displaystyle |}{\underset{\displaystyle CH_3}{}}}{\overset{2}{C}}} \overset{1}{CH_2OH}$$

2, 2-Dimethyl-1-propanol or
(2,2-Dimethylpropan-1-ol)

$$\overset{4}{CH_3} - \overset{3}{CH_2} - \overset{2}{CH_2} - \overset{1}{C}\overset{O}{\|} - OH$$

Butanoic acid

$$\overset{3}{CH_3} - \overset{2}{CH_2} - \overset{1}{C}\overset{O}{\|} - H$$

Propanal

$$\overset{3}{CH_3} - \overset{2}{\underset{\underset{\displaystyle OH}{|}}{CH}} - \overset{1}{CH_3}$$

Propan-2-ol

$$CH_3 \overset{\underset{\displaystyle |}{CH_3}}{\underset{\underset{\displaystyle |}{\underset{\displaystyle CH_3}{}}}{\overset{2}{C}}} \overset{1}{COCl}$$

2, 2-Dimethylpropanoyl chloride

$$\overset{5}{CH_3} - \overset{4}{CH_2} - \overset{3}{CH_2} - \overset{2}{\underset{\underset{\displaystyle C_2H_5}{|}}{CH}} - \overset{1}{CONH_2}$$

2-Ethylpentanamide

$$\overset{4}{CH_3} - \overset{3}{CH_2} - \overset{2}{CH_2} - \overset{1}{COOC_2H_5}$$

Ethyl butanoate

$$\overset{3}{CH_3} - \overset{2}{CH_2} - \overset{1}{CN}$$

Propanenitrile

$$CH_3 - CH_2 - CO$$
$$CH_3 - CH_2 - CO \Big\rangle O$$

Propanoic anhydride

$$CH_3COO^-NH_4^+$$

Ammonium ethanoate

1-Cyclohexylbutan-1-one

Cyclopentanethiol

$$CH_3 - O - \overset{1}{CH_2} - \overset{2}{CH_2} - \overset{3}{CH_3}$$

1-Methoxypropane

Ethoxycyclopentane

2.8.3 Nomenclature of Polyfunctional Compounds

The compounds which contain more than one functional group are known as polyfunctional compounds. If a compound contains several functional groups, the senior functional group will be considered as a principal functional group (suffix) while all other groups are treated as substituents. The order for preference of principal functional group along with prefix and suffix used is given in Table 2.1.

Some examples of compounds containing more than one type of functional groups:

$$\overset{3}{C}H_3 - \overset{2}{C}H(OMe) - \overset{1}{C}HO$$

2-Methoxypropanal

$$CH_3 - CH = CH - COOH$$

But-2-ene-1-oic acid

$$\overset{3}{C}H_3 - \overset{2}{C}H(OH) - \overset{1}{C}OOH$$

2-Hydroxypropanoic acid

$$\overset{4}{C}H_3 - \overset{3}{C}H(CH_3) - \overset{2}{C}(=O) - \overset{1}{C}OOH$$

3-Methyl-2-oxobutanoic acid

$$CN - \overset{3}{C}H_2 - \overset{2}{C}H_2 - \overset{1}{C}OOH$$

3-Cyanopropanoic acid

$$\overset{3}{C}H_2 = \overset{2}{C}(CH_3) - COOCH_3 \quad (CH_3)$$

3-Methyl 2-methyl prop-2-enoate

$$\overset{4}{C}N - \overset{3}{C}H_2 - \overset{2}{C}H_2 - \overset{1}{C}N$$

Butane-1, 4-dinitrile

$$\overset{1}{C}H_2(NH_2) - \overset{2}{C}H(CH_3) - \overset{3}{C}H_2 - \overset{4}{C}H_2(NH_2)$$

2-Methylbutane-1, 4-diamine

$$\overset{4}{O}HC - \overset{3}{C}H_2 - \overset{2}{C}H_2 - \overset{1}{C}(=O) - OH$$

4-Oxobutanoic acid

$$\overset{1}{C}H_2(NH_2) - \overset{2}{C}H(CH_3) - \overset{3}{C}H_2 - \overset{4}{C}H_2(NH_2)$$

2-Methylbutane-1, 4-diamine

$$\overset{2}{C}H_2(Cl) - \overset{1}{C}H_2(Br)$$

1-Bromo-2-chloroethane

$$\overset{4}{C}H_3 - \overset{3}{C}H = \overset{2}{C}(C(CH_3)_3) - \overset{1}{C}ONH_2$$

2-tert-Butylbut-2-enamide

2.8.4 Nomenclature of Aromatic Compounds

Aromatic compounds are cyclic compounds which contain one or more benzene rings. Benzene is the simplest hydrocarbon of aromatic series which has a planar cyclic ring of six carbon atoms having three alternate double bonds. Unsubstituted benzene can be numbered from any carbon as shown below:

Benzene

For monosubstituted benzene always start the numbering from the substituted carbon atom as shown below.

Ethyl benzene

Benzene forms only one monosubstituted derivative. However, it can form three disubstituted derivatives; namely 1, 2 or *ortho* (o-); 1, 3 or *meta* (m-) and 1, 4 or *para* (p-) derivatives.

ortho (or o-)   meta (or m-)   para (or p-)

Common name and IUPAC names of following substituted monocyclic aromatic hydrocarbons are same.

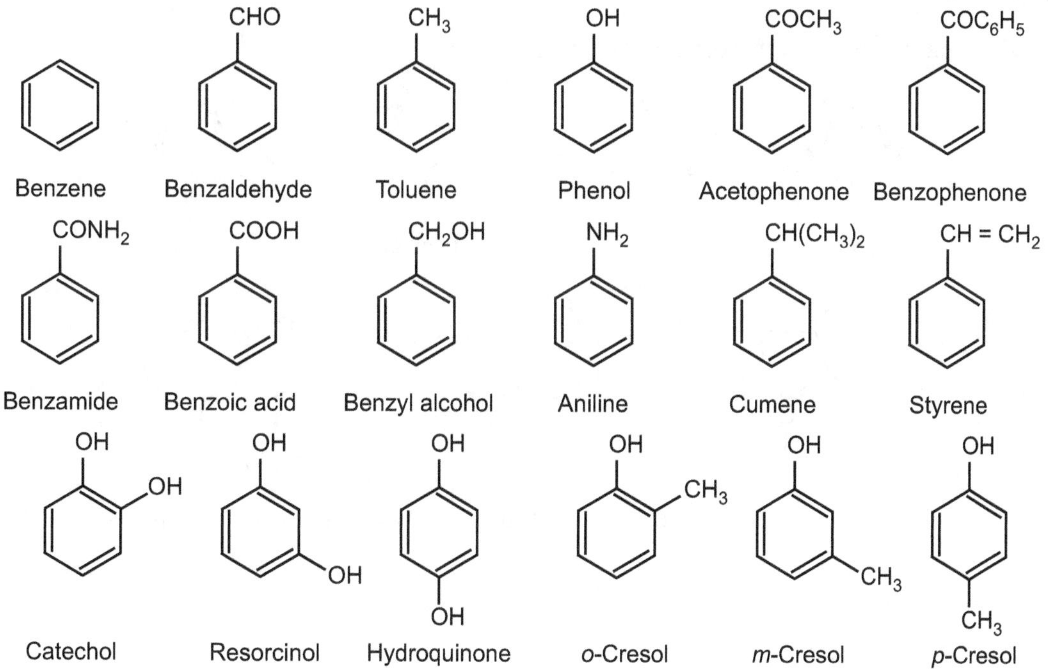

Benzene   Benzaldehyde   Toluene   Phenol   Acetophenone   Benzophenone

Benzamide   Benzoic acid   Benzyl alcohol   Aniline   Cumene   Styrene

Catechol   Resorcinol   Hydroquinone   *o*-Cresol   *m*-Cresol   *p*-Cresol

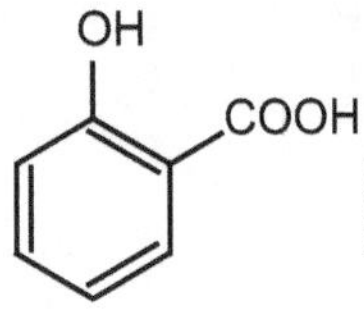

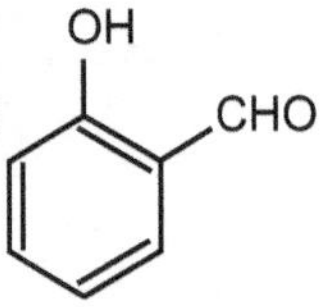

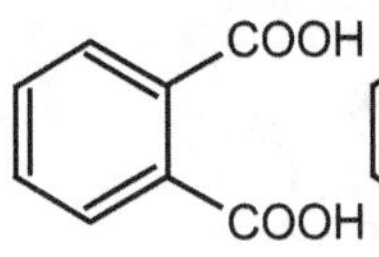

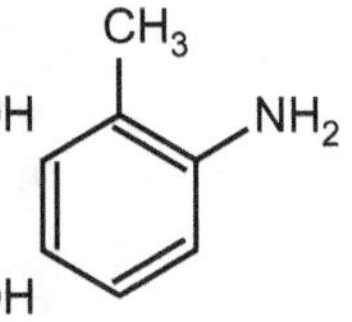

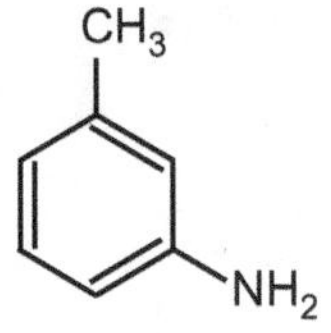

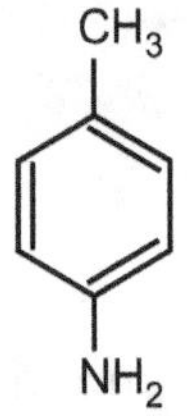

Salicylic acid   Salicylaldehyde   Phthalic acid   o-Toluidine   m-Toluidine   p-Toluidine

Common name and IUPAC name of following fused aromatic hydrocarbons are same:

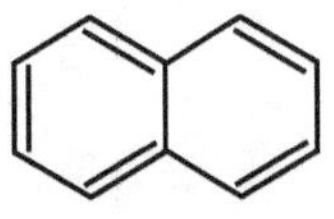

Naphthalene 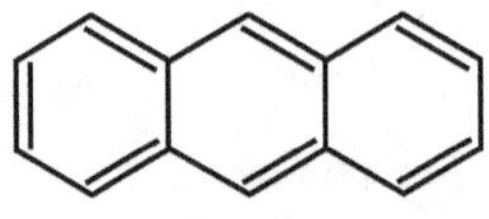   Anthracene 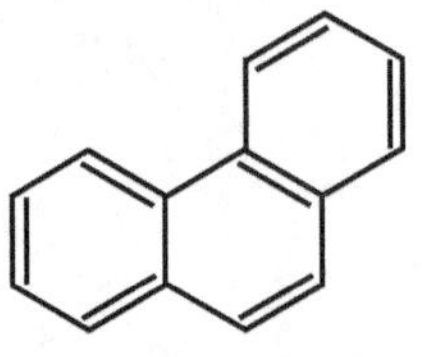   Phenanthrene

The root word of aromatic benzenoid compounds is derived from the name of ring it has.

e.g.

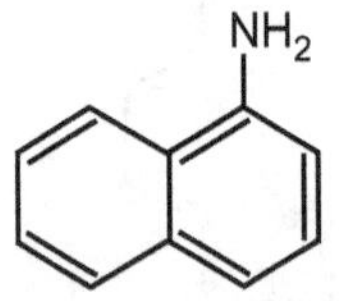

Root – derived from the name Naphthalene

Naphthaleneamine

The roots for following aromatic heterocyclic compounds are also derived from their parent rings.

IUPAC names of some heterocyclic compounds.

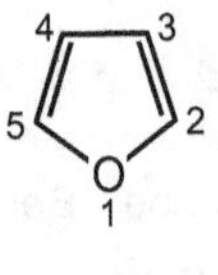

Furan 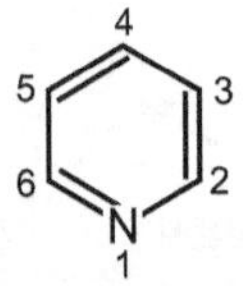   Pyridine 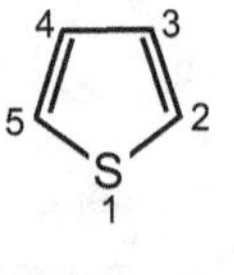   Thiophene 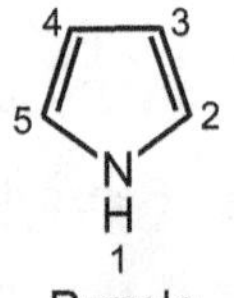   Pyrrole

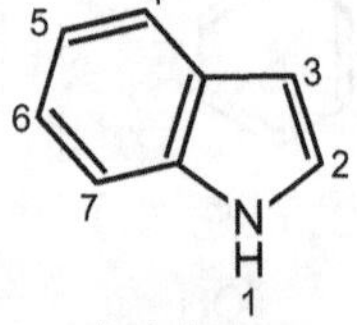

Indole 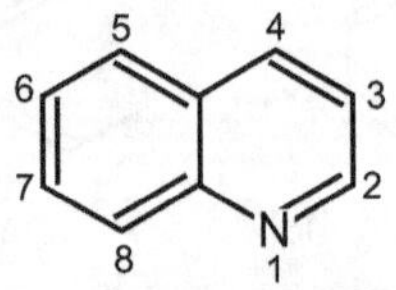   Quinoline 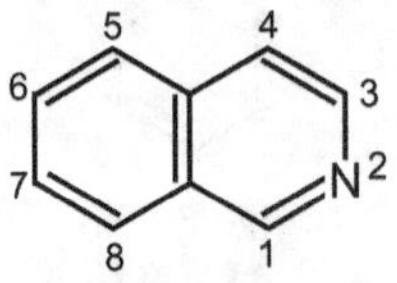   Isoquinoline

Thus the following compound is a derivative of pyrrole and its name is 5-Bromo-2-pyrrole carboxylic acid.

Prefix- 5-Bromo

Root word - Pyrrole

Suffix- Carboxylic acid

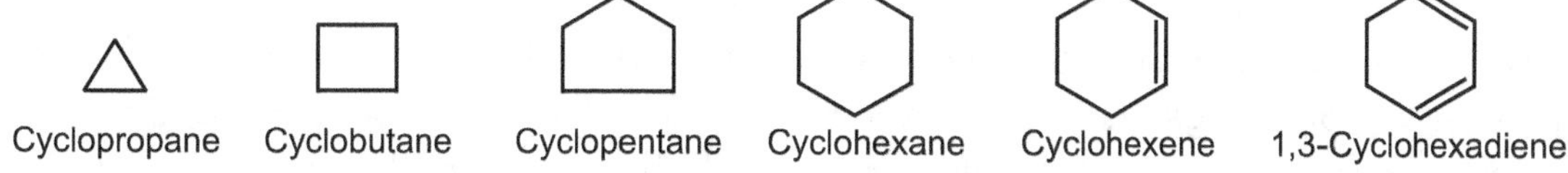

5-Bromo-2-pyrrole carboxylic acid

2.8.5 Nomenclature of Alicyclic Compounds

The name of the alicyclic compound is obtained by adding the prefix cyclo to the name of the corresponding straight chain hydrocarbons i.e. alkane, alkene or alkyne.

Cyclopropane   Cyclobutane   Cyclopentane   Cyclohexane   Cyclohexene   1,3-Cyclohexadiene

If only one substituent is present, there is no need to designate its position. If two or more substituents are present in the ring, their positions are indicated by numbering the carbon atoms of the ring (1, 2, 3, 4, ...). The numbering is done by using lowest number rule as discussed earlier.

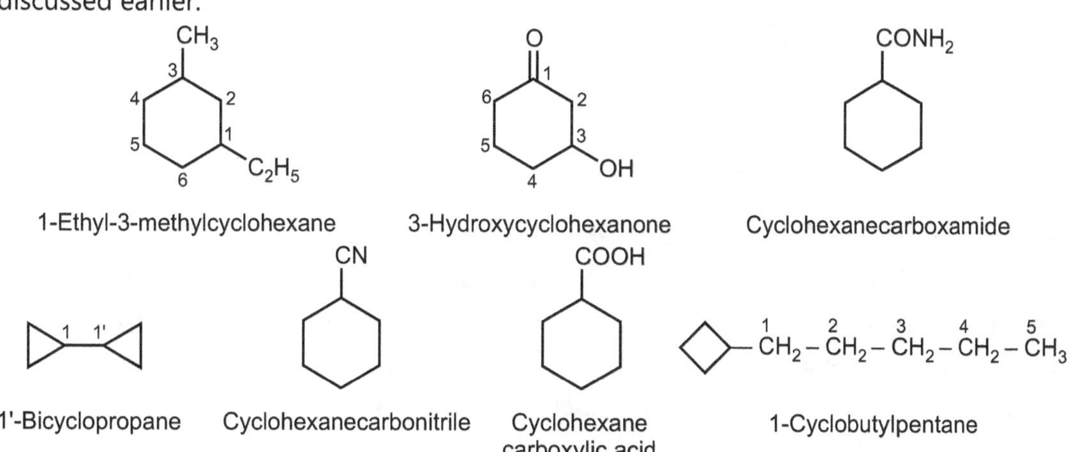

1-Ethyl-3-methylcyclohexane   3-Hydroxycyclohexanone   Cyclohexanecarboxamide

1-1'-Bicyclopropane   Cyclohexanecarbonitrile   Cyclohexane carboxylic acid   1-Cyclobutylpentane

2.8.6 Nomenclature of Bicyclic Compounds

Cycloalkanes consisting of two rings only and having two or more atoms in common are named by taking the prefix bicyclo followed by the number of carbon atoms representing the bridge (except bridge head positions) are written within bracket and then name of the alkane. The carbon atoms common to both the rings are called bridge heads and each bond or chain of atoms connecting the bridge head atoms is called a bridge.

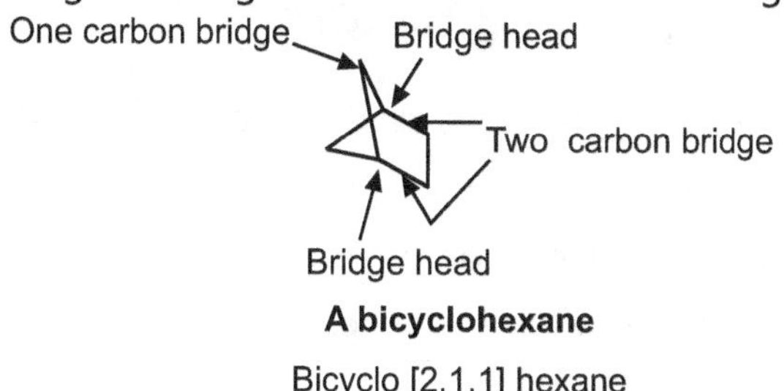

A bicyclohexane

Bicyclo [2.1.1] hexane

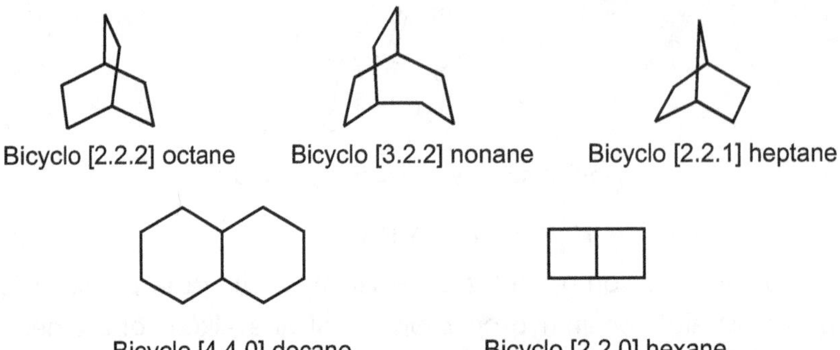

Bicyclo [2.2.2] octane   Bicyclo [3.2.2] nonane   Bicyclo [2.2.1] heptane

Bicyclo [4.4.0] decane   Bicyclo [2.2.0] hexane

For substituted bicyclic compounds number the bridged ring system beginning at one bridgehead, proceedings first along the lowest bridge to the other bridgehead, then along the next longest bridge back to the first bridgehead. The shortest bridge is numbered last.

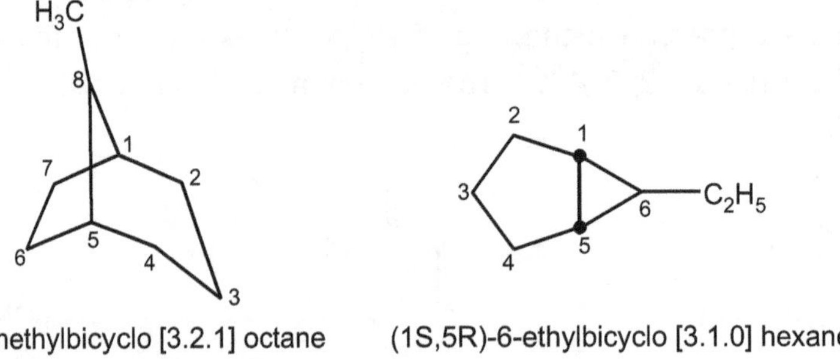

8-methylbicyclo [3.2.1] octane   (1S,5R)-6-ethylbicyclo [3.1.0] hexane

2.8.7 Nomenclature of Spiro Compounds

Two rings with one common atom is known as spiro ring system. In spiro ring system, the compound is indicated by the word 'spiro' followed by bracket indicating number of carbon atoms in each ring, ending with the alkane name describing number of carbons in the ring system including the spiro carbon. Numbering should start from smaller ring including the spiro carbon and then continued to the second ring.

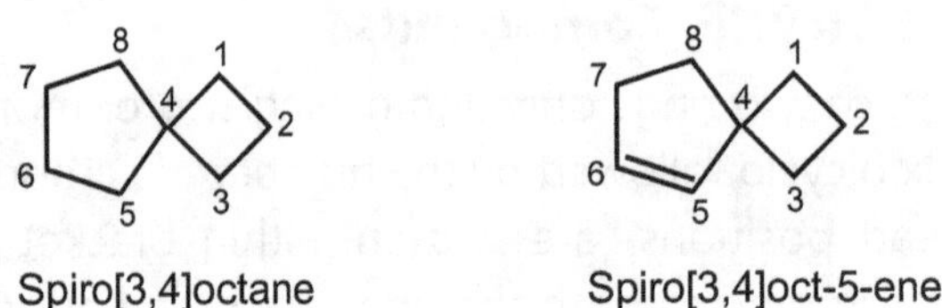

Spiro[3,4]octane   Spiro[3,4]oct-5-ene

QUESTIONS

Q.1   What are organic compounds ? Give classification of it in detail with examples.

Q.2   Define functional group. Give common functional groups used in organic chemistry.

Q.3   Draw the structures of following compounds:

(a)   2- Methyl N,N- dimethyl butanamine.

(b)   4- Amino-3-chloropentanenitrile.

(c)   Cyclopropane carboxylic acid.

(d)   4- Cyanobenzene sulphonic acid.

(e)   Methyl butenoate.

(f)   2(2-Methyl cyclobutyl) 2 butylnitrile.

(g)   1-Bromo-2-methyl propane.

(h)   1,2- Ethane diol.

(i)   2-Methyl-2-butane.

(j)   2-Methyl propanoic acid

(k)   1,3,5- Tribromobenzene

(l)   2-amino benzonitrile

(m)   Cyclohexane 1,4-dicarboxylic acid

(n)   Naphthalene 1,8-disulphonic acid

(o)   1,3,5- trichlorobenzene

(p)   2,2- Dichloropropionic acid

(q)   2,5- Hexanedione

(r)   3- Methylbutanamine

(s)   Ethanenitrile

(t)   2- Methyl-2-pentanol

(u)   2-Ethylbenzoic acid

(v)   3- Hydroxypentanal

(w)   4-Chloro-iodobenzene

(x)   Isopropyl benzene

(y)   4- Methyl pentanal

(z)   Ethyl propionate

(1)   4,4- Diphenyl-3- heptanone

(2)   1,2-Dichlorocyclopentane

(3)   Salicylic acid

(4)   3-oxobutanoic acid

(5)   Ethyl-4-amino benzoate

(6)   Cyclohexane 1,4-dicarboxylic acid

(7)   4-Chloro-3-nitropentanitrile

(8)   3-Phenyl-2-propenoic acid

Q.4 Write the IUPAC name of following compounds :

(a) $C_6H_5 - SO_3H$

(b) $CH_3 - CH_2 - \underset{\underset{\displaystyle CH_3}{|}}{CH} - CH_2 - OH$

(c) $CH_3 - \underset{\underset{\displaystyle CH_3}{|}}{\overset{\overset{\displaystyle CH_3}{|}}{N}} - CH - CH_2 - CH_3$

(d) cyclopropyl $- CH_3 - CH_2 - OH$

(e) 3-ethyl benzenethiol (ring with $-CH_2 - CH_3$ and HS)

(f) 8-hydroxyquinoline (quinoline ring with OH)

(g) cyclohexyl $-C(=O)-CH_2-CH_2-CH_3$

(h) cyclopentene $-C(=O)-\overset{-}{O}\overset{+}{N}H_4$

(i) $CH_3 - CH_2 - \overset{\displaystyle O}{C} - O - \overset{\displaystyle O}{C} - CH_2 - CH_3$

(j) $H_3C - \underset{\underset{\displaystyle CH_3}{|}}{\overset{\overset{\displaystyle CH_3}{|}}{C}} - OH$

(k) phenyl (with $COOH$) $- \underset{\underset{\displaystyle Br}{|}}{\overset{\overset{\displaystyle H}{|}}{C}} - \underset{\underset{\displaystyle H}{|}}{\overset{\overset{\displaystyle H}{|}}{C}} - CH_3$

(l) $H_3C - \overset{\overset{\displaystyle CH_3}{|}}{C} = CH_2$

(m) $H_3C - \underset{\underset{\displaystyle Br}{|}}{\overset{\overset{\displaystyle H}{|}}{C}} - \underset{\underset{\displaystyle Br}{|}}{\overset{\overset{\displaystyle H}{|}}{C}} - CH_3$

(n) $H_3C - \underset{\underset{\displaystyle CH_3}{|}}{\overset{\overset{\displaystyle CH_3}{|}}{C}} - Br$

(o) $C_6H_5CH_2CHO$

(p) $CH_3 - CH_2 - OCH_2 - CH_3$

(q) $H_3C - \underset{\underset{\displaystyle H}{|}}{\overset{\overset{\displaystyle NH_2}{|}}{C}} - COOH$

(r) phenyl (with $COOH$) $- CH_2 - CH_2 - CH_3$

(s) $CH_3 - CH_2 - \underset{\underset{CH_3}{|}}{CH} - CH_2 - OH$

(t) $CH_3 - SO_3H$

(u) $CH_3 - CH = CH - COOH$

(v) $CH_3 - \underset{\underset{CH_3}{|}}{CH} - CH_2 - CH_2 - \overset{\overset{H}{|}}{C} = O$

(w) $CH_3 - \underset{\underset{CH_3}{|}}{N} - CH_2 - CH_2 - C = O$

(x) $CH_3 - \overset{\overset{O}{||}}{C} - CH_2 - CH_2 - COOH$

(y) 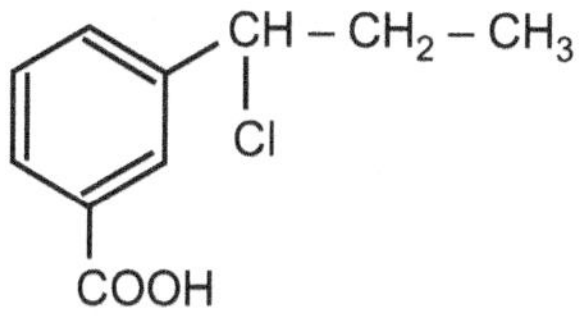   benzene ring with $CH(Cl)-CH_2-CH_3$ and $COOH$ substituents

(z) 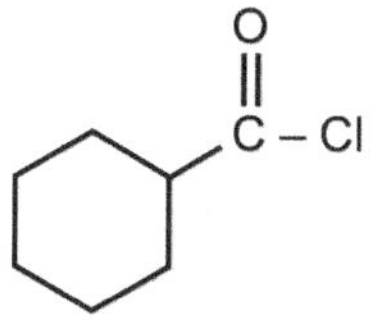   cyclohexane ring with $\overset{\overset{O}{||}}{C} - Cl$ substituent

(1) C_2H_5SH

(2) $CH_3 - CH_2 - CH_2 - CN$

(3) $CH_3 - \underset{\underset{CH_3}{|}}{CH} - CH_2 - \underset{\underset{OH}{|}}{CH} - CH_3$

(4) 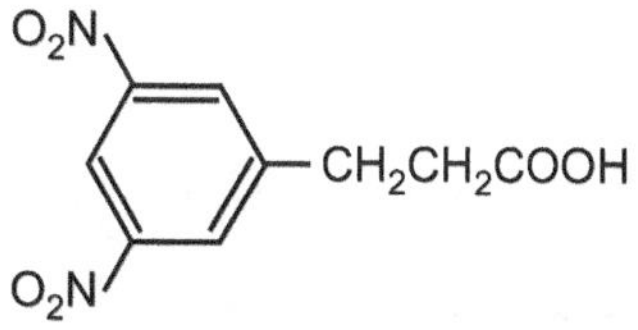   benzene ring with O_2N, O_2N and CH_2CH_2COOH substituents

(5) $(C_2H_5)CHCHO$

(6) $C_2H_5SO_3H$

(7) CH_3SH

(8) $CH_3COOC_6H_5$

(9) $CH_3CH_2OCH_2CH_2CH_3$

(10) $(CH_3)_2CHCHO$

(11) $CH_3CH_2OCH_2CH_2CH_3$

(12) CH_3SO_3H

(13) $C_2H_5COOC_6H_5$

(14) C_3H_7SH

(15) 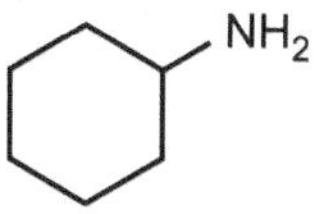 cyclohexane ring with NH_2 substituent

(16) 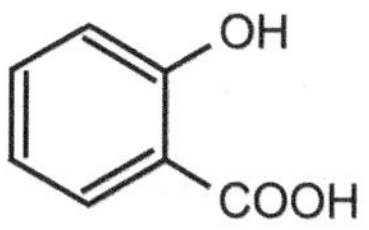 benzene ring with OH and $COOH$ substituents

(17) $CH_3 - CH_2 - \overset{\overset{\textstyle O}{\|}}{C} - CH_2 - COOH$

(18) [cyclohexane-COCl]

(19) [benzene ring with $CH_2 - \overset{\overset{\textstyle Cl}{|}}{CH} - CH_3$ and COOH]

(20) [cyclohexane with $\overset{\overset{\textstyle O}{\|}}{C} - NH_2$]

(21) [benzene ring with CN and Cl]

(22) $CH_3 - CH_2 - \overset{\overset{\textstyle O}{\|}}{C} - OCH_2CH_3$

(23) [benzene ring with CH_2 and $CH_2 - CH_2 - CH_2 - Cl$]

(24) [benzene ring with $\overset{\overset{\textstyle OH}{|}}{\underset{\underset{\textstyle CH_3}{|}}{C}} - COOH$]

(25) $CH_2COCH_2COOCH_3$

(26) [benzene ring with $N(CH_3)_2$ and two methyl groups]

(27) [cyclohexenone with CH_2OH]

(28) $\overset{\overset{\textstyle CH_2CH(CH)_3}{|}}{CH_2CH} - CH_2CH_2COCH_2CN$

(29) $CH_3CH_2OCH_2CH_2CH_3$

Q.5   Draw the structures of following compounds:

(1)   2-Methyl N,N-di-methyl butanamine, (2)   4-Amino-3-chloropentanenitrile

(3)   2,4-Hexadione   (4)   Methyl-2-butenoate

(5)   3-Methyl-4-penten-2-one,   (6)   3-Methyl-4-pentene-2-one

(7)   Cyclopropane carboxylic acid   (8)   3-Methyl-2-butenoic acid

(9)   2-Ethyl cyclopentene   (10) 2-Pentanone

(11) 3- Pentanol   (12) 1,2-Dichlorocyclopentane

(13) Cyclopropane carboxylic acid   (14) 3-(p-chlorophenyl) butanoic acid

(15) o-Amino benzoic acid   (16) 2-Pentene

(17) 2-Bromo-1-chloro propene

Chapter 3

STRUCTURE-PROPERTY RELATIONSHIP

3.1 INTRODUCTION

The structure of molecule determine its properties, which is a powerful concept in chemistry and in all fields in which chemistry is important. The structure of a molecule is described at various levels.

(i) The molecular formula, e.g., C_6H_7N, tells us which elements are present and in what ratio.

(ii) The relative overall size and 3-dimensional shape, known as the steric properties, give additional details.

(iii) Functional groups in the molecule indicate electrostatic properties (dipole moment, polarity, hydrogen bonding).

(iv) Chirality describes the spatial arrangement of atoms or groups.

Properties of compounds fall into following three general categories.

(a) Chemical properties: e.g., reaction rates, position of equilibria.

(b) Physical properties: e.g., odour, colour, taste, melting points, boiling points, solubility, spectra.

(c) Biological properties: e.g., drug action, toxicity.

3.2 DIPOLE MOMENT AND POLARITY OF MOLECULES

The nucleus of each atom has a certain ability to attract electrons. This is called as electronegativity. When two atoms of different electronegativities form a covalent bond, the electrons are not shared equally between them. The atom with greater electronegativity draws electron density closer to it as a result of which covalent bond becomes polar. This is referred as bond polarity. This is indicated in structure by putting partial positive ($\delta+$) and a partial negative ($\delta-$) charges above the atoms. Bond polarity in a molecule can often be measured by a dipole moment. When the centres of positive and negative charges in a molecule do not coincide, it is a dipole and the molecule is said to possess a dipole moment.

Dipole moment is defined as the product of the charge (e) in electrostatic units (esu) and the distance (d) in centimeters (cm) between the bonding atoms and is represented by μ. Dipole moment is commonly expressed in units called debyes (D).

$$\mu = e \times d$$

A dipole moment is designated by an arrow drawn in the direction of the dipole with arrowhead at the negative end. Dipole moment is a vector quantity i.e. it has both direction and magnitude.

For example:

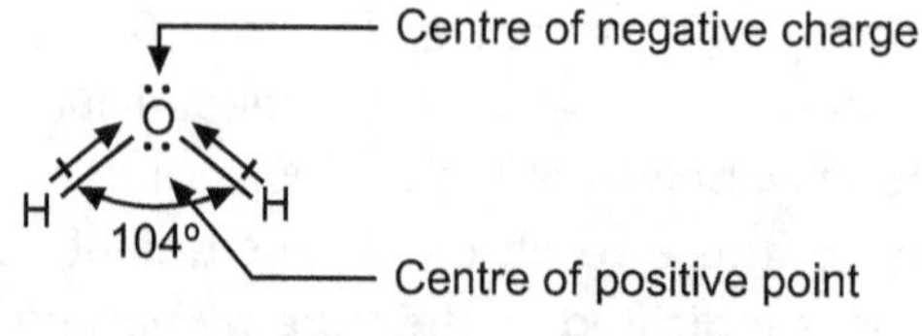

A molecule is said to be a polar molecule if it fulfils the following two conditions:

(1) The molecule must contain at least one or more polar bonds.

(2) The polar bonds must be so directed that there are separate centres of positive and negative poles in the molecule.

In a non-polar bond, the electric charge is equally distributed between the two identical atoms. e.g. N_2, Cl_2, Br_2, H_2 etc.

Thus, non-polar molecule have zero dipole moments. Whereas, a molecule like hydrogen fluoride (H-F) has large dipole moment of 1.75 D. Although H-F is a small molecule, the electronegative fluorine pulls the electrons strongly, although d is small, e is large and hence μ is large too.

$$\overset{\delta+}{H} \rightleftharpoons \overset{\delta-}{F}$$

$$\mu = 1.75\ D$$

Hydrogen fluoride

The net dipole moment of molecule is the vector sum of the dipole moments of the individual bond moments. For example, in water molecule two O–H bonds are polar. The H–O–H bond angle is 104°. The centre of the positive charge is between the hydrogen atoms. As the centre of positive charge and the centre of negative charge do not coincide, water molecule is polar.

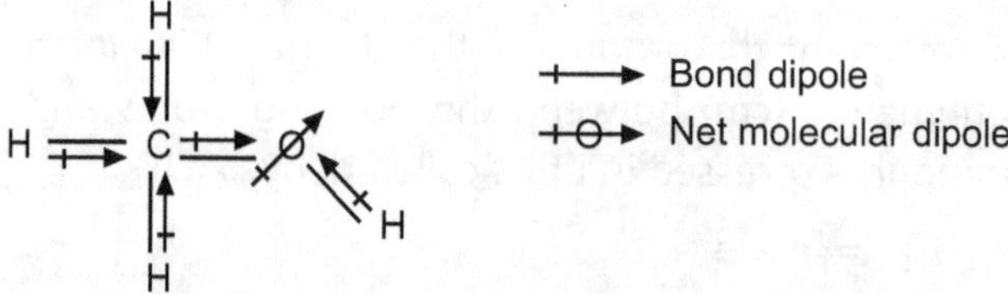

Dipole moment of water

Methanol has net dipole moment because the H–O–C bond angle is about 107° and oxygen is more electronegative than either carbon or hydrogen.

Dipole moment of methanol

In carbon tetrachloride, four polar C-Cl bonds are present, but still the molecule is non-polar. The CCl_4 is tetrahedral molecule with a bond angle of 109°28' and the centre of four negative charges is at the same place as the centre of positive charge i.e. at carbon atom. Therefore, even if a molecule has a polar bond, it may have no dipole moments.

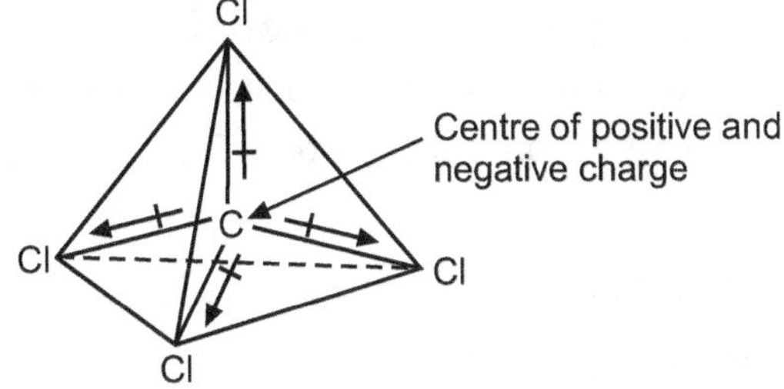

Structure of CCl_4

A molecule cannot have dipole moment if it has no polar covalent bonds. For example, hydrocarbons which do not contain polar bonds are non-polar.

Resonance is an important factor that influences dipole moment as it increases the distance between the charges of atoms. Let us see dipole moments of nitro compounds

Nitromethane (μ = 3.50 D)

Nitrobenzene (μ = 4.95 D)

p-nitroaniline (μ = 6.10 D)

Nitro compounds with decreasing order of dipole moment:

p-nitroaniline > Nitrobenzene > Nitromethane

p-nitroaniline has the highest value (6.10 D) of dipole moment because the electrons are transferred from the amino to the nitro group by resonance and this increases the distance of charge separation and as a result dipole moment increases. For the same reason CH_3Cl (μ = 1.87 D) has a large dipole moment than CH_3F (μ = 1.81 D) because the C-Cl bond is longer, though fluorine is more electronegative than chlorine. Dipole moment can give valuable information about the structure of a molecule. Dipole moment is very useful in determining the configuration of geometrical isomers.

3.3 INTERMOLECULAR FORCES OF ATTRACTION

The forces that hold molecules together are called intermolecular forces. These forces are electrostatic in nature, involving attraction of positive charge for negative charge. These intermolecular forces of attraction are also called as van der Waal's forces which are considerably important in liquid and solid states. There are three kinds of intermolecular forces:

(i) Dipole-dipole interaction.

(ii) van der Waal's forces.

(iii) Ion-dipole or ion-induced dipole forces.

3.3.1 Dipole-Dipole Interaction

Dipole-dipole interaction is the attraction of the positive end of one polar molecule for the negative end of another polar molecule (Fig. 3.1). These forces exist between polar molecules such as H_2O, NH_3, CH_3OH, HF etc.

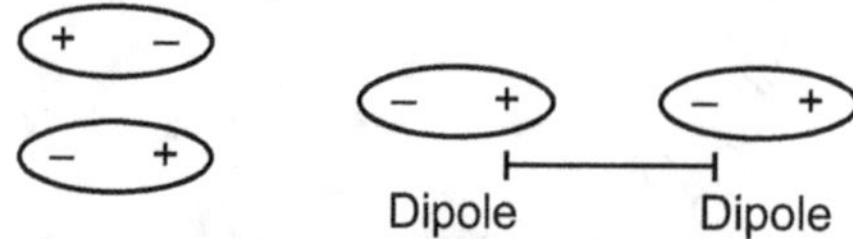

Fig. 3.1 : Dipole-dipole interaction

As a result of dipole-dipole interaction, polar molecules are generally held to each other more strongly than are non-polar molecules of comparable molecular weight; this difference in strength of intermolecular forces is reflected in the physical properties of the compound concerned. These forces increase the apparent molecular weight of compounds and increase its boiling point (B.P.).

Especially strongest dipole-dipole interaction is hydrogen bonding; (Refer chapter-1) in which a hydrogen atom acts as a bridge between two electronegative atoms (F, O and N) holding one by a covalent bond and the other by purely electrostatic forces. Hydrogen bonding is generally indicated by a broken line.

3.3.2 Van Der Waal's Forces

Since the electrons are always in motion, at any given instant, the charge may not be uniformly distributed in the molecule. Electrons may, in one instant, be slightly accumulated on one part of the molecule and as a result, a small temporary dipole will form. This temporary dipole in one molecule can induce opposite (attractive) dipoles in surrounding molecules (induced dipole). Thus, the temporary dipoles (instantaneous dipole) and the induced dipoles remain together by an attractive force or bonding known as instantaneous dipole-induced dipole interaction. These instantaneous dipoles and induced dipoles are changing constantly to the neutral state, till the attractive force so generated is able to bind the non-polar molecules together and is known as van der Waal's forces or London forces. These are attraction forces between atoms or molecules, named after Jobannes and van der Waal's (1837-1923).

These forces are much weaker than those arising from valence bonds and have a very short range. They act only between the portions of different molecules that are in close contact. That is, between the surfaces of molecules. van der Waal's forces increase rapidly with the increasing molecular weight. These forces exist between non-polar as well as polar molecules. These forces determine the melting point (M.P.) and boiling point (B.P.) of compounds.

3.3.2.1 Origin of van der Waal's forces

There are two factors causing such forces.

(i) Dipole-induced dipole interactions:

In dipole-induced dipole interactions the dipole of one polar molecule polarizes a neighbouring non-polar molecule so that the neighboring molecule also behaves as a dipole (Fig. 3.2). The polar molecule is said to have induced a dipole in the non-polar molecule.

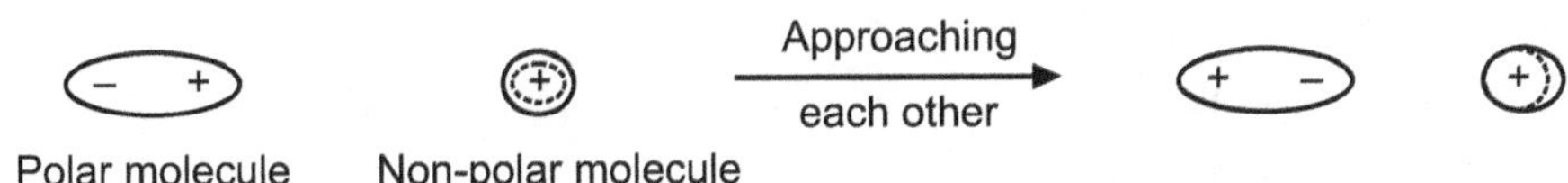

Fig. 3.2 : Dipole-induced dipole interaction

For example, picric acid with a large dipole moment induces a quite large dipole moment in naphthalene, which has no dipole moment. Thus, when these two molecules are brought together, they attract each other.

(ii) Instantaneous dipole-induced dipole interactions:

The non-polar molecules are electrically neutral. Any slight relative displacement of the nuclei or electrons in molecule, however, gives rise to an electrical dipole and it is known as instantaneous dipole (Fig. 3.3). These instantaneous dipole-induced dipole in the another adjacent molecule instantaneous dipole and induced dipole changing constantly to the neutral state still the attractive force so generated is able to bind.

Fig. 3.3

The bond dissociation energy of van der Waal's forces is about 4 kJ/mole.

3.3.2.2 Factors affecting strength of van der Waal's forces

(i) Molecular Weight:

van der Waal's forces increase rapidly with increase in molecular weight. Also, molecules with large size have large surface area. This increases the melting point (M.P.) and boiling point (B.P.) of a substance. For example, non-polar ethane (B.P. = –88.2°C) boils at higher temperature than methane (B.P. = –162°C) at a 1 atmospheric pressure. Boiling points (B.P.) of bigger molecules are higher because the surface area is large and more number of electrons which can move over longer distances. Therefore, the number of temporary dipoles that arise are greater, resulting in greater van der Waal's forces. Hence, greater thermal energy is required in order to break the force of attraction between the molecules.

(ii) Molecular shape :

Though n-pentane and neo-pentane both are structural isomers, van der Waal's forces are stronger in n-pentane than in neo-pentane. This is because, normal pentane has zig-zag chains which allow more interaction between the chains while neo-pentane has a closely packed structure which allows lesser interaction between the molecules. This leads to higher boiling point (B.P.) for n-pentane than neo-pentane.

$$CH_3{-}CH_2{-}CH_2{-}CH_2{-}CH_3$$

n-pentane

(B.P. = 36.1°C)

$$H_3C - \overset{\overset{\displaystyle CH_3}{|}}{\underset{\underset{\displaystyle CH_3}{|}}{C}} - CH_3$$

neo-pentane

(B.P. = 9.5°C)

Non-polar solutes dissolve in polar solvents or in non-polar solvents due to the van der Waal's force of attraction e.g. CCl_4 is soluble in benzene. Here both CCl_4 and benzene have van der Waal's forces or London forces.

3.3.3 Ion-Dipole and Ion-Induced Dipole Forces

Ion-dipole and ion-induced dipole forces are similar to dipole-dipole and induced-dipole interactions but involve ions, instead of only polar and non-polar molecules. Ion-dipole and ion-induced dipole forces are stronger than dipole-dipole interactions because the charge of any ion is much greater than the charge of a dipole moment. Ion-dipole bonding is also stronger than hydrogen bonding. An ion-dipole force results from an interaction between an ion and a polar molecule (Fig. 3.4). They align so that the positive and negative groups are next to one another, allowing for maximum attraction. Only water or highly polar solvents are able to dissolve ionic compounds appreciably due to this ion-dipole interaction. In solution, each ion is surrounded by a cluster of solvent molecules and is said to be solvated, if the solvent is water, the ion is said to be hydrated.

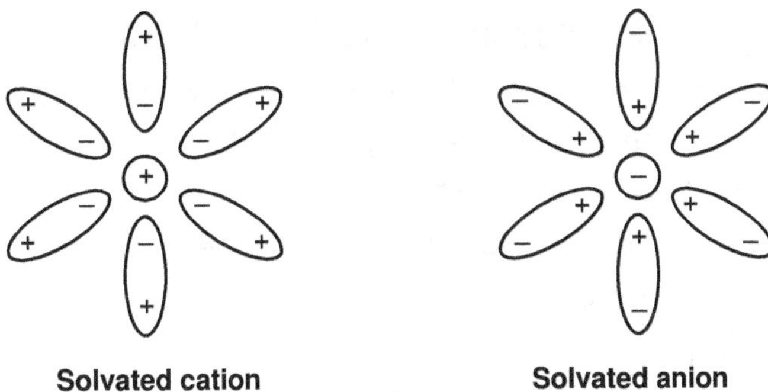

Solvated cation   **Solvated anion**

Fig. 3.4: Ion-dipole interactions

An ion-induced dipole force results from an interaction of an ion with a non-polar molecule. Like a dipole-induced dipole force, the charge of the ion causes distortion of the electron cloud on the non-polar molecule. This causes generation of weak force of attraction.

3.4 ISOMERISM

3.4.1 Introduction

The science of organic chemistry is based on the relationship between molecular structure and properties. The branch of science which deals with three dimensional structure of molecule is called stereochemistry. The molecular formula alone cannot completely describe the structure of the molecule. Information regarding the nature of linkage among atoms regardless of direction in space (bonding connectivity) and the relative orientation of atoms and groups in space (configuration) is necessary. Depending on these parameters, a certain combination of atoms can give rise to a number of molecular species known as isomers which are separated by energy barrier and differ in their chemical and physical properties.

Molecules that have the same molecular formula, but differ in arrangement of atoms or groups are called isomers and the phenomenon is termed as isomerism. That excludes any different arrangements which are simply due to the molecule rotating as a whole, or rotating about particular bonds.

3.4.2 Types of Isomerism

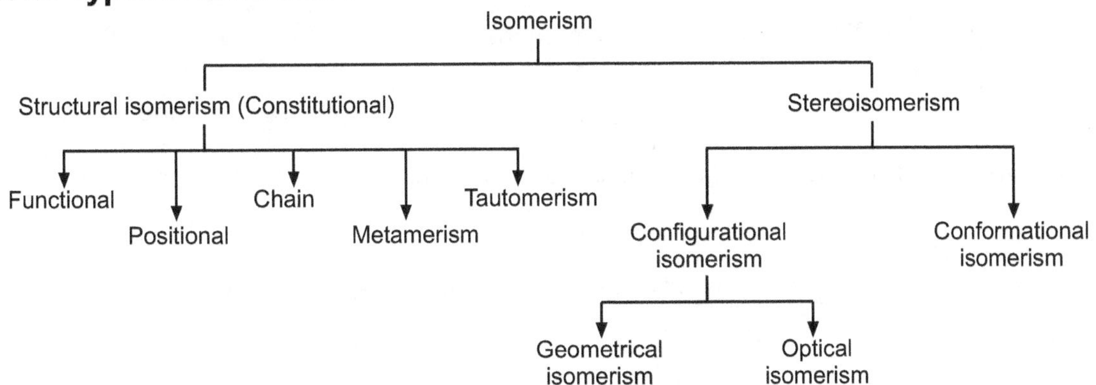

3.4.3 Structural Isomerism (Constitutional Isomerism)

When the isomerism is due to a difference in the arrangement of atoms within the molecule without any reference to space, they are said to be structural isomers and the phenomenon is termed as structural isomerism.

There are different kinds of structural isomerism as under :

(1) Chain or Nuclear isomerism.

(2) Position isomerism.

(3) Functional isomerism.

(4) Metamerism.

(5) Tautomerism.

(1) Chain or Nuclear isomerism:

Different compounds of the same class of organic compounds having the same molecular formula but differ in structure of carbon chain of the molecule are called the chain or nuclear isomers and the phenomenon is termed as chain or nuclear isomerism.

These isomers arise because of the branching in carbon chains.

For example,

(a) There are two isomers of butane, C_4H_{10}. In one of them, the carbon atoms lie in a straight chain whereas in the other the chain is branched.

$$CH_3-CH_2-CH_2-CH_3 \qquad\qquad CH_3-\overset{\overset{\displaystyle CH_3}{|}}{CH}-CH_3$$

n-Butane　　　　　　　　　　　Isobutane

(b) Pentane has three chain isomers (Molecular formula C_5H_{12})

$$CH_3-CH_2-CH_2-CH_2-CH_3 \qquad CH_3-CH_2-\overset{\overset{\displaystyle CH_3}{|}}{CH}-CH_3 \qquad H_3C-\overset{\overset{\displaystyle CH_3}{|}}{\underset{\underset{\displaystyle CH_3}{|}}{C}}-CH_3$$

n-Pentane　　　　　　Isopentane　　　　　　　　Neopentane

(c) n-Butanol and Isobutanol (Molecular formula $C_4H_{10}O$)

$$CH_3-CH_2-CH_2-CH_2-OH \qquad CH_3-\overset{\overset{\displaystyle CH_3}{|}}{CH}-CH_2OH$$

n-Butanol　　　　　　　　　　Isobutanol

(2) Positional isomerism:

When two or more isomers differ only in the position of the substituent atom or group on the identical base chain then they are called positional isomers and the phenomenon is termed as positional isomerism.

In positional isomerism, the basic carbon skeleton remains unchanged, but important groups are moved around on that skeleton.

For example:

(a) 1-Propanol and 2-Propanol (Molecular formula C_3H_8O)

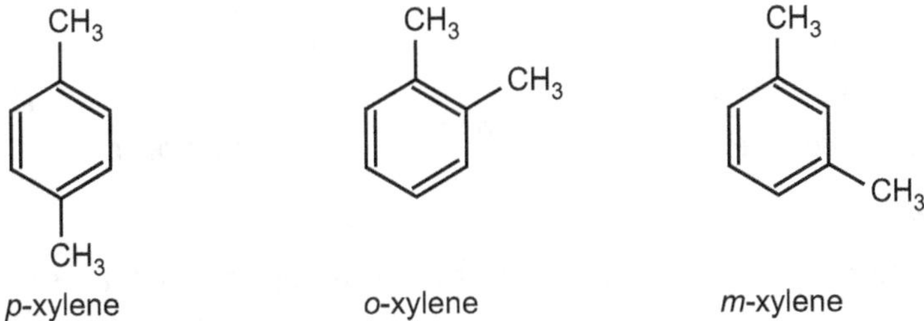

$$CH_3–CH_2–CH_2\text{-}OH$$
1-Propanol

$$CH_3 – CH – CH_3$$
$$|$$
$$OH$$
2-Propanol

(b) 1-Butene and 2-Butene (Molecular formula C_4H_8)

$$CH_2 = CH – CH_2 – CH_3 \qquad CH_3 – CH = CH – CH_3$$
1-Butene   2-Butene

(c) Position isomers on benzene rings. For example, xylene (Molecular formula C_8H_{10}).

p-xylene   o-xylene   m-xylene

(d) 1-Bromopropane and 2-Bromopropane (C_3H_7Br)

$$CH_3 – CH_2 – CH_2 – Br \qquad CH_3 – CH – CH_3$$
$$|$$
$$Br$$
1-Bromopropane   2-Bromopropane

(3) Functional isomerism:

Compounds with the same molecular formula but differing in the type of functional group they posses are called functional isomers and the phenomenon is termed as functional isomerism.

For example

(a) Ethyl alcohol and dimethyl ether (Molecular formula C_2H_6O)

$$CH_3 – CH_2 – OH \qquad CH_3 – O – CH_3$$
Ethyl alcohol   Dimethyl ether

(b) Propionaldehyde and acetone (Molecular formula C_3H_6O)

$$CH_3 - CH_2 - CHO$$
Propionaldehyde   and $$CH_3 - CO - CH_3$$
Propanone

(c) Propanoic acid (a carboxylic acid) and methyl ethanoate (an ester) (Molecular formula $C_3H_6O_2$).

$$CH_3 - CH_2 - \overset{\overset{\textstyle O}{\|}}{C} - OH$$ and $$CH_3 - \overset{\overset{\textstyle O}{\|}}{C} - O - CH_3$$

Propanoic acid   Methyl ethanoate

(4) Metamerism:

Isomerism is due to the unequal distribution of carbon atoms on either side of the functional group in molecule of compounds belonging to the same class is called as metamerism and the isomers are known as metamers.

For example:

(a) Diethyl ether and methyl propyl ether (molecular formula: $C_4H_{10}O$).

$$C_2H_5 - O - C_2H_5$$
Diethyl ether   and $$CH_3 - O - C_3H_7$$
Methyl propyl ether

(b) Diethyl ketone and methyl n-propyl ketone (molecular formula: $C_5H_{10}O$).

$$C_2H_5 - CO - C_2H_5$$
Diethyl ketone   and $$CH_3 - CO - C_3H_7$$
Methyl propyl ketone

(5) Tautomerism:

Compounds whose structures differ in the arrangement of atoms but which exist simultaneously in dynamic equilibrium with each other are called tautomers. In most of the cases, tautomerism is due to shifting of a hydrogen atoms from the carbon (or oxygen or nitrogen) to another with the rearrangement of single or double bonds. Tautomers are constitutional isomers existing in rapid equilibrium in a solution or in the liquid state and the equilibrium reaction is known as tautomerism. Tautomers are written with a sign of reversibility ($\rightleftharpoons$) between two tautomers. In tautomerism, the tautomers differ widely from each other in their structure.

For example:

(a)

Nitroethane   Aci-nitroethane

(b) Another example is a keto-enol tautomerism: In this case one isomer is a carbonyl compound and other is an enol and the equilibrium reaction is said to be keto-enol tautomerism.

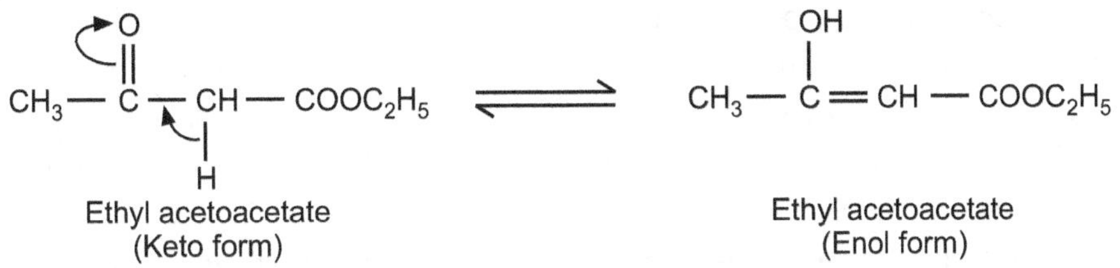

CH3—C—CH—COOC2H5
O
H
Ethyl acetoacetate
(Keto form)
OH
CH3—C=CH—COOC2H5
Ethyl acetoacetate
(Enol form)

3.4.4 Projection Formulae

The configuration is the three dimensional arrangement of atoms of a molecule in space. While studying stereochemistry of molecules the three dimensional formulae have to be drawn in two dimensions on paper. Therefore, the following projection formulae are used to represent the configurations of molecules on the plane of paper. While projecting the molecule it may be oriented in different ways with respect to the plane of paper.

(1) Fischer Projection Formula:

The Fischer projection formula is drawn according to the following conventions.

(i) The tetrahedral carbon atom is projected on a plane such that the horizontal bonds are above the plane and vertical bonds are below the plane of the paper.

(ii) Represent the asymmetric carbon(s) atom as the intersection of cross lines.

(iii) The longest chain of carbon atoms should be placed vertically, with the most oxidized group at the top or put carbon number 1 at the top.

The decreasing order of the oxidized state of some common groups is as follows.

$$-COOH > -CHO > -CH_2OH > -CH_3$$

For example

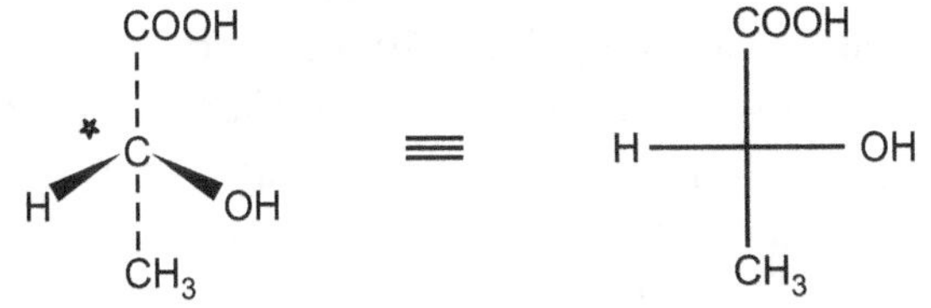

COOH
C
H
OH
CH3
≡
COOH
H
OH
CH3

(–) Lactic acid

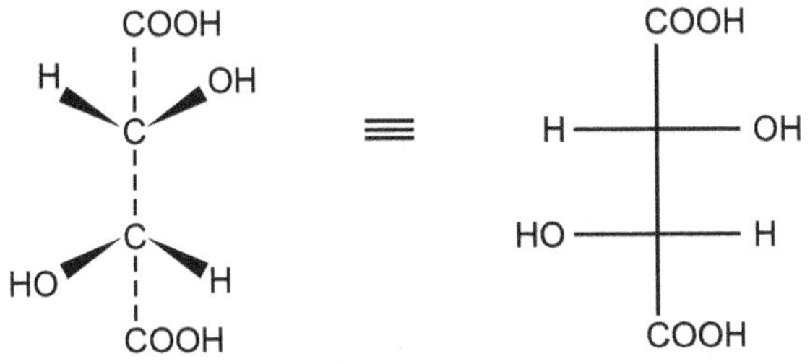

COOH
H
OH
C
C
HO
H
COOH
≡
COOH
H
OH
HO
H
COOH

(+) Tartaric acid

(2) Newman Projection Formula:

The formula can be drawn only for the molecules having two or more carbon atoms. The formula can be obtained by projecting the molecule such that the central C–C bond is perpendicular to the plane of paper. Thus the molecule is viewed along the C–C bond axis and hence the rear carbon atom cannot be seen as it is covered by the front carbon atom. The front carbon atom is represented by a point from which three bonds are drawn. The rear carbon atom is represented by a circle and three bonds radiate from its circumference. The central C–C bond is not visible (Fig. 3.5).

Due to rotation about the single bond the atoms or groups on an adjacent carbon atom can assume different relative positions.

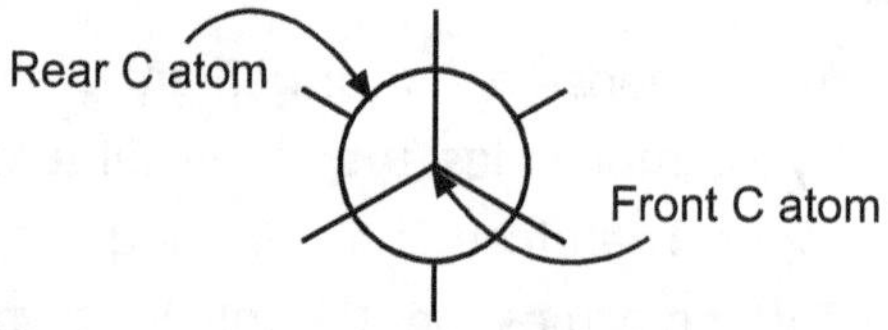

Fig. 3.5 : Newman projection formula

For example : Conformations of ethane

Staggered form

Eclipsed form

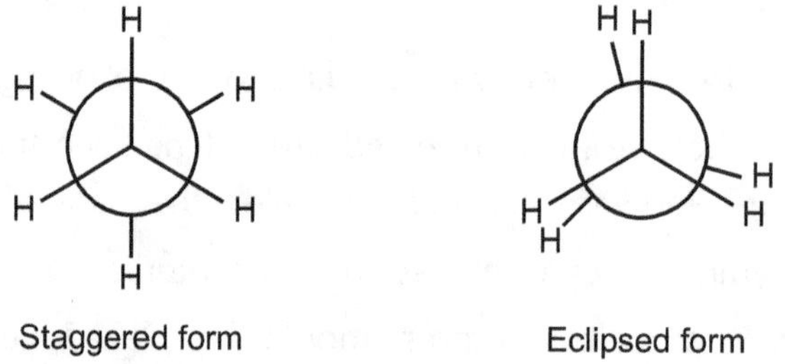

(3) Sawhorse Projection Formula:

In the sawhorse projection, the molecule is viewed from an angle. So the C–C bond is drawn obliquely.

In this method, the eclipsed groups are drawn parallel to each other on the same side of the oblique line; the staggered groups are also drawn parallel to each other, but on the opposite sides of the oblique line (Fig. 3.6). An eclipsed form gets converted into the staggered form when the carbon atom is rotated by a 180° angle around C–C bond. A skew form is generally drawn from a staggered or from an eclipsed form by rotating one of the C's in C–C bond around it through any angle other than 180° and 360°.

For example : Conformations of ethane

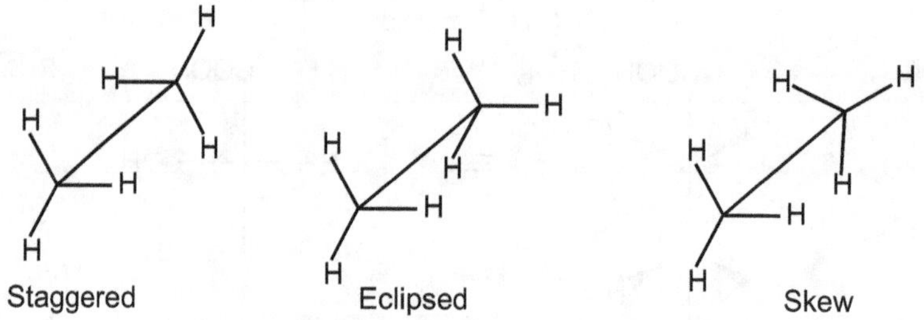

Fig. 3.6 : Sawhorse projection formula

(4) Flying-wedge projection:

The molecule is viewed sideways. So C–C bond is drawn horizontally. The common convention is that the solid lines represent bonds on the plane of the paper; the bonds directed behind the plane of the paper is projected by dotted lines and dark wedge represents bond above the plane of the paper (Fig. 3.7).

For example : Conformations of ethane

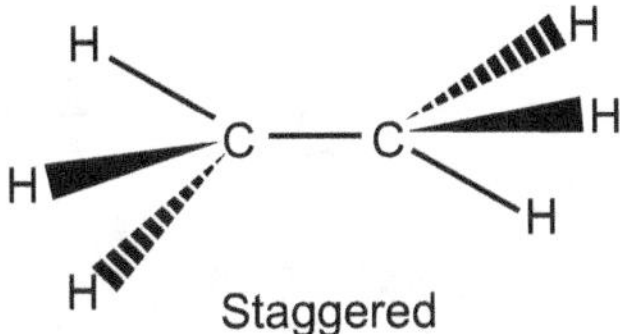

Fig. 3.7 : Flying-wedge projection formula

3.4.5 Stereoisomerism

Compounds with the same molecular formula and same bonding connectivity (constitution) but differing only in spatial arrangement of constituent atoms are called stereoisomers and the phenomenon of their existence is known as stereoisomerism. For example 2-butene (molecular formula C_4H_8) exists in nature in two forms: cis-2-butene and trans-2-butene.

  (i) cis-2-butene in which two CH_3 groups are on the same side of the carbon-carbon double bond (C=C).

  (ii) trans-2-butene in which two CH_3 groups are on the opposite side of the carbon-carbon double bond (C=C).

Stereoisomerism is of following different types.

  (1) Configurational isomerism

      (a) Optical isomerism (Enantiomerism)

      (b) Geometrical isomerism

  (2) Conformational isomerism

3.4.5.1 Configurational Isomerism

It arises due to different configurations at one or more stereocentre. The isomers are known as configurational isomers. These are non-interconvertible by rotation around single bonds. They can be interconverted only by breaking and making of bonds.

3.4.5.1.1 Optical Isomerism

Introduction: Optical isomerism is a type of stereoisomerism. Optical isomers have identical molecular and structural formula but the arrangement of groups in the space is different. Thus, because of molecular asymmetry, these compounds rotate the plane polarized light.

(A) Optical Activity:

Ordinary light vibrates in all possible directions in planes perpendicular to the direction of propagation. So ordinary light is called as unpolarized light. In plane polarized light (PPL) the vibrations takes place only in one plane, vibrations in other planes being cut off. Plane polarized light can be obtained by passing ordinary light through a nicol prism.

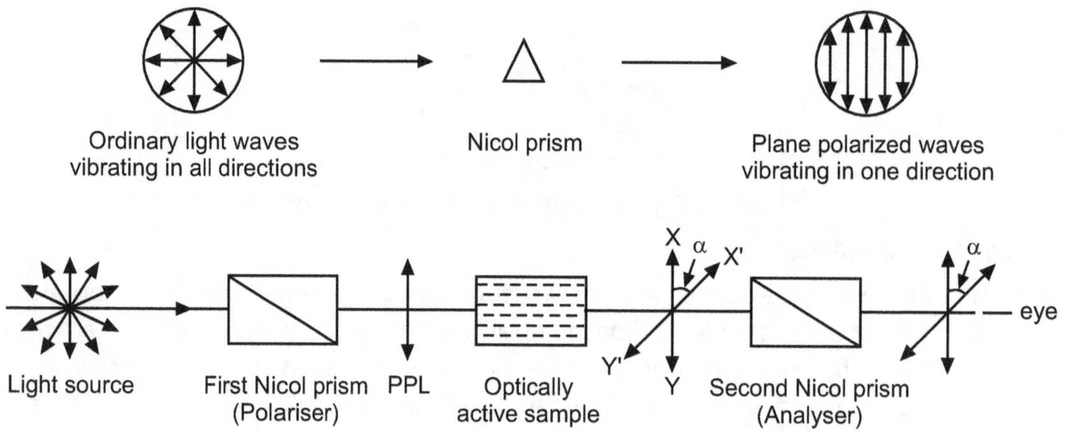

Fig. 3.8 : Components of a polarimeter

When solution of certain organic compounds are placed in the path of plane polarized light then they are able to rotate its plane through a certain angle which may be either to the left or to the right. If the polarized light has its vibrations in the plane XY before entering such a solution, the direction on leaving it will change to say X'Y', the plane having been rotated through the angle α (Fig. 3.8). This property of the substance of rotating the plane polarized light (PPL) is called optical activity and the substance possessing it is said to be optically active. e.g. isoamyl alcohol and lactic acid.

$$CH_3$$
$$|$$
$$C_2H_5 - CH - CH_2OH$$
Isoamyl alcohol

$$CH_3 - CH(OH) - COOH$$
Lactic acid

All molecules that do not have the capacity to rotate plane polarized light are said to be optically inactive. e.g. 2-chloropropane is optically inactive, it do not rotate PPL.

$$H$$
$$|$$
$$CH_3 - C - CH_3$$
$$|$$
$$Cl$$
2-Chloropropane

All optically active substances are known to exist in three forms.

The substance which rotate the PPL to the left or anticlockwise direction, this form is named as Laevorotatory (Latin, laevous = left). Laevorotation is designated as (–) or l.

The substance which rotate the PPL to the right or clockwise direction, this form is named as Dextrorotatory (Latin, dexter = right). Dextrorotation is designated as (+) or d.

A mixture containing equal quantities of (+) and (–) forms is not able to rotate the PPL. Hence it is optically inactive. It is called a racemic mixture and designated as ($\pm$ or dl).

For example : The three isomers of lactic acid, could be represented as:

COOH	COOH	COOH + COOH
H — C — OH	HO— C — H	H — C — OH + H — C — OH
CH_3	CH_3	CH_3 CH_3
D(–) Lactic acid	L(+) Lactic acid	dl-Lactic acid
Enantiomers		Racemic mixture

When the stereo isomers, which bear non-superimposable mirror image relationship, rotate PPL equally but in opposite direction, then such isomers are called as enantiomorphs (German word, enantio = opposite; morph = form) or enantiomers and the phenomenon is called as enantiomerism or enantiomorphism. Thus, optical isomerism is also referred to as enantiomerism.

For example: D(+)– glyceraldehyde and L(–)– glyceraldehyde.

CHO	CHO
H —— OH	HO —— H
CH_2OH	CH_2OH
D(+) Glyceraldehyde	L(–) Glyceraldehyde

Enantiomers

(B) Molecular Asymmetry and Optical Activity

(I) Asymmetric Carbon Atom (Chiral carbon):

The carbon atom to which all the four groups attached are different is called as asymmetric carbon or chiral carbon and molecule possessing asymmetric carbon atom is called as asymmetric molecule (Fig. 3.9). The compound possessing chiral carbon atom will always be dissymmetric or asymmetric and non superimposable on its mirror image. *This property of possessing chiral carbon atom and nonsuperimposability of an object with its mirror image is called as chirality.* Chirality is a necessary and sufficient condition for optical isomerism. Thus, it can be represented as

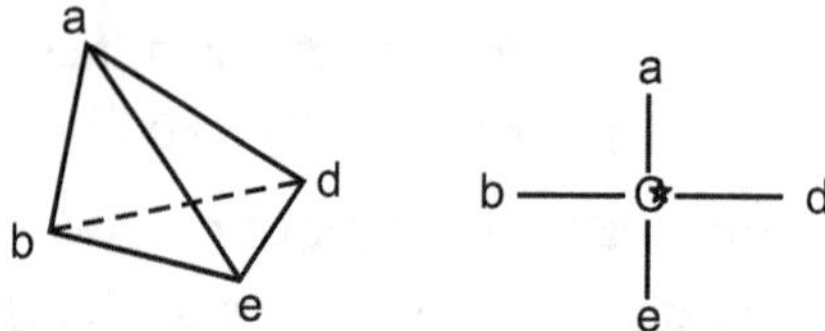

Fig. 3.9 : Asymmetric carbon or chiral carbon

It is indicated by (*) placed near it.

All organic compounds containing at least one asymmetric carbon atom are optically active.

For example: Lactic acid.

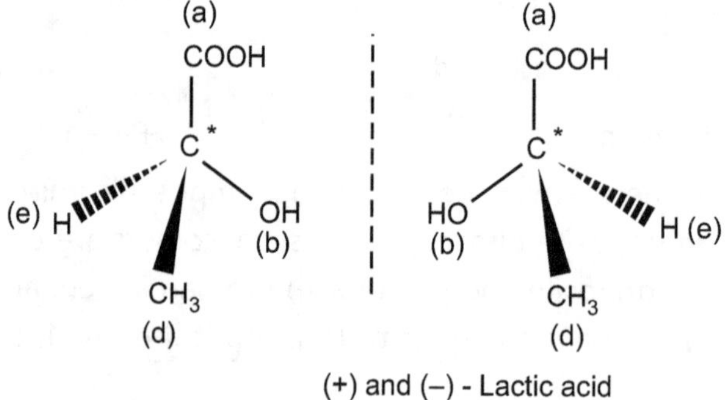

(+) and (−) - Lactic acid

D(−) and L(+) Tartaric acid.

D(−) Tartaric acid   L(+) Tartaric acid

The majority of optically active organic compounds contain one or more asymmetric carbon atoms. The essential requirement of optical activity is asymmetry of the molecule. A molecule containing two or more asymmetric carbon atoms may also show optical inactivity e.g. meso-tartaric acid. Though meso-tartaric acid contains two asymmetric carbon atoms, it is optically inactive because it possesses a plane of symmetry. Since meso-tartaric acid possesses plane of symmetry it is symmetric molecule and hence is achiral. Achiral refers to an object which can be superimposed on its mirror image and is optically inactive.

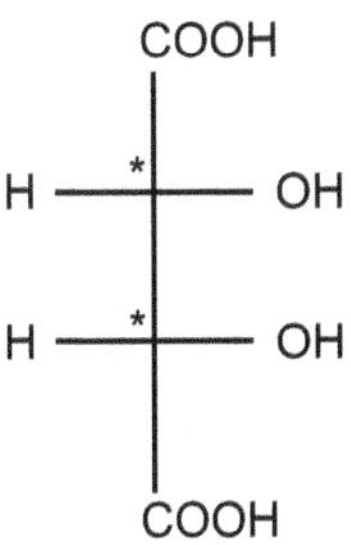

Meso Tartaric acid

The necessary condition for a molecule to exhibit optical isomerism is dissymmetry or chirality. Thus all organic compounds which contain an asymmetric carbon atom are chiral and exist in two tetrahedral forms. Although the two forms (I and II) shown in Fig. 3.10 have the same structure, they have different arrangements of groups a, b, d, e about the asymmetric carbon. In fact, they represent asymmetric molecules. They are related to each other as an object and mirror image and are nonsuperimposable. They are commonly called enantiomers.

The two forms of a molecule containing one asymmetric carbon are represented as follows.

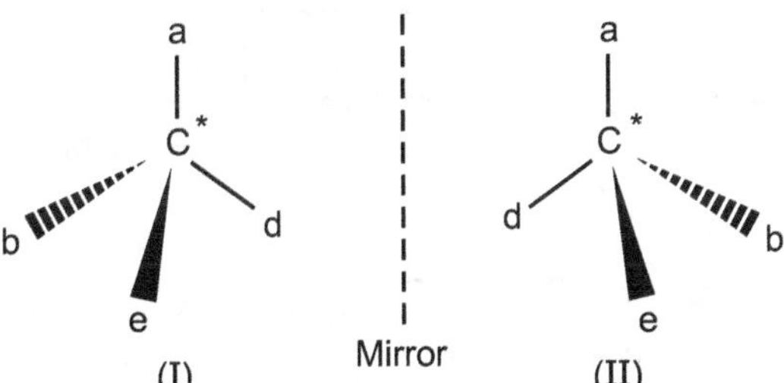

Fig. 3.10 : Mirror images of asymmetric molecule

(II) Asymmetric or Disymmetric Molecules

The molecule is said to be asymmetric or dissymmetric if it do not have following elements of symmetry.

    (1) Plane of symmetry

    (2) Centre of symmetry

    (3) Simple or proper axis of symmetry

    (4) Alternating axis of symmetry

A molecule which does not have any of these lines of symmetry is nonsuperimposable with its mirror image. Such a molecule is dissymmetric and optically active.

(1) Plane of Symmetry:

A plane of symmetry is an imaginary plane which divides an object in such a way that the part of it on one side of the plane is the mirror image of that on the other side of the plane. The plane is called σ- plane and operation is σ operation.

For example, meso-tartaric acid, benzene and meso-2, 3-dichlorobutane are optically inactive due to plane of symmetry as shown below.

For example

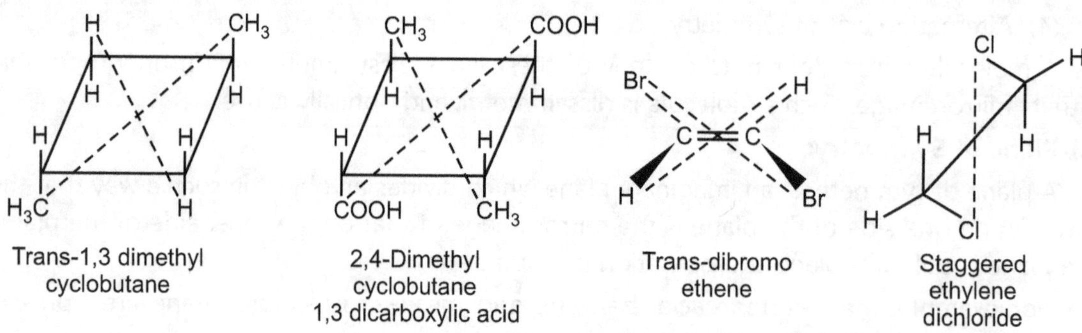

Meso tartaric acid   Benzene   Meso-2,3-dichlorobutane

Chiral molecules must have no internal plane of symmetry. Molecules that do have an internal plane of symmetry will be able to be split in half and each half will be a mirror image of the other. An example of this is 2-propanol (Fig. 3.11). If we construct a plane that cuts the molecule in half that would run through the hydrogen atom of the middle carbon and the hydroxyl group, the two halves would be mirror images of one another (Fig. 3.11). Such a molecule would be achiral that is, not capable of exhibiting chirality.

Achiral molecule

Fig. 3.11 : Achirality and internal plane of symmetry

(2) Centre of Symmetry:

The centre of symmetry of a molecule is defined as that point in the molecule, if the line is drawn from any atom to this point and equally extended on opposite side another identical atom is met. It is observed more satisfactorily in ring system. It is important to note that only even numbered rings can possess a centre of symmetry. It is designated as i and operation is called i- operation.

Trans-1,3 dimethyl cyclobutane   2,4-Dimethyl cyclobutane 1,3 dicarboxylic acid   Trans-dibromo ethene   Staggered ethylene dichloride

(3) Alternating axis of symmetry:

A molecule is said to possess one fold, two fold, three fold or four fold axis of symmetry. When a molecule is said to possess n fold axis of symmetry then if molecule is rotated through $360/n°$ around this, then reflected across the plane perpendicular to the plane of the paper, another identical structure results. It is designated as Sn.

For example: α-Truxilic acid has S_2 axis symmetry.

(4) Simple or Proper axis of symmetry:

An n-fold simple axis of symmetry is an axis such that, when a structure possessing this axis is rotated by an angle of $2\pi/n$ ($360/n°$) around the axis, another identical structure results. Rotation is usually taken as clockwise. The axis is designated as Cn and operation is called as Cn operation.

e.g. H_2O has two fold simple axis of symmetry (C_2) bisecting H-O-H angle.

Cis 1, 3-dimethyl cyclobutane has one C_2 axis.

Thus the molecule of bromochlorofluromethane is asymmetric because it is non super imposable on its mirror image.

Non-superimposable mirror images of bromochlorofluromethane

(C) Properties of Optical Isomers

The optical isomers will have the same chemical reactions with optically inactive substances and will be alike in all physical properties such as M.P., B.P., density etc. They can only be distinguished by their 'action on plane-polarized light'. This property is known as optical activity. Enantiomers have identical chemical properties towards optically inactive reagents. The rates of reaction of optically active reagent with two enantiomers different and sometimes one of the enantiomers does not react at all. Enantiomers rotate PPL to equal extent but in opposite direction.

The number of optical isomers will be equal to 2^n where n is the number of asymmetric carbon atoms. Thus the molecule with one asymmetric C atom will have two optical isomers; which are enantiomers or non-superimposable mirror images.

(D) Configuration of Optical Isomers

The optical isomers are of two types depending on the direction of rotation of PPL. Their specific rotation are given the signs (+) and (–) respectively.

However there is no definite relation between these signs and absolute configuration.

For example, (+) lactic acid when esterified, gives methyl (–) lactate. But there is no change in the configuration at the asymmetric C atom in this reaction.

$$CH_3OH, H_2SO_4$$
Esterification

(+) Lactic acid   Methyl (–) lactate

Thus, the signs d and *l* represent only the direction of optical rotation and not the absolute configuration. Hence, the configurations of different optical isomers are named according to the following systems.

(1) Relative configuration:

The configuration of a compound with reference to arbitrarily assigned configuration of a reference substance is known as its relative configuration.

(i) D, L-System:

This is one of the earliest attempts to name the configurations of optical isomers, made by Fischer (1891) and later by Rosanoff (1906). It is based on the Fischer projection formula of the molecule. It is suitable to name the isomers of a molecule having the structure

$$\begin{array}{c} R \\ | \\ X - \overset{*}{C} - H \\ | \\ R' \end{array}$$

where X may be halogen, $-OH$, $-OCH_3$, $-NH_2$, $-SH$, etc. The Fischer projection formula of the compound is drawn as per the conventions mentioned.

If the X is on the right hand side, then it is called D-isomer, whereas if X is on the left hand side then it is called L-isomer. The sign of optical rotation (+) or (−), is also written next to the D, L notations.

$$\begin{array}{c} R \\ | \\ X - \overset{*}{C} - H \\ | \\ R' \end{array} \qquad \begin{array}{c} R \\ | \\ H - \overset{*}{C} - X \\ | \\ R' \end{array}$$

L-Isomer   D-Isomer

For example

$$\begin{array}{c} COOH \\ | \\ H - \overset{*}{C} - OH \\ | \\ CH_3 \end{array} \qquad \begin{array}{c} COOH \\ | \\ HO - \overset{*}{C} - H \\ | \\ CH_3 \end{array} \qquad \begin{array}{c} CHO \\ | \\ H - \overset{*}{C} - OH \\ | \\ CH_2OH \end{array} \qquad \begin{array}{c} CHO \\ | \\ HO - \overset{*}{C} - H \\ | \\ CH_2OH \end{array}$$

D(-) Lactic acid   L(+) Lactic acid   D(+) Glyceraldehyde   L(−) Glyceraldehyde

Any compound that can be prepared from or converted to D–(+) glyceraldehyde belongs to D-series and similarly any compound that can be prepared from or converted into L(−) glyceraldehydes will belong to L-series.

e.g.,

$$\begin{array}{c} CHO \\ | \\ H - C - OH \\ | \\ CH_2OH \end{array} \quad \xrightarrow{\quad O \quad} \quad \begin{array}{c} COOH \\ | \\ H - C - OH \\ | \\ CH_2OH \end{array}$$

D(+) Glyceraldehyde   D(−) Glyceric acid

In case of compounds containing more than one asymmetric C atom, while representing relative configurational relationship, the asymmetric C atom of glyceraldehydes is always drawn at the bottom and the rest of the molecule is then built up.

D-series   L-series

Limitations:

(i)　It cannot be applied to compounds in which four groups attached to the asymmetric carbon atom are alkyl groups.

(ii)　If a molecule has more than one asymmetric C atom, then it will have more than two optical isomers. All these isomers cannot be distinctly named by the D, L system.

(ii) Erythro-threo System:

This type of nomenclature is used to name the isomers of a molecule of the following type, having two asymmetric carbon atoms.

$$R - \overset{\overset{\text{a}}{|}}{\underset{\underset{\text{X}}{|}}{C^*}} - \overset{\overset{\text{a}}{|}}{\underset{\underset{\text{Y}}{|}}{C^*}} - R'$$

It will have 4 optical isomers (2^2 = 4 isomers). The nomenclature is based on the notations derived fron the names of the sugars containing four C atoms called aldotetrose. In the isomer called erythrose, the hydroxyl groups are on the same side of the vertical C chain. In the isomer called threose, hydroxyl groups are on the opposite side.

Thus, in any other molecule, if the similar groups are on the same side of the vertical chain in the Fischer formula, then it is called erythro isomer. If the similar groups are on the opposite side of the chain then it is called threo isomer.

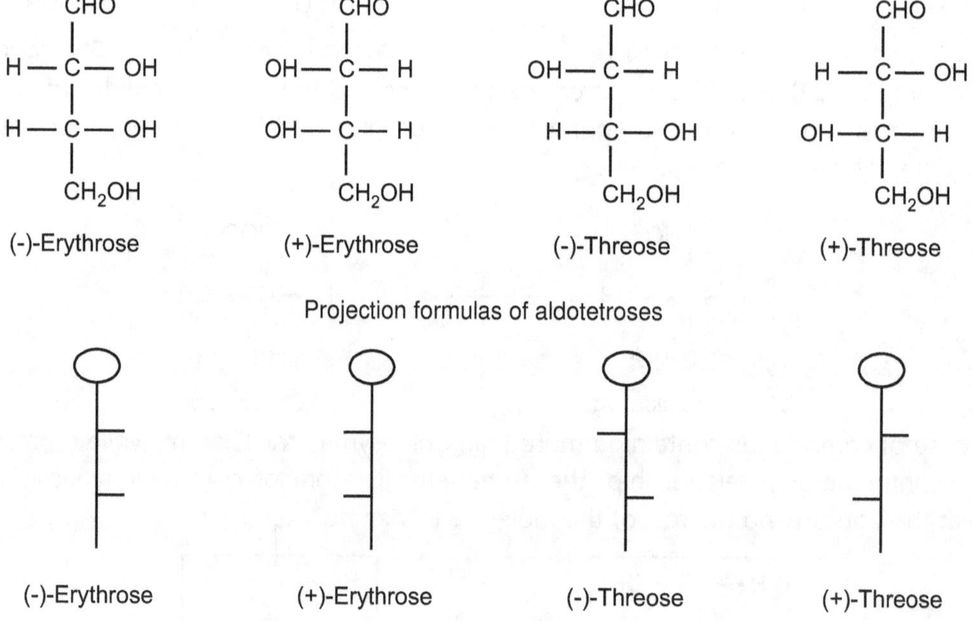

Projection formulas of aldotetroses

Abbreviated projection formulas for aldotetroses

The projection formulas of the (–) and (+)– erythrose shows that these molecules are mirror images of each other i.e. (–)– and (+)- erythrose are enantiomers and have identical physical and chemical properties except for the direction in which they rotate the plane of polarized light. Similarly, (–)– and (+)– threose are enantiomers. On the other hand, comparing either of the erythroses with either of the threoses, we find that, although stereoisomers, they are not mirror images of each other. Such molecules are called "diastereoisomers" (or diastereomers).

While enantiomers have identical properties in a symmetrical environment, diastereomers may differ widely in both physical and chemical properties in fact, many diastereomers differ among each other as much as ordinary (structural) isomers do.

(2) Absolute configuration:

The precise arrangement of the atoms or groups at a chiral centre is known as absolute configuration of the molecule and its stereochemical description is R or S.

R-S system: (Cahn, Ingold, Prelong system):

All enantiomers have a stereogenic centre carbon. This makes the molecule chiral, that is, having a non-superimposable mirror image. These enantiomers are differentiated by naming them differently. Each enantiomer in the pair has opposite configuration (the arrangement of the groups attached to a stereogenic centre).

To assign R and S configuration, the priority order of four groups or atoms bonded to chiral carbon as per CIP (Cahn, Ingold, Prelong) system is first determined. If in one enantiomer the arrangement is clockwise around the stereogenic carbon beginning with the highest priority atom or group, the enantiomer is said to have the "R" configuration. The letter "R" comes from the Latin Rectus meaning right. The other enantiomer of the pair being the non-superimposable mirror image, will always have an arrangement that proceeds anticlockwise around the stereogenic carbon. This is a different configuration and is called the "S" isomer. The letter "S" comes from the Latin Sinister meaning left. During the IUPAC nomenclature of these two, the letter "R" or "S" are written in parenthesis before the beginning of the IUPAC name.

R or S nomenclature is independent of nomenclature and numbering like D and L. It must be remembered that R and S have nothing to do with the signs of rotation.

Assignment of R and S configuration is done by the two rules:

(i)   The sequence rule – It consists of several standard sub rules and

(ii) Chirality rule.

(i) The sequence rule : The sequence rule arranges the four substituents of a chiral centre (Cabcd). In a priority sequence a>b>c>d ('a' having the highest priority and 'd' having the lowest) or ligands may be numbered 1>2>3>4 (1 having the highest priority and 4 having the lowest).

The sequence rule (standard sub rule) which determine the priority order are six in number have been stated under the headings 0-5. They must be applied in progression i.e. one after the other in the order stated.

Assign priority to the four groups or ligands as per the following rules;

Std. sub rule (0) Nearer end of an axis or a plane precedes the farthered end.

(1) Higher atomic number precedes lower. e.g. $S > F > O > N > C > H$

(2) Higher atomic mass number precedes lower. e.g. $T > D > H$

(3) Cis precedes trans or Z precedes E.

(4) Like pair RR or SS; precedes unlike pair RS or SR.

(5) R precedes S.

For the majority of the compounds only sub rules 1 and 2 are important. The other rules apply to special cases. Sub rule (1) is further elaborated below.

(1) Atoms directly attached to the central chiral atoms must be ranked first according to the sub rule (1). If the priority still remains undecided for some ligands, one passes over to the next atom in the ligand and the exploration continues until the decision is reached on the basis of the sub rules.

For example

$$- CH_2\underline{C}H_3 > CH_2\underline{H}; \qquad - CH_2\underline{O}H > - CH_2\underline{N}H_2; \qquad - CH_2CHF\underline{Br} > - CH_2CHF\underline{Cl}$$

(Decision is reached at the underlined atoms)

It may be noted that sub rule 2 must not be used until sub rule (1) is completely exhausted thus $CH_2CH_2CH_3 > CD_2CH_3$. But $CH_2CD_2CH_3 > CH_2CH_2CH_3$.

(2) In case a ligand bifurcates, one must proceed along the branch until a difference is encountered i.e. if a decision cannot be reached by ranking the first atoms in the substituents, look at the second, third, or fourth atom until a difference is found.

$$-CH_2-\underset{\underset{CH_3}{|}}{CH}-CH_2-Cl > -CH_2-\underset{\underset{CH_3}{|}}{CH}-CH_2-CH_3 ; \quad -CH_2-\underset{\underset{CH_3}{|}}{\overset{\overset{CH_3}{|}}{C}}-CH_3 > CH_2-\underset{\underset{CH_3}{|}}{CH}-CH_2-Cl$$

(3) When a central atom is a part of a ring system each branch is followed until a decision is reached as shown below.

(4) If there are multiple bondings like double or triple bonds involved, then for the sake of assigning priority, the double bond is split into two single bonds each with the atom on the far end of the multiple bond. Triple bonds would be split into three single bonds.

For example,

$$CH \equiv C— \quad \text{becomes} \quad H—\overset{\overset{\displaystyle C}{|}}{\underset{\underset{\displaystyle C}{|}}{C}}—\overset{\overset{\displaystyle C}{|}}{\underset{\underset{\displaystyle C}{|}}{C}}—$$

$$CH_2 = CH— \quad \text{becomes} \quad H—\overset{\overset{\displaystyle H}{|}}{\underset{\underset{\displaystyle C}{|}}{C}}—\overset{\overset{\displaystyle C}{|}}{\underset{\underset{\displaystyle H}{|}}{C}}—$$

$$CH_3—CH_2—$$

Hence priority order is

$$CH \equiv C— \quad > \quad CH_2 = CH— \quad > \quad CH_3—CH_2—$$

$$—CH = O \quad \text{becomes} \quad H—\overset{\overset{\displaystyle O}{|}}{\underset{\underset{\displaystyle C}{|}}{C}}—O$$

$$—\overset{\overset{\displaystyle O}{\|}}{C}—OH \quad \text{becomes} \quad —\overset{\overset{\displaystyle O}{|}}{\underset{\underset{\displaystyle O}{|}}{C}}—OH$$

$$—CH\begin{smallmatrix}\diagup OH \\ \diagdown OH\end{smallmatrix}$$

Hence priority order is

$$—\overset{\overset{\displaystyle O}{\|}}{C}—OH \quad > \quad —CH = O \quad > \quad —CH\begin{smallmatrix}\diagup OH \\ \diagdown OH\end{smallmatrix}$$

(ii) Chirality rule: Once the priority of the four ligands decided, the chiral centre is then viewed from the side away from the lowest ranking group (d or 4).

If from this point of view the arrangement a →— b →— c or (1 →— 2 →— 3) appears in the clockwise (right handed) direction, the configuration is R and if the arrangement appears in the anticlockwise (left hand) direction, the configuration is S, this is known as chirality rule.

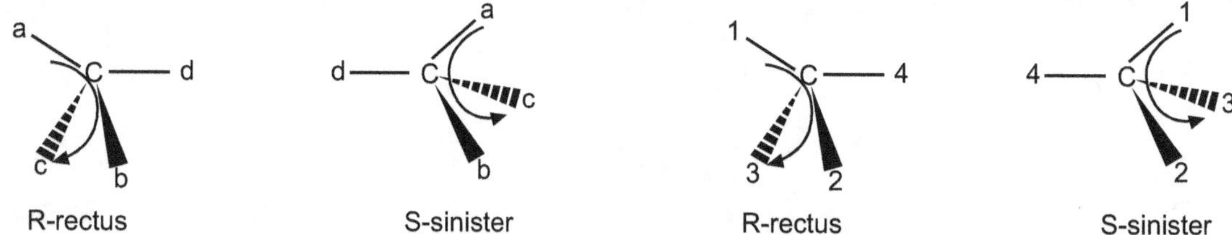

<table>
<tr><td align="center">R-rectus</td><td align="center">S-sinister</td><td align="center">R-rectus</td><td align="center">S-sinister</td></tr>
</table>

If the structure is a 3-D structure then determine the configuration in the following manner:

1. If the lowest priority group is already projected back behind the plane (dotted line) or is within the plane (solid line) then trace through the other three groups beginning with the highest priority group first as above (1, 2, 3 trace).

2. If on the other hand, the lowest priority group is projected infront of the plane (solid wedge) then trace through the other three groups beginning with the highest priority group first as above (1, 2, 3 trace). **Reverse** the trace so that if the trace was clockwise indicating "R" configuration make it "S" configured. If the trace was counter clockwise indicating "S" then **reverse** it and make it clockwise making it "R" configured.

    For example,

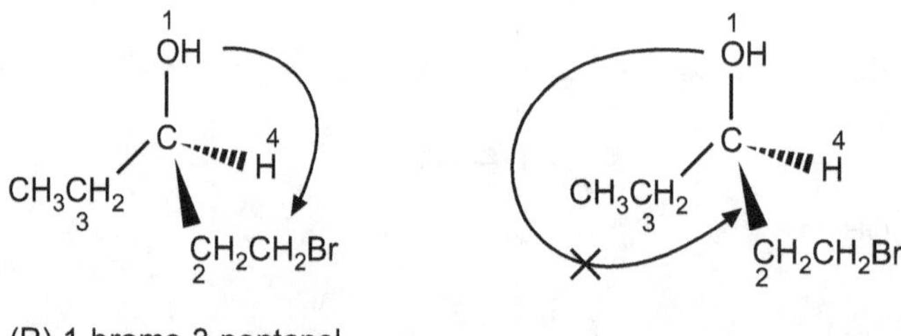

(R)-1-bromo-3-pentanol

R-S notations for Fischer formula:

Once the priority of ligands fixed, the lowest priority group or atom must have to the lower vertical position in the projection formula. If it is not so, the lowest priority group or atom should be brought to that position by making two interchanges or write reverse configuration.

For example,

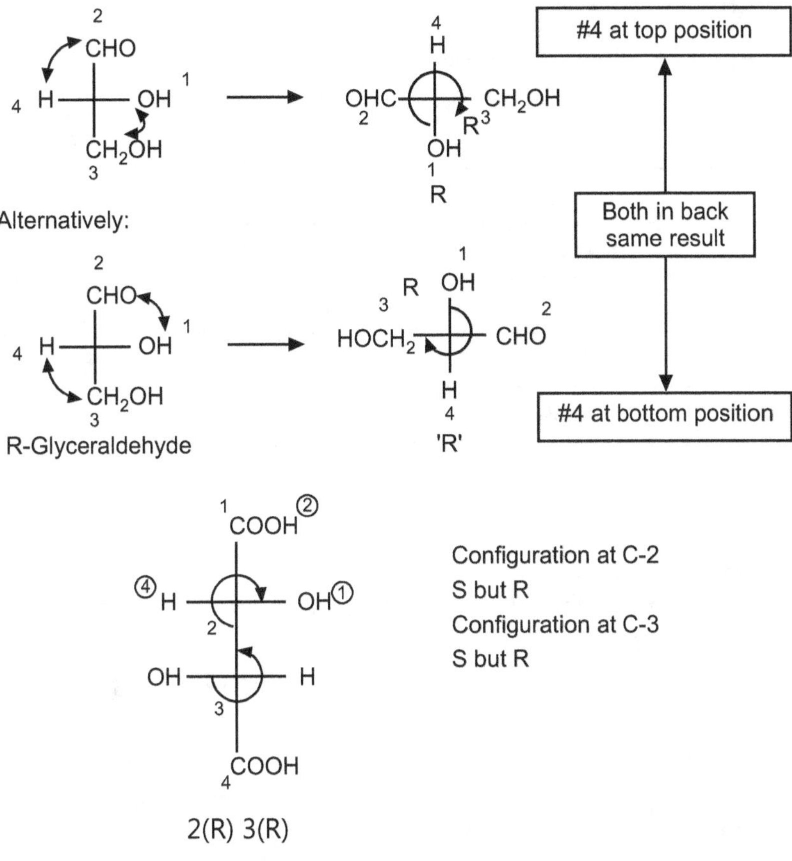

Configuration at C-2
S but R
Configuration at C-3
S but R

Table 3.1 : Cahn-Ingold-Prelog (CIP) system: Atoms and groups with increasing priority

Sr. No.	Atoms/Groups	Sr. No.	Atoms/Groups
1	H	19	COOR
2	D	20	NH_2
3	CH_3	21	$NHCH_3$
4	CH_2-CH_3	22	$N(CH_3)_2$
5	$CH_2(CH_2)nCH_3$	23	NO
6	$CH_2-CH=CH_2$	24	NO_2
7	$CH_2-C=CH$	25	OH
8	$CH_2-C_6H_5$	26	OCH_3
9	$CH(CH_3)_2$	27	OC_6H_5

Contd...

10	$CH=CH_2$	28	OCOR
11	$C(CH_3)_3$	29	F
12	$C=CH$	30	SH
13	C_6H_5	31	SR
14	CH_2OH	32	SOR
15	$CH=O$	33	SO_2R
16	$RC=O$	34	Cl
17	$CONH_2$	35	Br
18	COOH	36	I

More examples:

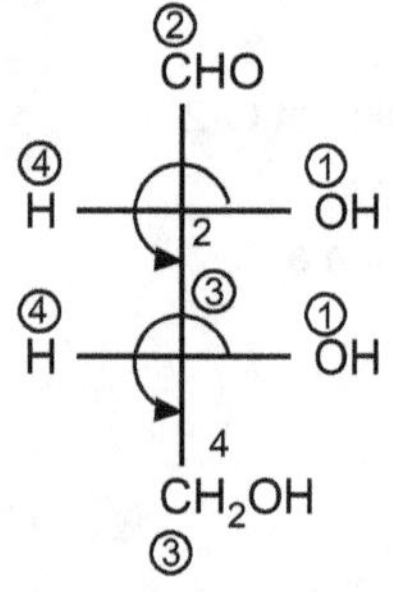

Configuration at C-2   'S' but 'R'
Configuration at C-3   'S' but 'R'
2R, 3R

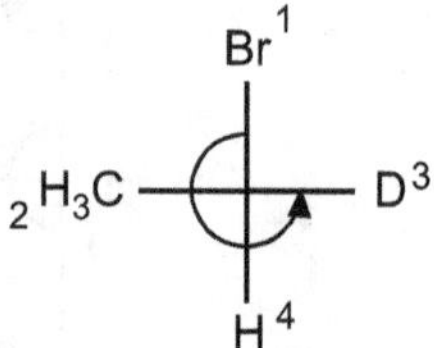

'S' configuration

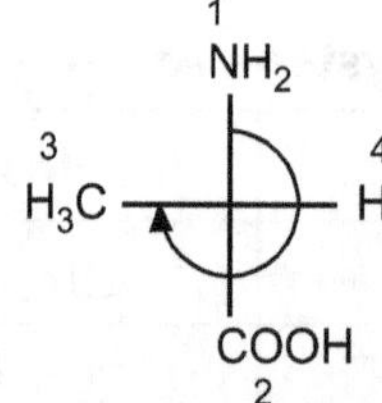

'R' but 'S' since (4) priority
group on horizontal position

3.4.5.1.2 Meso Compounds

The compounds containing two or more asymmetric carbon atoms but which possess plane of symmetry is called as meso compound. A molecule with two chiral carbons always have four possible stereoisomers. Sometimes there may be three only. This is because some molecules with chiral centres are overall achiral. To understand this let us consider an example of tartaric acid, which has two chiral carbons C-2 and C-3.

Example : Tartaric acid. (COOH – CH(OH) – CH(OH) – COOH)

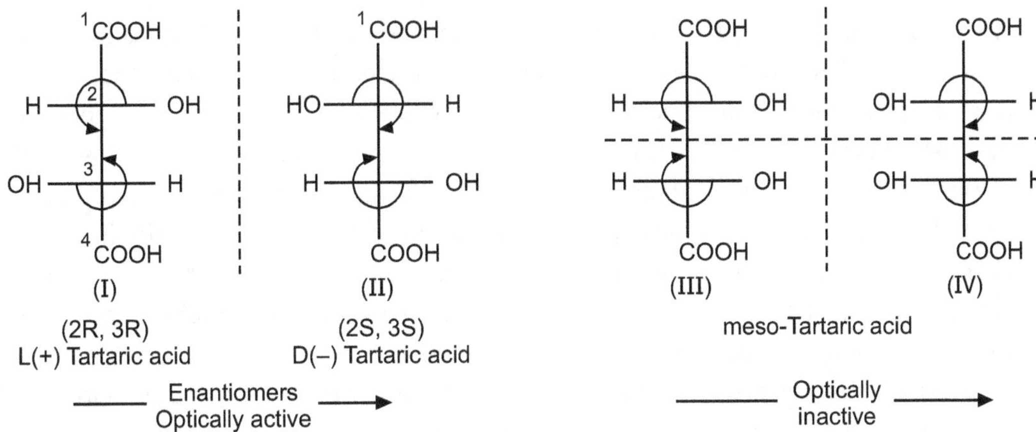

For the compounds to be optically active it should not posses any element of symmetry. Structures I and II are non- superimposable mirror images, hence represent a pair of enantiomers. Structures III and IV have a plane of symmetry and have super imposable mirror image. In these structures, arrangement of groups around C_2 and C_3 is such that two carbon atoms rotate plane of polarized to equal extent but in opposite direction. The rotation due to C_2 is compensated by C_3 and compound is optically inactive. Such compounds are called meso compounds. In a meso compound there is an internal compensation of optical rotation.

3.4.5.1.3 Geometrical Isomerism

It is the isomerism exhibited by compounds having the same molecular formula and structural formula but they differ in spatial arrangement of atoms around the doubly bonded carbon atoms. Geometrical isomerism arises due to restricted rotation of atoms or groups about a covalent bond.

Rotation, free or restricted, is a property of single bonds. Because the electron density in a sigma bond is cylindrically symmetrical, it is not altered by rotation around the bond. The situation is dramatically different in the case of double bonds. Here, in addition to the sigma bond, there is a pi bond, and the electron density in the pi bond is concentrated above and below the sigma bonded framework. Rotation around a double bond twists the p orbitals out of alignment, thereby reducing orbital overlap and raising the potential energy of the pi electrons. As a result, the atoms attached to these sp^2 carbons will always remain fixed in three dimensional space. Fig. 3.12 illustrates this idea.

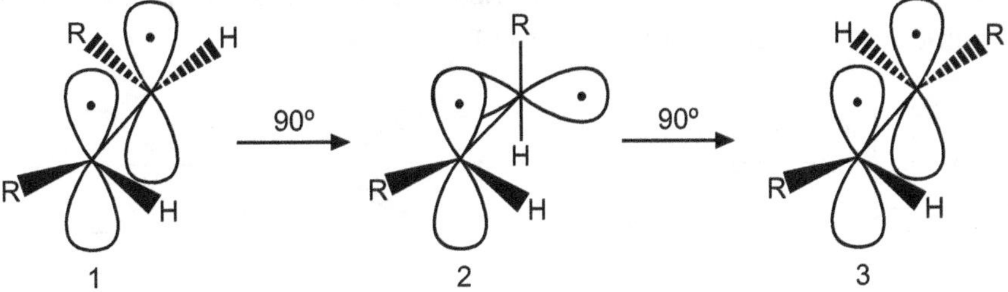

Fig. 3.12

In order to rotate around the double bond in structure 1, it is necessary to break the pi bond. In structure 2 the p orbitals are perpendicular (orthogonal) to each other and their overlap is zero. Typical C-C pi bond strength is approximately 65 kcal/mol. In other words, the potential energy barrier to rotation about a double bond in alkenes is at least 65 kcal/mol. The barrier to rotation around C-C bonds in alkanes is approximately 3-5 kcal/mol. Since the thermal energy available at room temperature is significantly less than 65 kcal/mol, rotation around a double bond does not occur. The lack of rotation gives rise to the possibility of geometric isomers. If the sp2 carbons have different atoms attached to themselves then we are able to differentiate between two like groups (one on each sp^2 carbon) being on the same side of the double bond and two similar groups being on the opposite sides of the double bond. For example, cis-1,2-dichloroethene would have two chlorines on the same side of the double bond. Trans-1,2-dichloroethene would have the two chlorines on opposite sides of the double bond.

Trans-1,2-dichloroethene   cis-1,2-dichloroethene

Compounds exhibiting geometrical isomerism:

Geometrical isomerism is exhibited by a wide variety of compounds and they may be classified into 3 groups.

(1) Compounds containing a double bond C=C, C=N, and N=N:

Example : Alkenes show geometric isomerism phenomenon

cis-isomer   Trans-isomer

Cumulene with odd number of double bonds and two different groups on end 'C's show diasteromerism (I). Since alternate double bonds are on the same plane, those with even number of double bonds show enantiomerism (II).

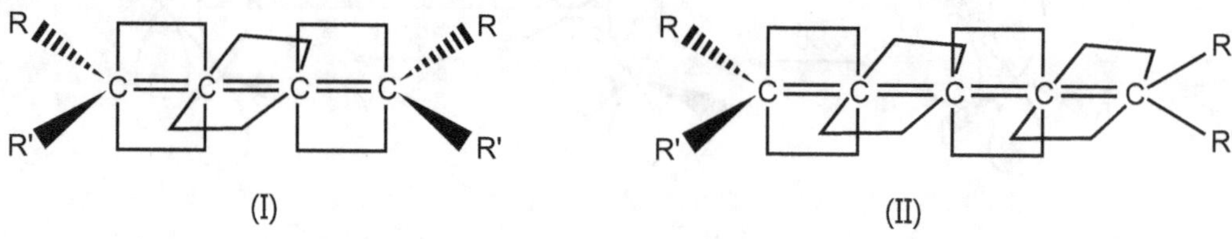

(I)   (II)

Compounds containing C=N exhibit diastereoisomerism.

e.g.

Syn or (E) - Benzaldoxime   Anti or (Z) - Benzaldoxime

(2) Compounds containing cyclic structure, homocyclic, heterocyclic and fused systems. The carbons found within the ring of a cyclic hydrocarbon also have restricted rotation. The carbons within the ring are sp^3 hybridized. If we attempt to rotate the carbons around each other, there will be a lessening of the overlap between two sp^3 orbitals. This, in turn, will cause instability if the overlap is decreased so there is a resistance to the rotation. Consequently, like the atoms attached to the sp^2 carbons in an alkene, the atoms attached to the sp^3 carbons within the ring become fixed as long as the ring remains intact. If two similar atoms or groups of atoms find them selves on opposite sides of the ring, then the groups are trans and the isomer is the trans form. If the two similar groups are on the same side of the ring then the groups are cis and the isomer is the cis isomer. For example, cis-1,2-dimethyl cyclohexane would have the two methyl groups on the same side of the six-membered ring system.

For example

Cis-1,2-dimethyl cyclohexane   Trans-1,2-dimethyl cyclohexane

(3) Compounds which may exhibit G.I. due to restricted rotation about a single bond.

e.g. N-Phenyl pyrrole

N-Phenyl pyrrole

There are no geometrical isomers for alkynes. That is because of the linear geometry around the sp hybrid carbons. The atoms attached to these carbons are in the same line as the carbons, so there is no difference in the geometrical orientation of these groups.

Criteria for the compound to exhibit geometric isomerism:

For a compound to show geometrical isomerism it should fulfill following criteria :

(i) Restricted rotation (often involving a carbon-carbon double bond for introductory purposes);

(ii) Two different groups on the left-hand end of the bond and two different groups on the right-hand end. It doesn't matter whether the left-hand groups are the same as the right-hand ones or not.

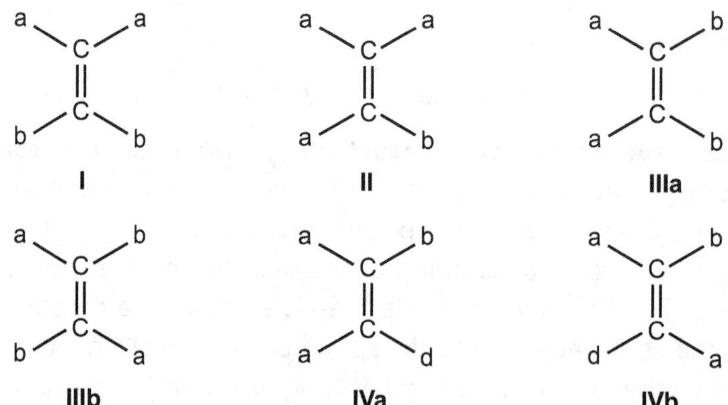

Inspection of these formulae shows that geometrical isomerism is not possible for I and II but is possible for III and IV. Thus double bond is not only condition for geometrical isomerism, the groups attached to the unsaturated carbon atoms must also be taken into consideration.

Number of geometrical isomers: If there are 'n' numbers of conjugated isolated double bonds there will be 2^n geometrical isomers provided all the substituents are different. If some of the substituents are identical, isomer number decreases.

Configuration of geometrical isomers:

E-Z configuration: The cis and trans- designation can be used only for the compounds in which two doubly bonded carbon atoms are having similar atoms or groups. But when the doubly bonded carbon atoms are having different atoms or groups attached to them it is not possible to assign them cis or trans configuration. To overcome this difficulty another system for designating the configuration of geometric isomers has been adopted. This system was developed by Cahn, Ingold and Prelong known as E and Z system, and is based on priority of attached groups. Assignment of configuration is done by following rules.

Rule-1: The atoms or groups attached to each carbon of the double bond, are assigned first and second priority. Priorities of atoms or groups are determined in the same way as for R and S configuration of optical isomers.

Rule-2: If the atoms or groups having higher priority attached to two carbons are on the same side of the double bond the configuration is designated as Z (derived from German word Zussamen meaning together) and if the atoms or groups of higher priority on opposite side of the double bond, the configuration is designated as E (derived from German word entgegen meaning across or opposite).

Rule-3: If in a compound, one of double bonded atom is not having any substituent, then while deciding priority, that vacant position is considered to have an atomic number zero.

For example, Benzaldoxime ($C_6H_5CH = N - OH$)

'E'   'Z'

Examples :

(a)

E-2 butene

(b)

Z-Z-2,4 hexadiene

(c)

E-3-methyl -2-al-2-pentenoic acid

(d)

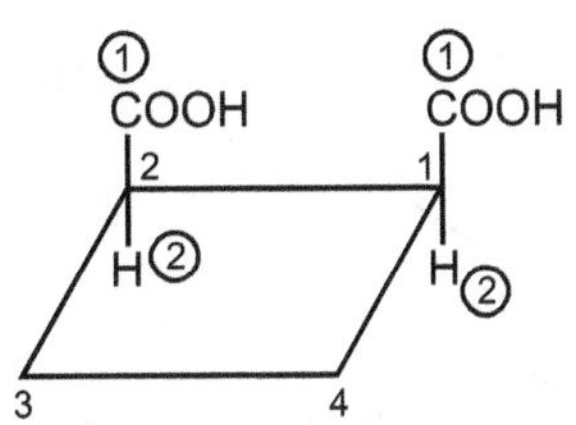

Z-1,2 cyclobutane dicarboxylic acid

(e)

Z-1,4-cyclohexane dicarboxylic acid

(f)

'E'

Properties of geometrical isomers:

Geometrical isomers have different physical and chemical properties. Comparison of the properties of cis and trans- isomers of known configuration shows certain regularities. The M. P. and stability of the cis isomers are lower than those of the trans isomer. The density, R.I., solubility, dipole moment, boiling point, heat of combustion and the dissociation constant (if the acid) of the cis- isomer are greater than those of the trans isomer. It can be seen from these properties that the cis-isomer is usually the labile form. It is possible by suitable means, to convert the labile, cis isomer into the stable trans isomer. For example, maleic acid may be converted to fumaric acid by heating the solid or solution of the solid in water or benzene, to a temperature above it's M.P. (130°C).

The effect of geometrical isomers on physical properties:

(1) Dipole moment: Generally cis isomers have greater dipole moment as compared to trans isomer. Both the isomers have exactly the same atoms joined up in exactly the same order. That means that the van der Waal's dispersion forces between the molecules will be identical in both cases. In case of cis isomer similar groups being on the same side of the double bond, the electronic effects are additive, while in case of trans-isomer, the similar groups being on opposite side, the electronic effects are cancel each other. The difference between the two is that the cis isomer is a polar molecule whereas the trans isomer is non-polar.

Example:

Cis-2-butene
$\mu = 0.4$

Trans-2-butene
$\mu = 0$

(2) Boiling point: Generally a cis isomer has a higher boiling point compared to the trans isomer. Because of higher dipole moment and higher polarity there must be stronger intermolecular forces (dipole-dipole interactions) between the molecules of the cis isomers than between trans isomers thus needing extra energy to break. This will raise the boiling point of the cis isomer than trans isomer.

For example, boiling point of cis-2- butene is higher than trans-2-butene. In case of cis-2- butene, similar methyl groups attached to the carbon-carbon double bond tend to "push" electrons away from themselves. Here electronic effects are additive and so we get a polar molecule. Thus, there is stronger dipole-dipole interaction and more energy is required to break and so their boiling points are higher. By contrast, although there will still be polar bonds in the trans isomers, overall the molecules are non-polar. The slight charge on the top of the molecule is exactly balanced by an equivalent charge on the bottom. This lack of overall polarity means that the only intermolecular attractions these molecules experience are van der Waal's dispersion forces. Less energy is needed to separate them, and so their boiling points are lower.

Cis-2-butene
B.P. = 277 K

Trans-2-butene
B.P. = 274 K

(3) Melting point: A cis isomer has a lower M.P. compared to the trans isomer. Here the factor that is important is the size of the molecule and intermolecular forces of attraction. It can be realized that a cis isomer will occupy a smaller volume compared to the trans isomer. The intermolecular forces of attraction lead to a higher melting point for cis isomers as well, but there is another important factor operating. In order for the intermolecular forces to work well, the molecules must be able to pack together efficiently in the solid. Trans isomers pack better than cis isomers. The "U" shape of the cis isomer doesn't pack as well as the straighter shape of the trans isomer. The poorer packing in the cis isomers means that the intermolecular forces aren't as effective as they should be and so less energy is needed to melt the molecule - a lower melting point.

e.g.

Maleic acid (cis)
M.P. = 403 K

Fumaric acid (trans)
M.P. = 575 K

3.4.5.1.4 Diastereomerism

Stereoisomers that are not related as an object and mirror image are called diastereomers and the phenomenon is called as diastereomerism.

e.g. 2-bromo-3-chlorobutane.

(I)	(II)	(III)	(IV)
Enantiomers		Enantiomers	

Here I and III, I and IV, II and III and II and IV are diastereomers. The enantiomers have opposed configuration on every chiral centre. In diastereomers one chiral centre has opposed configuration while the other has an identical configuration.

Optical isomers like erythro and threo isomers as well as geometric or cis-trans isomers are examples of diastereomers since they are not related to each other as an object and mirror image they are therefore, diastereomers. e.g. (Z)-2-butene and (E)-2-butene.

(Z) - 2 - butene   (E) - 2 - butene

Properties of diastereomers: Diastereomers show similar, but not identical, chemical properties (as they contain same functional group). Two diastereomers have different physical properties like melting points, boiling point, densities, refractive indices, specific rotations, solubilities etc. in a given solvent. Diastereomers also have different chemical reactivities toward given reagents. They can be separated by techniques like fractional crystallization, fractional distillation and chromatography.

QUESTIONS

Q.1   Explain factors affecting melting point, boiling point and solubility.

Q.2   Write anote on intermolecular forces, Dipol- Dipole interactions.

Q.3   Write a note on Geometrical isomerism. Explain it with suitable example.

Q.4   Define the terms Diastereomers, chiral center, Meso compound, Conformational isomer, Configurational isomer, enantiomers, racemic mixture.

Q.5   What is isomerism? Explain any four types of isomerism with examples.

Q.6   Write a note on Inter and Intra molecular forces of attraction.

Q.7   Write a note on Structural isomers

Q.8   Write a note on optical isomerism. Explain it with suitable example

Q.9   Explain enantiomerism with suitable example.

Q.10   Write a note on Geometrical isomerism.

Q.11   Give reason: Meso compounds do not show optical activity.

Q.12   Give reason: Cis and trans isomers differ in their melting and boiling points.

Q.13   Draw geometrical isomeric forms of the following

    1) 2- Pentene   2) 2- Methyl- 2- butene 3) 1- Bromopropene

Q.14   Write short note on

    1) Optical activity

    2) Enantiomerism

    3) Diastereomerism

    4) Dipole moment

Q.15   Assign E and Z configuration to following :

i)

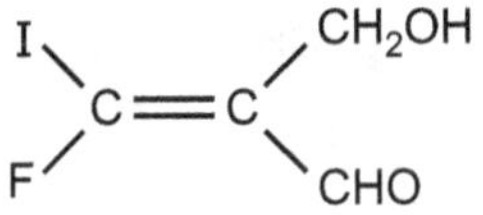

ii)

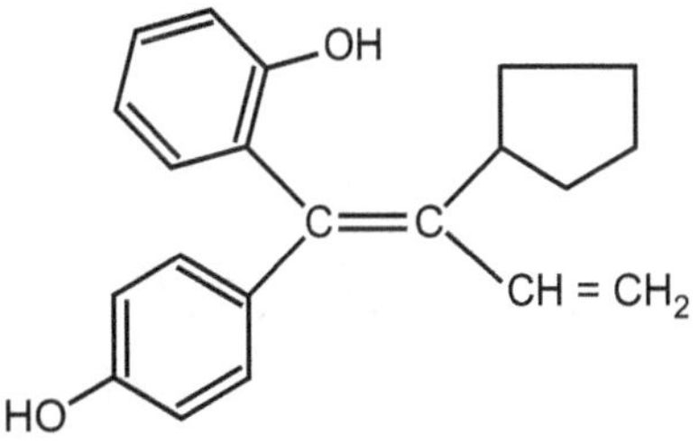

iii)

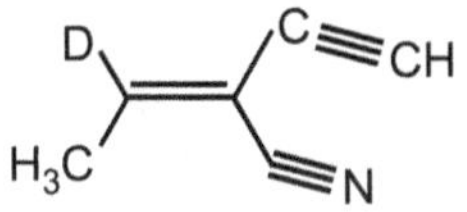

iv)

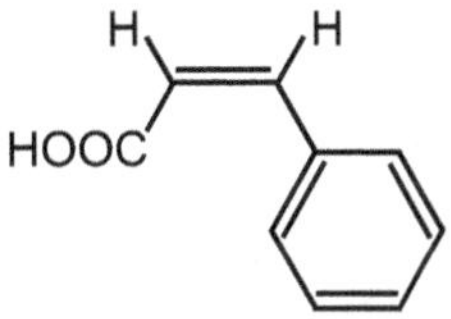

v)

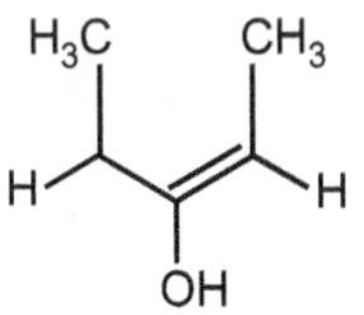

Q.16   Assign configuration to following :

i)

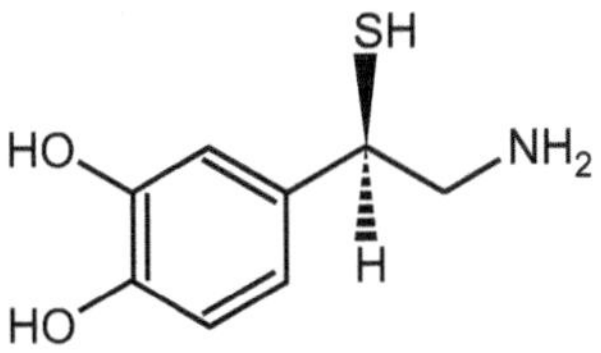

ii)

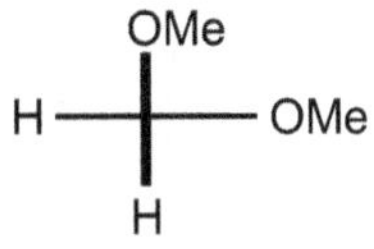

iii)

$$CH_2NH_2 \quad \overset{CH=CH_2}{\underset{OH}{\overset{|}{\underset{|}{C}}}} \quad CH_2OH$$

iv)

v)

$$H \overset{CH_3}{\underset{COOH}{\overset{|}{\underset{|}{C}}}} NH_2$$

vi)

Q.17 Assign R and S configuration to following :

i)

$$H \overset{CH_2OH}{\underset{CH_2OCH_3}{\overset{|}{\underset{|}{C}}}} OH$$

ii)

$$H \overset{CH_2OH}{\underset{CH_3}{\overset{|}{\underset{|}{C}}}} COOH$$

iii)

$$HS \overset{H}{\underset{NH_2}{\overset{|}{\underset{|}{C}}}} COOH$$

Q.18 Establish E and Z configuration to the following :

i)

ii)

iii)

iv)

REACTIONS AND REAGENTS

4.1 ORGANIC REACTION MECHANISM

The steps of an organic reaction depicting the breaking and making of new bonds of carbon atoms in the reactant called substrate leading to the formation of final products through transitory intermediates are called as its mechanism.

In brief, the mechanism of an organic reaction is the detailed step by step know - how of a chemical reaction taking place.

$$\text{Substrate} \longrightarrow \underset{\text{(Transitory)}}{\text{Reaction Intermediate}} \longrightarrow \text{Products}$$

Organic reaction mechanism may also be defined as the description of the path followed by the reactants as they are transformed into products.

4.2 NATURE OF THE FISSION OR CLEAVAGE OF COVALENT BONDS

Depending upon the nature of the given organic compound, the nature of attacking reagent and the reaction conditions, a covalent bond between two atoms of the given compound may be broken into two different ways forming different types of reaction intermediates. The different possibilities are illustrated below by considering a covalent bond between two atoms C and X.

4.2.1 Homolytic Cleavage or Homolytic Fission or Homopolar Fission

The breaking of a covalent bond in a manner so that each of the two species formed retains one electron of the shared pair is called a homolytic fission.

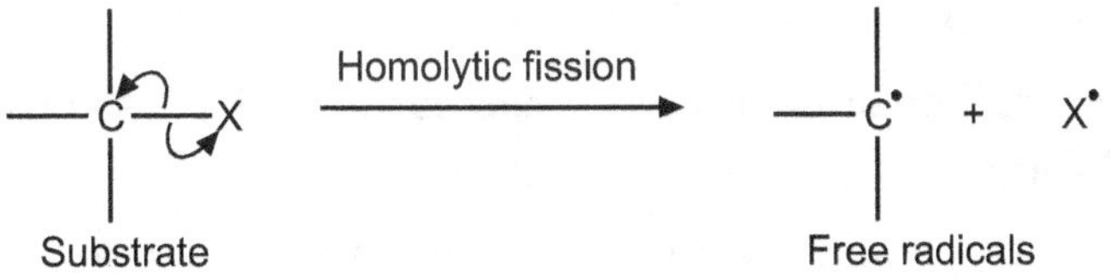

This leads to the formation of highly reactive neutral species containing odd or unpaired electron is known as free radicals.

The reactions which proceed through homolytic cleavage i.e. through the formation of intermediate free radicals are known as free radical reactions or homo reactions.

4.2.2 Heterolytic Cleavage or Heterolytic Fission or Heteropolar Fission

The breaking of a covalent bond in a manner in which ions are formed as reaction intermediates is called a heterolytic fission.

This involves a breaking of a bond in such a way that both the electrons of the shared pair are carried away by one of them. This can take place in two different ways:

(i) The C–X bond in the molecule $-\overset{|}{\underset{|}{C}}-X$ breaks up in such a way that C retains the covalently shared electron pair i.e. C^- ; leaving X as positively charged, i.e. X^+.

$$-\overset{|}{\underset{|}{C}}-X \quad\xrightarrow{\text{Heterolytic fission}}\quad -\overset{|}{\underset{|}{C}}{:}^{\ominus} \;+\; X^{\oplus}$$

$$\text{Substrate}\qquad\qquad\qquad\text{Nucleophile}\quad\text{Electrophile}$$

(ii) The C–X bond in the molecule $-\overset{|}{\underset{|}{C}}-X$ breaks up in such a way that X retains the covalently shared electron pair i.e. X^-; leaving carbon as positively charged, i.e. C^+.

$$-\overset{|}{\underset{|}{C}}-X \quad\xrightarrow{\text{Heterolytic fission}}\quad -\overset{|}{\underset{|}{C}}{}^{\oplus} \;+\; {:}\overset{\ominus}{X}$$

$$\text{Substrate}\qquad\qquad\qquad\text{Electrophile}\quad\text{Nucleophile}$$

The group which contains negatively charged 'C' atom as in the first type of heterolytic fission, is called as **carbanion** whereas the group which contains positively charged 'C' atom as in the second type of heterolytic fission is called a **carbocation** or **carbonium ion**.

The reactions which proceed through heterolytic fission i.e. in which electron pairs are transferred from one species to another in the substrates having at least one covalent bond, are called **polar or ionic reactions**.

Reactions in which carbonium ions are formed as intermediates are said to proceed by a carbonium ion mechanism.

On the other hand, reactions in which carbanion are formed as intermediates are said to proceed by a carbanion mechanism.

4.3 BOND FORMATION

Whenever a covalent bond in an organic reaction is cleaved, it is immediately followed by the bond formation which may occur (i) either in a next step (ii) or simultaneously with the help of bond fission.

i) H_3C—Cl $\xrightarrow{\text{Bond fission}}$ $CH_3^{\oplus}$ + $Cl^{\ominus}$

    Methyl chloride   Carbocation   Chloride ion

$CH_3^{\oplus}$ + $OH^{\ominus}$ $\xrightarrow{\text{Bond formation}}$ H_3C—OH

                               Methanol

ii) H_3C—Cl $\xrightarrow{\text{Bond fission}}$ H_3C—OH + $Cl^{\ominus}$

    $OH^{\ominus}$ Chloride ion

In case (ii) the half-life of the intermediate species is zero and is therefore, not formed.

Mechanism can be represented in a best manner as follows :

$$OH^{\ominus} + H_3C\text{—}Cl \longrightarrow \left[\overset{\delta\ominus}{HO} \cdots \underset{\underset{H}{|}}{\overset{\overset{H}{|}}{C}} \cdots \overset{\delta\ominus}{Cl} \right] \longrightarrow HO\text{—}CH_3 + Cl^{\ominus}$$

Bond making   Bond breaking

Transition state

4.4 TYPES OF ORGANIC REACTIONS

Depending upon the type of bond fission, organic reactions are classified into two main categories :

(a) Heterolytic reactions.

(b) Homolytic reactions.

Depending upon the nature of the reaction which the intermediate species (carbanion, carbonium ion or free radical) undergo, the various types of organic reactions are as follows :

(1) Substitution or displacement reactions.

(2) Addition reactions.

(3) Elimination reactions.

(4) Rearrangements.

(5) Molecular reactions.

(6) Polymerization reactions.

(7) Others.

4.4.1 Substitution or Displacement Reactions

In these reactions an atom or a group of atoms in a molecule is replaced by another atom or group. The incoming group or atom gets attached to the same carbon to which the leaving group or atom was attached.

The substituting species may be either an electrophile, a nucleophile or a free radical.

Electrophilic substitution: Nitration of benzene.

$$Benzene + NO_2^{\oplus} \longrightarrow Intermediate \longrightarrow Nitrobenzene + H^{\oplus}$$

Benzene   Nitronium ion (Electrophile)   Intermediate   Nitrobenzene

Nucleophilic substitutions:

$$R - X + Nu^{\ominus} \longrightarrow R - Nu + X^{\ominus}$$

Alkyl halide   Nucleophile

Free radical substitutions:

$$Cl_2 \longrightarrow 2Cl^{\bullet}$$

Chlorine   Chlorine free radicals

$$CH_4 + Cl^{\bullet} \longrightarrow CH_3Cl + H^{\bullet}$$

Methane   Methyl chloride

$$H^{\bullet} + Cl_2 \longrightarrow HCl + Cl^{\bullet}$$

4.4.2 Addition Reactions

The reactions in which two molecules combine to form a single molecule are called addition reactions. Addition reaction is common to compounds containing multiple bonds.

The attacking species may be a nucleophile, a electrophile or a free radical.

Addition by electrophile (Electrophilic addition) :

Ex. Formation of ethyl bromide from ethene.

$$H_2C = CH_2 \xrightarrow{HBr} H_3C - CH_2 - Br$$

Ethene   Ethyl bromide

Mechanism :

$$H_2C = CH_2 + H^{\oplus} \longrightarrow H_3C - CH_2^{\oplus} \longrightarrow H_3C - CH_2 - Br$$

Ethene

Addition by nucleophile (Nucleophilic addition):

Ex. Addition of hydrogen cyanide to acetone.

$$(H_3C)_2C = O \xrightarrow{HCN} (H_3C)_2C(OH)(CN)$$

Acetone   Cyanohydrin

Mechanism:

$$HCN \xrightarrow{\text{Base}} \overset{\oplus}{H} + \overset{\ominus}{CN}$$

Acetone → → Cyanohydrin

Addition by free radical (Free radical addition) :

Ex. Addition of HBr to double bond in the presence of peroxides.

$$H_2C = CH_2 \xrightarrow[\text{Peroxides}]{\text{HBr}} H_3C - CH_2 - Br$$

Ethene → Ethyl bromide

Mechanism:

$$HBr \xrightarrow{\text{Peroxides}} \overset{\bullet}{H} + \overset{\bullet}{Br}$$

$$H_2C = CH_2 + \overset{\bullet}{H} \longrightarrow H_3C - \overset{\bullet}{CH_2} \xrightarrow{\overset{\bullet}{Br}} H_3C - CH_2 - Br$$

Ethene

4.4.3 Elimination Reactions

The reactions in which two atoms or groups are removed from a single molecule without being replaced by other atoms or groups so that a new double or triple bond is formed are called as elimination reactions. The process is reverse of addition reaction.

There are two types of elimination reactions:

(i) α-elimination reaction: If elimination of two atoms happens to occur from one and the same atom of the substrate, it is known as α-elimination reaction.

Ex:

Chloroform → → Dichlorocarbene

(ii) β-elimination reaction: The process of elimination may occur from two adjacent atoms of the molecule and this is known as β-elimination. This results in the formation of multiple bonds.

Examples :

$$H_3C - CH - CH_2 + KOH \longrightarrow H_3C - CH = CH_2 + KBr + H_2O$$

Propylene

Propyl bromide

$$H_3C - CH_2 - OH \xrightarrow[160° - 170°C]{H_2SO_4} H_2C = CH_2 + H_2O + (H_2SO_4)$$

Ethyl alcohol   Ethylene

Elimination may also take place from atom separated by one, two or more atoms. These are called γ, δ, etc. elimination reactions. In such cases, usually rings are formed.

4.4.4 Rearrangement Reactions

The reaction in which there occurs the movement of an atom or a group from one atom to another within the molecule is called as rearrangement reaction.

The migrating groups are electrophile, nucleophile or free radicals.

Examples :

i)

Phenetole $\xrightarrow[\text{Anhydrous AlCl}_3]{150°C}$ o-Ethyl phenol + p-Ethyl phenol

ii)

1-Bromobutane $\xrightarrow[\text{Anhydrous AlCl}_3]{300°C}$ 2-Bromobutane

4.4.5 Molecular Reactions

The reactions in which the covalent bonds get reorganized either intramolecularly or intermolecularly through cyclic transition states but without involving ionic or radical intermediates are called molecular reactions.

These are not brought about by acids and bases. These reactions take place under the influence of heat or light and are characterized by a high degree of stereospecificity.

For example : Electrocyclic or cycloaddition reaction.

4.4.6 Polymerisation Reaction

The reactions in which a large number of species unite to form a macro species are called as polymerisation reactions.

Ex: A large number of ethane molecules unite to form polyethene.

These may be considered as reactions involving one/more substitution, addition or elimination type of reactions.

4.4.7 Other Reactions

(a) Condensation reaction: In which two or more molecules unite with or without the loss of small units.

Example: Aldol condensation

$$H_3C\text{——}CHO \; + \; H_3C\text{——}CHO \xrightarrow{\;\;OH^{\ominus}\;\;} H_3C\text{——}CH(OH)\text{——}CH_2\text{——}CHO$$

Acetaldehyde   Aldol

(b) Redox reaction: In which change in oxidation number of an atom or atoms occur.

$$\overset{-II}{H_3C}\text{——}OH \xrightarrow{\;\;Oxidation\;\;} \overset{0}{H}CHO$$

Methyl alcohol   Formaldehyde

4.5 CLASSIFICATION OF REAGENTS

When reaction takes place between two substances, one of the substance is generally regarded as the attacking reagent while the other is considered to be a substrate i.e. the substance which gets attacked. The substances formed as the result of the reaction are said to be products of the reaction.

$$\text{Substrate + Attacking reagent} \longrightarrow \text{Product}$$

4.5.1 Types of Reagents

The reagents are classified into three types depending upon their nature.

(i)   Electrophilic reagents

(ii) Nucleophilic reagents

(iii) Free radicals

4.5.1.1 Electrophilic Reagent or Electrophile (i.e Electron Loving)

It is the species having an atom with incomplete octet and attacks an atom of high electron density in the substrate.

These reagents are electron loving and they accept a share in an electron pair belonging to other atoms in a molecule. Therefore, these are also known as Lewis acids.

Types of Electrophiles:

These are classified into two types:

(1) Positive electrophiles: They are those species which carry a positive charge.

e.g. Protons, cations and carbons carrying a positive charge.

N^+, Br^+, Cl^+, NO_2^+, NO^+, NH_4^+, H_3O^+, R_3C^+, $Ar-N=N^+$

The positive electrophile attacks the substrate which is rich in electron and accepts an electron pair for sharing and forming a neutral molecule.

$$\underset{\text{Substrate}}{-\overset{|}{\underset{|}{C}}{:}^{\ominus}} \quad + \quad \underset{\text{Electrophile}}{\overset{\oplus}{E}} \quad \longrightarrow \quad \underset{\text{Product}}{-\overset{|}{\underset{|}{C}}-E}$$

(2) Neutral electrophiles: They are those species which lack positive charge.

e.g. BF_3, $AlCl_3$, $ZnCl_2$ and carbon having six electrons in the outermost orbit. All these behave as electron seeking reagents because they are short of a pair of electrons to attain stable configuration.

$$\underset{\text{Boron trifluoride}}{\overset{|}{\underset{|}{B}}-} \qquad \qquad \underset{\text{Dichlorocarbene}}{-\overset{..}{Cl}-}$$

Other examples:

$$FeCl_3, \quad AlCl_3, \quad \overset{*}{I}\text{-}Cl, \quad R-\overset{O}{\overset{||}{\underset{*}{C}}}-Cl, \quad R-\overset{O}{\overset{||}{\underset{*}{C}}}-O-\overset{O}{\overset{||}{C}}-R$$

* atoms accepting the substrate.

Sulphonium ion (SO_3) carries no net charge, but it acts as an electrophile for sulphonation in benzene rings. This is because of its structure. As the positive charge is concentrated and negative charge is scattered, it acts as an electrophile. The substances like $SnCl_4$ which have vacant d-orbitals would like to accommodate electrons in them. Thus such substances also act as electrophiles.

A neutral electrophile attacks the electron rich substrate, forming a negatively charged molecule.

$$\underset{\text{Substrate}}{-\overset{|}{\underset{|}{C}}{:}^{\ominus}} \quad + \quad \underset{\text{Electrophile}}{E} \quad \longrightarrow \quad \underset{\text{Product}}{-\overset{|}{\underset{|}{C}}-E^{\ominus}}$$

The reactions involving attack of electrophilic reagents are known as **electrophilic reactions**.

4.5.1.2 Nucleophilic Reagent or Nucleophile (i.e. Nucleus Loving)

It is a reagent having at least one unshared pair of valence electrons.

Such reagents are in search of an electron deficient site where it can share its electrons. Thus they behave as Lewis bases with unshared electron pair and which have a tendency to donate electron pair, are called nucleophiles.

As the nucleophiles are capable of donating electron pairs, they are considered as Lewis bases.

Types of Nucleophiles:

These are classified into two types.

(1) Negative nucleophiles: These are the species which carry an excess of electron pair and thus carry negative charge.

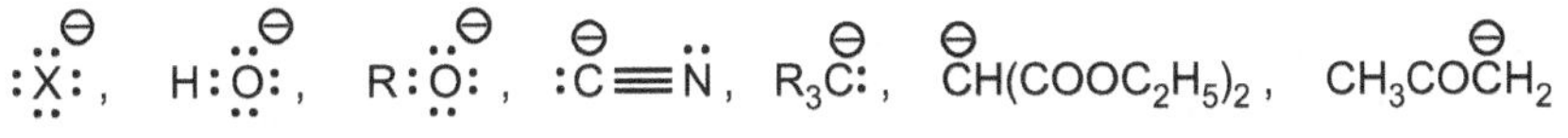

$$:\overset{\ominus}{\underset{..}{X}}:, \quad H:\overset{\ominus}{\underset{..}{O}}:, \quad R:\overset{\ominus}{\underset{..}{O}}:, \quad :C\equiv\overset{\ominus}{N}, \quad R_3\overset{\ominus}{C}:, \quad \overset{\ominus}{C}H(COOC_2H_5)_2, \quad CH_3CO\overset{\ominus}{C}H_2$$

Negative nucleophiles attack on positively charged substrate forming a neutral molecule. For example,

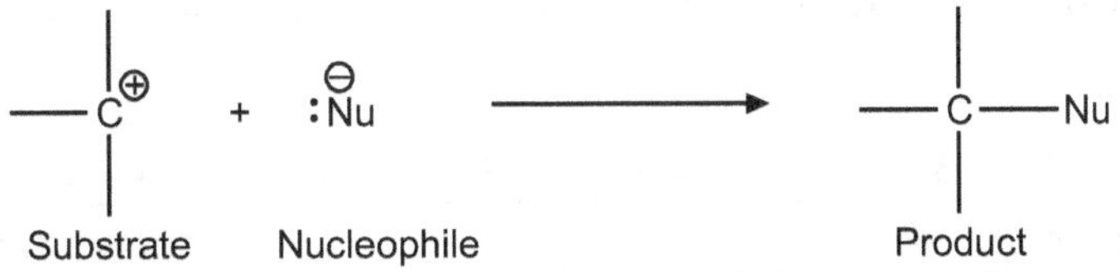

$$-\overset{|}{\underset{|}{C}}{}^{\oplus} \quad + \quad :\overset{\ominus}{Nu} \quad \longrightarrow \quad -\overset{|}{\underset{|}{C}}-Nu$$

$$\text{Substrate} \qquad \text{Nucleophile} \qquad\qquad\qquad \text{Product}$$

(2) Neutral nucleophiles: These are the species which are rich in electrons due to the presence of unshared electrons pair, but are electrically neutral.

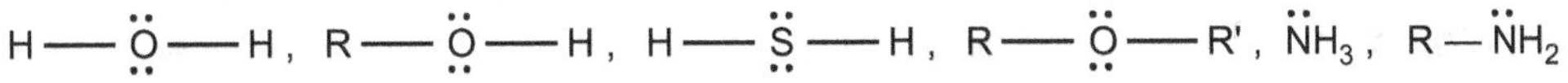

$$H-\overset{..}{\underset{..}{O}}-H, \quad R-\overset{..}{\underset{..}{O}}-H, \quad H-\overset{..}{\underset{..}{S}}-H, \quad R-\overset{..}{\underset{..}{O}}-R', \quad \overset{..}{N}H_3, \quad R-\overset{..}{N}H_2$$

Neutral nucleophiles attack on positively charged substrates forming positively charged products.

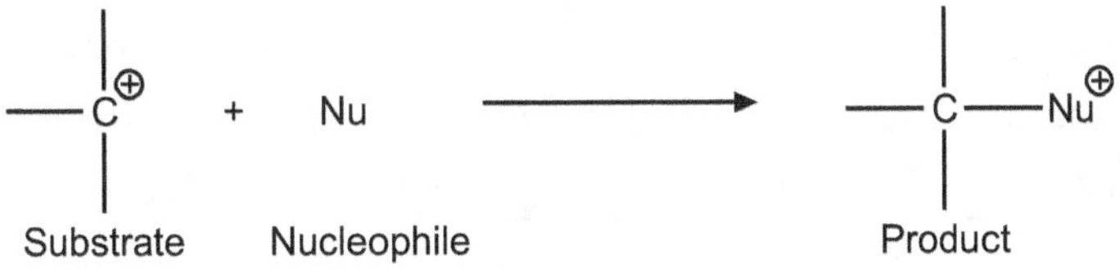

$$-\overset{|}{\underset{|}{C}}{}^{\oplus} \quad + \quad Nu \quad \longrightarrow \quad -\overset{|}{\underset{|}{C}}-Nu^{\oplus}$$

$$\text{Substrate} \qquad \text{Nucleophile} \qquad\qquad\qquad \text{Product}$$

The reactions which involve the attack of nucleophiles are known as **nucleophilic reactions.**

4.5.1.3 Free Radicals

These are the species having one or more unpaired electrons (odd electrons). Free radicals are neutral species which contain unpaired electrons in their valence shell.

4.6 DIFFERENCES BETWEEN FREE RADICAL AND IONIC REACTIONS

Free Radical Reactions	Ionic Reactions
(i) These are favored by light, high temperature and catalysts such as organic peroxides.	(i) These are unaffected by light, free radicals, peroxides.
(ii) These are inhibited by substances such as quinol which combine with free radicals, thereby stopping the chain mechanism.	(ii) These are catalysed by acids and bases which promote ionization. These are inhibited by quinol. They take place in polar solvents.
(iii) These reactions usually take place in vapour phase and non-polar solvents.	(iii) These reactions rarely take place in vapour phase. These are largely affected by nature of the solvent (polarity).
(iv) These are frequently autocatalytic and exhibit an induction period before the reaction commences.	(iv) These usually follow first / second order kinetics and are not autocatalytic. Rate of the reaction increases with temperature.
(v) Reactions of this type involving aromatic substances may not follow orientation rules.	(v) Aromatic substance of ionic type may follow orientation rules.

4.7 DIFFERENCES BETWEEN NUCLEOPHILES AND ELECTROPHILES

Nucleophiles	Electrophiles
(1) Electron rich species.	(1) Electron deficient species.
(2) Attack on electron deficient species.	(2) Attack on electron rich species.
(3) They have an unshared pair of electrons not holding too strongly to the atomic nucleus.	(3) They have an empty orbital which receives the electron pair from the nucleophile.
(4) They increase their covalency by one unit.	(4) They form an extra or alternative bond with the nucleophile.
(5) They are often anions.	(5) They are often cations.
(6) Serve as reducing agents.	(6) Serve as oxidizing agents.
(7) They act as bases.	(7) They act as acids.

QUESTIONS

1. Classify various types of chemical reactions with example.
2. Define the terms with examples : electrophiles, nucleophiles and radicals.
3. Classify various reagents used in organic synthetic reactions.
4. What do you mean by nucleophile and nucleophilicity?
5. Add a note on types of chemical reactions.

Chapter 5

REACTION INTERMEDIATES

5.1 INTRODUCTION

During organic synthesis most reactions do not proceed in a single step but rather take several steps to yield the desired product. In these multi-step reactions, short-lived intermediates can be generated that quickly convert into other intermediates, products or side products. Since these intermediates are very reactive, they cannot be isolated, but their existence and structure can be proved by experimental methods. Using the information obtained, researchers can better understand the underlying reaction mechanism of a certain organic conversion and thus develop novel strategies for efficient organic synthesis.

Reaction intermediates are formed by the breaking of bonds. These are short-lived and highly reactive species and are quickly converted to more stable molecules.

Types of reaction intermediates:

There are nine types of reaction intermediates.

1) Carbocations (Carbenium ion)   2) Carbanions   3) Free radicals

4) Carbenes   5) Nitrenes   6) Nitrenium ion

7) Benzynes   8) π-complexes   9) σ-complexes

5.2 CARBOCATIONS (CARBENIUM ION)

Carbocations are positively charged species in which a carbon atom bears a positive charge and six bonded electrons i.e. three bonds. Hence carbocations may be represented as:

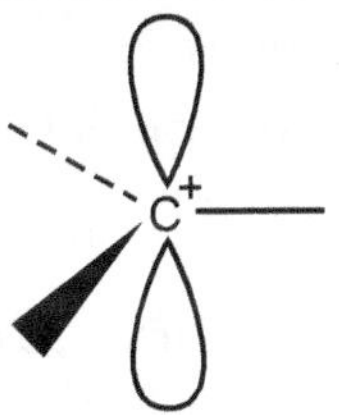

For example :

$^{\oplus}CH_3$ $H_3C — {}^{\oplus}CH_2$ $(CH_3)_2{}^{\oplus}CH$

Methyl cation   Ethyl cation   Isopropyl cation

5.2.1 Types of Carbocation

There are two types of carbocations.

(i) Classical carbocations : In classical carbocations the charge is localized on one carbon atom or delocalized by resonance involving an unshared pair of electrons or a double or triple bond in the allylic position. Carbenium ions are trivalent carbocations containing sp^2-hybridized electron deficient carbon atom and tend to be planar.

For example :

$$CH_2 = CH - {}^{\oplus}CH_2 \qquad\qquad {}^{\oplus}CH_2 - CH = CH_2$$

(ii) Non-Classical carbocations : Carbocations in which positive charge does not remain on a single carbon atom but spreads over at least three atoms and those three atoms form a cyclic cation are called bridged carbocation or non-classical carbocations.

For example

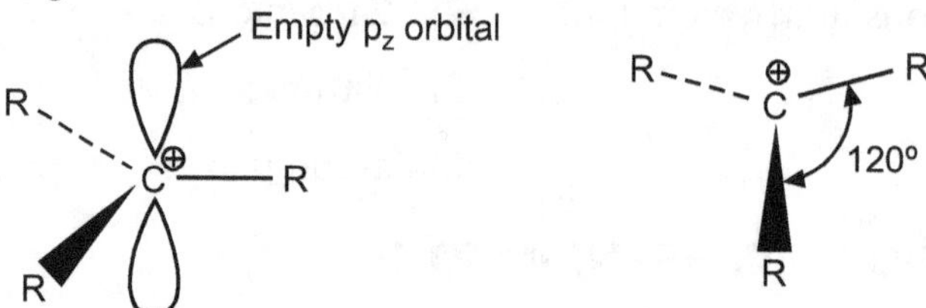

5.2.2 Stereochemistry

The carbon atom in a carbocation is sp^2-hybridized and it uses all its three sp^2 hybridized orbitals for forming bonds with other atoms. The remaining p_z orbital is empty and is perpendicular to the plane of the other three bonds. A carbocation has a triangular planar configuration with bond angle of 120° as shown below.

5.2.3 Generation of Carbocations

Following reactions generate carbocations :

(a) Direct ionization: A direct ionization in which a group attached to a carbon atom leaves with its pair of electrons.

$$R - X \longrightarrow R^{\oplus} + X^{\ominus} \text{ (may be reversible)}$$

For example :

$$CH_3 - Br \xrightarrow{\ Ag^{\oplus}\ } AgBr + {}^{\oplus}CH_3$$

(b) A proton or other positive species is added to one atom.

$$-\overset{|}{C} = Z + H^{\oplus} \longrightarrow -\overset{|}{\underset{|}{\overset{\oplus}{C}}} - Z - H$$

For example :

$$CH_2 = CH_2 \underset{\longleftarrow}{\overset{H^{\oplus}}{\rightleftharpoons}} CH_3 - {}^{\oplus}CH_2$$

Carbocations formed by any method mentioned above, are most often short-lived transient species and react further without being isolated.

5.2.4 Reactions of Carbocations

There are two chief pathways by which carbocations react to give stable products. They are :

(1) Combination with a negative species : The carbocations may combine with a species possessing an electron pair (a Lewis acid-base reaction).

$$R^+ \quad + \quad Y^- \longrightarrow \quad R-Y$$

The species (Y^-) may be OH^-, halides or any other negative ion or may be a neutral species with a pair to donate. In case of neutral species, the immediate product must bear a positive charge.

(2) Elimination of proton : The carbocations may lose a proton from the adjacent atom.

Carbocations can also adopt two other pathways that may not form stable products, but lead to the formation of other carbocations.

(3) Molecular Rearrangement : A carbocation undergoes molecular rearrangement to produce a more stable carbocation by any of the following ways:

A alkyl or aryl group or a hydrogen (sometimes another group) migrates with its electron pair to the positive centre, leaving another positive charge behind. This is illustrated below :

(i) Hydride shift :

1° carbocation   2° carbocation

(ii) Alkyl shift :

1° carbocation   3° carbocation

(iii) Ring expansion : Smaller rings like cyclopropyl and cyclobutyl rings are unstable due to angle strain. Hence, this type of rings having adjacent carbocation may undergo stabilization by ring expansion.

(iv) Addition : A carbocation may add to a double bond generating a positive charge at a new position.

5.2.5 Stability of Carbocations

The groups bonded to positively charged carbon determine the relative stability of carbocations. Electron releasing group bonded to carbocation increases the stability of carbocation while electron withdrawing group bonded to carbocation lowers the stability. Stability of carbocation may be ascertained by considering the following points:

1) Inductive effect
2) Hyperconjugative effect
3) Conjugative effect
4) Solvation effect

(1) Inductive effect (Field effect) :

Alkyl carbocations are stabilized by the electron-donation effect of alkyl groups. Alkyl group increases the electron density at the charge bearing carbon, reducing the net charge on the carbon and in effect spreading the charge over the α-carbons.

e.g. The more the effect on the 'C^{+}', the more stable is the carbocation.

$$CH_3-\overset{\overset{\displaystyle CH_3}{|}}{\underset{\underset{\displaystyle CH_3}{|}}{C}}\!\!\oplus \quad > \quad CH_3-\overset{\oplus}{\underset{\underset{\displaystyle CH_3}{|}}{CH}} \quad > \quad CH_3-\overset{\oplus}{CH_2} \quad > \quad \overset{\oplus}{CH_3}$$

       3º carbocation   2º carbocation   1º carbocation   Methyl carbocation

The more –I effect on the 'C' atom possessing the positive charge, the less stable is the carbocation.

(2) Hyperconjugative effect :

This effect is seen in primary, secondary and tertiary carbocations. More the number of canonical forms, greater is the stability.

Hyperconjugative effect in primary carbocation – Total 3 hyperconjugative forms.

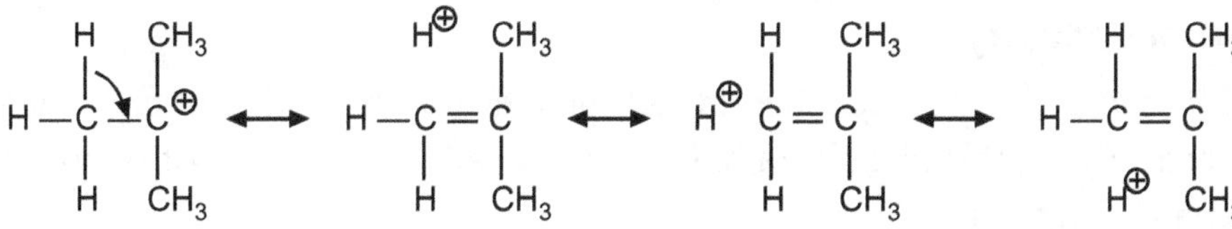

Hyperconjugative effect in t-butyl carbocation

Same hyperconjugative effect in 2 methyl groups. Total 9 hyperconjugative forms.

In the example shown above the primary carbocation has only three hyperconjugative forms. While the tertiary carbocation has nine. According to rule, greater the number of hyperconjugative forms, greater the resonance stability.

(3) Conjugative effect :

When the positive carbon is in conjugation with a double bond, the stability is greater because of increased delocalization of positive charge due to resonance and because the positive charge is spread over two atoms instead of being concentrated on one.

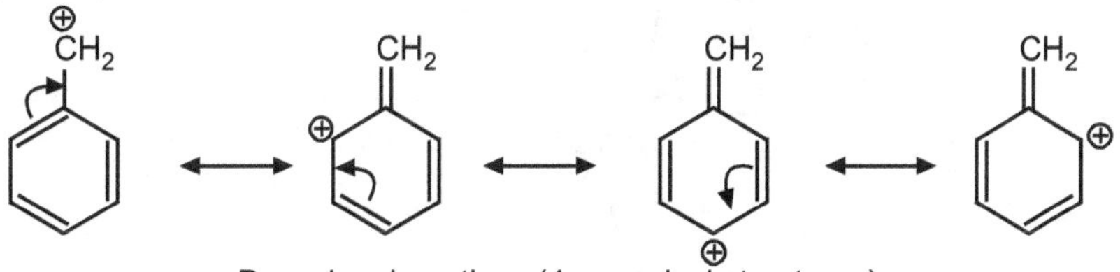

Benzyl carbocation (4 canonical structures)

Allyl carbocation (2 canonical structures)

(4) Solvation effect :

The more polar the solvent, the more stable is the carbocation through solvation, provided there is no chemical reaction between them.

5.3 CARBANIONS

Carbanions are anions i.e. negatively charged species in which a carbon atom carries three bonds and a lone pair of electrons, thus making the carbon atom negatively charged. Such carbon atoms have eight electrons in the outermost orbit.

Carbanion may be represented as :

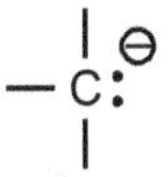

These all are strong Lewis bases and act as very strong nucleophile.

e.g.

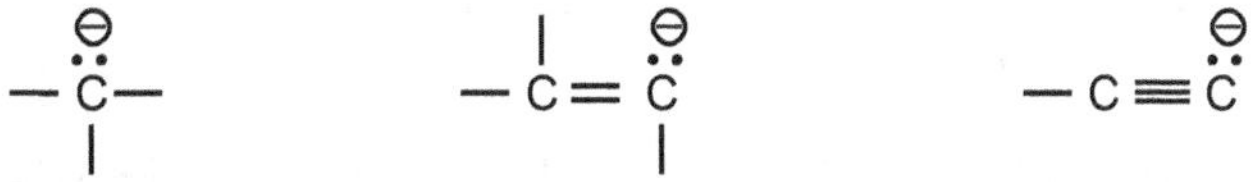

Alkyl carbanion   Vinyl carbanion   Acetylinic carbanion

5.3.1 Stereochemistry

The alkyl carbanion has sp^3 hybridized negatively charged carbon possessing an unshared electron pair. This gives pyramidal (non-planar) arrangement of bonds around the negatively charged carbon.

Tetrahedral sp^3 hybridized carbanion

However, when the carbanion is stabilized by delocalization, it assumes sp^2 hybridized for effective resonance. The lone pair electrons are considered to be present in unhybridized $2p$-orbital.

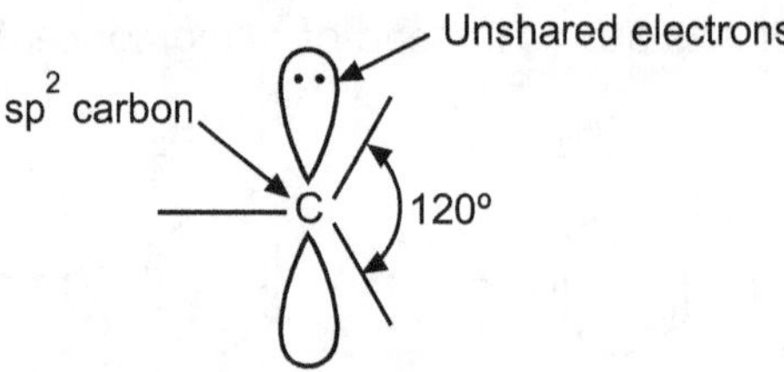

Planar sp^2 hybridized carbanion

5.3.2 Generation of Carbanion

Carbanions are generated by following methods.

(1) Elimination of proton (H⁺) :

A group attached to a carbon leaves without its bonding electron pair.

$$R\!-\!H \longrightarrow \ddot{R}^{\ominus} + H^{\oplus}$$

The leaving group is most often a proton. This is a simple acid-base reaction and a base is required to remove the proton.

(2) Decomposition of anion :

$$R\!-\!\underset{\underset{O}{\|}}{C}\!-\!\ddot{\underset{\cdot\cdot}{O}}{}^{\ominus} \xrightarrow{\;\Delta\;} \overset{\ominus}{\underset{\cdot\cdot}{R}} + C\!=\!\underset{O}{\overset{\|}{}}O$$

(3) Addition of negative ion to a C=C or C ≡ C :

$$-\overset{|}{\underset{|}{C}}\!=\!\overset{|}{\underset{|}{C}}- \; + \; Y^{\ominus} \longrightarrow -\overset{\ominus}{\underset{|}{C}}\!-\!\overset{|}{\underset{|}{C}}\!-\!Y$$

The addition of a negative ion to a carbon oxygen double bond does not give a carbanion since the positive charge resides on the oxygen.

5.3.3 Reactions of Carbanion

(1) Combination with a positive species :

The most common reaction of carbanions is the combination with a positive species usually a proton or with another species that has an empty orbital in its outer shell.

$$\overset{\ominus}{\underset{\bullet\bullet}{R}} \; + \; \overset{\oplus}{Y} \longrightarrow R - Y$$

(2) Displacement of a group or atom :

Carbanions may also form a bond with a carbon that already has four bonds, by displacing one of the four groups.

$$\overset{\ominus}{R} + -\overset{|}{\underset{|}{C}} - X \longrightarrow R - \overset{|}{\underset{|}{C}} - \; + \; \overset{\ominus}{\underset{\bullet\bullet}{X}}$$

(3) Addition to double bonds :

Like carbocation, carbanions can also react in different ways in which they are converted to species that are still not neutral molecules.

They can add to double bonds.

$$\overset{\ominus}{\underset{\bullet\bullet}{R}} \; + \; =\overset{\overset{\bullet\bullet}{O}}{\underset{}{C}} - \longrightarrow -\overset{:\overset{\ominus}{O}:}{\underset{\underset{R}{|}}{\underset{|}{C}}} -$$

(4) Rearrangement to most stable carbanion :

Primary carbanions rearrange to form tertiary carbanions. This is a rare rearrangement.

$$Ph - \overset{Ph}{\underset{Ph}{\overset{|}{\underset{|}{C}}}} - \overset{\ominus}{\underset{\bullet\bullet}{C}H_2} \longrightarrow Ph - \overset{\overset{\ominus}{\bullet\bullet}}{\underset{Ph}{\overset{|}{\underset{|}{C}}}} - CH_2 - Ph$$

5.3.4 Stability of Carbanion

The carbanions being electron rich are very reactive intermediates and are readily attacked by electrophiles. The stability of carbanion is increased if an electron attracting group like $C \equiv N$ or $- C = O$ or NO_2 is present in the molecule. However the stability is decreased if an electron releasing group is present in the molecule.

The stability of carbanions may be explained by the following effects.

(1) Conjugation: Conjugation of the unshared pair with an unsaturated bond:

$$Y = \overset{R}{\underset{R}{\overset{|}{\underset{|}{C}}}} - \overset{R}{\underset{R}{\overset{|}{\underset{\bullet\bullet}{C}}}} \longrightarrow \overset{\ominus}{\underset{\bullet\bullet}{Y}} - C = \overset{R}{\underset{R}{\overset{|}{\underset{|}{C}}}}$$

In case where a double or triple bond is located 'α' to the carbanionic carbon, the ion is stabilized by resonance in which the unshared pair overlaps with the π electrons of the double bond.

Allylic carbanion

Benzylic carbanion

(2) s-Character : Carbanions instability increases with an increase in the amount of 's' character at the carbanionic carbon. Thus the order of stability is :

$$R - C \equiv \overset{\ominus}{\ddot{C}} \; > \; R_2C = \overset{\ominus}{\ddot{C}H} \; \approx \; Ar^{\ominus} \; > \; R_3 - C - \overset{\ominus}{\ddot{C}H_2}$$

(3) Field effect : Most of the groups that stabilize carbanions by resonance effects have electron withdrawing field effects and thereby stabilize the carbanion further by spreading the negative charge.

Carbanions are stabilized by a field effect if there is any hetero atom (O, N or S) connected to the carbanionic carbon, provided that the heteroatom bears a positive charge in at least one important canonical form.

Alkyl anions have the following order of stability.

$$\overset{\ominus}{\ddot{C}H_3} \; > \; H_3C - \overset{\ominus}{\ddot{C}H_2} \; > \; (CH_3)_2 - \overset{\ominus}{\ddot{C}H} \; > \; (CH_3)_3 - \overset{\ominus}{\ddot{C}}$$

This order is explained by inductive effect : +I effect increases the electron density on the negatively charged carbon atom, thus if the +I effect group bonded to carbanion increases the stability of carbanion goes on decreasing. As shown above as the number of methyl group increases on the anionic carbon atom, the negative charge also increases on it and consequently the stability of species decreases. Therefore stability decreases down the series.

5.4 FREE RADICALS

A free radical may be defined as a species that contain one or more unpaired electrons. Free radicals are reactive intermediates. Free radical of a carbon atom consists of a carbon with three covalent bonds and an unpaired electron. Free radicals are electron deficient, highly reactive species and act as strong electrophiles in a chemical reaction.

e.g.

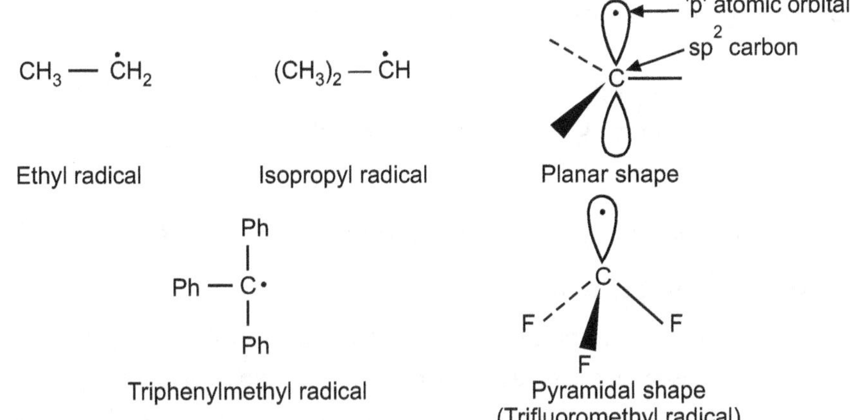

Homolytic fission of a bond gives rise to free radicals. This cleavage is initiated either by physical aids or by chemical reagents.

a)   Physical aids – Heat, light, radioactive radiation

b)   Chemical reagents -

   i)   Organic peroxides – Benzoyl peroxide

   ii) Azo compounds

   iii) Reductants and oxidants.

5.4.1 Generation of Free Radicals

Free radicals are formed from molecules by breaking a bond so that each fragment keeps one electron. The following methods can be used to generate free radicals.

1) Thermal cleavage :

Subjecting any organic molecule to a high enough temperature in the gas phase results in the formation of free radicals.

e.g.

$$R-\overset{\overset{\displaystyle O}{\|}}{C}-O-O-\overset{\overset{\displaystyle O}{\|}}{C}-R \xrightarrow{\Delta} 2R-\overset{\overset{\displaystyle O}{\|}}{C}-O^{\bullet}$$

$$R-N=N-R \longrightarrow 2R^{\bullet} + N_2$$

2) Photochemical cleavage :

The free radicals are also formed in the presence of light (energy of light of 600 nm to 300 nm).

$$Cl_2 \xrightarrow{h\nu} 2\,Cl^{\bullet}$$

$$R-\overset{\overset{\displaystyle O}{\|}}{C}-R \xrightarrow[\text{Vapour phase}]{h\nu} R-\overset{\overset{\displaystyle O}{\|}}{C}^{\bullet} + R^{\bullet}$$

Radicals are also formed from other radicals, either by reaction between radical and molecule or by cleavage of a radical to give another radical.

e.g.

$$Ph - C(=O) - O^{\bullet} \longrightarrow Ph^{\bullet} + CO_2$$

Radicals can also be formed by oxidation or reduction, including electrolytic methods.

5.4.2 Reactions of Free Radicals

Reactions of free radicals either give stable products (termination reaction) or lead to other radicals, which themselves must react further (propagation reactions)

a) Termination reaction : Free radical may combine with other free radical to form stable product.

$$R^{\bullet} \ + \ R^{\bullet \bullet} \longrightarrow R - R'$$

b) Propagation reaction : There are four main propagation reactions, of which first two are most common.

(1) Abstraction of another atom or group, usually a hydrogen atom :

$$R^{\bullet} \ + \ R' - H \longrightarrow R - H \ + \ R^{\bullet \bullet}$$

(2) Addition to a multiple bond :

$$R^{\bullet} \ + \ -C = C- \longrightarrow R - C - C^{\bullet}-$$

These radicals formed here may add to another double bond. This is one of the chief mechanisms of vinyl polymerization.

(3) Decomposition :

$$Ph - C(=R) - O^{\bullet} \longrightarrow Ph^{\bullet} \ + \ CO_2$$

(4) Rearrangement :

$$R - C(R)(R) - \overset{\bullet}{C}H_2 \longrightarrow R - C^{\bullet} - CH_2 - R$$

This is a less common reaction.

5.4.3 Stability of Free Radicals

The stability of free radicals depends upon the degree of delocalization of the odd electrons. As the delocalization increases, the stability of radicals increases.

The delocalization may take place in two ways.

(1) By hyperconjugation : As the number of α-hydrogens on free radicals increases, the stability of free radical increases in the order due to resonance.

Stability order of alkyl radicals is as given below.

Radical stability increases in the order methyl < primary < secondary < tertiary

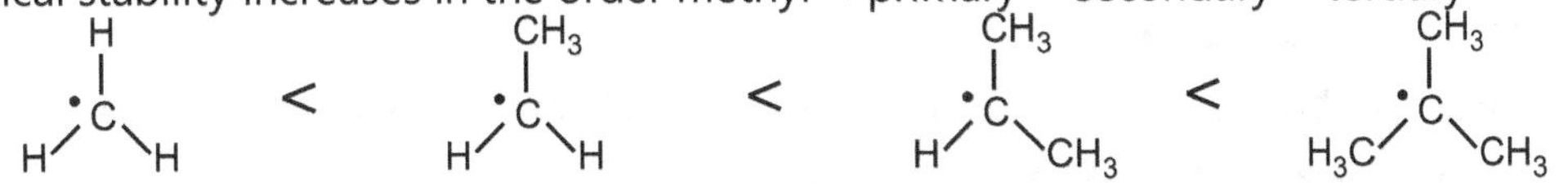

Methyl radical | Primary radical | Secondary radical | Tertiary radical
Least stable | | | **Most stable**

As we move away from the t-butyl radicals, we get decreasing number of no-bond resonating structures in their resonance hybrids and thus their stability falls down.

(2) By conjugation : The stability of allylic and benzylic radicals is explained by the p-π conjugation as given below.

For example

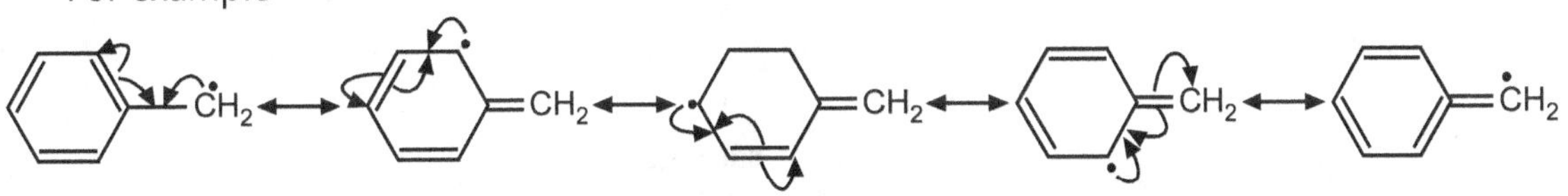

$$\text{e.g.} \quad Ph_3 \overset{\bullet}{C} > Ph_2 \overset{\bullet}{C}H > Ph\overset{\bullet}{C}H_2$$

Resonance effect due to conjugation stabilizes the free radicals.

It is found that with increasing number of phenyl groups, the probability of delocalization of electrons over a greater range increases. Hence the stability of triphenyl methyl radical is more as compared to diphenyl methyl and benzyl radical.

5.5 CARBENES OR METHYLENES

Carbenes are very short lived species in which one carbon atom possesses two bonds and two electrons, either paired or unpaired.

The simplest member of this class is methylene, a non-isolable species of the formula : CH_2.

The most common carbene is : CCl_2 (dichlorocarbene). Other carbenes are :

$$R_2C = C = \overset{..}{C} , \; C_6H_5 - \overset{..}{C} - C_6H_5, \; H\overset{..}{C} - \overset{O}{\overset{\|}{C}} - R$$

Usually carbenes are named as derivatives of : CH_2 (methylcarbene); $Ph_2\overset{..}{C}$ (diphenylcarbene); and

$$CH_3 - CO - \overset{..}{C}H \quad \text{(acetocarbene)}.$$

5.5.1 Methods of Preparation

(1) By elimination reaction :

$$CHCl_3 \xrightarrow[-HCl]{Alc.\ KOH} Cl_2C: \xleftarrow[-CO_2\ \&\ Cl^-]{\Delta} CCl_3COO^-$$

Chloroform   Trichloroacetate

(2) By decomposition reaction :

$$CH_2 = C = O \xrightarrow[or\ h\nu]{\Delta} :CH_2 \xleftarrow[or\ h\nu]{\Delta} CH_2 = \overset{\oplus}{N} = \overset{\ominus}{\overset{..}{N}:}$$

5.5.2 Types of Carbene

The two non-bonded electrons of carbene may be either unpaired or paired. Based on this there are following two types of carbene.

(a) Triplet carbene: When two non-bonded electrons are unpaired, the carbene is called a **triplet carbene. Triplet carbene has bent shape and bond angle around 136°.** Usually, a triplet carbene is more stable than the corresponding singlet carbene because in the latter, two electrons get accommodated in a single orbital though there is a one vacant orbital of almost same energy.

136°

Triplet carbene

(b) Singlet carbene: If non-bonded electrons are paired, then the carbene is called a singlet carbene. Singlet carbene has bent shape and bond angle is around 103°.

Vacant 'p' atomic orbital

sp^2 atomic orbital

103°

sp^2 hybridized carbon

Singlet carbene

Singlet carbenes having resonance stabilization are found to be more stable than the corresponding triplet state.

5.5.3 Stability of Carbene

Carbenes in which the carbene carbon is attached to two atoms, each bearing a lone pair of electrons are more stable due to resonance.

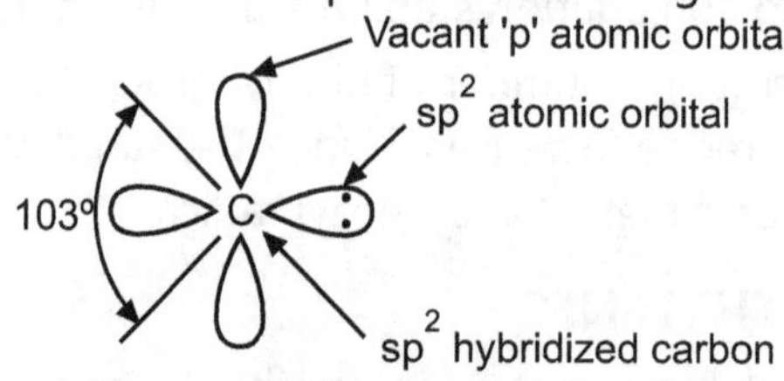

Triplet carbenes are more stable than singlet carbenes.

5.5.4 Reactions of Carbene

(1) Insertion : Singlet carbenes undergo unusual insertion reactions but triplet carbenes do not ; the reaction occurs mainly in C–H, O–H, C–Cl bonds but does not at all occur in a C–C bond.

$$H - CH_2 - CHOH - CH_3 \quad + \quad :CH_2 \longrightarrow \quad CH_3 - CH_2 - CHOH - CH_3$$

$$CH_3 - \underset{\underset{H}{|}}{C}(OH) - CH_3 \quad + \quad :CH_2 \longrightarrow \quad CH_3 - \underset{\underset{CH_3}{|}}{C}(OH) - CH_3$$

$$CH_3 - \underset{\underset{CH_3}{|}}{CH} - O - H \quad + \quad :CH_2 \longrightarrow \quad CH_3 - \underset{\underset{CH_3}{|}}{CH} - OCH_3$$

$$3\ CH_3 - CHOH - CH_3 \quad + \quad 3 :CH_2 \longrightarrow \quad CH_3CH_2CHOH - CH_3$$
$$+ \ (CH_3)_3 - C - OH$$
$$+ \ (CH_3)_2 - CH - OCH_3$$

(2) Addition : Both the singlet and the triplet carbenes undergo addition reaction. Addition to a multiple bond is a stereoselective and stereospecific reaction.

For example

(3) Rearrangement : Carbenes also take part in abstraction reactions and thus form free radicals e.g. methylene reacts with ethane and produces methyl and ethyl radicals.

$$CH_3 - CH_2 - H \quad + \quad :CH_2 \longrightarrow \quad CH_3 - \overset{\cdot}{C}H_2 \quad + \quad \overset{\cdot}{C}H_3$$

5.6 NITRENES

Nitrenes are non-isolable short-lived, highly reactive and electron deficient species having six electrons on a nitrogen atom.

Nitrenes are also called azenes, imenes, imidogens. The simplest nitrene is $H — \overset{..}{\underset{\cdot}{N}}:$

e.g.

$$R—\overset{\overset{\textstyle O}{\|}}{C}—\overset{..}{\underset{..}{N}} \qquad\qquad R—\overset{..}{\underset{..}{N}}$$

Acyl nitrene   Alkyl nitrene

Usually nitrenes are named as derivatives of $H — \overset{..}{\underset{\cdot}{N}}:$

5.6.1 Methods of Preparation

(i) α- elimination reaction :

$$R-\overset{\overset{O}{\|}}{C}-NHBr \xrightarrow{\ OH^{\ominus}\ } R-\overset{\overset{O}{\|}}{C}-\ddot{N}:$$

(ii) Pyrolysis :

$$R-\overset{\overset{O}{\|}}{C}-\ddot{N}=\overset{\oplus}{N}=\ddot{N}^{\ominus}: \longrightarrow R-\overset{\overset{O}{\|}}{C}-\ddot{N}: \ +\ N_2$$

Acylazide

(iii) Photolysis :

$$H-\overset{\ominus}{\underset{..}{\ddot{N}}}-\overset{\oplus}{N}\equiv N: \xrightarrow[\text{UV}]{\text{Hg, h}\upsilon} H-\ddot{N}: \ +\ N_2$$

Hydrazoic acid

$$R-\ddot{N}=C=\ddot{O}: \xrightarrow[\text{UV}]{\text{Hg, h}\upsilon} H-\ddot{N} \ +\ CO$$

Alkyl isocyanate

5.6.2 Types of Nitrenes

There are two types of nitrenes:

(1) Triplet nitrene

(2) Singlet nitrene

(1) Triplet nitrene: It is the ground state of nitrene since two degenerated orbitals accommodate one electron each. $H-\overset{\uparrow\uparrow}{N}:$

(2) Singlet nitrene: It has both the electrons in an orbital, i.e. they are paired.

$$H-\overset{\downarrow\uparrow}{N}:$$

5.6.3 Stability of Nitrenes

Nitrenes are very reactive species and can not be isolated. However, a nitrene has been trapped by its reaction with carbon monoxide to yield an isocyanate.

$$PhN_3 \xrightarrow{\ \Delta\ } Ph-\ddot{N}: \xrightarrow{\ CO\ } PhN=C=O$$

Phenyl isocyanate

Nitrene can also be trapped in the presence of ethylene.

$$H\ddot{N}: \ +\ CH_2=CH_2 \ \rightleftharpoons\ \underset{H}{\overset{\triangledown N}{}}$$

5.6.4 Reactions of Nitrene

Nitrenes behave as electrophiles and they undergo addition, insertion, rearrangement and H-abstraction reactions.

(a) Addition reaction : Nitrenes add to C=C.

For example :

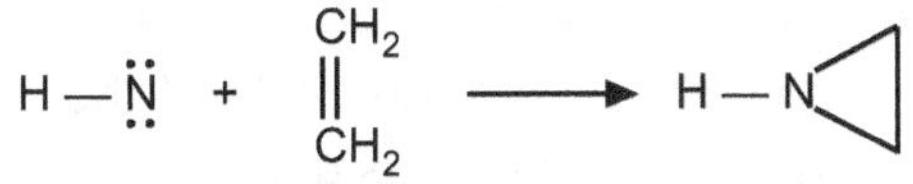

$$H-\ddot{N} \quad + \quad \begin{array}{c} CH_2 \\ \| \\ CH_2 \end{array} \quad \longrightarrow \quad H-N\!\!\triangleleft$$

Nitrene   Ethylene   Aziridine

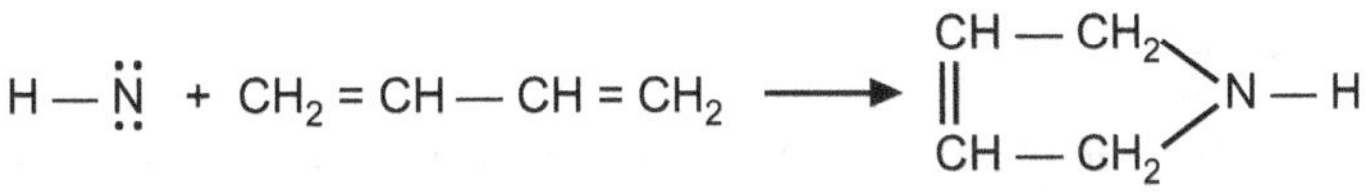

$$H-\ddot{N} \quad + \quad CH_2=CH-CH=CH_2 \quad \longrightarrow \quad \begin{array}{c} CH-CH_2 \\ \| \qquad\qquad\ N-H \\ CH-CH_2 \end{array}$$

Nitrene   1,4-Butadiene   3-Pyrroline

(b) Insertion reaction : Nitrenes are found to undergo insertion reaction in C–H bonds.

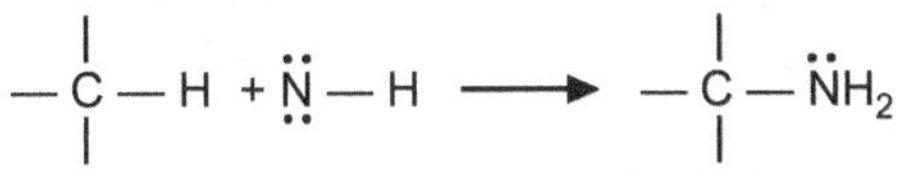

$$-\overset{|}{\underset{|}{C}}-H + \ddot{N}-H \quad \longrightarrow \quad -\overset{|}{\underset{|}{C}}-\ddot{N}H_2$$

Alkane   Nitrene   Amine

(c) Rearrangement reaction : The most easily formed nitrenes usually rearrange to give alkyl isocyanate. This rearrangement is involved in Curtius and Hofmann rearrangement.

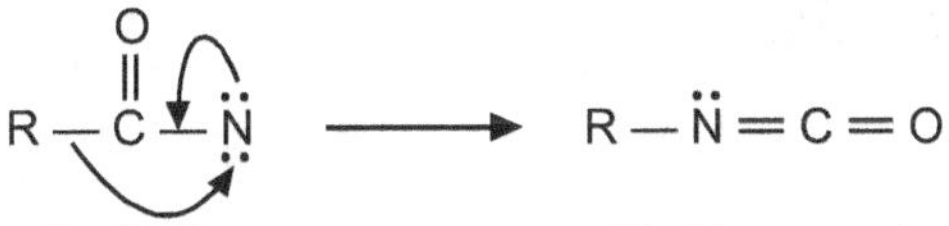

$$R-\overset{\overset{O}{\|}}{C}-\ddot{N} \quad \longrightarrow \quad R-\ddot{N}=C=O$$

Acyl nitrenes   Alkyl isocyanate

5.7 BENZYNES

1, 2-dehydrobenzene, C_6H_4 and its derivatives may be called benzynes or arynes, the simplest member is benzyne. It is neutral, non-isolable highly reactive species, in which the aromatic characters are not markedly disturbed.

It can be represented as:

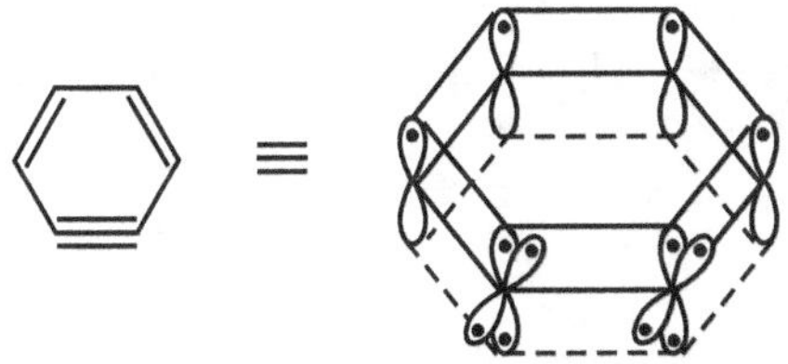

Fig. 5.1 : Structure of benzyne

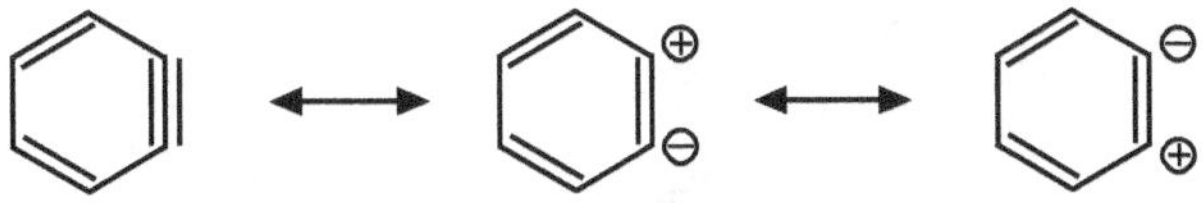

Benzyne has hexagonal planar ring structure with six delocalized π-electrons and two other additional π-electrons in a π-orbital formed by the side-on overlap of two sp^2 atomic orbitals (containing one electron each) covering two 'C' atoms only; these bond orbitals lie along the side of the ring and create deformation of the bond angle (120° to 180° as shown in Fig. 5.1). The deformation of the bond angle causes a strain and makes the species highly reactive. Its structure may also be looked upon as a resonance hybrid of some resonating structures, dipolar structures explain the electrophilic character of benzyne and the six membered ring structure containing a triple bond explains the instability and hence the high reactivity of the species. Thus, the structure tells us that these two additional electrons do not interact with the π-cloud involving Huckel number of π-electrons and hence they do not affect the aromaticity of the benzyne molecule.

5.7.1 Stereochemistry

Except for the two carbon atoms which are linked through a triple bond, all the other remaining carbon atoms are sp^2 hybridized. The carbon atoms linked through the triple bond are sp-hybridized. Due to these two sp-hybridized carbon atoms, the intermediate is highly strained and hence, is highly reactive. However the presence of sp-hybridization does not change its aromatic character. Hence the intermediate still consist of aromatic sextet.

5.7.2 Methods of Preparation

1)

Chlorobenzene $\overset{\ominus}{NH_2}$ (NaNH$_2$) in liq. NH$_3$ Benzyne + $\ddot{N}H_3$ + $Cl^{\ominus}$

2)

$\xrightarrow[50°C]{C_6H_6}$ + N_2 + CO_2

3)

o-dihalobenzene $\xrightarrow{Li/Hg}$

4)

o-Fluoroanisole $\xrightarrow[\text{(Phenyl lithium)}]{C_6H_5Li}$

5.7.3 Reactions of Benzyne

1) Benzynes being electrophilic, undergo nucleophilic addition reactions, which otherwise are not possible with benzene.

2) Benzynes undergo 1, 4 addition to conjugate dienes.

5.8 π-COMPLEXES

A weakly bonded charge transfer complex which exists in solution only and is formed by the association of an electrophilic species (E) and electron donating species (D) which utilizes its π-orbital electrons for association is known as a π-complex.

Alkenes, arenes, alkynes, cycloalkenes etc. are the electron donors and metal ions, molecular halogens, hydrogen halides etc. are common electrophilic reagents.

The structure of π-complex is not completely known. But it is said to be a resonance hybrid of the following resonating forms:

$$D + E \rightleftharpoons \overset{\delta+\ \ \delta-}{D\text{----}E} \longleftrightarrow \overset{\oplus\ \ \ominus}{D\text{---}E} \qquad \overset{\ominus\ \ \oplus}{D\text{---}E}$$

$$\text{(a)} \qquad\qquad \text{(b)} \qquad\qquad \text{(c)}$$

Form (a) contributes predominantly in the ground state of the complex, while form (b) and (c) contribute primarily in the excited state. Contribution of (c) is much less than that of (b) in most of the complexes. In the form (a) the components are held together by weak intermolecular forces like dipole-dipole, dipole-induced dipole, ion-dipole etc.

In form (b), the electrophile co-ordinates with the π-electrons of the donor without forming a strong σ-bond to any specific atom, instead there is a delocalized intermolecular co-ordinate covalent bond in which the bonding electron pair is provided by two or more atoms of the donor and is shared with two or more atoms in the electrophile.

For example, ethylene-silver ion π-complex is a resonance hybrid of the following forms:

Hybrid may be represented as :

Similarly toluene-bromine and benzene–hydrogen chloride π-complex may be represented as shown :

5.8.1 The Stability of a π-complex

Factors :

(i) The greater the polarisability of the donor component, the more stable is the π-complex.

(ii) The strength of the π-complex increases with decreasing ionization potential of the donor and increasing electron affinity of the electrophile.

(iii) Electron releasing groups which increase electron density in the donor species and electron withdrawing groups which decrease electron density in the electrophile increase the strength of the π-complex.

(iv) In a π-complex, the distance between the two planes of components is usually 0.3 nm to 0.35 nm. If either component is non-planar, the distance between the planes increases, which decrease the attractive force and thereby decrease the stability of the complex.

5.9 σ-COMPLEX

When an electrophile reacts with an arene usually in the presence of a catalyst, a salt is formed. This salt is composed of an anion and a complex resonance stabilized carbocation (arenium ion). Such a salt in which only two of the total π-electrons required for preservation of the aromaticity of the arene are utilized to form a σ-bond between a particular carbon atom of the ring and the electrophile, is called a σ-complex salt and the carbocation is called a σ-complex or Wehland intermediate.

For example, when benzene is treated with HCl in the presence of anhydrous $AlCl_3$, a Lewis acid, a salt of benzenium ion and $AlCl_4^-$, then σ-complex salt is formed.

A σ-complex is a resonance hybrid of several resonating structures. The benzenium ion may be represented as a resonance hybrid.

It is assumed that a σ-complex may form via a π-complex and equilibrium exists between the reactants, the π-complex and the σ-complex.

π-complex σ-complex

5.9.1 Reactions of a σ-complex

A σ-complex may undergo two kinds of reactions :

(1) Coupling with an anion　or

(2) Proton elimination reaction

If it undergoes proton elimination reaction, the product will be an aromatic compound; while the coupling product of a σ-complex is not an aromatic compound. Aromatic compounds being more stable than a non-aromatic compound having double bonds, σ-complexes give up proton to gain stability.

For example :

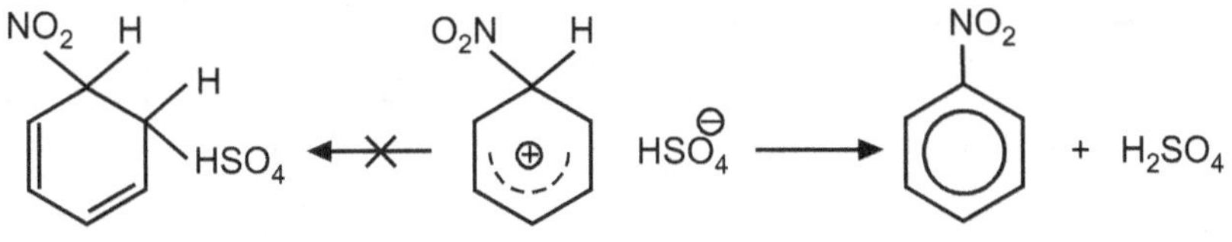

Non-aromatic compound　　　　Sigma complex　　　　Aromatic compound

5.9.2　Stability of a σ-complex

The stability of a σ-complex mainly depends on three factors : Inductive　effect, Resonance effect and Hyperconjugative effect.

An arenium ion (σ-complex), being a positively charged species, +I effect and hyperconjugative effect of alkyl groups increase its stability, while –I effect and –R effect decrease. If a group with +I or +R effect is situated at the o- or p- position instead of the m-position with respect to the tetrahedral carbon atom, the σ-complexes get extra stability.

For example:

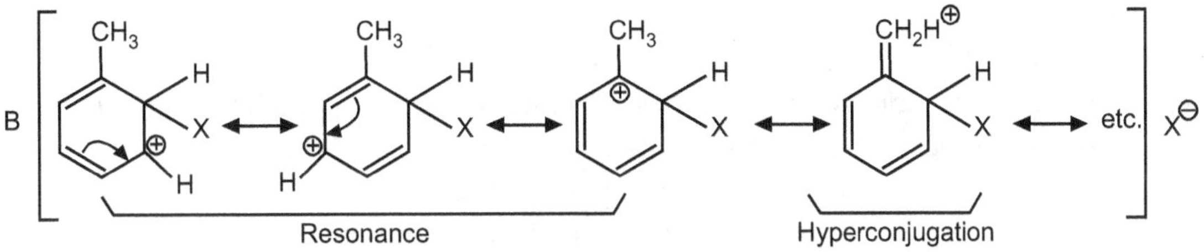

Resonance　　　　　　　Hyperconjugation

More stable σ-complex (A)

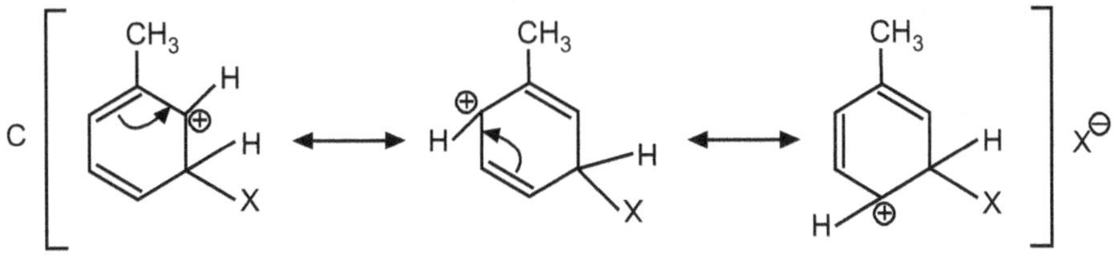

Less stable σ-complex (B)

Thus, in A, positive charge gets further delocalized by the hyperconjugative effect of the methyl group; whereas in B there is no such effect.

π-complex	σ-complex
1) Is a charge transfer type of complex which exists in solution.	1) Is a cyclic complex carbocation ion that can be isolated as salt.
2) It is an association of an electron donor species and an electrophile in which no covalent bond is formed between two species.	2) It contains a σ-bond between the electrophile and a particular carbon atom of the electron donor species. Substrate which utilizes its electrons for the formation of the σ-bond.
3) It is usually colourless / light yellow.	3) It is usually orange / deeper in colour.
4) It does not conduct electricity.	4) It conducts electricity.

QUESTIONS

Q.1   What is reaction intermediate? Enlist the types of reaction intermediates and discuss any one in brief.

Q.2   Compare the stability of primary, secondary and tertiary carbocations.

Q.3   Compare the stability of primary, secondary and tertiary carbanion ion.

Q.4   Define carbocation, electrophile, carbine, carbanion, nitrene, nitrenium ions, free radicals with example.

Q.5   Write a note on (a) Free radical, (b) Carbocation, (c) Free radical.

Q.6   Write a short note on Reaction intermediates.

Q.7   Arrange the following carbocations in the order of increasing stability and give reason.
$$Me - \overset{+}{C}H - Me, \quad CH_2 = CH - \overset{+}{C}H_2, \quad Me - CH_2 - \overset{+}{C}H_2$$

Q.8   What are free radicals? How are they generated? Discuss the stability of free radicals.

Q.9   Discuss carbocation, its formation, stability and reactions.
Compare the stability of the following pair of ions:
$$C_6H_5 - CH = CH - \overset{+}{C}H_2, \quad CH_3 - CH = CH - \overset{+}{C}H_2$$

Q.10 Tertiary carbocations are more stable than secondary carbocations. Explain.

Q.11 Write a note on Carbene, Nitrene and Nitrenium ions.

Chapter 6

ACIDITY AND BASICITY

6.1 INTRODUCTION

Acidity and basicity are based on the same chemical reaction and both happen simultaneously. In the following simple example the base, **B:**, removes a proton from the acid, **H–A**.

$$B: \quad H - A \quad \rightleftharpoons \quad {}^+B - H \quad + \quad {}^-:A$$

Base   Acid   Conjugate   Conjugate
                       acid   base

There are three theories used to describe acids and bases :

Theory	Acids	Bases
Arrhenius	Ionise to give H^+ in H_2O.	Ionise to give HO^- in H_2O.
Bronsted-Lowry	A proton donor.	A proton acceptor.
Lewis	An electron pair acceptor.	An electron pair donor.

Acidity: According to Bronsted-Lowry, acids are proton donors. The strength of an acid i.e. acidity is measured by the extent to which it can lose proton in a solvent which acts as a base. Water is the common solvent used for this purpose. The dissociation of a Bronsted-Lowry acid in water produces the conjugate base of the Bronsted acid, along with the hydronium ion. The equilibrium constant K for this dissociation measures the extent of hydronium ion formation and thus, effectively, how strong the Bronsted acid is. In this case, strength refers to the relative tendency of the acid to protonate water. For example dissociation of HA in water.

$$H - A + H_2O \longleftrightarrow A^- + H_3O^+$$

Here HA is the acid and A^- is its conjugate base. Now the equilibrium constant is given by the following equation

$$K_a = \frac{[A^-][H^+]}{[H-A]}$$

K_a is called the acid dissociation constant or acidity constant and is a measure of its acidity. The higher the value of K_a, the greater is the acidity. Thus in the aqueous medium the K_a value of benzoic acid is 6.1×10^{-5} and that of acetic acid is 1.75×10^{-5}; hence acetic acid is a weaker acid than benzoic acid.

The acidity is expressed as the negative logarithm of K_a with respect to the base 10 i.e. $-\log_{10} K_a$ and this is called pK_a.

The smaller the value of pK_a, the stronger is the acid and vice versa. Organic acids are weak acids, pK_a values are used to compare their relative strengths.

Basicity: According to Bronsted-Lowry, bases are proton acceptors. Basicity i.e. the strength of a base is measured by the extent to which it can gain proton in a solvent that acts as an acid. Water being amphoteric in nature, it is also a common solvent for the purpose of measuring basicity. For example, base in water.

$$B: + H_2O \longleftrightarrow BH^+ + OH^-$$

The ionization constant or equilibrium constant of the base (:B) is.

$$K_b = \frac{[BH^+][OH^-]}{[B:]}$$

K_b values of bases may be used to express and compare basicity of a series of bases. As K_b increases, the basicity increases. Thus K_b of pyridine is 2.3×10^{-9} and that of ammonia is 1.8×10^{-5}; this means ammonia is a stronger base than pyridine.

The basicity is expressed by pK_b naturally the greater the value of pK_b, the weaker is the base and vice versa.

6.2 THE EFFECT OF STRUCTURE UPON ACIDITY AND BASICITY

Acid/base reactions are of tremendous importance in organic chemistry, as they are also in inorganic and biochemistry. Further, the acidity of hydrogen containing compounds varies remarkably from one compound to another. In order to understand why acidities of Bronsted acids vary so widely, we will consider five main factors which affect the acidity and basicity of the compounds:

(i)　Atomic radius

(ii)　Electronegativity

(iii) Inductive effect

(iv) Resonance effect/Mesomeric effect

(v)　Steric effect

6.2.1 Atomic Radius

Atoms are most stable when their charges (positive or negative) are closest to neutral. In the case of a base, this neutrality can be achieved by sharing an electron pair (usually a lone pair) with a proton. The more concentrated the charge or electron density, the greater thermodynamic driving force there is to share electron density. This charge density is influenced by atomic radius. For an equal number of valence shell electrons, a smaller atom has greater charge density as measured by charge per unit of surface area or per unit of volume. Thus smaller atoms have a greater driving force to share electron density.

As we move down in the periodic table (i.e., second row to fifth row), atomic radius increases. Within a period (row) of the periodic table, atomic size does vary but not enough to have a significant influence on basicity.

6.2.2 Electronegativity

Electronegativity is the measure of an atom's attraction for electrons. The higher the electronegativity, the greater the attraction. Atoms with higher electronegativity will be less inclined to share their electrons with a proton. Thus, increasing electronegativity of the atom that shares an electron pair will decrease basicity. Weaker bases have stronger conjugate acids. As electronegativity of an atom increases the acidity of the attached proton also increases.

Example: The order of acidity is as follows.

$CH_4 < NH_3 < H_2O < HF.$

The lone pairs that are shared with a proton reside on C, N, O and F. Of these, carbon is the least electronegative (most willing to share electrons), so $-CH_3^-$ (methide ion) is the strongest base. Fluorine is the most electronegative, so F^- (fluoride ion) is the least willing to donate electrons (the weakest base). Overall, the electronegativity order is C (2.5) < N (3.0) < O (3.5) < F (4.0), so the order of basicity is $-CH_3^-$ (strongest base) > $-NH_2^-$ > HO^- > F^-. The relationship between conjugate basicity and acidity is an inverse one, so the order of acidity is: CH_4 (weakest acid) < NH_3 < H_2O < HF (strongest acid). The actual pK_a values are CH_4 with pK_a 51, NH_3 with pK_a 38, H_2O with pK_a 15.7 and HF with pK_a 3.2.

6.2.3 Inductive Effect

6.2.3.1 Inductive Effect and Acidity of Organic Acids

Acid on dissociation forms conjugate base and proton. A weaker H–A bond, favors acidity because the H–A bond is easy to break and stronger H–A bond tends to decrease the acidity because the bond is harder to break.

If the conjugate base of an acid is more stable than the acid itself, then the base strength i.e. basicity of a conjugate base is lower (weak base) than the acid strength of the acid. This means, weaker is the conjugate base, the stronger is the acid. So the factors which increase the stability of a conjugate base which will increase the acidity of organic acids.

The –I effect groups increase the acid strength of organic acids, because it favours dissociation of acid (H–A) by making H–A bond weak and also stabilize the conjugate base by electron withdrawing effect.

The +I effect groups makes H–A bond more stronger and also destabilize the conjugate base by electron donating effect.

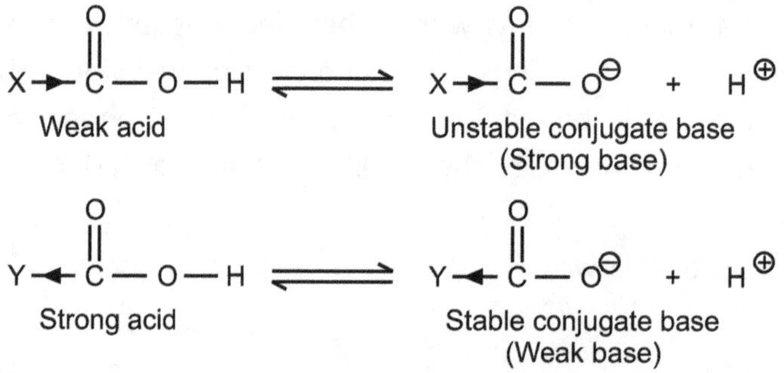

$$X \rightarrow \overset{\overset{O}{\|}}{C} - O - H \; \rightleftharpoons \; X \rightarrow \overset{\overset{O}{\|}}{C} - O^{\ominus} \; + \; H^{\oplus}$$

Weak acid   Unstable conjugate base
(Strong base)

$$Y \leftarrow \overset{\overset{O}{\|}}{C} - O - H \; \rightleftharpoons \; Y \leftarrow \overset{\overset{O}{\|}}{C} - O^{\ominus} \; + \; H^{\oplus}$$

Strong acid   Stable conjugate base
(Weak base)

(1) Formic acid is a stronger acid than acetic acid :

$$H - \overset{\overset{O}{\|}}{C} - \overset{\delta-}{O} \cdots \overset{\delta+}{H} \; \xrightarrow{\text{p}K_a = 3.77} \; H - \overset{\overset{O}{\|}}{C} - O^{\ominus} \; + \; H^{\oplus}$$

Formic acid   Formate ion

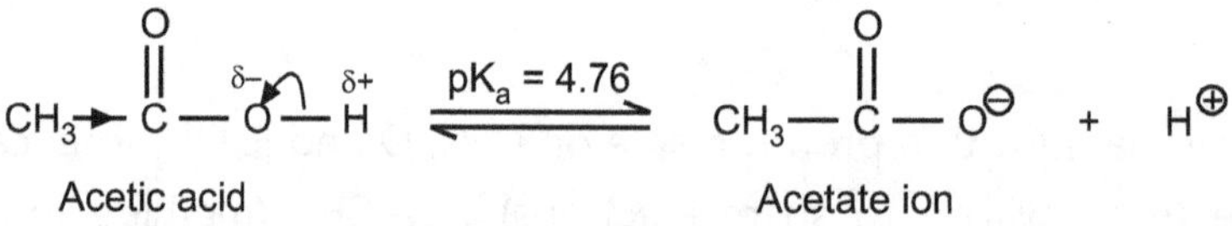

$$CH_3 \rightarrow \overset{\overset{O}{\|}}{C} - \overset{\delta-}{O} \cdots \overset{\delta+}{H} \; \xrightarrow{\text{p}K_a = 4.76} \; CH_3 - \overset{\overset{O}{\|}}{C} - O^{\ominus} \; + \; H^{\oplus}$$

Acetic acid   Acetate ion

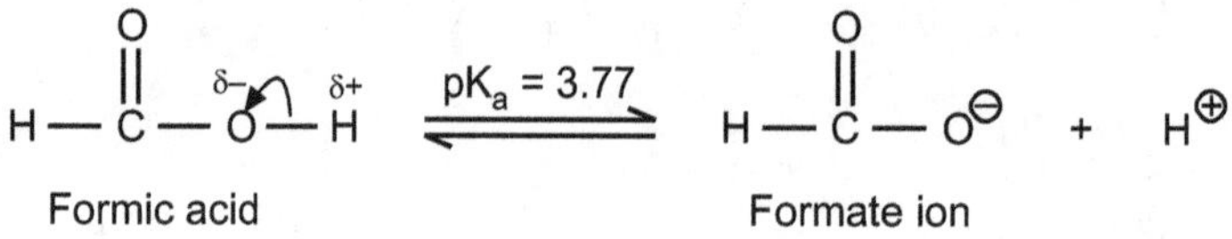

In case of acetic acid, the +I effect of methyl group will decrease the polarity of O–H bond and will not assist the dissociation of the O–H bond in the required direction. Similarly the conjugate base formed is also destabilized by the +I effect of methyl group.

In case of formic acid, such +I effect is absent. Therefore, the formate ion is more stable than acetate ion and this makes formic acid stronger than acetic acid.

Thus +I effect decreases the extent of dissociation of acid and stability of conjugate base and hence decreases the acid strength.

(2) Chloroacetic acid is a stronger acid than acetic acid :

$$CH_3 \rightarrow \overset{\overset{O}{\|}}{C} \rightarrow \overset{\delta-}{O} \cdots \overset{\delta+}{H} \; \xrightarrow{\text{p}K_a = 4.76} \; \overset{(+I)}{CH_3} \rightarrow \overset{\overset{O}{\|}}{C} - O^{\ominus} + H^{\oplus}$$

Acetic acid   Acetate ion

$$\overset{(-I)}{Cl} \leftarrow CH_2 \leftarrow \overset{\overset{O}{\|}}{C} \leftarrow \overset{\delta-}{O} \cdots \overset{\delta+}{H} \; \xrightarrow{\text{p}K_a = 2.81} \; \overset{(-I)}{Cl} \leftarrow CH_2 \leftarrow \overset{\overset{O}{\|}}{C} \leftarrow O^{\ominus} + H^{\oplus}$$

Chloroacetic acid   Chloroacetate ion

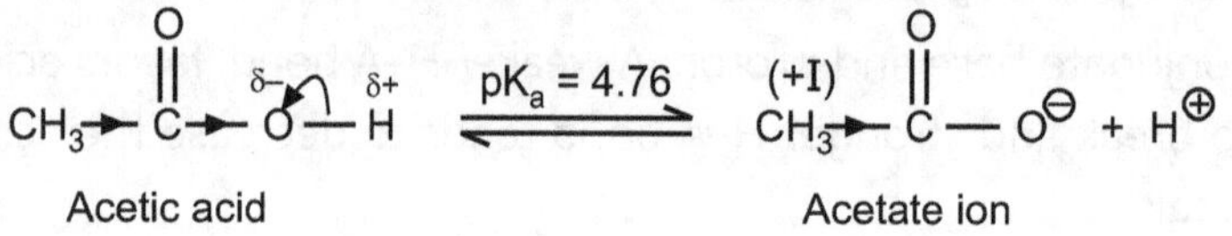

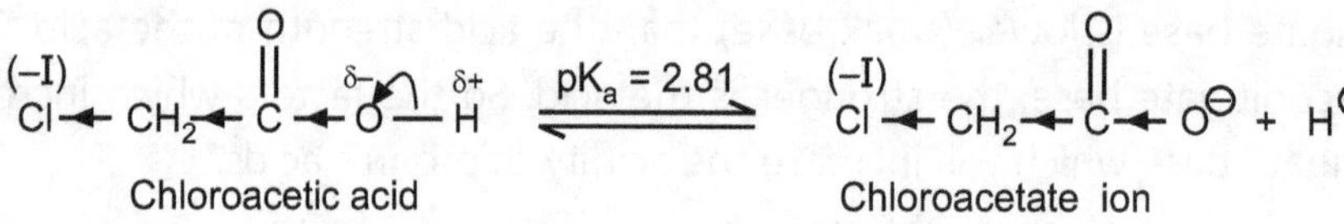

The –I effect of chlorine atom assists the dissociation of the O–H bond as well as it stabilizes the conjugate base. This makes monochloroacetic acid stronger than acetic acid.

As the number of chlorine atoms increases the − I effect increases and so the acid strength increases.

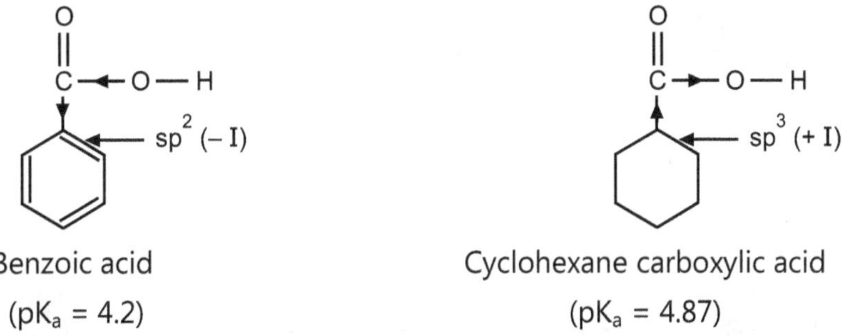

Trichloroacetic acid Dichloroacetic acid Monochloroacetic acid

(pK_a = 0.65) (pK_a = 1.29) (pK_a = 2.86)

(3) Benzoic acid is a stronger acid than cyclohexane carboxylic acid :

Benzoic acid Cyclohexane carboxylic acid

(pK_a = 4.2) (pK_a = 4.87)

In case of benzoic acid, the –COOH group is attached to sp^2 carbon atom, which exerts –I effect and increases the acid strength. In cyclohexane carboxylic acid, the –COOH group is attached to sp^3 carbon which exerts +I effect and decreases the acid strength.

6.2.3.2 Inductive Effect and Basicity of Bases

A base is a chemical entity which is capable of donating electron. Organic species containing N or O atom with donatable lone pair of electrons may be considered as organic bases. If any electron releasing group is attached to such an N or O atom in a base, it will increase the electron density on the atom and hence basicity of the base will increase.

If the lone pair of electrons gets delocalized, it is not readily available for donation and hence the entity will be of low basicity. As the delocalization of lone pair of electrons increases the basicity decreases and vice versa.

If the conjugate acid of an base is more stable than the base itself, the stronger is the base. So the factors which increase the stability of a conjugate acid will increase the basicity of organic bases and vice versa.

The +I effect groups increase the basicity of organic bases by the electron donating effect towards the O and N and also stabilize the conjugate acid formed.

The –I effect groups decrease the base strength of organic bases, by electron withdrawing effect from adjacent O or N and also by decreasing the stability of the conjugate acid formed.

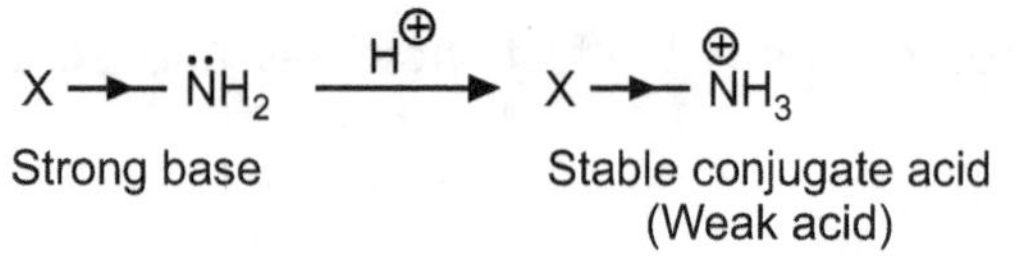

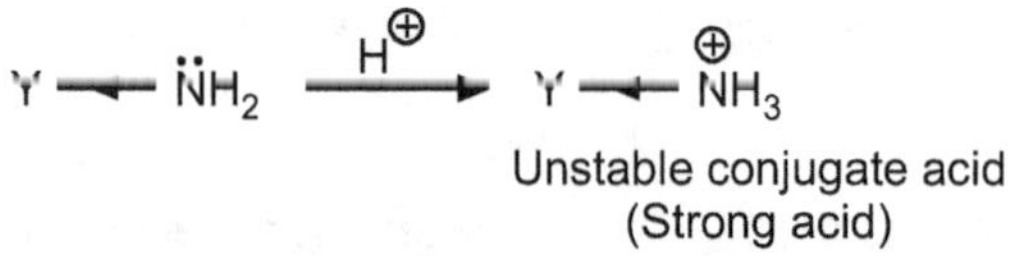

$$X \longrightarrow \overset{..}{N}H_2 \quad \xrightarrow{H^{\oplus}} \quad X \longrightarrow \overset{\oplus}{N}H_3$$

Strong base   Stable conjugate acid
(Weak acid)

$$Y \longleftarrow \overset{..}{N}H_2 \quad \xrightarrow{H^{\oplus}} \quad Y \longleftarrow \overset{\oplus}{N}H_3$$

Unstable conjugate acid
(Strong acid)

(1) Dimethylamine is stronger base than methyl amine :

(+I)
$$CH_3 \longrightarrow \overset{..}{N}H_2 \quad \xrightarrow{H^{\oplus}} \quad CH_3 \overset{\overset{H}{|}}{\underset{\underset{H}{|}}{\overset{\oplus}{N}}} H$$

Methyl amine   Conjugate acid

(+I)   (+I)
$$H_3C \longrightarrow \overset{..}{N} \longleftarrow CH_3 \quad \xrightarrow{H^{\oplus}} \quad H_3C \overset{\overset{H}{|}}{\underset{\underset{H}{|}}{\overset{\oplus}{N}}} CH_3$$

Dimethyl amine   Conjugate acid

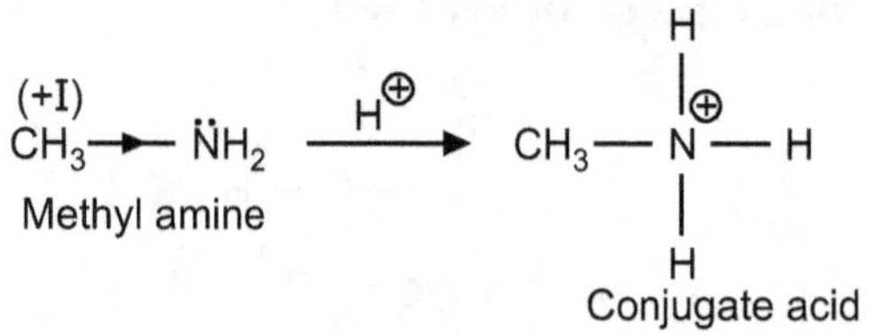

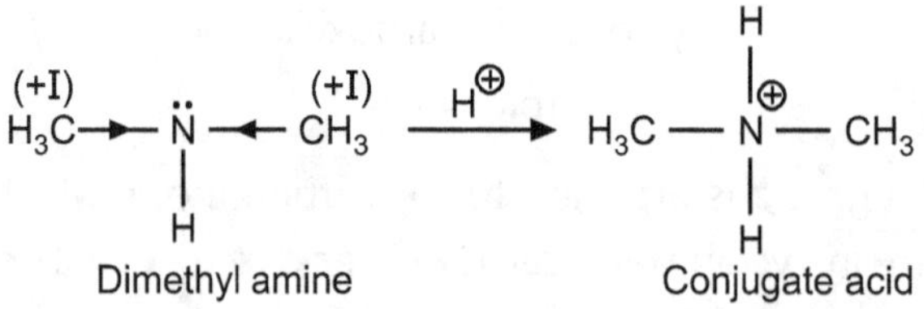

The methyl group is an electron donating group and has +I effect. It increases electron density on nitrogen, that accepts a proton and forms conjugate acid.

In dimethylamine, there are two – CH_3 groups attached to nitrogen atom which increase more electron density on nitrogen atom and the strength of base also increases. Therefore dimethylamine is stronger base than methyl amine.

Thus +I effect increases basicity while – I effect decreases basicity of organic bases.

(2) Methyl amine is a stronger base than ammonia :

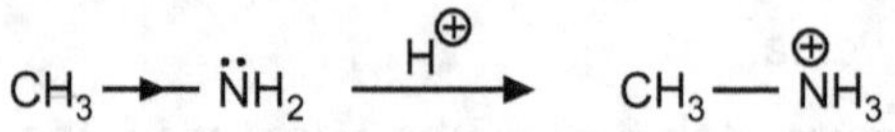

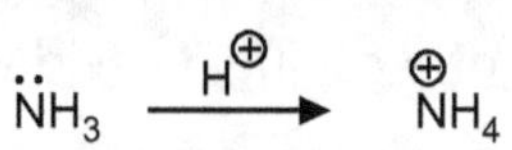

$$CH_3 \longrightarrow \overset{..}{N}H_2 \quad \xrightarrow{H^{\oplus}} \quad CH_3 \longrightarrow \overset{\oplus}{N}H_3$$

$$\overset{..}{N}H_3 \quad \xrightarrow{H^{\oplus}} \quad \overset{\oplus}{N}H_4$$

Due to +I effect of –CH_3 group, methyl amine is more basic than ammonia.

(3) Trifluoromethylamine is a weaker base than methylamine :

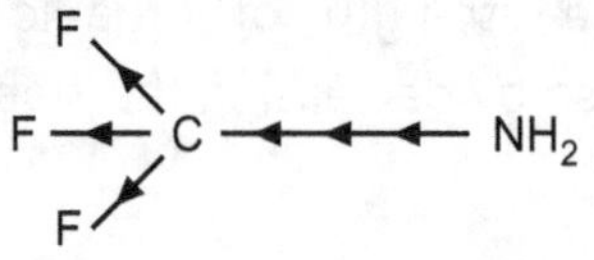

$$F_3C \longleftarrow NH_2 \quad \text{is less basic than } CH_3NH_2$$

Any electron withdrawing group attached to N or O atom in an organic base decreases the electron density on the atom and thereby decreases its basicity. Thus trifluoromethylamine has a very low basicity with respect to methylamine, this is because of –I effect of the three fluorine atoms.

6.2.4 Resonance Effect or Mesomeric Effect

6.2.4.1 Resonance Effect and Acidity of Organic Acids

Acid on dissociation forms conjugate base and proton. A weaker H–A bond, favours the acidity because the H–A bond is easy to break and stronger H–A bond tends to decrease the acidity because the bond is harder to break.

If the conjugate base of an acid is more stable than the acid itself, then the base strength i.e. basicity of a conjugate base is lower (weak base) than the acid strength of the acid. This means, weaker is the conjugate base, the stronger is the acid. So the factors which increase the stability of a conjugate base will increase the acidity of organic acids.

The –M (–R) effect groups increase the acid strength of organic acids, because it favours dissociation of acid, H–A by making H–A bond weak and also stabilizes the conjugate base by electron withdrawing effect.

The +M (+R) effect groups makes H–A bond more stronger and also destabilize the conjugate base by electron donating effect.

(1) Electron withdrawing groups having –I and –R effects present on benzene ring will increase the acid strength.

Benzoic acid	o-Nitrobenzoic acid	m-Nitrobenzoic acid	p-Nitrobenzoic acid
$pK_a = 4.2$	$pK_a = 3.2$	$pK_a = 3.45$	$pK_a = 3.40$

The –R effect is maximum in case of ortho isomer due to shortest distance, hence o-nitrobenzoic acid is stronger acid.

(2) If phenol contains electron withdrawing substituent such as NO_2 the acidity increases. All nitrophenols are stronger acids than phenol.

Phenol	o-Nitrophenol	m-Nitrophenol	p-Nitrophenol
$pK_a = 9.9$	$pK_a = 7.2$	$pK_a = 9.3$	$pK_a = 7.12$

As the number of NO_2 groups increases on the ring, the acidity goes on increasing.

2,4-dinitrophenol
$pK_a = 4.1$

Picric acid
$pK_a = 1.02$

(3) 4-methoxy benzoic acid is weaker acid than 4-nitro benzoic acid and 3-methoxybenzoic acid :

In substituted benzoic acids the mesomeric effect can be seen properly.

e.g.

4-methoxybenzoic acid   4-Nitrobenzoic acid   3-Methoxybenzoic acid

Let us consider each of the substance above:

(i)

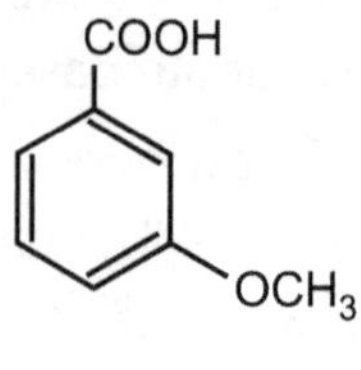

In 4-methoxy benzoic acid, electrons are pushed into the ring from the $-OCH_3$ group, hence the acid has excess electrons in the ring and the acid becomes less acidic; $pK_a = +4.5$, the +M effect is greater than the –I effect of the oxygen in the CH_3O- group.

(ii)

In 4– nitrobenzoic acid the NO_2 group has both an –M and –I effect on the benzoic acid hence the pK_a for this molecule is +3.4 and obviously more acidic.

(iii)

Because the OCH_3 is attached to position 3, it does not have access to the mesomeric effect, only the inductive effect plays a role here. The 3-methoxy benzoic acid is therefore more acidic pK_a = +4.0 than 4-methoxybenzoic acid.

(4) Alcohols are neutral while carboxylic acids are strong acids:

The ionization of molecules in the two cases may be depicted as follows.

Alkoxide ion

Carboxylate ion

As the carboxylate anion can undergo resonance in the following way, while the alkoxide ion cannot undergo, the former gets stabilized. Also it is observed that the resonance stabilizing occurs more in carboxylate ion than in the parent acid because in the latter case it gets decreased due to the charge separation.

(5) Phenols are acidic while alcohols are neutral:

Phenol

(–I effect of sp^2 carbon)

sp^3 carbon

Cyclohexanol

(+I effect of sp^3 carbon)

When phenol dissociates to form H^+, the conjugate base phenoxide ion is stabilised due to –R effect of phenyl ring.

But when cyclohexanol dissociates to produce H^+, the conjugate base formed i.e. cyclohexyl oxide cannot be stabilized by resonance (instead of it is destabilized due to +I effect of C) and hence it is unstable and dissociation is not favoured. Therefore phenols are acidic but alcohols are neutral.

6.2.4.2 Resonance Effect and Basicity of Bases

A base is a chemical entity which is capable of donating electron. Organic species containing N or O atom with donatable lone pair of electrons may be considered as organic bases. If any electron releasing group is attached to such an N or O atom in a base, it will increase the electron density on the atom and hence basicity of the base will increase.

If the lone pair of electrons gets delocalized it is not readily available for donation and hence the entity will be of low basicity. As the delocalization of lone pair of electrons increases the basicity decreases and vice versa.

If the conjugate acid of an base is more stable than the base itself, the stronger is the base. So the factors which increase the stability of a conjugate acid which will increase the basicity of organic bases and vice versa.

The +M (+R) effect groups increase the basicity of organic bases by the electron donating effect towards the O and N and also stabilize the conjugate acid formed.

The –M (–R) effect groups decrease the base strength of organic bases, by electron withdrawing effect from adjacent O or N and also by decreasing the stability of the conjugate acid formed.

(1) Aniline is a weaker base than cyclohexyl amine:

In aniline $-NH_2$ group is attached to the sp^2 carbon of the ring which exerts –I effect on the nitrogen. Similarly the lone pair of nitrogen is delocalized in the benzene ring due to the +R effect.

Thus the –I and –R effects of the phenyl ring reduce the chances of availability of lone pair on nitrogen atom. Secondly, the conjugate acid cannot be stabilized by resonance. This makes aniline a weak base.

Aniline	Conjugate acid (not stabilised)

On the other hand, cyclohexyl amine is a much stronger base because the –NH_2 group is attached to sp^3 carbon which has +I effect that stabilizes conjugate acid. There is no –R effect. Hence cyclohexyl amine is a stronger base.

Cyclohexyl amine	Conjugate acid (stabilised by +I effect)

(2) Aromatic amines are weaker bases than aliphatic amines:

In aromatic amines e.g. aniline, the lone pair of electrons on the nitrogen atom gets involved in resonance and is therefore lesser available for protonation than in aliphatic amines in which the phenomenon of resonance does not occur and hence lone pair of electrons will be readily available for donation.

Aniline (Aromatic amine)

Aliphatic amine

(3) Amides inspite of having –NH_2 group are found to be neutral.

This is because the lone pair on nitrogen is delocalized by –R effect of carbonyl group and is therefore not available for donation to H^+. Secondly the conjugate acid is destabilized due to electron withdrawing effect of carbonyl group.

6.2.5 Steric Effect

Steric effect arises due to the interaction in space, between the atoms or groups in the molecule.

When we try to put atoms or groups in space which is not sufficient to accommodate all of them, they try to push each other and try to go away from each other. These interactions are called as steric interactions.

The steric effects play vital role in determining the reactivity of the molecule. The effective delocalization via π orbital can only take place if the p or π orbital on the other atom involved in the delocalization can become parallel to each. If this is prevented, significant overlapping cannot take place and delocalization may be inhibited.

6.2.5.1 Steric Effect and Basic Strength

For example N, N-dimethyl aniline (A) is very much weaker base than its 2, 6-dimethyl derivative (B) :

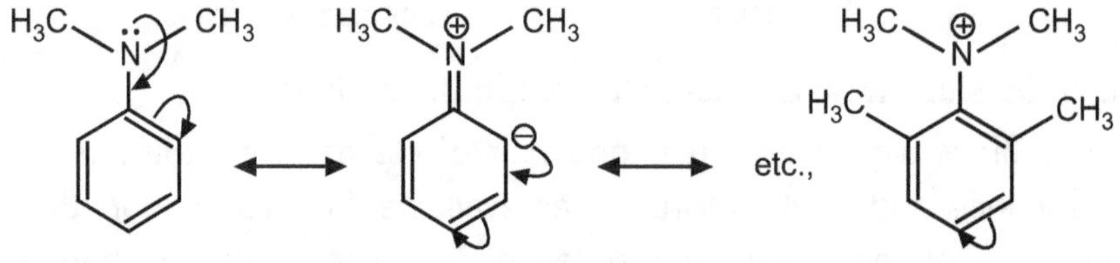

Fig. 6.1 : Resonance in N, N dimethyl aniline

In case of N, N-dimethylaniline (A) the 'sp^3' orbital of nitrogen which contains the non bonding electron pair is in the same plane as that of 'π' orbital of the benzene. Therefore electron pair on nitrogen is delocalized in the benzene ring as shown in Fig. 6.1 since lone pair is not readily available to accept H^+ ; it is a weak base.

In compound (B), the methyl groups at 2, 6 – positions and those on nitrogen are so closely placed that lot of steric interaction takes place. To avoid these interactions, the C–N bond rotates in such a way that the orbital containing non-bonding electron pair becomes perpendicular to the plane of the benzene ring. This reduces the steric interaction between the methyl groups attached to nitrogen and those attached to the ring. Since the orbital containing the electron pair on nitrogen is no longer parallel to those of benzene ring delocalization of this electron pair into the benzene ring is not possible. Thus the resonance is inhibited due to steric factors. This is known as steric inhibition of resonance. As the electron pair on nitrogen in compound (B) is not delocalized, it is readily available for donation to H^+ and therefore it is stronger base than (A).

6.2.5.2 Steric Effect and Acidic Strength

Let us consider the following two acids.

COOH   COOH

(A)   (B)

(A) is a stronger acid inspite of closeness of two electron donating methyl groups to –COOH. The significant factor affecting the acidic strength of this two compounds is –R effect of NO_2 group. In compound (B), NO_2 is surrounded by two bulky methyl groups and they sterically repel the NO_2 group. In order to minimize the steric repulsion by the two adjacent methyl groups, the $-NO_2$ group loses the planarity with ring, not able to resonate. This is known as steric inhibition of resonance. Thus, in B, $-NO_2$ is not increasing acidic strength of –COOH by –R effect on ring, hence weaker acid. Whereas in compound (A), $-NO_2$ group due to its –R effect increases the acid strength.

QUESTIONS

Q.1   Phenols are acidic in nature? Explain.

Q.2   Compare and explain the basicities of ethanalamine and aniline.

Q.3   Phenol is more acidic than alcohol. Explain.

Q.4   Ethyl amine is more basic than ammonia. Give reason.

Q.5   Explain the steric inhibition of resonance on physical properties, acidity and reactivity of organic compounds.

Q.6   Explain applications of resonance effects.

Q.7   Why α- chloro acetic acid is stronger than acetic acid?

Q.8   What is inductive effect? Discuss its applications.

Q.9   Give reason: Ammonia is stronger base over aniline.

Q.10   Give reason: p- Nitrophenol is a stronger acid than phenol.

Q.11   Give reason: Guanidine is one of the strongest organic base.

Q.12   Give reason: N, N- Dimethyl aniline is a stronger base than aniline.

Q.13   Give reason: Trifluoroacetic acid is a stronger acid than trichloroacetic acid.

Q.14   Monochloroacetic acid is more acidic than acetic acid but less acidic than trifluoroacetic acid. Why?

Q.15   What are steric effects? Give their effects on reactivity, rates of reaction and orientation with suitable examples.

Q.16　Give reason: Methylamine is a stronger base than ammonia and aniline is a weaker base than ammonia.

Q.17　Give reason: While benzamide is neutral, phthalimide is acidic.

Q.18　How will you account for the following giving reason.

a) Methyl amine is a stronger base as compared to ammonia, but aniline is a weaker base as compared to methyl amine.

Q.19　How will you account for the following

Following is the increasing order of acidity:

Propanoic acid, Acetic acid, Monochloroacetic acid.

❖ ❖ ❖

Chapter 7...

ALKANES

7.1 INTRODUCTION

Alkanes are saturated hydrocarbons with the general formula C_nH_{2n+2}. These are also called as paraffins (Parum means little, affins means affinity or reactivity). They can be categorized as acyclic or cyclic.

(a) Acyclic alkanes have the molecular formula C_nH_{2n+2} (where n = an integer) and contain only linear and branched chains of carbon atoms. They are also called saturated hydrocarbons because they have the maximum number of hydrogen atoms per carbon.

(b) Cycloalkanes contain carbons joined in one or more rings. Because their general formula is C_nH_{2n}, they have two fewer H atoms than an acyclic alkane with the same number of carbons.

All carbon atoms in an alkane are sp^3 hybridized surrounded by four groups.

The 3-D representations and ball-and-stick models for these alkanes indicate the tetrahedral geometry around each carbon atom.

Lewis structure   **3-D representation**   **ball and stick model**

Additionally, alkanes having more than 2 carbon atoms can be drawn in a variety of ways and still represent the same molecule. For example, three carbons of propane can be drawn in a horizontal row or with a bend. These representations are equivalent.

3 C's in a row   3 C's with a bend

There are two isomers for the alkanes containing four carbon atoms with molecular formula C_4H_{10}, named butane and isobutane. Butane and isobutane are constitutional or structural isomers – two different compounds with the same molecular formula but different structural formulae C_4H_{10}.

Two structural isomers of alkane having molecular formula C_4H_{10}.

$= CH_3CH_2CH_2CH_3$

Butane

Straight chain alkane

$$CH_3 - \underset{\underset{H}{|}}{\overset{\overset{CH_3}{|}}{C}} - CH_3 \quad =$$

Isobutane
(or 2-methylpropane)

Branched chain alkane

The maximum number of possible constitutional isomers increases as the number of carbon atoms in the alkane increases. Homologous series of alkanes obtained by increasing the number of carbons in an alkane by a CH_2 group, as shown below. The CH_2 group is called "methylene."

Table 7.1

Number of carbon atoms	Structural Formula	Name (n-Alkane)	Number of constitutional isomers
1.	CH_4	Methane	--
2.	$CH_3\text{-}CH_3$	Ethane	--
3.	$CH_3\text{-}CH_2\text{-}CH_3$	Propane	--
4.	$CH_3\text{-}(CH_2)_2\text{-}CH_3$	Butane	2
5.	$CH_3\text{-}(CH_2)_3\text{-}CH_3$	Pentane	3
6.	$CH_3\text{-}(CH_2)_4\text{-}CH_3$	Hexane	5
7.	$CH_3\text{-}(CH_2)_5\text{-}CH_3$	Heptane	9
8.	$CH_3\text{-}(CH_2)_6\text{-}CH_3$	Octane	18
9.	$CH_3\text{-}(CH_2)_7\text{-}CH_3$	Nonane	35
10.	$CH_3\text{-}(CH_2)_8\text{-}CH_3$	Decane	75

7.2 IUPAC NOMENCLATURE

The name of every organic molecule consists of 3 parts:

(i)   The parent name indicates the number of carbons in the longest continuous chain.

(ii) The suffix indicates what functional group is present.

(iii) The prefix tells us the location and number of substituents attached to the carbon chain.

For IUPAC nomenclature of alkanes

- First select longest continuous carbon chain (parent chain) i.e. "alkane".

- Then branches on the parent chain are named as "alkyl" groups.

- Number the parent chain starting from the end that gives the lower number for the first branch, assign "number" to the alkyl branches.

- If an alkyl group appears more than once use prefixes: di, tri, tetra, penta...; each alkyl group must have a number.

- The name is written as one word with the parent name last.

- The names and numbers for the alkyl branches are write in alphabetic order separating numbers with commas and letters from numbers with hyphens.

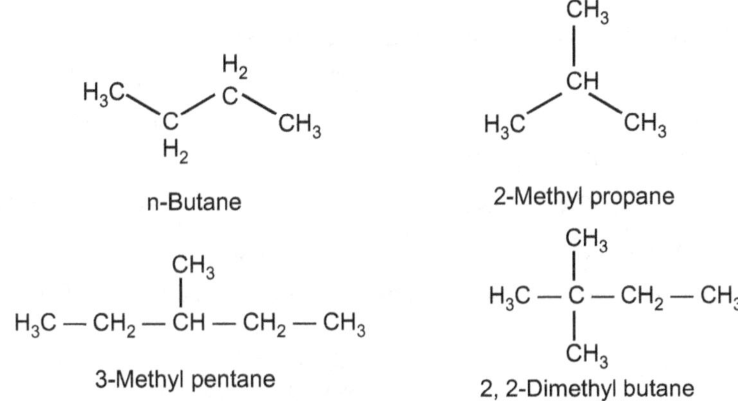

7.3 PREPARATION METHODS OF ALKANE

(1) By reduction of unsaturated hydrocarbons: Alkenes or alkynes on hydrogenation in the presence of metal catalyst such as nickel, platinum or palladium catalyst give alkanes. Hydrogenation in the presence of platinum or palladium takes place at room temperature but with nickel higher temperature (250 - 300°C) is required and the reaction is known as Sabatier-Senderens reaction. Methane cannot be prepared by this method.

$$CH_3—CH=CH_2 \;+\; 2H_2 \xrightarrow{\text{Ni/Pt/Pd}} CH_3—CH_2—CH_3$$

Propene   Propane

$$CH\equiv CH \;+\; 2H_2 \xrightarrow{\text{Ni/Pt/Pd}} CH_3—CH_3$$

Acetylene   Ethane

(2) By reduction of alkyl halides: Alkyl halides on reduction with zinc and HCl or HI, are converted to the corresponding alkanes in good yield.

$$CH_3—CH_2—I \;+\; H_2 \longrightarrow CH_3—CH_3 \;+\; HI$$

Ethyl iodide   Ethane

When alkyl halides are heated with sodium metal in ether solution they give higher alkanes. This reaction is known as Wurtz reaction.

$$2CH_3 - I \quad + \quad 2Na \quad \xrightarrow{\text{Dry ether}} \quad CH_3 - CH_3 \quad + \quad 2\,NaI$$

Methyl iodide   Ethane

Mechanism: Alkane formation is through the formation of an organometallic compound intermediate.

$$CH_3 - I \quad + \quad 2\overset{\bullet}{N}a \quad \longrightarrow \quad \overset{-}{C}H_3\overset{+}{N}a \quad + \quad NaI$$

Methyl iodide

$$\overset{-}{C}H_3\overset{+}{N}a \quad + \quad CH_3I \quad \longrightarrow \quad CH_3 - CH_3 \quad + \quad NaI$$

Ethane

(3) By decarboxylation of monocarboxylic acids: Sodium salts of fatty acids on heating with soda lime, remove a molecule of carbon dioxide and result in the formation of alkanes. Since in this molecule carbon dioxide is removed, it is known as decarboxylation process. It is laboratory method of preparation.

$$CH_3 - CH_2 - COONa \quad + \quad NaOH \quad \longrightarrow \quad CH_3 - CH_3 \quad + \quad Na_2CO_3$$

Sodium propionate   Ethane

Mechanism: Decarboxylation process initiates due to the attack of hydroxide ion from soda lime.

(4) By reduction of alcohols, ketones and carboxylic acids: In a sealed tube alcohols, ketones or carboxylic acids on reduction with hot HI and red phosphorus (150 - 200°C) they give alkanes.

From alcohol:

$$CH_3 - CH_2 - OH + 2HI \quad \xrightarrow{\text{red P}} \quad CH_3 - CH_3 \quad + \quad H_2O \quad + \quad I_2$$

Ethanol   Ethane

From ketone:

$$CH_3 - \overset{\overset{\displaystyle O}{\|}}{C} - CH_3 \quad + \quad 4\,HI \quad \xrightarrow{\text{red P}} \quad CH_3 - CH_2 - CH_3 \quad + \quad H_2O \quad + \quad 2I_2$$

Acetone   Propane

From carboxylic acids:

$$CH_3 - COOH \ + \ 6\,HI \ \xrightarrow{\text{red P}} \ CH_3 - CH_3 \ + \ 2H_2O \ + \ 3I_2$$

Acetic acid $\qquad\qquad\qquad\qquad\qquad$ Ethane

(5) By reaction of Grignard's reagent with active hydrogen: In the first step, Grignard reagent is prepared by reaction of an alkyl halide with magnesium metal in dry ether. In the second step, the treatment of Grignard's reagent (alkyl magnesium halides) with compounds containing active hydrogen such as water, amines, alcohol etc. give pure alkanes.

$$CH_3 - CH_2 - Br \ + \ Mg \ \xrightarrow{\text{red P}} \ CH_3 - CH_2\,MgBr$$

Ethyl bromide $\qquad\qquad\qquad$ Ethyl magnesium bromide
$\qquad\qquad\qquad\qquad\qquad\qquad$ (Grignard's reagent)

$$CH_3 - CH_2\,MgBr \ + \ H_2O \ \longrightarrow \ CH_3 - CH_3 \ + \ Mg(Br)OH$$

Ethyl magnesium bromide $\qquad\qquad\quad$ Ethane

$$CH_3 - CH_2\,MgI \ + \ CH_3OH \ \longrightarrow \ CH_3 - CH_3 \ + \ Mg(I)\,OCH_3$$

Ethyl magnesium iodide $\quad$ Methanol $\qquad\qquad$ Ethane

$$RMgX \ + \ R'.NH_2 \ \longrightarrow \ R - H \ + \ Mg(X)\,NH.R'$$

Ethyl magnesium halide $\quad$ Amine $\qquad\qquad$ Alkane

(6) By Kolbe's electrolytic method: When a concentrated solution of sodium or potassium salt of fatty acids or mixture of carboxylic acids is electrolysed, it results in the formation of alkanes. When dimethyl formamide is used as a solvent, the yield of alkane increases. This method has been used in the synthesis of natural compounds, particularly lipids.

$$R^1COO\bar{K}^+ + R^2COO\bar{K}^+ \ + \ 2H_2O \ \longrightarrow \ R^1 - R^2 \ + \ 2CO_2 \ + \ H_2 \ + \ 2KOH$$

Salt of carboxylic acid $\qquad\qquad\qquad$ Alkane

Mechanism: Free radical reaction mechanism

Step-I: Ionisation of sodium salt and formation of carboxylate anion which loses electron at the anode to form carboxylate radical.

Step-II: Carboxylate radical rapidly loses CO_2 to generate an alkyl radical.

$$R^1COOK \ \rightleftharpoons \ R^1COO^- \ + \ Na^+$$

Carboxylate ion

$$R^1COO^- \ \xrightarrow{-e^{\ominus}} \ R^1CO\dot{O} \ \xrightarrow{-CO_2} \ \dot{R}^1$$

Carboxylate radical $\qquad\qquad$ At anode

$$R^2COOK \rightleftharpoons R^2COO^- + Na^+$$

Carboxylate ion

$$R^2COO^- \xrightarrow{-e^{\ominus}} R^2CO\dot{O} \xrightarrow{-CO_2} \dot{R}^2$$

Carboxylate radical　　　　At anode

Step-III: Combination of two such alkyl radicals and formation of alkane.

$$\dot{R}^1 + \dot{R}^2 \longrightarrow R^1 - R^2$$

$$2\overset{+}{Na} + 2e^{\ominus} \longrightarrow 2\dot{N}a + 2H_2O \longrightarrow 2NaOH + H_2\uparrow \text{ (at cathode)}$$

This method is useful for the preparation of alkanes containing at least two carbon atoms. Methane cannot be prepared by this method.

7.4 PHYSICAL PROPERTIES OF ALKANES

(1) Boiling point: Alkanes have lower boiling points as compared to more polar compounds of comparable molecular weight.

	$CH_3-CH_2-CH_3$	CH_3-CHO	CH_3-CH_2-OH
Name	Propane	Acetaldehyde	Ethyl alcohol
M. Wt.	44	44	46
B.P.	–42°C	21°C	79°C

← Decreasing strength of intermolecular forces of attraction decreasing boiling point.

As the number of carbon atom increases in the normal alkane, boiling point increases because of increased surface area.

	$CH_3-CH_2-CH_2-CH_3$	$CH_3-CH_2-CH_2-CH_2-CH_3$	$CH_3-CH_2-CH_2-CH_2-CH_2-CH_3$
Name	n-Butane	n-Pentane	n-Hexane
B.P.	0°C	36°C	69°C

Increasing boiling point as the number of carbon atom increases →

The boiling point of branched isomers decreases because of decreased surface area.

	$CH_3-\overset{\overset{\displaystyle CH_3}{|}}{\underset{\underset{\displaystyle CH_3}{|}}{C}}-CH_3$	$H_3C-\overset{\overset{\displaystyle CH_3}{|}}{CH}-CH_2-CH_3$	$CH_3-CH_2-CH_2-CH_2-CH_3$
Name	Neopentane	iso-Pentane	n-Pentane
B.P.	10°C	28°C	69°C

Increasing surface area of isomers increases boiling point →

(2) Melting point: Alkanes have lower melting points as compared to more polar compounds of comparable molecular weight.

	$CH_3-CH_2-CH_3$	CH_3-CHO
Name	Propane	Acetaldehyde
M. Wt.	44	44
M.P.	$-187°C$	$-121°C$

Decreasing strength of intermolecular forces of attraction

decreasing metling point.

As the number of carbon atom increases in the normal alkane melting point increases because of increased surface area.

	$CH_3-CH_2-CH_2-CH_3$	$CH_3-CH_2-CH_2-CH_2-CH_2-CH_3$
Name	n-Butane	n-Hexane
M.P.	$-138°C$	$-95°C$

Increasing melting point as the number of carbon atom increases

(3) Solubility: Alkanes are insoluble in water and highly polar solvents but soluble in non-polar solvents such as benzene, chloroform and ether.

(4) Density: The relative density increases with size of the alkanes. All alkanes are less dense than water.

7.5 CHEMICAL REACTIONS OF ALKANES

Alkanes because of their saturated character are quite inert towards common reagents and thus they are fairly stable. A carbon-carbon and carbon- hydrogen linkage in alkanes is usually strong because of covalent nature of the linkage and there is no much difference in electronegativities of C and H. Thus there is no polarization in alkanes. This rules out the attack of electrophilic or nucleophilic reagents on the alkanes. Therefore most of the chemical reactions of alkanes are free radical substitution reactions as described below:

(1) Halogenation

(2) Nitration

(3) Sulphonation

(4) Oxidation

(5) Cracking or Pyrolysis

(6) Isomerisation

(7) Alkylation

(8) Aromatisation

(1) Halogenation: Halogenation is the replacement of one or more hydrogen atoms in an organic compound by a halogen (fluorine, chlorine, bromine or iodine). Since only two covalent bonds are broken (C–H and Cl–Cl) and two covalent bonds are formed (C–Cl and H–Cl), this reaction seems to be an ideal case for mechanistic investigation and speculation.

$$X-X \quad -\overset{|}{\underset{|}{C}}-H \quad \xrightarrow[\text{X = Br, Cl}]{\text{Light or heat}} \quad -\overset{|}{\underset{|}{C}}-X \quad H-X$$

Alkanes when treated with Br_2 or Cl_2, radical substitution of R–H generates the alkyl halide and HX.

General mechanism:

Step-I: Chain initiation:

In the presence of UV light or heat, homolytic fission of one molecule of halogen gives rise to two halogen free radicals.

$$\underset{\text{Halogen}}{X-X} \quad \xrightarrow[\text{or } \Delta]{\text{UV light}} \quad \underset{\text{Halogen free radical}}{2\overset{\bullet}{X}}$$

Step-II: Chain propagation:

The halogen free radical abstracts hydrogen from the alkane to form an alkyl free radical ($\overset{\bullet}{R}$). The alkyl free radical in turn abstracts a halogen atom from a halogen molecule to yield the alkyl halide and halogen radical.

$$\overset{\bullet}{X} \; + \; \underset{\text{Alkane}}{R-H} \quad \longrightarrow \quad H-X \; + \; \underset{\text{Alkyl radical}}{\overset{\bullet}{R}}$$

$$\overset{\bullet}{R} \; + \; X_2 \quad \longrightarrow \quad \underset{\text{Alkyl halide}}{R-X} \; + \; \overset{\bullet}{X}$$

Step-III: Chain termination:

If a radical undergoes a reaction which does not generate another radical, then the chain reaction given above slows and stops. If the free radical combine amongst themselves to form a neutral molecule.

$$\overset{\bullet}{X} \; + \; \overset{\bullet}{X} \quad \longrightarrow \quad X-X$$

$$\overset{\bullet}{R} \; + \; \overset{\bullet}{X} \quad \longrightarrow \quad R-X$$

$$\overset{\bullet}{R} \; + \; \overset{\bullet}{R} \quad \longrightarrow \quad \underset{\text{Higher alkane}}{R-R}$$

Characteristics of halogenations:

1. Reaction proceeds via a radical chain mechanism which involves radical intermediates.

2. The reactivity of halogens decreases in the following order: $F_2 > Cl_2 > Br_2 > I_2$.

3. The reactivity of alkane decreases in the following order : tertiary > secondary > primary > methyl.

4. Only chlorination and bromination are useful in laboratory, since fluorine is so explosively reactive it is difficult to control, and iodine is generally unreactive.

5. Chlorinations and brominations are normally exothermic.

6. Energy input in the form of heat or light is necessary to initiate these halogenations.

7. Halogenation reactions may be conducted in either the gaseous or liquid phase.

8. In gas phase chlorinations, the presence of oxygen (a radical trap) inhibits the reaction.

9. In liquid phase halogenations, radical initiators such as peroxides facilitate the reaction.

Kinetics and rate: The study of reaction rates, determining which products are formed fastest. It can also allow the prediction of how a reaction rate will change under different conditions. For reaction to occur, most reactions require the addition of energy. Energy is needed for molecules to pass over the energy barriers for to convert into the product. These energy barriers are called the **activation energy**, or **enthalpy of activation**, of the reactions. At room temperature, most molecules have insufficient kinetic energy to overcome the activation energy barrier. The average kinetic energy of molecules can be increased by increasing their temperature. The higher the temperature, the greater the fraction of reactant molecules that have sufficient energy to pass over the activation energy barrier. Thus, the rate of a reaction increases with increasing temperature.

A reaction rate is directly proportional to the concentration of reactants. The proportionality constant is called the **rate constant** for the reaction. Not every collision is effective in producing bond breakage and formation. For a collision to be effective, the molecules must have sufficient energy content as well as proper alignment.

For example, in the reaction of methane and chlorine, the molecules of each substance must "collide" with sufficient energy, and the bonds within the molecules must be rearranged for chloromethane and hydrogen chloride to be produced. As methane and chlorine approaches each other, old bonds are cleaved, and new bonds are formed. The cleavage of bonds requires a lot of energy, so as the reaction occurs, the reactant molecules must remain in high-energy states. When new bonds form, energy is released, and the resulting products possess less energy than the intermediates from which they were formed. When reactant molecules are at their maximum energy content (at the crest of potential energy curve), they are said to be in a **transition state.** The energy necessary to drive the reactants to the transition state is the **activation energy** (Fig. 7.1).

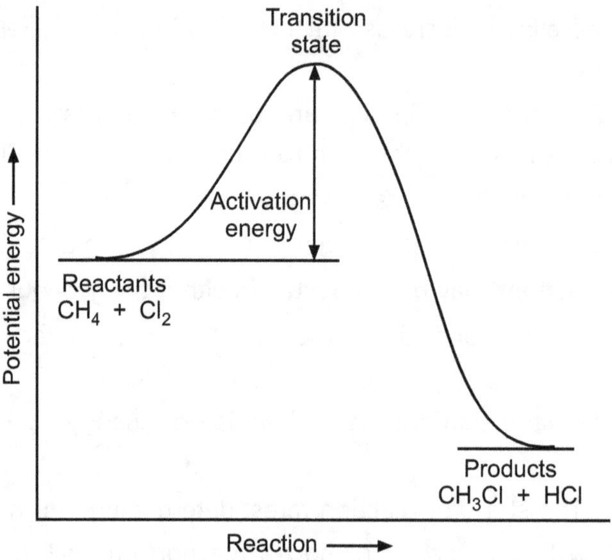

Fig. 7.1

The overall rate of the reaction is determined from the energy content by the transition state. This transition state, which is usually of the slowest step, controls the rate of reaction and is thus called the rate-determining step of the mechanism.

Energy of reaction: The energy of reaction is the difference between the total energy content of the reactants and the products (Fig. 7.2). In ordinary organic reactions, the products contain less energy than the reactants, and the reactions are therefore exothermic. The energy of reaction has no effect on the rate of the reaction. The greater the energy of reaction, the more stable the products.

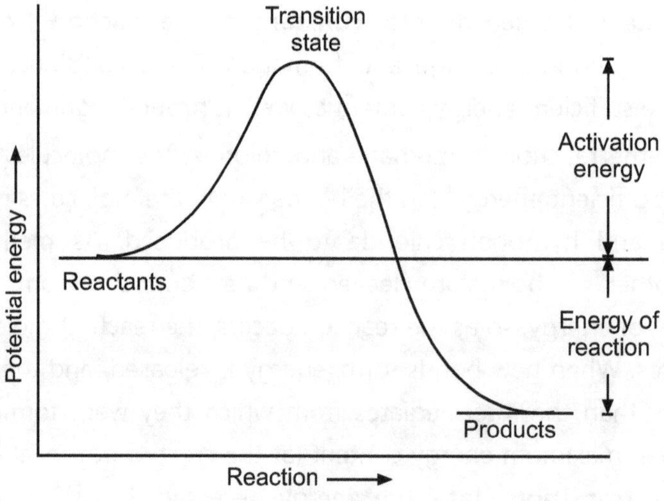

Fig. 7.2

Effects of temperature on rate of reaction: The rates of organic reactions approximately double with each 10°C rise in temperature.

For example the chlorination of methane: A study of the reaction revealed the following observations:

(1) Chlorination did not occur at room temperature or in the dark (heat or light is required to initiate the reaction).

(2) The most effective initiation is blue light of UV radiation. A chlorine molecule is known to absorb light of that wavelength. (The light is activating the chlorine molecule).

(3) The light-initiated reaction has a high quantum yield i.e. one photon gives more than one molecule of product. (The reaction is probably a Chain process).

$$CH_4 + Cl_2 \xrightarrow{\text{UV light or 400°C}} CH_3Cl + HCl$$

Methane　　　　　　　　　　　　　　　Methyl chloride

Mechanism:

Step I: Chain initiation

Chlorine molecules absorb UV light, whereas methane does not, it means it is the chlorine molecule that is being activated, and doing the initiation process. Blue light of UV contains the correct energy to split a chlorine molecule into two chlorine free radicals by homolytic cleavage of Cl_2 and starting the chain process (58 kcal/mol).

$$Cl:Cl \xrightarrow{\text{UV light}} Cl^{\bullet} + Cl^{\bullet}$$

Chlorine
free radicals

Step II: Chain propagation

(a) A chlorine radical abstracts a hydrogen to form HCl and a methyl radical, then

(b) the methyl radical abstracts a chlorine atom from another molecule of Cl_2 to form the methyl chloride product and ***another*** chlorine radical, which can then itself undergo reaction 2(a) creating a cycle that can repeat.

$$CH_4 + {}^{\bullet}Cl \longrightarrow CH_3{}^{\bullet} + H:Cl$$

Methane　　　Chorine　　　　Methyl　　　Hydrogen
　　　　　　 free radical　　free radical　chloride

$$H_3C\text{-}H + \cdot Cl \longrightarrow H_3C\text{-}Cl + Cl\cdot$$

Methyl　　Chorine　　　　Chloromethane　Chlorine
free radical　free radical　　　　　　　　　　free radical

Step III: (Termination)

Step-I and II are repeated till the termination of the chain by the combination of any two free radicals occur. This reaction remove radicals. Chain termination reaction between the possible pairs of radicals allow for the formation of ethane, Cl_2 or the product, methyl chloride. These reactions remove radicals.

Possible termination processes:

$$Cl\cdot + \cdot Cl \longrightarrow Cl\text{-}Cl$$

$$H_3C\cdot + \cdot Cl \longrightarrow H_3C\text{-}Cl$$

$$H_3C\cdot + \cdot CH_3 \longrightarrow H_3C\text{-}CH_3$$

Bromination of alkanes takes place in similar manner but less readily in different proportions. Iodination is reversible, but it may be carried out in the presence of an oxidizing agent such as HIO_3, HNO_3, HgO etc. which eliminate the hydrogen iodide as it is formed and drives the reaction to the right.

$$CH_4 + I_2 \longrightarrow CH_3I + HI$$

Methyl iodide

$$5HI + HIO_3 \longrightarrow 3I_2 + 3H_2O$$

(2) Nitration: The treatment of alkanes with fuming nitric acid at a very high temperature leads to the formation of nitroalkanes by the replacement of a hydrogen atom of alkane by nitro (NO_2) group.

$$R\text{-}H + HNO_3 \xrightarrow{425°C} R\text{-}NO_2 + H_2O$$

Alkane　　　　　　　　　　　Nitroalkane

Mechanism: Free radical reaction mechanism.

$$HO - NO_2 \xrightarrow{425°C} H\dot{O} + \dot{N}O_2$$

$$R - H + H\dot{O} \longrightarrow \dot{R} + H_2O$$

$$\dot{R} + \dot{N}O_2 \longrightarrow R - NO_2$$

Example: Nitration of propane

$$CH_3CH_2CH_3 + HNO_3 \longrightarrow \begin{cases} CH_3CH_2CH_2NO_2 \qquad\quad \underset{\overset{|}{NO_2}}{CH_3CHCH_3} \\ \text{1-nitropropane (25\%)} \qquad \text{2-nitropropane (40\%)} \\[2em] CH_3CH_2NO_2 \qquad\quad CH_3NO_2 \\ \text{1-nitropropane (10\%)} \quad \text{Nitromethane (25\%)} \end{cases}$$

Nitration of propane gives mixture of 1- nitropropane, 2- nitropropane, nitroethane and nitromethane. The yield and product distribution in nitration of alkanes is controlled as far as possible by the cautious addition of catalysts (e.g., oxygen and halogens), which are believed to raise the concentration of alkyl radicals. The products are separated from the mixtures by fractional distillation.

(3) Sulphonation: Sulphonation is the process of replacing a hydrogen atom of a molecule by a sulphonic acid ($-SO_3H$) group. It is carried out by treating alkane with fuming sulphuric acid. The ease of replacement of hydrogen atoms is decreasing in the following order: Tertiary > Secondary > Primary; replacement of a primary hydrogen atom in sulphonation is very low.

iso-Butane is readily sulphonated to give t- butylsulphonic acid.

$$\underset{\text{iso-Butane}}{\underset{\overset{|}{CH_3}}{\overset{\overset{CH_3}{|}}{H_3C-\underset{}{C}-H}}} \xrightarrow{\text{Oleum}} \underset{\text{t-Butylsulphonic acid}}{\underset{\overset{|}{CH_3}}{\overset{\overset{CH_3}{|}}{H_3C-\underset{}{C}-SO_3H}}} + H_2SO_4$$

Normal alkanes from hexane onwards when treated with oleum produce sulphonic acids. Concentrated sulphuric acid, enriched with sulphur trioxide is known as oleum. Lower hydrocarbons do not respond to sulphonation. Sulphonation is also a free radical reaction.

$$\underset{\text{n-Hexane}}{CH_3-CH_2-CH_2-CH_2-CH_2-CH_3} + H_2SO_4 \xrightarrow[400°C]{SO_3} \underset{\text{Hexane sulphonic acid}}{CH_3-CH_2-CH_2-CH_2-CH_2-CH_2-SO_3H} + H_2O$$

(4) Oxidation: Alkanes on oxidation under different conditions give different products. When alkanes are burnt completely in the presence of excess of oxygen, it gives CO_2 and H_2O. This process is known as combustion.

$$2\ CH_3 - CH_3\ +\ 7O_2\ \longrightarrow\ 4CO_2\ +\ 6H_2O\ +\ 736\ kcal$$

Ethane

It is an exothermic reaction and large amount of heat is evolved. For this reason, the hydrocarbons or alkanes are used as fuels in the form of petrol, diesel, kerosene oil, LPG etc.

Partial combustion of alkanes in limited supply of oxygen or at high pressure and in the presence of suitable catalyst, results in the formation on alcohols, aldehydes or fatty acids etc.

$$CH_4\ +\ [O]\ \xrightarrow[400°C/200\ atm.]{Cu}\ CH_3OH\ \xrightarrow{[O]}\ HCHO\ \xrightarrow{[O]}\ HCOOH$$

Methane　　　　　　　　　　　Methanol　　　Formaldehyde　　　Formic acid

Catalytic oxidation of alkanes is very useful for the commercial preparation of higher fatty acids used in soap and vegetable oil industry.

Alkanes are inert to oxidizing agents like $KMnO_4$ or $K_2Cr_2O_7$. However alkanes having a tertiary hydrogen are oxidized by these reagents to an alcohol, e.g *iso*-butane is oxidized to tert- butanol.

$$\underset{\text{iso-Butane}}{H_3C-\overset{\displaystyle CH_3}{\underset{\displaystyle CH_3}{C}}-H}\ \xrightarrow{KMnO_4}\ \underset{\text{ter-Butanol}}{H_3C-\overset{\displaystyle CH_3}{\underset{\displaystyle CH_3}{C}}-OH}$$

(5) Cracking or Pyrolysis: The alkane molecules are decomposed into a number of simpler smaller molecules by the action of heat. This thermal process of decomposition of a organic compound is called pyrolysis or cracking. This process involves the breaking up of C–H bonds of alkane, resulting in the formation of alkenes or by the breaking up of C–C bonds, resulting in the formation of a mixture of smaller alkanes.

For example:

$$\underset{\text{Ethane}}{CH_3-CH_3}\ \xrightarrow{\Delta}\ \underset{\text{Ethene}}{CH_2=CH_2}\ +\ \underset{\text{Methane}}{CH_4}\ +\ H_2$$

$$\underset{\text{Butane}}{CH_3-CH_2-CH_2-CH_3}\ \xrightarrow{\Delta}\ \underset{\text{1-Butene}}{CH_3-CH_2-CH_2=CH_2}\ +\ \underset{\text{Propene}}{CH_3-CH_2=CH_2}\ +\ \underset{\text{Propane}}{CH_3-CH_2-CH_3}$$

$$+\ \underset{\text{Ethane}}{CH_3-CH_3}\ +\ \underset{\text{Methane}}{CH_4}\ +\ H_2$$

Cracking process is used industrially to convert higher alkanes into smaller alkanes which are useful as fuels.

(6) Isomerisation: Isomerisation is the process of conversion of a compound into its isomer. Isomerisation of straight chain alkanes into branched alkanes is brought about by heating the alkane with anhydrous aluminium chloride and hydrochloric acid, at about $200^{\circ}C$, under a pressure of 35 atm. pressure.

For example:

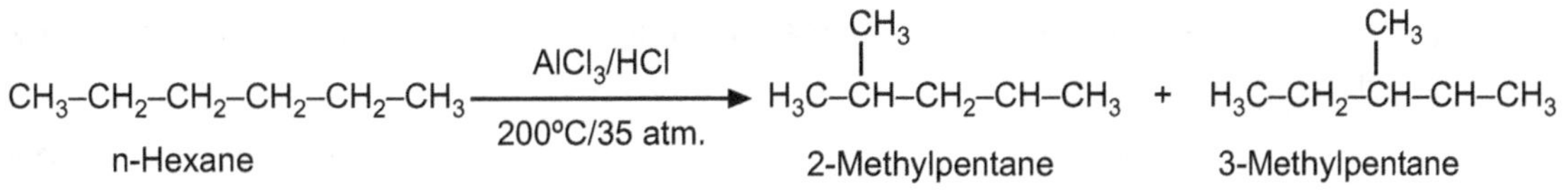

$$CH_3-CH_2-CH_2-CH_2-CH_2-CH_3 \xrightarrow[\text{200°C/35 atm.}]{\text{AlCl}_3/\text{HCl}}$$

n-Hexane

2-Methylpentane + 3-Methylpentane

Process of isomerisation is of immense importance in petroleum industry.

(7) Alkylation: Alkylation is the process of introducing an alkyl group in place of a hydrogen atom of the molecule. Branched chain alkanes are susceptible to alkylation when reacted with unsaturated hydrocarbons in the presence of catalyst like H_2SO_4, BF_3 etc.

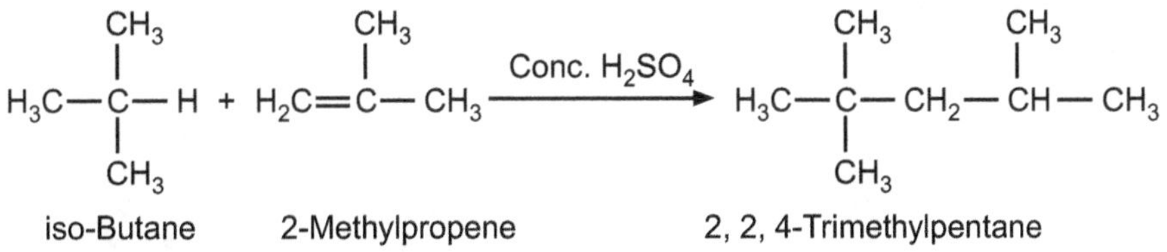

iso-Butane   2-Methylpropene   2, 2, 4-Trimethylpentane

(8) Aromatisation: Alkanes containing six or more carbon atoms may be catalytically cyclised on heating under pressure.

For example: n-Hexane under 15 atm. pressure passed over chromic oxide carried on alumina support and heated at $600^{\circ}C$, gives benzene.

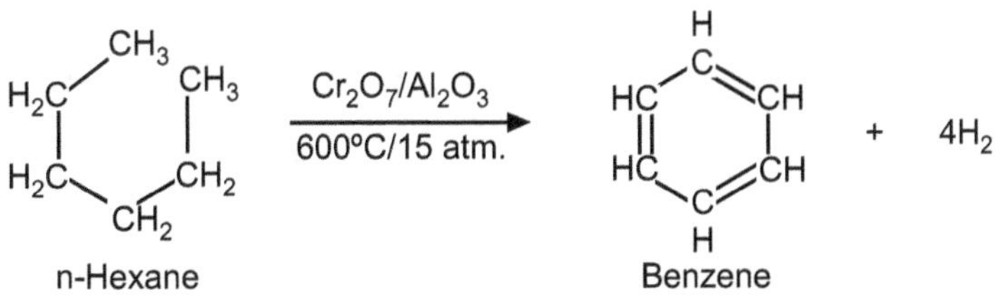

n-Hexane   Benzene $+$ $4H_2$

QUESTIONS

Q.1   Discuss in detail the reactions of alkanes.

Q.2   Comment on kinetics of halogenations of alkanes.

Q.3   Comment on physical properties of alkanes.

Q.4　Write a short note on :

(i)　Conformations of ethane and propane.

(ii)　Halogenation of alkanes and factors affecting it.

(iii)　Pyrolysis of alkanes.

Q.5　Give reasons:

(i)　Why straight chained alkanes have higher boiling point than the branched alkanes?

(ii)　In halogenation reaction of alkanes, bromine is more selective but less reactive than chlorine?

❖ ❖ ❖

Chapter 8

ALKENES AND ALKYNES

(A) ALKENES

8.1 INTRODUCTION

The class of organic compounds that contains a carbon-carbon double bonds (C=C) is called Alkenes or Olefins. Alkenes are hydrocarbons. They have the general formula C_nH_{2n} (n=number of carbon atoms). Alkenes contain two hydrogen atoms less than alkanes and are thus designated as unsaturated hydrocarbons. It occurs widely in nature from substances in petroleum to fats and oils to vitamins and hormones. Compounds containing several double bonds are of particular significance in biochemistry. e.g. β-carotene, the yellow colouring matter containing eleven conjugate double bonds is present in many plants such as carrots and tomatoes.

β-carotene

Ethylene is the first member of the series. Ethylene is the hormone that causes tomatoes and apples to ripe. Alkenes rarely occur free in nature. They are however produced in large amounts by cracking of petroleum.

8.2 STRUCTURE

According to the general formula of alkenes C_nH_{2n}, the first member should have been methylene CH_2. But methylene is very unstable and does not exist in stable form. Consequently the alkene family begins with two carbons containing member, ethylene C_2H_4. The structural formula and molecular orbital picture of ethylene is represented below.

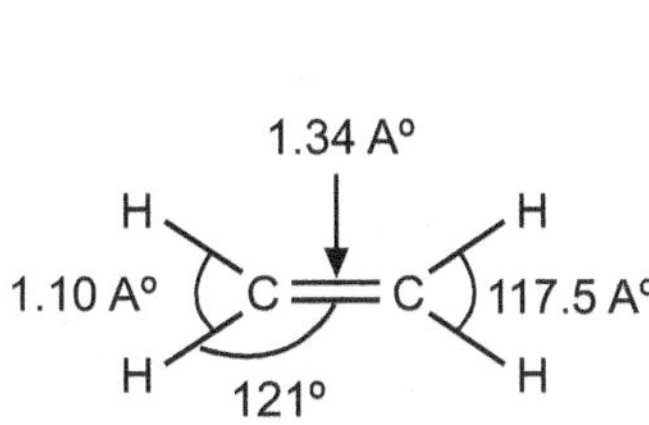

Structural formula of ethylene

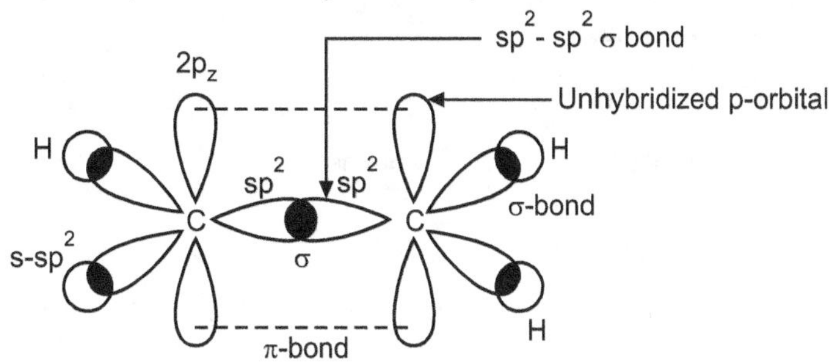

Molecular orbital picture of ethylene

Two carbon atoms in ethylene are connected by a σ-bond formed by overlapping one sp^2-hybrid orbital of each and by a π-bond which is formed by the parallel overlapping of $2p$-orbital of each carbon atom. Thus the double bond between the carbon atoms consists of one π-bond and one σ-bond. Four hydrogen atoms are connected by σ-bond formed by the overlapping of sp^2 orbital of carbons and s-orbital of hydrogen. The carbon–carbon double bond is thus made up of a stronger σ-bond and a weaker π-bond. The carbon–carbon double bond is the distinguishing feature of alkenes.

Alkenes are more reactive than alkanes. This is due to the availability of the more exposed π-electrons.

8.3 NOMENCLATURE OF ALKENES

Common names are rarely used except for simple alkenes: Ethylene, propylene and isobutylene. Depending on the presence of number of carbon atoms in alkenes are sometimes referred to collectively as the pentylenes, hexylenes, heptylenes and so on. Most alkenes are named by the IUPAC system.

IUPAC Nomenclature:

(i) Select the longest continuous chain of carbon atoms that contains the carbon-carbon double bond as the parent chain. The number of carbon atoms in the parent chain determines the word root. The carbon atoms which are not included in the parent chain are considered as alkyl substituent and determine the prefixes. Depending upon the number of carbon atoms each name is derived by changing the ending –ane of the corresponding alkane name to –ene.

If two equally long chains are possible, the chain with maximum number of side chains is selected as parent chain.

(ii) Give numbering to the longest hydrocarbon chain from the end of the chain nearest to the double bond i.e. indicate the carbon atoms involved in the double bond with the lowest number.

(iii) Indicate by numbers the positions of alkyl groups attached to the parent chain.

For example,

$CH_2 = CH_2$	$CH_3 - CH = CH_2$	$\overset{4}{C}H_3 - \overset{3}{C}H_2 - \overset{2}{C}H = \overset{1}{C}H_2$	$CH_3 - CH = CH - CH_3$
Ethene	Propene	1-Butene	2-Butene

2-Methylpropene   3, 3-Dimethyl-1-butene   3-Methyl-1-butene   2-Ethyl-3-methyl-1-butene

For the nomenclature of geometric isomers, a prefix is added: cis- or trans- or (Z)- or (E)-.

cis-2-butene   trans-2-butene

8.4 PHYSICAL PROPERTIES OF ALKENES

(i)   The alkenes possess physical properties similar to the saturated hydrocarbons, alkanes.

(ii) The melting points of highly substituted alkenes are higher compared to the straight chain alkenes.

(iii) Their boiling points increase gradually by 20-30° per carbon atom, as the carbon chain increases the length.

(iv) The cis-alkenes have a permanent dipole moment and thus boil at a higher temperature than the trans isomers **(Table 8.1)**. Alkenes are insoluble in water or ethanol but soluble in non-polar solvents.

Table 8.1 : Physical properties of alkenes

Name	Structure	M.P. (°C)	B.P. (°C)	Dipole moment (μ)
Ethylene	$CH_2=CH_2$	−169	−102	---
Propylene	$CH_2=CHCH_3$	−185	−48	---
1-Butene	$CH_2=CHCH_2CH_3$	---	−6.5	---
1-Pentene	$CH_2=CH(CH_2)_2CH_3$	---	30	---
1-Hexene	$CH_2=CH(CH_2)_3CH_3$	−138	−63.5	---
1-Heptene	$CH_2=CH(CH_2)_4CH_3$	−119	93	---
1-Octene	$CH_2=CH(CH_2)_5CH_3$	−104	122.5	---
1-Nonene	$CH_2=CH(CH_2)_6CH_3$	---	146	---
1-Decene	$CH_2=CH(CH_2)_7CH_3$	−87	171	---

Contd...

Name	Structure			
cis-2-butene	H_3C , CH_3 / H , H (C=C)	−139	4	0.33
trans-2-butene	H_3C , H / H , CH_3 (C=C)	−106	1	0
Isobutylene	CH_2 , H_3C , CH_3	−141	−7	---
cis-2-pentene	H_3C , H_2C-CH_3	−151	37	---
trans-2-pentene	H_3C , CH_3	---	36	---
cis-1-2-Dichloroethylene	Cl , Cl / H , H (C=C)	−80	60	1.85
trans-1-2-Dichloroethylene	Cl , H / H , Cl (C=C)	−50	48	0

8.5 PREPARATION OF ALKENES

Alkenes containing upto four carbon atoms can be obtained in pure form from the petroleum industry. Pure samples of more complicated alkenes should be prepared by following methods those outlined below.

The introduction of a carbon-carbon double bond into a molecule containing only single bonds must essentially involve the elimination of atoms or groups from two adjacent carbons.

$$-\underset{\underset{Z}{|}}{\overset{\overset{H}{|}}{C}}-\overset{|}{\underset{|}{C}}- \longrightarrow \overset{}{C}=\overset{}{C} \quad + \quad H-Z \qquad .... \text{Elimination}$$

Substrate   Alkene

8.5.1 Elimination Reactions

Definition: A reaction in which two atoms or group of atoms are removed from the substrate to form a product with higher degree of unsaturation is known as elimination reaction.

8.5.1.1 Types of Elimination Reactions

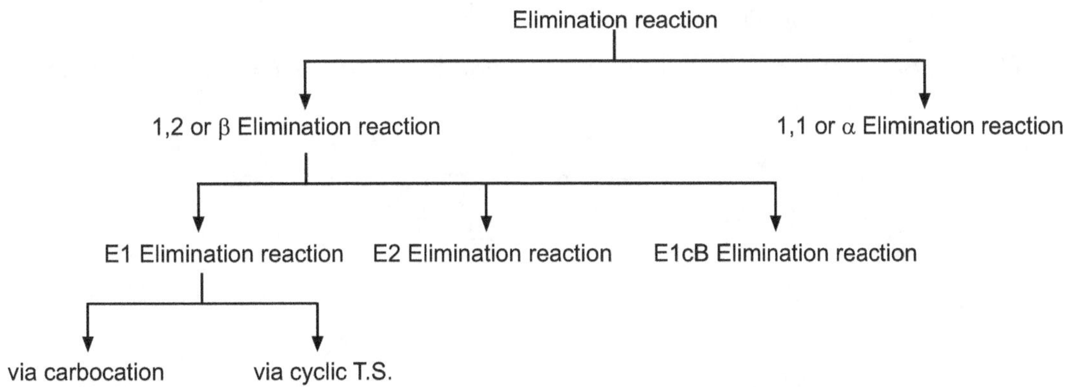

8.5.1.1.1 1,1-Elimination Reaction (α-Elimination Reaction)

When two atoms or groups are lost from the same carbon atom of the molecule, then the reaction is called 1,1- elimination reaction or α-elimination reaction. For example,

The carbene thus formed is not stable and immediately undergo further reaction so as to form stable molecule.

8.5.1.1.2 1,2- Elimination Reaction (β-Elimination Reaction)

When two atoms or groups are removed from the two adjacent carbon atoms so that a new double (or triple) bond is formed then the reaction is known as β-elimination.

It gives rise to a double or triple bond.

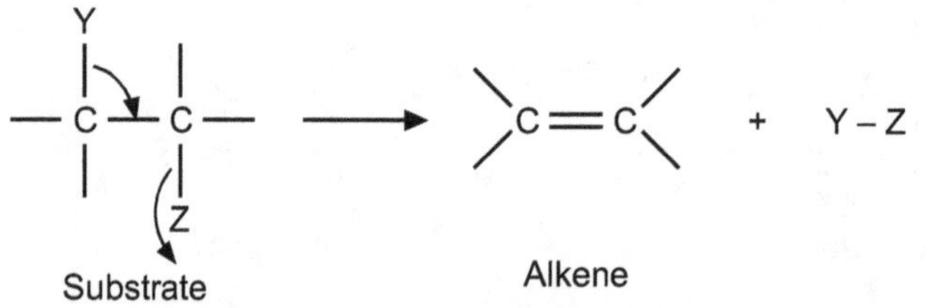
Y
C
C
Z
C=C
+
Y – Z
Substrate
Alkene

In most organic reactions, one of the eliminated group is hydrogen and other is a leaving group (Z^-) and sp^3 hybridised carbon changes to sp^2.

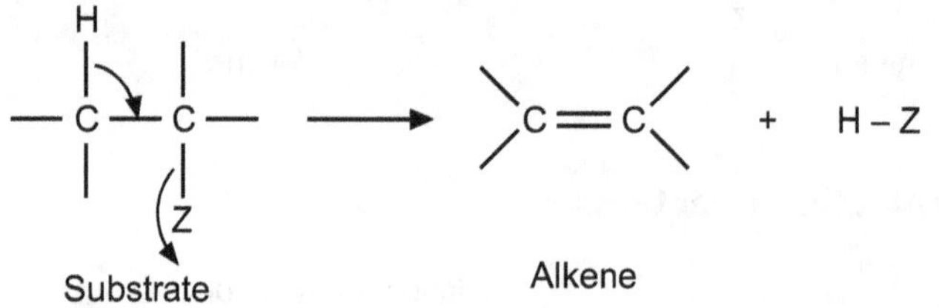
H
C
C
Z
C=C
+
H – Z
Substrate
Alkene

β-elimination reactions also lead to the formation of C=N, C≡N, C=O as shown below.

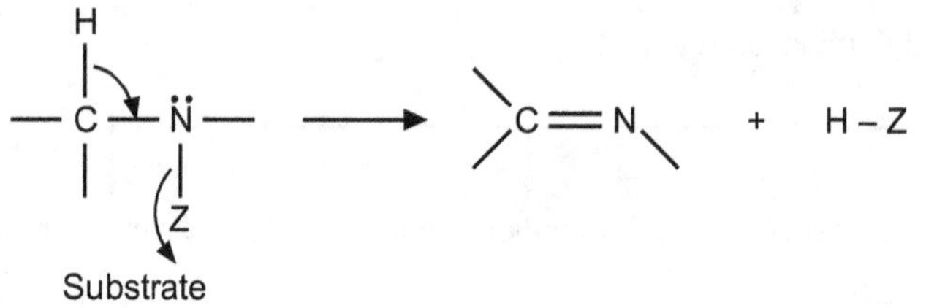
H
C
N
Z
C=N
+
H – Z
Substrate

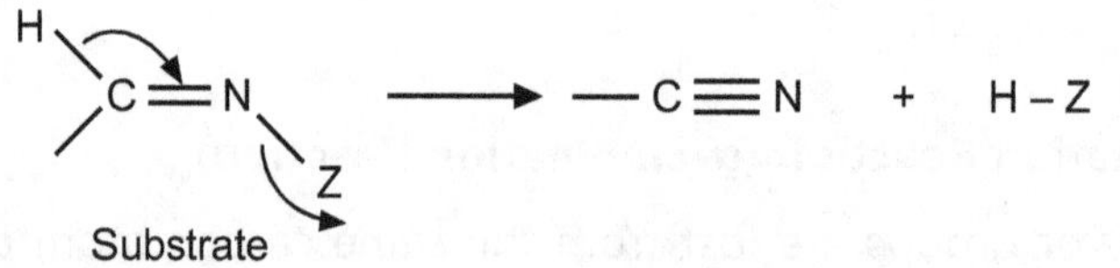
H
C=N
Z
—C≡N
+
H – Z
Substrate

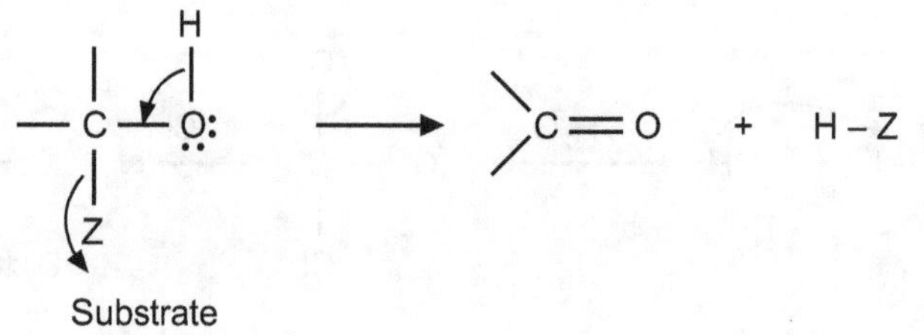
H
C
O:
Z
C=O
+
H – Z
Substrate

Similarly 1,3; 1,4; 1,5; and 1,6-eliminations are also known. Generally this elimination reaction results in the formation of cyclic molecules.

For example, 1,4-elimination:

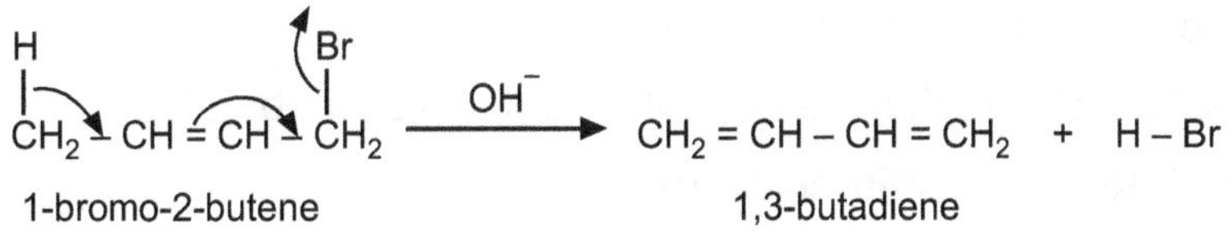
H
Br
CH_2 – CH = CH – CH_2
OH^-
CH_2 = CH – CH = CH_2 + H – Br
1-bromo-2-butene
1,3-butadiene

1,6-elimination:

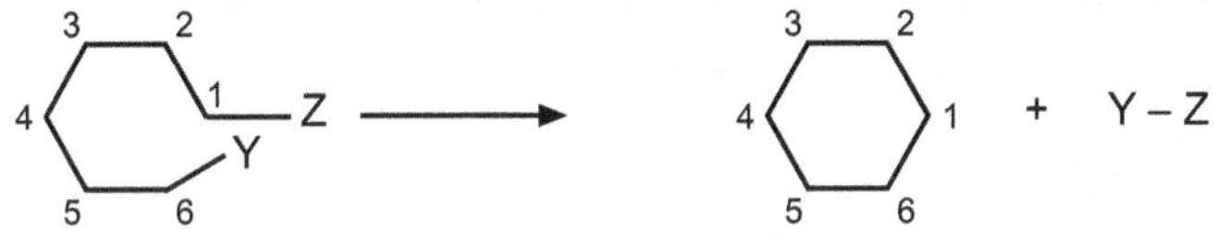
Z
Y
Y – Z

Cyclohexane

Mechanism of 1,2 or β-elimination reaction

Reactions which take place in basic medium are characterized by the following.

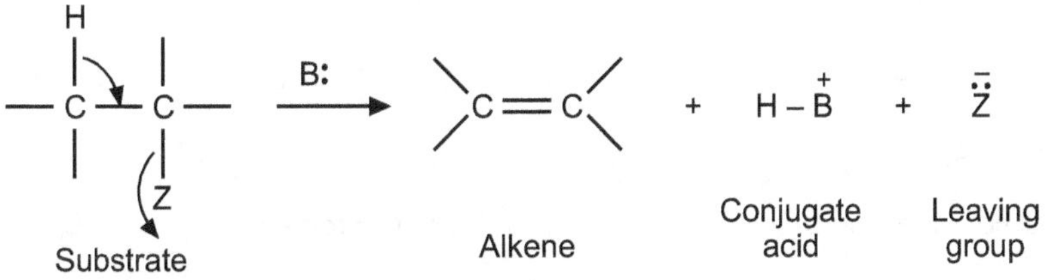
B:
Substrate
Alkene
Conjugate acid
Leaving group

Mechanism of β-elimination involving following steps:

Step-I: Breaking of C_α-Z bond : The substrate has a good leaving group Z^-. During the reaction C-Z bond breaks heterolytically, so that bonding pair of electrons is taken away with leaving group and formation of carbocation intermediate.

Step-II: Breaking of C_β-H bond : The base used abstracts the β-hydrogen as a proton; the bonding pair of electron is retained by the β-carbon. The electron pair retained by the β-carbon is used for the formation of a σ-bond between C_α and C_β.

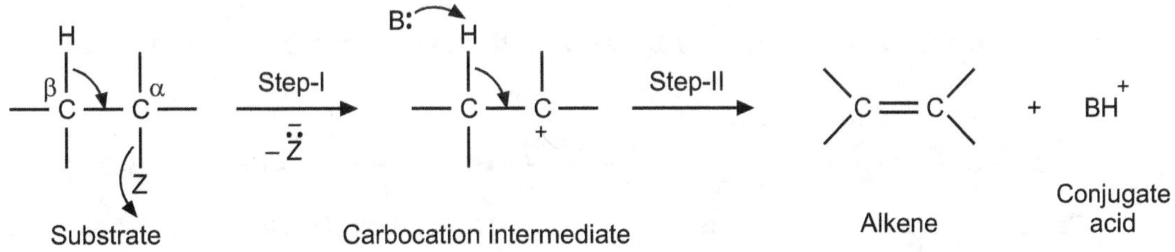
Step-I
Step-II
B:
BH^+
Substrate
Carbocation intermediate
Alkene
Conjugate acid

Bases used : OH^- (Hydroxide), CH_3O^- (Methoxide), $C_2H_5O^-$ (Ethoxide), $(CH_3)_3CO^-$ (t-butoxide) etc. Sometimes solvent itself acts as a base (H_2O, R-OH).

1,2- elimination reaction thus involves breaking of two σ-bonds and formation of one π-bond. Depending upon the timing or the sequence of bond breaking and bond formation, there are three types of β-elimination reactions.

(1)　E1 reaction (Elimination unimolecular)

(2)　E2 reaction (Elimination bimolecular)

(3)　E1cB reaction (Elimination unimolecular from conjugate base)

(1) E1 reaction (Elimination unimolecular) :

β-elimination reactions in which the T.S. of the rate determining step involves only one species i.e. substrate is known as E1 reaction. It follows first order kinetics. The mechanism of these reactions may be explained by two ways.

(a) E1 mechanism via carbocation :

The breaking of C_α–Z bond takes place in slow step to form a carbocation, which is then followed by fast breaking of C_β-H bond and formation of C_α- C_β σ-bond.

Reaction : Z-Br

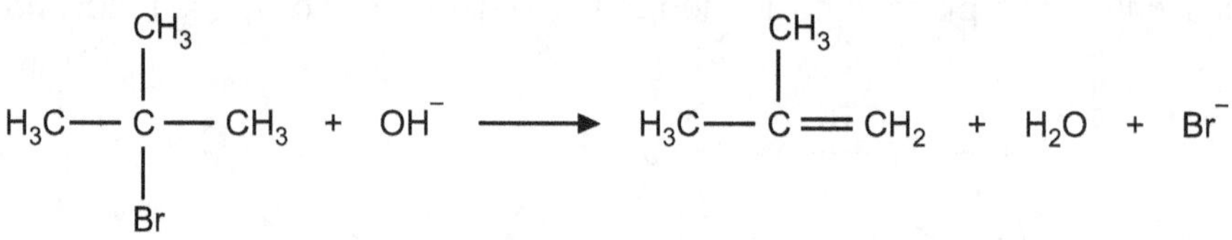

2-Bromo-2-methylpropane　　　　　　2-Methylpropene

A two step mechanism has been proposed for this type of elimination.

Step-I: The C-Br (Br⁻ is leaving group) bond is broken heterolytically to form a carbocation. It is a slow rate determining step.

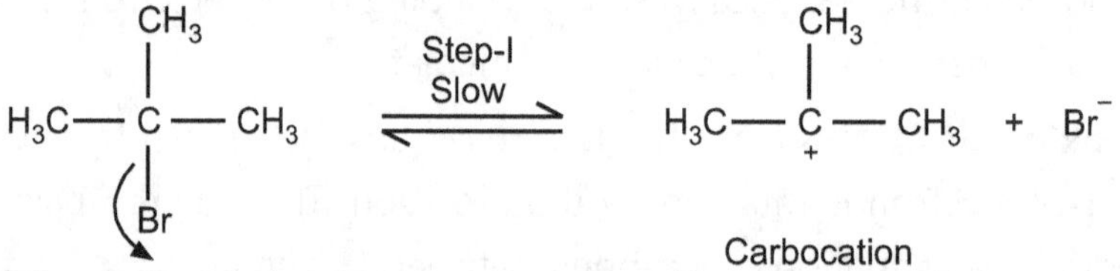

2-Bromo-2-methylpropane　　　Carbocation Transition state (I)

Step-II: Removal of a β-proton of carbocation with the help of a base to form a π-bond.

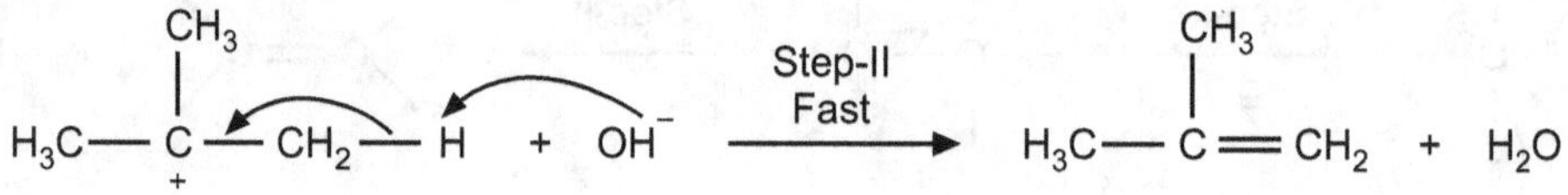

Carbocation Transition state (I)　　　Base　　　2-Methylpropene

Kinetics: Step-I is rate determining step in which Br⁻ (leaving group) is lost. In this reaction, rate of formation of the alkene i.e. 2-methyl propene is found to be proportional to the concentration of only alkyl halide and is independent of the concentration of the base i.e.

Rate of reaction = k [(CH₃)₃C-Br]

Therefore it is a first order i.e. unimolecular reaction.

In E1 reaction, the intermediate is carbocation and thus there can be rearrangement (leading to more stable carbocation) taking place before the proton is lost. For example,

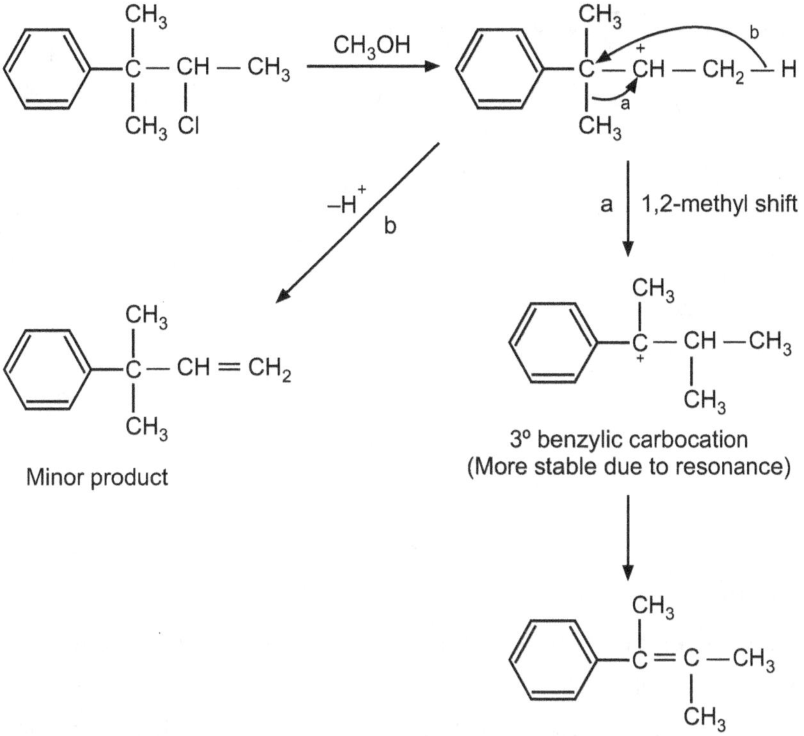

CH$_3$OH

−H$^+$

a | 1,2-methyl shift

3° benzylic carbocation
(More stable due to resonance)

Minor product

Major product

When two elimination products are formed, the major product is generally the one obtained by following Saytzeff's rule (the hydrogen atom is removed from the β-carbon bonded to the less number of hydrogens).

For example,

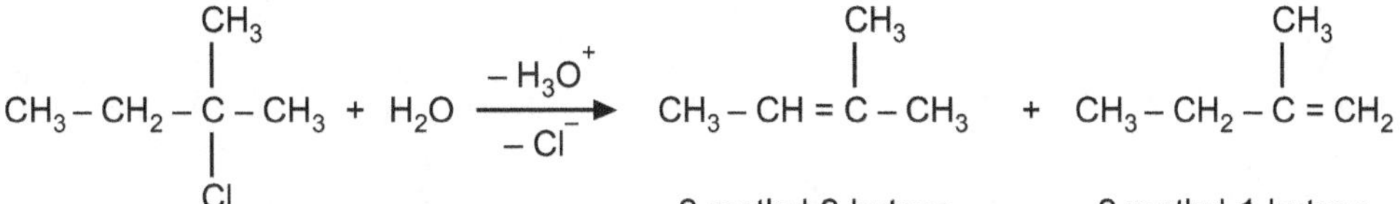

$$CH_3 - CH_2 - \underset{\underset{Cl}{|}}{\overset{\overset{CH_3}{|}}{C}} - CH_3 \ + \ H_2O \ \xrightarrow[- Cl^-]{- H_3O^+} \ CH_3 - CH = \underset{}{\overset{\overset{CH_3}{|}}{C}} - CH_3 \ + \ CH_3 - CH_2 - \overset{\overset{CH_3}{|}}{C} = CH_2$$

2-Chloro-2-methylbutane　　　　　　　2-methyl-2-butene　　　　2-methyl-1-butene
　　　　　　　　　　　　　　　　　　　　(Major product)　　　　　(Minor product)

(b) E1 mechanism via cyclic transition state:

It proceeds via cyclic transition state and produces cis product.

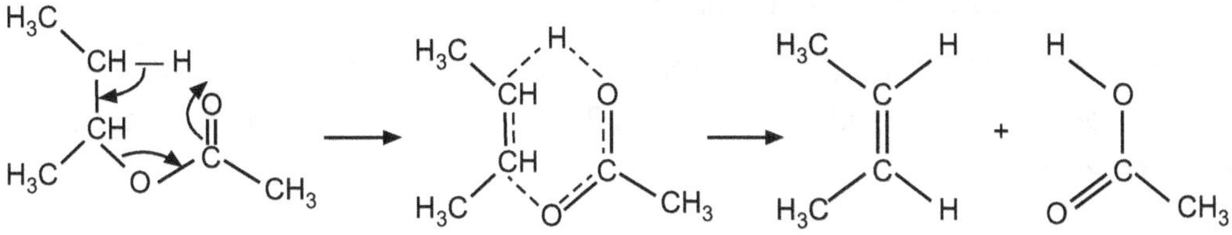

Butyl acetate　　　　　Cyclic transition state　　　　Cis-2-butene　　　　Acetic acid

Energy profile for E1 reaction:

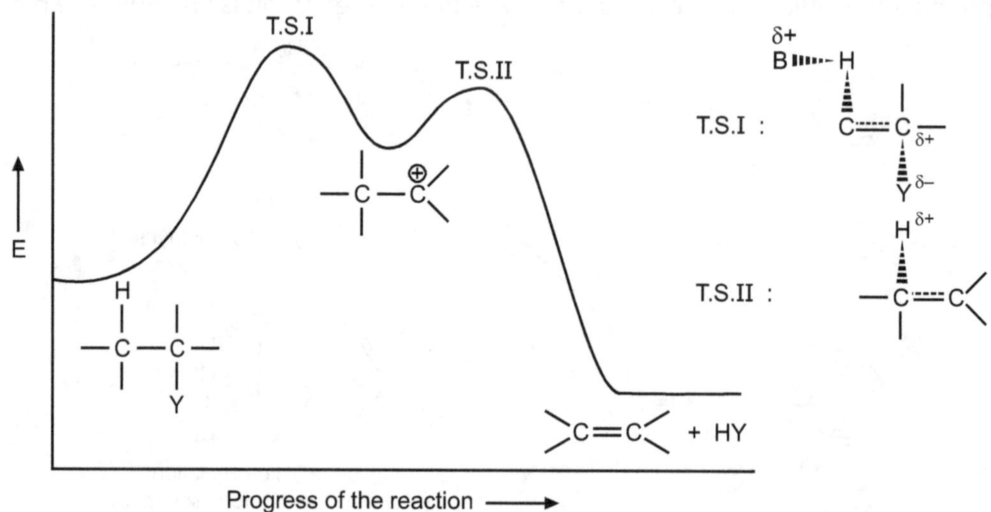

Fig. 8.1

Stereochemistry of E1 reaction:

An E1 reaction takes place in two steps : (i) The leaving group leaves in the first step (ii) a proton is lost from an adjacent carbon in the second step, following Saytzeff's rule in order to form the most stable alkene. If the β-carbon from which the proton is removed is bonded to two hydrogens the major product will be the one with the bulkier groups on opposite sides of the double bond.

The carbocation formed in the first step of an E1 reaction is planar. This means that electrons from a departing hydrogen can move towards the positively charged carbon from either side. Therefore both syn and anti-elimination can occur.

(2)　E2 reaction (Elimination bimolecular):

β-Elimination reactions in which the T.S. of the single concerted step involve two species i.e. substrate and base is called is known as E2 reaction. Generally the E2 reaction follows second order kinetics.

Reaction :

$$R—CH—CH_2 \longrightarrow R—CH{=\!=}CH_2 + H–B^+ + \ddot{Z}^-$$

with B: abstracting H, Z as leaving group; the starting species labelled Substrate, and the products labelled Alkene, Conjugate acid, Leaving group.

Mechanism :

The breaking of C_α-Z bond and C_β-H bond and formation of C_α-C_β σ bond take place simultaneously.

In this bimolecular elimination reaction, the two groups are lost simultaneously in a single concerted step.

$$R—CH—CH_2 \longrightarrow \left[R—CH{\cdots}CH_2 \right]^+ \longrightarrow R—CH{=\!=}CH_2 + H–B^+ + \ddot{Z}^-$$

with the Substrate (B: abstracting H, Z leaving group) converting through the Transition state (B⋯H, $Z^{\delta-}$) to the products Alkene, Conjugate acid, Leaving group.

Kinetics:

The rate of E2 reaction depends on the concentration of the substrate and the base. The reaction is of second order kinetics.

$$\text{Rate} = k[\text{substrate}]\,[\text{Base}]$$

For example, 2-bromopropane has two β-carbons from which a proton can be removed in an E2 reaction. Being symmetrical proton can be removed from either one to form propene.

$$H_3C—\underset{\underset{\text{2-Bromopropane}}{}}{\overset{\overset{Br}{|}}{CH}}—CH_3 \xrightarrow{CH_3O^-} \underset{\text{Propene}}{H_3C—CH{=\!=}CH_2} + CH_3OH + Br^-$$

But 2-bromobutane has two structurally different β-carbons from which a proton can be removed giving 1-butene and 2-butene. By Saytzeff rule substituted alkenes are more stable and thus 2-butene is predominant.

$$H_3C—\overset{\overset{Br}{|}}{CH}—CH_2—CH_3 \xrightarrow{CH_3O^-} H_3C—CH{=\!=}CH—CH_3 + H_3C—CH_2—CH{=\!=}CH_2 + CH_3OH + Br^-$$

2-Bromobutane → 2-butene (Major product) + 1-butene (Minor product)

Energy profile for E2 reaction:

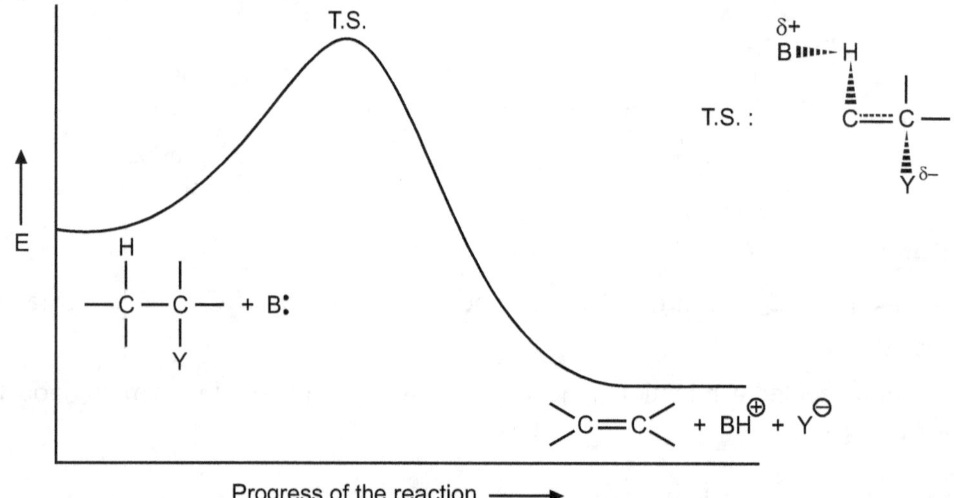

Fig. 8.2

Stereochemistry of E-2 reaction :

If an elimination reaction removes two substituents from the same side of the molecule, then the reaction is a syn elimination.

If the substituents are removed from opposite side of the molecule then the reaction is an anti elimination.

Anti elimination is favoured in an E2 reaction: syn elimination can occur, but it is a much slower reaction.

In antiperiplanar orientation the substrate is in staggered form instead of the eclipsed conformation, the energy content is less and the π-bond forming orbitals are very much parallel to each other. Because the staggered conformer is more stable the T.S. leading to the elimination from the staggered conformer is more stable than the T.S. leading to elimination from the eclipsed conformer. Consequently anti elimination occurs more readily.

For example, elimination of HBr from the meso comp (I) (1,2-dibromo-1,2-diphenyl ethane) gives *cis*-olefin (II) and its ($\pm$) –isomer (III) gives trans-olefin (IV).

1,2-dibromo-1,2-diphenyl ethane
(I)

cis-1-bromo-1,2-diphenylethene
(II)

($\pm$) isomer of I
(III)

trans-1-bromo-1,2-diphenylethene
(IV)

(3) E1 cB reactions

E1cB reactions involve an intermediate carbanion, the conjugate base (cB) of the substrate, which gives up a leaving group through a T.S. involving only one chemical species.

The breaking of C_β-H bond takes place first to produce a carbanion or conjugate base of the substrate, followed by simultaneously formation of C_α-C_β π–bond and breaking of C_α-Z bond.

Mechanism :

This is a two step-base catalysed 1,2-elimination reaction which involves a carbanion, the conjugate base of the substrate as the intermediate.

Step-I : The base abstracts the most acidic β-H from the substrate and a carbanion forms. This is a reversible and fast step.

Substrate

Conjugate base

Step-II : The leaving group leaves the carbanion and a C-C double bond forms. It is the slow and rate determining step.

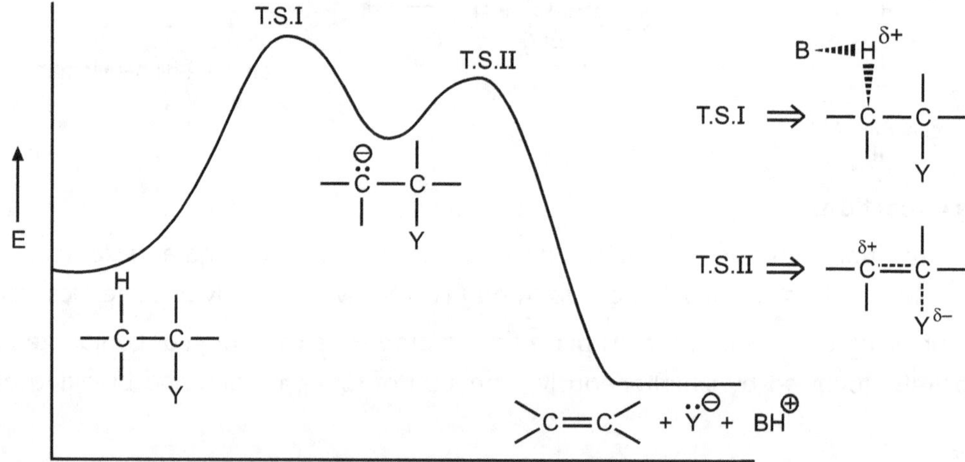

Kinetics: Since the T.S. for the slow step involves the conjugate base (cB) of the substrate only its conversion to the unsaturated compound follows the first order kinetics.

$$\text{Rate} = k\,[\text{conjugate base}]$$

$$\text{Rate} = k\,[\text{cB}]$$

So this mechanism is called E1cB mechanism (Elimination, unimolecular from conjugate base).

Energy Profile Diagram for E1cB reaction:

Fig. 8.3

The carbanion mechanism occurs only where the carbanion from the substrate is stabilized and where the leaving group is a poor leaving group.

For example,

1,2-dichloro-2,2,2-trifluoroethane   1,2-dichloro-2,2-difluoroethene

Stereochemistry of E1cB –elimination reaction:

Since carbanions are the intermediates in E1cB reactions and since a carbanion can adopt the most stable conformation the E1cB reactions are non-stereospecific.

8.5.2 Orientation in Elimination Reaction

The orientation of the product formed in elimination reaction is governed by two rules :

(1) Saytzeff's rule

(2) Hofmann rule

(1) Saytzeff's rule : In case of unsymmetrical alkyl halides, the course of elimination is determined by Saytzeff's rule.

Statement: This rule states that during dehydrohalogenation of unsymmetrical alkyl halide, hydrogen is eliminated preferentially from that carbon which has less number of hydrogen atoms and so that highly substituted alkene is formed as the major product.

For example,

$$H_3C - CH_2 - \overset{\overset{\textstyle Br}{|}}{C}H - CH_3 \xrightarrow{\text{Alc. KOH}} H_3C - CH = CH - CH_3 \ + \ H_3C - CH_2 - CH = CH_2$$

2-bromobutane   2-butene (80%)   1-butene (20%)

                              (Major product)   (Minor product)

These elimination reactions can take place either by E1 or by E2 mechanism.

(a) By E1 mechanism:

$$H_3C - CH_2 - \overset{\overset{\textstyle Cl}{|}}{\underset{\underset{\textstyle CH_3}{|}}{C}} - CH_3 \xrightarrow[-Cl^-]{OH^-} H_3C - CH_2 - \overset{+}{\underset{\underset{\textstyle CH_3}{|}}{C}} - CH_3$$

2-chloro-2-methyl butane

$$\xrightarrow{-H^+}$$

$$CH_3 - CH = \overset{\overset{\textstyle |}{\underset{\textstyle CH_3}{}}}{C} - CH_3 \qquad\qquad CH_3 - CH_2 - \overset{\overset{\textstyle |}{\underset{\textstyle CH_3}{}}}{C} = CH_2$$

2-methyl-2-butene   2-methyl-1-butene
Major (80%)   Minor (20%)

(b) By E2 mechanism:

$$H_3C - \overset{\overset{\textstyle Br}{|}}{C}H - \underset{\underset{\textstyle OH^-}{|}}{C}H - CH_3 \longrightarrow H_3C - \overset{\overset{\textstyle Br^-}{|}}{C}H = \underset{\underset{\textstyle OH - - - H}{\overset{\delta-}{|}}}{C}H - CH_3 \xrightarrow[-Br^-]{-H_2O} H_3C - CH = CH - CH_3$$

2-bromobutane   T.S.   2-butene (80%)

Whenever geometrical isomers are possible the *trans* isomer is found to be slightly more stable than the *cis*.

As the number of 'R' substituents attached to the C_α and C_β carbon increases, the energy of transition state (T.S.) goes on decreasing i.e. energy of activation (E_{act}) required to form T.S. decreases and hence more substituted alkene is formed at faster rate.

(2) Hofmann rule:

This rule is applicable for those substances in which α-carbon atom is attached to a positively charged atom.

Statement: It states that when positively charged species are decomposed by heating, then hydrogen is preferentially eliminated from that β-carbon atom, which is linked to the largest number of hydrogen atoms i.e. least substituted alkene is formed as a major product.

Positively charged species (leaving group) : For example,

–Ammonium bases [$-N^+(CH_3)_3$], –Sulphonium bases [$-S^+(CH_3)_2$]

For example,

$$CH_3 - \overset{\overset{\displaystyle CH_3\ OH^-}{|}}{\underset{\underset{\displaystyle CH_2 - CH_3}{|}}{N^+}} - CH_2 - CH_2 - CH_3 \xrightarrow{\Delta} CH_2 = CH_2 \ + \ CH_3 - CH = CH_2 \ + \ CH_3CH_2CH_2N(CH_3)_2$$

$$\text{Ethene (98\%)} \qquad \text{Propene (2\%)}$$

Ethyl dimethyl propyl
ammonium hydroxide

$$CH_3 - CH_2 - \overset{+}{S} - (CH_3)_2 \xrightarrow{C_2H_5O^-} CH_2 = CH_2 \ + \ S(CH_3)_2$$

$$\text{Ethene}$$

The hydroxide ion abstracts a proton from the β-carbon atom resulting in the formation of a double bond and the nitrogen atom is eliminated as trialkyl amine.

Kinetic studies have shown that this elimination reaction is a second order reaction.

$$\text{Rate} = k \ [\text{Oxonium ion}] \ [\text{OH}^-]$$

Whether a given elimination reaction will follow the Saytzeff's rule or Hofmann rule depends upon

(a) the nature of the leaving group

(b) the nature of base used.

(a) The effect of a leaving group (Z):

For example,

$$H_3C - \overset{\overset{\displaystyle H}{|}}{C}H - \overset{\overset{\displaystyle H}{|}}{\underset{\underset{\displaystyle Z}{|}}{C}}H - CH_2 \xrightarrow{B:} R - CH = CH - CH_3$$

$$\text{Saytzeff product}$$

Effect of size of leaving group on elimination

Sr. No.	Leaving group (Z)	Saytzeff product	Hofmann product
1.	$-Br$	80%	20%
2.	$-OTs$	60%	40%
3.	$-N^+(CH_3)_3$	5%	95%

These results indicate that as the size of leaving group increases, the % of Hofmann product increases and that of Saytzeff product decreases and vice versa with smaller leaving group.

(b) Effect of base:

As the size of attacking base increases, the T.S. for the Saytzeff elimination becomes more crowded than Hofmann elimination and hence less substituted alkene is obtained as a major product i.e. Hofmann product predominates.

For example,

$$C_2H_5 - \overset{\overset{H}{|}}{CH} - \underset{\underset{Br}{|}}{CH} - \overset{\overset{H}{|}}{CH_2} \xrightarrow{\text{Base}} C_2H_5 - CH = CH - CH_3 + C_2H_5 - CH_2 - CH = CH_2$$

2-pentene (Saytzeff product)   1-pentene (Hofmann product)

Effect of size of base on elimination

Sr. No.	Base	Saytzeff product	Hofmann product
1.	$C_2H_5O^-$	70%	30%
2.	$(CH_3)_3CO^-$	28%	72%
3.	$(C_2H_5)_3CO^-$	20%	80%

Mechanism of Hofmann elimination:

$$R - \overset{\overset{H}{|}}{CH} - \underset{\underset{Z}{|}}{CH} - \overset{\overset{H}{|}}{CH_2} \xrightarrow{\text{B:}} R - CH_2 - \underset{\underset{Z}{|}}{CH} = CH_2 \xrightarrow[-BH]{H---B} R - CH_2 - CH = CH_2$$

Less crowded T.S. required less energy   Hofmann product

8.5.3 Methods of Preparation of Alkenes

Most of the methods of alkene preparation involve elimination of atoms or groups from two adjacent carbon atoms.

(1) Dehydration of Alcohols:

$$R-\underset{\underset{H}{|}}{CH}-\underset{\underset{OH}{|}}{CH_2} \xrightarrow[\Delta]{H_2SO_4} R-CH=CH_2 + H_2O$$

Alcohol   Alkene

$$CH_3-CH_2-OH \xrightarrow[160°C]{H_2SO_4} CH_2=CH_2 + H_2O$$

Ethanol   Ethene

$$CH_3-CH_2-CH_2-OH \xrightarrow[180°C]{H_2SO_4} CH_3-CH=CH_2 + H_2O$$

Propanol   Propene

The ease of dehydration of alcohol is : 3° > 2° > 1°

Mechanism :

$$CH_3-CH_2-\overset{..}{\underset{..}{O}}H \underset{}{\overset{H^+, \text{fast}}{\rightleftharpoons}} CH_3-CH_2-\overset{\overset{H}{|}}{\underset{..}{O}}-H$$

Ethanol   (Oxonium ion)

Slow

$-H_2\overset{..}{\underset{..}{O}}$

$$H_3\overset{\oplus}{O} + CH_2=CH_2 \rightleftharpoons \underset{CH_2}{} \overset{\oplus}{\underset{CH_2}{}}$$

$-H_2\overset{..}{O}:$

$$CH_3-\underset{\underset{H}{|}}{CH}-\underset{\underset{OH}{|}}{CH}-CH_3 \xrightarrow[\Delta]{H_2SO_4} CH_3-CH=CH-CH_3$$

2-butanol   2-butene, 80%

+

$$CH_3-CH_2-CH=CH_2$$

1-butene, 20%

In unsymmetrical 2° or 3° alcohol, elimination takes place by Saytzeff rule.

Dehydrating agents which may be used are alumina (Al_2O_3), phosphorus pentoxide (P_2O_5) and phosphoric acid (H_3PO_4).

(2) Dehydrohalogenation of Alkyl Halides:

Alkenes can be prepared by heating an alkyl halide in the presence of alcoholic KOH solution. A molecule of hydrogen halide is lost and the process is known as dehydrohalogenation.

$$R-\underset{\underset{H}{|}}{CH}-\underset{\underset{X}{|}}{CH_2} + KOH \xrightarrow[\Delta]{\text{Alcohol}} R-CH=CH_2 + KX + H_2O$$

$$CH_3-CH-CH_2 + KOH \xrightarrow[\Delta]{Alcohol} CH_3-CH=CH_2 + KBr + H_2O$$

(with substituents H and Br on the carbon)

1-Bromopropane

$$H_3C-\underset{\underset{CH_3}{|}}{\overset{\overset{CH_3}{|}}{C}}-Br \xrightarrow[\Delta]{Alcohol\ KOH} \overset{H_3C}{\underset{H_3C}{>}}\overset{3}{C}=\overset{1}{C}H_2 + H_2O + KBr$$

t-Butyl bromide   2-methyl propene 90%

Mechanism : E2 mechanism

The ease of dehydrohalogenation of alkyl halides is : 3° > 2° > 1°

(3) Debromination of vicinal dibromides:

Vicinal dibromides are dihalo compounds in which bromine atoms are situated on adjacent carbon atoms. Vicinal dibromides are converted to alkenes by reaction with Zn / CH_3COOH or iodide ion.

$$CH_3-CH-CH_2 \xrightarrow[\Delta]{Zn\ /\ CH_3COOH} CH_3-CH=CH_2 + ZnBr_2$$

(with Br and Br on adjacent carbons)   Propene

1,2-Dibromopropane

Mechanism :

$$H_3C-\underset{H}{\overset{Br}{C}}-CH_2-Br \xrightarrow{Zn} H_3C-\underset{H}{\overset{Br}{C}}-\underset{H}{\overset{H}{C}}-Br \longrightarrow \ >C=C< + [ZnBr]^{\oplus} + Br^{\ominus}$$

$$\downarrow$$
$$ZnBr_2$$

(4) Controlled hydrogenation of alkynes:

Alkynes react with hydrogen in the presence of Lindlar's catalyst to give alkenes. Lindlar's catalyst is Pd poisoned with $CaCO_3$ and quinoline.

e.g.

$$CH_3-C\equiv CH + H_2 \xrightarrow[Quinoline]{Pd\ CaCO_3} CH_3-CH=CH_2$$

Propyne   Propene

$$H-C\equiv C-H + H_2 \xrightarrow{Lindlar's\ catalyst} CH_2=CH_2$$

Acetylene   Ethene

(5) Cracking of alkanes:

Petroleum is a complex mixture of large number of alkanes. Heating of petroleum above 500°C produces large quantities of mixture of alkenes. Alkanes when heated at 500-800°C in the absence of air decompose to yield lower molecular weight (M.Wt.) alkenes, alkanes and hydrogen.

e.g.

$$CH_3 - CH_2 - CH_2 - CH_3 \xrightarrow{\quad}
\begin{cases}
\xrightarrow{a} CH_4 + CH_2 = CH - CH_3 \\
\xrightarrow{b} CH_2 = CH_2 + CH_3 - CH_3
\end{cases}$$

8.6 REACTIONS OF ALKENES

Reactions of alkenes are of two kinds.

8.6.1 Addition Reactions

The reactions that take place at the double bond and destroy the double bond.

8.6.2 Allylic Substitution

The reactions that take place, not at the double bond, but at certain positions having special relationships to the double bond (Reactions at allylic position).

Halogenation (using NBS) :

$$H - \overset{|}{\underset{|}{C}} - C = C - \ + \ X_2 \ \xrightarrow{\Delta} \ X - \overset{|}{\underset{|}{C}} - C = C - \ + \ HX$$

Low concentration

$X_2 = Cl_2/Br_2$

Hydrogen halide   N-Halosuccinimide   Succinimide

8.6.1 Addition Reactions of Alkenes

A reaction in which the substrate and the reagents add up to form a product is called addition reaction.

The reactivity of alkene is due to the more exposed and easily available π-electrons to the electron–seeking (electrophilic) reagents. The typical reaction of an alkene is an electrophilic addition (AdE).

Addition reactions are divided into three classes depending upon the nature of the reagent.

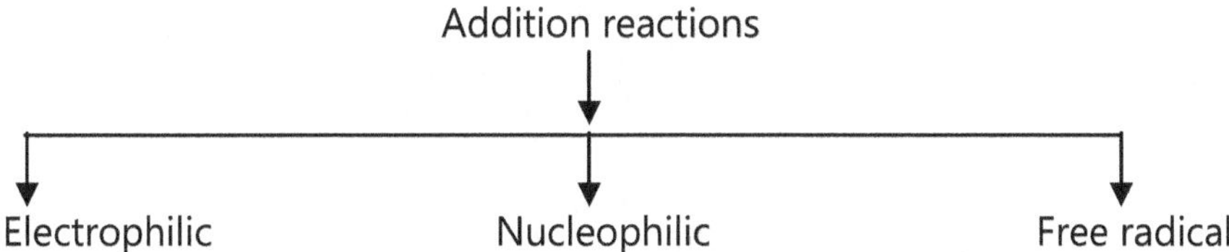

Alkenes easily undergo electrophilic addition reaction. When an electrophile (or positive pole of a dipole) initiates the process, the reaction is called as electrophilic addition. It is designated as AdE^2 (Addition electrophilic, bimolecular).

Reaction :

Alkene   Reagent   Product

E-Nu: HCl, HBr, HI, H_2SO_4, H_3O^+, Br_2 etc.

Nu : Cl^-, Br^-, I^-, HSO_4^-, H_2O, Br^- etc.

Mechanism : Two step mechanism.

Step-I :

Carbocation

Step-I involves the transfer of electrophile from reagent E-Nu to the alkene to form a carbocation. It is a slow or rate determining step.

Step-II :

It involves the combination of the carbocation with the nucleophile.

Kinetics : The rate of reaction depends upon the concentration of both, the alkene and reagent (E-Nu).

$$\text{Rate} = k\,[\text{Alkene}]\,[\text{E-Nu}]$$

The reaction requires an acidic reagent. If structure permits, reaction is accompanied by rearrangements.

Various reactions of alkenes are outlined as below.

(1) Hydrogenation (Addition of hydrogen) :

$$\text{C=C} \ + \ H_2 \ \xrightarrow{\text{Pt / Pd / Ni}} \ -\overset{|}{\underset{H}{C}}-\overset{|}{\underset{H}{C}}-$$

Alkane

(2) Halogenation (Addition of halogen) :

$$\text{C=C} \ + \ X_2 \ \xrightarrow{\text{CCl}_4} \ -\overset{|}{\underset{X}{C}}-\overset{|}{\underset{X}{C}}- \qquad X_2 = Cl_2/Br_2$$

1, 2-dihaloalkane

(3) Hydrohalogenation (Addition of hydrogen halide) :

$$\text{C=C} \ + \ HX \ \longrightarrow \ -\overset{|}{\underset{H}{C}}-\overset{|}{\underset{X}{C}}- \qquad HX = HCl, HBr, HI$$

Haloalkane

(4) Halohydrin formation [Addition of hypohalous acid (HO-X)] :

$$\text{C=C} \ + \ X_2 \ \xrightarrow[\text{HO}^{\delta-}-X^{\delta+}]{X_2 + H_2O} \ -\overset{|}{\underset{OH}{C}}-\overset{|}{\underset{X}{C}}- \qquad X_2 = Cl_2/Br_2$$

Haloalcohol
(halohydrin)

(5) Oxymercuration-Demercuration :

$$\text{C=C} \ + \ Hg(OAc)_2 \ + \ H_2O \ \longrightarrow \ -\overset{|}{\underset{OH}{C}}-\overset{|}{\underset{HgOAc}{C}}-$$

Mercuric acetate

Hydroxy mercurial compound

$$\downarrow NaBH_4$$

$$-\overset{|}{\underset{OH}{C}}-\overset{|}{\underset{H}{C}}-$$

(Markownikoff's addition)

(6) Hydroboration-Oxidation :

$$C=C \quad + \quad (BH_3)_2 \quad \longrightarrow \quad -\overset{|}{\underset{|}{C}}-\overset{|}{\underset{|}{C}}-$$

Diborane

Alkyl borane

$$\downarrow H_2O_2, \ OH^-$$

$$-\overset{|}{\underset{|}{C}}-\overset{|}{\underset{|}{C}}- \quad + \quad B(OH)_3$$

$$H \quad OH$$

(Anti Markownikoff's orientation)

(7) Hydroxylation (Glycol formation) :

$$C=C \quad + \quad KMnO_4 \ or \ HCO_3H \quad \longrightarrow \quad -\overset{|}{\underset{|}{C}}-\overset{|}{\underset{|}{C}}-$$

Or OsO_4

$$OH \quad OH$$

(8) Ozonolysis:

$$C=C \quad + \quad O_3 \ (ozone) \quad \longrightarrow$$

Ozonide

$$\downarrow H_2O, \ Zn$$

$$H-C=O \quad + \quad O=C-R$$

Aldehydes　　　　Ketones

Stereochemistry of addition reactions:

The electron density associated with the π–bond of an alkene is greatest above and below the plane of the double bond. Stereoelectronic considerations suggest that the most advantageous approach for the electrophile is along these electron-rich regions that are perpendicular to the plane of the double bond.

But the electrophilic reagent might be divided into an electrophilic and nucleophilic portion. Each part of the reagent may add to the double bond from the same side or from opposite sides of the reactant molecule.

When both parts add to the same side of the molecule, it is called *syn* addition (or *cis* addition) and when both parts add on the opposite sides of the double bond it is called anti (or *trans*) addition.

Several addition reactions are stereoselective and some others are even stereospecific.

(1) Addition of hydrogen (Hydrogenation) :

Hydrogen adds to the alkene under pressure and in presence of Ni, Pt or Pd catalyst to produce saturated hydrocarbons. A hydrogenation reaction carried out in this manner is called catalytic hydrogenation.

For example,

$$CH_2 = CH_2 \ + \ H_2 \ \xrightarrow[\Delta]{Ni} \ CH_3 - CH_3$$
  Ethylene   Ethane

$$CH_2 = CH - CH_2 - CH_3 \ + \ H_2 \ \xrightarrow[\Delta]{Ni} \ CH_3 - CH_2 - CH_2 - CH_3$$
   1-Butene   Butane

This reaction does not occur through the ionic mechanism. The reaction depends on high affinity of hydrogen gas for certain metals Ni, Pt or Pd. The hydrogen is adsorbed on the metal surface along with alkene molecules.

Hydrogenation is exothermic reaction because the two new σ–bonds (C–H) being formed are together stronger than σ–bond of H–H and one π–bond (C=C) being broken. The quantity of heat evolved when one mole of an unsaturated hydrocarbon converted into saturated hydrocarbon is called the heat of hydrogenation (ΔH).

It proceeds at a negligible rate in the absence of a catalyst, even at a elevated temperature, but the unsaturated reaction have a very large energy of activation. The function of the catalyst is to lower the energy of activation (E_{act}) so that the reaction can proceed rapidly at room temperature.

It is believed that surface of a solid catalyst breaks the σ-bond of the alkene prior to the reaction with hydrogen. The complex metal ion breaks the H–H bond and transfer the hydrogen atoms from the catalyst on the same side of the C=C (*cis*-addition). Finally dispersion of the product takes place immediately giving resultant alkanes.

Hydrogen adsorbed by catalyst

Dispersion of product

Some examples of hydrogenation :

Cis-1,2-dimethyl cyclohexane (meso)

Cis-1,2-dimethylstilbene

Meso-2,3-dimethyl butane

It is observed that *cis*-alkenes are usually hydrogenated much more rapidly than *trans* isomer. The rate of hydrogenation falls with increasing substituents in the alkene.

(2) Addition of halogen (Halogenation) :

Halogens F, Cl, Br, I undergo addition reaction with C=C in the absence of any catalyst.

Fluorine, chlorine and bromine undergo electrophilic addition reaction with C=C and convert unsaturated compound into saturated compound that contain two atoms of halogen attached to adjacent carbons to form dihalogen derivatives. Iodine generally fails to react.

Vicinal dihalide

e.g. (a) Addition of Bromine :

$$CH_2 = CH_2 + Br_2 \xrightarrow{\text{Inert solvent}} Br - CH_2 - CH_2 - Br_2$$

Ethylene   1, 2 - Dibromoethane

This reaction is a useful test for identifying unsaturated compounds, the red colour of the bromine being rapidly discharged as the colourless dibromo compound is formed.

Mechanism : Two step mechanism.

Step-I : Electrophilic attack by the reagent (Br_2) and formation of cyclic bromonium ion via a π-complex.

It is a slow step and hence the rate determining step.

Step-II : Nucleophilic attack by the Br^- ion from the sterically unhindered position i.e. from the opposite side of the ring on either carbon atom to produce *trans*-addition product.

Kinetics : The rate of reaction depends on concentration of alkene and concentration of bromine. It is a bimolecular electrophilic addition reaction (AdE^2).

$$\text{Rate = k [Alkene] [Br}_2\text{]}$$

Reactivity of alkenes :

Alkenes containing electron releasing substituents (+I, +R) activate an alkene and increase the rate of reaction and alkenes containing electron withdrawing substituents deactivate an alkene and decrease the rate of reaction.

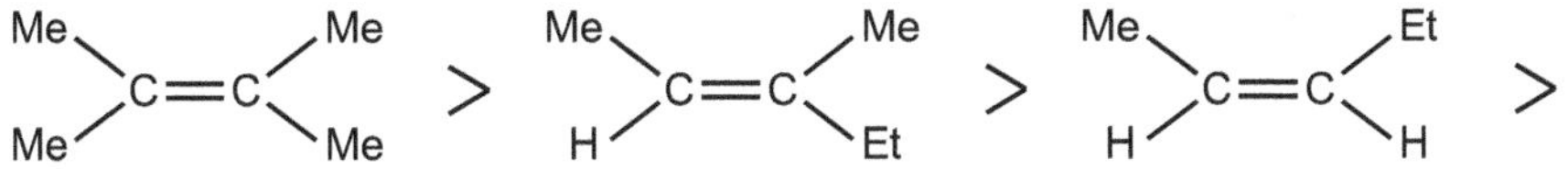

$Et-CH=CH_2 > CH_2=CH_2 > CH_2=CHBr$

Stereochemistry of addition : Anti addition

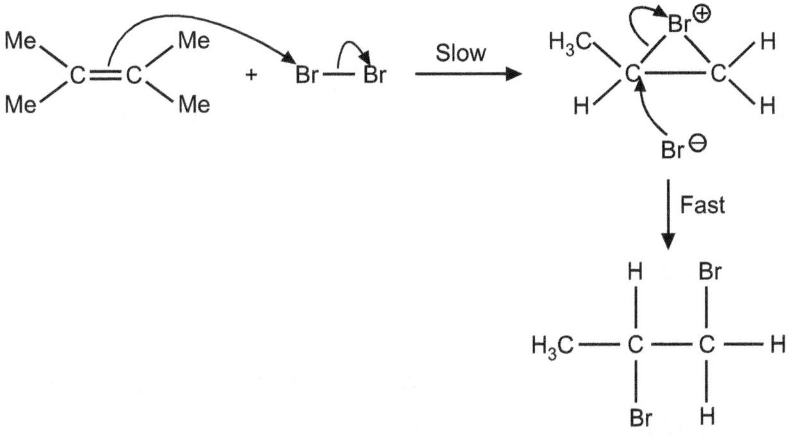

1, 2 - dibromopropane

The reaction is stereospecific.

(b) Addition of Chlorine : Same like Br_2 addition.

(c) Addition of Fluorine : This reaction is carried out at a very low temperature (–78°C) and xenon fluoride may be used as a reagent under controlled condition.

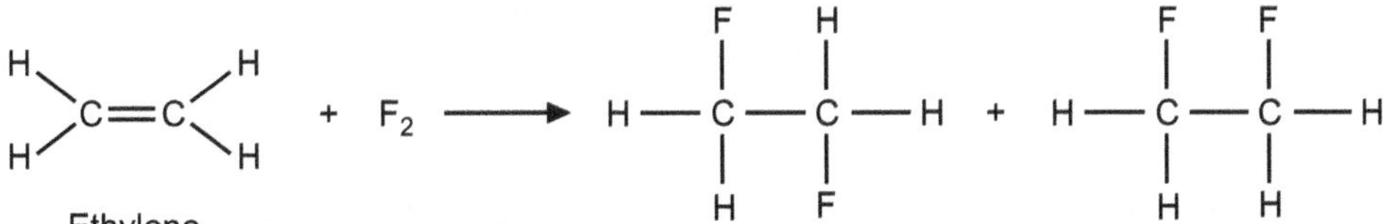

Ethylene

Difluoroethane (trans-product)

Difluoroethane (cis-product)

Mechanism : Two step mechanism

Step-I :

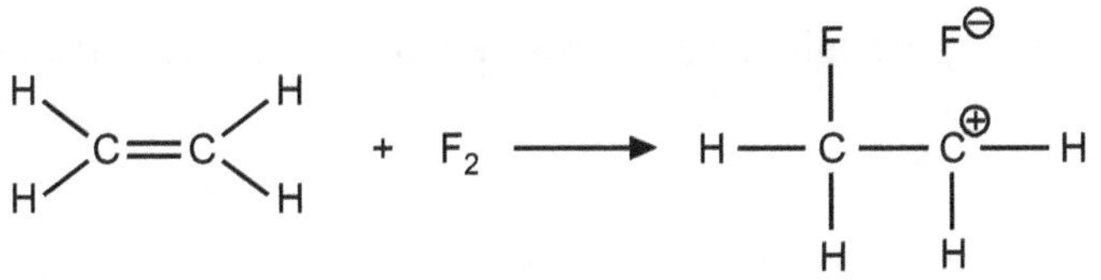

Ethylene

Acyclic carbocation

Bridged fluoronium ion is not formed because of small size and low electron donating tendency.

Step-II :

Intimate ion pair　　　　　　Cis-product (major)

Trans product (minor)

Trans-product formed by rotation of – C – F moiety about C – C bond axis.

(3) Addition of hydrogen halide (Hydrohalogenation) :

Addition of hydrogen halide to the C=C to form alkyl halide is called hydrohalogenation.

Alkenes react with halogen acids like HCl, HBr or HI to form alkyl chloride, alkyl bromide and alkyl iodide respectively.

Hydrogen halides add to the alkenes by polar mechanism usually to form 2° and 3° alkyl halides.

$$R - CH = CH_2 + HX \longrightarrow R - \underset{\underset{X}{|}}{CH} - CH_3$$

$$R - \underset{\underset{R'}{|}}{C} = CH_2 + HX \longrightarrow R - \underset{\underset{R'}{|}}{\overset{\overset{X}{|}}{C}} - CH_3$$

The reaction is usually carried out by passing dry hydrogen halide directly into the alkene or into a solution of the alkene in a polar solvent like acetic acid. Aqueous solutions of hydrogen halides are not generally used for the reaction because this may lead to hydration of alkene.

$$\underset{}{>}C=C\underset{}{<} \ + \ H_3O^{\oplus} \longrightarrow -\underset{\underset{H}{|}}{C} - \underset{}{C} - OH$$

Mechanism : Two step mechanism.

Step-I : Attack of electrophile i.e. H$^+$ to form a more stable carbocation.

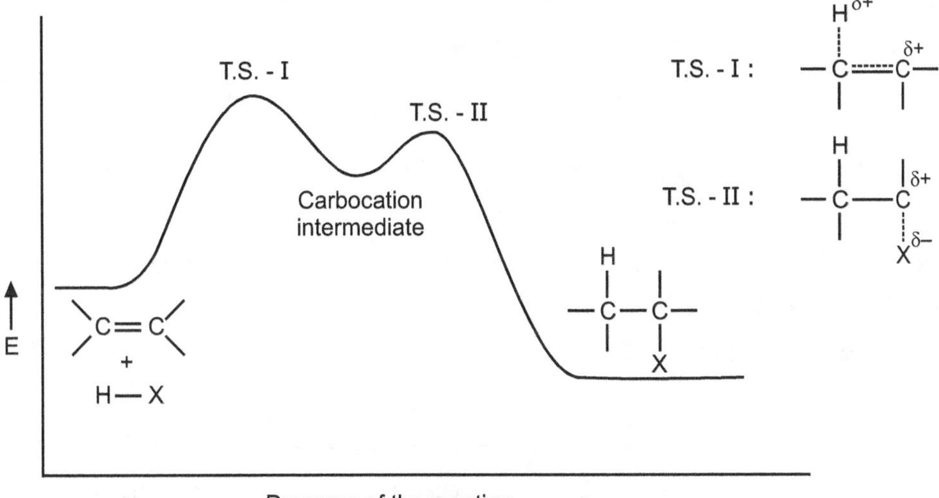

It is a slow step thus rate determining step.

Step-II : The fast attack of Nu$^-$ at the carbocation to give the addition product.

Kinetics : The rate of reaction depends on concentration of alkene and hydrogen halide both. Therefore it follows second order kinetics.

$$\text{The rate} = k\,[\text{alkene}]\,[\text{HX}]$$

Energy profile diagram :

Fig. 8.4

When hydrogen halide reacts with a symmetrical alkene, there is only one product possible, but in case of unsymmetrical alkene there is a possibility of forming two isomeric products.

For example,

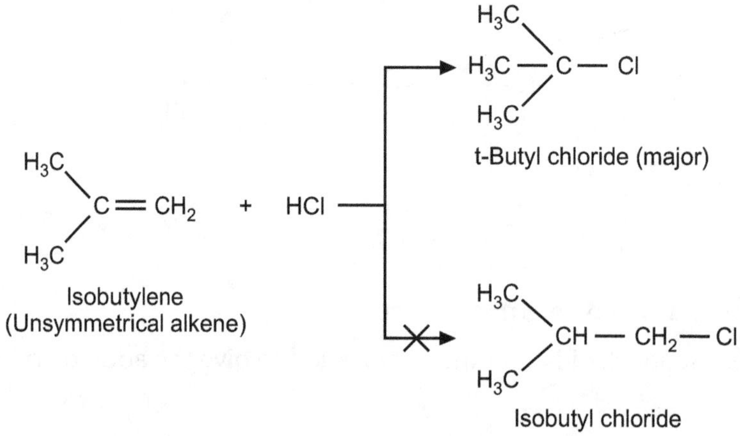

$$
\begin{array}{c}
H_3C \\
\ \ \diagdown \\
\ \ \ \ C = CH_2 \quad + \quad HCl \\
\ \ \diagup \\
H_3C
\end{array}
$$

t-Butyl chloride (major)

Isobutylene
(Unsymmetrical alkene)

Isobutyl chloride

In this case the formation of the major product is decided on the basis of a generalization called Markownikoff's rule.

Markownikoff's rule : *"This rule states that during the addition of unsymmetrical reagent to the unsymmetrical alkene, negative end of the reagent goes to the carbon atom containing lesser number of hydrogen atoms."*

However when both the doubly bonded carbons have same number of 'H' atoms a mixture of products are obtained.

$$CH_3 - CH_2 - CH = CH - CH_3 \ + \ HBr$$

2-Pentene

$$CH_3 - CH_2 - CH_2 - \overset{\overset{\textstyle Br}{|}}{CH} - CH_3 \quad + \quad CH_3 - CH_2 - \overset{\overset{\textstyle Br}{|}}{CH} - CH_2 - CH_3$$

2-Bromopentane   3-Bromopentane

Markownikoff's rule can be explained on the basis of relative stabilities of the intermediate carbocations.

For example,

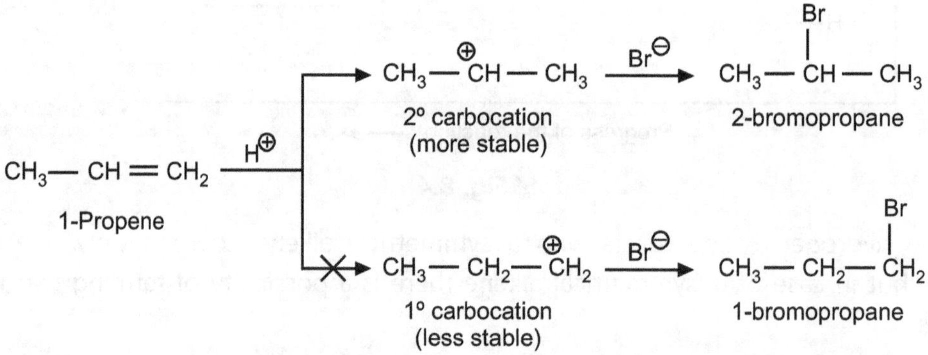

$$CH_3 - CH = CH_2$$

1-Propene

$$CH_3 - \overset{\oplus}{CH} - CH_3 \xrightarrow{\ Br^{\ominus}\ } CH_3 - \overset{\overset{\textstyle Br}{|}}{CH} - CH_3$$

2° carbocation
(more stable)

2-bromopropane

$$CH_3 - CH_2 - \overset{\oplus}{CH_2} \xrightarrow{\ Br^{\ominus}\ } CH_3 - CH_2 - \overset{\overset{\textstyle Br}{|}}{CH_2}$$

1° carbocation
(less stable)

1-bromopropane

In case of propene, due to +I effect of the methyl group, the π-electrons are displaced towards the terminal carbon atom which in turn acquires a partial negative charge. So the H^+ adds to the carbon atom which is farthest from the methyl group, followed by addition of halide ion to the formed 2° carbocation.

$$CH_3 - \overset{\delta+}{C}H = \overset{\delta-}{C}H_2 + HBr \xrightarrow{-Br^{\ominus}} CH_3 - \overset{\oplus}{C}H - CH_3$$

1-propene   2° carbocation

$$\downarrow Br^{\ominus}$$

$$CH_3 - CH - CH_3$$
$$|$$
$$Br$$

2 - bromopropane

The Markownikoff's addition is thus highly regioselective reaction. A regioselective reaction is the one which gives only one of the two possible constitutional isomers predominantly.

Addition of HBr (Peroxide effect or Anti-Markownikoff's rule) :

It is the addition of HBr to unsymmetrical alkene carried out in the presence of peroxide or light, the addition is against Markownikoff's rule. This is known as Anti-Markownikoff's addition or peroxide effect. This reaction takes place by free radical mechanism as shown below.

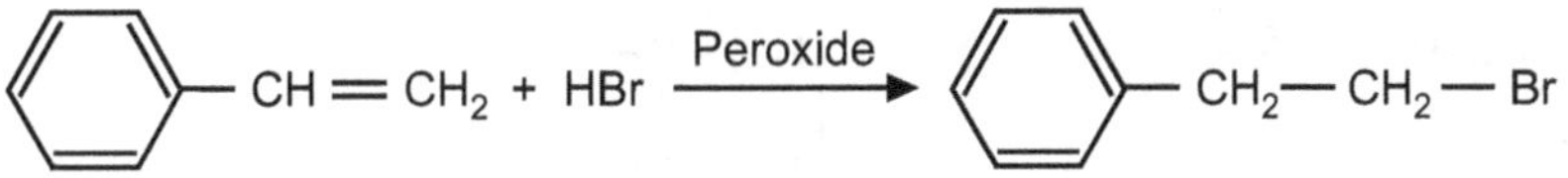

$$C_6H_5 - CH = CH_2 + HBr \xrightarrow{Peroxide} C_6H_5 - CH_2 - CH_2 - Br$$

Styrene   1-Phenyl-1-bromoethane

Mechanism : Free radical mechanism.

a) $H - O - O - H \longrightarrow 2HO^{\bullet}$

b) $H - Br + H\overset{\bullet}{O} \longrightarrow H - OH + \overset{\bullet}{B}r$

⎫ Chain initiating steps

Chain propagating steps

c) $C_6H_5 - CH = CH_2 + \overset{\bullet}{B}r \longrightarrow C_6H_5 - \overset{\bullet}{C}H - CH_2 - Br$

2° radical (more stable)

$$\downarrow H - Br$$

$$C_6H_5 - CH_2 - CH_2 - Br + \overset{\bullet}{B}r$$

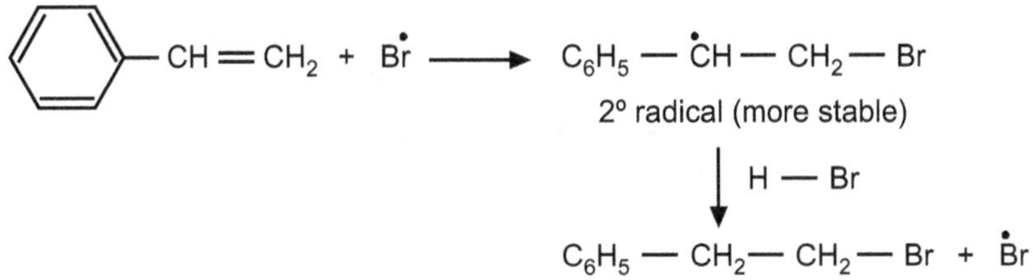

Chain termination steps

d) $H\overset{\bullet}{O}$ + $H\overset{\bullet}{O}$ ⟶ H — O — O — H

   $H\overset{\bullet}{O}$ + $\overset{\bullet}{Br}$ ⟶ HOBr

Free radical addition is faster than ionic addition of HBr.

Thus due to peroxide effect instead of secondary alkyl bromide, we get $1°$-alkyl bromide as a major product.

HCl and HI do not show peroxide effect and always add according to Markownikoff's rule.

(4) Addition of hypohalous acid (Halohydrin formation) :

Halohydrin are produced by the addition of aqueous solution of halogens (Cl_2 or Br_2) to the alkenes. Halohydrin means compounds with adjacent halogen and hydroxyl groups. Markownikoff's rule is followed in case of unsymmetrical alkenes. In these acids, halogen is the positive end (electrophile) and –OH group is the negative end (nucleophile).

e.g.

$$CH_2 = CH_2 \xrightarrow{Br_2,\ H_2O} \underset{\overset{|}{OH}\quad\overset{|}{Br}}{CH_2 - CH_2}$$

Ethylene

2-Bromoethanol
(Ethylene bromohydrin)

$$CH_3 - CH = CH_2 \xrightarrow{Cl_2,\ H_2O} \underset{\overset{|}{OH}\quad\overset{|}{Cl}}{CH_3 - CH - CH_2}$$

Propylene

1-chloro-2-propanol
(Propylene chlorohydrin)

Mechanism :

Halohydrins are not formed by addition of hypohalous acid, HOX, but by reaction of the alkene with successively halogen and water.

Two step mechanism :

Step-I : Halogen adds to form the halonium ion.

A halonium ion

Step-II : Halonium ion then reacts with water to yield the protonated alcohol.

where $X_2 = Cl_2$ or Br_2

Intermediate is not an open carbocation but a cyclic halonium ion.

Stereochemistry of addition : This addition takes place in a trans manner similar to the addition of halogens i.e. anti addition.

For example,

Cyclopentene　　　　　　Trans-2-chlorocyclopentanol

(5) Oxymercuration-Demercuration :

Alkenes react with mercuric acetate in the presence of water to give hydroxy mercuric addition product which on subsequent reduction with sodium borohydride yield alcohols.

Mechanism : Two step mechanism.

Step-I : Formation of a cyclic mercurinium ion, followed by attack of H_2O to give addition product [Oxymercuration step].

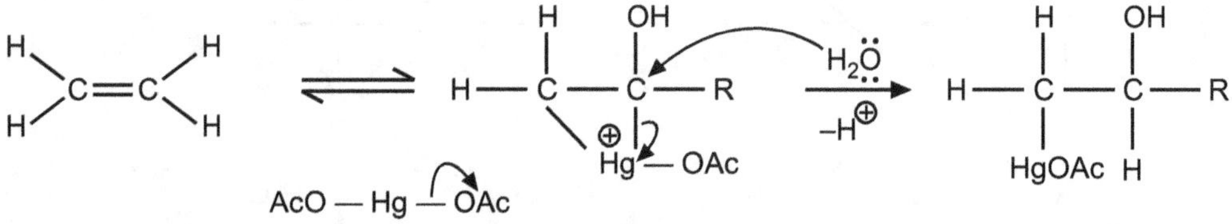

The reaction follows Markownikoff's rule, HgOAc attaches to the carbon atom containing the higher number of H atoms. It is a rapid step.

Step-II : Demercuration step : It involves alkaline reduction of the hydroxyl alkylmercury compound by $OH^-/NaBH_4$. In demercuration, –HgOAc is a replaced by –H.

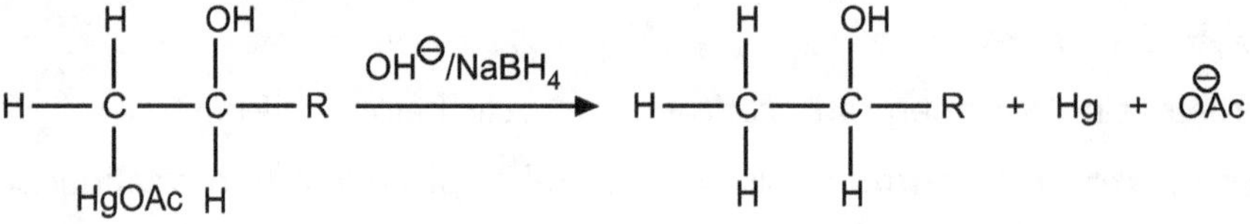

For example,

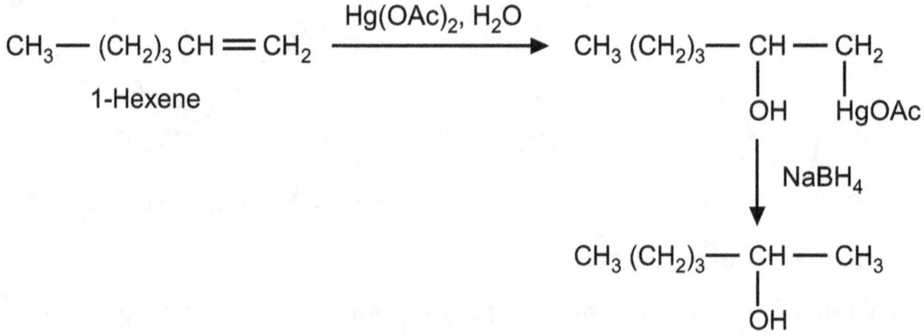

$$CH_3—(CH_2)_3 CH = CH_2 \xrightarrow{Hg(OAc)_2,\ H_2O}$$

1-Hexene

$$\xrightarrow{NaBH_4}$$

2-Hexanol

$$H_3C—\underset{CH_3}{\overset{H}{C}}—CH = CH_2 \xrightarrow{Hg(OAc)_2,\ H_2O}$$

$$\xrightarrow{NaBH_4}$$

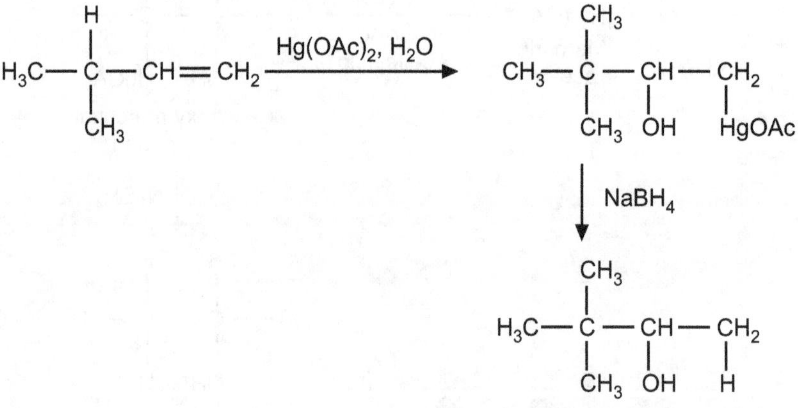

3, 3-dimethyl-2-butanol

(6) Hydroboration – Oxidation :

Hydroboration of alkenes is a two-step process for the preparation of alcohols. First the addition of borane across C = C by the action of diborane on an alkene to form alkylborane, which is subsequently oxidized (H_2O_2/OH^-) to an alcohol. The overall process is called hydroboration-oxidation.

Diborane, B_2H_6 is a dimer of borane (BH_3). When dissolved in ether, diborane dissociates to form a borane-ether complex. Diborane ether is the actual reagent in hydroboration.

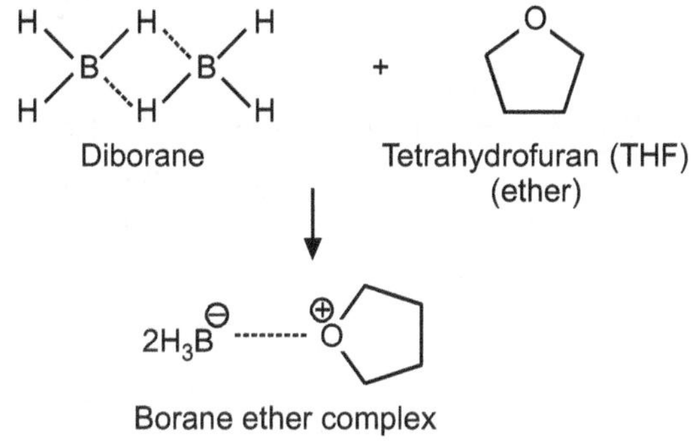

Diborane   Tetrahydrofuran (THF)
(ether)

Borane ether complex

Reaction :

$$3RCH_2 = CH_2 + B_2H_6 \xrightarrow{\text{Ether}} (RCH_2CH_2)_3B$$

Alkene   Trialkylborane

$$\xrightarrow[H_2O]{H_2O_2 / OH^-}$$

$$3R\,CH_2CH_2 - OH \ + \ B(OH)_3$$

$1°$ Alcohol

Mechanism : Two step mechanism.

Step-I : Formation of trialkyl borane

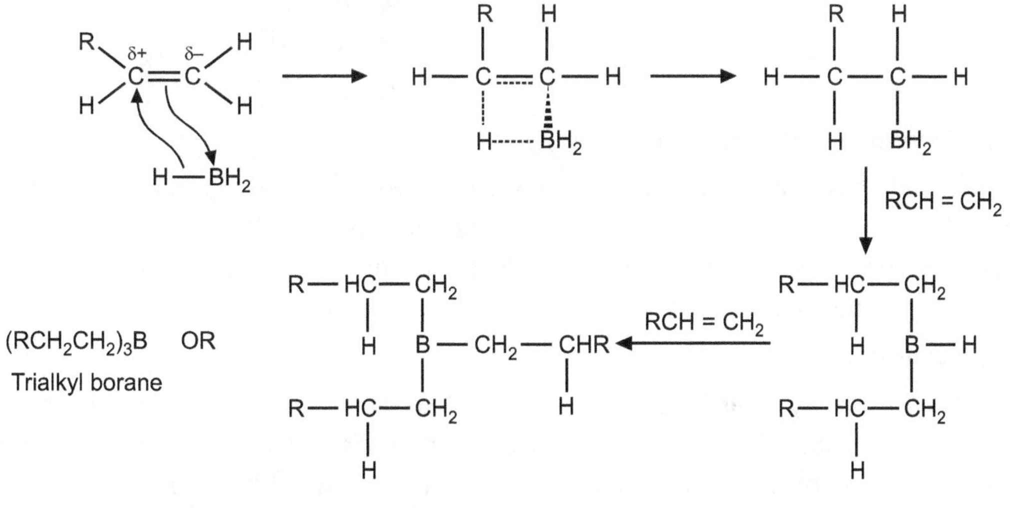

$(RCH_2CH_2)_3B$ OR

Trialkyl borane

Three molecules of alkenes react with one molecule of borane. Borane atom attaches to the less substituted carbon atom.

The addition takes place according to anti-Markownikoff's rule.

Step-II : The alkyle borane on oxidation with H_2O_2 /OH^- produces an alcohol.

$$(RCH_2CH_2)_3B + 3H_2O_2 + OH \longrightarrow 3\ RCH_2CH_2 - OH$$
$$1°\ Alcohol$$
$$+\ B(OH)_3$$
$$Boric\ acid\ (H_3BO_3)$$

For example,

$$CH_3 - CH = CH_2 + B_2H_6 \longrightarrow (CH_3CH_2CH_2)_3B$$

$$\text{Propene} \qquad\qquad\qquad\qquad \text{Tripropylborane}$$

$$\Big\downarrow H_2O_2/OH^-$$
$$H_2O$$

$$3CH_3CH_2CH_2 - OH + B(OH)_3$$
$$\text{1-propanol} \qquad \text{Boric acid}$$

Stereochemistry :

BH_3 adds from the same side of the alkene leading to syn-addition. It is highly regioselective. Addition is *cis* but the resulting alcohol is always *trans*.

1-Methyl cyclopentene $+$ Cl_2 $+$ H_2O $\xrightarrow{THF}$ [intermediate] $\xrightarrow{H_2O_2/OH^\ominus}$ product $+$ H_3BO_3

(7) Hydroxylation (Formation of 1,2-diols) :

Hydroxylation is a reaction in which two hydroxyl groups get added to an alkene to form 1,2-diol. The reagents like alkaline $KMnO_4$ and osmium tetra-oxide (OsO_4) are used for cis hydroxylation of alkenes while organic peracids (per acetic acid, CH_3CO_3H) are used for trans hydroxylation of alkenes.

Cis- hydroxylation :

Hydroxylation by $KMnO_4$: When cold, dilute and neutral solution of potassium permanganate is added, alkene is converted into a *cis*-glycol (*cis*-1,2-diol). Potassium permanganate solution is decolorized and a brown suspension of MnO_2 appears.

$$H_3C-C=C-CH_3 \text{ (Cis 2-butene)} + 2KMnO_4 \xrightarrow{4H_2O} 3H-C-C-H + 2MnO_2 + KOH$$

Cis 2-butene

Meso 1,2-diol

$$3CH_2=CH_2 + 2KMnO_4 + 4H_2O$$
$$\downarrow$$
$$3CH_2-CH_2 + 2KMnO_4 + 2KOH$$

(with OH, OH)

Mechanism :

Step-I : KMnO$_4$ add to the C=C of alkene and formation of cyclic intermediate.

Cis 2-butene

Cyclic intermediate

Step-II : Hydrolysis of cyclic intermediate and formation of diol.

Meso-1,2-diol

OR

Oxidation by permanganate is the basis of a very useful analytical test known as the Baeyer's test.

Baeyer's test is used for the identification of unsaturation in organic compounds.

Stereochemistry :

Oxygen atoms of KMnO$_4$ add to the double bond from the same side and cyclic intermediate results. The addition is syn or cis.

Hydroxylation with Osmium tetraoxide (OsO_4) :

OsO_4 also reacts by syn addition.

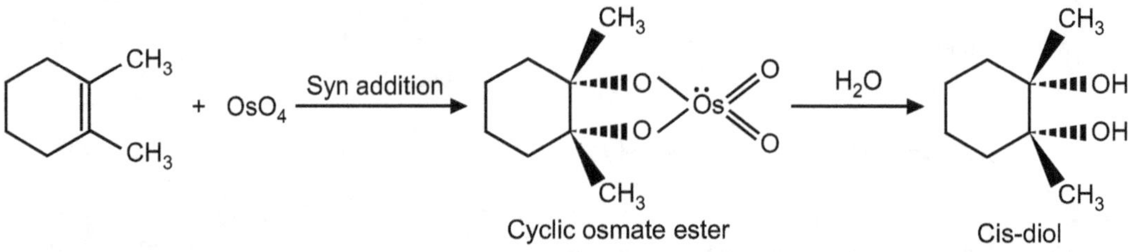

Cyclic osmate ester　　　　Cis-diol

Disadvantages of Hydroxylation by $KMnO_4$:

The resultant 1,2-diol is very susceptible to further oxidation by $KMnO_4$ to form ketones or carboxylic acids and it is somewhat difficult to stop the reaction at the diol stage.

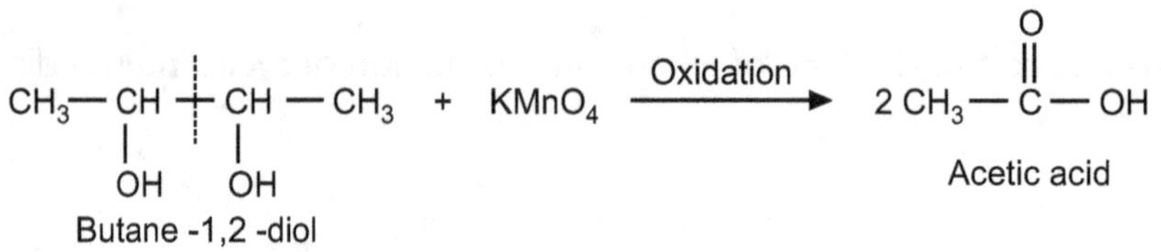

Butane -1,2 -diol

Acetic acid

Trans-hydroxylation : When an alkene is allowed to react with an organic per acid, three membered cyclic ether (epoxide) is formed. Epoxide on hydrolysis gives 1,2-diol.

The per acids like performic acid, per acetic acid, perbenzoic acid are generally used for trans-hydroxylation of alkenes. Hydroxylation is carried out by allowing the alkene to stand with a mixture of hydrogen peroxide (H_2O_2) and formic acid for few hours and then heating the product with H_2O to hydrolyse the cyclic ether to give 1,2-diol.

For example,

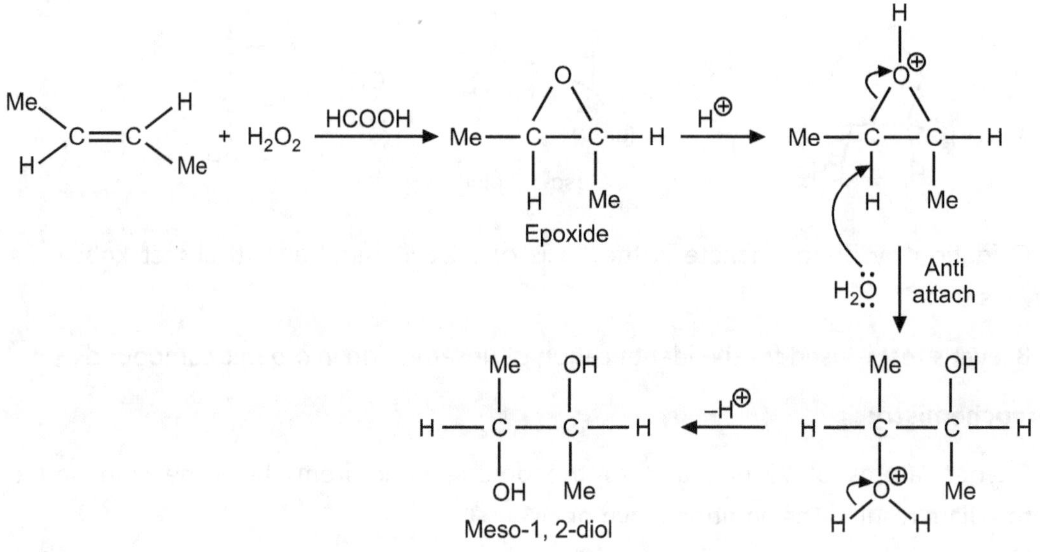

Epoxide

Anti attach

Meso-1, 2-diol

(8) Ozonolysis :

Ozonolysis is a cleavage reaction, in which the double bond of alkene is completely broken and the alkene molecule gets converted into smaller molecules. The reagent used for breaking the carbon-carbon double bond is ozone.

Process : The ozone (O_3) is passed through alkene in an inert solvent at room temperature, addition of ozone to alkene takes place to form an ozonide. Ozonide formed is not so stable that it could be isolated. They can be readily reduced to carbonyl compounds by the use of mild reducing agents like Zn/H_2O.

The whole process of formation of ozonides and their cleavage to yield carbonyl compounds is known as ozonolysis.

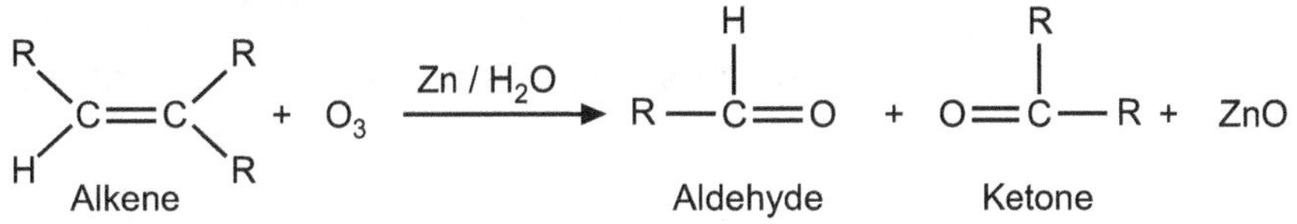

Mechanism :

Ozone resonating structures :

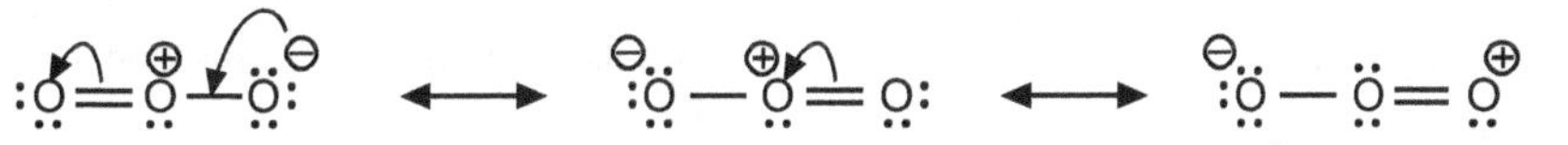

Electrophilic in nature

Two step mechanism :

Step-I : 1,3 dipolar addition of O_3 to the C=C of alkene and formation of ozonide.

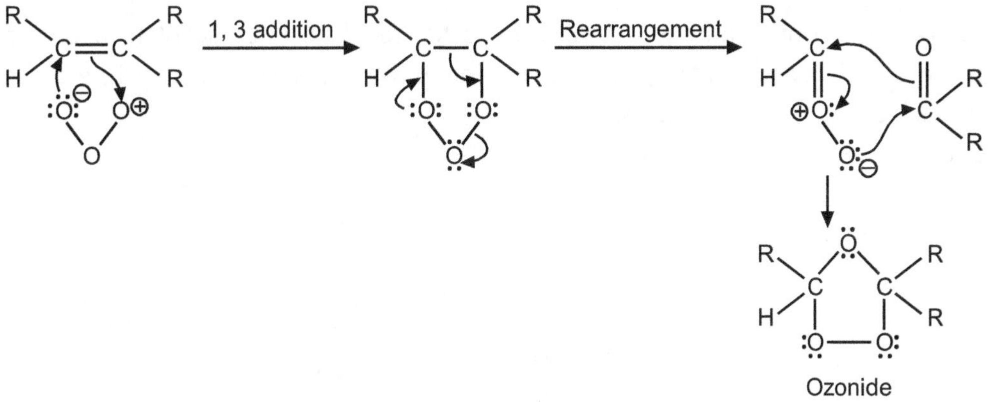

Ozonide

Step-II : Hydrolysis of the ozonide and formation of carbonyl compounds.

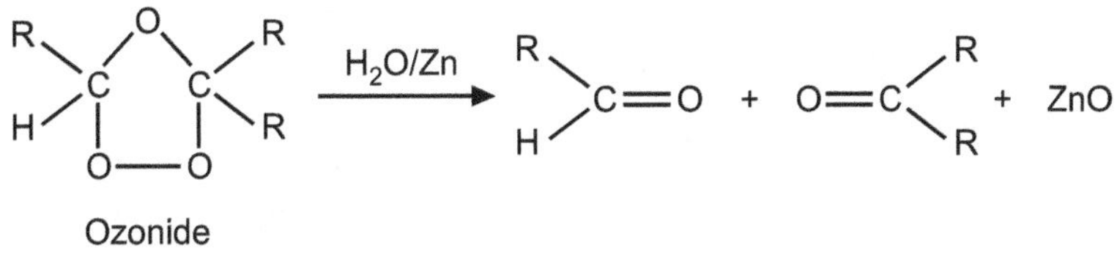

Ozonide

For example,

$$CH_3-CH_2 \quad C=C \quad C_2H_5 \xrightarrow[\text{(ii) Zn/H}_2\text{O}]{\text{(i) O}_3}$$

2 methyl-2 pentene　　　　　　　　Acetone　　　Propanaldehyde

If the double bonded carbon contains one and two substituents, we get mixture of aldehyde and ketone as shown above.

Propanaldehyde

If the double bond is at the terminal position, one of the product of ozonolysis will be formaldehyde.

For example,

Propene　　　　　　　　Acetaldehyde　　　Formaldehyde

8.6.2 Allylic Substitution (using NBS)

The compound N-bromosuccinimide (NBS) is a reagent used for the specific purpose of brominating alkenes at the allylic position. NBS functions by providing a constant, low concentration of bromine.

Hydrocarbons containing allylic carbon i.e. saturated carbon adjacent to a C=C can be brominated by refluxing with N-bromosuccinimide in the presence of benzoyl peroxide, heat or light which act as radical initiators.

For example,

$$CH_2=CH-CH_3 \quad + \quad \text{NBS}$$

Benzyol peroxide
CCl_4, reflux

$$CH_2=CH-CH_2-Br \quad + \quad \text{Succinimide}$$

Allyl bromide

Mechanism :

NBS provides a constant but very low concentration of bromine by reacting with HBr formed in the substitution reaction.

$$CH_2 = CH - CH_3 - \overset{\bullet}{B}r \longrightarrow CH_2 = CH - \overset{\bullet}{C}H_2 - HBr$$

$$CH_2 = CH - \overset{\bullet}{C}H_2 - Br_2 \longrightarrow CH_2 = CH - CH_2 - Br + \overset{\bullet}{B}r$$

Abstraction of an allylic hydrogen by Br gives a resonance stabilized allylic radical. The radical subsequently reacts with Br regenerating the Br radical.

For example,

8.7 DIENES

Alkenes that contain two double bonds are known as dienes. Two double bonds may be present in three different manners. Based on this there are three types of dienes.

(1) Conjugated dienes : Two double bonds may be separated by one single bond i.e. alternate double and single bond .

This type of diene is called as conjugated dienes.

For example,

$$H_2C = CH - CH = CH_2$$

1, 3 - Butadiene

1, 3 - Cyclohexadiene

(2) Isolated double bond : Two double bonds may be separated by more than one saturated carbon atom.

$$\text{>C=C-C-C=C<}$$

This type of diene is called as isolated diene.

For example,

$$CH_2 = CH - CH_2 - CH = CH_2$$

1, 4-pentadiene

(3) Cumulative diene : Both the double bonds may be present in two consecutive carbon atoms i.e.

$$\text{>C=C=C<}$$

Such type of diene is known as cumulative diene. The molecules containing two adjacent double bonds are called allenes.

e.g. $$H_2C = C = CH_2$$

Propadiene (Allene)

8.7.1 Structure of Conjugated Dienes

The representative member of conjugated dienes is 1, 3-butadiene. In 1, 3-butadiene σ-bonds in between carbon atoms involve sp^2-hybrid orbitals and covalent bonds between carbon and hydrogen atoms are due to overlapping of sp^2-s orbitals. Thus in each carbon there is one free p-orbital. All the carbon and hydrogen are in same plane and the π-orbitals are perpendicular to the plane of σ-bonds. Four p-orbitals one in each carbon atom can overlap each other in two different ways and so can form resonating structure.

Conjugated dienes are more stable than the non-conjugated dienes.

1, 3-butadiene

$$\equiv \quad H_2C = CH - CH = CH_2$$

1, 2 & 3, 4 overlapping

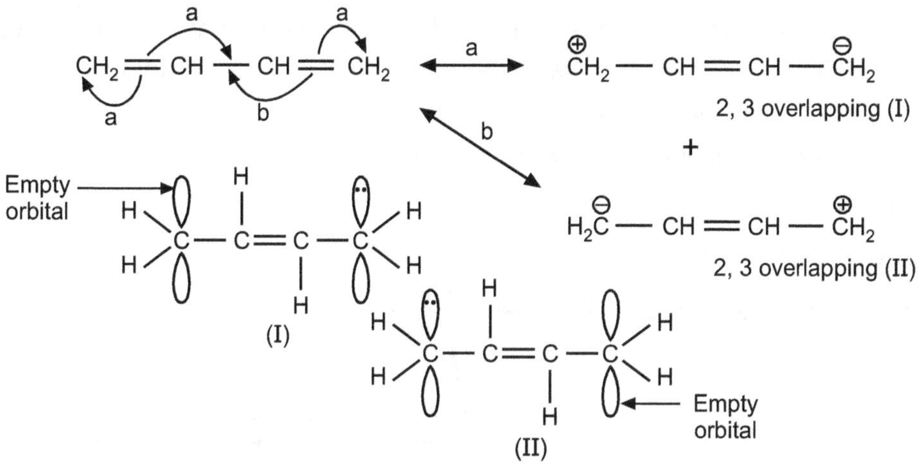

8.7.2 Electrophilic Addition to Conjugated Dienes

Addition reactions of dienes are to some extent unusual. The addition takes place at 1, 2 or at 1, 4-positions, very often the 1,4-product is the major one.

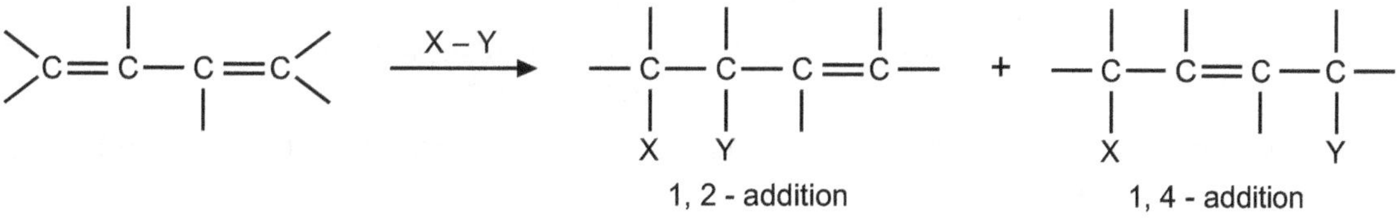

Mechanism : Two step mechanism

Step-I: Addition of electrophile to the C=C of diene to form most stable carbocation.

Step-II: Attack of nucleophile at the carbocation to form the product.

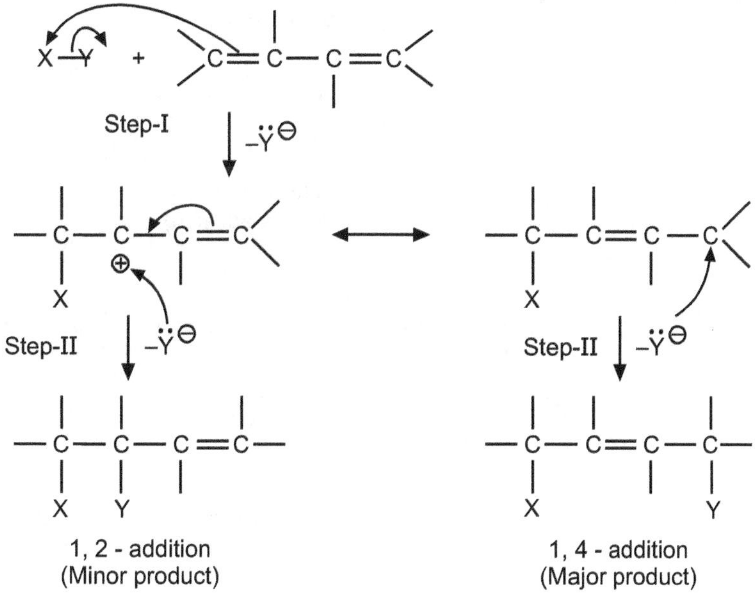

This unusual behavior of diene is a effect of the delocalized nature of the intermediate allylic cation. Different reagents that commonly take part in addition reaction with conjugated dienes are halogens and halogen acids.

Where XY = Br_2 (halogenation); HBr, HCl (hydrohalogenation)

For example :

1.   Addition of bromine :

$$CH_2 = CH - CH = CH_2 \quad \xrightarrow[-15°]{Br_2} \quad \overset{4}{C}H_2 - \overset{3}{C}H - \overset{2}{C}H = \overset{1}{C}H_2$$

with Br on carbon 4 and Br on carbon 3

2, 4 - dibromo-1-butene
(1, 2 addition) 54%

+

$$\overset{4}{C}H_2 - \overset{3}{C}H = \overset{2}{C}H - \overset{1}{C}H_2$$

with Br on carbon 4 and Br on carbon 1

1, 4 - dibromo-2-butene
(1, 4 - addition) 46%

At low temperature 1,2-addition product is major product and at high temperature 1, 4 - addition product is a major one

Addition of HCl :

$$CH_2 = CH - CH = CH_2 \xrightarrow[HCl]{25°C}$$

1, 3 butadiene

$CH_3 - CH - CH = CH_2$ with Cl

3-chloro-1-butene
78% (1, 2-addition)

$CH_3 - CH = CH - CH_2$ with Cl

1-chloro-2-butene
22% (1, 4-addition)

Addition of H-Br :

$$CH_2 = CH - CH = CH_2 \xrightarrow{HBr}$$

1, 3 butadiene

−80°C

$CH_3 - CH - CH = CH_2$ with Br + $CH_3CH = CH - CH_2$ with Br

(80%)   (20%)

40°C

$CH_3 - CH - CH = CH_2$ with Br + $CH_3CH = CH - CH_2$ with Br

(20%)   (80%)

8.8 DIELS-ALDER REACTION

Preparation of cyclic compounds from combination of two unsaturated molecules is called Diels-Alder reaction (D-A reaction).

This reaction involves a reaction between a conjugated diene and an unsaturated compound called a dienophile.

Butadiene or any conjugated diene serves a very good diene in Diels-Alder reaction for the synthesis of cycloalkenes. There are two possible planar conformations of 1,3-butadine, the S-*cis* and the S-trans. The diene can be in *cis* conformation to react in the Diels-Alder reaction

For example,

It is an example for 1,4-cycloaddition reaction. The addition occurs across carbons 1 and 4 of the diene. The product of Diels-Alder reaction is called an adduct.

The D-A reaction is an example of a cycloaddition reaction i.e. a reaction which leads to the formation of the ring.

Mechanism : Single step mechanism involving a cyclic T.S.

It is a pericyclic reaction. A concerted reaction that involves a cyclic flow of electrons is called a pericyclic reaction.

Kinetics : The reaction is second order and is not affected by the presence of polar solvents.

$$\text{Rate} = K\,[\text{Diene}]\,[\text{Dienophile}]$$

(B) ALKYNES

8.9 INTRODUCTION

Alkynes are unsaturated aliphatic hydrocarbons. The alkynes are characterised by the presence of a triple bond in between two carbon atoms $(C \equiv C)$. They are expressed by general molecular formula, C_nH_{2n-2}. The first and most important member of this series of hydrocarbon is acetylene $HC \equiv CH$ and hence these are also called the Acetylenes.

8.9.1 Structure

The simple hydrocarbon of this series is

$$H - C \equiv C - H$$

Acetylene

The carbon atoms in acetylene is in sp-hybridised state. The two carbon atoms are bonded by one σ-bond and two π-bonds. The C-H σ-bond is due to co-axial overlap of sp orbital of 'C' and s-orbital of 'H' atom. The π-bonds are formed from the parallel overlapping of the two p-orbitals from the two adjacent carbon atoms.

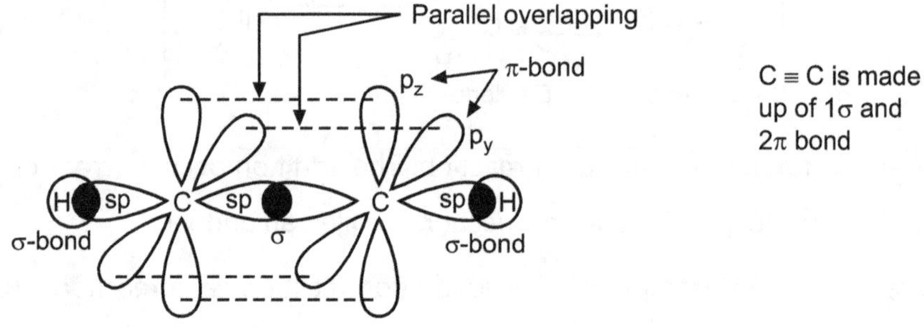

Molecular orbital picture of acetylene

Acetylene molecule
(Shape and size)

Acetylene is a linear molecule, all four atoms lying along a single straight line. The $C \equiv C$ is made up of one strong σ-bond and two weaker π-bonds. It has total strength of 198 kcal. It is stronger than the $C = C$ (163 kcal) and $C - C$ (88 kcal) and therefore is shorter than either.

8.9.2 Nomenclature of Alkynes

Alkynes are named according to two systems. In one system they are considered derived from acetylene by replacement of one or both hydrogen atoms by alkyl groups.

The more complicated alkynes are normally named by applying general rules of IUPAC system of nomenclature. The rules are same as for the naming alkenes except that the ending –yne replaces –ene.

A few examples are cited as below.

$$\overset{1}{H} - \overset{2}{C} \equiv \overset{3}{C} - C_2H_5 \qquad \overset{1}{CH_3} - \overset{2}{C} \equiv \overset{3}{C} - \overset{4}{CH_3} \qquad CH_3 - CH_2 - C \equiv C - CH_3$$

Ethylacetylene   Dimethylacetylene   Ethyl methyl acetylene
1-Butyne (But-1-yne)   2-Butyne (But-2-yne)   2-Pentyne (Pent-2-yne)

$$\begin{array}{c} CH_3 \\ | \\ H_3C - CH - CH_2 - CH_2 - C \equiv C - CH_3 \end{array}$$

Isopentyl methyl acetylene
6-Methyl-2-heptyne

8.9.3 Physical Properties of Alkynes

Alkynes have physical properties that are essentially same as those of alkanes and alkenes.

The first three members of series are gases, next eight are liquid and the higher alkynes are solids. The B.P. and M.P. of alkynes regularly increase with increase in molecular weights (Table 8.2). Alkynes have slightly higher B.P. than corresponding alkanes and alkenes. They are insoluble in water but quite soluble in the usual organic solvents of low polarity, such as ether, benzene, acetone, ethanol and carbon tetrachloride.

Table 8.2 : Physical Properties of Alkynes

Sr. No.	name	Structure	M.P. (°C)	B.P. (°C)
1	Acetylene	$HC \equiv CH$	– 82	– 75
2	Propyne	$HC \equiv C{-}CH_3$	– 101.5	– 23
3	1-Butyne	$HC \equiv C{-}CH_2{-}CH_3$	– 122	9
4	1-Pentyne	$HC \equiv C{-}CH_2{-}CH_2{-}CH_3$	– 98	40
5	1-Hexyne	$HC \equiv C{-}CH_2{-}CH_2{-}CH_2{-}CH_3$	– 124	72
6	1-Octyne	$HC \equiv C{-}CH_2{-}CH_2{-}CH_2{-}CH_2{-}CH_2{-}CH_3$	– 70	126
7	3-methyl-1-butyne	$HC \equiv C{-}\overset{\displaystyle CH_3}{\overset{\displaystyle |}{CH}}{-}CH_3$	–	29
8	3-Hexyne	$CH_3{-}CH_2{-}C \equiv C{-}CH_2{-}CH_3$	– 51	81
9	3, 3 - Dimethyl-1-butyne	$HC \equiv C{-}\overset{\displaystyle CH_3}{\overset{\displaystyle |}{\underset{\displaystyle |}{\underset{\displaystyle CH_3}{C}}}}{-}CH_3$	– 81	38

8.9.4 Preparation Methods of Alkynes

(1) Dehydrohalogenation of vicinal dihalides :

Vicinal dibromide $\xrightarrow[\Delta]{\text{Alc}}$ KOH Vinyl bromide (very unreactive)

Stronger base | $NaNH_2$

$R-C\equiv C-H$ + NaBr + $NH_3\uparrow$

Alkyne

Acetylene and propyne can be prepared by this method

(2) Dehalogenation of tetrahalides :

In this method, 1,1,2,2-tetrahalides are heated with zinc dust in alcohol, when halogens are removed as zinc halide and alkynes are formed.

$R-C-C-R$ → $2Zn$ $\xrightarrow[\Delta]{\text{Alcohol}}$ $R-C\equiv C-R$ + $2ZnX_2$

Tetrahalide   Alkynes

This method is not of much importance because the required tetrahalides are usually prepared from alkynes by the addition of halogens.

(3) Alkylation of acetylene :

In this method, acetylene or any alkyne having terminal hydrogen is converted to its salt by treatment with sodamide. These sodium salt of alkynes react with primary alkyl halides to form alkynes.

$R-C\equiv C-H$ + $NaNH_2$ → $R-C\equiv \overset{..}{C}\ \overset{\oplus}{Na}$ + $\frac{1}{2}H_2$

1-Alkyne   (Na in liq. NH_3)   Sodium acetylide

| R' – X

$R-C\equiv C-R'$ + NaX

For example,

$H-C\equiv C-H$ + $NaNH_2$ → $H-C\equiv \overset{..}{C}\ \overset{\oplus}{Na}$

Acetylene

| C_2H_5Br

$H-C\equiv C-C_2H_5$ + NaBr

1-Butyne

Advantages : It can be used to convert lower alkynes into higher alkynes.

Drawbacks : It proceeds smoothly with good yield, only in the case of primary alkyl halides.

(4) Reaction of calcium carbide with water :

Acetylene is prepared in the laboratory by reaction of calcium carbide with water.

$$CaC_2 \ + \ 2H_2O \longrightarrow H-C\equiv C-H \ + \ Ca(OH)_2$$

$$\text{Calcium carbide} \hspace{5cm} \text{Acetylene}$$

CaC$_2$ Preparation : Calcium carbide is readily obtained by heating a mixture of limestone and coke at 2000°C in an electric furnace.

$$CaCO_3 \longrightarrow CaO + CO_2$$

$$CaO + 3C \longrightarrow CaC_2 + CO$$

Drawback : The major drawback of this method is its high temperature.

8.9.5 Reactions of Alkynes

Alkynes give the same kind of reactions as do alkenes. However, with alkynes the addition may take place in one step or two steps.

The addition reactions occur due to the availability of the loosely held electrons.

Other reactions of alkynes result from acidic hydrogen atom in acetylene or 1-alkyne.

(1) Hydrogenation of Alkynes :

Alkynes adds up two molecules of H in presence of Ni, Pt or Pd forming the corresponding alkenes first and finally alkanes.

$$R-C\equiv C-H \xrightarrow{H_2/Ni} R-CH=CH_2 \xrightarrow{H_2/Ni} R-CH_2-CH_3$$

$$\text{Alkyne} \hspace{3.5cm} \text{Alkene} \hspace{3.5cm} \text{Alkane}$$

e.g.

$$CH_3-C\equiv CH \xrightarrow{H_2/Ni} CH_3-CH=CH_2 \xrightarrow{H_2/Ni} CH_3-CH_2-CH_3$$

$$\text{Propyne} \hspace{3.5cm} \text{Propene} \hspace{3.5cm} \text{Propane}$$

$$CH_3-C\equiv CH \xrightarrow[\text{quinoline}]{H_2 \mid Pd\text{-}BaSO_4}$$

$$CH_3-CH=CH_2$$

$$\text{Propene}$$

The reduction can be stopped at the alkene stage by using Pd poisoned with $BaSO_4$ + quinoline (Lindlar's catalyst). Almost entirely cis alkene is obtained if the hydrogenation of alkyne is carried out with Lindlar's catalyst.

$$CH_3-C\equiv C-CH_3 \xrightarrow[\text{catalyst}]{\text{Lindlar's}} \text{Cis 2-butene}$$

2-Butyne

(2) Addition of Hydrogen halide :

HCl, HI and HBr add to alkyne leading to the formation of gem-dihalide e.g. addition of HBr to acetylene yields a gem-dibromide.

$$H-C\equiv C-H + HBr \longrightarrow [H-C=C-H] \xrightarrow{HBr} H-C-C-H$$

Acetylene

Ethylidene dibromide
(gem-dihalide)

Mechanism :

$$H-C\equiv C-H + H-Br \longrightarrow H-C=C-H$$

Acetylene

$$CH_3-\overset{\oplus}{CH}-Br \xleftarrow{H-Br} CH_2=CH-Br$$

Vinyl bromide

$$\downarrow Br^{\ominus}$$

$$CH_3-CH-Br$$
$$|$$
$$Br$$

In case of unsymmetrical alkyne e.g. propyne the first molecule of HX adds according to Markownikoff's rule.

$$CH_3-C\equiv CH + H-X \longrightarrow CH_3-\overset{X}{\underset{}{C}}=CH_2$$

1-Propyne   2-Halo-1-propene

$$\downarrow HX$$

$$CH_3-\overset{X}{\underset{X}{C}}-CH_3$$

2, 2-dihalopropane

In the presence of free radical initiatiors, such as peroxides, anti-Markownikoff's addition of alkyl halide to alkyne is observed as with alkenes.

(3) Addition of Halogens :

Two moles of halogen react with one mole of alkyne to form tetrahalo derivatives as the final product. Halogen adds to alkyne first forming 1,2-dihaloalkane and then 1,1,2,2-tetrahaloalkane.

$$R - C \equiv C - R \xrightarrow[\text{CCl}_4]{\text{Br}_2} \left[\underset{Br}{\overset{R}{}} C = C \underset{R}{\overset{Br}{}} \right] \xrightarrow[\text{Br}_2]{\text{CCl}_4} R - \underset{Br}{\overset{Br}{C}} - \underset{Br}{\overset{Br}{C}} - R$$

Trans-product   Tetrabromo product

(4) Addition of Hypohalous acid :

Addition of two molecules of hypohalous acid (HOX) to alkynes take place in two steps. Addition follows Markownikoff's rule.

$$R - C \equiv C - H + 2 \overset{\ominus}{H}\overset{\oplus}{OX} \longrightarrow R - C - C - H \xrightarrow{-H_2O} R - \overset{O}{\overset{\parallel}{C}} - CHX_2$$

Alkyne   Unstable

(5) Hydration (Addition of water) :

$$R - C \equiv C - H + H - OH \xrightarrow[\text{H}_2\text{SO}_4]{\text{HgSO}_4} R - C = C - H \longrightarrow R - \overset{}{\underset{\overset{\parallel}{O}}{C}} - CH_3$$

Alkyne   [Unstable]   Ketone

Alkynes react with water in the presence of mercuric sulfate and sulfuric acid to form an aldehyde or a ketone.

(6) Oxidation with KMnO$_4$:

The oxidation of alkynes with alkaline KMnO$_4$ cleaves the molecules at the site of the triple bond to form carboxylic acids and CO.

$$R - C \equiv C - H + 4[O] \longrightarrow R - COOH + CO_2$$

1-Alkyne

$$R - C \equiv C - R' + 4[O] \longrightarrow R - \overset{O}{\overset{\parallel}{C}} - OH + R' - COOH$$

(7) Ozonolysis:

Alkynes react with ozone to give ozonides. These ozonides yield diketones on reaction with water, diketones oxidized to acids by H$_2$O$_2$ produced in the reaction.

$$R - C \equiv C - R' + O_3 \longrightarrow R - \underset{\underset{O-O}{|}}{C} \overset{O}{\triangle} \underset{|}{C} - R' \xrightarrow{H_2O} R - \overset{O}{\underset{||}{C}} - \overset{O}{\underset{||}{C}} - R' + H_2O_2$$

$$R - \overset{O}{\underset{||}{C}} - OH + R' - \overset{O}{\underset{||}{C}} - OH$$

Carboxylic acids

e.g. Propyne on ozonoysis gives acetic acid and formic acid.

(8) Salt formation :

Hydrogen in acetylene or 1-alkynes ($\equiv C - H$) are acidic. They can be replaced by metals to form salts known as acetylides.

$$R - C \equiv C - H + AgNO_3 + NH_4OH \longrightarrow R - C \equiv CAg + H_2O + NH_4NO_3$$

Alkyne   Alkynide

(9) Hydroboration-Oxidation :

Alkynes on hydroboration forms tri alkenyl borane intermediate, which can be oxidized to yield a ketone.

$$CH_3 - C \equiv C - CH_3 \xrightarrow[THF]{BH_3} \left(\underset{H}{\overset{H_3C}{}} C = C \overset{CH_3}{} \right)_3 B$$

2-Butyne

$\xrightarrow{H_2O_2 / OH^{\ominus}}$

$$CH_3 - CH_2 - \underset{\underset{O}{||}}{C} - CH_3 \xleftarrow{Tautomerism} CH_3 - CH = C - CH_3$$

2-Butanone

Whereas, terminal alkynes generally react a second time with BH_3 to give gem-diborane compound.

$$R - C \equiv CH \xrightarrow[THF]{BH_3} R - CH = CH - B \overset{H}{\underset{H}{}}$$

Alkenyl borane

$\downarrow BH_3$

$$R - H_2C - \underset{\underset{BH_2}{|}}{CH} - B \overset{H}{\underset{H}{}}$$

gem-Dibora compound

QUESTIONS

Q.1 What are elimination reactions? Write down E_1, E_2 and E_1CB reaction with respect to mechanism. Discuss factors affecting elimination reactions.

Q.2 What are elimination reactions? Discuss E_1, E_2 mechanism.

Q.3 What are elimination reactions? Discuss the mechanism, stereochemistry, kinetics and orientation involved in elimination reaction.

Q.4 What is Saytzeff rule? Explain.

Q.5 Write a note on Saytzeff and Hofmann elimination.

Q.6 Define elimination reaction. Differentiate E_1 and E_2 elimination and explain orientation of elimination.

Q.7 Explain orientation, reaction mechanism and stereochemistry of E_1 and E_2 reactions, add a note on factors affecting elimination reaction

Q.8 Give reason: Dehydrogenation of 1-bromo-1,2-diphenyl propane gives the expected product 1,2-diphenyl propene but, one pair of enantiomers yields only cis- alkene i.e. 1,2-diphenyl-1-propene.

Q.9 Depict and discuss the mechanism for the following reactions :

a) $CH_3\text{-}CH_2\text{-}\underset{\underset{CH_3}{|}}{CH}\text{-}CH_2OH \xrightarrow{H^+}$ $\underset{H_3C}{\overset{H_3C}{>}}C=C\underset{CH_3}{\overset{CH_3}{<}}$

Q.10 Write note on rules of double bond formation in elimination.

Q.11 Explain hydrogenation reaction with C=C bond.

Q.12 Explain hydrogenation reaction with C-C multiple bond.

Q.13 Explain hydrogenation and hydration reaction with C-C multiple bond.

Q.14 Write a note on

(i)   Ozonolysis

(ii) Peroxide effect

(iii) Hydroxylation

(iv) Markownikoff's and Anti-Markownikoff's rule

(v)   Oxymercuration-Demercuration

Q.15 What is electrophilic addition to olefins? Discuss addition reactions to olefins like hydrogenation, halogenations and ozonolysis.

Q.16 Give reason: Alkynes are less reactive than alkenes for electrophilic addition reaction.

Q.17 Explain addition of halogens and halogen acid to olefins.

Q.18   Predict the products of following reactions when ethylene reacts with Halogen, Halogen acid, Hydrogen.

Q.19   Explain Markownikoff and Anti-Markownikoff's rule with suitable examples.

Q.20   What are electrophiles? Explain the addition of halogen across double bond. Comment on orientation of the addition.

Q.21   Discuss hydroboration and ozonolysis reactions.

Q.22   Write a note on : (1) Ozonolysis, (2) Oxymercuration-Demercuration, (3) Peroxide effect, (4) Markownikoff's rule

Q.23   Predict the products and outline the mechanism for the following reactions:

(a) $CH_3 - \overset{\overset{\displaystyle H}{\displaystyle |}}{C} = CH_2 \ + \ Br_2 \ \xrightarrow{\ CCl_4\ }$

(b) $-\overset{|}{C} = \overset{|}{C} - \ + \ O_3 \ \longrightarrow$

❖ ❖ ❖

Chapter 9

BENZENE AND AROMATICITY

9.1 INTRODUCTION

In early 19th century the *"aromatic"* word was used to describe some fragrant compounds. Later they were grouped by chemical behavior. These chemical behaviors include the resistance to oxidation and addition and preference for substitution reactions over addition reaction etc. i.e. aromatic compounds that undergo substitution rather than addition.

Aromatic compounds are benzene and compounds that resemble in chemical behavior. Aromatic properties are those properties of benzene that distinguish it from aliphatic hydrocarbons. The compounds containing at least one benzene ring are known as benzenoid aromatic compounds while other compounds that exhibit aromatic behavior but do not contain benzene ring are called non-benzenoid aromatic compounds.

9.2 MOLECULAR ORBITAL STRUCTURE OF BENZENE

The structure of benzene is best explained on the basis of molecular orbital picture. All six carbon atoms in benzene are sp^2 hybridized. The sp^2 hybrid orbitals overlap with each other and with s orbitals of the six hydrogen atoms forming C-C and C-H σ-bonds.

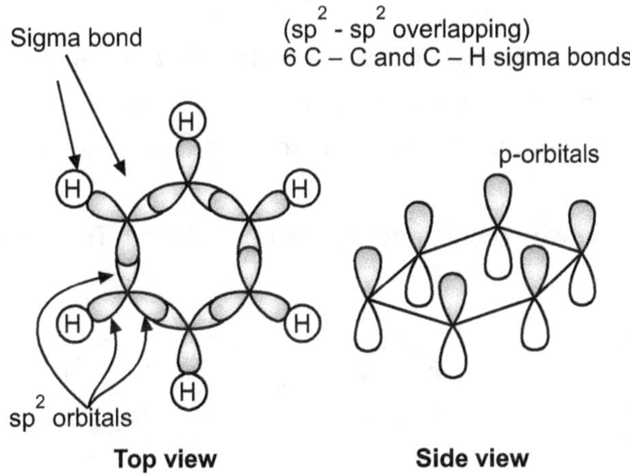

Fig. 9.1: Molecular orbital structure and formation of σ-bonds in benzene

Since the σ-bonds result from the overlap of planar sp^2 orbitals, all carbon and hydrogen atoms in benzene lie in the same plane. All σ-bonds in benzene lie in one plane and all bond angles are 120°.

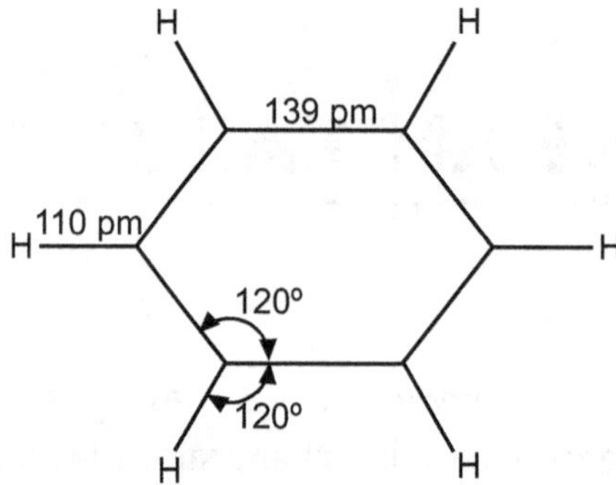

Fig. 9.2 : All σ-bonds in benzene lie in one plane

Also, each carbon atom in benzene possesses an unhybridised *p*-orbital containing one electron. These *p* orbitals are perpendicular to the plane of σ-bonds. The lateral overlap of these *p*-orbitals produces a π-molecular orbital containing six electrons. One half of this π-molecular orbitals lies above and the other half lies below the plane of σ-bonds.

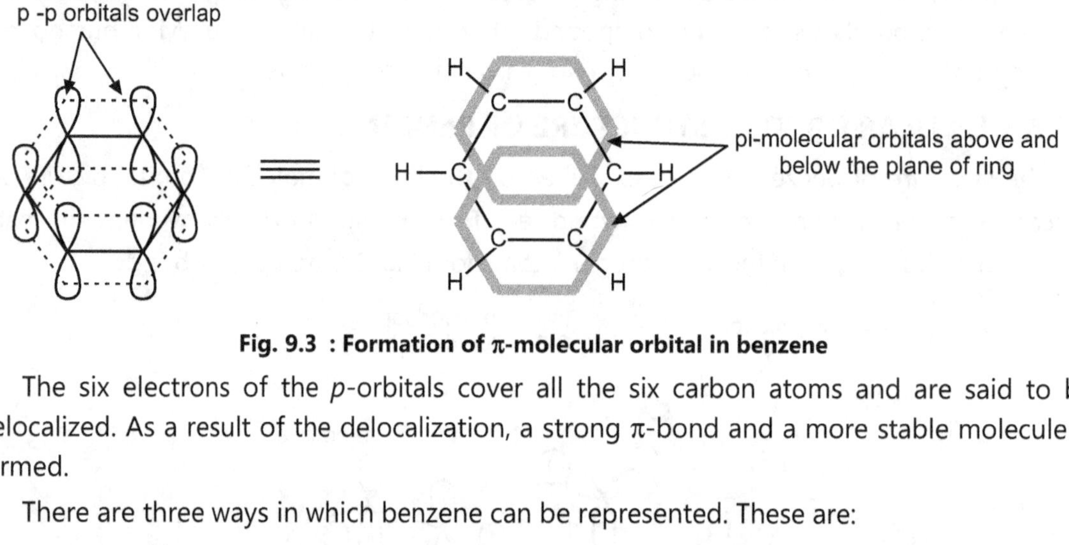

Fig. 9.3 : Formation of π-molecular orbital in benzene

The six electrons of the *p*-orbitals cover all the six carbon atoms and are said to be delocalized. As a result of the delocalization, a strong π-bond and a more stable molecule is formed.

There are three ways in which benzene can be represented. These are:

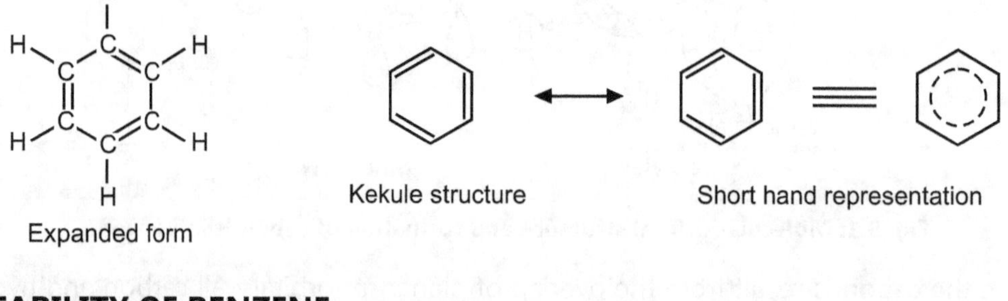

Expanded form　　　Kekule structure　　　Short hand representation

9.3 STABILITY OF BENZENE

The special stability of benzene is due to the formation of the delocalized π molecular orbitals. The magnitude of this extra stability can be estimated by measuring the changes in heat of hydrogenations that are associated with reactions. Hydrogenation of cyclohexene involves 28.6 kcal/mol, a typical value for hydrogenation of alkenes. About twice that amount is therefore expected for the hydrogenation of cyclohexadiene, i.e. about 57.2 kcal/mol. Experimentally, a reaction enthalpy of 55.4 kcal/mol is found for the hydrogenation of cyclohexadiene, which corresponds well to the theoretically expected value. This small difference may be due to the high stability of two conjugated double bonds compared to that of two isolated double bonds. The hydrogenation enthalpy of benzene may have been expected to be about 85.8 kcal/mol. The heat of hydrogenation of benzene actually amounts to only 49.8 kcal/mol. The 36 kcal difference between the heat evolved in the hydrogenation of benzene and that estimated for hydrogenation of a compound with the ordinary double bonds is the added stability. This difference (36.0 kcal/mol) is called **resonance energy**. Resonance energy is a measure of how much more stable a resonance hybrid structure is than its extreme resonance structures (Fig. 9.4).

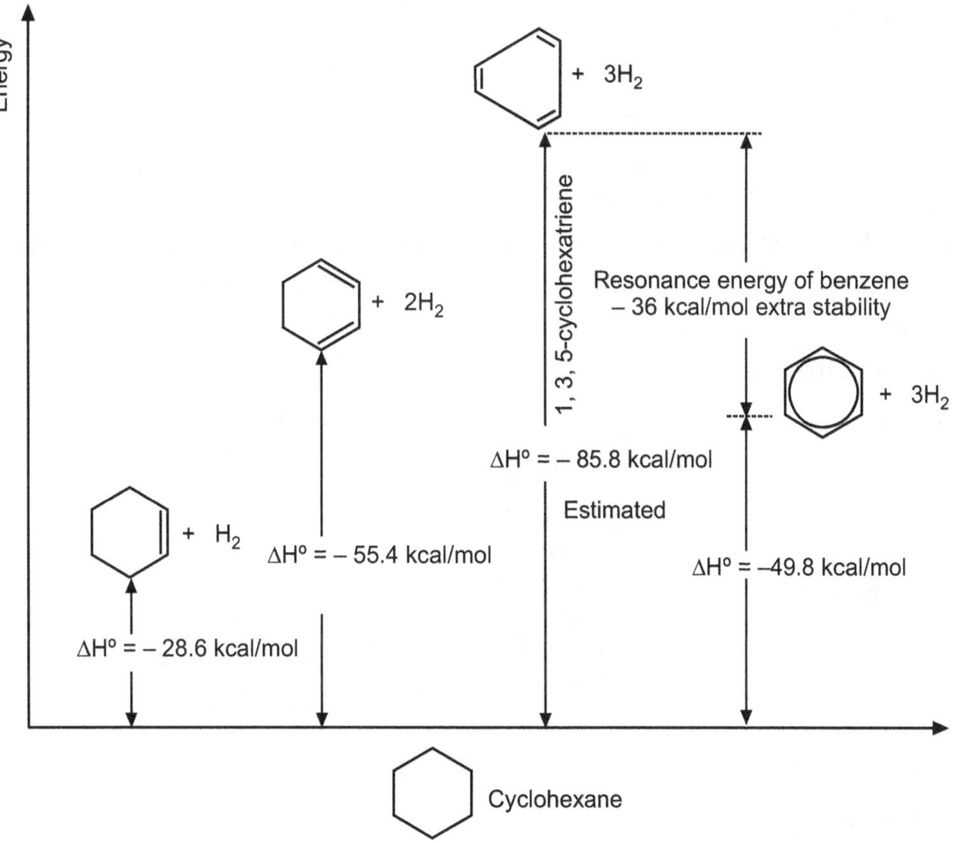

Fig. 9.4 : Heat evolved on hydrogenation of six membered cyclic compounds

9.4 AROMATICITY (HUCKEL RULE)

The aromatic compounds apparently contain alternate double and single bonds in cyclic structure and resemble benzene in chemical behavior. They undergo substitution rather than addition reactions. This characteristic behavior is called aromatic character or aromaticity.

Aromaticity is in fact a property of the sp^2 hybridized planar rings in which the p orbitals (one on each carbon atom) allow cyclic delocalization of π-electrons.

Criteria for aromaticity :

On the basis of above considerations, the following rules have been laid down which help us in knowing whether a particular compound is aromatic or non-aromatic.

(1) An aromatic compound is cyclic and planar.

(2) Each atom in an aromatic ring has a p orbital. These p orbitals must be parallel so that a continuous overlap is possible around the ring.

(3) The cyclic-molecular orbital (electron cloud) formed by overlap of p orbitals must contain $(4n + 2)$ π electrons, where $n = 0, 1, 2...$ This is known as **Huckel rule.**

e.g. Benzene, naphthalene, anthracene, pyrrole, furan, thiophene, pyridine etc.

Benzene :

$n = 1$

$(4 \times 1 + 2) \pi$

$= 6 \pi$ electrons

Benzene
(6 pi electrons)

It is a cyclic and planar compound. It has a p orbital on each carbon of the ring involved in a double bond. It has three double bonds and six π-electrons, which is in conformity with Huckel rule.

Naphthalene :

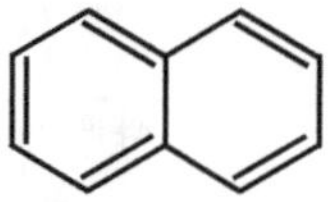

$n = 2$

$(4 \times 2 + 2) \pi$

$= 10 \pi$ electrons

Naphthalene
(10 π electrons)

Anthracene:

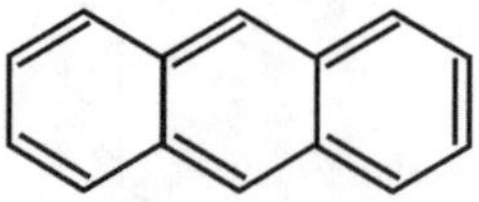

$n = 3$

$(4 \times 3 + 2) \pi$

$= 14 \pi$ electrons

Anthracene
(14 π electrons)

Pyrrole :

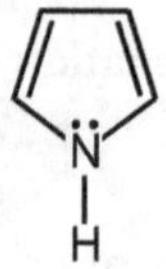

$n = 1$

$(4 \times 1 + 2) \pi$

$= 6 \pi$ electrons

Pyrrole
(6 π electrons)

Pyrrole is a heterocyclic, cyclic planar, aromatic compound. It has a p orbital on every ring atom and observes Huckel rule. In pyrrole there are *4p* orbitals on the 4 carbon atoms, containing one electron each. The N atom (also sp^2 hybridized) has an unused pair of electrons in a *p*-orbital parallel with the other 4p orbitals. The 4p electrons of carbon and the 2 electrons of N atom form a cyclic π molecular orbital.

All above compounds are aromatic because they obey Huckel's rule.

Cyclooctatetraene

(8π electrons)

We can never get 8π electrons by putting any number value of n in $(4n + 2)\pi$. Therefore it is non-aromatic.

9.5 RESONANCE IN BENZENE

Resonance is a way of describing the delocalized electrons within certain molecules. As stated previously benzene is stabilized by resonance. The theory of resonance was developed few years prior to the molecular orbital treatment. Thus resonance has provided a useful method of describing molecules like benzene. Benzene is represented as a resonance hybrid (III) of the following two equivalent resonance structures (I and II). Kekule structures involve identical positions of the atoms and differ only in their electronic arrangement. It is believed that the real structure of benzene is a resonance hybrid of the two structures and is not identical with either of the two. A hybrid structure (III) for benzene is represented using dotted line. The properties of hybrid are intermediate of the two equivalent structures but is of lower energy (about 35 to 36 kcal/mole) than either structures. The C-C bond is neither single nor double but is considered as a partial double bond. Resonance stabilizes the molecules against a number of chemical reactions.

(I)   (II)   (III)

Resonance structures   Resonance hybrid of benzene
(Kekule structures)

Resonance in derivatives of benzene:

(a) Phenol :

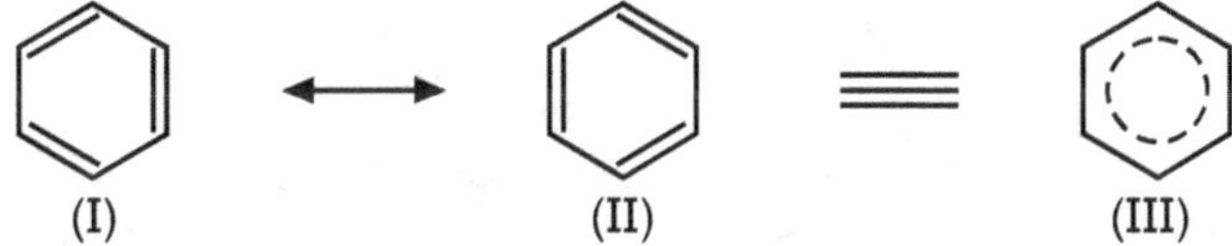

I   II   III   IV   V

(b) Aniline :

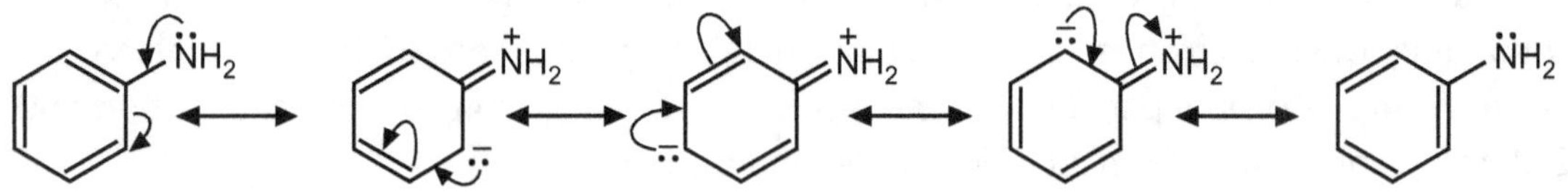

Aniline

(c) Benzaldehyde :

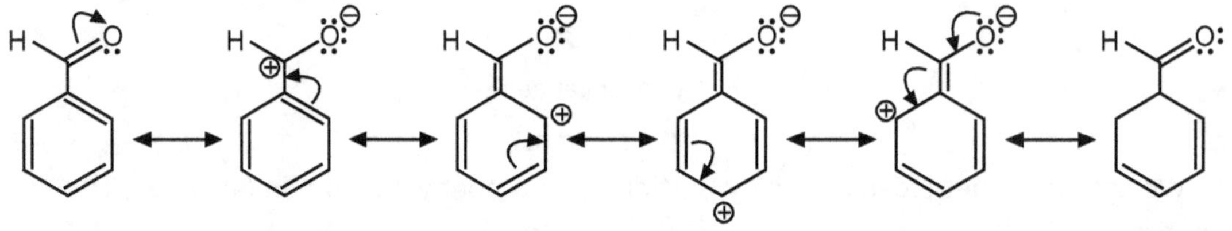

The *ortho* and *para* positions now have positive character on them. The *meta* position is not activated, but it is not deactivated either.

(d) Anisole :

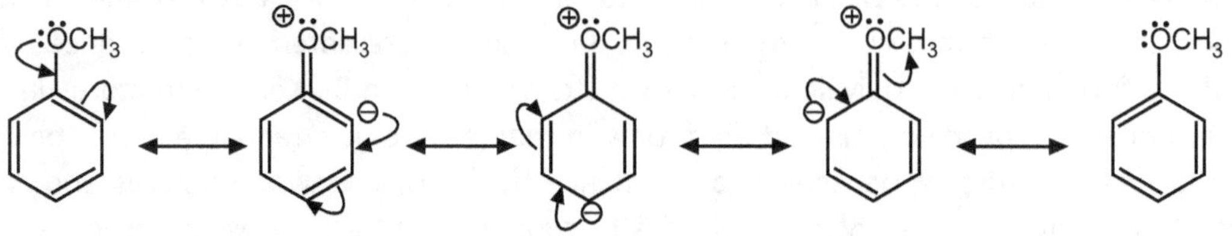

(e) Benzoic acid :

Let us look at the resonance contributors in benzoic acid to see where the most reactive and least reactive sites will be.

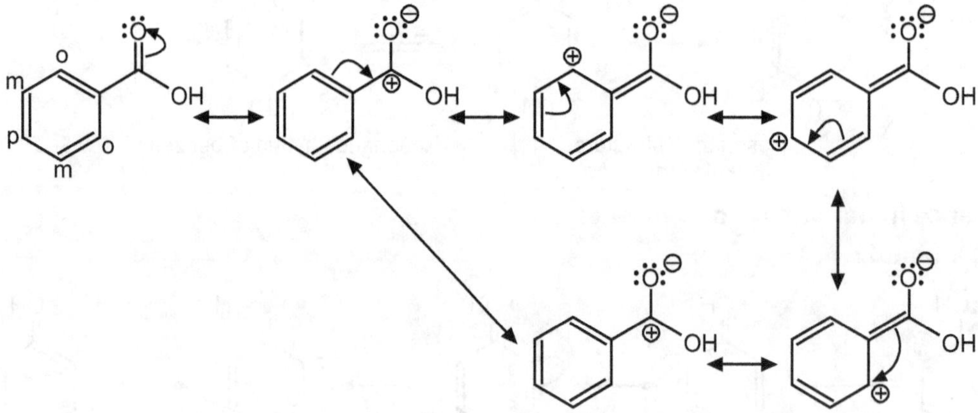

(f) Cyanobenzene:

(g) Benzene sulfonic acid:

(h) Nitrobenzene:

9.6 PHYSICAL PROPERTIES OF BENZENE

Benzene is a colourless liquid, B.P. 80.1°C, M.P. 5.5°C. It is insoluble in water, miscible with ether, alcohol and chloroform. Its vapours are highly toxic which on inhalation produce loss of consciousness. Benzene poisoning in the long run can prove fatal, destroying the red and white blood corpuscles. It burns with sooty flame, in contrast to alkanes and alkenes which usually burn with a bluish flame.

9.7 ELECTROPHILIC AROMATIC SUBSTITUTION

Benzene undergoes electrophilic substitution reactions. There is a cloud of π electrons above and below the plane of the benzene ring. The benzene ring with its delocalized π electrons is an electron-rich system. Through resonance, these π electrons are more involved in holding together carbon nuclei than the π electrons of a carbon- carbon double bond. Still, in comparison with σ electrons, these π electrons are loosely held and are available to a electrophilic reagent. Hence it is attacked by electrophiles, giving substitution products.

These reactions can be represented as

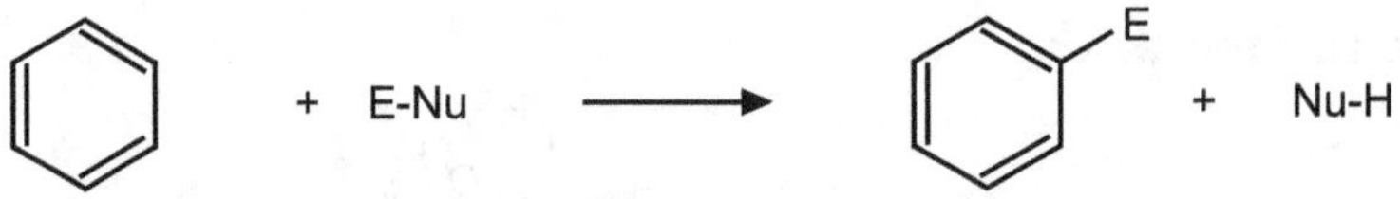

Benzene   Electrophilic reagent   Electrophile substituted product

where E is Electrophile e.g. NO_2^+, F^+, Cl^+, Br^+, I^+, $R - \overset{\overset{\textstyle O}{\textstyle \|}}{C}{}^+$, R^+, SO_3 etc.

Nu is nucleophile- e.g. NH_2^-, OH^-, F^-, Cl^-, Br^-, I^-, HSO_4^- etc.

Definition : The reactions in which the hydrogen atom of the aromatic ring is displaced by an electrophile are called aromatic electrophilic substitution reactions.

General mechanism :

All aromatic electrophilic substitution reactions follow the same three step mechanism which is as given below:

Step-I : Generation of an electrophile.

$$E\text{-NU} \longrightarrow \underset{\text{Electrophile}}{E^{\oplus}} + \underset{\text{Nucleophile}}{Nu^{\ominus}}$$

Step-II : Attack of electrophile on the aromatic ring and formation of resonance-stabilised σ-complex.

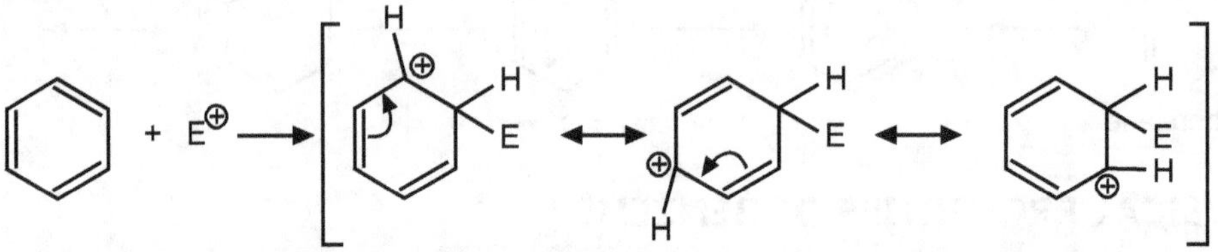

Resonance stabilized sigma complex (Arenium ion)

Step-III : Removal of a proton or aromatization to form the stable substitution product .

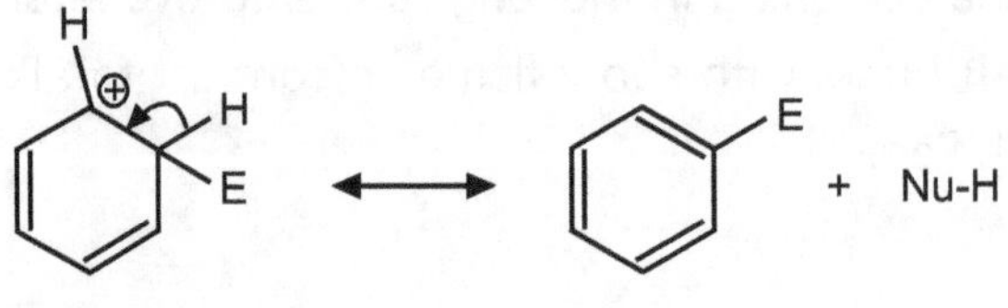

Arenes are much more stable and less reactive than alkenes. Unlike alkenes, arenes do not undergo electrophilic addition reactions.

Both benzene and alkenes are susceptible to electrophilic attack because of their exposed π electrons. Both react with electrophile to form stable carbocation. The carbocation produced from alkene usually combines with a nucleophile to give the overall addition product.

If this happens with benzene, the product would no longer be aromatic. The resonance energy of benzene would be lost. Instead the nucleophile removes a proton from the carbocation intermediate. The loss of proton allows the electrons from the C-H bond to go back into the ring and regenerate the aromatic π system. Net change is the replacement of a hydrogen atom by an electrophile.

A few of electrophilic aromatic substitution reactions are given below :

(1) Nitration

(2) Sulfonation

(3) Halogenation

(4) Friedel-Craft's alkylation reaction

(5) Friedel-Craft's acylation reaction

(6) Diazonium-coupling reaction

9.7.1 Nitration

Definition : Displacement of a hydrogen atom of an aromatic nucleus by a nitro group is called aromatic nitration reaction.

Nitrating agents used: The reaction may be carried out with several nitrating agents as given below :

(i)　Conc. HNO_3 in glacial acetic acid.

(ii)　HNO_3 in water.

(iii)　Conc. HNO_3 + Conc. H_2SO_4 (Mixed acid) .

(iv)　Fuming HNO_3 + Fuming H_2SO_4.

(v)　Fuming HNO_3 + Conc. H_2SO_4.

(vi)　Acyl nitrates, e.g. acetyl nitrate, benzoyl nitrate in organic solvents.

(vii)　N_2O_5 in carbon tetrachloride (CCl_4) in the presence of P_2O_5.

Among these the common reagent is the mixed acid and others are used depending on the nature of substrate.

Reaction :

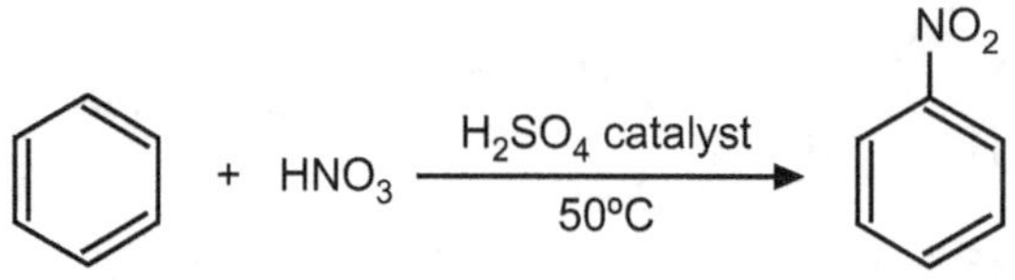

$$Benzene + HNO_3 \xrightarrow[50°C]{H_2SO_4 \text{ catalyst}} Nitrobenzene$$

Mechanism :

Step-I : Generation of electrophile (i.e. NO_2^+)

$$H_2SO_4 \rightleftharpoons \overset{+}{H} + HSO_4^-$$

$$H\ddot{O} - NO_2 + \overset{+}{H} \rightleftharpoons H_2\overset{+}{O} - NO_2 \rightleftharpoons H_2O + \overset{+}{N}O_2$$

$$H_2O + H_2SO_4 \rightleftharpoons H_3\overset{+}{O} + H_2SO_4^-$$

$$HNO_3 + 2HSO_4 \rightleftharpoons H_3\overset{+}{O} + 2HSO_4^- + \overset{+}{N}O_2$$

Nitric acid　　Sulfuric acid　　　　　　　　　　　Nitronium ion

Step-II : Formation of resonance stabilized σ-complex.

Because the nitronium ion ($\overset{+}{N}O_2$) is a good electrophile, it is attacked by aryl carbon to form resonance stabilized σ-complex.

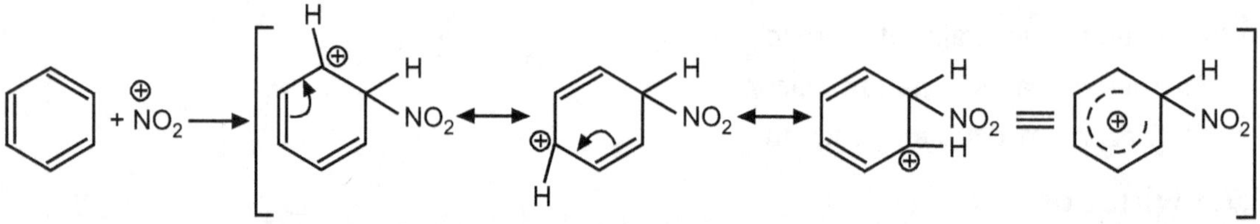

Sigma complex (nitroarenium ion)

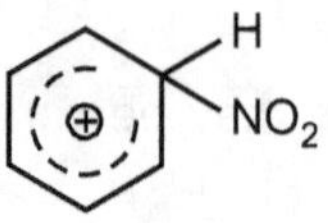

T.S. I

Step-III : Removal of a proton or aromatization. The σ-complex then gives up a proton to a base and gets aromatized to a nitroarene.

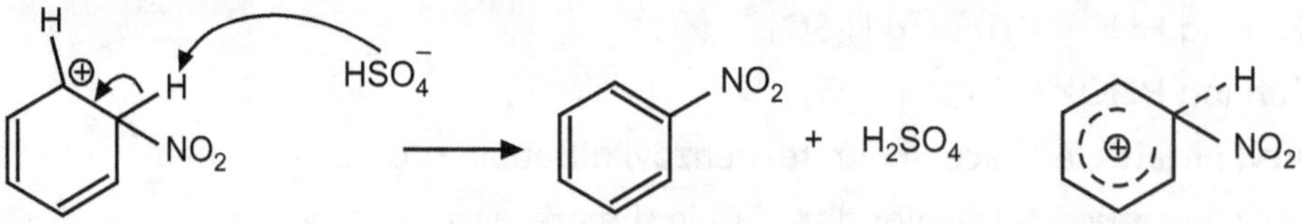

T.S. II

The base may be HSO_4^- in the case of mixed acid, or it may be a solvent molecule in the case of organic solvents.

Pathway for generation of NO_2^+ ion by different nitrating agents :

With most of the nitrating agents the attacking electrophile is the nitronium ion (NO_2^+).

In the case of dil. HNO_3 the attacking species is nitrosonium ion (NO^+). In this, nitrosation occurs at first and then the nitroso group gets oxidized to nitro group by the HNO_3. The pathway through which different nitrating agents give nitronium ion is given below.

(a) **When conc. HNO_3 is used as a nitrating agent :** In the case of conc. HNO_3 one molecule of the acid acts as a base and the other molecule as an acid. Thus acid-base reaction leads to the formation of NO_2^+ ions. When conc. HNO_3 is taken in an organic solvent, a very small amount of NO_2^+ forms by the reaction

$$HNO_3 \rightleftharpoons H^+ + NO_3^-$$

$$H^+ + HNO_3 \rightleftharpoons H_2O + NO_2^+$$

$$\overline{2HNO_3 \rightleftharpoons NO_3^- + H_2O + NO_2^+}$$

(b) **When N_2O_5 is used as a nitrating agent :** The nitronium ion forms through the spontaneous dissociation of N_2O_5.

$$N_2O_5 \rightleftharpoons NO_2^+ \; ; \; NO_3^- \rightleftharpoons NO_2^+ + NO_3^-$$

(c) **When dil. HNO_3 is used as a nitrating agent :** The nitrosonium ion (NO^+) is formed instead of NO_2^+ from HNO_2; the HNO_2 forms in the system through the minor redox reaction between the organic compound and HNO_3.

$$HNO_3 + \text{Organic compound} \longrightarrow HNO_2 + \text{Oxidized organic compound}$$

$$\text{Nitrous acid}$$

$$HNO_3 \rightleftharpoons H^+ + NO_3^-$$

$$H-\overset{..}{\underset{..}{O}}-N=O + H^+ \rightleftharpoons H_2\overset{+}{O}-N=O \rightleftharpoons \overset{+}{N}O + H_2O$$

$$\text{Nitrosonium ion}$$

Nitration in monosubstituted and disubstituted benzene :

The nitrating agents and conditions for reaction differ from substrate to substrate. The orientation is determined by the already present substituent. The compounds containing activating groups require mild nitrating agents and mild conditions, while compounds containing deactivating groups demand strong nitrating agents and vigorous conditions. Nitration is used to add nitrogen to a benzene ring, which can be used further in substitution reactions. The nitro group acts as a ring **deactivator**. Presence of nitrogen in a ring is very useful because it can be used as a directing group as well as a masked amino group. The products of aromatic nitration are very important intermediates in the industrial chemistry.

Examples :

(a) Substrates containing activating group :

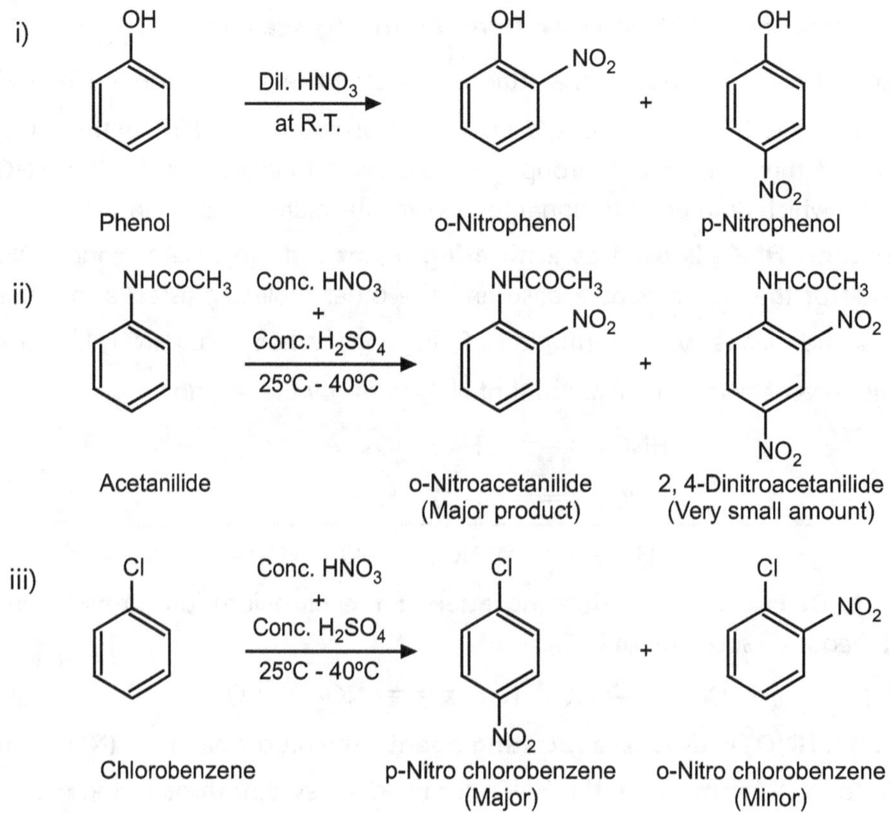

i)

Phenol   o-Nitrophenol   p-Nitrophenol

ii)

Acetanilide   o-Nitroacetanilide   2, 4-Dinitroacetanilide
(Major product)   (Very small amount)

iii)

Chlorobenzene   p-Nitro chlorobenzene   o-Nitro chlorobenzene
(Major)   (Minor)

(b) Substrate containing deactivating group :

Nitro benzene   m-Dinitrobenzene   1,3,5-Trinitrobenzene

9.7.2 Sulphonation

Definition : Displacement of a hydrogen atom of an aromatic nucleus by a SO_3H group is called aromatic sulphonation reaction.

Sulphonating agents used : conc. H_2SO_4 or fuming H_2SO_4 (Oleum, $H_2S_2O_7$ = SO_3 in H_2SO_4) or SO_3 in organic solvents (nitromethane, pyridine etc.) or chlorosulphonic acid in carbon tetra chloride.

Reaction :

SO$_3$H

Benzene $\xrightarrow[\text{25°C}]{\text{Fuming H}_2\text{SO}_4}$ Benzene sulfonic acid

Mechanism :

Aromatic sulphonation is a reversible reaction and takes place in the following way:

Step-I : Generation of electrophile (i.e. SO$_3$).

When the reagent for sulphonation is conc. H$_2$SO$_4$ or fuming H$_2$SO$_4$ or SO$_3$ in organic solvents, the electrophile is SO$_3$; the S atom is centre of positive charge.

$$H_2SO_4 \rightleftharpoons SO_3 + H_3O^+ + HSO_4^-$$

Sulfuric acid　　　Sulfur trioxide

$$H_2S_2O_7 \rightleftharpoons H_2SO_4 + SO_3$$

Oleum

Step-II : Formation of resonance stabilized σ-complex.

The sulfur in sulfur trioxide (SO$_3$) is electrophilic because the oxygens pull electrons away from it as oxygen is more electronegative than sulfur. The benzene attacks the sulfur to produce a resonance stabilized σ- complex.

Benzene

Sigma complex

Step-III : Removal of a proton or aromatization.

The σ-complex then gives up a proton to a base (HSO$_4^-$) and gets aromatized to a stable product. Deprotonation is the slow rate determining step.

$\xrightarrow{\text{Slow}}$　　$\xrightarrow{\text{Fast}}$

When the reagent is oleum the aromatization takes place as below.

At low temperature the reaction is practically irreversible. The reverse reaction is known as desulphonation reaction. Desulphonation is usually done by heating the sulphonic acid derivative with conc. HCl at an elevated temperature.

Sulphonation in monosubstituted and disubstituted benzene:

The orientation is determined by the already present substituent. Since the SO₃H is a bulky group there is a steric congestion at *o*-position. Because sulfonation is a reversible reaction, it can also be used in further substitution reactions in the form of a directing blocking group because it can be easily removed. The sulfonic group blocks the aryl carbon from being attacked by other substituents and once the reaction is completed it can be removed by reverse sulfonation.

Examples:

i) Benzene sulfonic acid → (Fuming H₂SO₄, 200°C - 400°C) → 1,3-benzene disulfonic acid → (Fuming H₂SO₄, 280°C - 300°C) → Benzene-1,3,5-trisulfonic acid

ii) Toluene → (Fuming H₂SO₄) → o-Toluenesulfonic acid (Minor) + p-Toluenesulfonic acid (Major)

iii) Phenol → (conc. H₂SO₄, 15°C - 20°C) → 2-Hydroxybenzene sulfonic acid (Minor) + 4-Hydroxybenzene sulfonic acid (Major)

Benzenesulfonic acids are used in the synthesis of detergents, dyes, and sulfa drugs. Benzenesulfonyl chloride is a precursor to sulfonamides, which are used in chemotherapy.

9.7.3 Halogenation

Definition : Displacement of a hydrogen atom of an aromatic nucleus by a halogen atom is called aromatic halogenation reaction.

Benzene　　　　Halogen　　　　Halobenzene

Where X : Cl or Br

Reagents used for halogenation :

When halogen is chlorine (chlorination) : Cl_2 + $FeCl_3$ or Cl_2 + Fe

When halogen is bromine (bromination) : Br_2 + $FeBr_3$ or Br_2 + Fe

Fluorination and iodination procedures differ from chlorination and bromination procedures.

Mechanism : General mechanism

Step-I : Generation of a electrophile (Halonium ion).

When halogen and Lewis acid is used:

Halogen　　　Ferric halide　　　　　　Halonium ion

When halogen and iron is used:

$$2Fe + 3X_2 \longrightarrow 2FeX_3$$

Halogen　　　Ferric halide　　　　　　Halonium ion

Step-II : Formation of resonance stabilized σ-complex.

Sigma complex

Step-III : Removal of a proton or aromatization and formation of halobenzene.

Halobenzene

Aromatic chlorination and bromination : Benzene reacts with chlorine and bromine in the presence of a Lewis acid catalyst such as $AlCl_3$, $FeCl_3$ or $FeBr_3$, leading to the substitution in the ring, a proton being lost as HCl or HBr.

Reactions :

Chlorination:

Benzene   Chlorine   Chlorobenzene

Bromination:

Benzene   Bromine   Bromobenzene

Mechanism for chlorination of benzene

Step-I : Generation of a electrophile (Chloronium ion).

Chlorine   Ferric halide   Chloronium ion

Step-II : Formation of resonance stabilized σ-complex.

Sigma complex

Step-III : Removal of a proton or aromatization.

Salt of sigma complex   Chlorobenzene

Iodination : The reactivity of iodine is very low and it reacts reversibly. The iodination procedure requires an acidic oxidizing agent, such as nitric acid.

Iodobenzene

The nitric acid is a strong **oxidizer** (i.e. removes electrons, converts iodine into I^+), this makes the iodine a much stronger electrophile.

$$2H^+ + 2HNO_3 + I_2 \longrightarrow 2I^+ + 2NO_2^+ + 2H_2O$$

The nitric acid is consumed in the reaction. It is therefore a **reagent**, not a catalyst.

However ICl may be used as a iodinating agent. Iodine being more electropositive than Cl, iodine becomes the positive pole and Cl becomes the negative pole of the I-Cl dipole. The species containing ring activating group such as phenols, amines etc. react with iodine in water. The *p*-product will the major product since OH or NH_2 group is quite large in size to create steric congestion.

Fluorination : The F-F bond energy is only 154.4 kJ/mol. When F is allowed to react with benzene, free radical addition takes place and forms polyfluorocyclohexane.

9.7.4 Friedel Craft's Reaction

Definition : Displacement of a hydrogen atom of an aromatic nucleus by an alkyl or an aryl or an acyl group in the presence of Lewis acid or a protonic acid as a catalyst is called Friedel-Craft's reaction.

For example:

i)

Benzene   Methyl bromide   Toluene

ii)

Benzene   Acetyl chloride   Acetophenone

The Friedel-Craft's reaction is discussed under the following two heads.

(i) The Friedel-Craft's alkylation.

(ii) The Friedel-Craft's acylation.

9.7.4.1 The Friedel-Craft's Alkylation

In Friedel-Craft's alkylation the displacement of a hydrogen atom of an aromatic nucleus is carried out by an alkyl or an aryl group in the presence of Lewis acid or a protonic acid as a catalyst.

In Friedel-Craft's alkylation reaction:

(a) The alkylating agents are alkyl halides, alkenes and alcohols. The order of reactivity among halides is $F^- > Cl^- > Br^- > I^-$.

(b) The substrates are aromatic hydrocarbons, haloarenes and phenols. Aromatic compounds with deactivating groups do not undergo this type of reaction, but if they contain activating groups also the reaction occurs.

(c) The acid catalysts are $AlBr_3 > AlCl_3 > FeCl_3 > SbCl_5 > SnCl_4 > BCl_3, BF_3$ etc.

Metal halides are generally used in case of alkyl halides and alkenes. When alcohols are used as alkylating agents, HF, BF_3, H_2SO_4 are used as acid catalysts.

(d) The solvents for solid substrates are carbon disulphide (CS_2) and nitrobenzene. For liquid substrates use of solvent is not essential; the excess of the substrate may play the role of solvent.

Reactions :

Benzene + R — Cl $\xrightarrow{AlCl_3}$ (R-substituted benzene) + HCl

Benzene   Alkyl chloride

Mechanism :

Step-I : Generation of an electrophile.

When alkyl halide and Lewis acid is used:

$$R - Cl: \; + \; AlCl_3 \rightleftharpoons R - Cl - AlCl_3 \rightleftharpoons RAlCl_4 \rightleftharpoons R^{\oplus} \; + \; AlCl_4^{\ominus}$$

Alkyl chloride   Aluminium chloride   Alkyl electrophile

Step-II : Formation of resonance stabilized σ-complex.

Benzene

Sigma complex

Step-III : Removal of a proton or aromatization.

Salt of sigma complex

Limitations of Friedel-Craft's Alkylation :

(i) Reaction is limited to alkyl halides only.

(ii) Reaction does not occur on rings containing strong electron withdrawing substituents.

(iii) Carbocation rearrangements generally occur with primary alkyl halides.

The Friedel-Craft's Acylation :

In Friedel-Craft's acylation the hydrogen atom of an aromatic nucleus is displaced by an acyl (RCO-) or benzoyl (ArCO–) group in the presence of a Lewis acid catalyst.

i)

$CH_3CH_2CH_2COCl$

Benzene   Butanoyl chloride   Propyl phenyl ketone

ii)

$CH_3(CH_2)_4COOH$

Resorcinol   Hexanoic acid   2,4-dihydroxyphenyl pentyl ketone

In this reaction the substrates are aromatic hydrocarbons including fused ring systems, derivatives of benzene containing *o, p*-directing groups such as hydroxyl, alkoxy, halo, acid-amido groups.

The reagents of reactions are usually acid halides (cyclic and acyclic) and carboxylic acids.

The solvents are nitrobenzene, carbon disulphide (CS_2) and tetrachloroethylene.

Reaction :

Benzene $R-C-Cl$ Acid chloride   Aryl ketone

Mechanism :

Step-I : Generation of an electrophile which is an acylium ion.

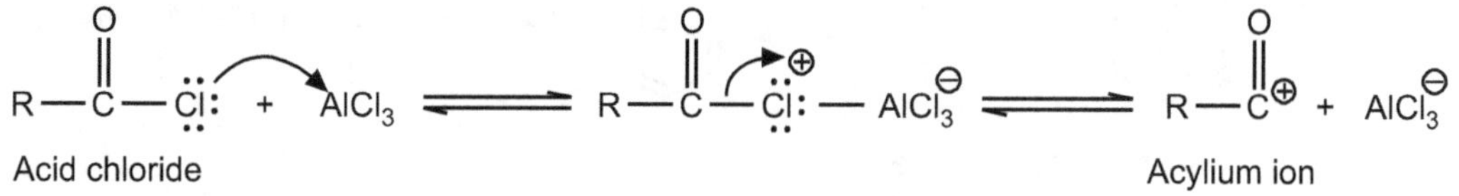

Acid chloride   Acylium ion

Step-II : Formation of resonance stabilized σ- complex.

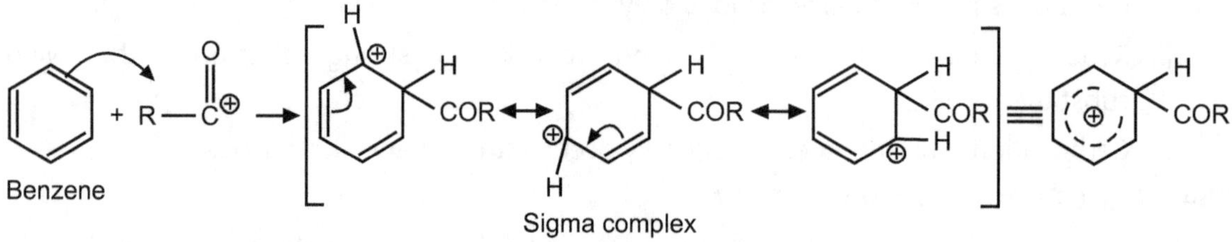

Benzene

Sigma complex

Step-III : Removal of a proton or aromatization and formation of aryl ketone.

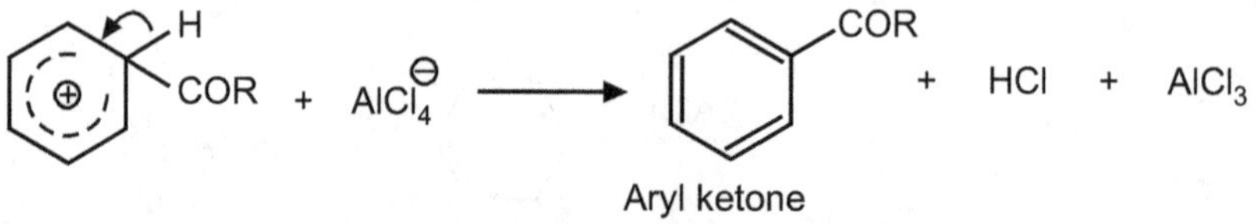

Aryl ketone

9.7.5 Diazonium Coupling Reaction

Definition : Aromatic diazonium ions combine with phenoxide ions and aromatic tertiary amine to form a large number of azo-dyes and these sort of reactions are known as diazonium coupling reactions.

The coupling reaction between a diazonium salt and phenol is usually carried out in the alkaline solution. Usually a strong acidic and cold solution of the diazonium salt is poured into an alkaline solution of phenol in cold and a good amount of azo dye forms rapidly. Thus benzene-diazonium ion may be coupled with alkaline β-naphthol and alkaline resorcinol.

i)

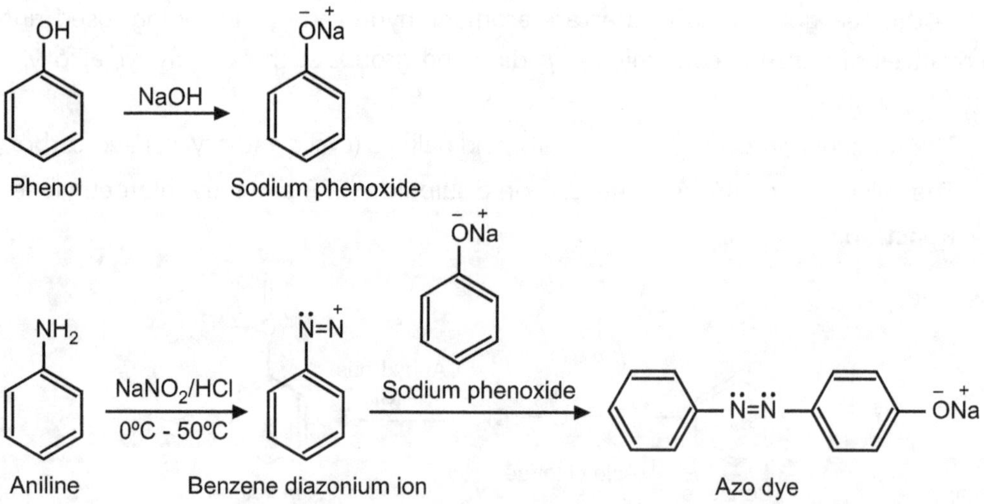

Phenol   Sodium phenoxide

Aniline   Benzene diazonium ion   Azo dye

ii)

Benzene diazonium ion + Sodium salt of beta naphthol → Azo dye

iii)

Benzene diazonium ion + Sodium salt of resorcinol → Azo dye

Depending on the nature of coupling component, the coupling reaction is carried out either in an alkaline or in a neutral or in slightly acidic medium. The coupling reactions are usually carried out in cold condition because of less stability of diazonium ions at normal condition.

When a primary aromatic amine is diazotized at a very low acid concentration, a certain amount of the amine forms the diazonium salt which then couple with the rest of the amine and forms diazonium compound; this on warming at $40^{\circ}C$ with the corresponding amine hydrochloride gives the azo dye.

Aniline $\xrightarrow[0^{\circ}C - 50^{\circ}C]{NaNO_2/HCl}$ Benzene diazonium ion + Aniline $\xrightarrow{CH_3COONa}$ Diazoamino compound

Diazoamino compound $\xrightarrow[40^{\circ}C]{\text{Aniline hydrochloride}}$

When a secondary amine couples with the diazonium ion, it forms N-substituted diazoaminobenzene as shown below.

Benzene diazonium ion + N-Methyl aniline $\xrightarrow{Na_2CO_3}$ N-methyl diazoamino benzene

However, a tertiary amine couples with the diazonium ion in a fairly acidic medium to form azo-dyes.

For example, when a diazotized solution of a sulphanilic acid is treated with N,N-dimethylaniline, an orange dye, called methyl orange is formed; this is orange in alkaline medium but red in acid solution. Since the colour of the dye is different in acid and in alkali media, this is used as an acid-base indicator.

Diazonium ion
of sulfanilic acid

N,N-Dimethyl aniline

Methyl orange

Methyl orange
in acidic solution (Red)

Methyl orange
in alkaline solution (Orange)

Mechanism :

The mechanistic steps of the reaction are given below :

Step-I : Generation of an electrophile.

$$NaNO_2 \; + \; HCl \xrightarrow{-\,NaCl} HONO \underset{}{\overset{H^+}{\rightleftharpoons}} \overset{+}{N} = O \; + \; H_2O$$

Sodium nitrite   Nitrous acid   Nitrosonium
                                                                ion

Aniline

Benzenediazonium
chloride (Electrophile)

Step-II : Coupling of diazonium ion with the coupling component : Attack of electrophile i.e. aromatic diazonium ion on the nuclear carbon of the coupling component and formation of resonance stabilized σ-complex.

Sigma complex

Step-III : Abstraction of a proton by base from the σ-complex and formation of stable azo dye as a final product.

Sigma complex　　　　　　　　　　　　　　　　Azo dye

The step-II is the slow step, the reaction then follows the second order kinetics.

The rate = k [Diazonium salt] [Phenoxide ion]

In most of the cases the diazonium coupling occurs at the para-position of the coupling component, when the *p*-position is blocked, *o*-coupling occurs. When the *o*- and *p*-positions are blocked by other groups, usually diazonium coupling does not take place; however there are reactions in which the coupling occurs at the *p*-position and the group occupying the *p*-position gets ejected.

The diazonium coupling reaction cannot take place with weak nucleophile.

$C_6H_5N_2^+$ is a very weak electrophile, much weaker than NO_2^+, Br^+ etc. Phenol itself being a weak nucleophile it does not couple with benzenediazonium ion. In alkaline medium its nucleophilicity is increased by conversion into phenoxide ion.

9.8 ORIENTATION AND REACTIVITY IN MONOSUBSTITUTED BENZENE

In benzene all the six hydrogens are chemically equivalent and a single product is obtained during an electrophilic substitution. But if a group is already occupying a position on the ring i.e. it is benzene derivative (monosubstituted benzene) the incoming electrophile may attack either of the ortho, meta or para positions to the attached group to yield a mixture of products.

It has been observed that substituents already attached to the benzene ring not only govern the orientation of further substitution but also affect the reactivity of benzene ring.

It is discussed as below:

(i) Effect of substituents on orientation : The nature of the group already attached to benzene ring determines the position of incoming group. These groups have been classified into following two categories.

(a) *Ortho-para* directing groups (Ring activating groups): A group or substituent present on the benzene ring can cause the benzene derivative to react faster than benzene itself by increasing the electron density on the ring is called ring activating group.

Ring activating groups which direct the incoming group (electrophile) towards *ortho-para* position are called *ortho-para* directing groups.

+I and +M effect groups are *ortho-para* directors.

For example, $-R$, $-OH$, $-SH$, $-OR$, $-NH_2$, $-NHR$, $-NR_2$, $-NHCOR$, $-F$, $-Cl$, $-Br$, $-I$ etc.

(b) Meta-directing groups (Ring deactivating groups): A group or substituent present on the benzene ring can cause the benzene derivative to react slower than benzene itself by decreasing the electron density on the ring is called ring deactivating group.

Ring deactivating groups which direct the incoming group (electrophile) towards meta position are called meta directing groups.

The ring deactivating groups are meta-directing groups. Electron withdrawing groups such as $-I$, $-M$ effect groups are meta directors.

For example, $-COOH$, $-CHO$, $-COR$, $-NO_2$, $-CN$, $-SO_3H$, $-SO_2R$, $-\overset{\oplus}{N}H_3$, $-\overset{\oplus}{N}R_3$, $-CF_3$, $-CCl_3$ etc.

(ii) Effect of substituents on reactivity: Reactivity of the benzene ring in electrophilic substitution reactions depends upon the tendency of the substituent group already present in the benzene ring to release or withdraw electrons.

A group that releases electrons activates benzene ring while the one which draws the electrons deactivates the benzene ring.

Explanation for why ring activators are *o/p*-directing and ring deactivators are *m*-directing: This phenomenon is explained by the following two ways.

(1) Stability of σ-complex : For this method draw the resonating structures of the three possible σ-complexes for the three products *o, m* and *p* and then relative stabilities to be determined. The greater the stability of σ-complex, the lower is the energy of activation and higher is the rate of reaction and higher is the yield of product.

Directing nature of ring activating groups:

Where X = –R, C_6H_5, –OH, –SH, –OR, –NH$_2$, –NHR, –NR$_2$, –NHCOR, –F, –Cl, –Br, –I etc.

As shown above *ortho* and *para* σ-complexes has extra resonating structures in their resonance hybrid, these two structures bring extra stability to the *ortho* and the *para* complexes. Therefore transition states for *o-* and *p*-positions will have lower activation energy than *m*-attack. As a consequence the rate of reaction at *o-* and *p-* positions will be greater than *m*-position which will tend to form *o-*/*p*-products predominantly.

Directing nature of ring deactivating groups :

For example,

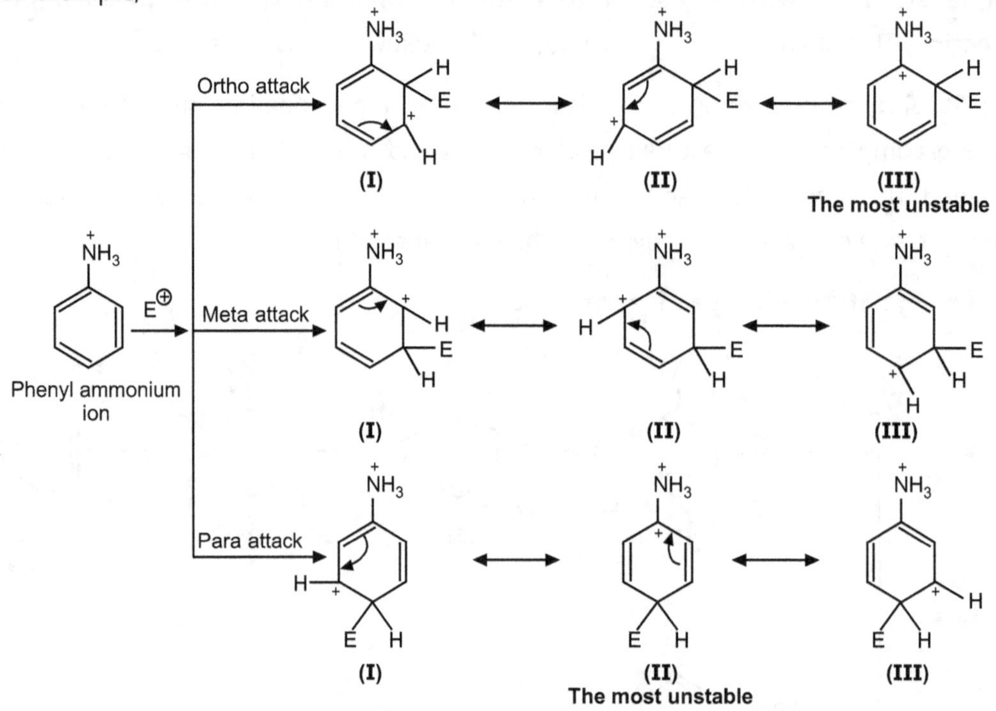

Phenyl ammonium ion

$E^{\oplus}$

Ortho attack

NH_3^+ ... H, E, H

(I) ⟷ (II) ⟷ (III)

The most unstable

Meta attack

(I) ⟷ (II) ⟷ (III)

Para attack

(I) ⟷ (II) ⟷ (III)

The most unstable

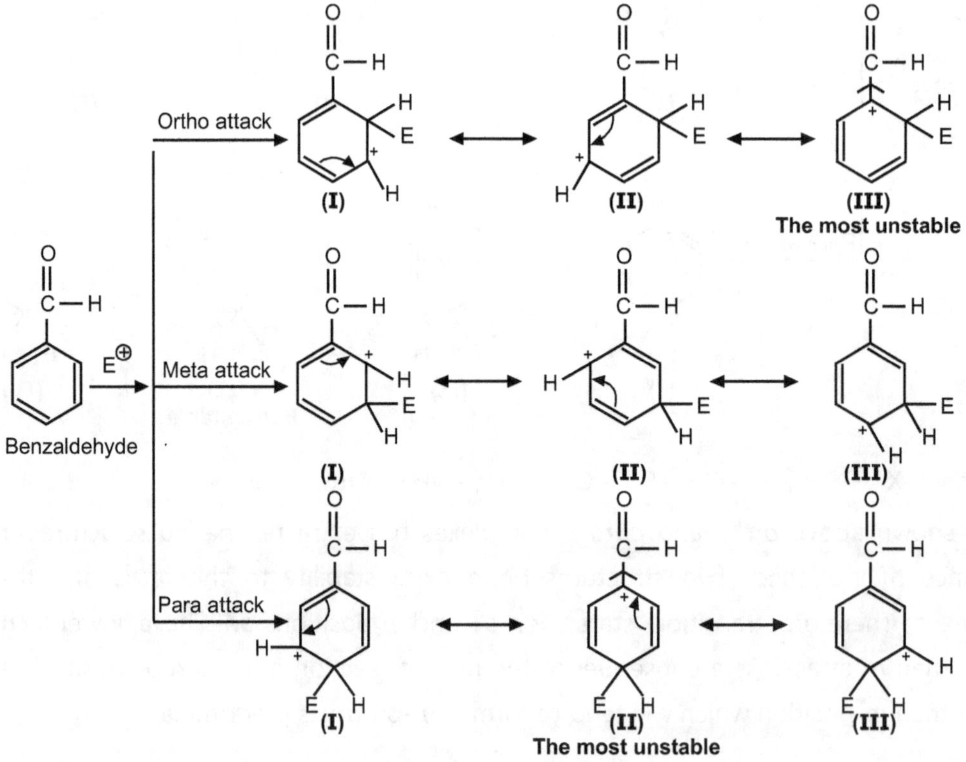

Benzaldehyde

$E^{\oplus}$

Ortho attack

(I) ⟷ (II) ⟷ (III)

The most unstable

Meta attack

(I) ⟷ (II) ⟷ (III)

Para attack

(I) ⟷ (II) ⟷ (III)

The most unstable

As shown in above resonating structures, *meta* σ-complex is more stable than the other two σ-complexes as the *o-* and *p-* σ-complexes contain one very unstable resonating structure because in phenyl ammonium, $-NH_3^+$ group and in benzaldehyde, CHO group will have to withdraw electron from an electron deficient positively charged carbon atom. Thus the *m-* product forms predominantly among the three products. Therefore ring deactivating groups are m-directing groups.

(2) Distribution of electronic charge :

Ring activating groups :

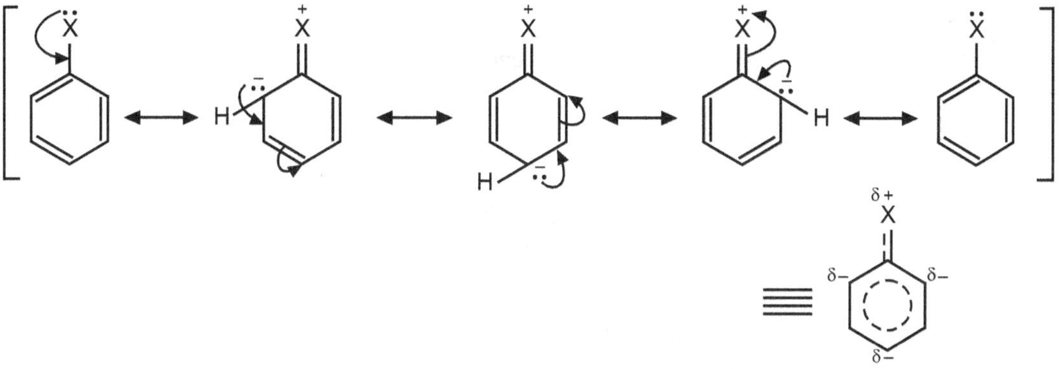

Note : Halo groups i.e. F, Cl, Br, I have deactivating effect due to –I effect yet they are *o-/p-* directing due to their +M (+R) effect.

These groups show –I effect (except O⁻) and +M effect of which +M effect predominates. The +M effect increases the electron density on the *o-/p-*positions. Therefore electrophilic attack will be on *o-* carbon and *p-*carbon. Hence electron releasing groups are *o-/p-* directing groups.

Ring deactivating groups : Ring deactivating groups such as

$$-NO_2, -CN, -SO_3H, -COOH, -COOR, -SO_3R, -CHO, -COR, \text{ etc.}$$

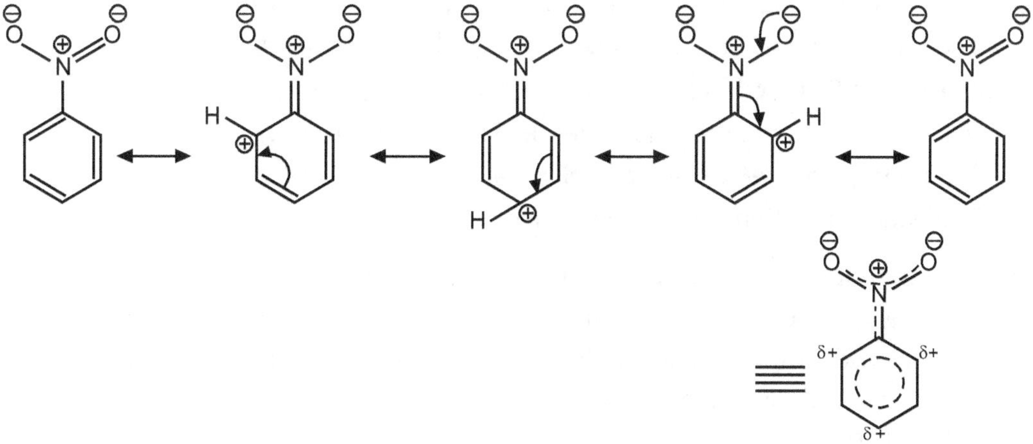

These groups have –I and –M effects; the –M effect is the predominant effect. The –M effect makes the *o-*/*p*-carbons less electron-dense than the *m*-carbons. Therefore the incoming electrophile will attack at the *m*-carbon and *m*-product will be obtained predominantly. Thus ring deactivating groups are *m*-directing groups.

Examples : Nitration of toluene gives mixture of *o*-nitro toluene and *p*-nitro toluene. Whereas nitration of nitrobenzene gives m-dinitrobenzene.

Toluene $\xrightarrow[\text{300°K}]{\text{Dilute HNO}_3/\text{H}_2\text{SO}_4}$ o-Nitro toluene + p-Nitro toluene

Nitrobenzene $\xrightarrow[\text{300°K}]{\text{Conc. HNO}_3/\text{H}_2\text{SO}_4}$ m-Dinitrobenzene

9.9 NUCLEOPHILIC AROMATIC SUBSTITUTION (AROMATIC S_N REACTION)

A nucleophilic aromatic substitution is a substitution reaction in which the nucleophile displaces a good leaving group, such as a halide, diazonium group etc. on an aromatic ring.

Every aromatic system has annular electronic cloud below and above its plane because of the presence of delocalized π-electron cloud. When a nucleophile approaches the nucleus of an aromatic system, repulsion takes place between them. The nucleophilic attack is very difficult on aromatic species. Under drastic conditions, i.e. under high temperature and pressure, strong nucleophiles may be substituted. Substituted aromatic compounds having properly placed strong electron withdrawing groups on aromatic nucleus undergo nucleophilic substitution with less difficulty as the electron withdrawing group draws electrons towards itself making the aromatic nucleus less electron dense.

Types of aromatic S_N reaction :

(1) Unimolecular via a carbocation intermediate (S_N1 aromatic).

(2) Bimolecular via intermediate complex anion (S_N2 aromatic).

(3) Elimination- addition via aryne intermediate.

9.9.1 Unimolecular via a Carbocation Intermediate (S_N1 Aromatic)

S_N1 reaction is possible but very unfavorable. Aromatic S_N1 reactions are very rare. The reaction would involve the loss of the leaving group and the formation of an aryl cation. Most common example is the displacement of N_2 in the reactions of diazonium salts in a stronger polar medium.

For example :

Benzene diazonium chloride   Aryl cation $+ \ N_2 \ + \ \bar{Cl}$ Conc. HCl   Chlorobenzene

Benzene diazonium chloride   Aryl cation H_2O, $-N_2$, $-\bar{Cl}$ Oxonium ion $-\overset{+}{H}$ Phenol

Mechanism :

Step-I : Removal of leaving group and formation of aryl cation.

Benzene diazonium chloride   Slow   Aryl cation $+ \ N_2 \ + \ \bar{Cl}$ Conc. HCl   Chlorobenzene

It is reversible and slow rate determining step.

The aryl cation so formed is very unstable since the positive charge cannot get delocalized. This is because the breaking of C-N σ-bond leaves a vacant sp^2 atomic orbital with the cationic carbon. This vacant sp^2 atomic orbital is perpendicular to π orbital, so delocalization of charge is not possible.

Step- II : Nucleophilic attack on the aryl cationic carbon atom.

$+ \ \bar{Nu}$ Rapid   Nu

Where, Nu = $\bar{Cl}$

Kinetics : The first step being slow rate determining step. The reaction is found to follow the first order kinetics.

$$\text{Rate} = k \ [ArN_2^+]$$

9.9.2 Bimolecular via Intermediate Complex Anion (S_N2 Aromatic)

It is the most common type of aromatic S_N reaction. For example 2,4-dinitrochlorobenzene will undergo reaction with nucleophiles such as ammonia and hydroxide, where the chloro group is displaced.

2, 4-Dinitrochlorobenzene $\xrightarrow[\text{Heat}]{\text{NaOH}}$ 2, 4-Dinitrophenol

$\xrightarrow[]{\text{Heat} \mid NH_3}$

2, 4-Dinitroaniline

Mechanism : The mechanism consists of two steps.

Step I : Nucleophilic attack on an aryl carbon and formation of resonance stabilized intermediate complex carbanion via a T.S. which involves the substrate and the incoming nucleophile. This is a slow rate determining step.

Step II : Loss of the leaving group from the intermediate anion to produce the product.

Since step-I is the slow rate-determining step and its T.S. involves both the nucleophile and the substrate, it is a bimolecular reaction. The kinetics of the reaction follows the second order rate equation.

The mechanism of this nucleophilic substitution does not proceed by the S_N2 mechanism seen with alkyl halides because the aryl halide cannot provide a suitable geometry for back side attack of the nucleophile (aryl ring blocks the attack of the nucleophile). Yet the S_N1 mechanism also cannot operate since the reaction is not found to be unimolecular, and strong nucleophiles are required.

Consider the reaction of hydroxide ion with 2, 4-dinitrochlorobenzene.

Step 1 : Attack by hydroxide gives a resonance-stabilized sigma complex.

Step 2 : Loss of chloride ion leads to the formation of final stable product.

Sigma complex   2, 4-Dinitrophenol

9.9.3 Elimination - Addition via Aryne Intermediate

The previous addition-elimination reaction mechanism required powerfully electron withdrawing groups on the benzene ring. However, under forceful conditions, inactivated halo benzenes with at least one *ortho*-hydrogen are treated with a strong base like $NaNH_2$ or NaOH, the halogen group gets displaced by the amino or hydroxyl group respectively and thus aryl amines or phenols are formed. Being arynes as intermediate in these reactions, these type of reactions are known as aromatic nucleophilic reactions involving aryne as an intermediate.

Chlorobenzene   Phenol   ;   Chlorobenzene   Aniline

Mechanism : This is a two stage reaction.

Stage-1 : Elimination :

In this stage, aryne intermediate results by the elimination of hydrogen halide from the vicinal positions. Elimination takes place in two steps. Step I involves abstraction of proton from the aryl halide by the base from the *ortho* position with respect to the halogen atom. Then in next step (Step-II) removal of the halide ion results into aryne intermediate.

Carbanion　　　　Benyne

Stage-2 : Addition :

Addition of the base i.e. NH_2 occurs to the aryne intermediate. Addition also takes place in two steps. In step-III base attacks at any one of the triple bonded carbons and in the last step-IV protonation of the carbanion intermediate by the solvent leads to the formation of product.

Benzyne　　　　Carbanion

Step IV

QUESTIONS

Q.1　What are substitution reactions? Explain the mechanism involved in Freidel-Craft acylation and sulphonation of benzene.

Q.2　Explain Huckel's rule for aromaticity with suitable example.

Q.3　Write the synthesis of following compounds starting with benzene and suitable reagents :

　　a)　meta nitro toluene

　　b)　1, 3- dinitro benzene

　　c)　para nitro toluene

Q.4　Define the following terms and give any two suitable examples of each.

　　a)　Activating group

　　　b)　Deactivating group

　　　c)　Ortho and para director

Q.5　Aniline is more reactive than acetanilide for electrophilic substitution reaction. Give reason.

Q.6　Give definition, reaction, mechanism of nitration, sulphonation, halogenations, Friedel Craft's reaction.

Q.7　How will you synthesize following compounds from benzene?

　　　a)　4-Nitroacetanilide

　　　b)　Phenol

Q.8　Explain nitro group is meta directing, while amino group is ortho and para-directing in orthosubstituted benzene.

Q.9　Explain the mechanism involved in Friedel-Craft alkylation and nitration of benzene.

Q.10　Methyl group in toluene is ortho para directing. Explain.

Q.11　Explain mechanism of sulphonation and nitration on benzene. What is the role of H_2SO_4 in each reaction?

Q.12　Explain why halogens though electron withdrawing are ortho/para directors?

Q.13　Give reasons: Halogens though deactivators are o, p, directors in electrophilic aromatic substitution.

Q.14　Give reason: Electron donating groups are o, p directors in electrophilic aromatic substitution.

Q.15　Write a note on Nitration of Benzene.

Q.16　Which reagent should be used to carry out the following reactions: .

(i)　benzene $\rightarrow$ bromobenzene (Br) $\rightarrow$ phenylmagnesium bromide (MgBr) $\rightarrow$ phenol (OH)

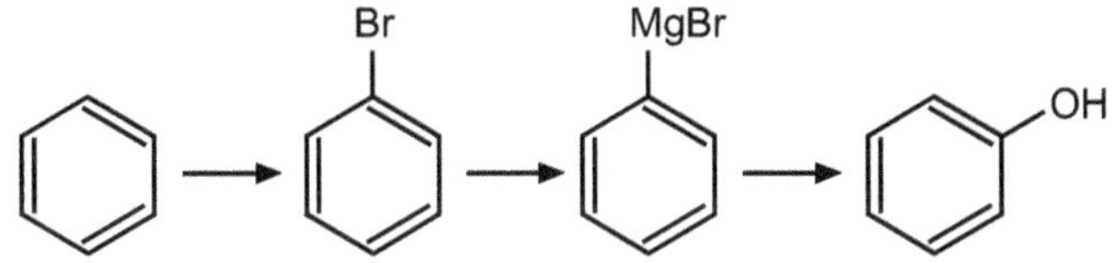

(ii)　benzene $\rightarrow$ nitrobenzene (NO_2) $\rightarrow$ aniline (NH_2) $\rightarrow$ acetanilide (NH–CO–CH_3)

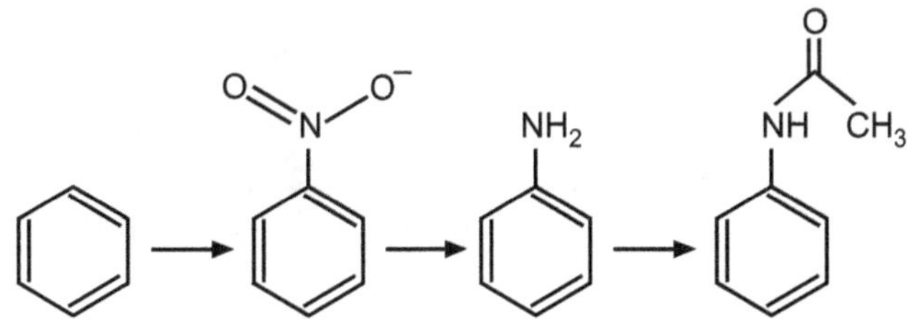

Q.17　Write short note on benzene and aromaticity.

Q.18　Predict the products:

　　　Acetanilide　+　Br_2 water　$\longrightarrow$　?

Q.19　Explain electrophilic aromatic substitution with respect to nitration and halogenations.

Q.20　Write a short note on orientation in monosubstituted benzene.

Q.21　Give reason: Nitrobenzene when reacted with nitrating mixture gives m-dinitrobenzene.

Q.22　Explain Friedel-Craft acylation.

Q.23　Describe mechanism of the nitration of benzene with conc. H_2SO_4 and conc. HNO_3. Explain the effect of substitution on nitration of benzene.

Q.24　Predict the products giving equation when

Toluene + HNO_3, H_2SO_4 $\longrightarrow$?

Q.25　Describe mechanism of nitration of benzene with conc. H_2SO_4 and conc. HNO_3. Enlist different nitrating reagents. Add a note on effect of substituents on nitration of benzene.

Q.26　How will you bring out the following conversions from benzene :

i)　m-Bromophenol

ii)　p-Bromoacetanilide

Q.27　List out electron releasing groups and electron withdrawing groups. Discuss in detail about the effect of substituent in electrophilic substitution of benzene.

Q.28　Write a note on nucleophilic aromatic substitution.

Q.29　Write a note on reactions involving benzyne intermediates.

❖ ❖ ❖

Chapter 10...

ALDEHYDES AND KETONES

10.1 INTRODUCTION

Aldehydes and ketones are simple organic compounds which contain a ***carbonyl group*** - a carbon-oxygen double bond ($-C=O$). The other two bonds of the carbon may be occupied by hydrogen or alkyl or aryl substituents. If at least one of these substituents is hydrogen, the compound is an **aldehyde**. If neither is hydrogen, the compound is a **ketone**.

Aldehydes

A ketone

Aldehydes and ketones are commonly found in nature. A few examples of aldehydes obtained from plant and animal sources are given below.

Cinnamaldehyde

Vanillin

Citral

Aldehydes from plants

Curvone

Camphor

Ketones from plants

Muscone

Testosterone

Ketone from animals

Male sex hormone-a ketone

Aldehydes (R–CHO) are attractive building blocks for the synthesis of molecules due to their ability to easily react with many nucleophiles. Because of their high chemical reactivity, aldehydes are important intermediates for the manufacture of resins, plasticizers, solvents, dyes, and pharmaceuticals.

Aromatic aldehydes (e.g. benzaldehyde, C_6H_5CHO) are also known. They undergo a number of chemical reactions that are not shown by aliphatic aldehydes.

10.2 NOMENCLATURE

Aldehydes are named by replacing -*ic* acid of the corresponding carboxylic acids by -aldehyde for the common names. The branching if present, is referred to as α-, β-, γ-, δ- etc. to indicate the point of attachment of the side chain/group; the α-carbon being the one to which the –CHO group is attached.

For IUPAC nomenclature, the longest chain carrying the –CHO group is chosen as the parent structure and is named by replacing the -*e* of the corresponding alkane by –*al*. The carbonyl carbon is always considered to be C-1 and the position of substituent is accordingly stated.

Numbering used in IUPAC names:

Symbols used in common names

Let us see some examples to understand the nomenclature:

Aliphatic aldehydes:

Formaldehyde
Methanal

Acetaldehyde
Ethanal

Butyraldehyde (common name)
Butanal (IUPAC name)

3-Methylpentanal

3-Methylpent-4-enal

4-Hydroxybutanal

Ketones:

In the IUPAC system of nomenclature, a characteristic suffix of *-one* is assigned to ketones. Location of the ketone carbonyl function is usually given by a location number. Chain numbering normally starts from the end nearest to the carbonyl group so that the carbonyl carbon group gets the lowest possible number. Very simple ketones, such as propanone and phenylethanone do not require a locator number, since there is only one possible site for a ketone carbonyl function.

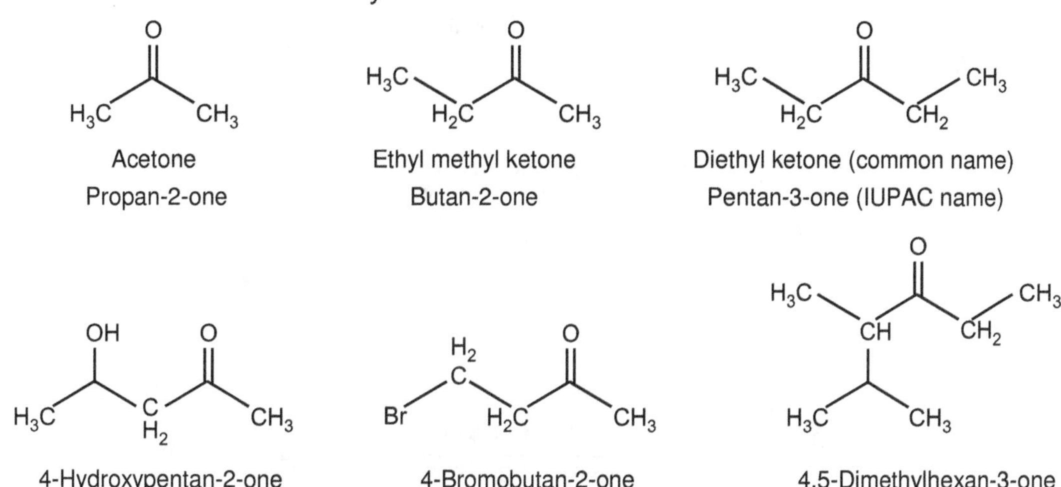

Acetone
Propan-2-one

Ethyl methyl ketone
Butan-2-one

Diethyl ketone (common name)
Pentan-3-one (IUPAC name)

4-Hydroxypentan-2-one

4-Bromobutan-2-one

4,5-Dimethylhexan-3-one

10.3 METHODS OF PREPARATION OF ALDEHYDES

Aldehydes can be prepared by the following methods:

1. From alcohols:

Oxidation of primary alcohols with a mild oxidizing reagent like pyridinium chlorochromate gives aldehydes. Other oxidizing reagents that can be used for oxidizing primary alcohols to aldehydes are: X_2, $K_2Cr_2O_7$, MnO_2, aluminium tertiary butoxide (Al(tBuO)$_3$) etc. The reaction can be written as:

$$RCH_2 - OH \xrightarrow{[O]} RCHO$$

Alcohol   Aldehyde

Example:

$$H_3C - CH_2OH \xrightarrow{[O]} CH_3CHO$$

Ethanol   Acetaldehyde

Dehydrogenation of primary alcohols by Cu or Ag at 300°C also yields aldehydes.

2. From acid chlorides:

Aliphatic and aromatic acid halides are partially reduced to give aliphatic and aromatic aldehydes respectively. Rosenmund reduction reduces an acid halide to an aldehyde using hydrogen gas over palladium-on-carbon poisoned with barium sulfate. Reduction with metal hydrides like aluminium hydride (AlH_3) and sodium borohydride ($NaBH_4$) in presence of pyridinium chlorochromate (PCC) also gives good yield.

$$RCOCl \text{ or } ArCOCl \xrightarrow[\text{Pd-BaSO}_4]{H_2} RCHO \text{ or } ArCHO \text{ (Rosenmund reduction)}$$

$$RCOCl \text{ or } ArCOCl \xrightarrow{NaBH_4, PCC} RCHO \text{ or } ArCHO$$

Acid chloride	Aldehyde

Example:

4-Nitrobenzoyl chloride	$\xrightarrow[\text{NaBH}_4, \text{ PCC, THF}]{H_2/\text{Pd-BaSO}_4 \text{ or}}$	4-Nitrobenzaldehyde

Butyryl chloride	$\xrightarrow[\text{NaBH}_4, \text{ PCC, THF}]{H_2/\text{Pd-BaSO}_4 \text{ or}}$	Butyraldehyde

3. **By hydration of alkynes:**

Ethyne on hydration with $HgSO_4$/dil. H_2SO_4 at 333 K forms acetaldehyde.

$$HC \equiv CH + H-OH \xrightarrow[333 \text{ K}]{Hg^{2+}/H^+} CH_2=C-H$$

$$\underset{\text{Ethyne}}{} \qquad \overset{|}{OH}$$

$$\Big\updownarrow \text{Isomerisation}$$

$$CH_3-C-H$$
$$\overset{||}{O}$$

Ethanal

4. **By reduction of ester:** Esters are reduced to aldehydes in the presence of DIBAL-H (Diisobutylaluminium hydride).

$$CH_3(CH_2)_3-\overset{\overset{O}{||}}{C}-OC_2H_5 \xrightarrow[\text{2. } H_2O]{\text{1. DIBAL-H}} CH_3(CH_2)_3-\overset{\overset{O}{||}}{C}-H$$

Ethyl pentanoate	Pentanal

5. Methods of preparation of only aromatic aldehydes are as follows:

(i) Oxidation of methylbenzenes: Following reagents can convert methylbenzenes to aromatic aldehydes.

$$Ar-CH_3 \xrightarrow[\text{i) CrO}_3,\ \text{CH}_3(\text{CO})_2\text{O ii) H}_2\text{O, H}_2\text{SO}_4]{\text{i) Cl}_2,\ \text{heat ii) CaCO}_3,\ \text{H}_2\text{O or}} Ar-CHO$$

Example:

Toluene $+ CrO_3 + (CH_3CO)_2O \xrightarrow{273\text{-}283K}$ [CH(OCOCH$_3$)$_2$] $\xrightarrow[\Delta]{H_3O^+}$ Benzaldehyde (CHO)

Toluene (CH$_3$) $\xrightarrow{Cl_2/h\nu}$ Benzyl dichloride (CHCl$_2$) $\xrightarrow[373\ K]{H_2O}$ Benzaldehyde (CHO)

Etard reaction uses chromyl chloride (CrO_2Cl_2) to convert toluene to benzaldehyde.

Toluene (CH$_3$) $+ CrO_2Cl_2 \xrightarrow{CS_2}$ Chromium complex [CH(OCrOHCl$_2$)$_2$] $\xrightarrow{H_3O^+}$ Benzaldehyde (CHO)

(ii) Gattermann-Koch reaction: Aromatic hydrocarbons and halobenzenes give this reaction.

Benzene $\xrightarrow[\text{Anhy. AlCl}_3/\text{CuCl}]{\text{CO, HCl}}$ Benzaldehyde (CHO)

Toluene (CH$_3$) $\xrightarrow[\text{Anhy. AlCl}_3/\text{CuCl}]{\text{CO, HCl}}$ Benzaldehyde (CHO)

Formylation with $Zn(CN)_2$ and HCl is called **Gattermann** reaction. It can be applied to alkylbenzenes, phenols and their ethers and many heterocyclic compounds.

(iii) Reimer-Teimann reaction: Phenols give phenolic aldehydes in this reaction:

Phenol (OH) $+ CHCl_3 \xrightarrow{OH^-}$ (O$^-$, CHO) $\xrightarrow{H^+}$ Phenolic aldehyde (OH, CHO)

This method is only useful for phenols and some heterocyclic compounds. The incoming –CHO group is directed to *ortho* position. If both *ortho* positions are blocked then it occupies the *para* position.

10.4 METHODS OF PREPARATION OF KETONES

Ketones are prepared by using the following methods :

1.   **By oxidation of secondary alcohols:** CrO_3 or $K_2Cr_2O_7$ oxidize secondary alcohols to give ketones. Also, on heating with Cu at 300°C secondary alcohols yield ketones.

Secondary alcohol $\xrightarrow[\text{or Cu, 300°C}]{CrO_3 \text{ or } K_2Cr_2O_7}$ Ketone

Example:

Propan-2-ol $\xrightarrow{K_2Cr_2O_7, \text{ dil } H_2SO_4}$ Propan-2-one

2.   **From acid chlorides:** Acid chlorides can be conveniently converted to ketones by the following reactions:

Friedel Crafts acylation: Aromatic ketones having a carbonyl group attached to an aromatic ring can be readily prepared using this method.

Benzene   Aryl or alkyl acid chloride $\xrightarrow{\text{Anhyd. } AlCl_3}$

Example:

Benzene $\xrightarrow{AlCl_3}$ Acetophenone

Acid chlorides undergo nucleophilic substitution reaction with dialkyl cadmium (R_2Cd) or dialkyl lithium. Dialkyl cadmium is prepared by reaction of cadmium chloride ($CdCl_2$) with Grignard reagent.

$$2R - Mg - X \; + \; CdCl_2 \longrightarrow R_2Cd + 2Mg(X)Cl$$

Grignard reagent

$$2R'-C-Cl \; + \; R_2Cd \longrightarrow 2R'-C-R \; + \; CdCl_2$$

(with $\|$ O below each carbonyl carbon)

Acid chloride

Example:

Butyryl chloride   n-Butyl isopropyl ketone

Acid chlorides on reaction with Grignard reagent give ketones.

$$R-CO-Cl + R'-Mg-X \text{ excess} \longrightarrow RCOR'$$

3. From carboxylic acids: Good yield of ketones can be obtained by treatment of lithium salt of a carboxylic acid (RCOOLi) with alkyl lithium reagent (RLi), followed by hydrolysis. As illustrated below, in the product, one alkyl group comes from the acid while the other comes from the alkyl lithium. R may be alkyl or aryl and R' may be aryl, primary, secondary or tertiary alkyl.

$$RCOOLi + R'Li \longrightarrow R-\underset{\underset{OLi}{|}}{\overset{\overset{OLi}{|}}{C}}-R' \xrightarrow{H_2O} R-\underset{\underset{O}{\|}}{C}-R'$$

Example :

$$C_6H_5COOLi + CH_3Li \longrightarrow C_6H_5-\underset{\underset{OLi}{|}}{\overset{\overset{OLi}{|}}{C}}-CH_3 \xrightarrow{H_2O} C_6H_5-\underset{\underset{O}{\|}}{C}-CH_3$$

Lithium benzoate   Methyl lithium   Acetophenone

4. From ethyl acetoacetate: It is a very useful method for preparing aliphatic and complicated ketones. In this synthesis, ethyl acetoacetate is reacted with an alkyl halide in the presence of a base to give an intermediate which on hydrolysis and decarboxylation gives the ketone.

$$H_3C-\underset{\underset{O}{\|}}{C}-CH_2-COOC_2H_5 \xrightarrow[\text{ii) RX}]{\text{i) Base}} H_3C-\underset{\underset{O}{\|}}{C}-\underset{\underset{R}{|}}{CH}-COOC_2H_5 \xrightarrow[-CO_2]{H^+ / \text{dil. } OH^-} H_3C-\underset{\underset{O}{\|}}{C}-CH_2-R$$

Ethyl acetoacetate   Ketone

5. Ozonolysis of alkenes: Compounds containing double bonds when treated with ozone at low temperature are converted to ozonides which can be decomposed with zinc and acetic acid or catalytic hydrogenation to give 2 moles of aldehyde, or 2 moles of ketone, or 1 mole of each, depending on the groups attached to alkene.

2-Methylbut-2-ene   Ozonide   Acetaldehyde   Acetone

10.5 PROPERTIES OF ALDEHYDES AND KETONES

(i) Physical :

Aldehydes and ketones are polar compounds due to the presence of polar carbonyl group. However, they are not capable of forming hydrogen bonds and thus show lower boiling points than alcohols and carboxylic acids having the corresponding number of carbon atoms. Lower aldehydes and ketones (number of carbon atoms less than five) are quite soluble in water. Aldehydes and ketones are soluble in the usual organic solvents like alcohol, chloroform, toluene etc.

The simplest aldehyde, formaldehyde is a gas with b.p. of −21°C. It is available either as an aqueous solution or as solid polymers i.e. paraformaldehyde, $(CH_2O)_n$ or trioxane, $(CH_2O)_3$. Acetaldehyde has a b.p. of 20°C and is available as a trimer, paraldehyde which can be converted back to acetaldehyde by heating with acid.

Aldehydes are very prone to oxidation and thus must be stored with great care.

(ii) Chemical:

Nucleophilic addition to the carbonyl carbon is a characteristic of this class of compounds and most of the reactions shown by aldehydes and ketones follow this mechanism. Aldehydes and ketones undergo nucleophilic addition reaction due to presence of the carbonyl group which contains oxygen doubly bonded to carbon. Oxygen being very electronegative in comparison to the carbon pulls the *pi* electrons towards it. This creates an electron deficiency at the carbonyl carbon while oxygen becomes electron rich. This polarized group is flat and is thus easily accessible to attack by reagents from either side. This property of the group makes the molecules very reactive towards nucleophilic reagents (or bases).

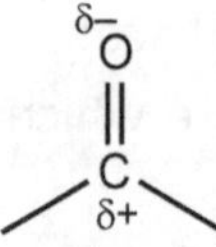

Aldehydes are more reactive than ketones. Both steric and electronic factors can be used to explain this difference. During the transition state, ketones having two alkyl groups show greater crowding as compared to aldehydes that contain only one alkyl group. Also, since the alkyl groups are electron releasing, they destabilize the transition state by increasing the negative charge on the oxygen.

Aromatic aldehydes and ketones are less reactive than their aliphatic counterparts. Since aryl ring is electron withdrawing it may be expected to stabilize the transition state by decreasing the charge over oxygen, thus assisting its conversion to product. However, the resonance effect of these groups stabilizes the reactants even more so that they become less receptive to the nucleophile and hence less active.

Less crowding in aldehydes   Crowding in aldehydes

Nucleophilic addition reaction to carbonyl compounds is enhanced by presence of acids. The hydrogen ion of the acid gets attached to the oxygen. Oxygen is then able to pull the *pi* electrons without getting negatively charged, hence stabilizing the transition state and thus decreasing the $E_{act.}$ of the reaction. Thus acids (sometimes Lewis acids also) are used to catalyze the nucleophilic addition reaction of aldehydes and ketones. The mechanism is clearly explained in the section on reactions of aldehydes and ketones.

10.6 REACTIONS OF ALDEHYDES AND KETONES

1. Oxidation:

Aldehydes can be readily oxidized to carboxylic acids using mild oxidizing agents while ketones require vigorous conditions. This is because aldehydes contain hydrogen that can be abstracted during oxidation while ketones do not have any hydrogen attached to the carbonyl carbon.

Typical oxidizing agents for aldehydes include either potassium permanganate ($KMnO_4$) or potassium dichromate ($K_2Cr_2O_7$) in acid solution and Tollen's reagent (ammoniacal silver nitrate).

Benzaldehyde   Benzoic acid

Cyclohexanecarbaldehyde   Cyclohexanoic acid

Silver ions are very mild oxidizing agents but require a basic media for the reaction. Ammonia is added to the reagent to prevent precipitation of silver oxide. This reagent is called Tollen's reagent. As the oxidation of aldehydes proceeds, the silver ions get reduced to give free silver which forms a mirror along the wall of the test tube. This reaction is useful identification test that distinguishes aldehydes from ketones and is also referred to as "silver mirror test".

$$R - \overset{\overset{\displaystyle O}{\|}}{C} - H \quad + \quad 2Ag(NH_3)_2(OH)_2 \longrightarrow R - \overset{\overset{\displaystyle O}{\|}}{C} - O^-NH_4^+ \quad + \quad 3NH_3 + 2Ag + H_2O$$

Aldehyde   Tollen's reagent   A carboxylate salt   Silver

$$R - \overset{\overset{\displaystyle O}{\|}}{C} - R \quad + \quad 2Ag\,(NH_3)_2(OH)_2 \longrightarrow \text{No reaction}$$

Ketone   Tollen's reagent

Ketones can be oxidized only with the help of a strong oxidizing agent under vigorous conditions. Peroxyacids like peroxybenzoic acid oxidize ketone to acid. During the reaction, a C – C bond is broken to yield the corresponding acids.

Site of bond breaking

Heptan-4-one
(Symmetrical ketone)

[O]

Butyric acid   +   Propionic acid

Octan-4-one
(Unsymmetrical ketone)

[O]

Bond breaks at the site containing more number of alkyl groups (Poff's rule)

Butyric acid

Ketones can be smoothly oxidized by hypohalide in the haloform reaction.

$$\underset{\text{Ketone}}{R-\overset{\overset{\displaystyle O}{\|}}{C}-CH_3} \xrightarrow[\text{(ii) } H^+]{\text{(i) } X_2,\ OH^-} \underset{\text{Carboxylic acid}}{R-COOH} \ + \ \underset{\text{Haloform}}{CHX_3}$$

Example :

$$\underset{\text{Propan-2-one}}{H_3C-\overset{\overset{\displaystyle O}{\|}}{C}-CH_3} \xrightarrow[\text{(ii) } H^+]{\text{(i) } I_2,\ OH^-} \underset{\text{Acetic acid}}{H_3C-COOH} \ + \ \underset{\text{Iodoform}}{CHI_3}$$

The above reaction is also a confirmatory test for ketones.

2. Reduction:

(a) Reduction to alcohols:

Aldehydes are reduced to primary alcohols while the ketones are reduced to secondary alcohols. The reduction can be carried out catalytically (H_2 and Ni/Pt/Pd) as well as chemically (LiAlH$_4$ or NaBH$_4$).

$$\underset{\text{Aldehyde}}{R-\overset{\overset{\displaystyle O}{\|}}{C}-H} \xrightarrow[\text{LiAlH}_4 \text{ or NaBH}_4]{\overset{H_2 \text{ and Ni/Pt/Pd}}{\text{or}}} \underset{1^\circ \text{ alcohol}}{R-CH_2OH}$$

$$\underset{\text{Ketone}}{R-\overset{\overset{\displaystyle O}{\|}}{C}-R} \xrightarrow[\text{LiAlH}_4 \text{ or NaBH}_4]{\overset{H_2 \text{ and Ni/Pt/Pd}}{\text{or}}} \underset{2^\circ \text{ alcohol}}{R-\overset{\overset{\displaystyle OH}{|}}{C}H-R}$$

Reduction using metal hydrides like LiAlH$_4$ proceed through the nucleophilic addition reaction. The hydride ion H^- is first transferred from the metal to the electron deficient carbon followed by attachment of the metal to the carbonyl oxygen. Finally acid releases the reduced molecule from the complex.

Reduction using LiAlH$_4$

Reduction using NaBH$_4$

Example:

Cyclohexanone　　　　　　　　　　　Cyclohexanol

Butyraldehyde　　　　　　　　　　　Butan-1-ol

LiAlH$_4$ or NaBH$_4$ are selective reducing agents as they do not reduce carbon-carbon double bonds present in the substrate aldehyde or ketone and hence are called selective reducing agents. LiAlH$_4$ however is able to reduce groups like NO$_2$, CN and COOR while NaBH$_4$ does not affect these groups.

Complex metal hydride reactant like 9-borabicyclo-[3.3.1]-nonane (9-BBN) reduces aldehyde selectively in the presence of a ketone. This is called a chemoselective reduction. The same reagent is also regioselective. That is, if an aldehyde is containing a C-C double bond also, then 9-BBN reduces only the carbonyl group leaving the double bond intact.

(b) Reduction to hydrocarbons:

Clemmensen reduction (involving amalgated zinc and conc. HCl) and Wolff-Kishner reduction (involving hydrazine and a strong base like KOH or potassium tert-butoxide) can reduce aldehydes and ketones to hydrocarbons.

(i) Clemmensen reduction:

Ketone　　　　　　　　　　　Hydrocarbon

The reduction takes place at the surface of the zinc catalyst. In this reaction, alcohols are not proposed to be the intermediate because if the corresponding alcohols are subjected to the same reaction conditions they do not form alkanes. Since the reaction is carried out in strongly acidic media, only acid stable aldehydes and ketones can be reduced by this method. The following mechanism has been proposed to explain the reduction:

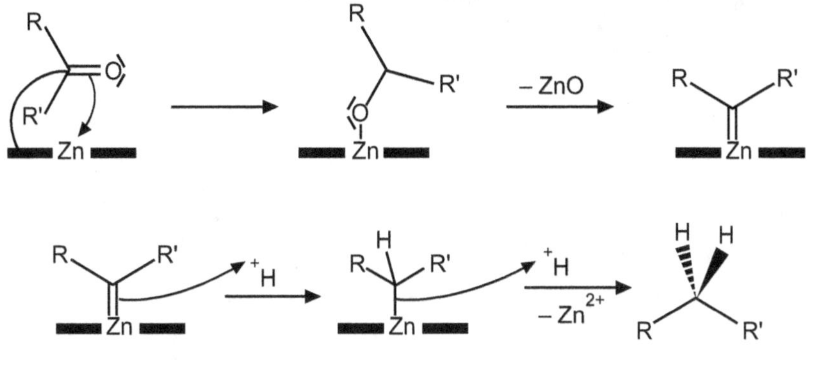

Example:

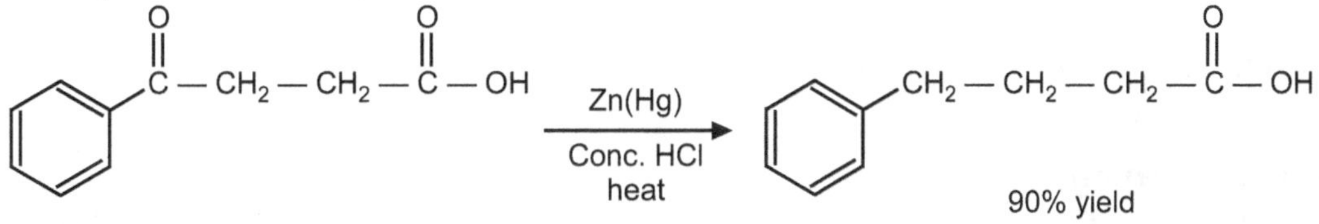

4-Oxo-4-phenylbutanoic acid   4-Phenylbutanoic acid

This method is the least preferred method of reduction compared to Wolff-Kishner and desulfurization methods.

(ii) Wolff-Kishner reduction:

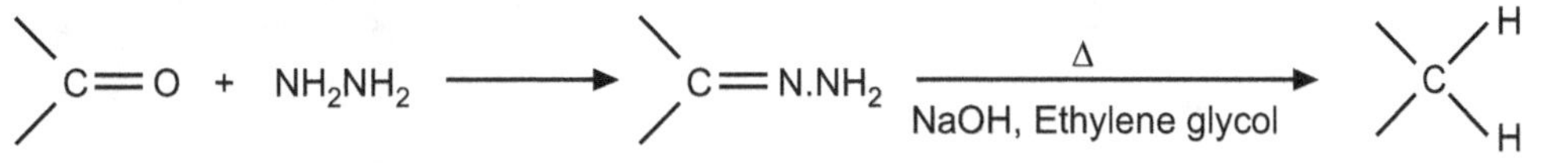

Aldehyde/Ketone   Hydrazine   Hydrazone   Hydrocarbon

The Wolff-Kishner reduction is useful for the reduction of carbonyl compounds that are stable in strong base. The mechanism involved is:

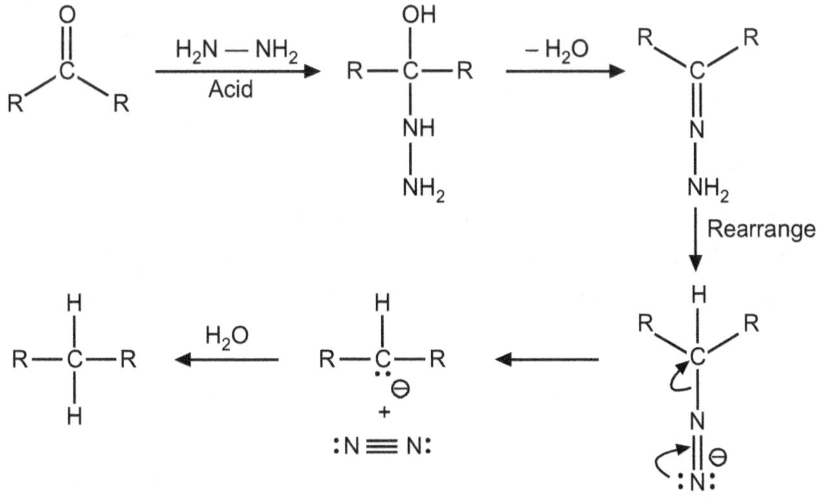

Example:

Isatin

75% yield

In the above reaction, sodium ethaoxide ($NaOCH_2CH_3$) has been used as the base and ethanol as a solvent.

(iii) Desulfurization:

Aldehydes and ketones can form thioacetals and thioketals respectively on reaction with excess thiol. These compounds then can be reduced using Raney Ni to give hydrocarbons.

Pentan-3-one

Raney Ni, H_2

Pentane

(iv) Cannizzaro reaction:

This is a special type of reaction involving self-oxidation and reduction by aldehydes not containing any α-hydrogen to yield a mixture of an alcohol and salt of a carboxylic acid. This reaction takes place in the presence of aqueous or alcoholic sodium hydroxide.

Formaldehyde   Methanol   Sodium formate

$$2 \; \underset{C_6H_5 \quad H}{\overset{O}{\|}} \quad \xrightarrow{\text{50\% NaOH}} \quad \underset{C_6H_5}{H_2C-OH} \;+\; \underset{C_6H_5}{\overset{O}{\|}}C-\overset{-\;+}{ONa}$$

Benzaldehyde   Benzyl alcohol   Sodium benzoate

Crossed Cannizzaro reaction: A mixture of two different aldehydes will produce all the possible products. This type of reaction is called a crossed Cannizzaro reaction. However, an interesting fact to note is that if one of the two aldehydes is formaldehyde, almost exclusive formation of sodium formate and alcohol corresponding to the other aldehyde is produced. This type of reaction is called a crossed Cannizzaro reaction.

$$\underset{\substack{\text{4-Methoxybenzaldehyde}\\\text{(Anisaldehyde)}}}{\overset{CHO}{\bigcirc}\!\!-\!OCH_3} \;+\; HCHO \xrightarrow{\text{35\% NaOH}} \underset{\text{4-Methoxybenzyl alcohol}}{\overset{CH_2OH}{\bigcirc}\!\!-\!OCH_3} \;+\; HCOO^-Na^+$$

Mechanism of Cannizzaro reaction can be written as follows:

Step 1 :

$$\underset{Ar}{\overset{H}{\diagdown}}C=O \;\; \overset{\text{OH}^-}{\rightleftharpoons} \;\; H-\underset{\underset{(A)}{Ar}}{\overset{\overset{O^-}{|}}{C}}-OH$$

In this step the hydroxide ion gets added to give an intermediate (A).

Step 2 :

$$\underset{Ar \quad H}{\overset{O}{\|}} \;+\; H-\underset{\underset{(A)}{Ar}}{\overset{\overset{O^-}{|}}{C}}-OH \longrightarrow H-\underset{Ar}{\overset{\overset{O^-}{|}}{C}}-H \;+\; \underset{Ar}{\overset{O}{\|}}C-OH$$

$$\downarrow +H^+ \qquad\qquad \downarrow -H^+$$

$$\underset{\underset{Ar}{|}}{\overset{\overset{OH}{|}}{H-C-H}} \;+\; \underset{\underset{Ar}{|}}{\overset{O}{\|}}C-O^-$$

                                        Alcohol   Acid

The intermediate (A) gets added to a second molecule of aldehydes to give the products.

3. Addition of hydrogen cyanide:

Hydrogen cyanide adds to the carbonyl group of aldehydes and ketones to give cyanohydrin. The addition follows the nucleophilic addition to carbonyl group mechanism. This reaction is useful in the synthesis of α-hydroxyacids which are obtained after hydrolysis of cyanohydrins. The source of cyanide can be potassium cyanide, sodium cyanide or trimethylsilyl cyanide. With aromatic aldehydes such as benzaldehyde, the benzoin condensation is a competing reaction.

Ketone   Cyanohydrin   2-Hydroxy acid

Example :

Acetaldehyde   2-Hydroxypropanenitrile

Acetone   2-Hydroxy-2-methyl propanenitrile

4. Addition of ammonia derivatives:

Aldehydes and ketones react with primary amines to form a class of compounds called imines. The mechanism involved is nucleophilic addition to carbonyl group.

The amino group being nucleophilic due to unshared pair of electrons on the nitrogen, attacks the electron deficient carbonyl carbon.

A proton is transferred from the nitrogen to the oxygen anion.

The hydroxy group is then protonated to yield an oxonium ion, which is a good leaving group.

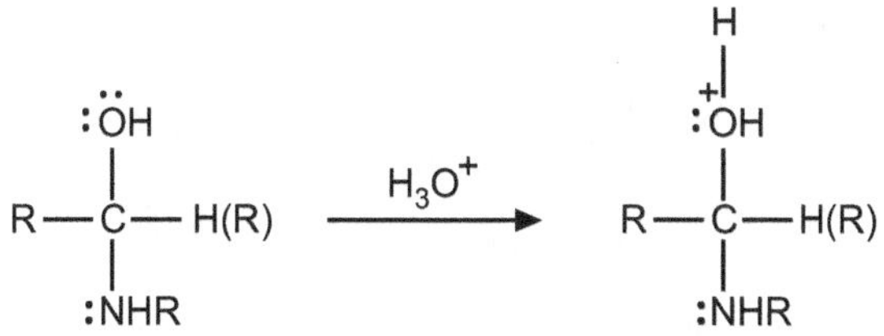

An unshared pair of electrons on the nitrogen migrates toward the positive oxygen, causing the loss of a water molecule.

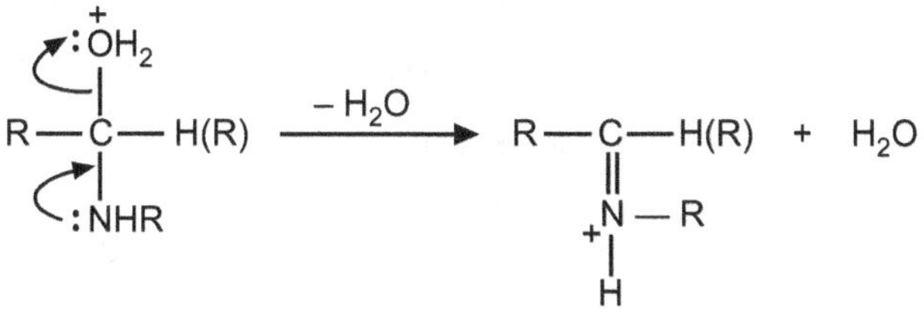

A proton from the positively charged nitrogen is transferred to water, leading to the imine's formation.

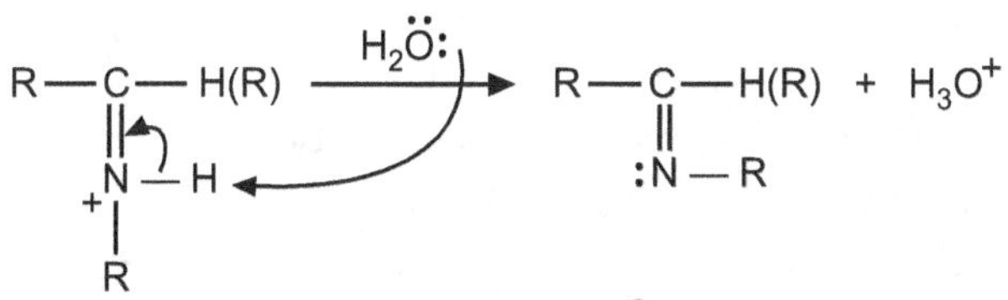

Imines

Imines of aldehydes are relatively stable while those of ketones are unstable. Derivatives of imines that form stable compounds with aldehydes and ketones include phenylhydrazine, 2, 4–dinitrophenylhydrazine, hydroxylamine, and semicarbazide. The reactions can be written as:

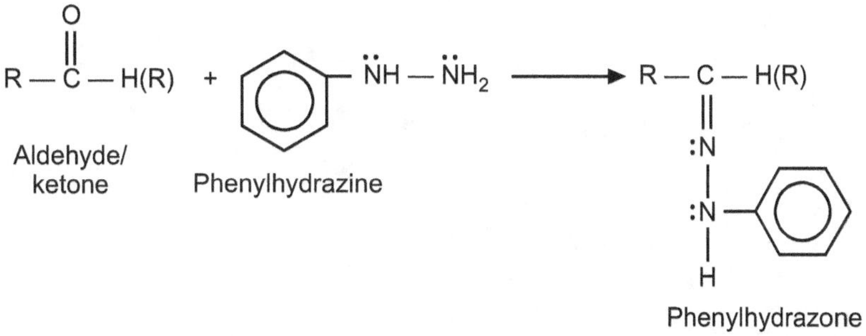

Aldehyde/ketone + Phenylhydrazine $\longrightarrow$ Phenylhydrazone

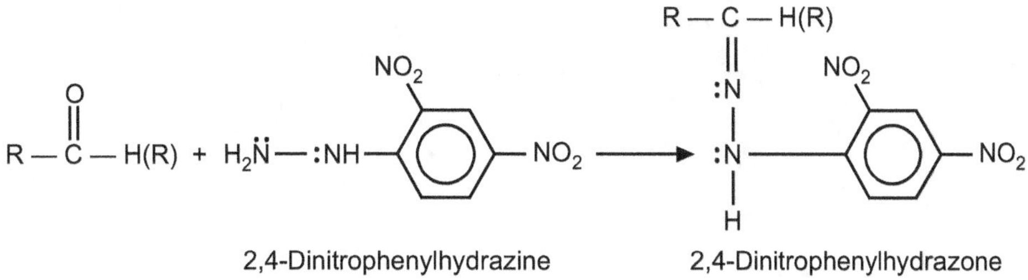

2,4-Dinitrophenylhydrazine $\longrightarrow$ 2,4-Dinitrophenylhydrazone

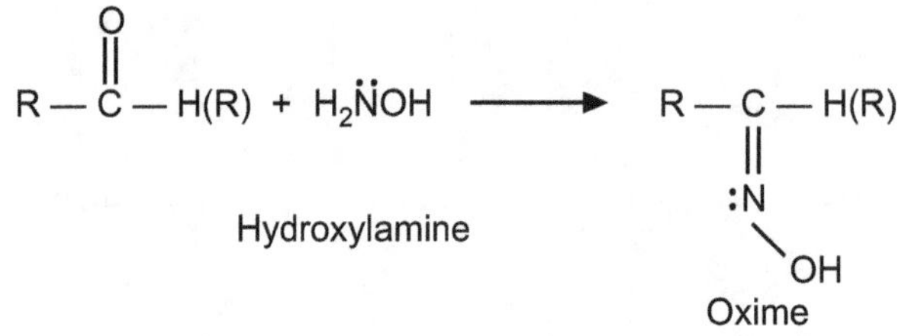

$$R-\overset{\overset{\displaystyle O}{\|}}{C}-H(R) \; + \; H_2\ddot{N}OH \longrightarrow R-\underset{\underset{\displaystyle OH}{|}}{\underset{\displaystyle :N}{\overset{\displaystyle \|}{C}}}-H(R)$$

Hydroxylamine

Oxime

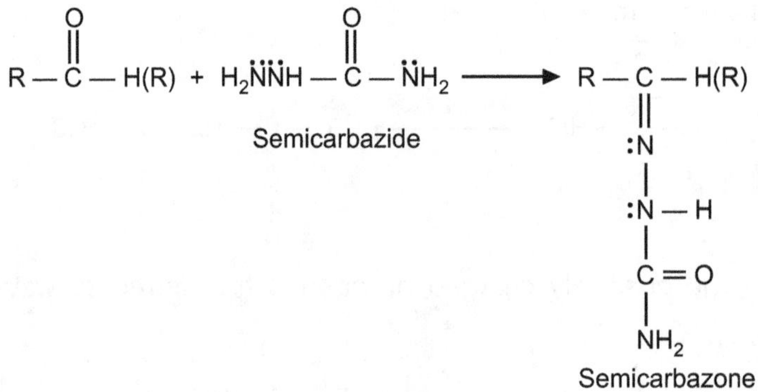

$$R-\overset{\overset{\displaystyle O}{\|}}{C}-H(R) \; + \; H_2\ddot{N}\ddot{N}H-\overset{\overset{\displaystyle O}{\|}}{C}-\ddot{N}H_2 \longrightarrow R-C-H(R)$$

Semicarbazide

Semicarbazone

Oximes, 2, 4-dinitrophenylhydrazones, and semicarbazones are often used in qualitative organic chemistry as derivatives for aldehydes and ketones.

Imines formed from secondary amines can lose a proton from the α-carbon to form an **enamine**.

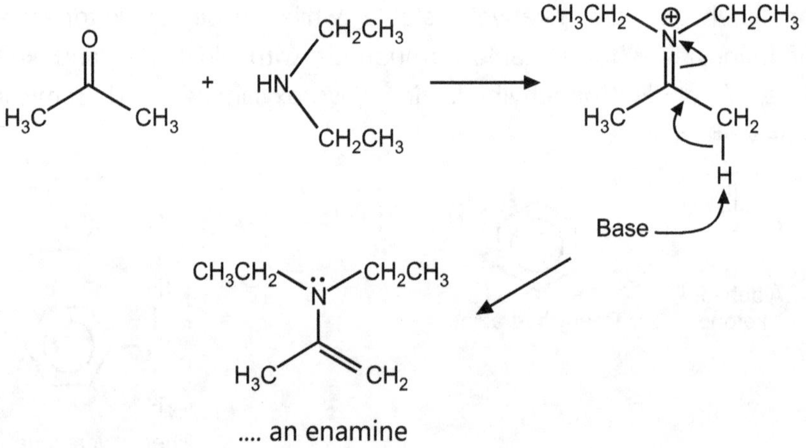

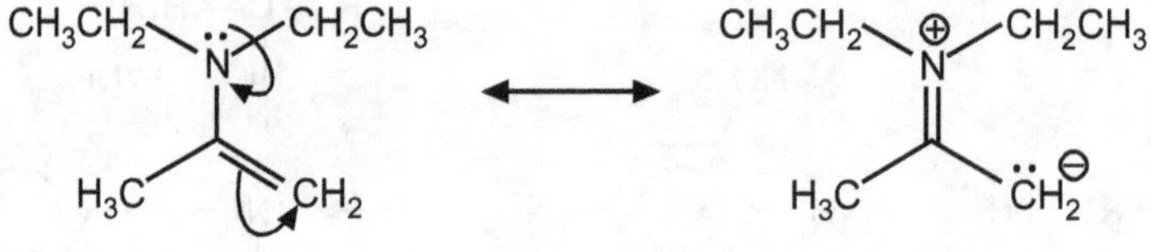

.... an enamine

5. Addition of sodium bisulphite (NaHSO$_3$):

Aldehydes and ketones undergo addition of NaHSO$_3$ through the usual nucleophilic addition mechanism to give bisulphite product.

$$\text{C=O} + \text{NaHSO}_3 \rightleftharpoons \text{(intermediate)} \xrightarrow{\text{Proton transfer}} \text{(bisulphite addition compound)}$$

Bisulphite addition compound (crystalline)

Example :

$$CH_3-CHO + Na^+ HSO_3^- \longrightarrow CH_3-C(OH)(H)-SO_3^- Na^+$$

Acetaldehyde → Sodium 1-hydroxyethanesulfonate

$$CH_3-CO-CH_3 + Na^+ HSO_3^- \longrightarrow CH_3-C(OH)(CH_3)-SO_3^- Na^+$$

Acetone → Sodium 2-hydroxypropane-2-sulfonate

6. Addition of water:

Aldehydes can add water to give stable hydrates.

$$CH_3-CO-H \xrightarrow[H^+]{H_2O} CH_3-C(OH)(H)-OH$$

Acetaldehyde → Hydrate (ethane-1,1-diol)

The reaction can be catalyzed using small quantities of acids or bases, as addition of water follows nucleophilic addition mechanism. The mechanism can be written as:

Oxonium ion

Water, acting as a nucleophile, is attracted to the partially positive carbon of the carbonyl group, generating an oxonium ion. The oxonium ion liberates a hydrogen ion that is picked up by the oxygen anion in an acid - base reaction.

7. Addition of alcohols:

Aldehydes and ketones undergo nucleophilic addition reaction with alcohols in the presence of acid to give acetals and ketals respectively. The proton from acid protonates the carbonyl oxygen followed by nucleophilic attack of the alcohol. The intermediate thus formed loses a proton to form a hemiacetal (or hemiketal). The hemiacetal undergoes protonation and loss of water to give an oxocarbonium ion, which undergoes attack by another mole of alcohol and loss of a proton to give the final product. The complete process of acetal and ketal formation is a reversible process. Thus, acetals and ketals can convert back to aldehydes and ketones respectively in the presence of acids. However, they are stable in basic medium.

Examples :

8. Addition of ylides (the Wittig reaction):

Ketones and aldehydes react with phosphorus ylides to form alkenes. Ylide is a neutral dipolar molecule containing a formally negatively charged atom (usually a carbanion) directly attached to a heteroatom with a formal positive charge (usually nitrogen, phosphorus or sulfur). Phosphorus ylides are prepared by reacting a phosphine with an alkyl halide, followed by treatment with a strong base like butyl lithium (buLi).

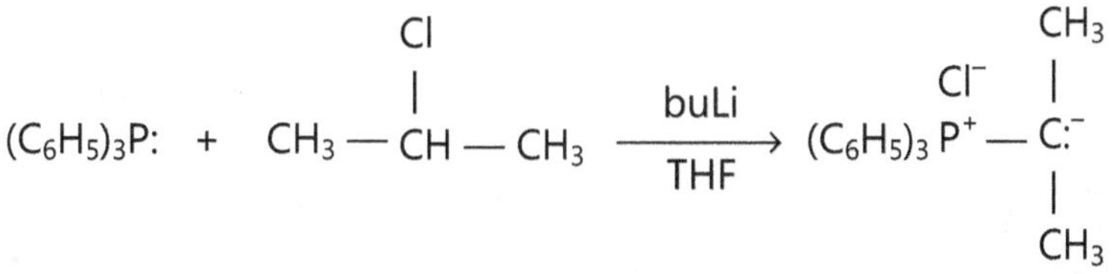

$$(C_6H_5)_3P: \ + \ CH_3-\underset{\underset{Cl}{|}}{CH}-CH_3 \xrightarrow[THF]{buLi} (C_6H_5)_3 \ \overset{Cl^-}{P^+}-\underset{\underset{CH_3}{|}}{\overset{\overset{CH_3}{|}}{C:^-}}$$

Triphenylphosphine   2-Chloropropane   Ylide

The mechanism of the Wittig reaction involves nucleophilic addition of ylide to the carbonyl group to give an intermediate betaine, which decomposes to give the alkene and triphenylphosphine oxide. The Wittig reaction works well to prepare mono-, di- and tri-substituted alkenes; tetra-substituted alkenes cannot be prepared by this method.

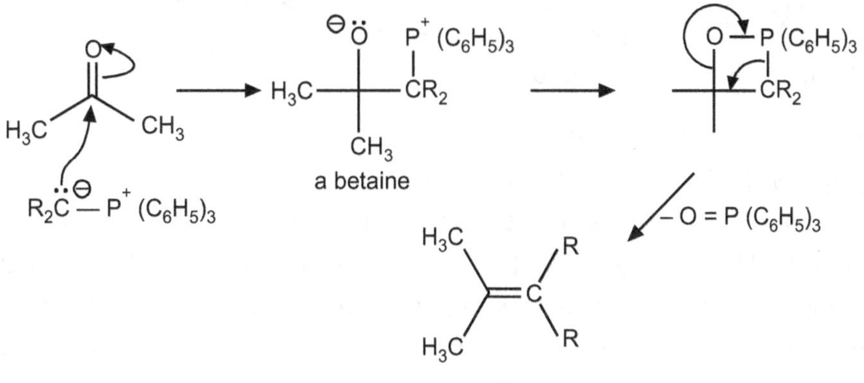

a betaine

$-O = P (C_6H_5)_3$

Alkene

Example:

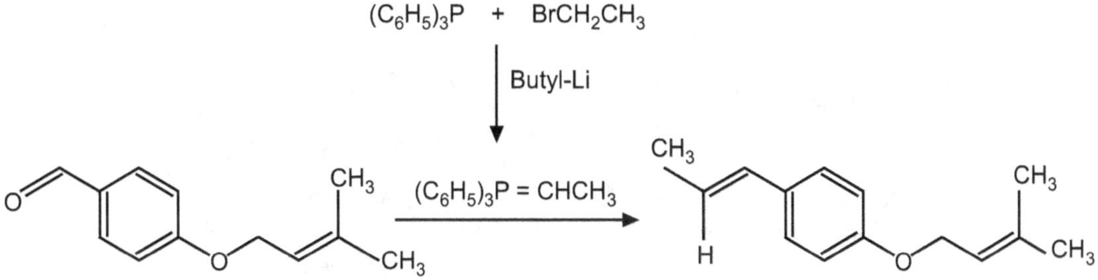

$$(C_6H_5)_3P \ + \ BrCH_2CH_3$$

Butyl-Li

$(C_6H_5)_3P = CHCH_3$

Feniculun

9. Addition of Grignard reagent:

Grignard reagents react with formaldehyde to produce primary alcohols, all other aldehydes to produce secondary alcohols and ketones to produce tertiary alcohols.

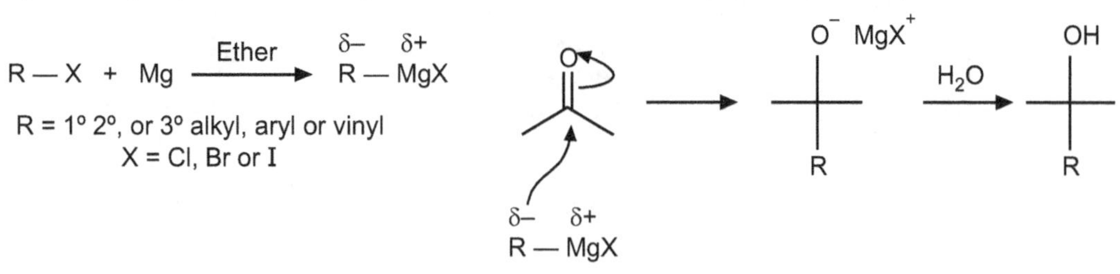

$$R-X \ + \ Mg \xrightarrow{Ether} \overset{\delta-}{R}-\overset{\delta+}{MgX}$$

R = 1° 2°, or 3° alkyl, aryl or vinyl
X = Cl, Br or I

$\overset{\delta-}{R}-\overset{\delta+}{MgX}$

Example :

Benzaldehyde   + CH_3Br $\xrightarrow[\text{2. }H_3O^+]{\text{1. Mg/ether}}$ α-Methyl benzyl alcohol

Bromobenzene   +   Acetone $\xrightarrow[\text{2. }H_3O^+]{\text{1. Mg/ether}}$ α,α-Dimethyl benzyl alcohol

10. Reactions involving alpha-hydrogen:

Hydrogen atoms attached to carbons alpha (adjacent) to the carbonyl group are referred to as α hydrogens, and the carbon to which they are bonded is an α carbon. These hydrogens are weakly acidic (K_a 10^{-19} to 10^{-20}) due to electron withdrawing nature of the adjacent carbonyl group and can react with strong bases to form anions. In ethanal, there is one α carbon and three α hydrogens, while in acetone there are two α carbons and six α hydrogens.

Ethanal

Acetone

The anion formed by the loss of an α hydrogen can be resonance stabilized because of the mobility of π electrons that are on the adjacent carbonyl group. This resonance creates two resonance structures - an enol and a keto form. In most cases, the keto form is more stable.

Keto   Enol

The following reactions involve the formation of carbanion as explained above.

(i) Aldol condensation:

Aldehydes having α hydrogens react with themselves in the presence of a dilute aqueous acid or base resulting in the formation of β-hydroxy aldehydes or aldols. Such reactions are called aldol condensation reactions. Aldols are compounds that contain both an aldehyde and alcohol functional group.

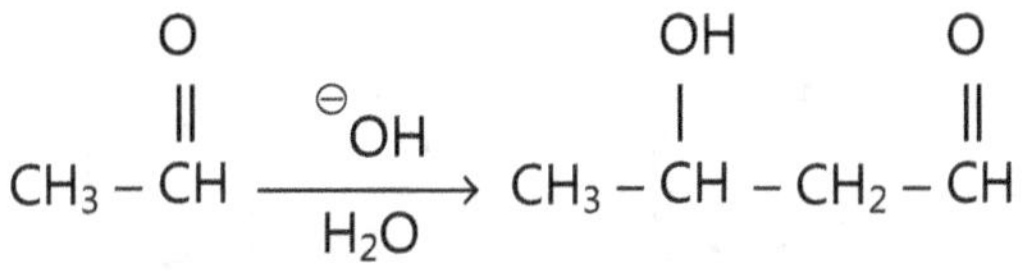

$$CH_3-CH\overset{O}{\overset{\|}{}} \xrightarrow[\ H_2O\ ]{\ ^{\ominus}OH\ } CH_3-\overset{OH}{\overset{|}{C}H}-CH_2-\overset{O}{\overset{\|}{C}}H$$

Ethanal   3-Hydroxybutanal

Mechanism :

Base catalyzed aldol condensation:

Step 1: The relatively acidic hydrogen on the α-carbon is deprotonated by a base to form the enolate.

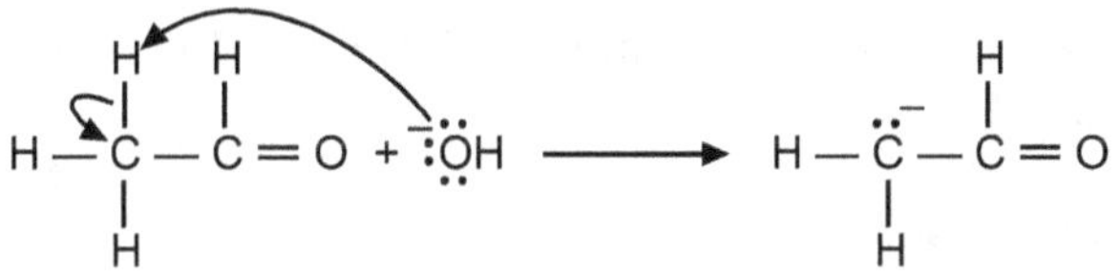

Step 2: The enolate reacts as a carbon nucleophile and undergoes addition at the carbonyl group of another aldehyde molecule.

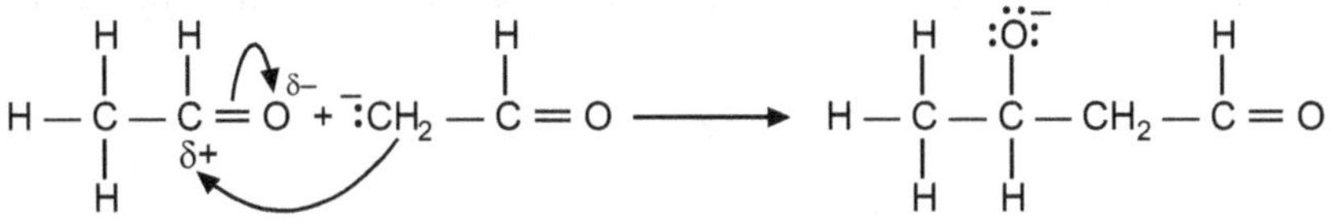

Step 3: The alkoxide ion produced above gains a proton from water to give the product, i.e. an aldol.

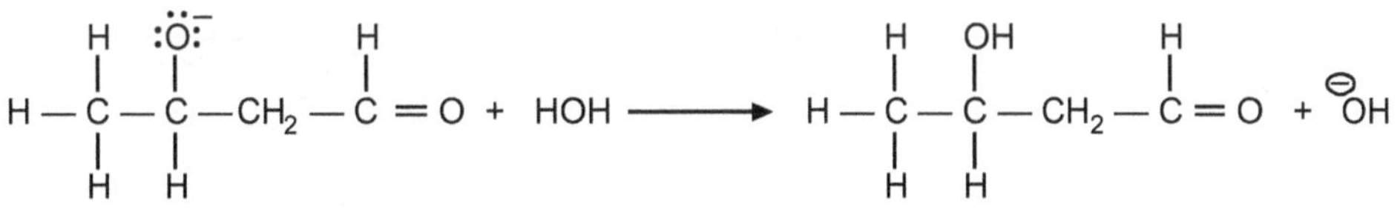

The aldol when heated in a base can undergo dehydration (removal of water molecule) to give an α, β-unsaturated aldehyde.

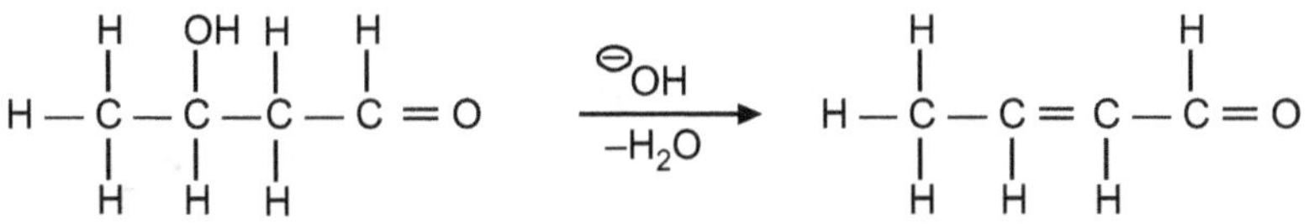

α, β-unsaturation aldehyde
(Elimination product)

Ketones also undergo base catalysed aldol condensation though not as readily as aldehydes. The following reaction shows aldol condensation involving acetone, a symmetrical ketone.

Acetone

Enolate ion of acetone

Second molecule of acetone

'Aldol' product form acetone 4-hydroxy -4-methylpentan-2-one

Whether a reaction will give an aldol or the elimination product is dependent partly on the conditions (the more vigorous conditions like stronger base, higher temperatures, longer reaction time) tend to give the elimination product and partly on the structure of the reagents (some combinations are easy to stop at the aldol stage, while some almost always give the elimination product).

Acid catalyzed aldol condensation:

Aldol condensation can also be acid catalyzed. In this case dehydration usually follows. Mechanism involves first the protonation of carbonyl oxygen followed by attack of this positively charged species at the α carbon of the enol form of the other molecule.

"Mixed" or "crossed" aldol condensations occur when two different molecules containing carbonyl groups are combined. If two different aldehydes are used, a mixture of four products is generally obtained. Thus, such type of reaction is not useful synthetically. However, a mixed aldol condensation is practical if one of the compounds has no α hydrogens – thus only one enol or enolate is generated and so there is only a single nucleophile formed. Generally, the mixed aldol reaction is performed between an aldehyde that has no α-hydrogens, and a ketone. Thus, the nucleophile is generated only from the ketone. The aldehyde is usually more reactive towards nucleophiles than the ketone, further reducing the possibility of the ketone undergoing unwanted self-condensation. This reaction is also called *Claisen-Schmidt reaction*. Reactions between two different ketones are rarely performed.

Aldehyde with no   Ketone with   Aldol condensation
α-hydrogen α-hydrogen   product

Similar to all reversible steps in aldol condensation, the dehydration step of an aldol condensation is also reversible in the presence of acid and base catalysts. Thus, on heating with aqueous solutions of strong acids or bases, many α, β-unsaturated carbonyl compounds fragment into smaller aldehydes or ketones in a process known as **retro-aldol reaction.**

Examples :

Acetone   4-Methylpent-3-en-2-one

Butanal   2-Ethylhex-2-enal

Acetophenone   1,3-Diphenylbut-2-en-1-one

(ii) Nitroaldol reaction:

In the nitroaldol reaction, condensation between a nitroalkane and an aldehyde or a ketone yields a nitroalcohol that can undergo dehydration to yield a nitroalkene. It is also known as Henry reaction.

Nitroalkene

Dehydration

Nitroalkane   Ketone/   β-Nitro   α-Nitro
                 Aldehyde   alcohol   ketone

Base solvent

Oxidation
if R_2 = H

Reduction

β-Amino
alcohol

The Henry reaction begins with the deprotonation of the nitroalkane on the α-carbon position forming a resonance stabilized anion. This is followed by alkylation of the nitroalkane with the carbonyl containing substrate to form a diastereomeric β-nitro alkoxide. The protonation of the alkoxide by the previously protonated base will yield the respective β-nitro alcohol as a product. All the steps in this reaction are reversible.

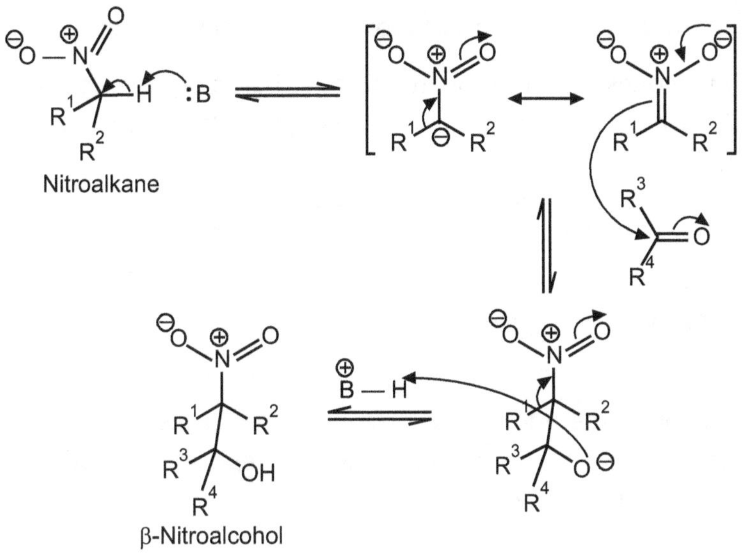

Nitroalkane

β-Nitroalcohol

(iii) Halogenation of aldehydes and ketones:

Aldehydes and ketones can be halogenated in the α position with bromine, chlorine or the iodine in the presence of an acid or a base. The reaction is not successful with fluorine. The purpose of acid or base catalyst is to provide a small amount of enol or enolate. The mechanism can be written as:

Acid catalyzed mechanism:

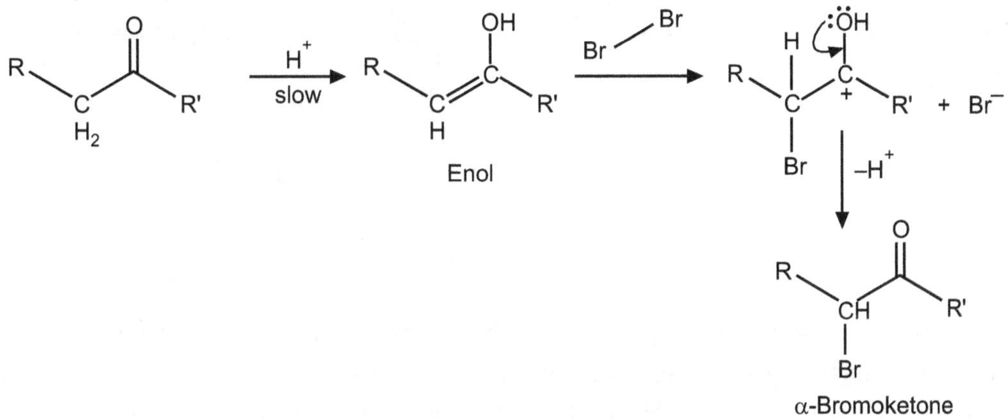

Enol

α-Bromoketone

The first step involves formation of enol which then attacks bromine. Proton is then lost to give α-bromo derivative.

Base catalyzed mechanism: Removal of α hydrogen by base leads to the formation of enolate which then attacks bromine to give the α-bromo derivative

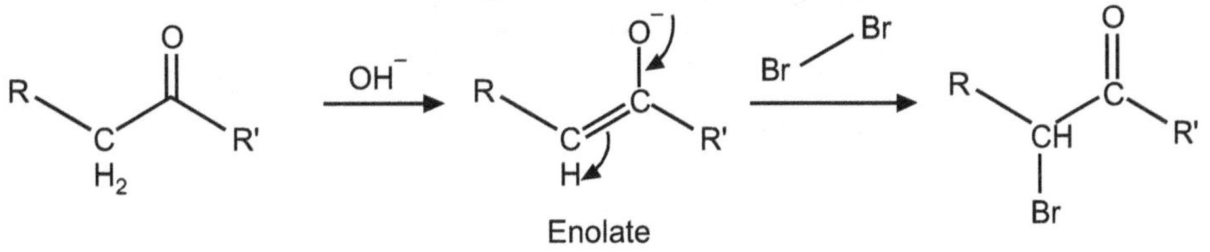

Enolate

(iv) Homologation of aldehydes and ketones with diazomethane:

Aldehydes and ketones can be converted to their homologs with diazomethane. Epoxide is formed as a side reaction. The reaction is a rearrangement reaction.

Aldehyde/Ketone   Diazomethane

Mechanism:

The first step involves the addition of diazomethane to the carbonyl group to form an intermediate called betaine. Betaine can undergo either epoxide formation or rearrangement to give the homologous aldehyde or ketone.

Ketone   Diazomethane   Betaine   Homologous ketone

Epoxide

Aldehydes give fairly good yield of methyl ketones; that is, hydrogen migrates in preference to alkyl. However, addition of methanol increases the yield of aldehyde in preference to methyl ketone. In aldehydes containing an electron withdrawing group, the side reaction, that is, formation of epoxides is increased and ketones are formed in smaller amounts. Cyclic ketones can also undergo this reaction in the following manner.

Cyclopentanone   Cyclohexanone

11. Haloform reaction:

The haloform reaction involves the reaction of a methyl ketone with chlorine, bromine, or iodine in the presence of hydroxide ions to give a carboxylate ion and a haloform (trihalomethane). Other than acetaldehyde, no other aldehyde gives this reaction. When the halogen used is iodine, the product iodoform is yellow and has a characteristic odour. This reaction has been used in qualitative analysis to indicate the presence of a methyl ketone. Haloform reaction can be used for the oxidative demethylation of methyl ketones if the other substituent on the carbonyl groups has no enolizable α-protons.

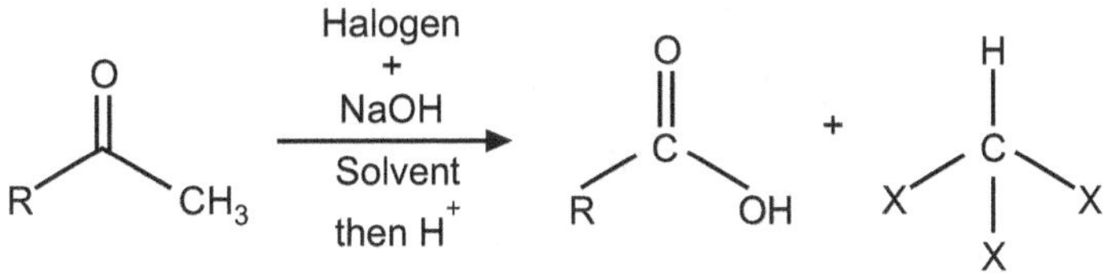

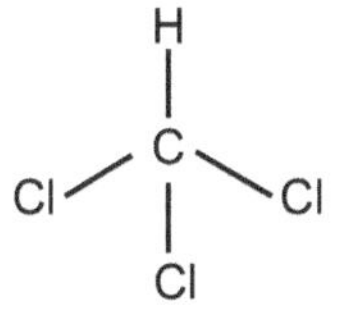

Chloroform 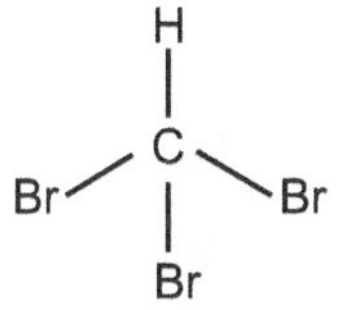   Bromoform 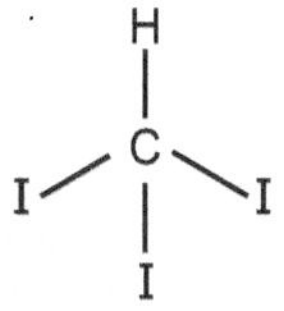   Iodoform

Mechanism:

Step I :

In presence of a base, the ketone undergoes keto-enol tautomerization. This enolate then undergoes exhaustive halogenations to give the tri α-halomethyl ketone.

Methyl ketone   Enolate

Tri α-halomethyl ketone

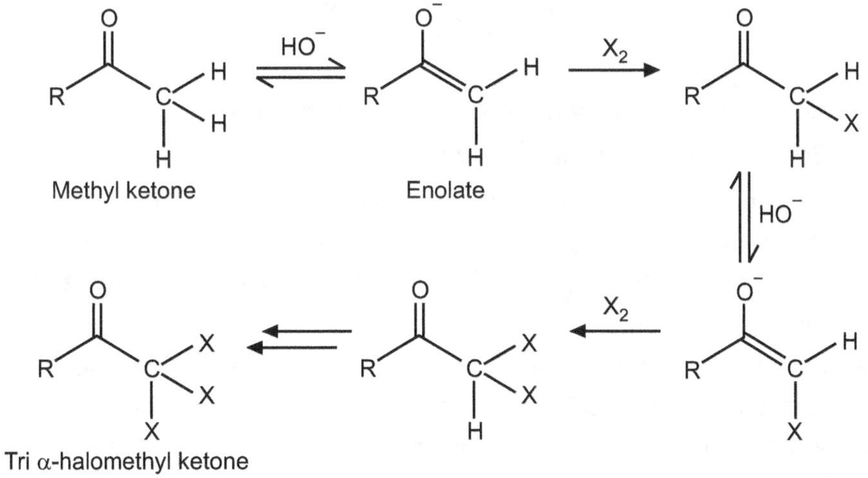

Step II :

The tri α-halomethyl ketone undergoes a nucleophilic acyl substitution by hydroxide, with $-CX_3$ being the leaving group. The $-CX_3$ anion abstracts a proton from either the solvent or the carboxylic acid formed in the previous step, and forms the haloform.

Tri α-halomethyl

Carboxylate   Haloform

Example:

Bromoform

12. Some named reactions involving aldehydes and ketones:

(i) Claisen - Schmidt condensation reaction:

The condensation of an aromatic aldehyde (with no α hydrogen) with an aliphatic aldehyde or ketone (having a α hydrogen) in the presence of a base or an acid to form an α,β-unsaturated aldehyde or ketone with high chemoselectivity is generally known as Claisen–Schmidt condensation.

The mechanism is very similar to aldol condensation as seen above. The base abstracts a α hydrogen from the ketone resulting in the formation of an enolate ion which acts as a nucleophile and attack the electron deficient carbonyl to give a β-hydroxy carbonyl compound. This compound undergoes loss of water in the presence of a base to form a conjugated system composed of a double bond and the carbonyl group (α, β-unsaturated aldehyde or ketone). Formation of benzalacetophenone can be used to illustrate the reaction mechanism.

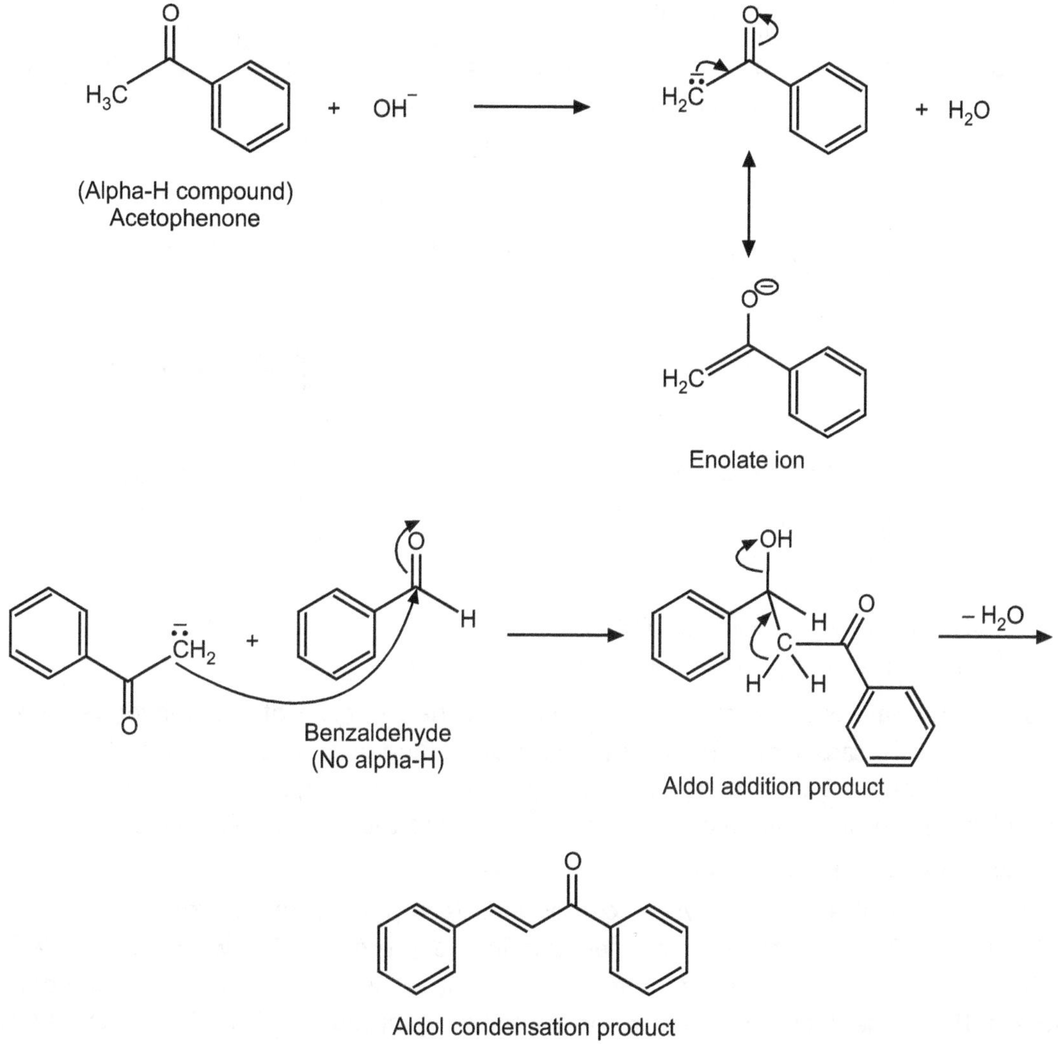

(Alpha-H compound)
Acetophenone

Enolate ion

Benzaldehyde
(No alpha-H)

Aldol addition product

Aldol condensation product

(ii) Perkin reaction:

The condensation of aromatic aldehydes with anhydrides is called Perkin reaction. Anhydrides containing two α hydrogens always show dehydration of the product. The β-hydroxy acid salt is thus never isolated. The base used in Perkin reaction is always the salt of the acid corresponding to the anhydride.

Mechanism:

$$C_6H_5CHO + (CH_3CO)_2O \xrightarrow[170\text{ - }175^\circ C]{CH_3COONa} C_6H_5CH = CHCOOH + CH_3COOH$$

Benzaldehyde   Cinnamic acid   Acetic acid

$$CH_3COONa \rightleftharpoons CH_3COO^{\ominus} + Na^{\oplus}$$

Sodium acetate

$$CH_3COO^{\ominus} + H-CH_2-\overset{\overset{O}{\|}}{C}-O-\overset{\overset{O}{\|}}{C}-CH_3 \rightleftharpoons {}^{\ominus}CH_2-\overset{\overset{O}{\|}}{C}-O-\overset{\overset{O}{\|}}{C}-CH_3 + CH_3COOH$$

Acetic anhydride   I

$$C_6H_5\overset{\overset{H}{|}}{C}=O \ + \ {}^{\ominus}CH_2COOCOCH_3 \longrightarrow C_6H_5-\overset{\overset{H}{|}}{\underset{\underset{O^{\ominus}}{|}}{C}}-CH_2COOCOCH_3$$

I   II

$H^{\oplus}$ from CH_3COOH

$$C_6H_5CH=CH.CO.O.COCH_3 \ \overset{-H_2O}{\rightleftharpoons} \ C_6H_5C-\overset{\overset{H}{|}}{\underset{\underset{OH}{|}}{C}}CHCOOCOCH_3$$

III

Hydrolysis H^+/H_2O

$$C_6H_5CH=CHCOOH \ + \ CH_3COOH$$

Cinnamic acid   Acetic acid

The carboxylate anion abstracts a proton from the α-carbon of the anhydride to form carbanion I. This carbanion undergoes nucleophilic addition to carbonyl carbon of the aldehyde. The anion II so formed takes up a proton to form a hydroxy compound III which first undergoes dehydration before getting hydrolyzed to the α, β-unsaturated acid.

(iii) Knoevenagel condensation:

The reaction of active methylene compounds (compounds of the form Z – CH$_2$ – Z' or Z – CHR – Z') with ketones or aldehydes in the presence of a weak base to afford α, β-unsaturated dicarbonyl or related compounds is known as the **Knoevenagel condensation**. The Z groups are electron withdrawing groups, such as CHO, COR, COOH, COOR, CN, NO$_2$, SOR, SO$_2$R, SO$_2$OR or similar groups. The reaction is named after Emil Knoevenagel who first reported this reaction in 1894.

Ketone   Diketone   α, β-unsaturated
dicarbonyl compound

The Knoevenagel condensation uses a weak amine base. The mechanism can be written as on next page :

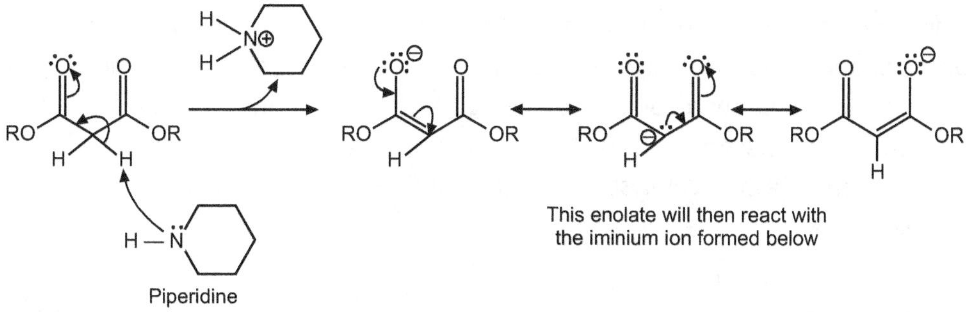

Piperidine
This enolate will then react with
the iminium ion formed below
Proton transfer 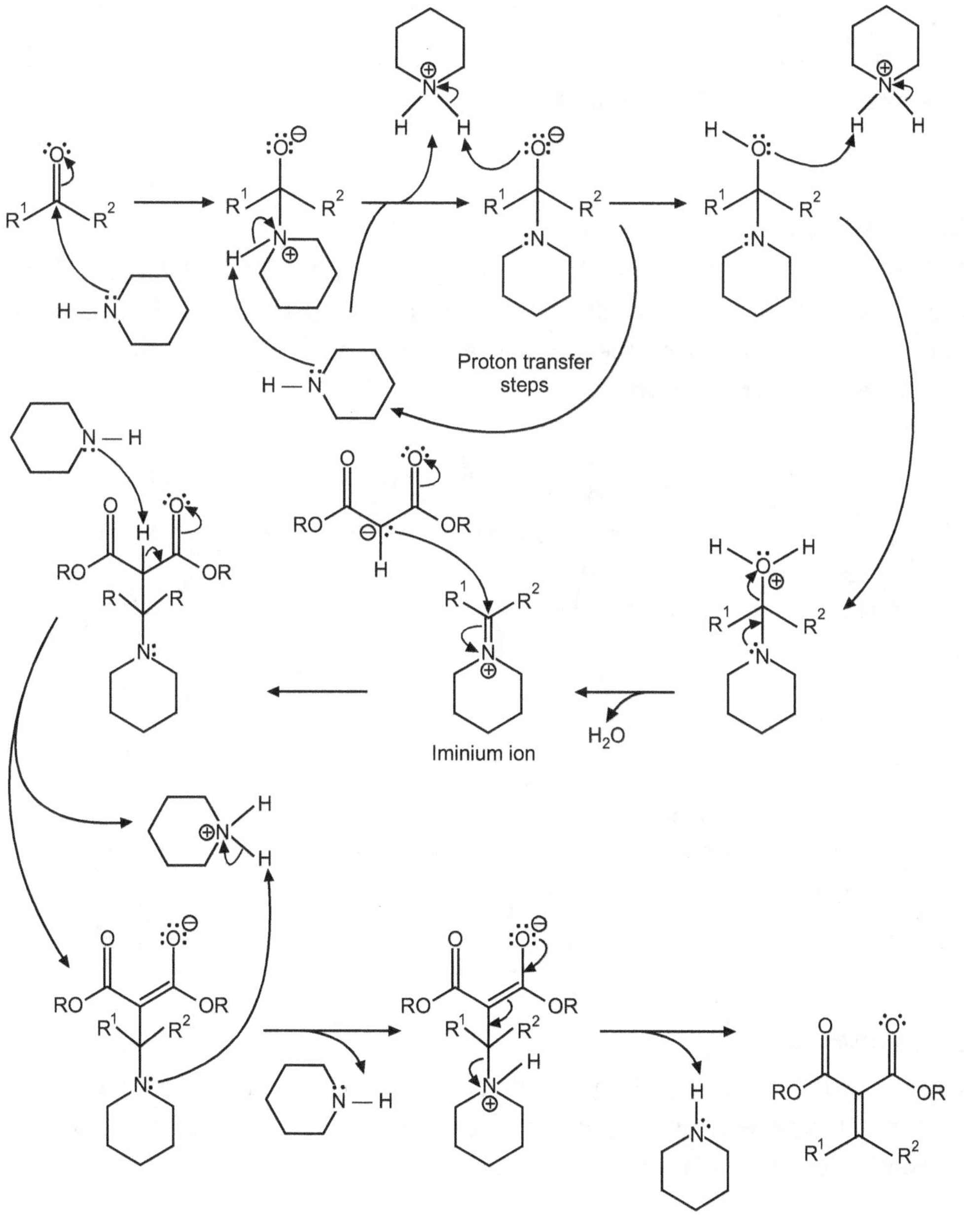
steps
H₂O
Iminium ion

In this mechanism the base reacts with both reagents to form an enolate of the dicarbonyl reagent and an immine salt of the ketone or aldehyde. The intermediate compound formed gets deprotonated by the base to give another enolate while the amine of the intermediate gets protonated. A rearrangement then takes place which releases the amine base, regenerates the catalyst, and yields the final olefin product.

Example:

Benzaldehyde + Ethyl 3-oxobutanoate $\xrightarrow[-H_2O]{\text{2,6-diethylpiperidine}}$ Ethyl 2-benzylidene-3-axobutanoate

Aldehydes undergo this reaction much faster than ketones. The choice of solvents is critical for the reaction with polar aprotic solvents (DMF, acetonitrile) favouring the reaction.

When malonic acid is used as the compound with active methylene compound, in presence of pyridine as the base, the product can lose a carboxylic group. This modification is called the **Doebner modification**.

Acrylaldehyde + Malonic acid

Pent -2,4-dienoic acid

$CO_2\uparrow$ +

(iv) Reformatsky reaction:

Zinc induced formation of β-hydroxyalkanoates from the reaction of α-halocarbonyl compounds with aldehydes and ketones is called the Reformatsky reaction. It was discovered by the scientist Sergey Nikolaevich Reformatsky.

X = Cl, Br, I

M = Sn, In, Zn

Solvent = THF, Et_2O, CH_2Cl_2

The organozinc reagent, also called a 'Reformatsky enolate', is prepared by treating an alpha-halo ester with zinc dust. Reformatsky enolates are less reactive than lithium enolates or Grignard reagents and hence nucleophilic addition to the ester group does not occur.

Mechanism:

Initially zinc reacts with α-halo ester to give an organozinc reagent called Reformatsky enolate. It is just like the Grignard reagent.

It is added to the carbonyl group of aldehyde or ketone to furnish β- hydroxy ester.

The organozinc reagents are less reactive and hence the nucleophilic addition to the ester group seldom occurs. Some of them are quite stable to be isolated and their structure can be elucidated by techniques like X-ray analysis.

Example:

$$CH_3CHO + Br\text{-}CH_2\text{-}COOC_2H_5 \xrightarrow{\text{(i) Diethyl ether, Zn (ii) Water}} CH_3CH(OH)\text{-}CH_2COOC_2H_5$$

Acetaldehyde Ethyl bromo acetate   Ethyl 3-hydroxybutyrate

(v) Benzoin Condensation:

The Benzoin Condensation is a coupling reaction between two aromatic aldehydes that leads to the formation of α-hydroxyketones (benzoins). The condensation involves addition of one molecule of aldehyde to the C = O of another. The reaction can be carried out only with some aromatic aldehydes.

$$2ArCHO + KCN \longrightarrow$$

Alpha-hydroxy ketone

One molecule of the aldehyde is called a *donor* and the other molecule of aldehyde is called the *acceptor*. *Donor* is the molecule that has given its hydrogen to the *acceptor* molecule. Some aldehydes can perform only one of these functions and therefore cannot undergo self condensation but can be condensed with other aldehydes. For example, *p*-dimethylaminobenzaldehyde can only act as a donor but not acceptor. Thus it cannot undergo self condensation but can condense with benzaldehyde. Benzaldehyde, on the other hand can perform both functions though it is a better acceptor than it is a donor.

Mechanism:

The reaction is reversible.

Addition of the cyanide ion to the electrophilic aldehyde carbon makes it more acidic and now it can be easily deprotonated by a strong base to yield the nucleophile. A second equivalent of aldehyde reacts with this carbanion; elimination of the catalyst (cyanide ion) regenerates the carbonyl compound at the end of the reaction.

Certain thiazolium salts can also catalyze the reaction. In this case aliphatic aldehyde can also be used (the products are called acyloins). Mixtures of aliphatic and aromatic aldehydes give mixed α-hydroxy ketones.

(vi) Baeyer - Villiger Oxidation (Baeyer - Villiger Rearrangement):

Baeyer-Villiger oxidation is the oxidation of ketones to carboxylic acid esters using a peroxyacid or hydrogen peroxide as the oxidizing agent.

Mechanism:

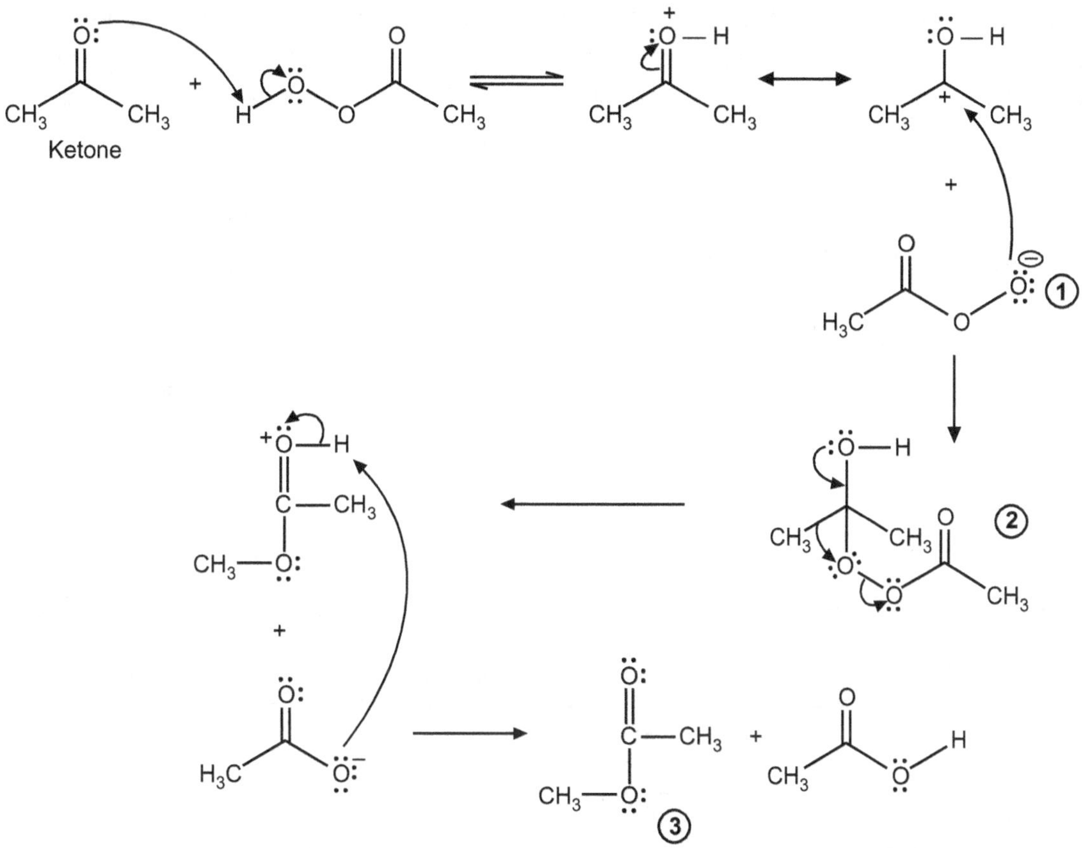

The peracids donate a proton to the carbonyl oxygen thereby themselves getting converted to a nucleophile (1). This nucleophile then attacks the electron deficient carbon of the protonated ketone. The intermediate (2) then loses carboxylate ion followed by migration of alkyl group from the α-carbon with its bonding electrons to the oxygen. This creates a positive charge on the α-carbon. Proton is finally lost to regenerate the carbonyl group and the ester (3) is formed. In case of unsymmetrical ketone, Baeyer-Villiger oxidation is regioselective. Of the two alpha carbons in the ketone, the one that can stabilize a positive charge more effectively i.e. one which is the more highly substituted, migrates from carbon to oxygen preferentially. Thus, the order of preference is: tert. alkyl > cyclohexyl > sec. alkyl > phenyl > prim. alkyl > CH_3.

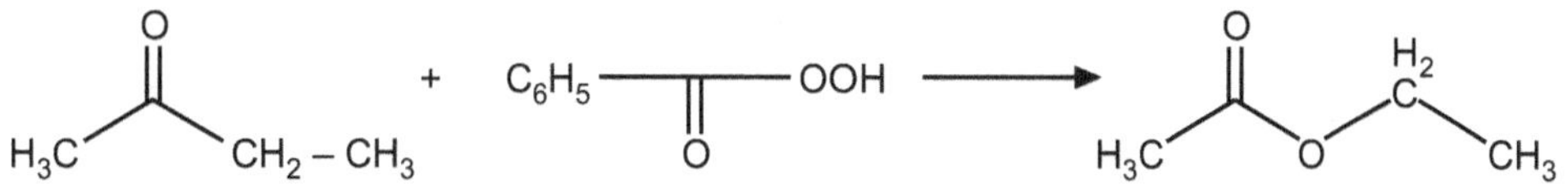

Ethyl methyl ketone   Perbenzoic acid   Ethyl acetate

(vii) Stobbe condensation:

Diethyl succinate and its derivatives condense with aldehydes and ketones in presence of bases like NaOEt and NaH. This reaction is called Stobbe condensation. During the reaction one or both of the ester groups may get hydrolyzed. The mechanism can be written as:

Diethylsuccinate

Aldehyde/ketone

2-Step tetrahedral mechanism

$C_2H_5O^-$

(viii) Willgerodt Reaction:

The Willgerodt rearrangement or Willgerodt reaction involves converting an aryl alkyl ketone to the corresponding amide by reaction with ammonium polysulfide. The formation of the ammonium salt of corresponding carboxylic acid is a side reaction. When the alkyl group is an aliphatic chain (n typically 0 to 5), multiple reactions take place with the amide group always ending up at the terminal end. Thus,

Arylalkyl ketone

However, yields are lowered as the length of the chain increases.

When sulfur and a dry primary or secondary amine (morpholine) or ammonia is used as the reagent, it is called the Kindler Modification of the Willgerodt reaction. The product is a thioacetamide which can be hydrolyzed to the acid.

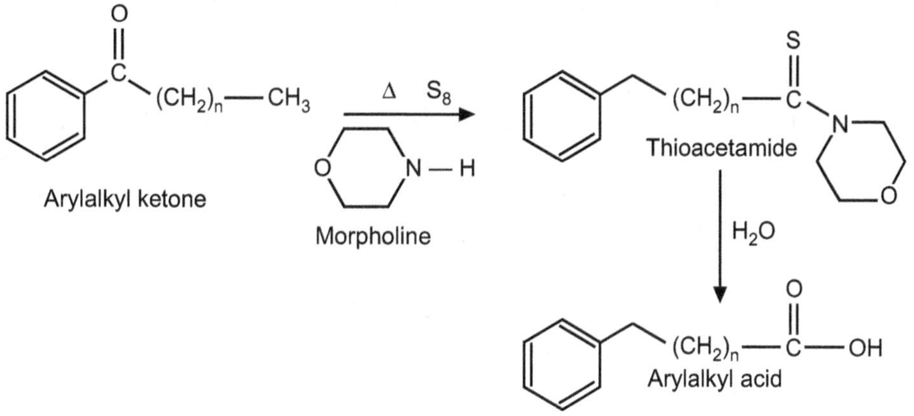

The Willgerodt reaction mechanism is not clear. However the mechanism for the Kindler modification can be written as:

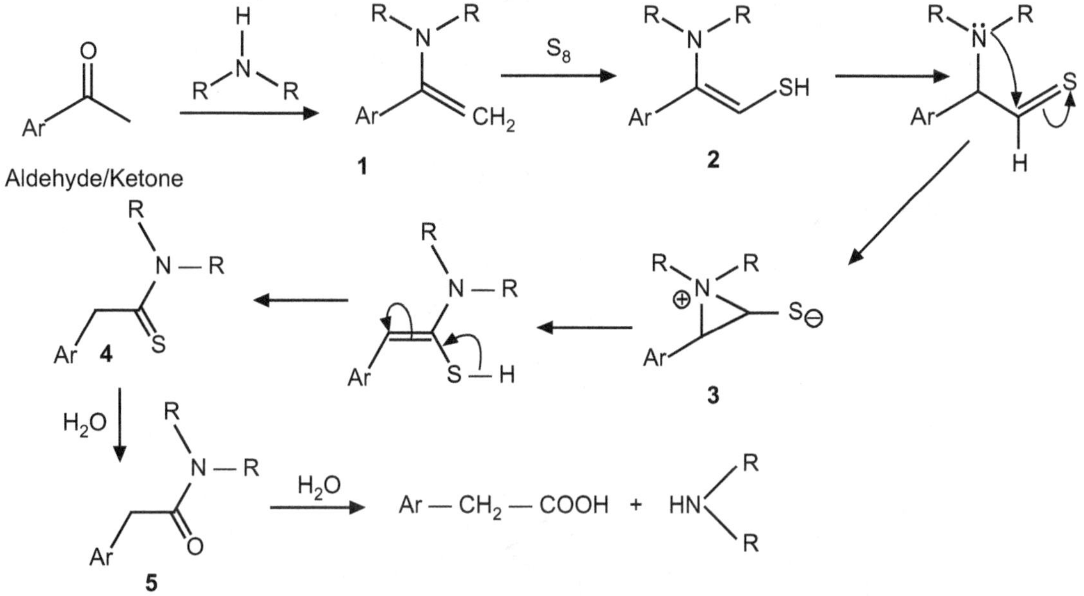

The first stage of the reaction involves imine formation by the addition of morpholine to the ketone group and then loss of α-hydrogen by this imine to form the enamine **1** (see under addition of amines). Enamine reacts in a conjugate addition with sulfur to form the sulfide **2**. The rearrangement follows when the amine group attacks the thiocarbonyl in a nucleophilic addition temporarily forming an aziridine **3** and the thioacetamide **4** by tautomerization. Hydrolysis of **4** then gives the amide **5**. Further hydrolysis yield the corresponding acid.

(ix) Favorskii reaction

The Favorskii reaction (or rearrangement) is a base-induced rearrangement of α-halo ketones to the corresponding carboxylic acid derivatives (e.g., acids, esters, and amides) with the same number of carbon atoms in the skeleton. The bases used can be hydroxide, alkoxide, or amines.

The mechanism involves first, the abstraction of hydrogen attached to the carbon containing the halogen atom followed by loss of halide leading to cyclization to give a cyclopropane derivative. In presence of a base, cyclopropanone derivative undergoes rearrangement to give the corresponding acid (if alkali is used), amide (if ammonia is used as a base) or an ester (if an alkoxide is used).

Cyclopropanone derivative

Acid derivative

Example:

α-chlorocyclohexanone

Cyclopentanoic acid

(x) Mannich reaction

The Mannich reaction involves condensation of two carbonyl compounds (one non-enolizable and one enolizable) with a primary or secondary amine to give a β-amino carbonyl compound, also known as a Mannich base. An acid is used as a catalyst.

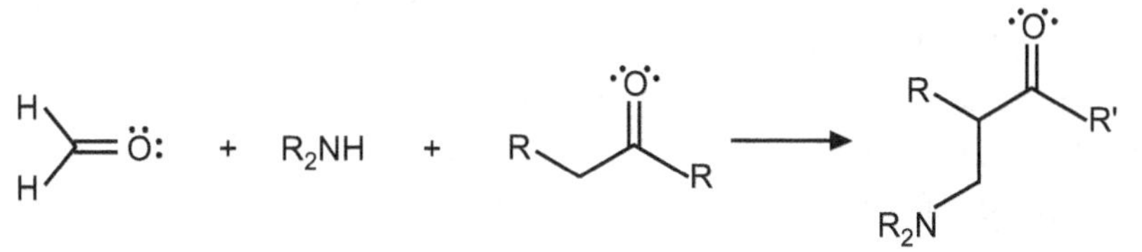

Formaldehyde	Amine	Compound containing carbonyl functional group	Amino methylated product

Mechanism of acid catalyzed reaction involves protonation of oxygens of both the carbonyl compounds. The enolizable carbonyl compound, which has an α hydrogen, then gets deprotonated to form an enol intermediate. The other, non-enolizable carbonyl compound reacts with the amine to form an iminium ion. The enol intermediate then attacks the iminium ion which after deprotonation provides the final Mannich base product.

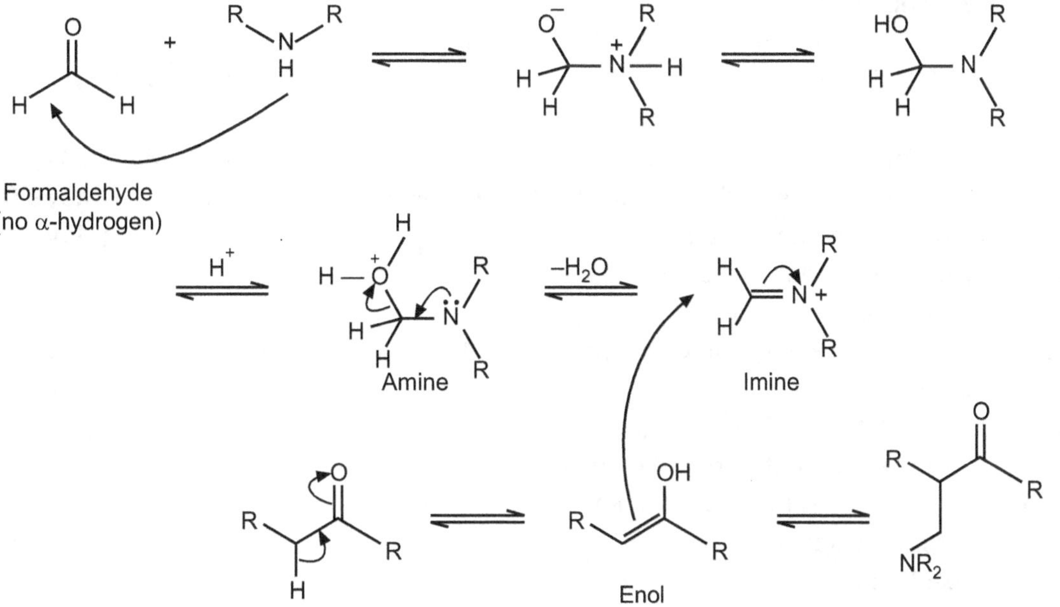

Formaldehyde
(no α-hydrogen)

Amine

Imine

Enol

Example:

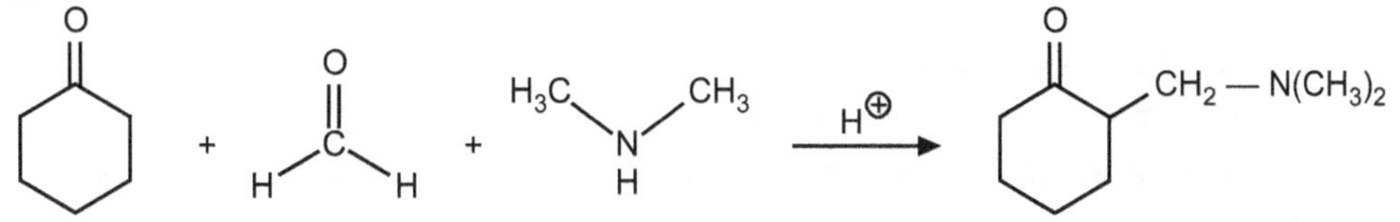

Cyclohexanone	Formaldehyde	Dimethylamine	2-Dimethylaminomethyl cyclohexanone

QUESTIONS

Q.1 Explain why aldehydes are more reactive than ketones for nucleophilic addition reaction and add a note on addition of water to aldehydes and ketones.   **(10M)**

Q.2 Explain why aldehydes are more reactive than ketone for nucleophilic addition reaction and add a note on Cannizzaro reaction.   **(10M)**

Q.3 What are nucleophilic addition reactions? Explain in brief addition of Grignard reagents to aldehydes.   **(May-2015) (10M)**

Q.4 Write method of preparation and uses of the following: **(Dec-2015) (10M)**
(a) Acetals   (b) Oximes   (c) Imines   (d) Semicarbazone.

Q.5 Aldehydes and ketones are susceptible for nucleophilic addition reactions explain. Write any two methods of preparation of aldehydes and write a note on aldol condensation.   **(May-2014) (10M)**

Q.6 Give reaction, mechanism and applications of Perkin reaction and Mannich reaction.   **(May-2014) (10M)**

Q.7 What are condensation reactions? Explain mechanism of Aldol condensation.   **(Dec-2014) (10M)**

Q.8 Write notes on
1) Haloform reaction
2) Cannizzaro reaction   **(May-2014, Dec-2014)**
3) MPV reduction
4) Knoevenagel condensation   **(May-2015, May-2014) (5M)**

Q.9 Write any two methods of preparation of aldehydes and ketones.   **(May-2015)**

Q.10 Explain Oppenaur oxidation.   **(May-2015)**

Q.11 Write a note on Oppenauer oxidation.   **(Dec-2015)**

Q.12 Explain Perkin reaction.   **(Dec-2015)**

Q.13 Write the reactions of Grignard's reagent and Hydride ions with aldehydes and ketones.   **(Dec-2015)**

Q.14 Explain Reformatsky reaction.   **(May-2014)**

Q.15 Explain addition of Grignard reagent and alcohol to aldehydes.   **(Dec-2014)**

Q.16 Draw structures from IUPAC names of the following :
2-bromopentanal   **(Dec-2015)**
2-pentanone
2-Hydroxycyclopentanone   **(May-2014)**
4-Methyl-2-pentanone   **(Dec-2014)**

Q.17 Write method of preparation and uses of hydrazone.

Q.18. Write preparation and uses of enamine.

Q.19. Explain why aldehydes are more reactive than ketones for nucleophilic addition reaction.

Q.20. What are enamines? How are they prepared?   **(Dec-2015)**

❖❖❖

Chapter 11

PHENOLS

11.1 INTRODUCTION

Phenols are molecules having a **hydroxyl group** (OH) attached to the carbon atom of an aromatic ring. The general formula for representing phenols is Ar–OH, where Ar is a phenyl, substituted phenyl or any other aryl group. Phenols are very common in nature and are a part of our daily life. Examples include tyrosine, one of the standard amino acids found in most proteins; epinephrine (adrenaline), a stimulant hormone produced by the adrenal medulla; and serotonin, a neurotransmitter in the brain. Many of the more complex phenols are used as flavouring agents and are obtained from essential oils of plants. For example, vanillin, the principal flavouring in vanilla, is isolated from vanilla beans, and methyl salicylate, which has a characteristic minty taste and odour, is isolated from wintergreen. Other phenols obtained from plants include thymol, isolated from thyme, and eugenol, isolated from cloves.

Tyrosine

Epinephrine

Serotonin

Vanillin

11.2 NOMENCLATURE

Phenols are usually named as derivatives of the simplest member of the family, that is, phenol. The other substituents are listed in an alphabetical order. In IUPAC nomenclature, the parent molecule is called benzenol, and substituents are always numbered with the OH group being given the first position. For the compounds below, the first name listed is the common name and the second is the IUPAC name. However, phenol has become an accepted word even for the systematic nomenclature.

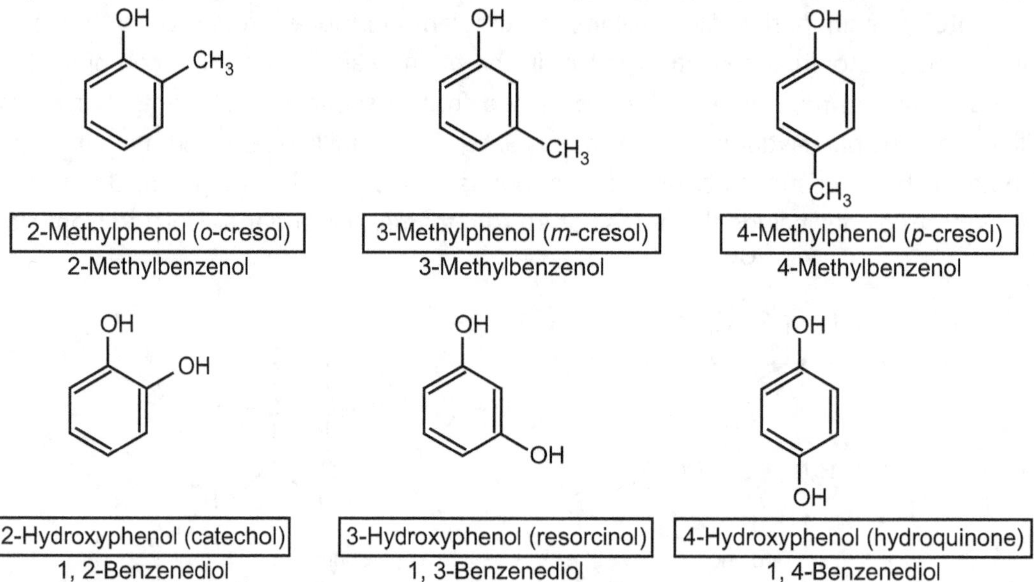

Phenol / Benzenol

p-Chlorophenol / 4-Chlorobenzenol

m-Nitrophenol / 3-Nitrobenzenol

3, 5-Dinitrophenol / 3, 5-Dinitrobenzenol

Common names are also popular for certain phenols. For example, methyl phenols are called *cresols*. Similarly, hydroxyphenols also have common names. In the examples given below, the common names are listed in the brackets, while the IUPAC names are listed last.

2-Methylphenol (*o*-cresol) / 2-Methylbenzenol

3-Methylphenol (*m*-cresol) / 3-Methylbenzenol

4-Methylphenol (*p*-cresol) / 4-Methylbenzenol

2-Hydroxyphenol (catechol) / 1, 2-Benzenediol

3-Hydroxyphenol (resorcinol) / 1, 3-Benzenediol

4-Hydroxyphenol (hydroquinone) / 1, 4-Benzenediol

11.3 METHODS OF PREPARATION OF PHENOLS

Either of the methods given below can be used to synthesize phenols.

1. Reaction of sulfonic acids with hydroxide:

In this process, benzene sulfonic acid is reacted with aqueous sodium hydroxide. The resulting salt is mixed with solid sodium hydroxide and fused at high temperature. The product of this reaction is sodium phenoxide, which is acidified with aqueous acid to yield phenol.

Benzene sulfonic acid — Sodium benzene sulphonate — Sodium phenoxide — Phenol

This is one of the oldest methods for industrial preparation of phenols.

2. From chlorobenzene (Dow process):

In Dow process, chlorobenzene is reacted with dilute sodium hydroxide at 300°C and 3000 psi pressure.

$$\text{Chlorobenzene} \xrightarrow[\text{300°C/3000 psi}]{\text{dilute NaOH}} \text{Phenol}$$

This method is also useful for industrial preparation of phenols.

3. From cumene:

The air oxidation of cumene (isopropyl benzene) leads to the production of both phenol and acetone, as shown in the following figure. The reaction involves formation and degradation of cumene hydroperoxide.

$$\text{Cumene} \xrightarrow[\text{100 - 130°}]{O_2} \text{Cumene hydroperoxide} \xrightarrow{H_3O^+} \text{Phenol} + CH_3-\overset{O}{\underset{\|}{C}}-CH_3 \ (\text{Acetone})$$

This method has become the most popular method for synthesizing phenol and acetone on an industrial scale.

4. From aryl diazonium salts:

This is one of the most versatile methods for synthesizing phenols on a laboratory scale. Aryl diazonium salts which are prepared by reaction of aryl amines with nitrous acid (HNO_2) are converted to phenols by the action of aqueous acid and heat.

$$\text{Aniline} \xrightarrow{NaNO_2/H^+} \text{Benzene diazonium salt} \xrightarrow[\text{100°C}]{H_2O, H_2SO_4} \text{Phenol}$$

11.4 PROPERTIES OF PHENOLS

Physical

Low molecular weight phenols are normally liquids or low melting solids. Since they are capable of hydrogen bonding, most low molecular weight phenols are water soluble. Phenols tend to have higher boiling points than alcohols of similar molecular weight because they have stronger intermolecular hydrogen bonding. Phenols are colourless, though they are easily oxidized to coloured compounds.

Chemical

Phenols can undergo a number of synthetically useful reactions which can be easily categorized under two classes, that is, those involving the phenolic hydrogen, and those involving the aromatic ring.

11.5 REACTIONS INVOLVING PHENOLIC HYDROGEN

1. Acidity of phenols:

Phenols show appreciable acidity and therefore are converted into salts by aqueous hydroxides, but not by aqueous bicarbonates.

$$(pK_a = 10^{-10})$$

Thus, though phenols are much stronger acids than alcohols, they are much weaker acids than the carboxylic acids ($pK_a = 10^{-5}$). Let us see why phenols are acidic and alcohols are neutral compounds.

Alcohols on ionization give alkoxide ion, which is unstable and quickly combines with the proton to give original alcohol.

$$R-OH \rightleftharpoons H^+ + RO^-$$

Now let us have a look at the ionization of phenol:

In the above reaction, both phenol, as well as the phenoxide ion, formed are stabilized by resonance due to presence of the benzene ring. To understand why the equilibrium shifts towards right, let us compare the stability of two molecules, that is, the phenol and the phenoxide ion.

Phenol is stabilized by the following resonating structures:

I   II   III

While the phenoxide ion is stabilized by these structures:

$$\text{IV} \quad\longleftrightarrow\quad \text{V} \quad\longleftrightarrow\quad \text{VI}$$

Comparing the stability offered by these structures, we find that structures I, II and III (resonating structures of phenol), have both positive and negative charges. Especially structures I and III have two opposite charges very near to each other and therefore have high energy states. However, resonating structures of phenoxide ions IV, V and VI have only a negative charge and thus are at a lower energy level than those of I, II and III. Hence, we can say that resonance is stabilizing the phenoxide ion more than the phenol, and thus ionization of phenol is favoured.

2. Esterification of phenol:

Phenols form esters with acid anhydrides, acid chlorides and sulfonyl chlorides.

Phenol + Acetic anhydride $\xrightarrow{CH_3COONa}$ Phenylacetate + Ethanoic acid (CH_3COOH)

Phenol + Acetyl chloride $\xrightarrow{NaOH}$ Phenylacetate + HCl (Hydrochloric acid)

2-Bromophenol + 4-Methyl benzenesulphonic acid $\xrightarrow{Pyridine}$ Phenyl 4-methylbenzenesulfonate

3. Williamson ether synthesis:

Phenols can be converted to ethers by their alkaline solutions with alkyl halides. This method of synthesis of ethers is known as Williamson ether synthesis. The reaction takes place via a nucleophilic substitution mechanism.

The phenoxide ion acts as a nucleophile and displaces the halide ion from the alkyl halide.

Anisole, phenylmethyl ether, can also be prepared by using methyl sulfate, which is much cheaper, in place of alkyl halide.

11.6 REACTIONS INVOLVING PHENOLIC BENZENE RING

The benzene ring of phenols undergoes electrophilic substitution. The hydroxy group in a phenol molecule has a strong activating effect on the benzene ring because it provides a ready source of electron density for the ring (as seen in the resonating structures of phenols). This effect is so strong that substitutions on phenols can be achieved without the use of a catalyst.

The electrophilic substitution reactions can be summarized as:

Reaction	Reagent used
Nitration	dil. HNO_3 in H_2O or CH_3CO_2H
Sulfonation	conc. H_2SO_4
Halogenation	X_2
Alkylation	ROH / H^+ or $RCl / AlCl_3$
Acylation	$RCOCl / AlCl_3$
Nitrosation	aq. $NaNO_2 / H^+$

1. Halogenation:

Phenols react with halogens to yield mono-, di-, or tri-substituted products, depending on reaction conditions. For example, an aqueous bromine solution brominates all *ortho* and *para* positions on the ring. On the other hand mono bromination is achieved by running the reaction at extremely low temperatures in carbon disulfide (CS_2) as the solvent.

2, 4, 6-Tribromophenol

4-Bromophenol

2. Nitration:

Phenol when treated with dilute nitric acid at room temperature, forms *ortho*- and *para*-nitrophenol.

Phenol   o-Nitrophenol   p-Nitrophenol

With concentrated nitric acid, more nitro groups substitute around the ring to give 2, 4, 6-trinitrophenol.

Phenol   2, 4, 6-Trinitrophenol

3. Nitrosation:

Phenols when reacted with nitrous acid yield *p*-nitrosophenols. Phenols are one of the few classes of compounds reactive enough to undergo attack by the weakly electrophilic nitrosonium ion, NO^+. Nitrosophenol can be oxidized to nitrophenol by nitric acid.

4-Nitrosophenol
80% yield

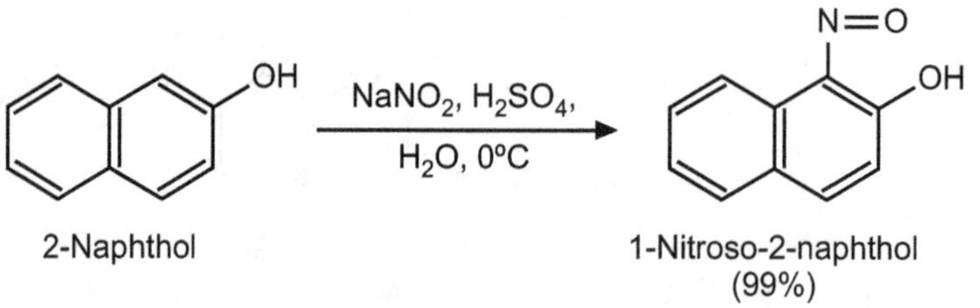
N=O
OH
OH
NaNO2, H2SO4,
H2O, 0°C
2-Naphthol
1-Nitroso-2-naphthol
(99%)

If the reaction is allowed to proceed at a higher temperature a further reaction takes place coupling the nitrosophenol with phenol.

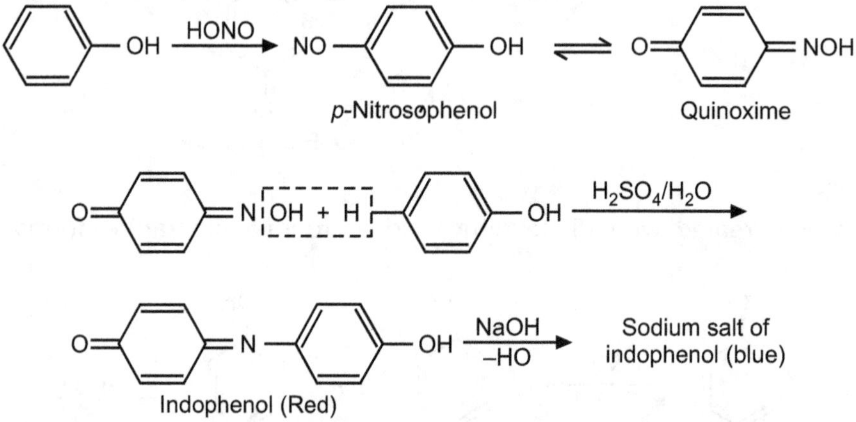
OH
HONO
NO
OH
O
NOH
p-Nitrosophenol
Quinoxime
O
N OH + H
OH
H2SO4/H2O
O
N
OH
NaOH
–HO
Sodium salt of
indophenol (blue)
Indophenol (Red)

The above reaction is called the Liebermann nitroso reaction, the uncharged indophenol is red; but in alkali the compound becomes deep blue again. This can be used as a test for phenols.

4. Sulfonation:

The reaction of phenol with concentrated sulfuric acid is thermodynamically controlled. At 25°C, the *ortho* product predominates while at 100°C, the *para* product is the major product.

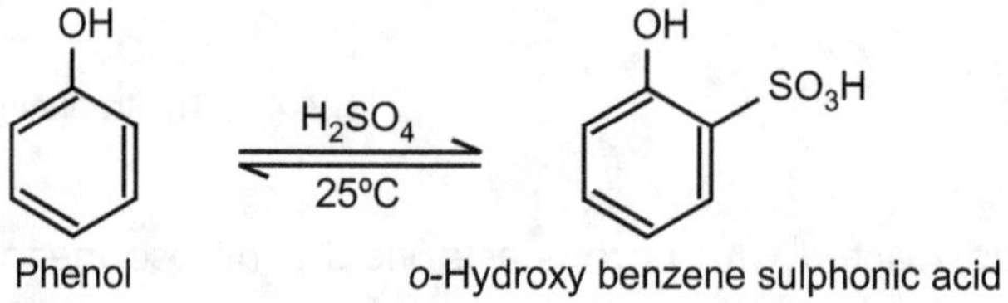
OH
OH
SO3H
H2SO4
25°C
Phenol
o-Hydroxy benzene sulphonic acid

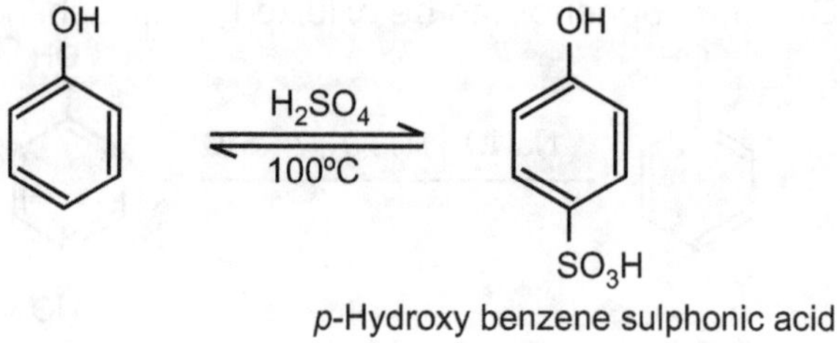
OH
OH
H2SO4
100°C
SO3H
p-Hydroxy benzene sulphonic acid

p-Hydroxy benzene sulphonic acid

At both 25°C and 100°C, initially an equilibrium is established. However, at higher temperature, the equilibrium is destroyed and the more thermodynamically stable product is produced exclusively.

5. Kolbe reaction:

When the sodium salt of a phenol is treated with cabon dioxide, a carboxyl group, -COOH is substituted on the ring by replacing a ring hydrogen.

Sodium phenoxide

Salicylic acid
(*o*-hydroxybenzoic acid)

The reaction proceeds through the following mechanism:

keto-enol tautomerization

In this reaction, the electron deficient carbon atom in carbon dioxide is attracted to the electron rich π system of the phenol. The resulting compound undergoes keto-enol tautomerization to create the product.

6. Alkylation:

The benzene ring of phenols can be alkylated using Friedel Craft reaction, just like any other aromatic compound.

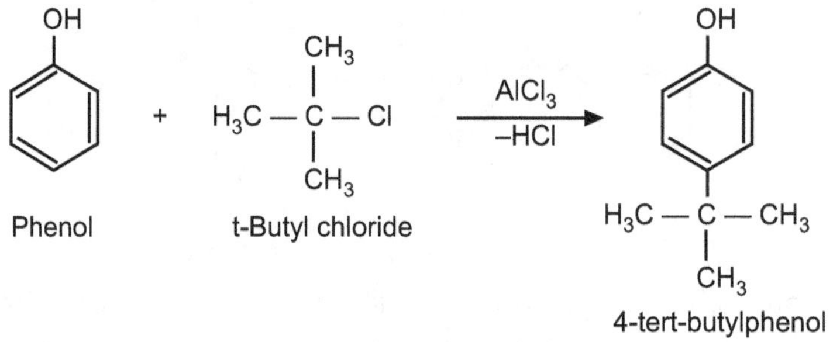

7. Acylation of phenols:

Phenols can react with acid chloride in the following two ways:

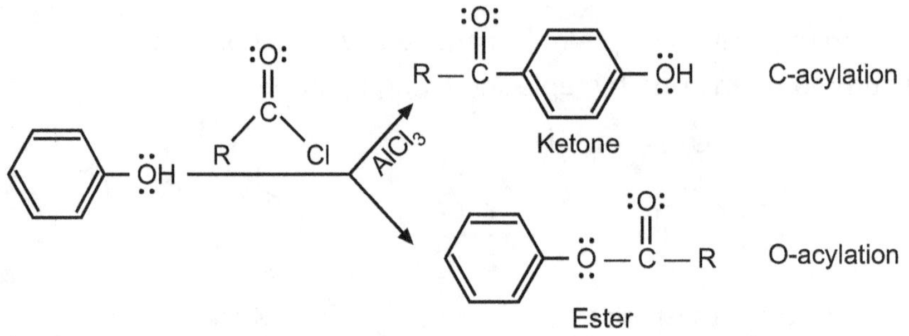

C-Acylation: C-acylation or the ring acylation of phenols is achieved by Friedel-Craft acylation reaction, involving the use of $AlCl_3$. Acylation can also be performed using an acid anhydride in place of an acyl chloride. This reaction is an electrophilic substitution reaction.

O-Acylation: Phenols react with acid chlorides in absence of $AlCl_3$ to give a phenolic ester. This reaction proceeds via nucleophilic substitution mechanism. The reaction can be enhanced by use of an acid or a base catalyst. The acid catalyst protonates the acylating oxygen, making the agent more electrophilic, while a base deprotonates the phenol and converts it into a stronger nucleophile. The phenolic esters when heated in presence of $AlCl_3$ can rearrange to give ketones. This reaction is known as Fries Rearrangement.

8. Fries rearrangement:

Esters of phenols when heated with $AlCl_3$ undergo a rearrangement in which the acyl group migrates from the phenolic oxygen to an *ortho* or *para* position of the ring to yield a ketone.

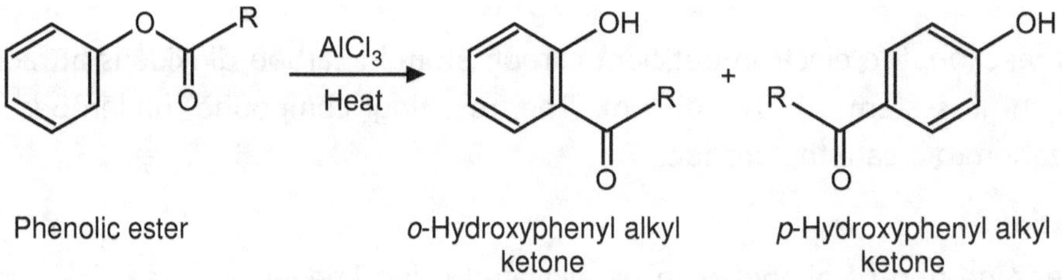

This reaction is called the Fries rearrangement, and is used to perform direct acylation for the synthesis of phenolic ketones.

Phenol　+　Butyryl chloride　⟶　Phenyl butanoate

$$\downarrow AlCl_3$$

1-(4-Hydroxyphenyl) butane-1-one

9. Claisen rearrangement:

Phenolic allyl ethers on heating undergo a sigmatropic rearrangement to give *o*-allyl phenols. However, if both the *ortho* positions are blocked, then *para*-allyl phenols are formed.

Phenolic allyl ether　—Heat→　*o*-allyl phenol

A sigmatropic rearrangement is a reaction in which a σ bond migrates from one end of a π system to the other.

10. Formylation of phenols:

Phenols can be formylated (introduction of formyl group, –CHO) using the following reactions:

(a) Reimer-Tiemann reaction:

The Reimer-Tiemann reaction is used to convert a phenol to an *o*-hydroxy benzaldehyde using chloroform and a base.

Phenol　$\xrightarrow[\text{3 KOH}]{\text{CHCl}_3}$　*o*-hydroxy benzaldehyde

The reaction involves electrophilic substitution on the highly activated benzene ring. The mechanism involves abstraction of the proton from chloroform by the base (KOH) to form a trichlorocarbanion which spontaneously loses a chloride ion to form a neutral dichlorocarbene. The base also ionizes the phenol to penoxide which then attacks the carbene. A series of steps and a final acidification result in the formation of *o*-hydroxy benzaldehyde.

Chloroform   Trichlorocarbene   Dichlorocarbene

Phenol   Phenoxide

o-hydroxybenzaldehyde
(salicylaldehyde)

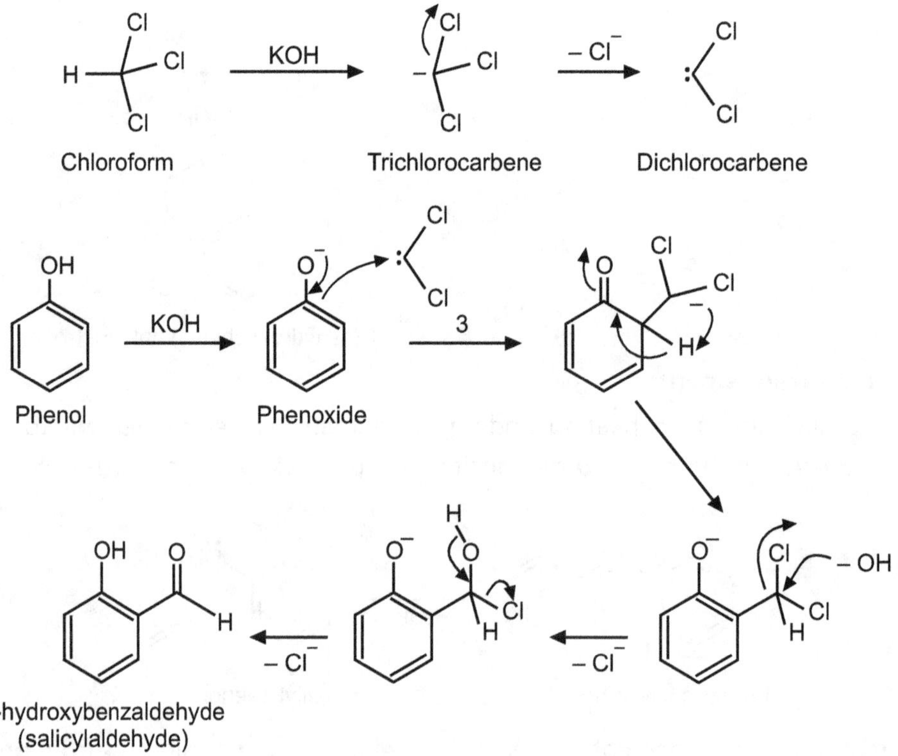

(b) Gattermann aldehyde synthesis:

The Gattermann synthesis of hydroxy aldehydes involving saturating an anhydrous ether solution of phenols and anhydrous hydrogen cyanide with dry hydrogen chloride in the presence of anhydrous zinc chloride, gives excellent yields of products which are readily purified. The method has proved to be invaluable for the preparation of certain intermediates in the synthesis of many natural compounds, and is still the only available process for preparing many representative hydroxy aldehydes.

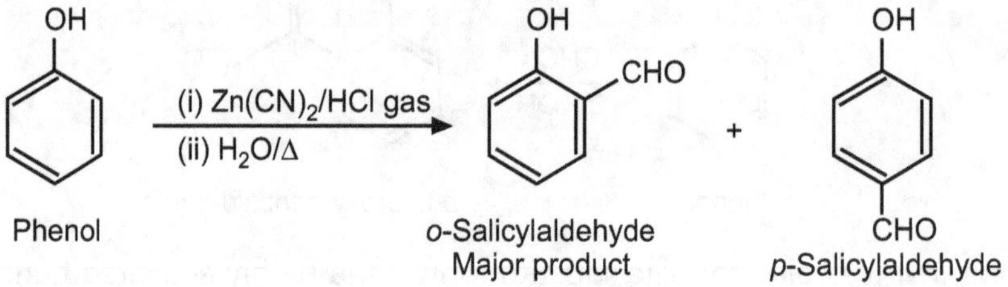

Phenol   *o*-Salicylaldehyde   *p*-Salicylaldehyde
                          Major product

(c) Duff reaction:

The reaction uses hexamine ($C_6H_{12}N_4$) and alkali for formylation of phenols at *ortho* and *para* positions.

OH   i) $C_6H_{12}N_4$/KOH   OH   O

Phenol   ii) H_2O/H^+/Heat   *o*-salicylaldehyde

11. Houben-Hoesch reaction:

Synthesis of acylphenols from phenols or phenolic ethers by the action of organic nitriles in the presence of hydrochloric acid and aluminium chloride as a catalyst is called as Houben-Hoesch reaction.

OH   RCN / HCl, $AlCl_3$ OH   Ether   OH

OH   OH, RC = NH . HCl   OH, COR

Resorcinol   2, 4-dihydroxy aryl ketone

12. Coupling with diazonium salts:

When reacted with a cold solution of diazonium salt, phenols, dissolved in an alkaline solution undergo a coupling reaction where the aromatic diazonium ion acts as an electrophile and undergoes substitution on the benzene ring of phenols. The substitution normally occurs at the **para** position. When this position is already occupied **ortho** position is favoured. The mechanism involved in the reaction has been explained under the chapter on amines. Amines also undergo a similar coupling reaction. Coupling with phenols is carried out in mildly alkaline solution while amines are coupled in mildly acidic solution. No coupling takes place at very low pH.

$\overset{+}{N_2}\overset{-}{Cl}$ +   OH $\xrightarrow{OH^-}$ N = N   OH + HCl

Benzenediazonium chloride   Phenol   *p*-Hydroxyazobenzene (Orange solid)

QUESTIONS

Q.1   What are phenols? Explain acidity of phenols. Discuss any three methods of prepration and any three reactions of phenol.

Q.2   Explain acidity of phenols.   **(May-2015, Dec-2014)**

Q.3   Give any two methods of preparation and reactions of phenol.   **(May-2014)**

Q.4   Explain Kolbe- Schimidt reaction of phenols.   **(May-2015, Dec-2014)**

Q.5   Give any two reactions of phenols.   **(Dec-2015)**

Q.6   Give any two methods of preparation of phenols.   **(Dec-2015, Dec-2014)**

Q.7   Phenols are acidic in nature, explain.   **(May-2014)**

Chapter 12

SULPHONIC ACIDS

12.1 INTRODUCTION

Sulphonic acids are a group of organic acids containing a sulphonic acid group ($-SO_3H$) attached to an alkyl or an aryl skeleton. Thus, they can be written as:

R = alkyl, aryl

Taurine

Taurine, a bile acid, is one of the few sulphonic acids present in nature. Though both, alkyl and aryl sulphonic acids exist, aryl sulphonic acids are in general more useful synthetically than the alkyl sulphonic acids. Examples of some synthetically available and important alkyl and aryl sulphonic acids are:

CH_3SO_3H

Benzenesulphonic
acid

4-methylbenzenesulphonic acid
or
p-toluenesulphonic acid

Methanesulphonic acid

12.2 NOMENCLATURE

Sulphonic acids are named by naming the carbon group as a separate word followed by the word sulfonic acid as illustrated in the above examples.

12.3 METHODS OF PREPARATION OF SULPHONIC ACIDS

1. Sulfoxidation: Alkyl sulphonates are prepared easily by sulfoxidation of hydrocarbons. Sulfoxidation involves use of a mixture of sulphur dioxide and oxygen in the presence of an initiator which could be UV light, γ-radiation, dichlorine, peroxides or ozone. The reaction is written as:

$$\text{R—H} + SO_2 + 0.5\, O_2 \xrightarrow{\text{Initiator}} \text{R — } SO_3H$$

2. Direct sulphonation: Arenes react with fuming sulphuric acid at room temperature to form sulphonic acids. However, if concentrated sulphuric acid is used, the sulphonation reaction requires heating.

Benzene $+$ Fuming $H_2SO_4 \longrightarrow$ Benzene sulphonic acid

Toluene $+$ $H_2SO_4 \xrightarrow{\Delta}$ 4-methylbenzene sulphonic acid

Sulphonation reaction is a type of electrophilic aromatic substitution reaction in which SO_3 (sulphur trioxide) is the electrophile. Since fuming sulphuric acid contains dissolved SO_3, the reaction can be easily carried out at room temperature.

$$2H_2SO_4 \rightleftharpoons H_3O^+ + HSO_4^- + SO_3$$

3. From sulphonyl chloride: Arenes are reacted with excess of chlorosulphonic acid to form sulphonyl chlorides, which on acid hydrolysis yield sulphonic acids.

$$\text{Ar} - \text{H} \quad + \quad \text{ClSO}_3\text{H} \longrightarrow \text{ArSO}_2\text{Cl} \xrightarrow{H_2O/H^+} \text{ArSO}_3\text{H}$$

Arene   Chlorosulphonic acid   Arene sulphonyl chloride   Arene sulphonic acid

The reaction can also be carried out in carbon tetrachloride with equimolar quantity of chlorosulphonic acid, in which case, pure sulphonic acid is obtained directly.

$$\text{ArH} + \text{ClSO}_3\text{H} \longrightarrow \text{ArSO}_3\text{H} + \text{HCl}$$

For example,

$$C_6H_6 + ClSO_3H \longrightarrow C_6H_5SO_3H \quad + \quad HCl$$

Benzene   Benzenesulphonic acid

4. From thiophenols: Oxidation of thiophenols with alkaline $KMnO_4$ results in the formation of arenesulphonic acids.

Benzenethiol/thiophenol　　　　　　Benzene sulphonic acid

12.4 PHYSICAL PROPERTIES OF SULPHONIC ACIDS

While alkylsulphonic acids occur as thick liquids, the arenesulphonic acids are crystalline solids. They are deliquescent in nature and do not possess a sharp melting point. These compounds are highly polar in nature and completely ionize in water. This property makes them very water soluble. However, solubility in organic solvents is very poor.

12.5 CHEMICAL PROPERTIES OF SULPHONIC ACIDS

1. Reactions of –OH or –SO₃H Group :

(i) Acidity of sulphonic acids: Sulphonic acids are strong acids, about as strong as sulphuric acid, and much stronger than carboxylic acids. In the sulphonic acid group, the sulphur is forming double bonds with two oxygen atoms and forms a single bond with one oxygen atom, which in turn is bound to the hydrogen. The doubly bonded oxygens, due to their electronegativity pull the electrons towards themselves making the hydrogen bonded to the third oxygen very acidic, that is, it is easily lost. Further, the sulphonate ion formed is quite stable as it is resonance stabilized.

The acidic nature of these compounds makes it possible for them to form salts with bases. Thus, alkyl and arylsulphonic acids can form salts with bases like hydroxides, carbonates and oxides to form soluble salts called sulphonates.

$$CH_3SO_3H \;+\; NaHCO_3 \longrightarrow CH_3SO_3Na \;+\; CO_2 \;+\; H_2O$$

Methanesulphonic　　　Sodium　　　　　　Sodium
acid　　　　　　bicarbonate　　　methanesulphonate

Benzenesulphonic acid + NaOH → Sodium benzenesulphonate + H_2O

(ii) Reaction with PCl₅ or SOCl₂: Sulphonic acids and their salts are converted to sulphonyl chloride by heating them with phosphorous pentachloride (PCl_5) or thionyl chloride ($SOCl_2$). The sulphonyl chlorides in turn can be reacted with ammonia to be conveniently converted to sulphonamides. Unlike the sulphonic acids, the sulphonamides have definite melting points and thus can be used in identification of the parent sulphonic acids. Sulphonamides are an important class of drugs with a wide range of therapeutic actions.

Benzenesulphonic acid → (PCl₅ or SOCl₂) → Benzenesulphonyl chloride → (NH₃) → Benzenesulphonamide

The sulphonyl chlorides can also be converted to sulphonic esters by reacting with alcohol. Direct conversion of sulphonic acids to esters is not possible.

$$Ar-SO_3H \xrightarrow{PCl_5 \text{ or } SOCl_2} Ar-SO_2Cl \xrightarrow{ROH} Ar-SO_2OR$$

Arene sulphonic acid   Arenesulphonyl chloride   Arenesulphonate ester

4-Methylbenzenesulphonic acid/ *p*-toluenesulphonic acid → (PCl₅ or SOCl₂) → 4-Methylbenzenesulphonyl chloride/ *p*-toluenesulphonyl chloride

(CH₃OH) →

Methyl 4-methylbenzenesulphonate/ methyl *p*-toluenesulphonate

2. Reactions in which $-SO_3H$ is replaced

(i) Hydrolysis: An arenesulphonic acid when boiled with dilute hydrochloric acid or dilute sulphuric acid, loses SO_3H group to give the parent arene.

Benzenesulphonic acid   Benzene

(ii) Nucleophilic substitution reactions: Due to the electron withdrawing nature of the sulphonic acid group, the carbon to which it is attached becomes electron deficient, and thus becomes prone to the nucleophilic replacement. It must be noted that ordinarily the aromatic compounds show only electrophilic substitution. Thus, replacement of sulphonic acid group with nucleophilic groups offers an important way to synthesize phenols, amines, nitriles etc. In such reactions, the salts of sulphonic acids are fused with appropriate reagents providing the nucleophilic group.

$C_6H_5SO_2ONa$
Sodium benzenesulphonate

Fuse

NaOH → C_6H_5ONa + Na_2SO_3
Sodium phenoxide
→ C_6H_5OH
Phenol

NaNH$_2$ → $C_6H_5NH_2$ + Na_2SO_3
Aniline   Sodium sulfite

NaCN → C_6H_5CN + Na_2SO_3
Benzonitrile

NaSH → C_6H_5SH + Na_2SO_3
Benzenethiol/
thiophenol

3. Reactions Involving Benzene Ring

(i) Electrophilic aromatic substitution: The $-SO_3H$ group being a deactivating group, directs the incoming group to the meta position during the electrophilic aromatic substitution reactions. Also, the reaction requires more vigorous conditions than required for unsubstituted benzene.

QUESTIONS

Q.1 What are aromatic sulphonic acids? Explain acidity of benzene sulphonic acid and write laboratory method of preparation of benzene sulphonic acid.   **(May-2015)**

Q.2 What are sulphonic acids? Explain their nature. Explain any three methods of preparation and three reactions of sulphonic acids.   **(Dec-2015)**

Q.3 Write a note on preparation of sulphonic acid.

Q.4 Write a note on reaction of sulphonic acid.

Q.5 Give any two reactions of benzene sulphonic acid.   **(May-2015, May-2014)**

Q.6 Explain acidity of benzene sulphonic acid.   **(Dec-2014)**

Q.7 How will you distinguish between phenols and ethyl alcohol?   **(May-2015)**

❖ ❖ ❖

Chapter 13

ALCOHOLS AND ETHERS

13.1 INTRODUCTION

13.1.1 Alcohols

Alcohols are organic compounds containing a hydroxyl group (OH) as the functional group attached to the carbon. The general formula for alcohols is R–OH. Depending upon the kind of carbon attached to the –OH group, the alcohols can be classified as primary, secondary or tertiary. Also the R group may be cyclic, may contain additional functional groups etc. Thus, though the functional group –OH determines the characteristic properties of this class of compounds, the variation in structure of R will determine the rate at which the alcohol will undergo a certain reaction. Sometimes R may also affect the type of reaction.

$1°$ alcohol $2°$ alcohol $3°$ alcohol

Examples:

Ethanol   Propan-2-ol   2-Methylbutan-2-ol
$1°$ alcohol $2°$ alcohol $3°$ alcohol

Alcohols may also be classified on the basis of number of hydroxyl groups present. Thus, compounds containing one hydroxyl group are called monohydric (e.g. ethanol), those with two hydroxyl groups are called dihydric alcohols or glycols (e.g. ethylene glycol) and those containing more than two hydroxyl groups are called polyhydric alcohols (e.g. glycerol).

Ethylene glycol
Dihydric alcohol

Glycerol
Polyhydric alcohol

Alcohols are an important class of organic compounds having great use in synthetic chemistry as well as day to day life. Alcohols like methanol, isopropanol and butanol are important solvents while ethanol is the main component of alcoholic beverages. Menthol, an alicyclic alcohol is a very popular flavouring agent and is also used as a counter irritant and local anaesthetic.

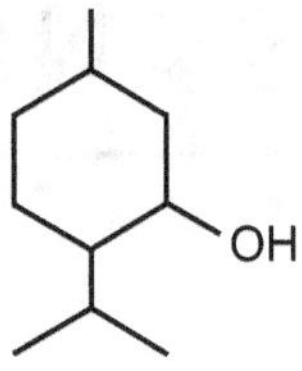

Menthol

13.1.2 Ethers

Ethers are organic compounds characterized by an oxygen atom bonded to two alkyl or aryl groups. The general formula for ethers is R-O-R, Ar-O-R, or Ar-O-Ar, where Ar is phenyl or other aromatic group. Some of the most important ethers are diethyl ether, dimethyl ether and anisole. Diethyl ether is a useful inhalation general anaesthetic and an important solvent.

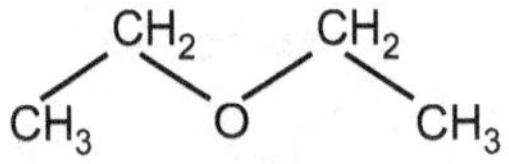

Diethyl ether 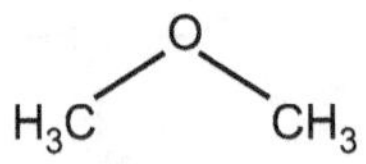   Dimethyl ether 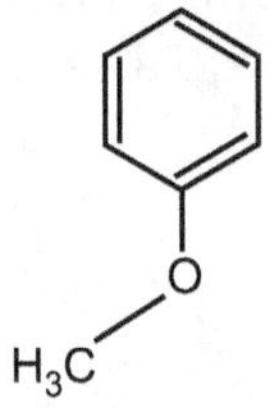   Anisole

13.2 NOMENCLATURE

13.2.1 Alcohols

Common names of alcohols are derived by naming the alkyl group that bears the hydroxyl substituent (–OH) and then adding alcohol as a separate word. The following rules are followed while naming alcohols:

1. Select the longest chain containing the –OH group. Replace the -e ending of the corresponding alkane by the suffix -ol.

2. Indicate the position of hydroxyl group by number generally giving the lowest possible number to the carbon to which the –OH group is attached.

3. Indicate the positions of other groups attached to the parent chain by numbers.

Given below are some examples to understand the nomenclature:

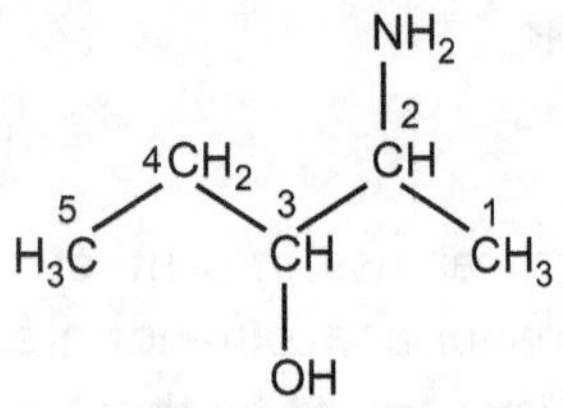

2-Aminopentan-3-ol 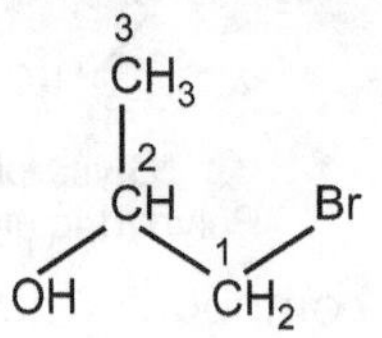   1-Bromo-2-propanol 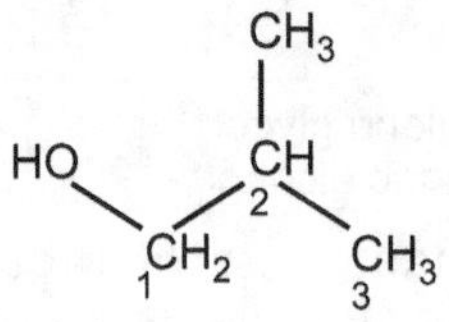   2-Methyl-1-propanol 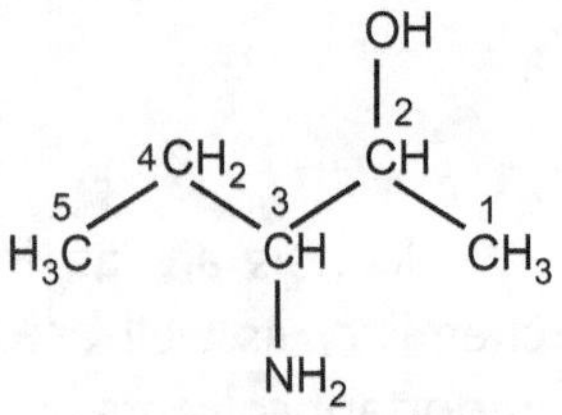   3-Aminopentan-2-ol

13.2.2 Ethers

Ethers can be named by naming each of the two carbon groups as a separate word followed by a space and the word ether. The –OR group can also be named as a substituent using the group name, alkoxy. For example, CH_3–CH_2–O–CH_3 is called ethyl methyl ether or methoxyethane. The smaller, shorter alkyl group becomes the alkoxy substituent. The larger, longer alkyl group side becomes the alkane base name. Each alkyl group on each side of the oxygen is numbered separately. The numbering priority is given to the carbon closest to the oxygen. The alkoxy side (shorter side) has an "-oxy" ending with its corresponding alkyl group. For example, $CH_3CH_2CH_2CH_2CH_2$-O-$CH_2CH_2CH_3$ is 1-propoxypentane.

Ethers having two identical groups are called **symmetrical ethers** (diethyl ether) while those having different groups are called **unsymmetrical ethers** (ethyl methyl ether). Given below are some examples:

Diethyl ether	tert-butyl methyl ether	
Symmetrical	Unsymmetrical	
Ethoxyethane	**2-Methoxy-2-methylpropane**	**3-Ethoxy-2-methylbutan-1-ol**

13.3 METHODS OF PREPARATION

13.3.1 Alcohols

1. From alkanes:

Alkanes having tertiary carbon can be oxidized with cold $KMnO_4$ to give tertiary alcohols.

$$\text{Alkane} \xrightarrow{\text{cold } KMnO_4} \text{tert-alcohol}$$

2. From alkenes:

Alkenes can be converted to alcohols by number of reagents. These are given below:

Reactant	Reagents	Product
alkene	**Oxidation** (i) conc. H_2SO_4 (ii) HOH	secondary alcohol

Contd...

	Oxymercuration-demercuration (i) Hg(OCOCH₃)₂/HOH (ii) NaBH₄ 　　(mercuric acetate)　(sodium borohydride)	
	Hydroboration-oxidation (i) (BH₃)₂/THF　　　　　(ii) H₂O₂/OH⁻ (diborane in tetrahydrofuran)　(alkaline hydrogen peroxide)	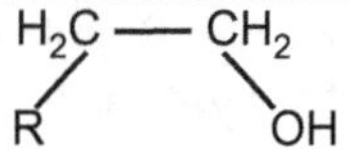 H_2C — CH_2 R　　　OH Primary alcohol
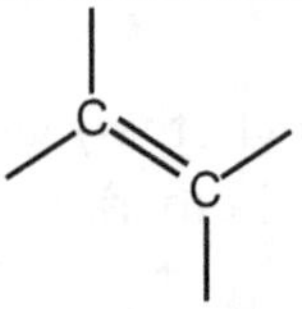 alkene	**Hydroxylation** KMnO₄ (Potassium permanganate)	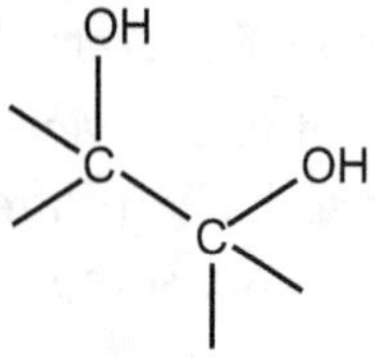 OH ... OH A diol (*syn-hydroxylation*)
	Hydroxylation RCO₂OH (Organic peracid)	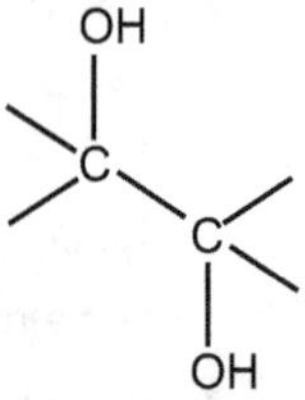 OH ... OH A diol (*anti-hydroxylation*)

3. From Akyl Halides

Alkyl halides (R-X) can be converted to alcohols with aqueous base or with moist silver oxide (Ag₂O).

$$R - X \xrightarrow[\substack{or \\ wet\ Ag_2O}]{HOH/NaOH} R - OH$$

4. From Aldehydes and Ketones:

Aldehydes are reduced to primary alcohols and ketones are reduced to secondary alcohols:

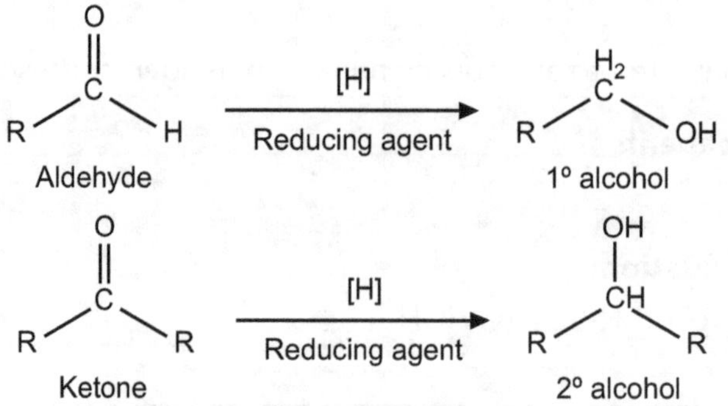

$$\underset{\text{Aldehyde}}{R-\overset{\overset{\textstyle O}{\|}}{C}-H} \xrightarrow[\text{Reducing agent}]{[H]} \underset{1°\ \text{alcohol}}{R-\overset{H_2}{C}-OH}$$

$$\underset{\text{Ketone}}{R-\overset{\overset{\textstyle O}{\|}}{C}-R} \xrightarrow[\text{Reducing agent}]{[H]} \underset{2°\ \text{alcohol}}{R-\overset{\overset{\textstyle OH}{|}}{C}H-R}$$

Various reagents used in reduction and their characteristics are given below:

Name of reducing agents	Formula of reducing agent	Characteristics
Lithium aluminium hydride	$LiAlH_4$	Does not reduce C-C double or triple bond if present in the molecule.
Sodium borohydride	$NaBH_4$	Only reduces carbonyl group. No effect on other reducible groups.
Aluminium isopropoxide, isopropyl alcohol	$Al(OC_3H_7)_3$	Also called Meerwein-Ponndorf Verley (MPV) reduction. Only reduces carbonyl group. No effect on other reducible groups.
Sodium in ethanol	Na/C_2H_5OH	Benzaldehyde cannot be reduced as it undergoes coupling reaction
Metals like zinc, iron or tin along with acids like hydrochloric, dil sulphuric acid and acetic acid	Zn, Fe or Sn HCl, dil H_2SO_4 or CH_3COOH	Non selective reducing agents. They reduce other reducible groups present in the molecule besides reducing the carbonyl group.

5. From Grignard Reagent:

Aldehydes and ketones on reaction with Grignard reagent undergo addition reaction followed by hydrolysis to give alcohols.

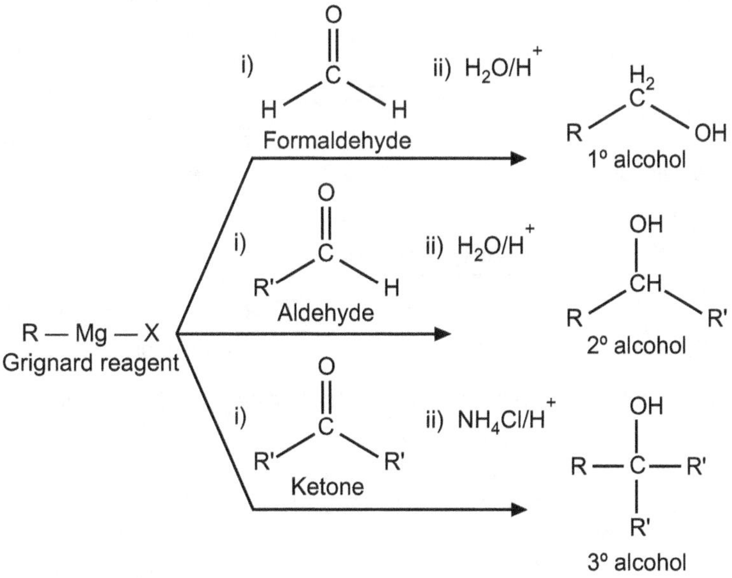

Grignard reagent also reacts with **acid chlorides** and **esters** to give alcohol.

R — Mg — X (Grignard reagent)

i) Acid chloride (R'—CO—Cl) ii) H_2O/H^+ → 3° alcohol (R'—C(R)(R)—OH); if R' = H, no reaction

i) Formate ester (H—CO—OR) ii) H_2O/H^+ → 2° alcohol (R—CH(OH)—R')

i) Ester (R'—CO—OR") ii) H_2O/H^+ → 3° alcohol (R'—C(R)(R)—OH)

6. By Reduction of Carboxylic Acids, Acid Chlorides and Esters:

Lithium aluminium hydride ($LiAlH_4$) can reduce carboxylic acids, esters and acid chlorides to give primary alcohol. However, esters on reduction may also yield 1°, 2° or 3° alcohol along with a primary alcohol. The reaction is illustrated below:

R—CO—OH (Acid) $\xrightarrow{\text{i) } LiAlH_4 \text{ ii) } H_2O/H^+}$ R—CH_2—OH (1° alcohol) + H_2O

R—CO—Cl (Acid chloride) $\xrightarrow{\text{i) } LiAlH_4 \text{ ii) } H_2O/H^+}$ R—CH_2—OH (1° alcohol) + HCl

R—CO—OR' (Ester) $\xrightarrow{\text{i) } LiAlH_4 \text{ ii) } H_2O/H^+}$ R—CH_2—OH (1° alcohol) + R'OH

Carboxylic acids and esters are also reduced to primary alcohol by borohydride (BH_3).

R—CO—OH (Acid) $\xrightarrow{\text{i) } BH_3/THF \text{ ii) } H_2O/H^+}$ R—CH_2—OH (1° alcohol) + H_2O

i) BH$_3$/THF ii) H$_2$O/H$^+$

Ester → $1°$ alcohol + R'OH

13.3.2 Ethers

1. From Alcohols:

Alcohols can be dehydrated (removal of water) when heated with sulphuric acid to give ethers. However, if the temperature of this reaction is not controlled properly, the alcohol may undergo another type of dehydration, involving elimination, to give alkenes. Thus, if ethyl alcohol is heated with conc. H$_2$SO$_4$ at 180°C, it gives ethylene, while if the same reaction is carried out at 140°C, diethyl ether is obtained. Only primary alcohol can be used as secondary and tertiary alcohols give elimination products. This method is routinely used in industrial scale preparation of ethers.

$$2R\text{—OH} \xrightarrow{\text{H}_2\text{SO}_4,\ heat} R\text{—O—R}$$

Alcohol → Ether

It is important to note that this method is generally limited to preparation of symmetrical ethers, as use of two different alcohols will give a mixture of three ethers.

2. Williamson Synthesis:

In this synthesis an alkyl halide is reacted with a sodium alkoxide to give ether. The method is useful for synthesis of both symmetrical as well as unsymmetrical ethers.

R'—OH (Alcohol) $\xrightarrow{Na^+}$ R'—O$^-$Na$^+$ (Alkoxide) $\xrightarrow[\text{Alkyl halide}]{R\text{—X}}$ R—O—R' (Dialky ether)

or

Ar—OH (Phenol) $\xrightarrow{NaOH}$ Ar—O$^-$Na$^+$ (Aryl oxide) $\xrightarrow{R\text{—X}}$ R—O—Ar (Aryl alkyl ether)

Example:

Phenol + CH$_3$CH$_2$Br $\xrightarrow{\text{aq. NaOH}}$ 1-Ethoxybenzene or Ethyl phenyl ether

3. Alkoxymercuration-Demercuration:

This reaction converts alkenes into ethers. Alkene is reacted with mercuric acetate and alcohol in the first step, followed by treatment with sodium borohydride in the next step.

$$\underset{\text{Alkene}}{\text{C}=\text{C}} \xrightarrow[\text{2. NaBH}_4]{\text{1. Hg(OAc)}_2/\text{ROH}} \underset{\text{Ether}}{\text{H}-\text{C}-\text{C}-\text{OR}}$$

The addition follows Markovnikov's rule. Given below is an example:

$$\underset{\text{Propene}}{\text{CH}_3\text{CH}=\text{CH}_2} + \underset{\text{Ethanol}}{\text{C}_2\text{H}_5\text{OH}} + \underset{\substack{\text{Mercuric} \\ \text{trifluoro acetate}}}{\text{Hg(OCOCF}_3)_2} \xrightarrow{\text{THF}} \underset{\text{OC}_2\text{H}_5}{\text{CH}_3\text{CHCH}_2}-\text{HgOCOCF}_3 \xrightarrow{\text{NaBH}_4} \underset{\substack{\text{OC}_2\text{H}_5 \\ \text{2-Ethoxypropane}}}{\text{CH}_3\text{CHCH}_3}$$

13.4 PHYSICAL PROPERTIES

13.4.1 Alcohols

Alcohols are liquids with a peculiar odour. Alcohols (R–OH) can be considered derivatives of water (H–OH) and also of alkanes (R-H). While the –OH group mostly determines the physical properties of alcohols, the alkyl group (R) modifies it. Presence of a hydroxyl group (–OH) makes the alcohols capable of forming hydrogen bonds. This property of forming hydrogen bonds is responsible for the following physical properties shown by alcohols:

1. **Boiling points:** Alcohols have higher boiling points than the hydrocarbons having similar molecular masses. This is because higher energy is required to break the hydrogen bonds present in alcohols as compared to the van der Waals forces present in the hydrocarbons. This is evident from the table given below:

Formula	Name	Molar Mass	Boiling Point (°C)
CH_4	methane	16	–164
H_2O	water	18	100
C_2H_6	ethane	30	–89
CH_3OH	methanol	32	65
C_3H_8	propane	44	–42
CH_3CH_2OH	ethanol	46	78
C_4H_{10}	butane	58	–1
$CH_3CH_2CH_2OH$	1-propanol	60	97

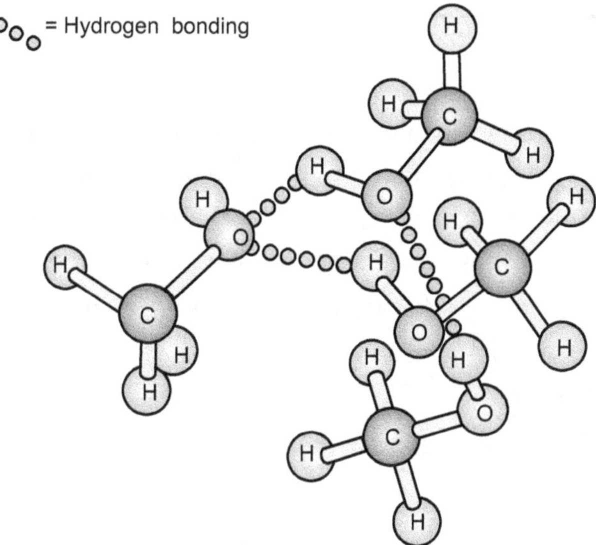

2. Solubility: Unlike hydrocarbons, lower alcohols are miscible with water. This property is again due to the formation of hydrogen bond between the alcohol and water molecules. Thus, while the hydrocarbons are insoluble in water, alcohols with one to three carbon atoms are completely soluble. As the length of the chain increases, however, the solubility of alcohols in water decreases; the molecules become more like hydrocarbons and less like water. The alcohol 1-decanol ($CH_3CH_2CH_2CH_2CH_2CH_2CH_2CH_2CH_2CH_2OH$) is essentially insoluble in water. The borderline of solubility in a family of organic compounds is usually considered at four or five carbon atoms.

13.4.2 Ethers

Dimethylether and ethyl methyl ether are gases at ordinary temperature. The other lower homologues are colourless, pleasant smelling, volatile liquids with typical ether smell. Since the C–O–C bond angle is not 180°, the dipole moments of the two C–O bonds do not cancel each other giving a small net dipole moment to ethers. The weak polarity of ethers however, does not appreciably affect their boiling points which are comparable to those of the alkanes of comparable molecular mass. Ethers have much lower boiling points as compared to isomeric alcohols. This is because alcohol molecules are associated by hydrogen bonds while ether molecules are not.

$$R \overset{\displaystyle O}{\underset{110°}{\diagup \diagdown}} R'$$

Ethers containing upto three carbon atoms are soluble in water which is thought to be due to their hydrogen bond formation with water molecules. The unshared electron pairs on oxygen can form a hydrogen bond with hydrogen of the water molecule. The solubility decreases with increase in the number of carbon atoms. The relative increase in the hydrocarbon portion of the molecule decreases the tendency of H-bond formation.

Ethers are appreciably soluble in organic solvents like alcohol, benzene, acetone etc.

13.5 CHEMICAL PROPERTIES

13.5.1 Alcohols

Just like the physical properties, the chemical properties of alcohols are also based on the hydroxyl group. The alkyl group in turn may modify certain properties. The chemical reactions shown by alcohols can be studied under the following categories:

1. Reactions involving breaking of carbon-oxygen (C–O) bond.

2. Reactions due to acidic character of alcohols (i.e. due to breaking of oxygen-hydrogen (O–H) bond).

3. Oxidation of alcohols.

Now let us see each type of reaction in detail.

1. Reactions Involving Breaking of Carbon-Oxygen (C–O) Bond

(i) Nucleophilic substitution (SN) reactions: Alcohols undergo nucleophilic substitution reactions when treated with following reagents:

$$R-OH \xrightarrow[\Delta]{HCl,\ ZnCl_2} R-Cl\ (Alkyl\ chloride)$$

$$R-OH \xrightarrow[\Delta]{PCl_3\ or\ PCl_5} R-Cl\ (Alkyl\ chloride)$$

$$R-OH \xrightarrow[\Delta]{P,\ Br_3\ or\ PBr_3} R-Br\ (Alkyl\ bromide)$$

$$R-OH \xrightarrow[\Delta]{P,\ I_2\ or\ PI_3} R-I\ (Alkyl\ iodide)$$

$$R-OH \xrightarrow[or\ SOCl_2,\ ether]{SOCl_2,\ Pyridene} R-Cl + SO_2 + HCl$$

Alcohols cannot undergo nucleophilic substitution with a halide ion from NaX because -OH is a strongly nucleophilic, poor leaving group and thus cannot be replaced by a weakly basic halide ion i.e X^-. However, if strong acid is used in the reaction, the –OH is converted to $-OH_2^+$, which is a good leaving group and thus can be replaced with a halide ion from NaX.

$$R-OH + H^+ \longrightarrow R-OH_2^+ \xrightarrow{Na^+X^-} R-X + H_2O$$

Reactivity: The reactivity of alcohols towards the above reactions is in the following order:

primary < secondary < tertiary, allyl, benzyl

Some examples of nucleophilic substitution are:

Isopropyl alcohol (2°) $\xrightarrow[\text{reflux}]{\text{conc. HBr or NaBr, H}_2\text{SO}_4}$ Isopropyl bromide

n-Pentyl alcohol (1°) $\xrightarrow[\text{Heat}]{\text{HCl, ZnCl}_2}$ n-Pentyl chloride

tert-Butyl alcohol (3°) $\xrightarrow[\text{Room temperature}]{\text{Conc. HCl}}$ tert-Butyl chloride

2-Methyl-1-butanol $\xrightarrow{\text{PBr}_3}$ 1-Bromo-2-methylbutane

(ii) Dehydration: Alcohols can be dehydrated by various reagents like conc. H_2SO_4, $KHSO_4$, H_3PO_4, anhy. Al_2O_3, anhy. PCl_5, anhy. $ZnCl_2$, BF_3 and P_2O_5 to give an alkene.

Alcohol $\xrightarrow[-\text{H}_2\text{O}]{\text{Dehydrating agent}}$ Alkene

Dehydration of alcohols generally results in the formation of a mixture of alkenes, the major product being the Saytzeff product (i.e. double bond goes to the carbon which is more substituted).

Pentan-2-ol $\xrightarrow[-\text{H}_2\text{O}]{\text{H}_2\text{SO}_4}$ Pent-2-ene (major product) + Pent-1-ene (minor product)

2. Reactions due to Breaking of Oxygen-Hydrogen (O–H) Bond

(i) Acidity of alcohols:

Alcohols possess weak acidic and basic properties just like water. These properties are due to the presence of the –OH group. Presence of oxygen with unshared electron pair makes the alcohol basic enough to accept a proton from strong acids like hydrochloric acid and sulfuric acid. Similarly alcohols can dissociate to give a proton in the presence of a strong base. Alcohols are much stronger acids (by roughly 1030 times) than alkanes. However, alcohols are weaker acids than water (only methanol being an exception), and much weaker than phenols.

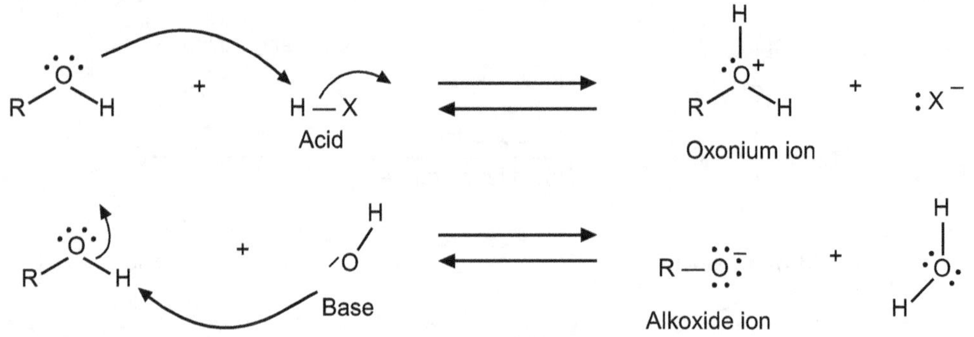

Dissociation of alcohols

The nature of the alkyl group can affect the acidity of alcohols. Acidity of alcohols decreases as the carbon attached to oxygen changes from primary to tertiary. This is because the alkoxide ion generated from a primary alcohol is more stable than that from secondary and tertiary alcohol. The increasing order of +I effect of alkyl group from primary to tertiary, increases the negative charge on oxygen, thereby decreasing the stability of the corresponding alkoxide. The unstable alkoxide combines with the hydrogen ion to revert back to its undissociated form.

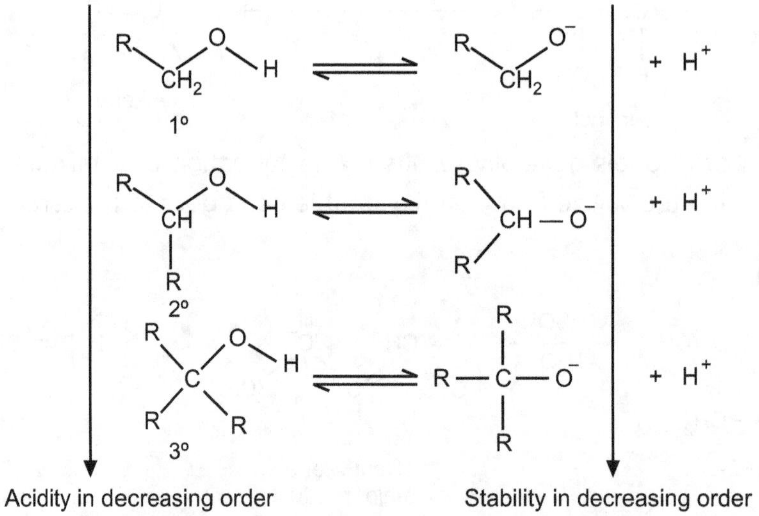

Acidity in decreasing order　　　　　Stability in decreasing order

(ii) Salt formation:

Alcohols react with heavy metals to form metal alkoxide and evolve H_2. This reaction is an acid base reaction.

$$2R-O-H \;+\; M \longrightarrow 2RO^-M^+ \;+\; 1/2H_2$$

Alcohol (acid)   metal (base)   metal salt of alcohol (metal alkoxide)

Thus, reaction with sodium can be written as:

$$2R-O-H \;+\; 2Na \longrightarrow 2\,RO^-Na^+ \;+\; H_2$$

Al, Mg and Zn can also react with alcohols to form metal oxides but the most reactive of the three is aluminium. Aluminium has great affinity for oxygen, and aluminium isoproxide is a very popular reagent for reduction of carbonyl group (MPV reduction).

Isopropanol

Aluminium isopropoxide

(iii) Ester formation with carboxylic acids and chlorides:

Alcohol behaves as a nucleophile and gives addition reaction with the carbonyl group of carboxylic acid. The adduct formed undergoes loss of water to form an ester. Mineral acid is used to facilitate the nucleophilic attack of the alcohol by protonating the carbonyl oxygen.

Isopropanol   Ethanoic acid   Ethyl ethanoate

The mechanism can be written as:

Rapid proton transfer

Ester formation with acid chlorides does not require acid catalysis as the carbonyl carbon of acid chloride is sufficiently electron deficient to attract the nucleophilic alcohol.

Ethanol + Acetyl chloride → ($-HCl$) → Ethyl ethanoate

Alcohols can also react in a similar manner with acetic anhydride to form an acetylated derivative. This reaction is mainly used for the determination of number of hydroxyl groups in the given compounds.

(iv) Ester formation with sulfonic acids and sulfonyl chlorides:

Sulfonic acids and sulfonyl chlorides undergo ester formation readily with alcohols.

Ethanol + Methanesulfonic acid → ($-H_2O$) → Ethyl methanesulfonate

Ethanol + Methanesulfonyl chloride → ($-H_2O$) → Ethyl methanesulfonate

Alcohols also react with derivatives of p-toluenesulfonylchloride (TsCl) to form the respective sulfonate esters. p-Toluene sulfonyl chloride is also called tosyl chloride and the esters formed are called tosylate esters. The tosyl group is a very good leaving group and thus the reaction has a lot of synthetic importance.

Isopropanol + p-toluenesulfonylchloride (tosyl chloride TsCl) → ($-HCl$) → Isopropyl p-toluenesulfonate (tosylate ester)

(v) Ester formation with proton acids having –OH group:

Alcohols react with nitric, sulphuric and phosphoric acids to give inorganic esters.

Alcohol + Nitric acid (OHNO$_2$) → ($-H_2O$) → Nitrate ester

Example:

Glycerine + 3 OHNO$_2$ $\xrightarrow{-3H_2O}$ Glyceryl trinitrate/nitroglycerine (antianginal agent)

Alcohol + Sulfuric acid $\xrightarrow{-H_2O}$ Sulfonate ester

Alcohol + Phosphoric acid $\xrightarrow{-H_2O}$ Phosphonate monoester

The above reaction can repeat once or twice to produce diesters and triesters, respectively.

Phosphonate monoester + Alcohol $\xrightarrow{-H_2O}$ Phosphonate diester

Phosphonate diester + Alcohol $\xrightarrow{-H_2O}$ Phosphonate triester

Phosphate esters play important roles in biological systems:

Phosphodiesters make up the structural "backbones" of the nucleic acids (RNA and DNA).

Phosphate esters are key intermediates in carbohydrate metabolism (glycolosis), also phosphate esters (and anhydrides) provide the "high energy bond" construct in ATP.

(vi) Alkylation of alcohols:

Replacement of –H of the –OH group of alcohols by an alkyl group is known as alkylation reaction. Ether is obtained as the product. The reagent used in this reaction is called an alkylating agent. Methylation is the most important reaction of this class. Reagents like dimethyl sulphate ($(CH_3)_2SO_4$) and sodium hydroxide or methyl iodide (CH_3I) and potassium carbonate (K_2CO_3) are used for the reaction.

$$R-O-H \xrightarrow[\;CH_3I,\; K_2CO_3\;]{(CH_3)_2SO_4,\; NaOH\; or} R-O-CH_3$$

Alcohol   Ether

3. Oxidation of Alcohols

All alcohols containing α-hydrogen can undergo oxidation reaction. The reaction involves dehydrogenation (removal of hydrogen) and is 1, 2-elimination type of reaction. Reactivity of alcohols towards oxidation is directly proportional to the number of hydrogens on the α-carbon. Thus, methanol (CH_3OH) is most readily oxidized while tertiary alcohols are not oxidized at all. A number of oxidizing agents are available to oxidize alcohols into a variety of products.

(i) Oxidation by mild oxidizing agents:

Primary alcohols are oxidized to aldehydes by mild oxidizing agents while secondary alcohols are oxidized to ketones. The reagents used are:

Halogens (like Cl_2, Br_2 and I_2); Fenton reagent (H_2O_2 and $FeSO_4$); chromic acid ($K_2Cr_2O_7/H_2SO_4$); Jone's reagent (CrO_3/H^+, Me_2CO); potassium permanganate ($KMnO_4/H_2O$) ; HNO_3 ; CuO/Δ or Ag/Δ.

$$R-\underset{\underset{H}{|}}{\overset{\overset{H}{|}}{C}}-OH \xrightarrow{\text{Mild oxidizing agent}} R-\overset{\overset{O}{\|}}{C}-H$$

1° alcohol   Aldehyde

$$R-\underset{\underset{R'}{|}}{\overset{\overset{H}{|}}{C}}-OH \xrightarrow{\text{Mild oxidizing agent}} R-\underset{\underset{R'}{|}}{C}=O$$

2° alcohol   Ketone

$$R-\underset{\underset{R'}{|}}{\overset{\overset{R''}{|}}{C}}-OH \xrightarrow{\text{Mild oxidizing agent}} \text{No reaction}$$

3° alcohol

However, tertiary alcohols may undergo dehydration to give an alkene when heated with copper.

$$R-\underset{\underset{CH_3}{|}}{\overset{\overset{CH_3}{|}}{C}}-OH \xrightarrow{\text{Cu, 300°C}} R-\underset{\underset{CH_3}{|}}{\overset{CH_2}{\overset{\|}{C}}} + H_2O$$

3° alcohol   Alkene

(ii) Oxidation by strong oxidizing agents:

Since the primary alcohols contain two α-hydrogens, strong oxidizing agents are able to remove both the hydrogens, leading to formation of an acid. The secondary alcohols are oxidized only to ketones as they contain only one α-hydrogen.

$$R-\underset{\underset{H}{|}}{\overset{\overset{H}{|}}{C}}-OH \xrightarrow{\text{Strong oxidizing agent (SOA)}} \underset{R}{\overset{O}{\overset{\|}{C}}}OH$$

1° alcohol   Carboxylic acid

$$R-\underset{\underset{R'}{|}}{\overset{\overset{H}{|}}{C}}-OH \xrightarrow{\text{Strong oxidizing agent (SOA)}} R-\underset{\underset{R'}{|}}{C}=O$$

2° alcohol   Ketone

SOA = $KMnO_4$, OH^-, heat; $KMnO_4$, H^+, heat; $K_2Cr_2O_7$, H^+, heat; conc. HNO_3, heat

(iii) Miscellaneous oxidations:

(a) **Oxidation with O_2 and Pt:** This reagent oxidizes only primary alcoholic groups into carboxylic groups without affecting the secondary and tertiary hydroxyl groups.

(b) **Oxidation of 1° and 2° alcohols having β-CH$_3$ group with halogens in basic medium (haloform reaction):** The halogen disproportionates in the presence of hydroxide to give the halide and hypohalite. For example,

$$Br_2 + 2OH^- \rightarrow Br^- + BrO^- + H_2O$$

The hypohalite then oxidizes the primary alcohol to an aldehyde and a secondary alcohol to a ketone. The β-CH$_3$ is then exhaustively halogenated to form $-CX_3$, which being a good leaving group leaves the molecule to form haloform (CHX_3) and a carboxylic acid.

$$\underset{R}{\overset{OH}{\overset{|}{\underset{\diagdown CH_3}{CH}}}} \xrightarrow{OH^-,\ OBr^-} \underset{R}{\overset{O}{\overset{\|}{\underset{\diagdown CH_3}{C}}}}$$

2° alcohol   Ketone

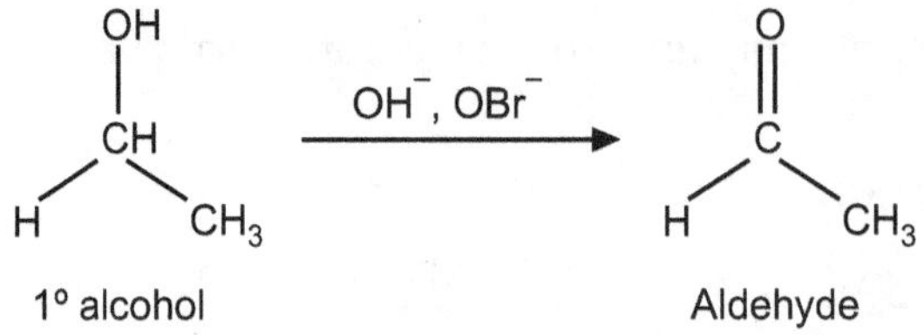
OH⁻, OBr⁻
1° alcohol
Aldehyde

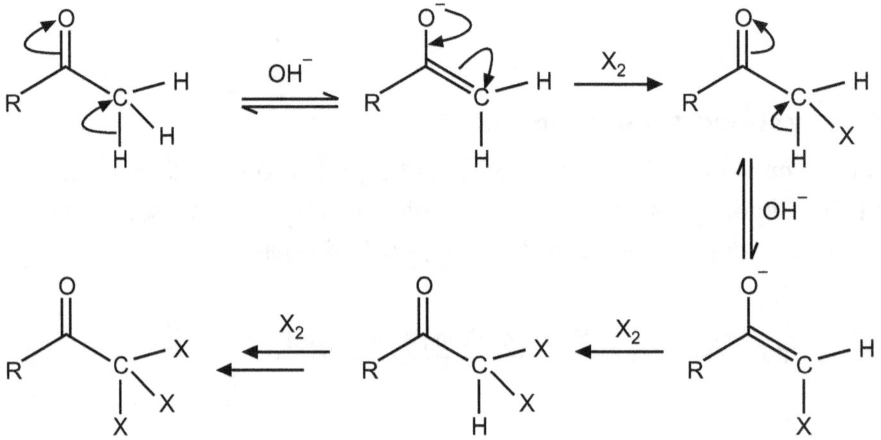

Tri α-halomethyl ketone

Tri α-halomethyl aldehyde (R=H)

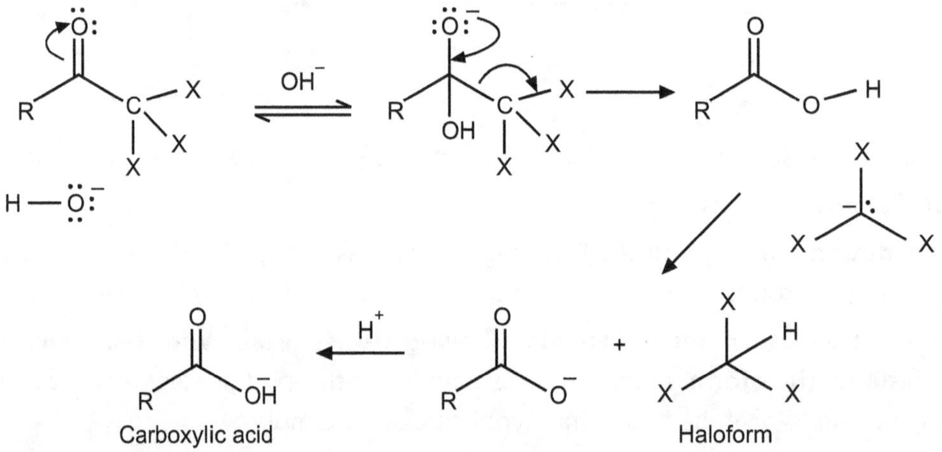
Carboxylic acid
Haloform

4. Reduction of Alcohols

The alcohols are not normally reduced directly to alkanes. However, they may be first dehydrated to form alkenes, which then can be reduced to alkanes. The other method is to first form the tosyl ester and then reduce it to give alkanes.

For example,

$$\underset{\text{Alcohol}}{CH_3CH(OH)CH_3} \xrightarrow{H_2SO_4} \underset{\text{Alkene}}{CH_2=CHCH_3} \xrightarrow[Pt]{H_2} \underset{\text{Alkane}}{CH_3CH_2CH_3}$$

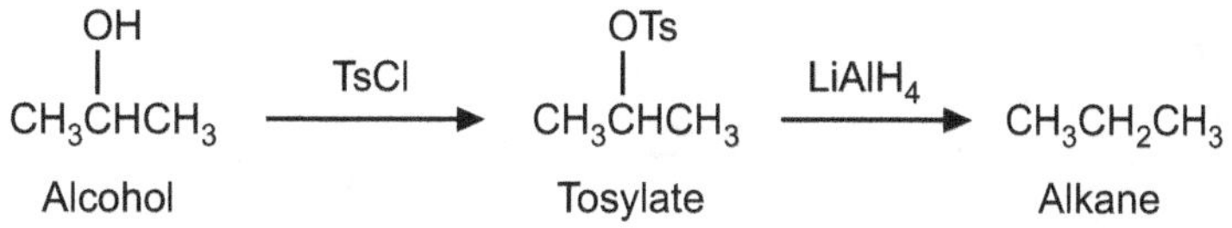

$$\underset{\text{Alcohol}}{\overset{\overset{\displaystyle OH}{|}}{CH_3CHCH_3}} \xrightarrow{\text{TsCl}} \underset{\text{Tosylate}}{\overset{\overset{\displaystyle OTs}{|}}{CH_3CHCH_3}} \xrightarrow{\text{LiAlH}_4} \underset{\text{Alkane}}{CH_3CH_2CH_3}$$

13.5.2 Ethers

Ethers are relatively unreactive compounds and thus react with very few reagents other than acids. The only site for other reagents are the C–H bonds of the alkyl groups. Ethers are resistant to attack by nucleophiles and bases as they themselves are nucleophilic. The oxygen of ether is able to donate electrons to electrophiles. Thus, electrophiles can be solvated by ether thereby acting as solvents for many reactions.

When ethers are treated with strong acid in the presence of a nucleophile, they can be cleaved to give alcohols and alkyl halides. If the ether is on a primary carbon this may occur through an S_N2 pathway while, the tertiary alkyl group tends to undergo S_N1 displacement.

Common acids for this purpose are HI and other hydrogen halides, as well as H_2SO_4 in the presence of H_2O.

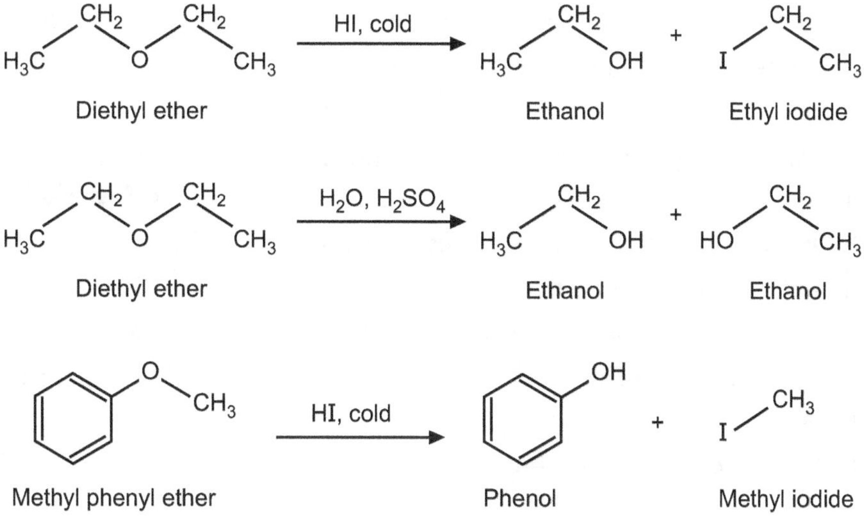

The mechanism involves two steps. In step I, the ether oxygen being basic gets protonated and in step II, this protonated ether undergoes substitution with the nucleophile through either S_N1 or S_N2 mechanism.

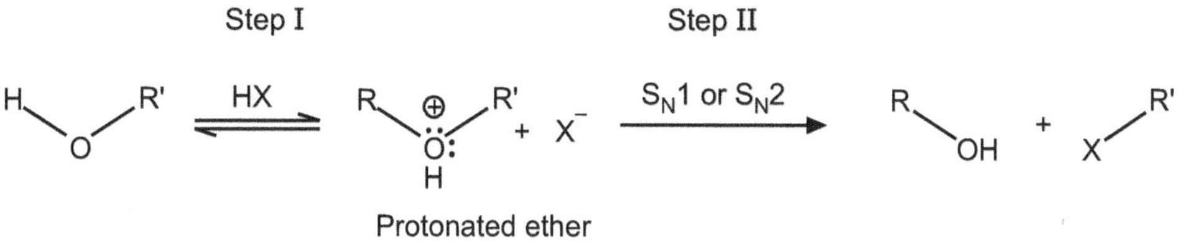

S_N1 Mechanism:

$$R\overset{\oplus}{\underset{H}{O}}R' \xrightarrow{\text{Slow}} R^+ + HOR'$$

Protonated ether   Carbocation   Alcohol

$$R^+ + X^- \xrightarrow{\text{Fast}} R-X$$

Halide   Alkyl halide

S_N2 Mechanism:

$$R\overset{\oplus}{\underset{H}{O}}R' \xrightarrow{X^-} \left[\overset{\delta-}{X}\text{--}R\text{--}\underset{\delta+}{\overset{H}{O}}\text{--}R'\right] \longrightarrow R-X + HOR'$$

Protonated ether   Alkyl halide   Alcohol

QUESTIONS

Q.1   What are alcohols? Explain why boiling point of alcohols are much higher than those of corresponding alkanes. Discuss preparation methods and reactions of alcohols.

Q.2   Write a note on preparation of alcohols and ethers.

Q.3   Write a note on reactions of alcohols and ethers.

Q.4   Explain why boiling point of alcohols are much higher than those of corresponding alkanes.   **(May-2015, Dec-2014)**

Q.5   Write distinguishing test of primary, secondary, tertiary alcohols.   **(May-2015)**

Q.6   Comment of Williamson's ether synthesis.   **(Dec-2015, May-2014)**

Q.7   Discuss two methods for the preparation of alcohols.   **(Dec-2015, May-2014)**

Q.8   How will you distinguish among primary, secondary and tertiary alcohols by a chemical test?   **(May-2014)**

Q.9   Write about Lucas test of alcohols.   **(Dec-2014)**

AMINES

14.1 INTRODUCTION

Amines are derivatives of ammonia in which one or more hydrogens have been replaced one at a time by hydrocarbon groups.

Amines fall into different classes depending on how many of the hydrogen atoms are replaced.

Primary amines:

In primary amines, only one of the hydrogen atoms in the ammonia molecule has been replaced. Thus, the formula of the primary amine is RNH_2 where "R" is an alkyl group.

For example :

$$CH_3-NH_2, \quad CH_3-CH_2-NH_2, \quad CH_3-CH_2-CH_2-NH_2, \quad CH_3-\overset{\overset{\textstyle NH_2}{\textstyle |}}{C}H-CH_3$$

Secondary amines:

In a secondary amine, two of the hydrogens in an ammonia molecule have been replaced by hydrocarbon groups. The two alkyl groups could be same or different.

For example:

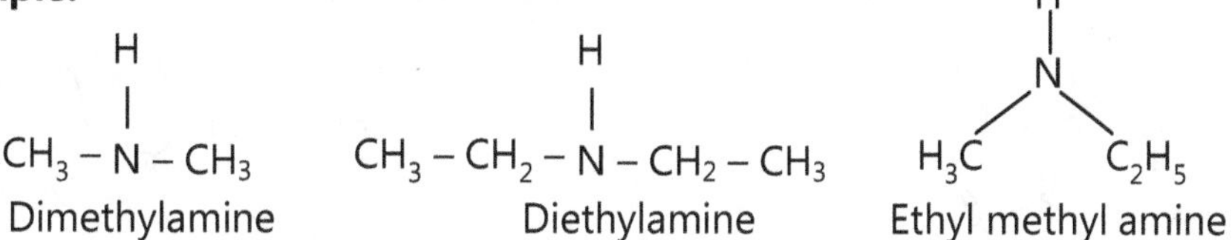

$$CH_3-\overset{\overset{\textstyle H}{\textstyle |}}{N}-CH_3 \qquad CH_3-CH_2-\overset{\overset{\textstyle H}{\textstyle |}}{N}-CH_2-CH_3$$

Dimethylamine · · · · · · · · · Diethylamine · · · · · · · · · Ethyl methyl amine

There are other ways of naming, but this is the commonest and simplest way of naming these small secondary amines.

Tertiary amines:

In a tertiary amine, all of the hydrogens in an ammonia molecule have been replaced by hydrocarbon groups. Again, there can be simple ones where all three of the hydrocarbon groups are the same alkyl groups or one or more alkyl groups may be different.

The naming is similar to secondary amines.

For example :

$$CH_3-\overset{\overset{\textstyle CH_3}{\textstyle |}}{N}-CH_3$$

Trimethylamine

14.2 NOMENCLATURE

Amines are named in a number of different ways.

1. The IUPAC system names amine functions as substituents on the largest alkyl group. The simple -NH$_2$ substituent found in 1°-amines is called an **amino group**. For 2° and 3°-amines a compound prefix (e.g. dimethylamino is the fourth example) includes the names of all but the root alkyl group.

2. The Chemical Abstract Service (CAS) has adopted a nomenclature system in which the suffix -**amine** is attached to the root alkyl name e.g. butanamine (first example). The additional nitrogen substituents in 2° and 3°-amines are designated by the prefix N- before the group name (third example).

3. A common system for simple amines names for each alkyl substituent on nitrogen in alphabetical order, followed by the suffix -**amine**.

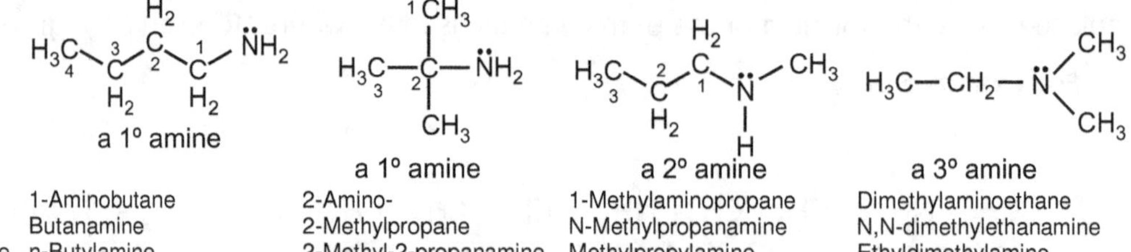

	a 1° amine	a 1° amine	a 2° amine	a 3° amine
IUPAC name	1-Aminobutane	2-Amino-2-Methylpropane	1-Methylaminopropane	Dimethylaminoethane
CA name	Butanamine	2-Methyl-2-propanamine	N-Methylpropanamine	N,N-dimethylethanamine
Common name	n-Butylamine	tert-butylamine	Methylpropylamine	Ethyldimethylamine

There are many examples of 1°, 2°, 3° and even 4° amines in nature. They are mostly present in plants as secondary metabolites called alkaloids. There are several amines present in human body as neurotransmitters and hormones. Some examples are listed below:

Caffeine
(3º amine-A constituent of tea and coffee)

Serotonin
an important neurochemical
(1º amine)

14.3 METHODS FOR PREPARATION OF AMINES

Methods for preparing amines on an industrial scale are quite different from those used for laboratory scale preparation of amines.

14.3.1 Industrial Methods

Following are a couple of methods used for preparation of aniline on an **industrial scale**:

1. **By reduction of nitrobenzene:**

    (a) Iron and hydrochloric acid: Nitrobenzene is treated with 30% hydrochloric acid in the presence of iron and the mixture is heated to give ammonium chloride which when treated with sodium carbonate gives aniline.

(b) By catalytic hydrogen using molecular hydrogen: A solution of nitrobenzene in alcohol is shaken with finely divided nickel or platinum under hydrogen gas.

$$R - NO_2 \xrightarrow{\text{metal/H}^+ \text{ or } H_2/\text{catalyst}} R - NH_2$$

$$Ar - NO_2 \longrightarrow Ar - NH_2$$

2. **Treatment of chlorobenzene with ammonia** at high temperatures and high pressures in the presence of a catalyst like cuprous oxide. This process involves a nucleophilic replacement reaction.

$$\text{Chlorobenzene} \quad C_6H_5-Cl \xrightarrow{NH_3,\ Cu_2O,\ 200°C,\ 900\ lb/m^2} C_6H_5-NH_2 \quad \text{Aniline}$$

14.3.2 Laboratory Methods Used in Preparation of Amines

The laboratory methods used in preparation of amines are as follows :

1. Reduction of nitrogen containing compounds: Various nitrogen containing compounds can be reduced to give amines. The following table lists the starting compounds and the reagents used in the reduction of these compounds.

Table 14.1

Type of compounds	Reagents used	Product formed
$R - NO_2$ $Ar - NO_2$ Nitro compounds	Metal/acid or H_2/Ni or Na/C_2H_5OH or $LiAlH_4$	$R - NH_2$
$R - CO - NH_2$ Amides	$LiAlH_4$ or Na/C_2H_5OH BH_3/THF	$R - CH_2 - NH_2$
$R - C \equiv N$ Cyanides	$LiAlH_4$ or Na/C_2H_5OH H_2/Ni	$R - CH_2 - NH_2$
$R - N^+ \equiv C^-$ Isocyanides	$LiAlH_4$ or Na/C_2H_5OH $H_2/Ni/\Delta$	$R - NH - CH_3$
$\underset{R'}{\overset{R}{>}}C = N - OH$ Oximes	$LiAlH_4$ or Na/C_2H_5OH $H_2/Ni/\Delta$	$\underset{R'}{\overset{R}{>}}CH - NH_2$

2. Reaction of alkyl halides with ammonia (Ammonolysis of halides): Alkyl halides can be converted to amines by treating them with ammonia. This involves the nucleophilic substitution reaction. Major disadvantage of this method is that a mixture of different classes of amines is obtained. The primary amine formed on reaction of alkyl halide with ammonia may attack a second molecule of alkyl halide thus yielding a secondary amine. This secondary amine in turn can further attack a third molecule of alkyl halide to form a tertiary amine. Finally a tertiary amine can attack another molecule of alkyl halide to form a quaternary ammonium salt.

$$NH_3 \xrightarrow{RX} R-NH_2 \xrightarrow{RX} R-\overset{R}{\underset{}{N}}H \xrightarrow{RX} R-\overset{R}{\underset{R}{N}} \xrightarrow{RX} R-\overset{R}{\underset{R}{\overset{\oplus}{N}}}-R \quad X^{\ominus}$$

$$\text{1° amine} \qquad \text{2° amine} \qquad \text{3° amine} \qquad \text{4° ammonium salt}$$

RX = alkyl halide or aryl halide

$$C_2H_5Cl \xrightarrow{NH_3} C_2H_5NH_2 \xrightarrow{CH_3Cl} C_2H_5 - \overset{H}{\underset{}{N}} - CH_3$$

$$\text{Ethyl chloride} \qquad \text{Ethylamine} \qquad \text{Ethylmethylamine}$$

Benzyl chloride　　　Benzylamine　　　Benzyldimethylamine

Another drawback of the reaction is that elimination reaction competes with the substitution reaction. Thus, a primary halide gives highest yields as substitution dominates in this reaction, while tertiary halides mainly yield an elimination product.

3. Reductive amination of aldehydes and ketones : Many aldehydes and ketones can be converted to amines by treating with ammonia to first form an imine and then reducing the carbon nitrogen double bond to give the amine. Reduction can be carried out either by molecular hydrogen and a catalyst like nickel or chemically by use of sodium cyanoborohydride, $NaBH_3CN$. Both aliphatic and aromatic amines can be prepared using this method.

$$\overset{}{\underset{}{\big\rangle}}C=O + NH_3 \xrightarrow{-H_2O} \big\rangle C=NH \xrightarrow[\text{or } NaBH_3CN]{H_2/Ni} \big\rangle CH-NH_2$$

Aldehyde/Ketone　　　　　　　Imine　　　　　　　1° Amine

$$\big\rangle C=O + R-NH_2 \xrightarrow[\substack{\text{or } NaBH_3CN \\ -H_2O}]{H_2/Ni} \big\rangle CH-NH-R$$

2° Amine

$$\big\rangle C=O + R_2NH_2 \xrightarrow[\substack{\text{or } NaBH_3CN \\ -H_2O}]{H_2/Ni} \big\rangle CH-\overset{}{\underset{R}{N}}-R$$

3° Amine

Acetone   Ammonia   Hydrogen   Isopropylamine

Acetaldehyde   Ammonia   Hydrogen   Dimethylethylamine

4. From amides using Hofmann Degradation Reaction: Amides can be converted into primary amines with one carbon atom less using Hofmann Bromamide reaction. The reaction involves a rearrangement taking place in the presence of sodium hypobromite solution.

Phthalimide   Anthranilic acid

Benzamide   Aniline

5. From carboxylic acids and acid chlorides : Carboxylic acids can be converted to primary amines with one carbon less by Schmidt, Curtius or the Lossen rearrangement. In all these reactions, isocyanate is formed as an intermediate which on hydrolysis yields the primary amine.

Schmidt rearrangement

$$R-COOH \xrightarrow[\text{conc. } H_2SO_4]{N_3H} [R-N=C=O] \xrightarrow{H_2O} R-NH_2$$

Carboxylic acid $1°$ amine

Curtius rearrangement

$$R-COOH \xrightarrow{SOCl_2} R-COCl \xrightarrow{NaN_3/heat} [R-N=C=O] \xrightarrow{H_2O} R-NH_2$$

Carboxylic acid   Acid chloride $1°$ amine

Lossen rearrangement

$$R-COOH \xrightarrow{SOCl_2} R-COCl \xrightarrow{NH_2OH} R-CONHOH \xrightarrow[\text{heat}]{OH^-} [R-N=C=O] \xrightarrow{H_2O} R-NH_2$$

Carboxylic acid   Acid chloride   Hydroxamic acid   1° amine

6.   The Gabriel synthesis: Synthesis of primary amines from phthalimide without any formation of secondary and tertiary amines is known as Gabriel synthesis. Phthalimide is first converted to potassium salt which then undergoes nucleophilic substitution, S_N2 to give N-substituted phthalimide. The latter on alkaline hydrolysis gives the primary amine.

Phthalimide   Potassium salt   N-substituted   Phthalate
                                              phthalimide

The alkyl halide should be methyl, primary or secondary whose beta carbon is not 3° or 4° as the crowding will prevent the S_N2 reaction to proceed smoothly.

14.4 PROPERTIES OF AMINES

14.4.1 Physical

Amines being derivatives of ammonia are polar in nature and can form hydrogen bonds with water. Thus, smaller amines like methyl amine and ethylamine are soluble in water. But as the number of carbon atoms increases, the solubility decreases. Lower amines like methylamine and ethylamines have ammonia like smell while higher amines have a characteristic fishy smell.

Amines: H-bonding

14.4.2 Chemical

The amino group is the most common functional group found in drug molecules. Basicity of amino group is the main physicochemical property of importance in the drug chemistry of amines. Because most amines are basic, salts can be easily prepared to facilitate water solubility or solubility in other vehicles for drug administration. Many drugs contain a protonated amino which is thought to provide a cationic centre required for binding to drug targets like receptors and enzymes. In addition to basicity, amines are capable of functioning as nucleophiles and participating in displacement reactions with electrophilic compounds.

R — N̈ — R   H⁺   ⇌   R — N⁺ — R

Amine (base)   Conjugate acid

Aromatic amines like aniline are very prone to oxidation and become coloured on standing. They are also very toxic. Direct contact with skin must be avoided as they are easily absorbed through the skin and can be very harmful.

14.4.3 Reactions of Amines

All the three types of amines viz. 1°, 2° and 3° amines contain nitrogen that has an unshared pair of electrons. The property of sharing these unshared electrons makes the amines nucleophilic as well as basic. Even the aromatic amines show this property and are highly reactive.

1.   Basicity or Salt formation:

All aliphatic and aromatic amines can react with mineral as well as organic acids to form a salt.

HX → R' — N⁺ — R"   Mineral acid salt

R' — N̈ — R"

RCOOH → R' — N⁺ — R"   Organic acid salt

Amine (Free base)

An aliphatic amine is more basic than ammonia as the alkyl groups have a +I effect and therefore the unshared electrons of nitrogen are more available. Also, the alkyl group is able to disperse the positive charge of the quaternary ammonium ion, stabilizing it better than the unsubstituted ammonium ion. Thus, for the same reason, secondary amines are more basic than primary amines as they contain two alkyl groups. Tertiary amines though contain three alkyl groups are less basic than secondary as their bulky structure prevents efficient solvation. This reduction in pK_a thus, is a result of steric factors. The attachment of large and/or multiple substituents to the basic nitrogen of amines hinders bond formation with a proton and thereby reduces basicity.

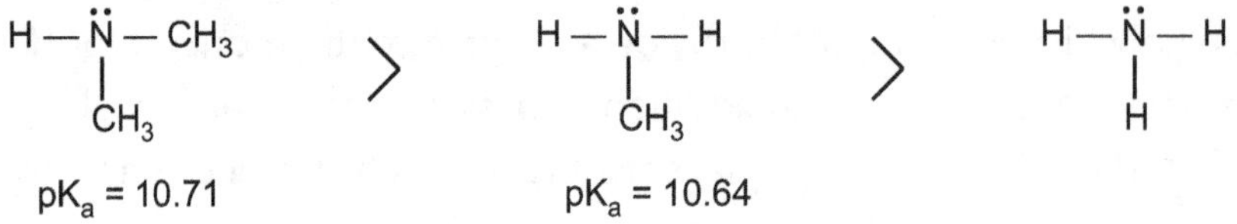

$$H-\ddot{N}(CH_3)-CH_3 \quad > \quad H-\ddot{N}(CH_3)-H \quad > \quad H-\ddot{N}(H)-H$$

$$pK_a = 10.71 \qquad\qquad pK_a = 10.64$$

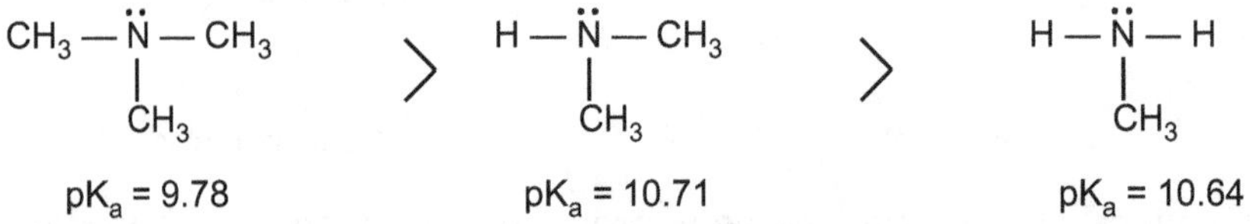

$$CH_3-\ddot{N}(CH_3)-CH_3 \quad > \quad H-\ddot{N}(CH_3)-CH_3 \quad > \quad H-\ddot{N}(CH_3)-H$$

$$pK_a = 9.78 \qquad\qquad pK_a = 10.71 \qquad\qquad pK_a = 10.64$$

However, aniline, an aromatic amine is less basic than ammonia as the unshared electrons are shared by the benzene ring and thus participate in the resonance stabilization of the molecule. However this kind of resonance stabilization is not possible for anilinium ion as the unshared electrons are now no longer available with nitrogen. Resonance thus lowers the energy content of the aniline more than it does for ammonium ion, thus shifting the equilibrium towards less ionization. Thus, we can say that aniline is a weaker base than ammonia because the unshared pair of nitrogen is now partly shared with the ring and is thus less available for sharing it with hydrogen during a reaction with acid. This tendency however makes the aromatic rings substituted with $-NH_2$ group more active towards an electrophilic attack.

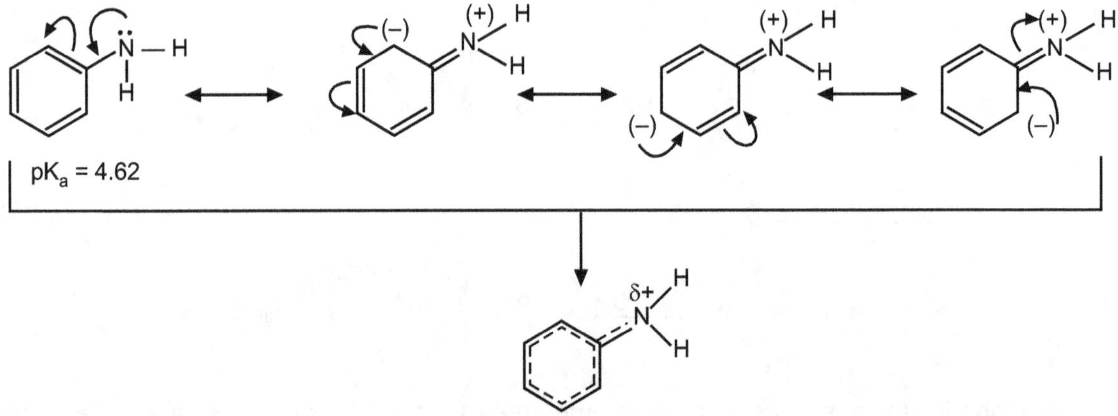

$$pK_a = 4.62$$

Composite resonance structure

Basicity of aromatic amines can be increased by substituting the ring with electron releasing groups like $-NH_2$, $-OCH_3$ and $-CH_3$. Electron withdrawing groups like $-NO_2$, $-CN$, $-COOH$, $-SO_3$ and halogens on the other hand decrease the basicity of aromatic amines. This is because the groups with $+I$ effect push electrons towards nitrogen and make the lone pair more available for sharing with acid, while groups with $-I$ effect pull electrons away from nitrogen and thus make it more difficult for nitrogen to share the lone pair with acid.

p-Methoxyaniline (+R group)
pK_a about 7

Increased basicity of anisidine (*p*-methoxyaniline) due to +R effect of $-OCH_3$.

Reduced basicity of *para*-Nitroaniline due to electron pair delocalization

2. Alkylation:

Alkylation of amines is a nucleophilic substitution reaction. An amine can react with an alkyl halide to give an amine of the next higher class. Alkyl halide undergoes substitution with the basic amine acting as the nucleophilic reagent. Since in this reaction one hydrogen attached to the nitrogen is replaced by an alkyl group, the reaction is called as alkylation of amines. All types of amines that is, primary, secondary, tertiary and aromatic can undergo this reaction.

$$RNH_2 \xrightarrow{R-X} R_2NH \xrightarrow{R-X} R_3N \xrightarrow{R-X} R_4N^+X^-$$

$$1° \qquad\qquad 2° \qquad\qquad 3° \qquad\qquad 4° \text{ salt}$$

$$\boxed{S_N2 : R - X \text{ must be } 1° \text{ or } CH_3}$$

$$CH_3CH_2CH_2NH_2 \xrightarrow{CH_3Cl} CH_3CH_2CH_2NHCH_3$$

n-Propylamine   Methyl-*n*-propylamine

Aniline   N, N-Diethylaniline

Benzylamine   Benzyltrimethylammonium iodide

3. Acetylation:

Ammonia reacts with acid chlorides of carboxylic acids and that of sulfonic acids to yield amides and sulfonamides respectively. This again is a nucleophilic reaction where the ammonia acts as a nucleophilic reagent, attacking the carbonyl carbon or sulfur displacing chloride ion. Primary and secondary amines behave in a similar fashion with acid chlorides to form substituted amides, the –Cl of acid chloride being replaced by –NHR or –NR$_2$ group. Tertiary amines fail to react in this manner as the nitrogen does not have replaceable hydrogen. Substituted amides thus obtained are named as derivatives of unsubstituted amides as illustrated below:

Conversion to amides:

$$R - NH_2 + RCOCl \longrightarrow RCONHR \quad + \quad HCl$$

1° Amine   N-substituted amide

$$R_2NH + RCOCl \longrightarrow RCONR_2 \quad + \quad HCl$$

2° Amine   N, N-disubstituted amide

$$R_3N + RCOCl \longrightarrow \text{No reaction}$$

3° Amine

Examples :

Aniline   Acetic anhydride   N-phenylacetamide (Acetanilide)

Diethylamine   Benzoyl chloride   N,N-Diethyl benzamide

N, N-Dimethylaniline   Acetyl chloride

Substituted amides of aromatic carboxylic acids or of sulfonic acids are prepared by the Schotten-Baumann reaction. The reaction in which an amine is reacted with the acid chloride in presence of base to give a substituted amide is called Schotten-Baumann reaction. Acetylation (substitution with an acetyl group) is generally carried out by using acetic anhydride rather than acetyl chloride as acetyl chloride if reacted with a primary amine can lead to disubstituted amides.

Conversion to sulfonamides:

$$R - NH_2 + ArSO_2Cl \quad \rightarrow \quad ArSO_2NHR \; + \; HCl$$

1° Amine　　Aryl sulfonylchloride　　　　N-substituted sulfonamide

$$R_2NH \; + \; ArSO_2Cl \quad \rightarrow \quad ArSO_2NR_2 \; + \; HCl$$

2° Amine　　　　　　　　　　　N, N- disubstituted sulfonamide

$$R_3N \; + \; ArSO_2Cl \quad \rightarrow \quad \text{No reaction}$$

3° Amine

4.　Ring substitution in aromatic amines:

As stated above, $-NH_2$, $-NHR$, and $-NR_2$ groups when substituted on an aromatic ring act as powerful activators for electrophilic substitution on the aromatic ring. They are thus - *ortho*, - *para* directors in an electrophilic aromatic substitution. This is possible as one of the resonating structures have a positive charge on the nitrogen while all the carbon atoms of the ring have a complete octet. However, the main problem with aromatic amines is that they are very reactive and thus undergo multiple substitution on the ring. For example, bromination of aniline yields 2, 4, 6-tribromoaniline.

Aniline　　　　　　　　　　　　2, 4, 6-Tribromoaniline

Similarly, nitric acid not only nitrates but also oxidizes the highly reactive ring leading to loss of much material as tar. Also, in the strong acidic nitration medium, the amine is converted into the anilinium ion. Nitrogen in the anilinium ion has no unshared electrons and thus instead of activation, it causes deactivation of the ring. The electrophilic substitution in such cases will now be directed to *meta* position. This problem can be overcome by substituting the amino group of the aromatic amine with $-COCH_3$. The acetamido group, - $NHCOCH_3$ thus formed remains an activating group but is less powerful than a free amino group. Electron withdrawal by oxygen of the carbonyl group makes the nitrogen of an amide a much weaker source of electrons than the nitrogen of an amine. Thus, amides are much weaker bases than amines and are also less activators in electrophilic aromatic substitution. Rings containing a $-NHCOCH_3$ group therefore, undergo monosubstitution, that too mostly at *para* position as $-NHCOCH_3$ offers steric hinderance at *ortho* position for an incoming group. Thus, acetylation has become an important method in protecting the amino group as well as directing the incoming electrophile to *para* position thus avoiding polysubstitution as seen with $-NH_2$ group. Acetamido group can be easily hydrolysed to release the $-NH_2$ after the required substitution on the ring has been made.

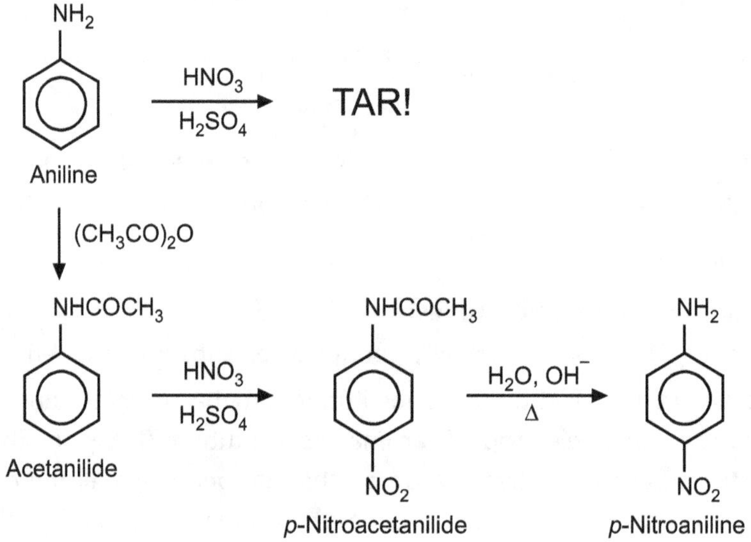

5. Sulfonation of aromatic amines:

Aniline reacts with sulfuric acid to give the salt, anilinium hydrogen sulfate which on heating at 180-200°C yields a major -*para* product called sulfanilic acid i.e. *p*-aminobenzenesulfonic acid. Sulfanilic acid is a high melting compound and exists as a zwitterion in water, in which it is insoluble. It dissolves in alkaline solution as the $-OH$ ion pulls a hydrogen atom from quaternary nitrogen making it neutral while the sulfonic acid group remains charged.

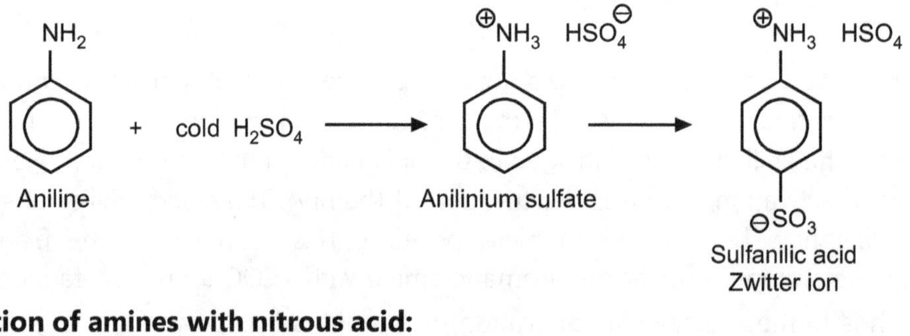

6. Reaction of amines with nitrous acid:

Nitrous (HONO) acid is an unstable acid generated by the action of mineral acid (HCl, H_2SO_4) on sodium nitrite ($NaNO_2$). Nitrous acid reacts with all types of amines to yield different products.

Primary aromatic amines react with nitrous acid to yield diazonium salts. This is very important reaction intermediate in synthetic organic chemistry and is discussed in the following sections in details. Primary aliphatic amines also react with nitrous acid to form diazonium salts. However these are very unstable and break down to yield a complicated mixture of organic compounds and thus are of hardly any synthetic value.

1° Aromatic amine

$$C_6H_5-NH_2 + HONO \longrightarrow C_6H_5-\overset{\oplus}{N}\equiv N \quad \text{Diazonium salt}$$

1° Aliphatic amine

$$R-NH_2 + HONO \longrightarrow N_2 + \text{Mixture of alcohols and alkenes}$$

Both aliphatic and aromatic secondary amines react with nitrous acid to yield N-nitrosamines.

Secondary aromatic amine + HONO ⟶ N-nitrosamine

Tertiary aromatic amines undergo ring substitution with nitroso group, –N=O. Thus, N, N–dimethylaniline yields mainly *p*-nitroso-N, N-dimethylaniline. In this reaction, nitrosonium ion, which is weak electrophile is substituted on a highly activated ring. Substitution of a nitroso group on the aromatic ring is called nitrosation. The nitrosation reaction can take place only in rings containing powerfully activating groups like dialkylamino, $-NR_2$ or hydroxyl, –OH group.

Tertiary amine + HONO ⟶ p-Nitrosocompound

All the above reactions of amines with nitrous acid involve attack of nitrosonium ion as the first step. In primary and secondary amines the attack takes place at nitrogen, the site of maximum electron availability while in case of tertiary amines, the attack occurs at the activated ring as there is no replaceable hydrogen on nitrogen.

7. Carbylamine reaction:

This reaction is given only by primary amines.

Primary amines when heated with chloroform and alcoholic caustic potash give isocyanides (carbylamines) having very unpleasant smell, which can be easily detected.

$$C_2H_5NH_2 + CHCl_3 + 3KOH \longrightarrow C_2H_5NC + 3KCl + 3H_2O$$

Ethylamine → Ethyl isocyanide

$$C_6H_5NH_2 + CHCl_3 + 3KOH \longrightarrow C_6H_5NC + 3KCl + 3H_2O$$

Aniline → Phenyl isocyanide

14.5 QUATERNARY AMMONIUM SALTS

As discussed earlier, an amine reacts with alkyl halides to give an amine of higher class. Thus, quaternary ammonium salts are the products of the final stage of alkylation of nitrogen. They contain four covalently bounded organic groups and the positive charge on the nitrogen is balanced by some negative ion. They are represented as $R_4N^+X^-$. On reaction with silver oxide, they give compounds called quaternary ammonium hydroxides. Silver halide is obtained as a precipitate in this reaction. On heating strongly, (to 125°C or higher) quaternary ammoinium hydroxide decomposes to give water, a tertiary amine and an alkene. This reaction is called the **Hofmann elimination**.

Tertiary amine   Quaternary ammonium iodide   Quaternary ammonium hydroxide Alkene Tertiary amine

The elimination reaction mostly follows E_2 mechanism that involves first a loss of hydrogen by carbon to hydroxide ion followed by expulsion of a tertiary amine molecule. This loss creates a double bond leading to the formation of an alkene. Some reactions showing E_1 elimination are also known. Also, nucleophilic substitution reactions, S_N1 and S_N2 compete with the elimination reaction.

Butan-2-amine   Methyliodide

In Hofmann elimination reaction, the double bond goes to the carbon that is least substituted in contrast to the alkene obtained by other E_2 reactions like dehydrohalogenation in which the preferred product is the more highly branched alkene (which is also the more stable one).

14.6 SEPARATION OF PRIMARY, SECONDARY AND TERTIARY AMINES : HINSBERG METHOD

Hinsberg test or method is an important test in finding out the nature of amines, whether primary, secondary or tertiary. The procedure involves shaking the amine with benzenesulfonyl chloride (A) in the presence of aqueous potassium hydroxide. Since the tertiary amines have no replaceable hydrogen, they fail to react with the reagent while the primary and secondary amines form substituted sulfonamides.

The nitrogen of the monosubstituted sulfonamide (B) obtained from the primary amine is acidic enough to lose the hydrogen and form a salt (C) with the base i.e. potassium hydroxide and therefore dissolves in the alkaline medium. The free sulfonamide can be precipitated on acidification.

The disubstituted sulfonamide (D) obtained from the secondary amine however does not possess any acidic hydrogen and thus remain undissolved in the alkaline medium. Thus, when an amine is treated with benezenesulfonyl chloride and excess potassium hydroxide, a primary amine yields a clear solution which on acidification gives an insoluble material. A secondary amine yields an insoluble compound which remains unaffected by acid. A tertiary amine yields an insoluble material (the unreacted amine itself) that dissolves on acidification.

Example :

14.7 DIAZONIUM SALTS

14.7.1 Preparation

Diazonium salts are prepared by suspending a primary aromatic amine in cold aqueous mineral acid and then reacting it with sodium nitrite. Although some diazonium salts have been isolated, they mostly decompose on standing, even at ice-bath temperatures. The solution is thus used immediately after preparation.

$$NaNO_2 \ + \ HCl \ \xrightarrow{0-5°C} \ HONO$$

Mechanism involved:

Step 1:

Step 2:

14.7.2 Reactions

The variety of reactions shown by diazonium salts can be classified into two types:

1. **Reactions in which both nitrogen are lost (replacement reactions):** In these reactions the nitrogen is lost as N_2 and its place is taken by another atom or group.

   Such reactions are helpful in introducing –F, –Cl, –Br, –CN, –OH besides other groups like $-NO_2$, –OR, $-SO_2Cl$, –NCS, NCO etc.

2. **Reactions proceeding without loss of nitrogen:** Nitrogen is retained in these reactions. The main reactions of this type are: (i) Reaction with NaOH, (ii) Reduction to hydrazines and (iii) Coupling to electron rich rings such as phenols and amines.

1. Reactions in which both nitrogen are lost (replacement reactions):

(i) Sandmeyer reaction (replacement by –Cl, –Br and –CN):

The diazonium group of the freshly prepared diazonium salt can be replaced by treating the solution with cuprous chloride or cuprous bromide. The reaction involving use of cuprous halides for replacing diazonium group with the halide group is called Sandmeyer reaction. Procedure involving use of copper powder and hydrogen halide to give the required halide is called Gattermann reaction.

Reaction:

$$\text{Ar-}N_2^+ + CuX \longrightarrow \text{Ar-}X + N_2 + Cu^+$$

Introduction of –I does not require presence of cuprous salts or copper. Thus, the diazonium group can be easily replaced by –I by mixing the diazonium salt solution with potassium iodide. Mechanism involved in this reaction is as shown below:

Mechanism :

$$\text{Ar-}N_2^+ + Cu^+ \xrightarrow{-N_2} \text{Ar}^{\bullet} + Cu^{2+}$$

$$\text{Ar}^{\bullet} + X^- \longrightarrow \text{Ar-}X + e^-$$

$$e^- + Cu^{2+} \longrightarrow Cu^+$$

For the introduction of –F group, fluoroboric acid, HBF_4 is added to the solution of diazonium salt. This leads to the precipitation of diazonium fluoroborate, ArN_2BF_4 which can be filtered, washed and dried. The dry diazonium fluoroborate on heating decomposes to give the aryl fluoride. The diazonium fluoroborates are quite stable and can be stored in dry state.

$$\underset{\text{Aniline}}{\text{C}_6\text{H}_5\text{NH}_2} \xrightarrow[\text{NaNO}_2]{\text{HBF}_4} \underset{\substack{\text{Benzenediazonium} \\ \text{fluoroborate}}}{\text{C}_6\text{H}_5\text{N}_2^+\,{}^-\text{BF}_4} \xrightarrow{\Delta} \underset{\text{Fluorobenzene}}{\text{C}_6\text{H}_5\text{F}} + N_2 + BF_3$$

These procedures are valuable synthetically as iodination and fluorination of benzene cannot be carried out directly.

Diazonium group can be replaced by –CN by reacting the diazonium salt with cuprous cyanide CuCN. The diazonium salt solution is neutralized with sodium carbonate before the reaction in order to prevent the loss of cyanide as HCN. This reaction is very useful in the synthesis of aryl carboxylic acids as hydrolysis of nitriles yields carboxylic acids.

(ii) Replacement by –OH:

Diazonium salts when treated with water undergo replacement of the diazonium group by the hydroxyl group to give phenols. The reaction can take place in cold conditions though a little slowly. This explains why diazonium salts must be reacted immediately to give the required product. If they are allowed to stand they will yield phenols.

Diazonium salt　　　$\xrightarrow[100°C]{H_2O,\ H_2SO_4}$　　　Phenol

Diazonium salts also undergo coupling with phenols, as will be illustrated in the following section. To minimize the chances of diazonium salt undergoing coupling with the formed phenol, the diazonium solution is slowly added to a large volume of boiling dilute sulfuric acid. It has been observed that coupling reaction slows down as the acidity of the reaction medium increases.

(iii) Replacement by –H (Hydrogenolysis):

A number of reducing agents, like alcohol, zinc, formaldehyde etc. can be used to bring about a replacement of the diazonium group by –H. However, hypophosphorous acid is mostly used for replacing the diazo group with –H. The diazonium salt can be treated with hypophosphorous acid and allowed to stand at room temperature to give the product. The diazonium group leaves as nitrogen and the hypophosphorous acid is oxidized to give phosphorous acid. This reagent is specific, that is, it does not reduce any other group present in the diazonium salt. If hypophosphorous acid itself is used for diazotisation, then the diazotised salt can be immediately reduced in the same reaction mixture.

Benzenediazonium chloride $+$ H_3PO_2 Hypophosphorous acid $+$ H_2O $\xrightarrow{\Delta}$ Benzene $+$ N_2 $+$ H_3PO_3 Phosphorous acid $+$ HCl

2. Reactions proceeding without loss of nitrogen: Nitrogen is retained in these reactions:

(i) Coupling reaction of Diazonium salts (Azo coupling):

Azo coupling is the most widely used industrial reaction in the production of dyes, paints and pigments. Aromatic diazonium ion acts as an electrophile when reacted with activated aromatics such as anilines or phenols. The substitution normally occurs at the ***para*** position. When this position is already occupied, ***ortho*** position is favoured. The pH of solution is quite important. Coupling with phenols is carried out in mildly alkaline solution while amines are coupled in mildly acidic solution. No coupling takes place at very low pH.

Coupling of diazonium salts with phenols is carried out in mildly alkaline medium as phenols dissociate in alkaline medium to give phenoxide ion which is a better ring activator than phenol itself towards electrophilic substitutions. However, if the concentration of hydroxide ion is large, that is in highly alkaline medium, the diazonium salts get converted to species that do not couple. Similarly, highly acidic medium converts the amine to which the diazonium salts need to be coupled, into its ion with the nitrogen carrying a positive charge. The ring is deactivated because of this positive charge towards the electrophilic substitution of the diazonium salt.

Benzenediazonium chloride + Phenol $\xrightarrow{OH^-}$ p-Hydroxyazobenzene (Orange solid) + HCl

Benzenediazonium chloride + Dimethylaniline $\xrightarrow{H^+}$ N, N-Dimethyl p-aminoazobenzene (Yellow solid) + HCl

Benzenediazonium chloride + Aniline $\xrightarrow{CH_3CO_2Na}$ Diazoaminobenzene

Azo compounds are usually coloured compounds because azo group (–N=N–) is a chromophoric group and two benzene rings are in conjugation with azo group. Such compounds absorb light in the visible light. Azo compounds are used as dyes. Coupling reaction is used as the identification test for primary aromatic amines and is called the dye test.

Mechanism involved in the reaction can be written as follows:

Coupling with phenols:

Diazonium salt   Penoxide ion   p-Hydroxyazobenzene
(Phenol in alkaline medium)

Coupling with primary aromatic amines:

Aniline   Diazoaminobenzene

Coupling with tertiary aromatic amines:

N,N-Dimethylaniline   Diazonium salt   N,N-dimethylaminoazobenzene

(ii) Reaction with alkali:

Benzene diazonium chloride reacts with sodium hydroxide to form sodium phenyldiazonate.

$$C_6H_5\overset{+}{N}_2Cl^- \quad + \quad NaOH \quad \rightleftharpoons \quad C_6H_5N_2 - OH$$

Benzenediazonium chloride   Phenyldiazoic acid

$$C_6H_5 - \overset{\ominus}{O}Na^{\oplus}$$

Sodium phenyldiazonate

(iii) Reduction to hydrazines:

Benzene diazonium salt is reduced to hydrazines either by $SnCl_2/HCl$ or by $NaHSO_3$ (Sodium bisulfite).

$$C_6H_5 - \overset{+}{N}_2X^- \xrightarrow{NaHSO_3} C_6H_5 - N = N - SO_3H \longrightarrow C_6H_5 - NH - NH - SO_3H$$

Benzene diazonium salt

$$H_2SO_4 \;+\; C_6H_5 - NH - NH_2$$

Phenylhydrazine

QUESTIONS

Q.1   What are amines? Explain separation methods of amines from primary, secondary and tertiary amine mixtures.   **(Dec-2014, May-2015)**

Q.2   What are amines? Give any three methods of preparation and any three reactions of amines. Discuss action of nitrous acid on primary, secondary and tertiary amines.

(May-2014)

Q.3   What are diazonium salts? Write reaction and mechanism of diazotization. Discuss uses of diazonium salts.

Q.4   Explain Hoffmann's degradation of amides.   **(May-2015)**

Q.5   Write a note on preparation of amines.   **(Dec-2015)**

Q.6   Write any two methods of preparation of amines.   **(Dec-2014)**

Q.7   Write a note on separation methods of amines.

Q.8   How will you differentiate between primary, secondary and tertiary amines by chemical test?   **(May-2015)**

Q.9   Compare basicity between cyclohexylamine and aniline.   **(Dec-2014, May-2015)**

Q.10   Ethyl amine is more basic than ammonia. Give reasons.   **(Dec-2015)**

Q.11   Compare and explain the basicities of ethanalamine and aniline.   **(Dec-2015)**

Q.12   How will you separate primary, secondary and tertiary amines by suitable chemical test ?   **(Dec. 2015)**

Q.13   Aromatic amines are less basic than aliphatic amines. Explain.   **(May- 2014)**

Q.14   What are diazonium salts? How are they prepared?   **(May-2014)**

Q.15   Write any two reactions of amines.   **(Dec-2014)**

Q.16.   Explain why acetamide is feeble base.   **(Dec-2014)**

Chapter 15

CYANIDES AND ISOCYANIDES

15.1 INTRODUCTION

Cyanides are organic compounds containing a carbon nitrogen triple bond ($-C\equiv N$) as the functional group. Cyanides are also referred to as nitriles. These compounds contain a CN group linked by a covalent bond to a carbon-containing group, such as methyl (CH_3) in methyl cyanide (acetonitrile).

Isocyanides are the isomers of cyanides (therefore the prefix *–iso*) with the functional group of (–N=C). An isocyanide is also called as isonitrile or a carbylamine. Cyanide is more stable than the corresponding isocyanide. On **heating** isocyanide isomerizes into cyanide.

$$H-C\equiv N \quad \rightleftharpoons \quad H-\overset{+}{N}\equiv \overset{-}{C}$$

Hydrogen cyanide Hydrogen isocyanide

$$R-C\equiv N \quad \rightleftharpoons \quad R-\overset{+}{N}\equiv \overset{-}{C}$$

Alkyl cyanide Alkyl isocyanide

$$Ar-C\equiv N \quad \rightleftharpoons \quad Ar-\overset{+}{N}\equiv \overset{-}{C}$$

Aryl cyanide Aryl isocyanide

In nature cyanides are produced by bacteria, fungi, and algae and are found in a number of plants. Certain seeds and fruit stones, e.g., those of apricots, apples, and peaches also contain cyanides.

On the other hand, isocyanides are far less common than cyanides. The first isocyanide (isonitrile) compound was obtained by Lieke in 1859. Ivar Ugi (1930-2005) is credited with discovery of many important isocyanides. Isocyanide is a useful synthetic building block.

15.2 NOMENCLATURE

15.2.1 Cyanides

The cyanides can be named by substitutive nomenclature by one of the following methods:

1. Compounds of RCN type, in which $\equiv N$ replaces H_3 at the end of the main chain of an acyclic hydrocarbon are denoted by adding "-nitrile" or "-dinitrile" to the name of this hydrocarbon.

For example,

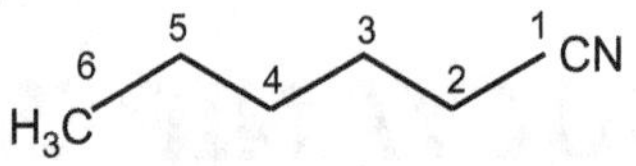

Hexanenitrile 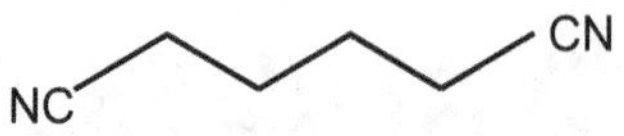   Hexanedinitrile

Thus, "nitrile", here denotes the triply bound nitrogen atom, ≡N and not the carbon atom attached to it. Numbering begins with the carbon atom containing the nitrogen.

2.   Compounds of the type RCN, when considered as derived from acids R-COOH whose systematic names end in "-carboxylic acid", are named by changing this ending to "-carbonitrile".

It must be noted that "carbonitrile" denotes the group –C≡N, including the carbon atom contained therein. That carbon atom is excluded from the numbering of a chain to which that group is attached.

For example,

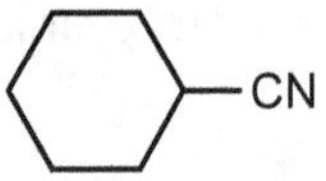

Cyclohexane carbonitrile 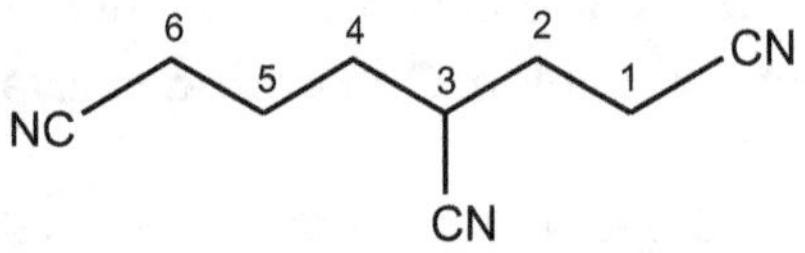   1, 3, 6-Hexanetricarbonitrile 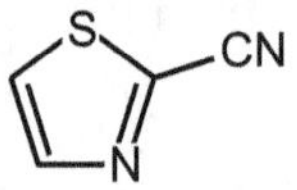   2-Thiazolecarbonitrile

3. Names of compounds RCN, when considered as derived from acids R–COOH having trivial names, are formed by changing the suffix "-oic acid" to "-onitrile", or, if the name of the acid does not end in "-oic acid", then by changing "-ic acid" to "-onitrile".

For example,

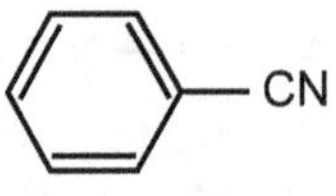

Benzonitrile    Propionitrile

4.   By the radico functional procedure, compounds RCN are named by stating the name of the radical R, followed by the name "cyanide" for the group -CN.

For example,

Ethyl cyanide 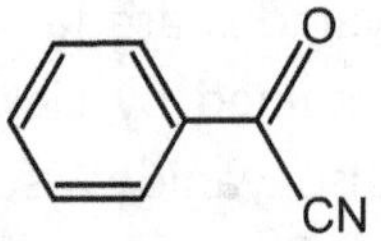   Benzoyl cyanide

5.   When a compound also contains a group that has priority over –CN for citation as principal group, the -CN group is named by the prefix "cyano-".

For example,

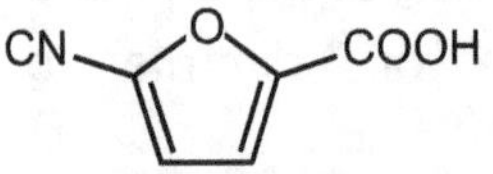

5-Cyano-2-furoic acid 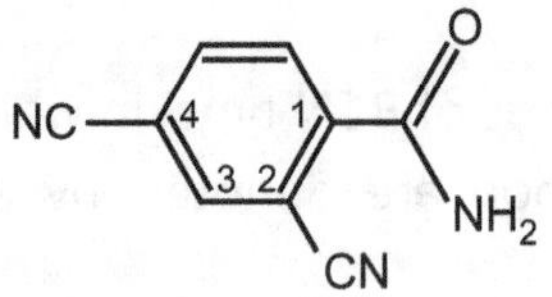   2, 4-Dicyanobenzamide

15.2.2 Isocyanides

The methods used in nomenclature of cyanides can be applied to isocyanides also. For example,

Phenyl isocyanide   Cyclohexyl isocyanate

p-isocyanobenzoic acid p-Tolylisothiocyanate

15.3 METHODS OF PREPARATION

15.3.1 Cyanides

1. **From alkyl halides:** Primary alkyl nitriles are generally prepared by the reaction of potassium or sodium cyanide with a primary alkyl halide. Secondary and tertiary nitriles cannot be formed by this route.

$$R\text{–}X \quad + \quad KCN \longrightarrow R\text{–}CN + KBr$$

$$CH_3CH_2CH_2Br \quad + \quad KCN \longrightarrow CH_3CH_2CH_2CN \ + \ KBr$$

Propyl bromide   Potassium cyanide   Propyl cyanide

2. **From amides:** Primary, secondary and tertiary cyanides can be conveniently prepared from amides by carrying out their dehydration by thionyl chloride or phosphorous (V) oxide. High molecular weight amides can simply be dehydrated to cyanides by heating.

$$RCONH_2 \xrightarrow[-\ H_2O]{SOCl_2 \ or \ P_2O_5} R-CN$$

$$CH_3(CH_3)_6CONH_2 \longrightarrow CH_3(CH_2)_6CN$$

Octanamide   Octanenitrile or heptycyanide

3. **From Grignard reagent and cyanogen chloride:** Grignard reagents react with cyanogen chloride to give alkyl cyanides. This method is especially useful for preparation of tertiary cyanides.

$$R - MgX + \ Cl\text{–}CN \xrightarrow{dry\ ether} R - C \equiv N$$

$$(CH_3)_3CMgCl \quad + \quad Cl\text{-}CN \xrightarrow{dry\ ether} (CH_3)_3CCN + MgCl_2$$

3° Butyl magnesium   Cyanogen chloride   3° Butyl cyanide
    chloride

4. **From aryl diazonium salts:** This method is suitable only for preparation of aryl cyanides. In this the aryl diazonium salt is heated with potassium cyanide and copper (I) cyanide (or copper powder) to give the corresponding cyanide.

KCN / C_1 packet

Benzene diazonium halide   Phenyl cyanide

5. **From aldoximes:** Aldoximes, like amides, can be dehydrated by phosphorous (V) oxide or acetic anhydride or by heating to yield the cyanides. Aldoximes are obtained when aldehydes are reacted with hydroxylamine hydrochloride.

P_2O_5, heat

Aldehyde   Hydroxylamine   Aldoxime   Alkyl cyanide

15.3.2 Isocyanides

1. **From alkyl halides:** Alkyl halides react with metal cyanides like silver cyanide (AgCN) or copper (I) cyanide (CuCN) to give an alkyl isocyanide.

Alkyl iodide   or   Alkylisocyanide

AgI
or
CuI

2. **From amines:** Amines are converted into isocyanides by **carbylamine reaction**. In this, a mixture of primary amine and chloroform with ethanolic potassium hydroxide is heated to give the corresponding isocyanide.

$$RNH_2 \ + \ CHCl_3 \ + \ 4KOH \longrightarrow RNC \ + \ 3KCl \ + \ 3H_2O$$

1°Amine   Chloroform   Potassium hydroxide   Alkyl isocyanide   Potassium chloride

$+ \ CHCl_3 \ + \ 3KOH \longrightarrow \quad + \ 3KCl \ + \ 3H_2O$

Aniline   Phenyl isocyanide

15.4 PHYSICAL PROPERTIES

15.4.1 Cyanides

The small cyanides are liquids at room temperature. The smallest organic nitrile is ethanenitrile, CH_3CN (methyl cyanide or acetonitrile). These compounds have high boiling points in relation to their size. They are very polar molecules. The nitrogen is very electronegative and the electrons in the triple bond are very easily pulled towards the nitrogen end of the bond. Nitriles therefore have strong permanent dipole-dipole attractions as well as van der Waals dispersion forces between their molecules thus displaying high boiling points.

Cyanide (nitrile)	Name	Boiling point (°C)
CH_3CN	Methyl cyanide (Ethanenitrile)	82
CH_3CH_2CN	Ethyl cyanide (Propanenitrile)	97
$CH_3CH_2CH_2CN$	Propyl cyanide (Butanenitrile)	116 - 118

Ethanenitrile is completely soluble in water. The solubility falls as chain length increases. The solubility in water is because although cyanides do not form hydrogen bonds with themselves, they can form hydrogen bonds with water. One of the slightly positive hydrogen atoms in a water molecule is attracted to the lone pair on the nitrogen atom in a nitrile and a hydrogen bond is formed.

$$CH_3 - C \equiv \overset{\delta-}{N}: \text{------} \overset{}{H}_{\delta+} \cdots O - H$$

Hydrogen bond

Dispersion forces and dipole-dipole attractions also exist between the nitrile and water molecules. However, as the chain length increases the hydrocarbon parts of the nitrile molecules force themselves between water molecules, breaking the relatively strong hydrogen bonds between water molecules and the cyanide molecules thus making higher cyanides insoluble in water.

15.4.2 Isocyanides

Alkyl isocyanides are poisonous, unpleasant smelling, with lower boiling points than isomeric cyanides. They are not very soluble in water, as unlike cyanides the nitrogen atoms of isocyanides lack a lone pair of electrons required for hydrogen bonding.

$$R - \overset{+}{N} \equiv \overset{-}{C}:$$

Unable to form
hydrogen bond

Being stable carbenes, isonitriles are highly reactive compounds that can react with almost any type of reagents (electrophiles, nucleophiles and even radicals).

15.5 CHEMICAL PROPERTIES

15.5.1 Cyanides

Alkyl cyanides undergo two types of reactions: **A.** reactions due to cyano group and **B.** due to α-hydrogen.

(A) Reactions due to cyano group:

1. Partial hydrolysis : Cyanides on partial hydrolysis form amides. This can be carried out by shaking the cyanide with cold conc. HCl or by dissolving in conc. H_2SO_4 and then pouring into water.

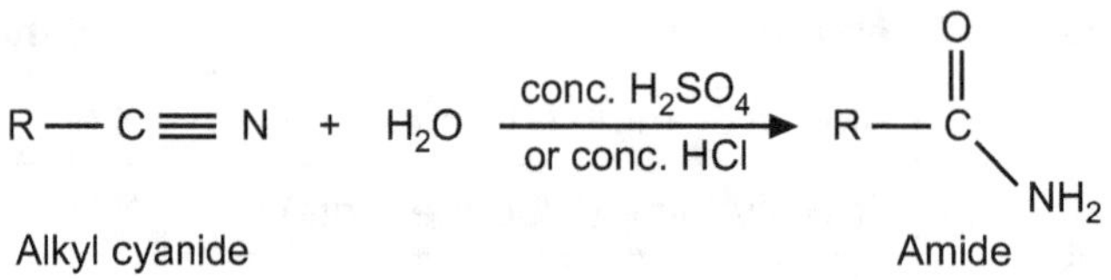

$$R-C \equiv N \ + \ H_2O \xrightarrow[\text{or conc. HCl}]{\text{conc. } H_2SO_4} R-\overset{\overset{\displaystyle O}{\|}}{C}-NH_2$$

Alkyl cyanide   Amide

The mechanism can be illustrated as:

Step 1: Protonation of nitrogen making it an electrophile.	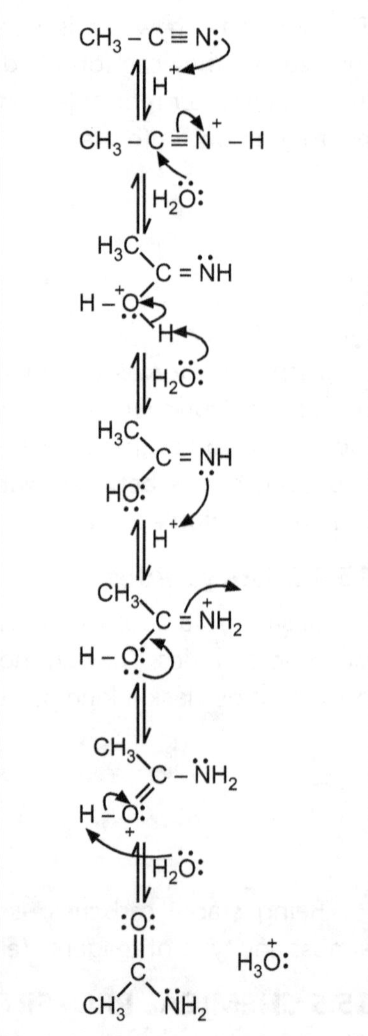 $CH_3 - C \equiv N:$ $\downarrow H^+$ $CH_3 - C \equiv \overset{+}{N} - H$
Step 2: Electrons from carbon move towards nitrogen thus inviting an attack of water, a nucleophile.	$H_2\ddot{O}:$
Step 3: Deprotonation of oxygen.	$H_2\ddot{O}:$
Step 4: Protonation of **N** leads again to a positively charged nitrogen.	H^+
Step 5: Electrons of an adjacent **O** are used to neutralise the positive at the **N** and form the π bond in the **C=O**.	
Step 6: Deprotonation of the oxonium ion leads to the formation of the amide,	$H_2\ddot{O}:$

2. Total hydrolysis: Cyanides can be hydrolysed to carboxylic acids by heating with water in the presence of an acid or a base as a catalyst.

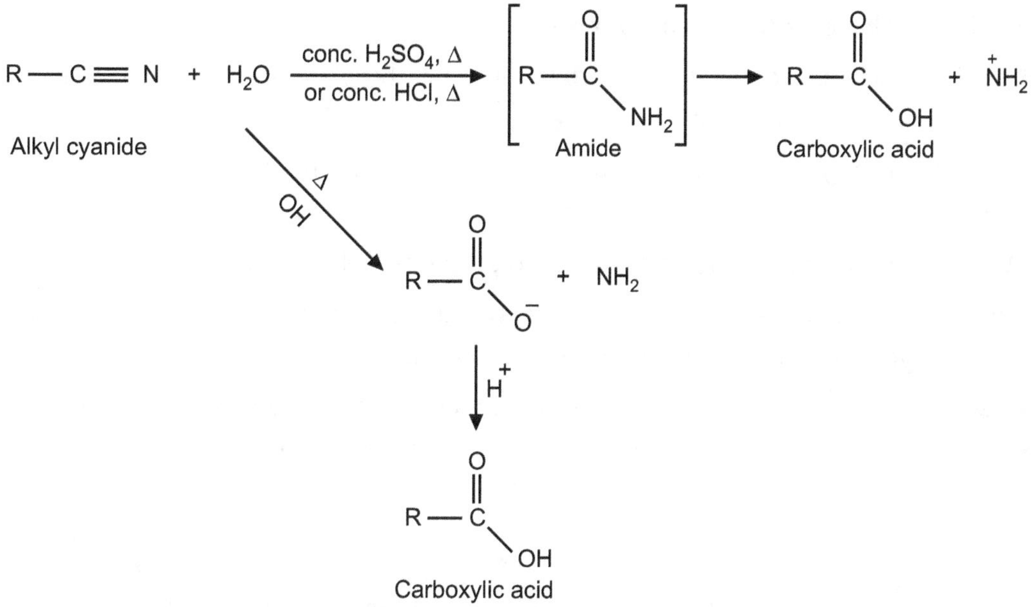
R—C≡N + H2O
conc. H2SO4, Δ
or conc. HCl, Δ
Alkyl cyanide
Amide
Carboxylic acid
OH Δ
H+
Carboxylic acid

Mechanism involved in the acid catalysed hydrolysis of nitriles can be written as:

As seen above, partial hydrolysis of cyanides with acids yields amides. If the procedure is allowed to continue, amides get hydrolysed to give carboxylic acid. The further mechanism involving the amide formed above thus can be written as:

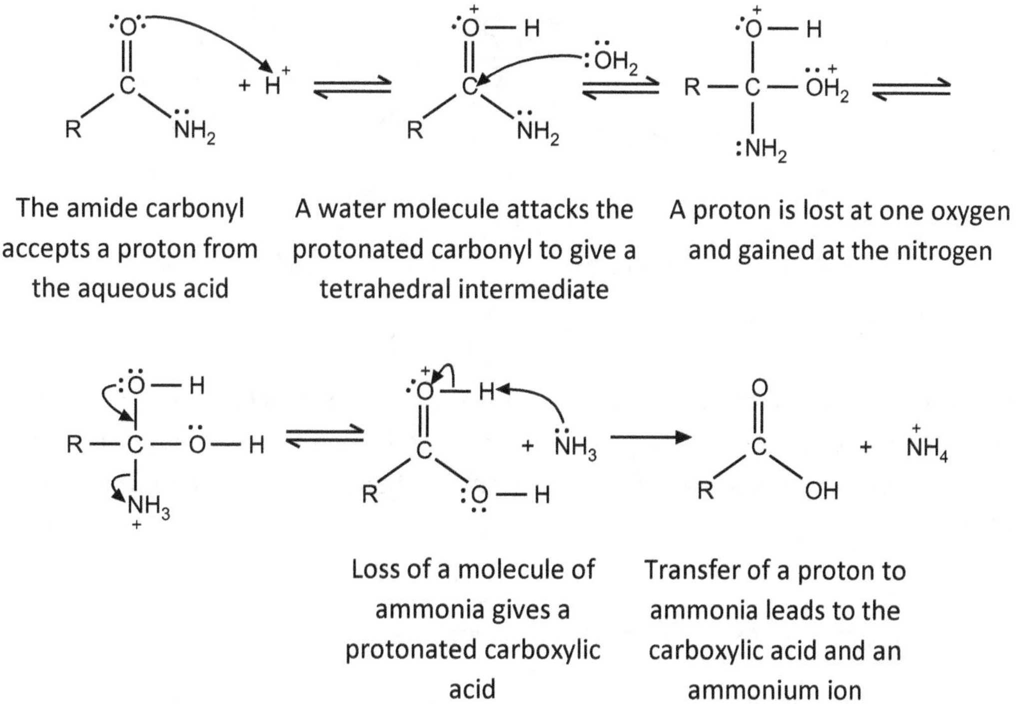
The amide carbonyl accepts a proton from the aqueous acid
A water molecule attacks the protonated carbonyl to give a tetrahedral intermediate
A proton is lost at one oxygen and gained at the nitrogen
Loss of a molecule of ammonia gives a protonated carboxylic acid
Transfer of a proton to ammonia leads to the carboxylic acid and an ammonium ion

Mechanism for base hydrolysis of cyanides:

Step 1 : Nucleophilic attack of hydroxide ion on the electron deficient nitrile carbon, generating a negative charge on the nitrogen.

Step 2 : This negatively charged nitrogen acquires a proton from the surrounding water molecule.

Step 3 : A proton transfer from oxygen to nitrogen reveals an amide.

Step 4 : The carbonyl carbon of amide being electron deficient is attacked by the nucleophilic hydroxide ion forming a tetrahedral intermediate.

Step 5 : This intermediate loses a molecule of ammonia assisted by the loss of proton in a simultaneous reaction leading to the formation of a carboxylate ion.

3. **Addition with alcohols:** Cyanides undergo addition reaction with alcohols in the presence of dry HCl gas to give an adduct known as imidate ester. This reaction is called **Pinner synthesis.** The imidate ester is an excellent synthetic intermediate for the preparation of amides, esters and ortho esters.

Ethyl benzimidate → Δ → $C_6H_5-\overset{\overset{\displaystyle O}{\|}}{C}-NH_2$ + C_2H_5Cl
Benzamide

Ethyl benzimidate → $H_2O\ \Delta$ → $C_6H_5-\overset{\overset{\displaystyle O}{\|}}{C}-OC_2H_5$
Ethyl benzoate

Ethyl benzimidate → C_2H_5OH → $\left[C_6H_5-\overset{\overset{\displaystyle NH_2}{|}}{\underset{\underset{\displaystyle OC_2H_5}{|}}{C}}-OC_2H_5\right]$ → $C_6H_5-\overset{\overset{\displaystyle OC_2H_5}{|}}{\underset{\underset{\displaystyle OC_2H_5}{|}}{C}}-OC_2H_5$

1-(Triethoxymethyl) benzene
(ortho ester)

4. Addition of ammonia: A molecule of ammonia gets added to the cyano group of alkyl cyanides in dry state to yield amidine.

Alkyl cyanide + $\ddot{N}H_3$ → → Amidine

5. Reaction with Grignard reagents: Cyanides react with Grignard reagent to yield ketones.

1) R'–MgX
2) Aqueous acid
e.g. $H_3O^{\oplus}$

Nitrile → Ketone + NH_3 + Mg salt

Phenyl cyanide → 1) CH_3MgBr 2) Water, acid → Acetophenone

Cyclohexyl cyanide → 1) CH_3CH_2MgBr 2) Water, acid → 1-Cyclohexylpropan-1-one

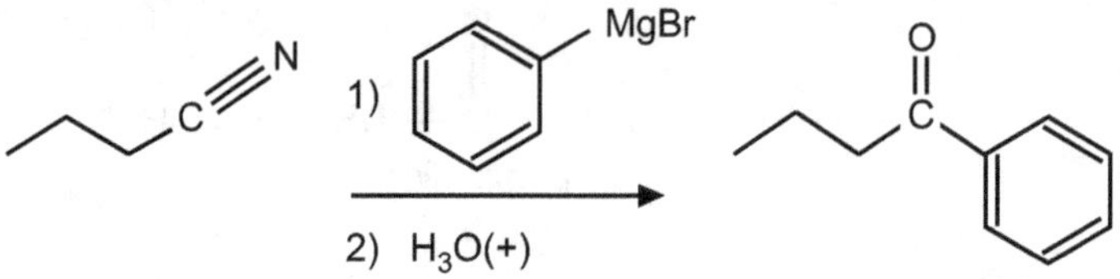

Propyl cyanide → 1) PhMgBr 2) $H_3O(+)$ → Butyrophenone

6. Reduction: Cyanides are reduced to amines in the presence of reducing agents like H_2, Ni, and heat; metal and acid; $LiAlH_4$; or Na, C_2H_5OH (Mandius reaction). However, when $SnCl_2$ and HCl is used, the cyanide is reduced to an aldehyde. This reaction is called Stephen reaction.

Example:

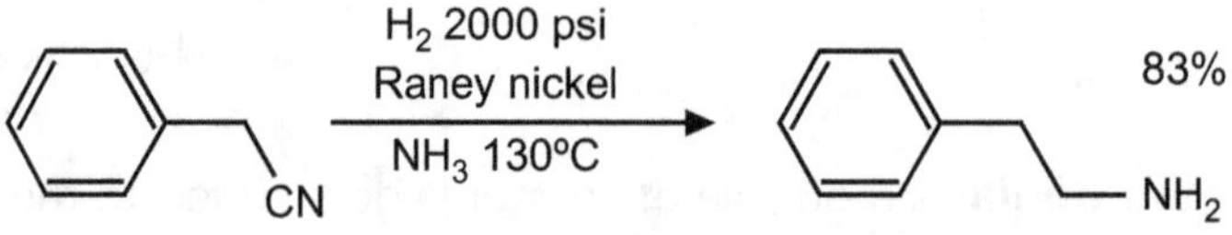

Benzyl cyanide $\xrightarrow[\text{NH}_3\ 130°C]{\substack{H_2\ 2000\ psi \\ \text{Raney nickel}}}$ 2-phenylethyl amine   83%

7. Stephen reaction: This reaction involves reaction of nitriles with tin(II) chloride ($SnCl_2$), hydrochloric acid (HCl) to produce aldehydes (R-CHO). The iminium salt ($[R-CH=NH_2]^+Cl^-$) formed in the first step is treated with water (H_2O) to yield aldehyde. During the synthesis, ammonium chloride is also produced.

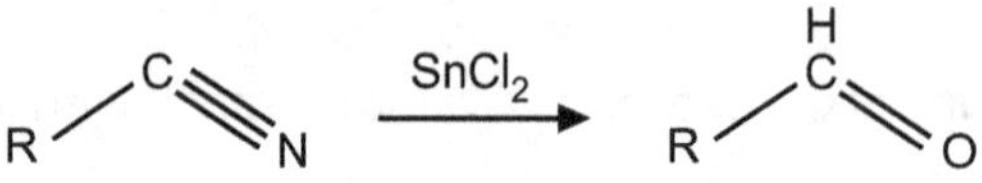

Nitrile $\xrightarrow{SnCl_2}$ Aldehyde

The reaction can be written in two steps:

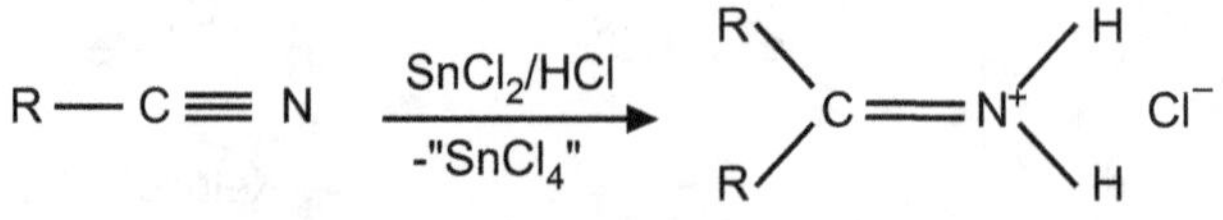

$R-C\equiv N$ $\xrightarrow[\text{-"SnCl}_4\text{"}]{SnCl_2/HCl}$ Iminium salt

Iminium salt $\xrightarrow[-NH_4^+]{H_2O}$ aldehyde

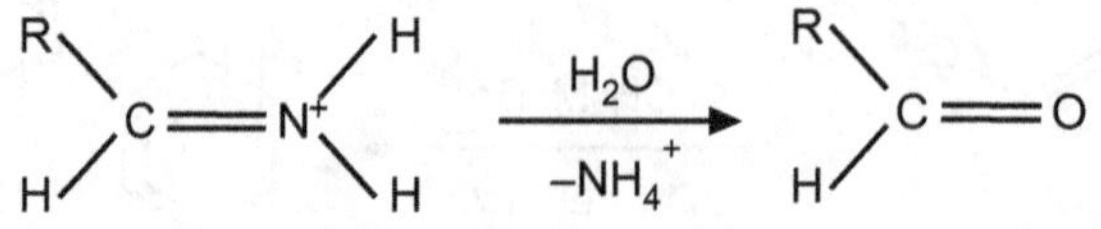

(B) Reactions due to α-hydrogens: Nitriles having at least one α-hydrogen react with strong base to form anions. These anions are similar to the enolates obtained from carbonyl compounds.

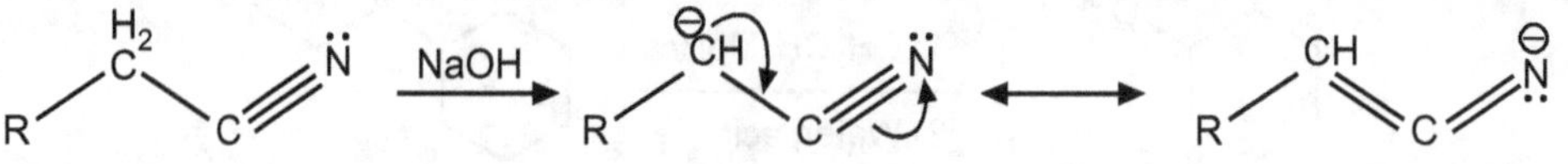

$\xrightarrow{NaOH}$

Nitrile anions are good nucleophiles and readily undergo alkylation on carbon in preference to nitrogen.

1. Alkylation at α-carbon : Alkyl cyanides when reacted with alkyl halides undergo alkylation at the α-hydrogen in presence of a base like liquid ammonia or the sodamide (NaNH$_2$).

R–CH$_2$–C≡N $\xrightarrow[\text{ii) R'X}]{\text{i) NaNH}_2/\text{NH}_3(1)}$ R–CH(R')–C≡N

Nitrile   α-Substituted nitrile

2. Thorpe Nitrile Condensation: Two moles of alkyl cyanides undergo self-condensation in the presence of a base (an alkoxide) to yield iminonitriles. This reaction is called "Thorpe Nitrile Condensation". The mechanism can be written as:

N≡C–CHR–H $\xrightarrow[-\text{C}_2\text{H}_5\text{OH}]{^-\text{OC}_2\text{H}_5}$ N≡C–C$^-$HR ⟶ N≡C–C(R)(H)–C(=N$^-$)–CH$_2$–CH$_3$

Alkyl cyanide

$\updownarrow$ H$^+$

N≡C–C(R)(H)–C(=NH)–CH$_2$–CH$_3$

Iminonitrile

15.5.2 Isocyanides

1. Hydrolysis: Alkyl isocyanides are hydrolysed by dilute acids to form 1° amine and formic acid.

:C≡N$^+$–CH$_3$ + H$_2$O $\xrightarrow{\text{dil. acid}}$ CH$_3$NH$_2$ + HCOOH

Methyl isocyanide   Methyl amine   Formic acid

2. Reduction: Though cyanides on reduction give primary amines, the isocyanides on reduction yield secondary amines.

:C≡N$^+$–CH$_3$ $\xrightarrow{\text{LiAlH}_2}$ H$_3$C–NH–CH$_3$

Methyl isocyanide   Dimethyl amine

3. Addition reaction: Isocyanides react with halogens, sulphur, mercuric oxide etc. to give addition products. The significant feature of these addition reactions is that both the electrophilic and nucleophilic part add to the same carbon unlike as seen with addition reactions of carbon-carbon and carbon heteroatom (C=O) bonds where the addition takes place at different atoms.

(a) Cl₂ gives alkyliminocarbonyl chloride:

$$:\bar{C}\equiv\overset{+}{N}-CH_3 \ + \ Cl_2 \longrightarrow \ \underset{Cl}{\overset{Cl}{>}}C=N-CH_3$$

Methyl isocyanide   Methyliminocarbonyl chloride

(b) Sulphur gives sulphur isothiocyanate:

$$:\bar{C}\equiv\overset{+}{N}-CH_3 \ + \ \frac{1}{8}S_8 \longrightarrow \ S=C=N-CH_3$$

Methyl isocyanide   Methyl isothiocyanate

(c) Mercuric oxide gives isocyanate:

$$:\bar{C}\equiv\overset{+}{N}-CH_3 \ + \ HgO \longrightarrow \ O=C=N-CH_3$$

Methyl isocyanide   Methyl isocyanate

QUESTIONS

Q.1	Write a note on reactions of cyanides and isocyanides.	**(Dec-2015)**
Q.2	Explain any two reactions of alkyl cyanide.	**(May-2015, Dec-2014)**
Q.3	How to distinguish nitriles from isonitriles?	**(May-2014)**

❖ ❖ ❖

Chapter 16

ESTERS AND AMIDES

16.1 INTRODUCTION TO ESTERS

Esters are derivatives of carboxylic acids in which the –OH has been replaced by –OR. Thus, esters are neutral derivatives of carboxylic acids, which themselves are weak acids. Esters are known for their distinctive odors and are commonly used for food aroma and fragrances. The general formula of an ester is RCOOR'. One of the most commonly discussed ester is ethyl ethanoate. The structure can be written as:

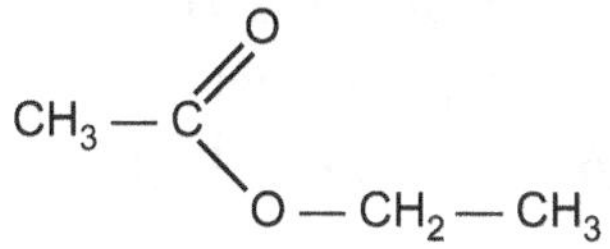

Ethyl ethanoate

Esters are widespread in nature. They occur naturally in plants and animals. Small esters, in combination with other volatile compounds, produce the pleasant aroma of fruits. In general, a symphony of chemicals is responsible for specific fruity fragrances. Esters, thus are popular as flavouring agents.

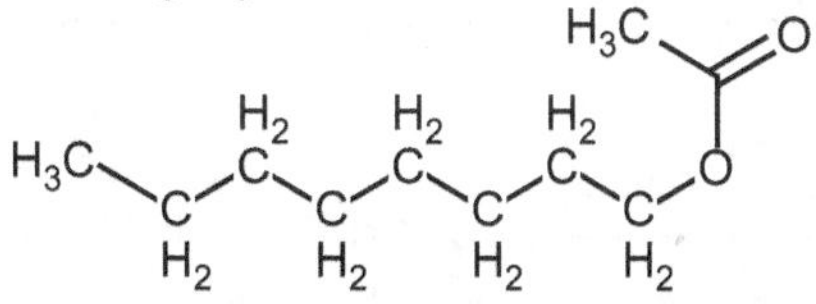

Octyl acetate-a constituent of orange

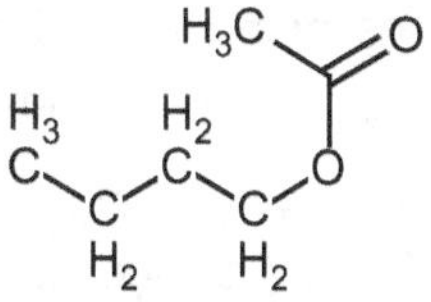

Butyl acetate-a constituent of apple

There are many drugs which also contain an ester functional group. Examples are;

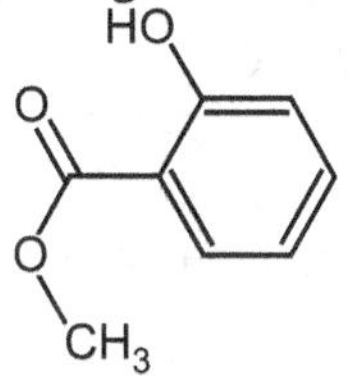

Methyl salicylate-counter irritant

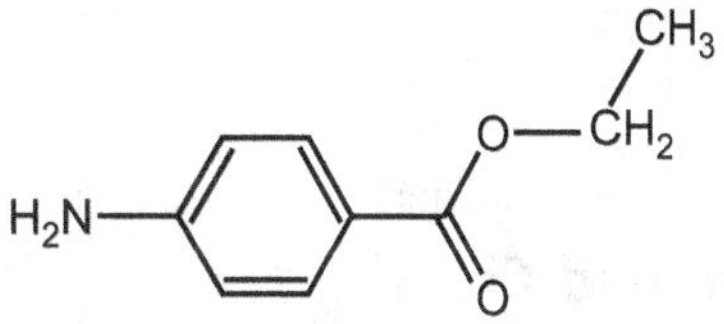

Benzocaine-local anesthetic

16.2 NOMENCLATURE OF ESTERS

Esters are formed through reactions between an acid and an alcohol with the elimination of water. The first step towards naming an ester is to identify the carboxylic acid and the alcohol from which they have been prepared. The general ester, RCO_2R' can be said to be derived from the carboxylic acid RCO_2H and the alcohol R'OH. The first component of an ester name, the alkyl is derived from the alcohol, R'OH. The second component of an ester name, the -oate is derived from the carboxylic acid, RCO_2H. For the alcohol component, the root name is based on the longest chain containing the -OH group. The chain is numbered so as to give the –OH the lowest possible number. Similarly, for the **carboxylic**

acid component, the root name is based on the longest chain including the carbonyl group. Since the carboxylic acid group is at the end of the chain, it is numbered 1. The "e" of the hydrocarbon is replaced by the suffix for the acid e.g. -ane + –oate = –anoate etc. The complete ester name is therefore, **alkyl alkanoate.**

$$CH_3-C(=O)-O-H \quad + \quad HO-CH_2-CH_3 \quad \longrightarrow \quad CH_3-C(=O)-O-CH_2-CH_3$$

　　　　Ethanoic acid　　　　　　　　　Ethanol　　　　　　　　　　Ethyl ethanoate

Propanol + Ethanoic acid $\Rightarrow$ Propyl ethanoate

Butanol + Ethanoic acid $\Rightarrow$ Butyl ethanoate

Ethanol + Propanoic acid $\Rightarrow$ Ethyl propanoate

Ethanol + Benzoic acid $\Rightarrow$ Ethyl benzoate

16.3 METHODS OF PREPARATION OF ESTERS

1. From Carboxylic Acids

Esters are produced when carboxylic acids are heated with alcohols in the presence of an acid catalyst. The catalyst is usually concentrated sulphuric acid. This method of acid catalyzed esterification is called Fischer Esterification. This is a reversible reaction and unless a product is removed, for example, removal of water by azeotropic distillation or absorption by molecular sieves or an excess of reactant (mostly alcohol, because it is cheap) is used, the reaction does not undergo completion.

$$R-COOH \quad + \quad R'-OH \quad \underset{}{\overset{H^+, \text{ reflux}}{\rightleftharpoons}} \quad RCOOR' \quad + \quad H_2O$$

　　　　Carboxylic acid　　　　Alcohol　　　　　　　　　　Ester

Example:

$$CH_3-C(=O)-OH \quad + \quad C_2H_5OH \quad \underset{}{\overset{H_2SO_4}{\rightleftharpoons}} \quad H_3C-C(=O)-O-C_2H_5 \quad + \quad H_2O$$

　　　Ethanoic acid　　　　　　Ethanol　　　　　　　　　Ethyl ethanoate

2. From Acid Chlorides

Acid chlorides can be reacted with alcohols or phenols to prepare esters readily.

$$CH_3-C(=O)-Cl \quad + \quad CH_3CH_2OH \quad \longrightarrow \quad CH_3-C(=O)-O-CH_2CH_3 \quad + \quad HCl$$

　　　Acetyl chloride　　　　　　Ethanol　　　　　　　　Ethyl acetate

$$CH_3-C(=O)-Cl \quad + \quad C_6H_5OH \quad \longrightarrow \quad CH_3-C(=O)-O-C_6H_5 \quad + \quad HCl$$

　　　Acetyl chloride　　　　　Phenol　　　　　　　　Phenyl ethanoate

Less reactive acid chlorides can be reacted with phenol only in the presence of a strong base like sodium hydroxide to yield the corresponding ester, e.g. phenyl benzoate. Sodium hydroxide is used to first ionize phenol to a phenoxide ion which then reacts with benzoyl chloride to displace the chloride in a nucleophilic displacement reaction.

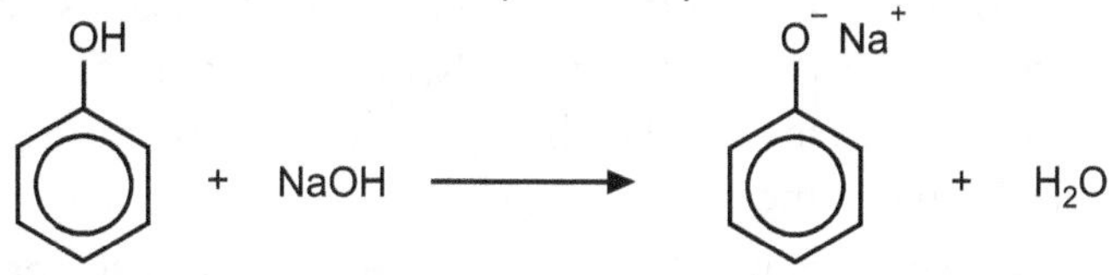

Phenol Sodium phenoxide

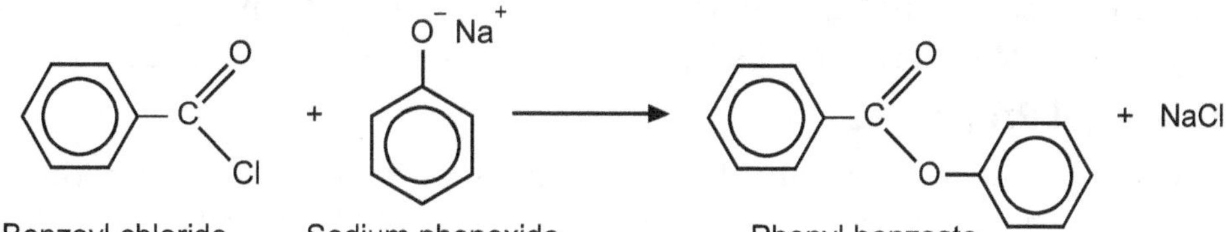

Benzoyl chloride Sodium phenoxide Phenyl benzoate

3. From Anhydrides

Acid anhydrides can be reacted with both phenols and alcohols to give esters. This reaction is slower than that with acid chlorides and requires presence of a mineral acid for catalyzing the reaction. The reaction is irreversible. One molecule of acid (from the anhydride) is obtained as the side product. Given below is an example in which acetic anhydride is reacted with an alcohol to form the acetate ester and one molecule of acetic acid as the side product.

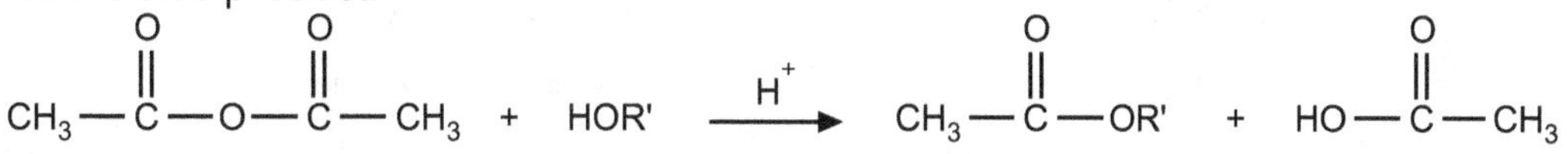

Acetic anhydride Alcohol An acetate ester Acetic acid

Phenols can also be reacted in a similar manner.

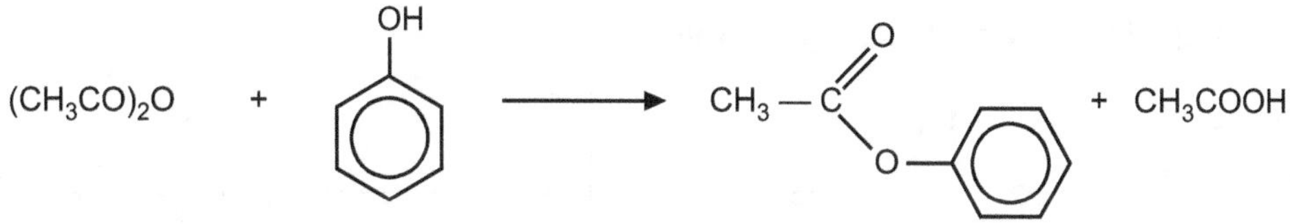

Acetyl anhydride Phenol Phenyl acetate Acetic acid

4. From Esters: Transesterification

Transesterification is the conversion of a carboxylic acid ester into a different carboxylic acid ester. The most common method of transesterification is the reaction of the ester with an alcohol in the presence of an acid catalyst.

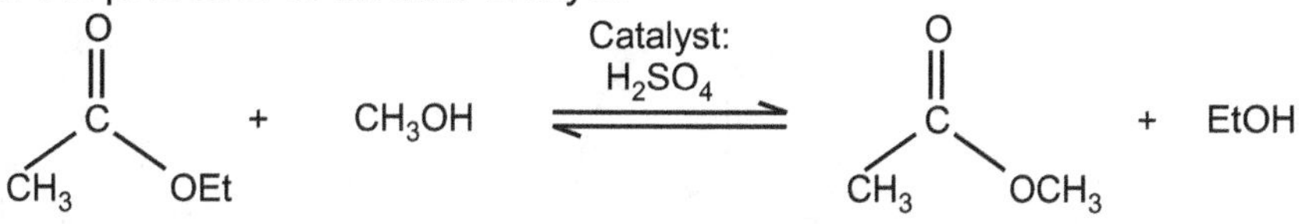

Ethyl ethanoate Methanol Methyl ethanoate Ethanol

This reaction has been explained in detail under "reactions of esters".

16.4 PROPERTIES OF ESTERS

16.4.1 Physical Properties

The small esters have boiling points which are similar to those of aldehydes and ketones with the same number of carbon atoms. They are polar molecules and therefore show dipole-dipole interactions as well as van der Waals dispersion forces. However, unlike carboxylic acids, they do not form intermolecular hydrogen bonds, and so their boiling points are lower than the acid with the same number of carbon atoms.

Small esters are quite water soluble because of their tendency to form hydrogen bonds with water molecules. The hydrogen of water molecule can easily form a hydrogen bond with the carbonyl oxygen of the ester. As the hydrocarbon part increases, the solubility decreases.

16.4.2 Chemical Properties

Esters undergo nucleophilic substitution reactions as shown by other carboxylic acid derivatives. The $-OR'$ is replaced by groups like $-OH$, $-OR''$ or $-NH_2$. The site of the nucleophilic attack is the electron deficient carbonyl carbon. Such reactions are usually catalyzed by a mineral acid. The proton, H^+ attaches itself to the carbonyl oxygen, making the carbonyl carbon more reactive towards a nucleophilic attack.

1. Hydrolysis of Esters

Esters can be hydrolyzed to give the corresponding carboxylic acids by both, acid and base catalysis.

$$RCOOR' + H_2O \xrightarrow{\;H^+/OH^-\;} RCOOH + R'OH$$

Ester   Acid   Alcohol

$$CH_3COOCH_2CH_3 + H_2O \xrightarrow{\;H^+/OH^-\;} CH_3COOH + CH_3CH_2OH$$

Ethyl ethanoate   Ethanoic acid   Ethanol

Mechanism for acid catalyzed hydrolysis:

In step 1 the carbonyl oxygen is protonated by the mineral acid used as a catalyst. This makes the carbonyl oxygen more prone to attack by the nucleophile (here, water) in step 2. In step 3 the tetrahedral intermediate formed after the attachment of water, loses a proton to water, which is also the solvent in the reaction. The alkoxy group, $-OR'$ is protonated in step 4, which converts it into a good leaving group. The group thus leaves in step 5, along with the bonding electrons to form an alcohol. The deficiency created due to loss of the alkoxy group is overcome in step 6 by loss of proton by the oxygen so that the electrons can be shared with the carbon leading to the formation of a carboxylic acid.

Mechanism for alkaline hydrolysis of esters:

Carboxylate ion   Alcohol

In step 1 the hydroxide nucleophile attacks at the electrophilic carbon of the ester, C=O, breaking the π bond and creating the tetrahedral intermediate. The intermediate loses the alkoxide ion in step 2 followed by loss of proton in step 3 to form a carboxylate ion. Treatment with a mineral acid then converts the carboxylate salt to carboxylic acid.

Alkaline hydrolysis of esters is also referred to as saponification and is used in preparation of soaps.

2. Ammonolysis of Esters

When esters are treated with ammonia, generally in an alcoholic solution, amides are formed. The mechanism involved is nucleophilic substitution as the $-OR'$ is replaced by $-NH_2$.

Ester   Amide

Example:

Methyl benzoate   Benzamide   Methanol

The mechanism involved is very similar to that of alkaline hydrolysis, and can be written as:

Tetrahedral
intermediate

Methyl acetate ⇌ Acetamide + CH_3OH

3. Reduction of Esters

Esters are reduced by lithium aluminium hydride ($LiAlH_4$) to yield primary alcohols.

$$R - \overset{\overset{O}{\|}}{C} - OR' \xrightarrow[\text{ether}]{LiAlH_4} RCH_2OH \ + \ R'OH$$

Ester   Primary alcohol

$LiAlH_4$ is selective for the carbonyl group. Thus, esters containing a C=C bond can be reduced without the bond getting affected.

$$CH_3CH = CH\overset{\overset{O}{\|}}{C} - OCH_2CH_3 \xrightarrow[\text{2. H}_2\text{O, H}^+]{\text{1. LiAlH}_4} CH_3CH = CHCH_2OH \ + \ CH_3CH_2OH$$

Ethyl 2-butenoate   2-Buten-1-ol   Ethanol

The mechanism involved in the reduction is the same as that for reduction of aldehyde and ketones by $LiAlH_4$, that is, by hydride transfer. Aldehyde is formed as an intermediate but cannot be isolated.

$$R - \overset{\overset{O}{\|}}{C} - OR' \xrightarrow{H - \bar{A}lH_3} R - \overset{O \ \bar{A}lH_3}{\underset{H}{\overset{|}{C}}} - OR' \xrightarrow{- \bar{A}lH_3 (OR')} R - \overset{\overset{O}{\|}}{C} - H \xrightarrow{H - \bar{A}lH_2 (OR')}$$

Ester   Aldehyde

$$R - \overset{O \ \bar{A}lH_2 (OR')}{\underset{H}{\overset{|}{C}}} - H \xrightarrow[\text{H}^+]{- H_2O} RCH_2OH \ + \ R'OH$$

1° alcohol

4. Hydrogenolysis of Esters

Hydrogenolysis means cleavage by hydrogen. Hydrogenolysis of an ester requires rigorous conditions. High temperature and pressures are used. The catalyst used normally is copper chromite, a mixture of oxides with an approximate composition of $CuO.CuCr_2O_4$. The product is a primary alcohol.

$$CH_3(CH_2)_{10}COOCH_3 \xrightarrow[\text{150°C, 5000 lb/in}^2]{H_2, CuO.CuCr_2O_4} CH_3(CH_2)_{10}CH_2OH$$

Methyl laurate   Lauryl alcohol

5. Reaction with Grignard reagent

Carboxylic esters react with 2 equivalents of organolithium or Grignard reagents to give tertiary alcohols. The tertiary alcohol thus formed contains two identical alkyl groups (from R in the scheme). The reaction proceeds via a ketone intermediate which then reacts with the second equivalent of the organometallic reagent. However, the reaction cannot be used in preparation of ketones, as the ketone formed is more reactive than the ester and immediately reacts to form an alcohol.

$$2\,R\,Li \;\; \text{or} \;\; 2\,R\,MgX \;+\; \underset{R'\quad\quad OR''}{\overset{O}{\underset{\|}{C}}} \longrightarrow R\!-\!\underset{\underset{R}{|}}{\overset{\overset{OH}{|}}{C}}\!-\!R'$$

The mechanism involved is nucleophilic substitution, followed by nucleophilic addition reaction. The nucleophilic carbon of the Grignard reagent attacks the electrophilic carbonyl carbon of the ester. Electrons from the **C=O** move to the electronegative **O** creating the tetrahderal intermediate **(1)**, a metal alkoxide complex. This tetrahedral intermediate loses the alcohol portion of the ester, in the form of the alkoxide, **RO–**. This produces a *ketone* **(2)** as an intermediate. A second molecule of the reagent then adds to the carbonyl group of the ketone, in a manner similar to above to give another intermediate **(3)** which on treatment with water leads to the formation of the alcohol **(4)**.

$$CH_3\!-\!\overset{\overset{O}{\|}}{C}\!-\!OC_2H_5 \xrightarrow{CH_3MgI} \left[CH_3\!-\!\underset{\underset{CH_3}{|}}{\overset{\overset{OMgI}{|}}{C}}\!-\!OC_2H_5\right] \xrightarrow{-C_2H_5OMgI} \underset{CH_3}{CH_3\!-\!C\!=\!O}$$

Ester   1   2

$$CH_3\!-\!\underset{\underset{CH_3}{|}}{\overset{\overset{OH}{|}}{C}}\!-\!CH_3 \xleftarrow{HOH} \left[CH_3\!-\!\underset{\underset{CH_3}{|}}{\overset{\overset{OMgI}{|}}{C}}\!-\!CH_3\right] \xleftarrow{CH_3MgI}$$

Tert-butyl alcohol   3
4

6. Transesterification:

An ester on reaction with an alcohol can displace the original alcohol portion to form a different ester. This cleavage of an ester with alcohol (alcoholysis), to yield another ester is called as transesterification.

$$R'-CO-OR'' \;+\; ROH \;\rightleftharpoons\; R'-CO-OR + R''OH$$

The mechanism of transesterification is very similar to that involved in hydrolysis of an ester, except that the nucleophile in this case is not a water molecule but an alcohol, R"OH.

Similar to hydrolysis of esters, this reaction is also best catalyzed by an acid. Acid enhances the attack of the nucleophile (alcohol) on the carbonyl carbon. The reaction is reversible, therefore, a large excess of alcohol is used to shift the equilibrium to the right, that is, formation of the new ester. Another way to ensure completion of reaction is to remove the product (newly formed ester) from the reaction as soon as it is formed.

16.5 INTRODUCTION TO AMIDES

Amides are one of the derivatives of carboxylic acids in which the –OH group has been replaced by the $-NH_2$. Substituted amides are those in which the hydrogen/hydrogens of nitrogen have been replaced by groups like alkyl, aryl etc. Since there is no acidic hydrogen, the amides are neutral compounds. Though the amides contain amino, $-NH_2$ group, they are not basic as the amino group is joined to an electron withdrawing carbonyl –C=O. The carbonyl group, being electron withdrawing (–I effect), pulls the unshared electrons of the nitrogen towards itself, making them unavailable for accepting a proton. This effect of the carbonyl group is also responsible for shortening of the C-N bond length in amides in comparison to the CN bond length in amines. The bond length measured for amides is about half way between that typical for C-N single bonds and C=N double bonds.

The following figure can be used to explain the phenomenon:

The above structure also explains the planar nature of the molecule without any free rotation around C-N bond.

The simplest amide is ethanamide, also known commonly as acetamide.

Ethanamide

Amides are widespread in nature. All proteins contain amino acids linked through amide linkage.

Capsiacin-a constituent or red, green chilli peppers

There are many popular drugs also containing amide functional group. Some of the examples are given on the next page :

Lignocaine-local anesthetic　　　　　Diazepam CNS depressant

16.6 NOMENCLATURE OF AMIDES

In simple amides the name is derived from the acid by replacing the "oic acid" ending by "amide". If the molecule is branched, the carbon in the $-CONH_2$ group counts is numbered as first carbon atom. For example:

3-Methylbutanamide

In case of substituted amides, the substituents on the nitrogen are named first followed by the name of the longest chain containing the functional group. Following examples illustrate the same:

N-methylpropanamide   N,N-dimethylpropanamide   N-ethyl-N-methyl-propanamide

16.7 PREPARATION OF AMIDES

Following methods can be used in preparation of amides:

1. From carboxylic acids :

Carboxylic acids when reacted with ammonia or a source of ammonia give amides. The carboxylic acid is first converted into an ammonium salt which then produces an amide on heating. The ammonium salt is formed by adding solid ammonium carbonate to an excess of the acid.

For example, ammonium ethanoate is made by adding ammonium carbonate to an excess of ethanoic acid.

$$2CH_3COOH \quad + \quad (NH_4)_2CO_3 \longrightarrow 2CH_3COO^-NH_4^+ \; + \; H_2O + CO_2$$

Ethanoic acid   Ammonium carbonate   Ammonium ethanoate

When the reaction is complete, the mixture is heated and the ammonium salt dehydrates producing ethanamide.

$$CH_3COO^-NH_4^+ \longrightarrow CH_3CONH_2 + H_2O$$

Ammonium ethanoate   Ethanamide

The excess of ethanoic acid prevents dissociation of the ammonium salt before it dehydrates.

A N-substituted amide is prepared by reacting an acid with a primary amine.

$$CH_3-CH_2-\overset{O}{\overset{\|}{C}}-OH \xrightarrow[\Delta]{CH_3\ddot{N}H_2} CH_3-CH_2-\overset{O}{\overset{\|}{C}}-NHCH_3 \; + \; NH_4Cl$$

Propanoic acid   N-Methyl propanamide

2. From acid halides, acid anhydrides and esters :

Acid halides, acid anhydrides and esters also can be readily converted into amides as compared to acids by reacting with ammonia (unsubstituted) or amines (substituted).

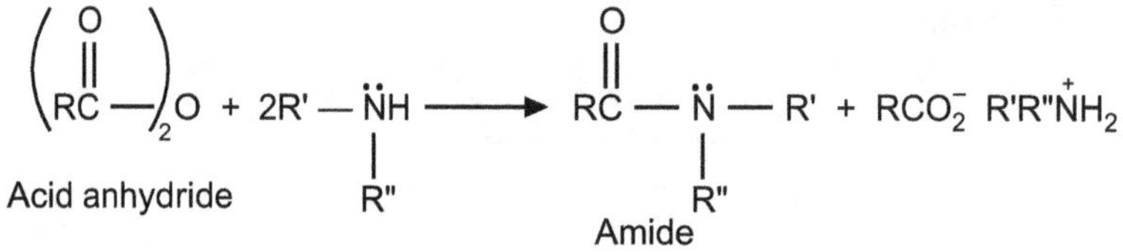

$$\left(\underset{RC}{\overset{O}{\|}}\right)_2 O + 2R'-\ddot{N}H \longrightarrow \underset{R''}{\overset{O}{\underset{|}{\|}}}RC-\ddot{N}-R' + RCO_2^- \; R'R''\overset{+}{N}H_2$$

Acid anhydride   R''   R''
                                   Amide

R', R" can be H, alkyl or aryl.

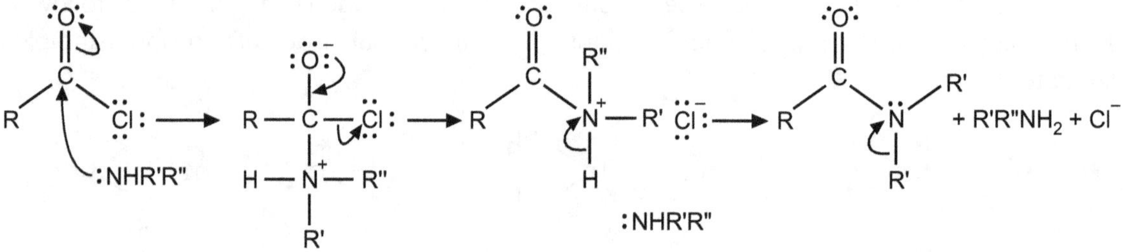

Reactant	**Product**

Ammonia; R', R" = H   Unsubstituted amide; R', R" = H

1º Amine; R' = H, R" = alkyl, aryl   N-Substituted amide; R' = H, R" = alkyl, aryl

2º Amine; R', R" = alkyl, aryl   N, N-Disubstituted amide; R', R" = alkyl, aryl

16.8 PROPERTIES OF AMIDES

16.8.1 Physical Properties

The amides have high melting points in relation to their size because they can form hydrogen bonds. The hydrogen atoms in the $-NH_2$ group are sufficiently positive to form a hydrogen bond with a lone pair on the oxygen atom of another molecule.

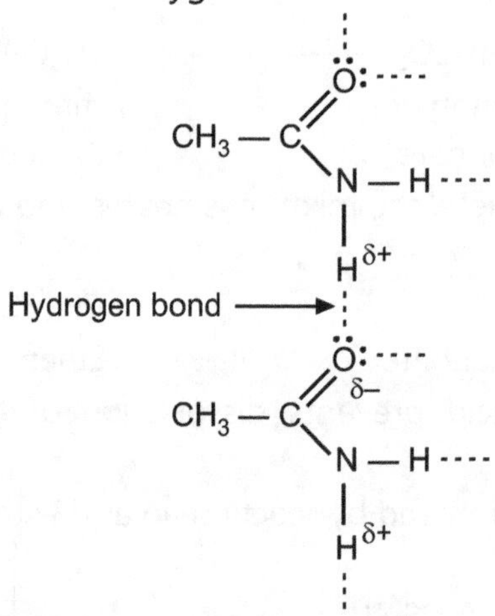

The ability of smaller amides to form hydrogen bonds with water makes them water soluble. However, as the alkyl chain gets longer, solubility decreases.

16.8.2 Chemical Properties

Amides are synthetically important compounds as they can be converted into a number of other functional groups through simple reactions.

1. Hydrolysis:

Like other derivatives of carboxylic acids, amides can be hydrolyzed under acidic or basic conditions to give the parent acid. However, amides are more slowly hydrolyzed than the esters or anhydrides. This is a nucleophilic substitution reaction in which the $-NH_2$ group is replaced by $-OH$.

Acid hydrolysis

Alkaline hydrolysis

Mechanism of acid hydrolysis:

The amide carbonyl accepts a proton from the aqueous acid

A water molecule attacks the protonated carbonyl to give a tetrahedral intermediate

A proton is lost at one oxygen and gained at the nitrogen

Loss of a molecule of ammonia gives a protonated carboxylic acid

Transfer of a proton to ammonia leads to the carboxylic acid and an ammonium ion

Mechanism of alkaline hydrolysis:

A hydroxide ion attacks the acyl carbon of the amide

A hydroxide ion removes a proton to give a dianion

The dianion loses a molecule of ammonia (or an amine); this step is synchronized with a proton transfer from water due to the basicity of NH_2^-.

2. Conversion to imides:

Cyclic anhydrides on reaction with ammonia yield a product containing both the –COOH and the $-NH_2$ groups. This product when heated cyclizes to give a product containing two carbonyl groups attached to a nitrogen. Such compounds are called imides.

Phthalic anhydride

Ammonium phthalamate (94%)

Phthalamic acid (81%)

Phthalamic acid

Phthalimide (~100%)

3. Hofmann degradation of amides:

In this synthetically important reaction, amides are converted to primary amines with one carbon less than the starting amide.

Amide → 1º Amine

(reagents: Br_2, KOH or NaOH)

Example:

$$CH_3CONH_2 + Br_2 \xrightarrow{\text{NaOH or KOH}} CH_3NH_2$$

Acetamide Methyl amine

This reaction occurs in three steps:

$$CH_3-\overset{\overset{\displaystyle O}{\|}}{C}-NH_2 + Br_2 + KOH \rightarrow CH_3CONHBr + KBr + H_2O$$

Acetobromamide

$$CH_3-\overset{\overset{\displaystyle O}{\|}}{C}-NHBr + KOH \rightarrow CH_3NCO + KBr + H_2O$$

Methylisocyanate

$$CH_3NCO + 2KOH \rightarrow CH_3NH_2 + K_2CO_3$$

Methylamine

$$CH_3CONH_2 + Br_2 + 4KOH \rightarrow CH_3NH_2 + 2KBr + K_2CO_3 + 2H_2O$$

The mechanism can be written as:

Isocyanate

Carbamate ion

$$RNH_2 + CO_2 + OH^-$$

1º Amine

The reaction starts by removal of a proton from amide nitrogen by the hydroxide ion. The electron rich nitrogen thus created attacks a molecule of bromine. In the next step the hydroxide ion removes the second hydrogen from the nitrogen, leading to the formation of a species that gets converted to isocyanate by loss of the bromide. Isocyanate undergoes alkaline hydrolysis to yield the primary amine. The carbonyl carbon is therefore lost as carbon dioxide.

As is clear from the mechanism, mono- and di-substituted amides cannot undergo Hofmann degradation reaction as they have no replaceable hydrogen.

4. Conversion to nitrile:

Heating an unsubstituted amide with a dehydrating agent like P_2O_5 on boiling acetic anhydride results in the formation of the corresponding nitrile.

$$R-C(=O)(NH_2) \xrightarrow[\text{Heat} \ (-H_2O)]{P_2O_5 \ \text{or} \ (CH_3CO)_2O} R-C \equiv N: + H_3PO_4 \ \text{or} \ CH_3CO_2H$$

A nitrile

5. Reduction of amides:

Reducing agents like lithium aluminium hydride, $LiAlH_4$ and diborane, B_2H_6 can reduce amides into corresponding amines.

$$\underset{\text{Amide}}{R-C(=O)-NH_2} \xrightarrow{LiAlH_4 \ \text{or} \ B_2H_6} \underset{\text{Amine}}{R-CH_2-NH_2}$$

QUESTIONS

Q.1   Give reaction, mechanism and application of Claisen and Dieckmann reactions.

(Dec-2015)

Q.2   Write synthetic uses of ethylacetoacetate.   **(May-2015)**

Q.3   Explain Dieckmann condensation.   **(May-2015, May-2014, Dec-2014)**

Q.4   Write a note on Michael addition.   **(May-2015)**

Q.5   Write a note on synthetic uses of diethyl malonate.

Q.6   Write a note on synthetic uses of malonic ester.

Q.7   Why esters are less reactive towards nucleophile than aldehydes?   **(Dec-2015)**

Q.8   Explain acidity of benzene sulphonic acid.   **(Dec-2014)**

Q.9   Explain ammonolysis of esters.   **(May-2014)**

Q.10 Explain addition of Grignard reagent to unsaturated compounds.

Chapter 17

ALKYL HALIDES

17.1 INTRODUCTION

Alkyl halides (or haloalkanes) are a class of compounds derived from alkanes containing one or more halogen atoms and are represented as R–X (where –X is a halogen atom). Alkyl halides are widely used commercially as refrigerants (CF_2Cl_2-freon 12), solvents ($CHCl_3$-chloroform), fire extinguishers ($BrCF_3$-bromotrifluoromethane) and pharmaceuticals ($CF_3CHClBr$-halothane). Methyl iodide is one of the simplest naturally occurring alkyl halide. Alkyl halides are used primarily as industrial and household solvents. Carbon tetrachloride was once used for dry cleaning, spot removing, and other domestic cleaning however, being toxic, has been replaced with 1,1,1-trichloroethane and other solvents instead. Methylene chloride and chloroform are also good solvents for cleaning and degreasing work. Chloroform was once a popular general anesthetic but has been replaced by halothane ($CF_3CHClBr$), a mixed alkyl halide. The freons (also called chlorofluorocarbons, or CFCs) are fluorinated haloalkanes that were developed to replace ammonia as a refrigerant gas. Lindane (hexachlorocyclohexane) is used to kill lice.

Lindane (used to kill lice)

17.2 NOMENCLATURE

Alkyl halides can be classified as primary (1°), secondary (2°) or tertiary (3°).

According to IUPAC nomenclature, alkyl halides are treated as alkanes with a halogen (Halo-) substituent. The halogen prefixes are Fluoro-, Chloro-, Bromo- and Iodo-. For example, ethane with bromine becomes bromoethane, methane with four chlorine groups becomes tetrachloromethane. In common nomenclature, simple alkyl halides are named as alkyl derivatives of the corresponding halogens. The name of the alkyl group then precedes the name of the halide. However, many of these compounds have an established trivial name which is endorsed by the IUPAC nomenclature for example, chloroform (trichloromethane) and methylene chloride (dichloromethane). Given below are some illustrations.

$H_3C - Cl$

Chloromethane

Methyl chloride

1º halide

Chloroethane

Ethyl chloride

2º halide

2-Fluorobutane

2-Butyl fluoride

1, 2-Dichloroethane

Ethylene dichloride

3º halide

2-Bromo-2-methylpropane

Tertiary butyl bromide

Other types of halides are:

1. Geminal (gem) dihalide: it has two halogens on the same carbon and

2. Vicinal dihalide has halogens on adjacent carbon atoms.

Gem dibromide

Vicinal dichloride

17.3 METHODS OF PREPARATION OF ALKYL HALIDES

1. Free Radical Halogenation

(a) Halogenation of alkanes:

Alkanes on reaction with chlorine (Cl_2) or bromine (Br_2) in the presence of UV light yield alkyl halides. If the reaction is not controlled, polyhalogen derivatives are obtained. Thus, under uncontrolled conditions, methane reacts with chlorine to give carbon tetrachloride. This method is therefore an inefficient method for synthesis of alkyl halides. Free radical mechanism is involved in this reaction. Therefore, the method is also known as free radical halogenation.

Methane Chloromethane Dichloromethane Chloroform Carbon tetrachloride

Alkyl iodide (R-I) and alkyl fluoride (R-F) cannot be synthesized using this method.

(b) Allylic Bromination:

Hydrocarbons containing an allylic carbon (carbon adjacent to a C = C double bond), can be brominated by refluxing with N-bromosuccinimide (NBS) in the presence of a radical initiator like benzoyl peroxide, heat or light.

Prop-1-ene　　　　N-Bromosuccinimide　　　　3-Bromoprop-1-ene　　Succinimide
or
Allyl bromide

Cyclohexene　　　　　　　　　　　3-Bromocyclohex-1-ene

The above reaction is known as Wohl-Ziegler reaction.

NBS is used as a substitute for Br_2 in these cases since Br_2 in high concentrations tends to react with double bonds to form dibromides. The advantage of NBS is that it provides a low-level concentration of Br_2, and bromination of the double bond does not compete as much. N-bromosuccinimide (NBS) continually generates small amounts of Br_2 through reaction with HBr, trace amounts of which are normally present in NBS.

Once bromine is formed, the reaction follows a free radical mechanism.

2. Addition of Hydrogen Halide to Alkenes

Halogen acids like HCl, HBr and HI add to alkenes to yield the alkyl halides. These additions follow the *Markovnikov rule* (for addition of hydrogen halides to alkenes, the H atom adds to the C having the most H atoms) except for the addition of HBr in the presence of organic peroxides (R – O – O – R).

$$CH_2 = CH_2 + HX \longrightarrow H_2C - CH_3$$

Ethene　　　　　　　　　　　　　　　Haloethane
where X = F, Cl, Br, I

$$R - CH = CH_2 \ + \ HX \longrightarrow R - \underset{\underset{H}{|}}{\overset{\overset{X}{|}}{C}} - CH_3$$

Unsymmetrical	Hydrogen	Alkyl halide
alkene	halide	(Anti-Markovnikov rule)

Gem-dihalides can be obtained by reacting an alkyne with two moles of hydrogen halide.

$$R - C \equiv C - R \ + \ 2HX \longrightarrow H - \underset{\underset{H}{|}}{\overset{\overset{R}{|}}{C}} - \underset{\underset{X}{|}}{\overset{\overset{R}{|}}{C}} - X$$

Alkene	Gem-dihalide

3. Addition of Halogens to Alkenes

Vicinal dihalides are obtained by the addition of halogens to alkenes.

$$H_2C = CH_2 \ + \ 2HCl \longrightarrow \underset{Cl}{H_2C} - \underset{Cl}{CH_2}$$

Ethene	1, 2-Dichloroethane

4. From Alcohols

Various reagents like PCl_5, PBr_3, $SOCl_2$ are used to convert alcohols into corresponding halides. PBr_5 and PI_5 cannot be used as they are unstable.

With Et_3N or pyridine and $SOCl_2$:

$$-\overset{|}{\underset{|}{C}}-OH \longrightarrow -\overset{|}{\underset{|}{C}}-Cl \ + \ SO_2 \ + \ HCl$$

Alkyl chloride

With Et_3N or pyridine and PCl_5:

$$-\overset{|}{\underset{|}{C}}-Cl \ + \ H_3PO_3 \ + \ HCl$$

Alkyl chloride

With Et_3N or pyridine and PBr_3:

$$-\overset{|}{\underset{|}{C}}-Br \ + \ H_3PO_3 \ + \ HBr$$

Alkyl bromide

In the above reaction, triethyl amine (Et_3N) or pyridine (C_6H_5N) is used to neutralize the halogen acid formed.

Similarly HBr and HCl also react with alcohols to produce alkyl bromides or alkyl chlorides respectively.

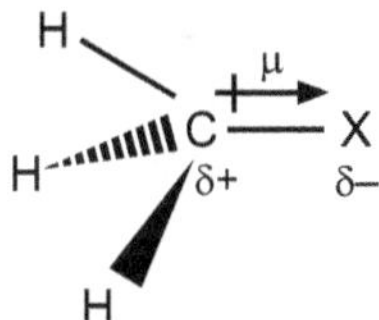

$$-\overset{|}{\underset{|}{C}}-OH \;+\; HX \;\xrightarrow{\;X = Cl,\, Br\;}\; -\overset{|}{\underset{|}{C}}-X \;+\; H_2O$$

Alcohol   Hydrogen halide   Alkyl halide   Water

17.4 PROPERTIES OF ALKYL HALIDES

17.4.1 Physical Properties

Halogens (F, Cl and Br) are more electronegative than carbon. Therefore, carbon atoms attached to halogens are charged partially positive while the halogen is charged partially negative. The polarity of the C–X bond causes a measurable dipole moment. As a result of the partial positive charge, the carbon atom displays an electrophilic character.

The electronegativities decrease in the following order: $F>Cl>Br>I$ while the carbon-halogen bond lengths increase in the order: $F<Cl<Br<I$. This is due to the larger size of Br and I.

Table 17.1 : Bond distance and dipole moments of methyl halides

Compound	Bond length	Dipole moment μ_D
CH_3F	1.385	1.82
$CH_3\text{-}Cl$	1.784	1.94
$CH_3\text{-}Br$	1.929	1.79
$CH_3\text{-}I$	2.139	1.64

Boiling point: Alkyl halides show much higher boiling points than those of the corresponding alkanes. The dipole moment of alkyl halides leads to attractive dipole-dipole interactions in liquid alkyl halides leading to high boiling points. Polyhalogenation further increases the boiling point. For example: CH_3Cl boils at −24°C, CH_2Cl_2 at 40°C, $CHCl_3$ at 61°C; and CCl_4 at 77°C. Multiple fluorine substitution is an exception, however: CH_3CH_2F boils at −32°C, CH_3CHF_2 at −25°C, CH_3CF_3 at −47°C, and CF_3CF_3 at −78°C. The boiling points of different alkyl halides containing the same halogen increase with increasing chain length. For a given chain length, the boiling point increases as the halogen is changed from fluorine to iodine. For isomers of the same compound, the compound with the more highly-branched alkyl group normally has the lowest boiling point. By reducing the molecular polarizability, multiple fluorine substitution weakens the strength of induced dipole-induced dipole attractive forces between molecules. In the liquid state these weakened intermolecular forces are reflected in unusually low boiling points, and in the solid state they are responsible for the novel properties of fluorocarbon polymers.

Solubility: Though more polar than alkanes, the alkyl halides are insoluble in water as they cannot form hydrogen bonds with water. However, they are soluble in organic solvents.

17.4.2 Chemical Properties

1. Aliphatic Nucleophilic Substitution: The halogen atom of alkyl halides can be easily displaced by a large variety of nucleophilic reagents. This is due to the planar nature of the carbon-halogen bond.

Some examples are given below:

Nucleophile	Product	Class of product
OH^-	ROH	Alcohol
NH_3	$RNH_3^+X^-$	Amine salt
CN^-	RCN	Cyanide
SH^-	RSH	Thiol (mercaptan)
OR^-	ROR	Ether
SR'^-	RSR'	Thioether
N_3^-	RN_3	Azide
$R'NH_2$	RNHR'	Secondary amine

Details of the mechanism of this reaction are given in the later part of the chapter.

2. Elimination Reaction: Alkyl halides undergo loss of a halide and a hydrogen atom to form alkenes under basic conditions. Sometimes the elimination and substitution reactions compete with each other. These eliminations are called dehydrohalogenations because a hydrogen halide has been removed from the alkyl halide.

Alkyl halide   Base   Alkene

In the elimination, the reagent B⁻ acts as a base, abstracting a proton from the alkyl halide. Most nucleophiles are also basic and can engage in either substitution or elimination, depending on the alkyl halide and the reaction conditions.

3. Formation of Grignard Reagents: Alkyl halides on treatment with magnesium metal in the presence of dry ether form alkyl magnesium halides also known as Grignard reagent. This reagent is an important reagent in synthetic chemistry.

$$R-X \ + \ Mg \xrightarrow{\text{Dry ether}} RMgX$$

Alkyl halide ⟶ Alkyl magnesium bromide

$$C_2H_5-Br \ + \ Mg \xrightarrow{\text{Dry ether}} C_2H_5\,MgBr$$

Ethyl bromide ⟶ Ethyl magnesium bromide

4. Friedel-Crafts Reaction: Alkyl halides provide the alkyl group for alkylation of an aromatic ring. This reaction requires $AlCl_3$, a Lewis acid, as a catalyst.

$$Ar \ + \ R-X \xrightarrow{AlCl_3} Ar-R \ + \ HCl$$

Benzene + CH_3Cl $\xrightarrow{AlCl_3}$ Toluene (CH_3) + HCl

5. Reduction: Alkyl halides can be reduced to alkanes in the presence of nascent hydrogen.

$$C_2H_5I \ + \ H_2 \xrightarrow{Ni} C_2H_6 \ + \ HI$$

Ethane   Hydrogen iodide

The nascent hydrogen may be obtained by any one of the following:

(i)   Zn + HCl

(ii) Zn + CH_3COOH

(iii) Zn-Cu couple in ethanol

(iv) Red P + HI

(v)   Al-Hg + ethanol

Alkyl halides can also be reduced catalytically to alkane by H_2/Pd or $LiAlH_4$ or by H_2/Ni.

17.5 NUCLEOPHILIC SUBSTITUTION REACTIONS

Nucleophilic substitution reactions involve replacement of a group by a nucleophile. It can be represented as:

$$R-L + :Nu^- \longrightarrow R-Nu + :L^-$$

Where L is a leaving group and Nu is an incoming nucleophile. Nucleophile is a species having either a negative charge or may be an uncharged species with an unshared pair of electrons. Examples of nucleophiles are: NO_2^-, N_3, $RCOO^-$, CN^-, I^-, Br^-, Cl^-, OH^-, OMe^-, H_2O, ROH, NH_3, RNH_2 etc.

Alkyl halides are easily converted to many other functional groups. Since the halogen atom can leave with its bonding pair of electrons to form a stable halide ion we say that a halide is a good leaving group. When another atom replaces the halide ion, the reaction is a substitution. When the halide ion leaves with another atom or ion (often) and forms a new *pi* bond, the reaction is elimination. The elimination reaction has been discussed in the chapter on Alkenes.

A useful reaction involving nucleophilic substitution reaction is the formation of alcohol from alkyl halide.

$$C_2H_5Br \xrightarrow{\quad OH^- \quad} C_2H_5OH \; + \; Br^-$$

$$\text{Ethyl bromide} \qquad\qquad \text{Ethanol}$$

In the above reaction, Br^- is the leaving group while OH^- is the nucleophile.

Nucleophilic substitution reactions may proceed through two different mechanisms, S_N1 and S_N2, based on the reaction condition and the substrate used. These two mechanisms differ in the molecularity involved.

17.5.1 The Second-Order (Bimolecular) Nucleophilic Substitution (S_N2) Reaction

A nucleophilic substitution reaction on a sp^3 carbon in which both the substrate and the reactant are involved in the transition state of the rate-determining step is known as nucleophilic substitution reaction bimolecular and is designated as S_N2.

$$:Nu^{\ominus} + R-L \longrightarrow \left(Nu \text{........} R \text{......} L\right)^{\ominus} \longrightarrow Nu-R + :L^-$$

$$\text{Transition state}$$

To understand the reaction better, let us again consider the reaction of ethyl bromide with a hydroxide ion:

Hydroxide	Ethyl bromide	Ethanol	Bromide
(nucleophile)	(substrate)	(product)	(leaving group)

In the above reaction, hydroxide ion is a strong nucleophile (donor of an electron pair) because the oxygen atom has unshared pairs of electrons and a negative charge. Bromoethane or ethylbromide is called the substrate, that is, the compound that is attacked by the reagent. The carbon atom of bromoethane is electrophilic because it is bonded to an electronegative bromine atom. The halogen being electronegative, the charge is drawn away from carbon by the halogen atom, giving the carbon atom a partial positive charge. The negative charge of hydroxide ion is attracted to this partial positive charge.

Hydroxide (nucleophile)   Ethyl bromide (substrate)   Transition state   Ethanol (product)   Bromide (leaving group)

Mechanism: It was proposed by Ingold that the nucleophile, OH⁻ (hydroxide ion) attacks the back side of the electrophilic carbon atom, donating a pair of electrons to form a new bond. Carbon can accommodate only eight electrons in its valence shell, so the carbon-bromine bond must begin to break as the carbon-oxygen bond begins to form. Bromide ion is the leaving group; it leaves with the pair of electrons that once bonded it to the carbon atom. Thus, the transition state (T.S.) is a structure in which both OH and Br are partially bonded shown with a dotted line (shown above). The T.S. possesses higher energy and breaks to give the products. The negative charge of the hydroxide ion starts to decrease because it is starting to share its electrons with the carbon atom while bromine carries a negative charge because it has started removing its shared pair of electrons from the carbon atom. At the same time the ion dipole bonds with the solvent molecules and the hydroxide ion are being broken and the dipole bonds between the bromide ion are being formed. The energy for breaking the C–Br bond is partially supplied by formation of C–OH bond. Thus, the bond breaking and bond forming are taking place simultaneously i.e. it is a concerted process.

In the T.S., the carbon atom is bonded to five groups (i.e. H, Br and OH). The –OH and –Br are located as far as possible. The three C–H bonds are in a plane while the C–OH and C–Br bonds are perpendicular to the plane of C–H bonds.

The nucleophile, OH⁻ always approaches from the backside of C–Br bond. The attack from the front is not possible because of repulsion between a partially negatively charged bromine atom and the negatively charged hydroxide ion.

Kinetics of S$_N$2 reaction: Since the reaction results from collision between a –OH⁻ ion and a methyl bromide molecule, the rate of reaction, as expected, depends on the concentration of both these reactants. Thus,

i)   doubling the concentration of either the substrate or the nucleophile, doubles the rate of reaction.

ii)   if either concentration is reduced to half, the collision frequency and consequently the rate should be halved.

$$\text{Rate} \propto [C_2H_5Br][OH^-]$$

The reaction therefore is said to follow the second order kinetics. The rate of the reaction is dependent upon the concentration of both, the substrate as well as the nucleophile. The rate equation can be written as:

$$\text{Rate} = k_2[C_2H_5Br][OH^-]$$

where k_2 is the rate constant.

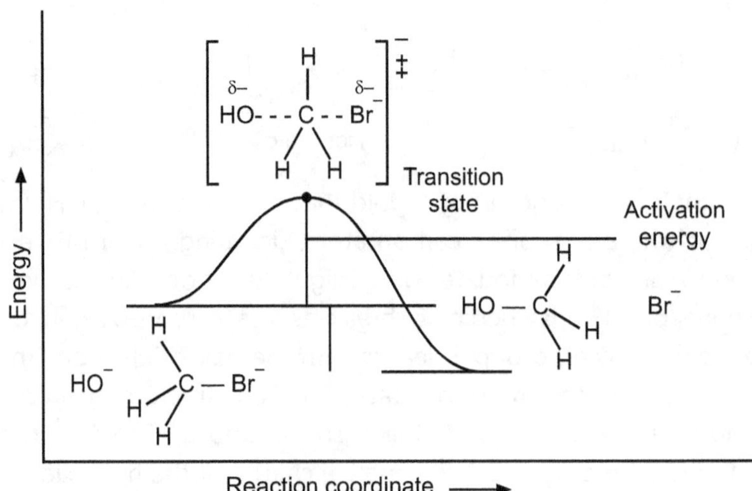

Fig. 17.1

Stereochemistry of S_N2 reaction-inversion of configuration

In a S_N2 reaction, since the attack of nucleophile (e.g. –OH⁻) takes place from the side opposite to that of the leaving group (e.g. – Br⁻), such a reaction is always accompanied with the inversion of configuration in an optically active compound. This phenomenon is called **Walden inversion.**

(S)-2-Bromobutane   Transition state   (R)-2-Butanol

(S)-2-Chlorosuccinic acid   (R)-2, 3-Dihydroxypropanoic acid
(maleic acid)

Most of the primary aliphatic halides undergo hydrolysis by this mechanism. Some examples of S_N2 reactions are summarized below:

$$Nu:^- \ + \ R-X \ \longrightarrow \ Nu-R \ + \ X^-$$

Nucleophile		Product	Class of Product
$R-X$ + $\ddot{I}:^-$	$\longrightarrow$	$R-\ddot{I}:$	Alkyl halide
$R-X$ + $^-:\ddot{O}H$	$\longrightarrow$	$R-\ddot{O}H$	Alcohol
$R-X$ + $^-:\ddot{O}R'$	$\longrightarrow$	$R-\ddot{O}R'$	Ether
$R-X$ + $^-:\ddot{S}H$	$\longrightarrow$	$R-\ddot{S}H$	Thiol (mercaptan)
$R-X$ + $^-:\ddot{S}R'$	$\longrightarrow$	$R-\ddot{S}R'$	Thioether (sulfide)
$R-X$ + $:\ddot{N}H_3$	$\longrightarrow$	$R-\overset{+}{\ddot{N}}H_3 \ X^-$	Amine salt
$R-X$ + $:\ddot{N}=\overset{+}{N}=\ddot{N}:^-$	$\longrightarrow$	$R-\ddot{N}=\overset{+}{N}=\ddot{N}:^-$	Azide
$R-X$ + $^-:C\equiv C-R'$	$\longrightarrow$	$R-C\equiv C-R'$	Alkyne
$R-X$ + $^-:C\equiv N:$	$\longrightarrow$	$R-C\equiv N:$	Nitrile
$R-X$ + $^-:\ddot{O}-\overset{\displaystyle \ddot{O}}{\overset{\|}{C}}-R'$	$\longrightarrow$	$R-\ddot{O}-\overset{\displaystyle \ddot{O}}{\overset{\|}{C}}-R'$	Ester
$R-X$ + $:\ddot{P}Ph_3$	$\longrightarrow$	$[R-\ddot{P}Ph_3]^+ \ ^-X$	Phosphonium salt

17.5.2 The First-Order (Unimolecular) Nucleophilic Substitution (S_N1) Reaction

A nucleophilic substitution reaction on a sp^3 Carbon in which only one species is involved in the transition state of the rate-determining step is known as nucleophilic substitution reaction unimolecular and is designated as S_N1. The general reaction can be written as:

$$R-L \ \rightleftharpoons \ R^{\oplus} + \overset{\ominus}{L}$$

$$:Nu^{\oplus} + R^{\oplus} \longrightarrow Nu-R$$

Mechanism: As seen above, the reaction occurs in two steps:

Step I: At this step slow ionization of the substrate occurs; a carbenium ion and the leaving group (in case of alkyl halides, the halide ion) get separated.

$$R-X \ \underset{}{\overset{Slow}{\rightleftharpoons}} \ R^{\oplus} + X^{\ominus}$$

Step II: The carbenium ion so formed invites the incoming nucleophile and subsequently a bond between them forms rapidly.

$$R^{\oplus} + :Nu^{\ominus} \xrightarrow{\text{Fast}} Nu\text{-}R$$

Step I being the slowest, is also the rate determining step. The overall reaction may be represented as:

$$R\text{—}X \underset{\text{Slow}}{\rightleftharpoons} \left[\overset{\delta+}{R}\text{----}\overset{\delta-}{X}\right] \underset{\text{Slow}}{\rightleftharpoons} R^{\oplus} + :X^{\ominus} \xrightarrow{\text{Fast}} R\text{-}Nu + :X^{\ominus}$$

$$\text{T.S.}$$

Kinetics of S$_N$1 reaction: From the energy profile diagram given below it is clear that the first step involving formation of the carbenium ion (carbocation) is endothermic while the second step involving attack of the nucleophile is exothermic.

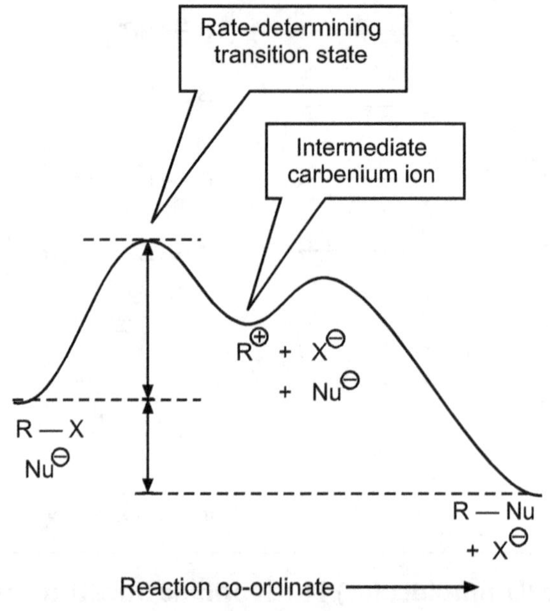

Fig. 17.2

Therefore, step I being the slowest step in this reaction, it is said to be the rate determining step in this reaction.

$$\text{Rate} \propto [R\text{—}X]$$

$$\text{Rate} = k_1[R\text{—}X]$$

Since the rate determining step of the reaction is dependent only on the concentration of the substrate, the reaction is unimolecular in nature that is, it follows first order kinetics.

Stereochemistry of S$_N$1 reaction:

In S$_N$1 reaction, the species being attacked by the nucleophile is the carbenium ion having sp^2 hybridized state. Since the carbenium ion is planar, the nucleophile can attack from either of the two sides that is, front or back. If the substrate is achiral, the product formed from the two types of attack is the same. However, if the alkyl halide is chiral (optically active), then the products obtained from the front and the back attack would give two compounds that are enantiomers (mirror images) of each other.

Back-side attack — Front-side attack — Retention of configuration — Inversion of configuration

Thus, an optically active compound after undergoing S_N1 reaction should theoretically yield a racemized product since the chances of front-side and back-side attack on the carbocation are equal. However, 100% racemization is rarely achieved. Most of the reactions display varying degrees of inversion e.g. (R)1-phenyl ethyl chloride on hydrolysis with aqueous NaOH gives 75% (S) 1-phenylethanol (inversion) and 25% (R) 1-phenylethanol.

(R)-1-Phenyl ethylchloride — Carbenium ion

(S)-1-Phenylethanol inversion (75%)   (R)-1-Phenylethanol retention (25%)

It is found that most of the S_N1 reactions are accompanied with higher proportion of inversion than retention. Higher proportion of inversion indicates that even though the carbocation is planar in nature, the back-side attack is predominant over the front-side attack. Following factors affect the stereochemistry of S_N1 reaction:

1. Stability of carbocation: If the carbocation is stable enough, there will be an equal chance of attack from both sides and will result in racemizaion. However, if the carbocation is unstable, the back-side attack will be preferred as on the front side the leaving group will still be lying near even after dissociation. The negatively charged leaving group will therefore repel the negatively charged nucleophile and thus prevent the back-side attack. The back attack will thus be favoured, leading to higher percentage of inverted product. Thus, it can be said that *as the stability of carbocation increases, proportion of racemization also increases and as the stability of carbocation decreases, percentage of inversion increases.*

2. **Solvation of ions:** The solvation in a S_N1 reaction can be shown as follows:

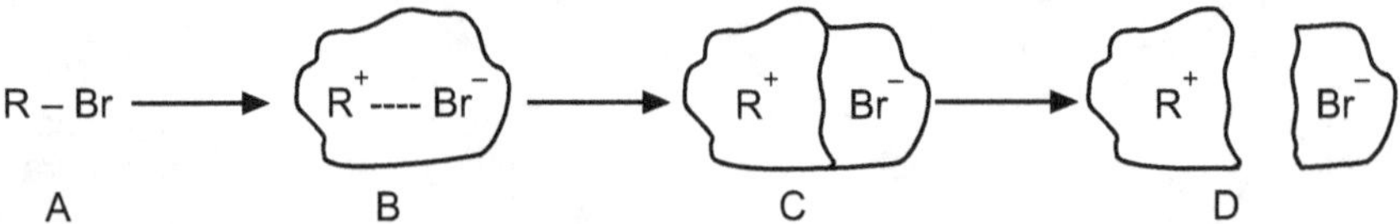

At the time of dissociation, the solvent molecules surround the dissociating molecule (B). Dissociation leads to formation of ion pairs that are separated by the solvent (C). Finally complete solvation of ions is achieved (D). Thus, following are the possibilities of the nucleophilic attack:

i)   If the nucleophilic attack takes place at the stage (B), the front attack will be blocked by the leaving group, while the back attack will be favoured. This back-side attack will thus lead to inversion.

ii)   At stage (C) also, the back-side attack is favoured as the leaving group is still nearby.

iii)   At stage (D) the R^+ can be attacked from front as well as the back as the two ions are nicely separated by the solvent. Attack of nucleophile at this stage will result in complete racemization.

As the stability of carbocation R^+ increases, so will be the proportion of stage (D) of solvation, leading to racemization. When the stability of the carbocation is low, the proportion of stage (B) will be more, thus, inversion will predominate. Reactions where the solvent itself is a nucleophile, then even in stage C and D there will be equal chances of attack by the solvent on both sides of the carbocation. However, in stage D, the back-side attack will certainly be favoured over the front-side attack and hence inversion will predominate.

3. **Leaving group:** Incomplete racemization is also observed often when substrates with a relatively poor leaving group (e.g. chloride) are used. A back-side attack of the nucleophile on the substrate can then take place before the C–X bond is completely cleaved. That is, the S_N1 reaction may display a partial S_N2 characteristic. In contrast to the chloride anion, the bromide anion is a very good leaving group. Therefore, complete racemization is more easily obtainable when bromine is exchanged in a nucleophilic substitution. This can be experimentally illustrated in the formation of R- and S-1-phenylethanol. Incomplete racemization is obtained in the hydrolysis of 1-chloroethylbenzene. In the hydrolysis of 1-bromoethylbenzene, however, complete racemization is obtained.

S	S		R
if X = Br:	50%		50%
if X = Cl:	41%		59%

17.5.3 Factors Affecting S_N1 and S_N2 Reactions

The following factors have been found to affect the rate of nucleophilic substitution reactions:

1. **Nature of substrate**: The structure of the substrate has a profound effect on the type of substitution reaction (S_N1 or S_N2) it will undergo. Two factors are important for the substrate. They are the steric hindrance and the nature of the leaving group.

    (i) Steric hindrance: Different alkyl halides undergo reactions at vastly different rates. The structure of the substrate is the most important factor in its reactivity toward displacement.

    S_N2 **reaction** goes rapidly with methyl halides and with most primary halides but decreases with secondary halides. Tertiary halides fail to react at all by the mechanism. The table given below shows the effect of alkyl substitution on the rate of S_N2 displacements.

Table 17.1

Class of Halide	Example	Relative Rate
Methyl	$CH_3 - Br$	> 1000
Primary (1°)	$CH_3CH_2 - Br$	50
Secondary (2°)	$(CH_3)_2CH - Br$	1
Tertiary (3°)	$(CH_3)_3C - Br$	<0.001
n-butyl (1°)	$CH_3CH_2CH_2CH_2 - Br$	20
Isobutyl (1°)	$(CH_3)_2CHCH_2 - Br$	2
Neopentyl (1°)	$(CH_3)_3CCH_2 - Br$	0.0005

This is because in the T.S of S_N2 reaction, the back side of the electrophilic carbon atom is crowded by the presence of bulky groups. Tertiary halides are more hindered than secondary halides, which are more hindered than primary. This can be represented as below:

Ethyl bromide   Isopropyl bromide   *ter*-Butyl bromide

S_N2 attack on a simple primary alkyl halide is unhindered. Attack on a secondary halide is hindered, and attack on a tertiary halide is impossible.

The above structures show the reaction of hydroxide ion with ethyl bromide (1°), isopropyl bromide (2°), and *tert*-butyl bromide (3°). The nucleophile can easily approach the electrophilic carbon atom of ethyl bromide. In isopropyl bromide, the approach is hindered, but still possible. In contrast, approach to the tertiary carbon of tert-butyl bromide is impossible because of the steric hindrance of the three methyl groups. Therefore the reactivity of alkyl halides towards S_N2 substitution reaction can be written as:

$$1° > 2° > 3°$$

However, in case of S_N1 reaction, the crowding at electrophilic carbon increases the rate of reaction. The rate-limiting step of the S_N1 reaction is ionization to form a carbocation, consequently, rates of reactions depend strongly on carbocation stability. The alkyl groups stabilize carbocations by donating electrons through sigma bonds (the inductive effect) and through overlap of filled orbitals with the empty *p*-orbital of the carbocation (hyperconjugation). Highly substituted carbocations are therefore more stable. Reactivity toward S_N1 substitution mechanism follows the stability of carbocations:

$$3° > 2° > 1°$$

Resonance stabilization of the carbocation can also promote the S_N1 reaction. For example, allyl bromide is a primary halide, but it undergoes the S_N1 reaction about as fast as a secondary halide. The carbocation formed by ionization is resonance stabilized, with the positive charge spread equally over two carbon atoms.

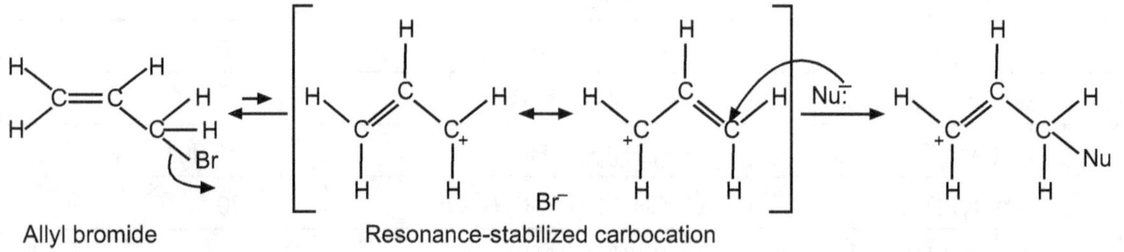

Allyl bromide   Resonance-stabilized carbocation

(ii) Nature of leaving group: The leaving group is breaking its bond to carbon in the rate-limiting ionization step of both, the S_N1 and the S_N2 mechanism. A highly polarizable leaving group helps stabilize the rate-limiting transition state through partial bonding as it leaves. The leaving group should be a weak base, very stable after it leaves with the pair of electrons that bonded it to carbon. Fig. 17.3 shows the transition state of the ionization step of the S_N1 reaction. The leaving group is taking on a negative charge while it stabilizes the new carbocation through partial bonding. A good leaving group is just as necessary in the S_N1 reaction as it is in the S_N2. As a result, the nature of the leaving group has little effect on which mechanism, S_N1 or S_N2 is predominant.

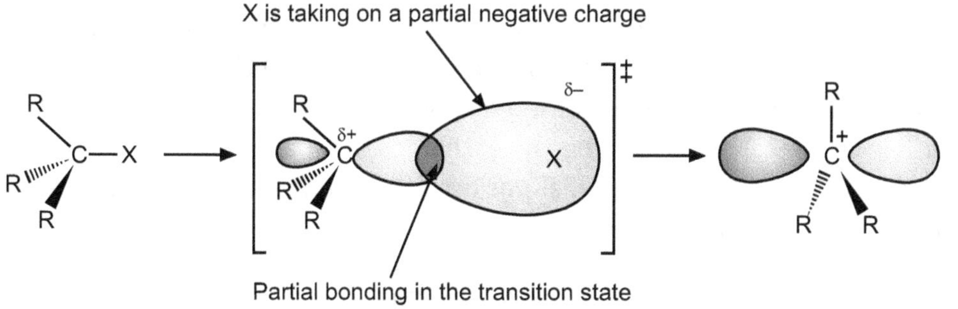

Fig. 17.3

In the transition state of the S_N1 ionization, the leaving group is taking on a negative charge. The C–X bond is breaking, and a polarizable leaving group can still maintain substantial overlap.

A group that leaves easily (energy required to break the bond between carbon and the leaving group is small) is termed as a good leaving group. Presence of a good leaving group increases the rate of reaction. A good leaving group has following qualities:

i)   The bond between the carbon and the leaving group is weak

ii) The leaving group is stable that is, after leaving the molecule it does not recombine with carbon.

Good leaving groups should be weak bases; therefore, they are the conjugate bases of strong acids. The hydrohalic acids HCl, HBr, and HI are strong acids, and their conjugate bases (Cl^-, Br^- and I^-) are all weak bases. Other weak bases, such as sulfate ions (SO_4^{2-}), sulfonate ions (SO_3^{-}), and phosphate ions (HPO_4^{2-}), can also serve as good leaving groups. Hydroxide ion (OH^-), alkoxide ions (OCH_3^-), and other strong bases are poor leaving groups for reactions. For example, the –OH group of an alcohol is a poor leaving group because it would have to leave as hydroxide ion (OH^-), a strong base.

2. Nature of the nucleophile: The basic difference between the S_N1 and S_N2 reactions is that in S_N1 the nucleophile is involved in the second step of the mechanism (fast step i.e. after the rate determining step) while in the S_N2 mechanism it is involved in the rate determining step. Therefore, changing the nature of the nucleophile changes the rate of reaction in S_N2 but not the S_N1 mechanism. There are three factors about the nucleophile that need to be considered: (i) strength of the nucleophile, (ii) concentration of the nucleophile and (iii) structure of nucleophiles. Moreover, the strength of the nucleophile is also dependent on the solvent in which the reaction is being carried out. Let us discuss these factors one by one.

(i) Strength of the nucleophile: Stronger the nucleophile, faster it will react with the alkyl halide. Generally, negatively charged species are much better nucleophiles than analogous neutral species. Consider methanol (CH_3OH) and methoxide (CH_3O^-) reacting with CH_3I. It is found that methoxide reacts about a million times faster in S_N2 reactions than methanol. This is because methoxide ion has nonbonding electrons that are readily available for bonding. In the transition state, the negative charge is shared by the oxygen of methoxide ion and by the halide leaving group therefore decreasing the energy of activation, E_a. However, since methanol has no negative charge; the transition state has a partial negative charge on the halide but a partial positive charge on the methanol oxygen atom. This transition state thus requires higher E_a.

Conjugate base
(stronger nucleophile)   Lower E_a

Conjugate acid
(weaker nucleophile)   Higher E_a

Following generalizations can be made for the strength of nucleophiles:

1. A species with a negative charge is a stronger nucleophile than a similar neutral species. In particular, a base is a stronger nucleophile than its conjugate acid.

    $$^-OH \; > \; H_2O \qquad ^-SH \; > \; H_2S \qquad ^-NH_2 \; > \; NH_3$$

2. Nucleophilicity decreases from left to right in the periodic table, following the increase in electronegativity from left to right. The more electronegative elements have more tightly held nonbonding electrons and are less reactive towards forming new bonds.

    $$^-NH_2 \; > \; ^-OH \; > \; ^-F \qquad NH_3 \; > \; H_2O \qquad (CH_3CH_2)_3P \; > \; (CH_3CH_2)_2S$$

3. Nucleophilicity increases down the periodic table, following the increase in size and polarizability, and the decrease in electronegativity.

    $$^-I \; > \; ^-Br \; > \; ^-Cl \; > \; ^-F \qquad ^-SeH \; > \; ^-SH \; > \; ^-OH \qquad (CH_3CH_2)_3P \; > \; (CH_3CH_2)_3N$$

As we go down a column in the periodic table, the atoms become larger, with more electrons at a greater distance from the nucleus. The electrons are more loosely held, and the atom is more polarizable: Its electrons can move more freely towards a positive charge, resulting in stronger bonding in the transition state. The increased mobility of its electrons enhances the atom's ability to begin to form a bond at a relatively long distance.

(ii) Concentration of the nucleophile: As the S_N2 reaction is a second order reaction, the increase in concentration of the nucleophile increases the rate of reaction. We have seen above that:

$$\text{Rate} \propto [C_2H_5Br][OH^-]$$

However, the change in concentration has no effect on the rate of S_N1 reaction. Thus, other things being equal, a high concentration of nucleophile favours S_N2 reaction, and a low concentration favours S_N1 reaction.

(iii)　Structure of the nucleophile: To replace the leaving group (halide), the nucleophile, must come closer to the electron deficient carbon atom. If bulky groups are present on the nucleophile, the attack on the carbon atom will be hindered and thus slow down the reaction rate. For example, while the *tert*-butoxide ion is a stronger base (for abstracting protons) than ethoxide ion, it is weaker nucleophile as it has three methyl groups that hinder any close approach to a more crowded carbon atom. Therefore, ethoxide ion is a stronger nucleophile than tert-butoxide ion.

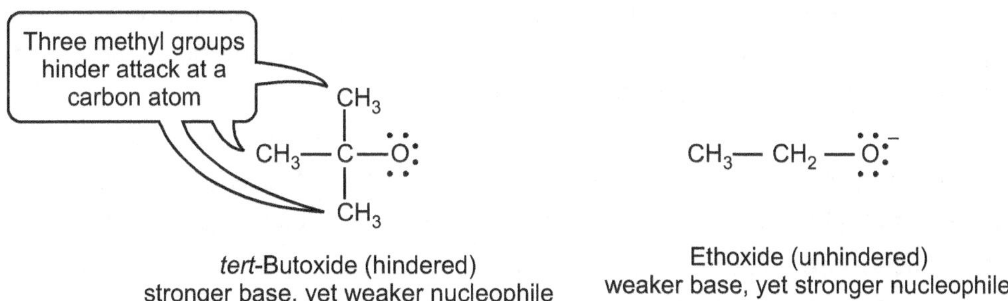

tert-Butoxide (hindered)
stronger base, yet weaker nucleophile

Ethoxide (unhindered)
weaker base, yet stronger nucleophile

(iv) Effect of solvent: Choice of solvent for a reaction can also affect the nucleophilicity of nucleophiles. A protic solvent is one that has acidic protons, usually in the form of O–H or N–H groups. These groups form hydrogen bonds with negatively charged nucleophiles. Protic solvents, especially alcohols, are convenient solvents for nucleophilic substitutions because the reagents (alkyl halides, nucleophiles, etc.) tend to be quite soluble in these. Small anions are solvated more strongly than large anions in a protic solvent because the solvent approaches a small anion more closely and forms stronger hydrogen bonds. When an anion reacts as a nucleophile, energy is required to remove some of the solvent molecules, breaking some of the hydrogen bonds that stabilize the solvated anion. More energy is required to remove solvent from a small, strongly solvated ion such as fluoride than from a large, diffuse, less strongly solvated ion like iodide. The enhanced solvation of smaller anions in protic solvents, requiring more energy to get rid of their solvent molecules, reduces their nucleophilicity. The poor nucleophilicity will thus result in poor rates of S_N2 reactions.

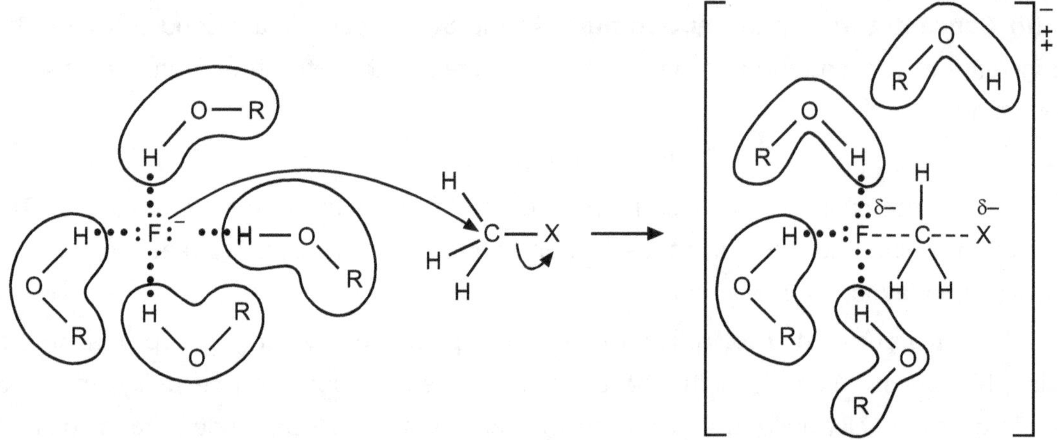

Solvent partially removed
off in the transition state

In contrast with protic solvents, aprotic solvents like dimethyl sulfoxide (DMSO) and dimethyl formamide (DMF) enhance the nucleophilicity of anions. An anion is more reactive in an aprotic solvent because it is not so strongly solvated. There are no hydrogen bonds to be broken when the nucleophile approaches an electrophilic carbon atom. However, the relatively weak solvating ability of aprotic solvents is also a disadvantage as most polar, ionic reagents are insoluble in simple aprotic solvents such as alkanes.

On the other hand, polar aprotic solvents have strong dipole moments to enhance solubility, yet they have no –NH or –OH groups to form hydrogen bonds with anions. Acetonitrile, dimethylformamide, and acetone are examples of useful polar aprotic solvents.

3. Solvent effect: The S_N1 reaction goes much faster in polar solvents. The rate limiting step of S_N1 reaction forms two ions, and ionization is taking place in the transition state. The dipole moment of polar solvents interact with the charge of the ion. Protic solvents such as alcohols and water are even more effective solvents because anions form hydrogen bonds with the –OH hydrogen atom, and cations complex with the nonbonding electrons of the –OH oxygen atom. Ionization of an alkyl halide requires formation and separation of positive and negative charges, therefore reactions require highly polar solvents that strongly solvate ions.

Ionization

Solvated ions

The effect of solvent on the rate of S_N2 reaction has already been discussed in the previous section (strength of nucleophile).

17.6 REARRANGEMENTS IN S$_N$1 REACTIONS

Carbocations (carbenium ions), the reaction intermediates in S$_N$1 reactions, frequently undergo structural changes, called rearrangements, to form more stable ions. A rearrangement may occur after a carbocation has formed or it may occur as the leaving group is leaving. Since S$_N$2 reactions do not involve formation of carbocations, no rearrangements are seen in these reactions. An example of a reaction with rearrangement is the reaction of 2-bromo-3-methylbutane in boiling ethanol. The product is a mixture of 2-ethoxy-3-methylbutane (not rearranged) and 2-ethoxy-2-methylbutane (rearranged).

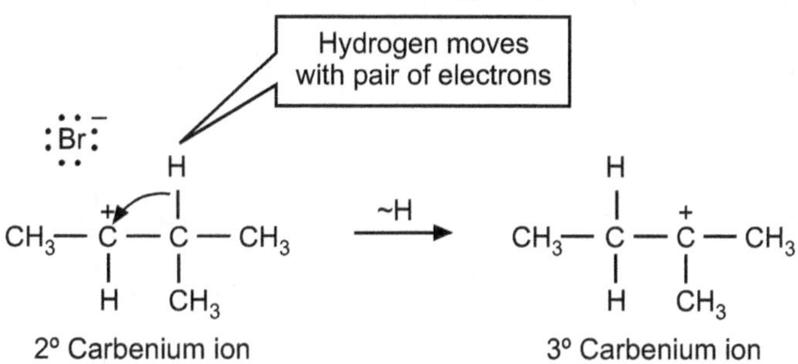

These rearrangements may involve any one of the two phenomena: the hydride shift (shifting of hydrogen with its bonding electrons) or a methyl shift. In either case, the driving force behind the rearrangement is the formation of a more stable carbocation. Let us discuss them one by one.

1. Hydride shift: In this mechanism, the hydrogen shifts with its bonding electrons (–H⁻). Let us take the example of 2-bromo-3-methylbutane to illustrate the mechanism. Following steps are involved:

Step 1: Formation of a carbenium ion following ionization.

Step 2: Hydride shift leading to a more stable carbenium ion.

Step 3: The solvent (weak nucleophile) attacks the stable carbocation.

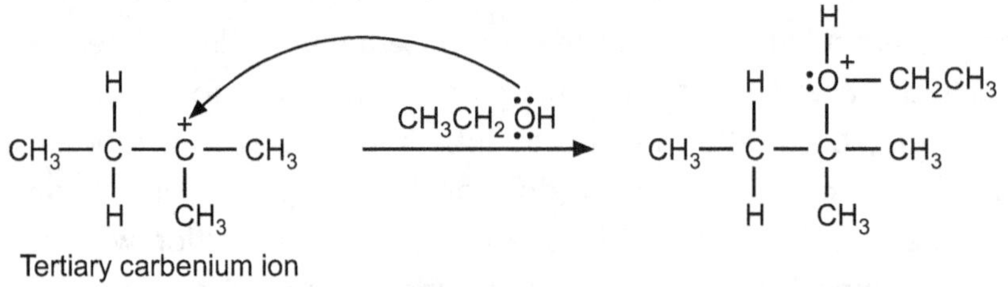

Tertiary carbenium ion

Step 4: Loss of a proton (deprotonation) to give the rearranged product.

Rearranged product

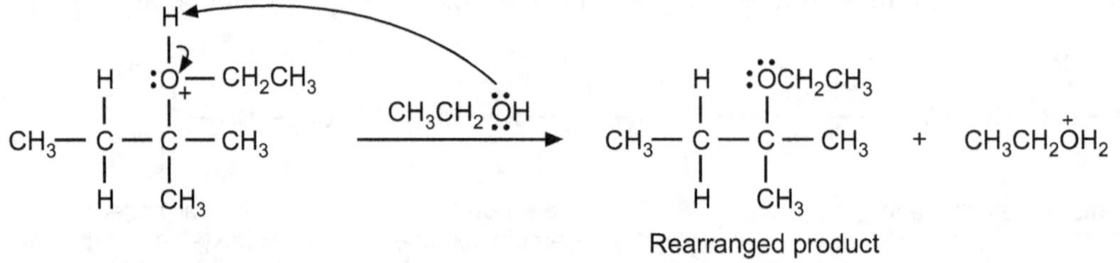

2. Methyl shift: When neopentyl bromide is boiled in ethanol, it gives only a rearranged substitution product. This product results from a methyl shift, that is, the migration of a methyl group together with its pair of electrons. Without rearrangement, ionization of neopentyl bromide would give a very unstable primary carbocation. Methyl shift occurs only while the bromide is leaving therefore forming only the rearranged product.

Neopentyl bromide　　　　　　1° Carbenium ion

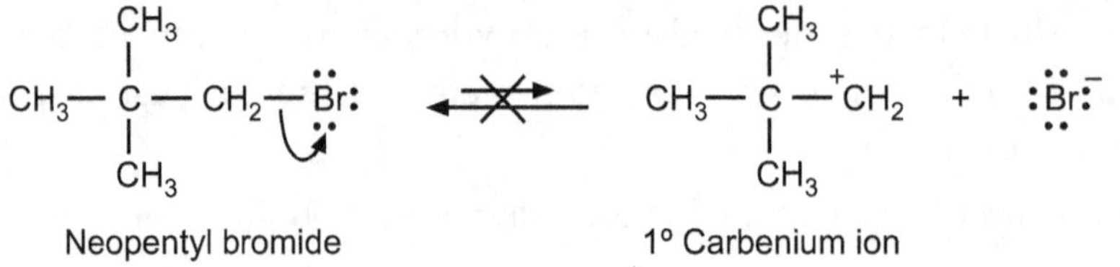

Let us see the mechanism involved:

Step 1: Ionization occurs with a methyl shift.

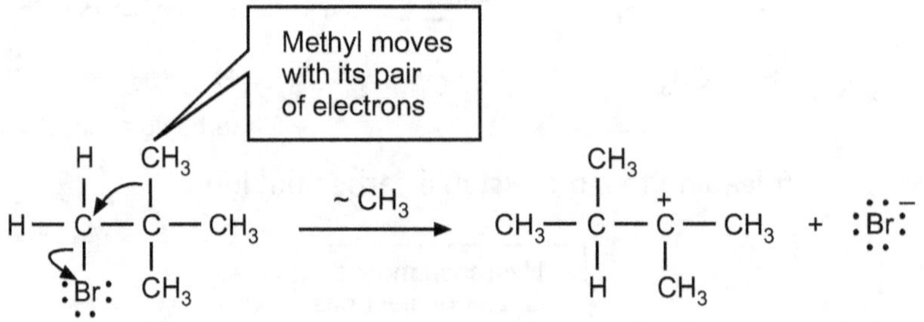

Methyl moves with its pair of electrons

Step 2: Attack of the solvent.

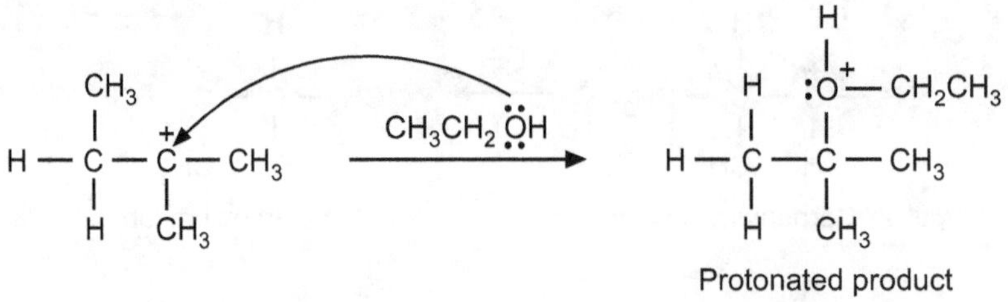

Protonated product

Step 3: Loss of proton to give a stable rearranged product.

Rearranged product

In the above case, only the rearranged product is formed as rearrangement is required for ionization.

Let us now summarize the facts we have learnt about the two types of nucleophilic reactions shown by the alkyl halides in the form of a table.

S_N1 reactions	S_N2 reactions
Follow unimolecular kinetics rate = k r [R → X]	Follow bimolecular kinetics. rate = k r [R → X][Nu⁻]
Strength of nucleophile is not important (weak nucleophile is normally used)	Strong nucleophile is required
The substrate is a tertiary or a secondary alkyl halide (3° > 2°). A primary substrate or CH_3X generally do not react.	Tertiary substrates are not suitable. $CH_3X > 1° > 2°$
Good ionizing solvent required.	May go faster in a less polar solvent.
Mixture of retention and inversion; racemization.	Complete inversion.
Rearrangements are common.	Rearrangements are impossible.

17.6 ELIMINATION REACTIONS

Halide of the alkyl halide when leaves the molecules taking with itself another atom, the reaction is called elimination reaction.

Since like nucleophilic substitution reaction, this reaction is also catalysed by a base, elimination may compete the substitution reaction. Elimination reaction is discussed in detail in the chapter on Alkenes. However, following is the comparison between the two reactions.

Nucleophilic substitution versus Elimination :

Factor	Substitution	Elimination
1. Type of alkyl halide		
Primary	Favoured	
Secondary	Possible	Possible
Tertiary		Mainly elimination
2. Solvent		
Water	Favoured	
Ethanol		Favoured
3. Temperature		
High		Favoured
4. Concentration of base		
High concentration		Favoured

QUESTIONS

Q.1 What is S_N1 and S_N2 reaction? Explain mechanism and factors affecting S_N1 reactions. **(May-2015)**

Q.2 Discuss reaction mechanism and factors affecting S_N1 and S_N2. **(Dec-2015)**

Q.3 Explain the substitution nucleophilic unimolecular reaction (S_N1) with mechanism and stereochemistry giving suitable examples. **(May-2014)**

Q.4 What are nucleophilic substitution reactions? Explain mechanism and stereochemistry of S_N1 reactions **(Dec-2014)**

Q.5 What is S_N1 and S_N2 reaction mechanism? Discuss factors affecting on S_N1 and S_N2 reaction mechanism. **(Oct/Nov-2011)**

Q.6 Explain substitution nucleophilic unimolecular reaction mechanism with stereochemistry and add note on factors affecting on it. **(April/May-2010)**

Q.7 Explain S_N2 reaction mechanism with its stereochemistry and add a note on factors affecting on it. **(April/May-2009)**

Q.8 Compare and contrast between substitution and elimination. **(May-2015, Dec-2014)**

Q.9 Write any two reactions of ethers and alcohols each. **(Dec-2015)**

Q.10 Write a note on substitution nucleophilic unimolecular reaction. **(Dec-2015, 2014)**

Q.11 Write short on elimination versus substitution. **(May-2014)**

Write about substitution nucleophilic reaction. **(Dec-2014)**

Q.12 Write any two methods of preparation of alkyl halides. **(Dec-2014, May-2015)**

Q.13 Give any two chemical reactions of alkyl halides. **(May-2014)**

❖ ❖ ❖

Chapter 18

CARBOXYLIC ACIDS

18.1 INTRODUCTION

Molecules having a carboxylic group (–COOH) are called carboxylic acids. Carboxylic acid is one of the most common class of compounds in organic chemistry as well as biochemistry. These compounds are weakly acidic in nature, though stronger than phenols. Carboxylic acids can react with organic bases (amines) as well as inorganic bases (Na_2CO_3, NaOH, etc.) to form corresponding salts. Being polar in nature, the carboxyl group can form hydrogen bond with water molecules. Thus, lower carboxylic acids are easily soluble in water but the solubility decreases as the number of carbon atoms increases. Thus, five carbon carboxylic acid is partly soluble in water while benzoic acid or hexanoic acid or higher acids are insoluble in water. However, the salts of these acids made by reacting them with bases, are water soluble. Besides being abundant in nature, carboxylic group or its derivatives (carboxamido, ester, etc.) are also frequently encountered in pharmaceuticals. Carboxylic acids are a very popular class of non-steroidal analgesic and anti-inflammatory (NSAID) compounds. Some examples are given below:

Formic acid
from ants

Acetic acid
or vinegar

Acetyl salicylic acid
or aspirin

Maleic acid
(various fruits)

Pyruvic acid
(a metabolic intermediate)

Niacin
(a vitamin)

Citric acid
(from citrus fruits)

18.2 NOMENCLATURE

Substituted carboxylic acids are named either by the IUPAC system or by common names which are mostly derived from the source of the acids as exemplified in the table given below:

Table 18.1

Formula	Common Name	Source	IUPAC Name
HCO_2H	formic acid	ants (*L. formica*)	methanoic acid
CH_3CO_2H	acetic acid	vinegar (*L. acetum*)	ethanoic acid
$CH_3CH_2CO_2H$	propionic acid	milk (Gk. *protus prion*)	propanoic acid
$CH_3(CH_2)_2CO_2H$	butyric acid	butter (*L. butyrum*)	butanoic acid
$CH_3(CH_2)_3CO_2H$	valeric acid	valerian root	pentanoic acid
$CH_3(CH_2)_4CO_2H$	caproic acid	goats (*L. caper*)	hexanoic acid
$CH_3(CH_2)_5CO_2H$	enanthic acid	vines (Gk. *oenanthe*)	heptanoic acid
$CH_3(CH_2)_6CO_2H$	caprylic acid	goats (*L. caper*)	octanoic acid
$CH_3(CH_2)_7CO_2H$	pelargonic acid	pelargonium (a herb)	nonanoic acid
$CH_3(CH_2)_8CO_2H$	capric acid	goats (*L. caper*)	decanoic acid

In the IUPAC system of nomenclature, a characteristic suffix is added to these classes. The ending **–e** is removed from the name of the parent chain and is replaced by **-anoic acid**. Since a carboxylic acid group always lies at the end of a carbon chain, it is always given the first position in numbering and it is not necessary to include the number in the name.

In common names, the carbon atoms near the carboxyl group are often designated by Greek letters. The atom adjacent to the carbonyl function is alpha, the next is beta and so on.

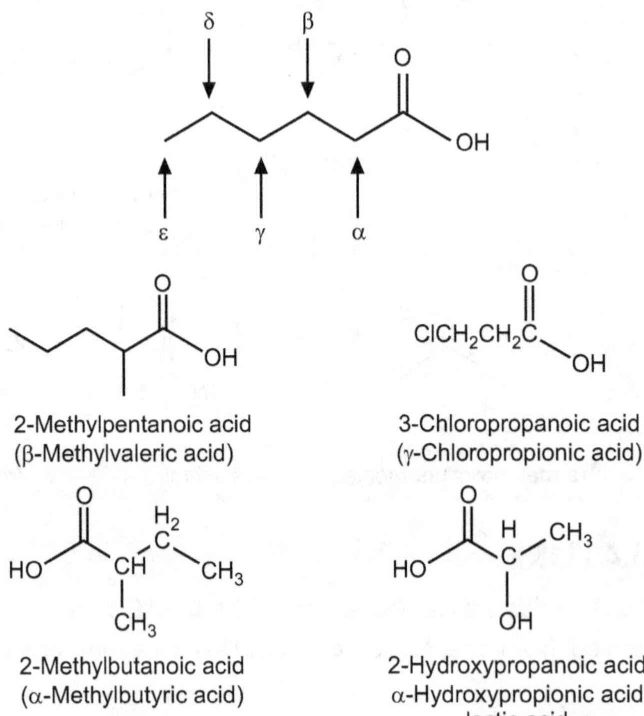

2-Methylpentanoic acid
(β-Methylvaleric acid)

3-Chloropropanoic acid
(γ-Chloropropionic acid)

2-Methylbutanoic acid
(α-Methylbutyric acid)

2-Hydroxypropanoic acid
α-Hydroxypropionic acid
lactic acid

Trans-3-pentenoic acid   (E)-2-Methyl-2-butenoic acid

Aromatic acids are usually named as derivatives of the parent acid, benzoic acid, C_6H_5COOH. The methyl benzoic acids are called *toluic acids*.

3-Nitrobenzoic acid
m-Nitrobenzoic acid

3-Methylbenzoic acid
m-Toluic acid

18.3 METHODS OF PREPARATION OF CARBOXYLIC ACIDS

The carboxylic acids can be prepared using the following methods. Oxidation of a variety of compounds yields carboxylic acids. These methods are described below:

1. **Oxidation of primary alcohols and aldehydes:**

Primary alcohols and aldehydes can be oxidised with potassium permanganate to give carboxylic acids.

$$CH_3 - CH_2 - OH \xrightarrow[\substack{^-OH \\ heat \\ 2.\ H_2O}]{1.\ KMnO_4} CH_3 - \overset{\overset{O}{\|}}{C} - OH$$

Ethanol   Ethanoic acid

$$CH_3 - \overset{\overset{OH}{|}}{CH_2} \xrightarrow[\substack{H^+ \\ warm \\ 2.\ H_2O}]{1.\ KMnO_4} CH_3 - \overset{\overset{O}{\|}}{C} - OH$$

Ethanol   Ethanoic acid

Other strong oxidizing agents like potassium dichromate, and chromium trioxide can easily oxidize the alcohols to aldehydes and then the aldehydes to carboxylic acids. However, mild oxidizing reagents like manganese dioxide (MnO_2) and Tollen's reagent [$Ag(NH_3)_2$ $^+OH^-$] are only able to oxidize alcohols to aldehydes but are unable to oxidize the aldehydes to carboxylic acids.

2. **Oxidation of alkyl benzenes:**

Alkyl groups containing **benzylic hydrogens** (hydrogen(s) on a carbon α to a benzene ring) can be oxidized using strong oxidizing agents to give aromatic acids.

Propylbenzene $\xrightarrow[\substack{OH^- \\ heat \\ 2.\ H_2O}]{1.\ KMnO_4}$ Benzoic acid

Isopropylbenzene $\xrightarrow[\substack{OH^- \\ heat \\ 2.\ H_2O}]{1.\ KMnO_4}$ Benzoic acid

t-Butylbenzene $\xrightarrow[\substack{OH^- \\ heat \\ 2.\ H_2O}]{1.\ KMnO_4}$ No reaction

As seen above, no matter how long is the alkyl chain attached to benzene, the product is always benzoic acid. However, presence of at least one α-hydrogen (benzylic) is must for oxidation to take place. Thus, as t-butylbenzene contains no benzylic hydrogen, it cannot be oxidized.

3. Hydrolysis of nitriles:

Nitriles which are organic molecules containing a cyano group, can be hydrolysed in acidic or basic media to give carboxylic acids.

$$CH_3 - CH_2 - C \equiv N \xrightarrow[heat]{H_3O^+} CH_3 - CH_2 - \overset{\displaystyle O}{\underset{\displaystyle }{C}} - OH$$

Propanenitrile   Propanoic acid

Propylbenzene $\xrightarrow[\substack{H_2O \\ heat \\ 2.\ H_3O}]{1.\ OH^-}$ Benzoic acid

4. Carbonation of Grignard reagents:

Grignard reagents react with carbon dioxide to yield acid salts, which upon acidification, produce carboxylic acids.

$$\begin{array}{l} R-X \\ Ar-X \end{array} \xrightarrow{Mg} RMgX \xrightarrow{CO_2} R-COOMgX \xrightarrow{H^+} \begin{array}{l} R-COOH \\ Ar-COOH \end{array}$$

Phenyl magnesium bromide → Benzoic acid

2-Chloro-2-methyl-butane
t-pentylchoride

2,2-Dimethylbutanoic acid
ethyldimethylacetic acid

As seen in above examples, there is an increase in number of carbon atoms in the final compound by one.

5. Synthesis of substituted acetic acids via acetoacetic ester:

Acetoacetic ester is an ester formed by the self–condensation of ethyl acetate via a Claisen condensation. It has a methylene unit located between the two carbonyl functional groups. The hydrogens of this methylene unit are acidic due to the electron withdrawing effects of the carbonyl groups. Either or both of these hydrogens can be removed by reaction with strong bases to give carbanions which can act as nucleophiles and can undergo placement of alkyl group.

$$CH_3 - \overset{O}{\overset{\|}{C}} - CH_2 - \overset{O}{\overset{\|}{C}} - OCH_2CH_3 + Na^+\bar{O}C_2H_5 \longrightarrow CH_3 - \overset{O}{\overset{\|}{C}} - \underset{Na^+}{\overset{\bar{}}{C}H} - \overset{O}{\overset{\|}{C}} - OCH_2CH_3 + C_2H_5OH$$

Acetoacetic ester   Carbanion

Step 1:

$$CH_3 - \overset{O}{\overset{\|}{C}} - \underset{Na^+}{\overset{..}{C}H} - \overset{O}{\overset{\|}{C}} - OCH_2CH_3 + CH_3Cl \longrightarrow CH_3 - \overset{O}{\overset{\|}{C}} - \underset{CH_3}{\overset{|}{C}H} - \overset{O}{\overset{\|}{C}} - OCH_2CH_3 + Na^+Cl^-$$

Step 2:

The resulting product on hydrolysis with sodium hydroxide liberates the sodium salt of the substituted acid. Acidification of the salt solution gives the free acid.

$$CH_3 - \overset{O}{\overset{\|}{C}} - \underset{CH_3}{\overset{|}{C}H} - \overset{O}{\overset{\|}{C}} - OCH_2CH_3 + NaOH \xrightarrow[\text{Heat}]{H_2O} CH_3 - \overset{O}{\overset{\|}{C}} - \bar{O}Na^+ + CH_3CH_2\overset{O}{\overset{\|}{C}} - \bar{O}Na^+ + CH_3CH_2OH$$

Step 3:

$$CH_3CH_2\overset{O}{\overset{\|}{C}}-\bar{O}Na^+ + CH_3\overset{O}{\overset{\|}{C}}-\bar{O}Na^+ \xrightarrow[H_2O]{HCl} CH_3CH_2\overset{O}{\overset{\|}{C}}-OH + CH_3\overset{O}{\overset{\|}{C}}-OH + NaCl$$

Propionic acid

(monosubstituted acid)

Step 4:

The second hydrogen on the methylene unit of acetoacetic ester can also be replaced by an alkyl group, creating a disubstituted acid. For this, the reaction product in step 2 above is reacted again with a very strong base to create a carbanion which is further alkylated. Other steps follow in the same manner to give a disubstituted acid.

$$CH_3-\overset{O}{\overset{\|}{C}}-\underset{\underset{CH_3}{|}}{CH}-\overset{O}{\overset{\|}{C}}-OCH_2CH_3 + (CH_3)_3CO^-K^+ \longrightarrow CH_3-\overset{O}{\overset{\|}{C}}-\underset{\underset{CH_3}{|}}{\overset{K^+}{\overset{..}{C}}}-\overset{O}{\overset{\|}{C}}-OCH_2CH_3 + (CH_3)_3COH$$

$$CH_3-\overset{O}{\overset{\|}{C}}-\underset{\underset{CH_3}{|}}{\overset{K^+}{\overset{..}{C}}}-\overset{O}{\overset{\|}{C}}-OCH_2CH_3 + CH_3CH_2Cl \longrightarrow CH_3\overset{O}{\overset{\|}{C}}-\underset{\underset{CH_3}{|}}{\overset{CH_2CH_3}{\overset{|}{C}}}-\overset{}{\underset{O}{\overset{\|}{C}}}-OCH_2CH_3 + KCl$$

$$CH_3\overset{O}{\overset{\|}{C}}-\underset{\underset{CH_3}{|}}{\overset{CH_2CH_3}{\overset{|}{C}}}-\underset{O}{\overset{\|}{C}}-OCH_2CH_3 + NaOH \xrightarrow[Heat]{H_2O} CH_3\overset{O}{\overset{\|}{C}}-\bar{O}Na^+ + \underset{\underset{CH_3}{|}}{\overset{CH_2CH_3}{\overset{|}{CH}}}-\overset{O}{\overset{\|}{C}}-\bar{O}Na^+ + CH_3CH_2OH$$

$$H-\underset{\underset{CH_3}{|}}{\overset{CH_2CH_3}{\overset{|}{C}}}-COO\bar{N}a^+ \xrightarrow[HCl]{H_2O} H\underset{\underset{CH_3}{|}}{\overset{CH_2CH_3}{\overset{|}{C}}}-COOH$$

2-Methyl butanoic acid

It is important to use strong solution of sodium hydroxide in the hydrolysis step as dilute solutions tend to give a methyl ketone rather than the acid. This happens because dilute sodium hydroxide has sufficient strength to hydrolyze the ester functional group but insufficient strength to hydrolyze the ketone functional group. Concentrated sodium hydroxide is strong enough to hydrolyze both the ester functional group and the ketone functional group and, therefore, forms the substituted acid rather than the ketone.

A reaction between a disubstituted acetoacetic ester and dilute sodium hydroxide forms the following products:

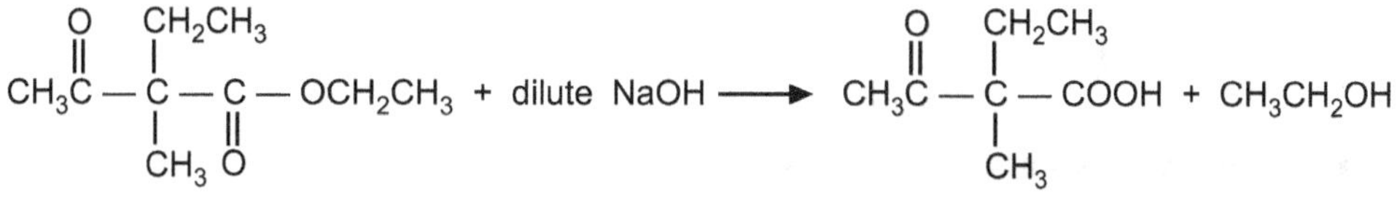

$$CH_3\overset{\overset{O}{\|}}{C} - \overset{\overset{CH_2CH_3}{|}}{\underset{\underset{CH_3}{|}}{C}} - \overset{\overset{O}{\|}}{C} - OCH_2CH_3 + \text{dilute NaOH} \longrightarrow CH_3\overset{\overset{O}{\|}}{C} - \overset{\overset{CH_2CH_3}{|}}{\underset{\underset{CH_3}{|}}{C}} - COOH + CH_3CH_2OH$$

β-ketoacid

Upon heating, the β ketoacid becomes unstable and decarboxylates, leading to the formation of the methyl ketone.

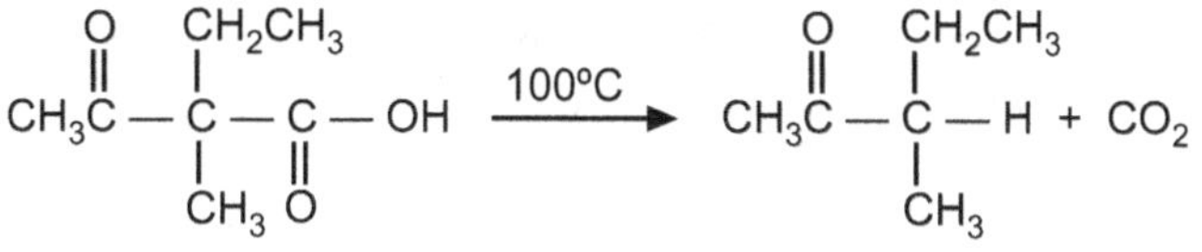

$$CH_3\overset{\overset{O}{\|}}{C} - \overset{\overset{CH_2CH_3}{|}}{\underset{\underset{CH_3}{|}}{C}} - \overset{\overset{O}{\|}}{C} - OH \xrightarrow{100°C} CH_3\overset{\overset{O}{\|}}{C} - \overset{\overset{CH_2CH_3}{|}}{\underset{\underset{CH_3}{|}}{C}} - H + CO_2$$

Ketone

6. From malonic ester:

Malonic ester is an ester formed by reacting an alcohol with malonic acid (propanedicarboxylic acid). Following is the structure of diethyl malonate:

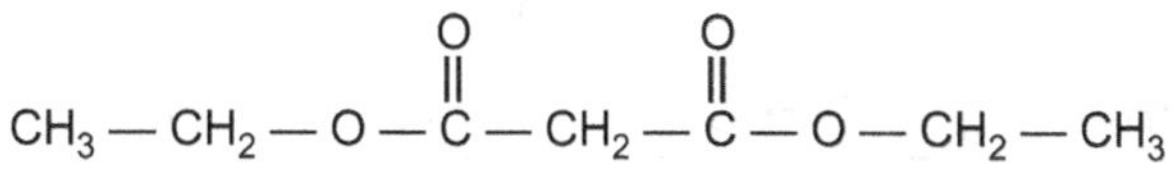

$$CH_3 - CH_2 - O - \overset{\overset{O}{\|}}{C} - CH_2 - \overset{\overset{O}{\|}}{C} - O - CH_2 - CH_3$$

The hydrogen atoms on the methylene unit between the two carboxyl groups are acidic like those in acetoacetic ester. Strong bases can remove these acidic hydrogens. The steps followed in the synthesis of the monosubstituted or disubstituted acids are same as seen above. Thus, a disubstituted malonic ester upon hydrolysis with sodium hydroxide gives:

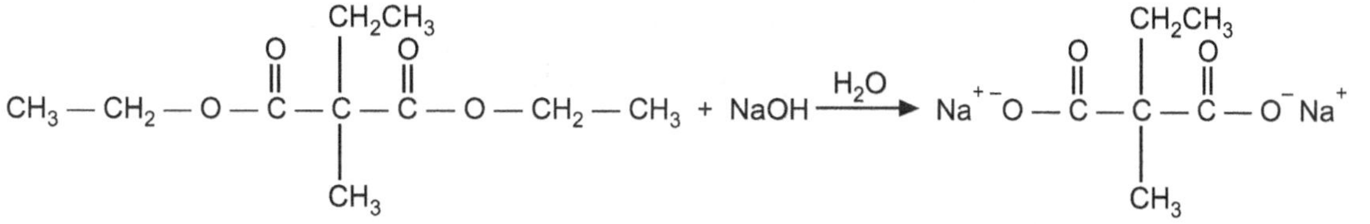

$$CH_3 - CH_2 - O - \overset{\overset{O}{\|}}{C} - \overset{\overset{CH_2CH_3}{|}}{\underset{\underset{CH_3}{|}}{C}} - \overset{\overset{O}{\|}}{C} - O - CH_2 - CH_3 + \text{NaOH} \xrightarrow{H_2O} Na^+{}^-O - \overset{\overset{O}{\|}}{C} - \overset{\overset{CH_2CH_3}{|}}{\underset{\underset{CH_3}{|}}{C}} - \overset{\overset{O}{\|}}{C} - O^- Na^+$$

Addition of aqueous acid converts the salt into its conjugate acid.

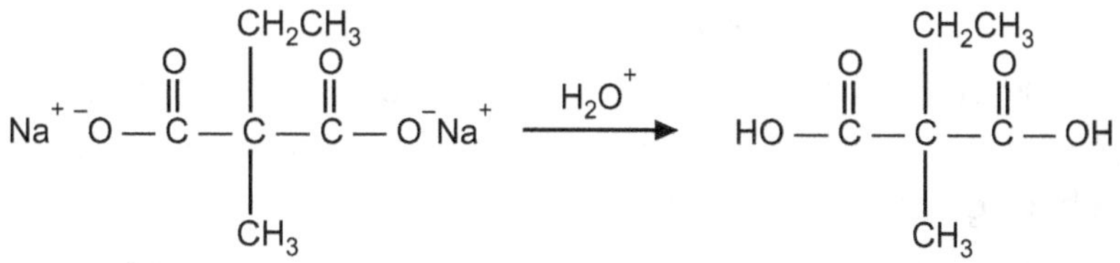

$$Na^+{}^-O - \overset{\overset{O}{\|}}{C} - \overset{\overset{CH_2CH_3}{|}}{\underset{\underset{CH_3}{|}}{C}} - \overset{\overset{O}{\|}}{C} - O^- Na^+ \xrightarrow{H_2O^+} HO - \overset{\overset{O}{\|}}{C} - \overset{\overset{CH_2CH_3}{|}}{\underset{\underset{CH_3}{|}}{C}} - \overset{\overset{O}{\|}}{C} - OH$$

Upon heating, the β ketoacid becomes unstable and decarboxylates, forming a disubstituted acetic acid.

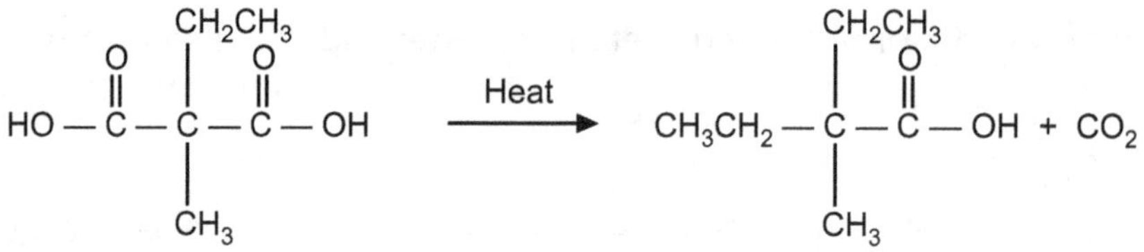

$$HO-\overset{\overset{\displaystyle O}{\|}}{C}-\overset{\overset{\displaystyle CH_2CH_3}{|}}{\underset{\underset{\displaystyle CH_3}{|}}{C}}-\overset{\overset{\displaystyle O}{\|}}{C}-OH \quad \xrightarrow{\text{Heat}} \quad CH_3CH_2-\overset{\overset{\displaystyle CH_2CH_3}{|}}{\underset{\underset{\displaystyle CH_3}{|}}{C}}-\overset{\overset{\displaystyle O}{\|}}{C}-OH \;+\; CO_2$$

7. Oxidative cleavage of alkenes and alkynes :

Alkenes and alkynes when heated in the presence of an oxidizing agent like potassium permanganate, yield two molecules of the carboxylic acid. However the two doubly bonded carbons of the alkene must have a hydrogen attached to them.

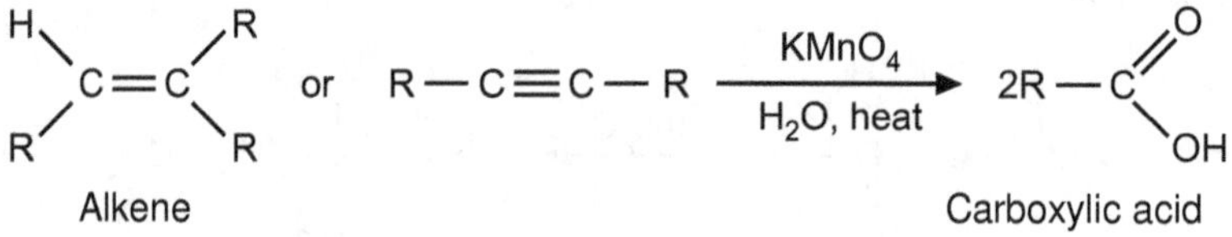

$$\underset{\text{Alkene}}{\overset{\displaystyle H}{\underset{\displaystyle R}{}}\!\!\!\!\!C=C\!\!\!\!\!\overset{\displaystyle R}{\underset{\displaystyle R}{}}} \quad \text{or} \quad R-C\equiv C-R \quad \xrightarrow[\text{H}_2\text{O, heat}]{\text{KMnO}_4} \quad \underset{\text{Carboxylic acid}}{2R-C\overset{\displaystyle O}{\underset{\displaystyle OH}{}}}$$

18.4 PHYSICAL PROPERTIES OF CARBOXYLIC ACIDS

Similar to alcohols, the physical properties (for example, boiling point and solubility) of carboxylic acids are governed by their ability to form hydrogen bonds. When comparing carboxylic acids and alcohols having similar molecular masses, the carboxylic acids have higher boiling points than alcohols as shown below:

Name	Formula	Molecular weight	B.P.
propan-1-ol	$CH_3CH_2CH_2OH$	60.1	97.2°C
ethanoic acid	CH_3COOH	60.05	118°C

In a pure carboxylic acid, hydrogen bonding can occur between two molecules of acid to produce a **dimer**.

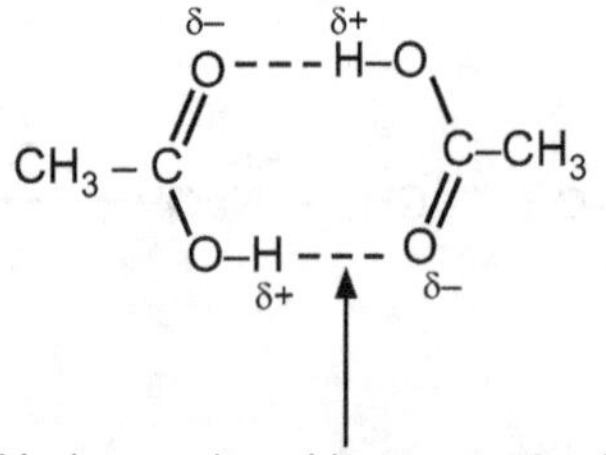

Hydrogen bond between the fairly
positive hydrogen atom and a lone pair
on the fairly negative oxygen atom

This immediately doubles the size of the molecule and therefore there is an increase in the van der Waals dispersion forces between one of these dimers and its neighbours. This results in a high boiling point.

However, the carboxylic acids do not dimerise in the presence of water. Instead, hydrogen bonds are formed between water molecules and individual molecules of acid. Carboxylic acids with upto four carbon atoms can be mixed with water in any proportion. On mixing, energy is released due to formation of new hydrogen bonds between the carboxylic acid and water molecules. This energy is nearly equal to that needed to break the hydrogen bonds in pure liquids.

The solubility of the bigger acids decreases very rapidly with size. This is because the longer hydrocarbon "tails" of the molecules get between water molecules and break hydrogen bonds. In this case, these broken hydrogen bonds are only replaced by much weaker van der Waals dispersion forces.

18.5 CHEMICAL PROPERTIES OF CARBOXYLIC ACIDS

I.   Acidity of carboxylic acids:

Carboxylic acids are weak acids as they ionize only partially in water. Ionization constant (K_a) is used to measure the acidity of an acid. The expression for calculating K_a can be written as:

$$H-A + H_2O \rightleftharpoons H_3O^{\oplus} + A^{\ominus} \qquad K_{eq} = \frac{[H_3O^{\oplus}][A^{\ominus}]}{[HA][H_2O]}$$

$$pK_a = -\log K_a = \log\left(\frac{1}{K_a}\right)$$

The equilibrium equation for the ionization of acetic acid can be written as:

$$CH_3COOH_{(aq)} + H_2O_{(l)} \rightleftharpoons CH_3COO^-_{(aq)} \quad + \quad H_3O^+_{(aq)}$$

Acetic acid   Acetate ion (conjugate base)

$$K_a = \frac{[CH_3COO^-][H_3O^+]}{[CH_3COOH][H_2O]}$$

The concentration term for water is neglected since it is not affected by the ionization of acid.

$$K_a = \frac{[CH_3COO^-][H_3O^+]}{[CH_3COOH]}$$

We know that equilibrium favours the thermodynamically more stable side, and that the value of the equilibrium constant is related to the energy difference between the components of each side. In an acid-base equilibrium, the equilibrium always favors the weaker acid and base (these are the more stable components). Water is the standard base used for pK_a measurements; thus, anything that stabilizes the conjugate base (A^-) of an acid will make that acid (H–A) stronger and shift the equilibrium to the right. Both the carboxyl group and the carboxylate anion are stabilized by resonance, but the stabilization of the anion is much greater than that of the neutral function, as shown in the following diagram. In the carboxylate anion the two structures contribute equally in the hybrid, and the C–O bonds are of equal length (between a double and a single bond). This stabilization leads to a markedly increased acidity.

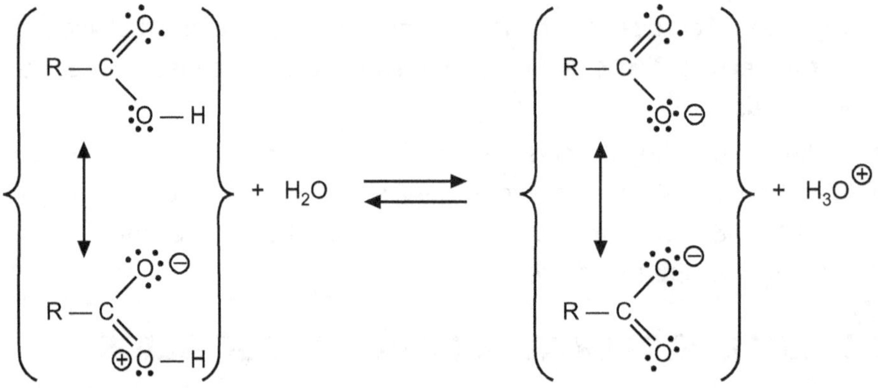

Small
resonance stabilization
(only charge separation)

Large
resonance stabilization
(charge delocalization)

The pKₐ's of some typical carboxylic acids are listed in **Table 18.1**. The resonance effect described above is the major contributor to the exceptional acidity of carboxylic acids. However, inductive effects also play a role. From the table it is evident that electronegative substituents (Cl^-, Br^-, F^- etc.) near the carboxyl group tend to increase the acidity while the electropositive groups ($-CH_3$) decrease the acidity. Thus, trichloroacetic acid containing three electron withdrawing chloro groups is most acidic (lowest pKₐ, highest ionization) while butanoic acid with only electropositive groups, is least acidic.

Table 18.2 : pKₐ of organic acids

Compound	pKₐ	Compound	pKₐ
HCO_2H	3.75	$CH_3CH_2CH_2CO_2H$	4.82
CH_3CO_2H	4.74	$ClCH_2CH_2CH_2CO_2H$	4.53
FCH_2CO_2H	2.65	$CH_3CHClCH_2CO_2H$	4.05
$ClCH_2CO_2H$	2.85	$CH_3CH_2CHClCO_2H$	2.89
$BrCH_2CO_2H$	2.90	$C_6H_5CO_2H$	4.20
ICH_2CO_2H	3.10	$p\text{-}O_2NC_6H_4CO_2H$	3.45
Cl_3CCO_2H	0.77	$p\text{-}CH_3OC_6H_4CO_2H$	4.45

II. Reactions of carboxylic acids:

A carboxylic group actually is a combination of two functional groups, that is, the carbonyl group ($-C=O$) and the hydroxyl group ($-OH$). Thus, the reactions of carboxylic acids can roughly be studied under three categories:

   (i) Reactions involving the $-OH$ group

   (ii) Reactions involving the carbonyl group

(iii) Reactions involving the –COOH group

(iv) Reactions involving the alkyl moiety, –R

Let us see these reactions one by one.

(i) Reactions Involving the –OH Group :

1. Salt Formation:

Being acidic, carboxylic acids can react with bases to form ionic salts. Salts with ammonia, simple amines and alkali hydroxides are usually soluble in water. However, heavy metals such as silver, mercury and lead form salts having more covalent character, and the water solubility is reduced, especially for acids composed of four or more carbon atoms.

$$RCO_2H \ + \ NaHCO_3 \ \longrightarrow \ RCO_2^- \ Na^+ \ + \ CO_2 \ + \ H_2O$$

$$RCO_2H \ + \ (CH_3)_3N{:} \ \longrightarrow \ RCO_2^- \ (CH_3)_3NH^+$$

$$RCO_2H \ + \ AgOH \ \longrightarrow \ RCO_2^- \ Ag^+ \ + \ H_2O$$

Carboxylic acids and salts having alkyl chains longer than six carbons exhibit unusual behavior in water due to the presence of both hydrophilic (CO_2) and hydrophobic (alkyl) regions in the same molecule. Such molecules are termed as **amphiphilic** (Gk. amphi = both) or **amphipathic**. Depending on the nature of the hydrophilic portion, these compounds may form monolayers on the water surface or sphere-like clusters, called micelles in solution. The sodium or potassium salts of long chain fatty acids are called soaps.

2. Substitution of the Hydroxyl Group:

In this type of reactions, the hydroxyl group, –OH, of the carboxylic group is replaced by another nucleophilic functional group. These reactions are important in preparation of functional derivatives of carboxylic acids, like acid halides, esters, amides and anhydrides.

(a) Formation of acid halides: Carboxylic acids react with phosphorous trichloride (PCl_3), phosphorous pentachloride (PCl_5), thionyl chloride ($SOCl_2$), and phosphorous tribromide (PBr_3) to form acyl halides. The acid halides are very reactive in comparison to carboxylic acids and can be more easily converted to amides and esters.

$$RCOOH \ \xrightarrow{PCl_5 \text{ or } PCl_3 \text{ or } SOCl_2 \text{ or } PBr_3} \ RCOCl$$

Some examples are given below:

$$Cl{-}CH_2{-}\underset{\displaystyle \parallel O}{C}{-}OH \ \xrightarrow{PCl_2} \ Cl{-}CH_2{-}\underset{\displaystyle \parallel O}{C}{-}Cl \ + \ POCl_3 \ + \ HCl$$

2-Chloroacetic acid   2-Chloroacetyl chloride

p-Nitrobenzoic acid　→ (SOCl₂, heat) → p-Nitrobenzoyl chloride + HCl + SO₂

Benzoic acid → (PCl₃) → Benzoyl chloride + P(OH)₃

(b) Formation of esters: Carboxylic acids are converted to esters by refluxing with alcohol and mineral acid. This method of acid catalyzed esterification is called Fischer Esterification. This is a reversible reaction and unless a product is removed, for example, removal of the water by azeotropic distillation or absorption by molecular sieves or an excess of reactant (mostly alcohol, because it is cheap) is used, the reaction does not undergo completion.

$$R-COOH \ + \ R'-OH \ \underset{}{\overset{H^+,\ reflux}{\rightleftharpoons}} \ RCOOR' \ + \ H_2O$$

Carboxylic acid　　Alcohol　　　　　　　　　　　　　Ester

The mechanism of Fischer esterification involves protonation of the carbonyl oxygen by the mineral acid leading to a more reactive electrophile. Nucleophilic attack of the alcohol at the electron deficient carbon gives a tetrahedral intermediate in which there are two equivalent hydroxyl groups. One of these hydroxyl groups is eliminated after a proton transfer (tautomerism) to give water and the ester.

Example:

$$H_3C-COOH + C_2H_5OH \xrightarrow{H_2SO_4} H_3C-COO-C_2H_5 + H_2O$$

Ethanoic acid　　　Ethanol　　　　　　　　　　Ethyl ethanoate

Alternatively, acid chlorides can be converted to esters by reacting them with alcohol. In this reaction hydrochloric acid is formed instead of water.

$$CH_3-COCl + CH_3CH_2OH \longrightarrow CH_3-COO-CH_2CH_3 + HCl$$

Acetyl chloride　　　Ethanol　　　　　　　　　　Ethyl acetate

(c) Formation of amides: Carboxylic acids when reacted with ammonia or a source of ammonia give amides. The carboxylic acid is first converted into an ammonium salt which then produces an amide on heating. The ammonium salt is formed by adding solid ammonium carbonate to an excess of the acid.

For example, ammonium ethanoate is made by adding ammonium carbonate to an excess of ethanoic acid.

$$2CH_3COOH + (NH_4)_2CO_3 \longrightarrow 2CH_3COONH_4 + H_2O + CO_2$$

Ethanoic acid　　Ammonium carbonate　　　　　　Ammonium ethanoate

When the reaction is complete, the mixture is heated and the ammonium salt dehydrates producing ethanamide.

$$CH_3COONH_4 \longrightarrow CH_3CONH_2 + H_2O$$

Ammonium ethanoate　　　　　　Ethanamide

The excess of ethanoic acid is used to prevent dissociation of the ammonium salt before it dehydrates.

An N-substituted amide is prepared by reacting an acid with a primary amine.

$$CH_3-CH_2-COOH \xrightarrow[\Delta]{CH_3NH_2} CH_3-CH_2-CONHCH_3 + NH_4Cl$$

Propanoic acid　　　　　　　　　　N-methyl propanamide

(d) Formation of acid anhydrides: Heating of a carboxylic acid gives a symmetrical anhydride after loss of water. A dehydrating agent, like acetic anhydride, phosphorous pentaoxide, aluminium trioxide is used to remove water.

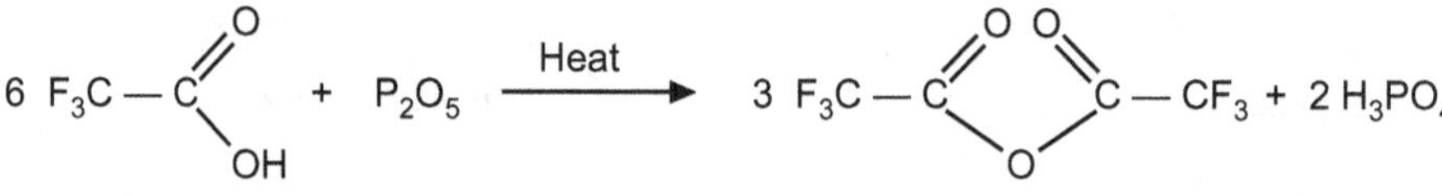

$$6\ F_3C-\overset{O}{\underset{OH}{C}} \ +\ P_2O_5 \xrightarrow{\text{Heat}} 3\ F_3C-C \underset{O}{\overset{O\ \ O}{\diagup \diagdown}} C-CF_3\ +\ 2\ H_3PO_4$$

Trifluoroacetic acid   Trifluoroacetic anhydride

(e) Reaction with diazomethane: Carboxylic acids react with diazomethane to yield esters. Acids first lose a proton to diazomethane to form a carboxylate ion and CH_3-N_2. Attack on the carbon of CH_3-N_2 by the carboxylate ion gives methyl ester.

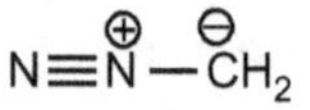

$$N\equiv\overset{\oplus}{N}-\overset{\ominus}{C}H_2$$

Diazomethane (CH_2N_2)

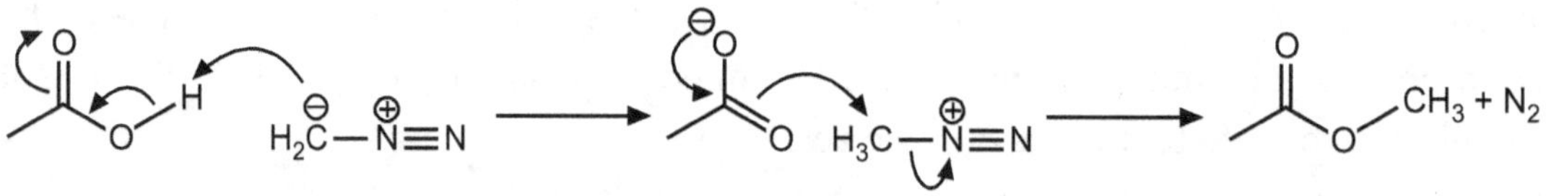

(ii) Reactions Involving the Carbonyl Group:

The reactions normally displayed by the carbonyl ($-C=O$) group of aldehydes and ketones are not shown by the carbonyl group of the carboxylic acids as the carboxylic group also contains a hydroxyl ($-OH$) group besides the carbonyl. Thus, the nucleophilic addition reactions shown by the carbonyl group of aldehydes and ketones are not displayed by the carboxylic acids. The reactions undergone by the carbonyl group of the carboxylic acids are the following:

1. Reduction: Carboxylic acids can be reduced to yield primary alcohols by lithium aluminium hydride ($LiAlH_4$). Sodium borohydride ($NaBH_4$), that is normally used for reducing aldehydes and ketones is unable to reduce the carboxylic acids.

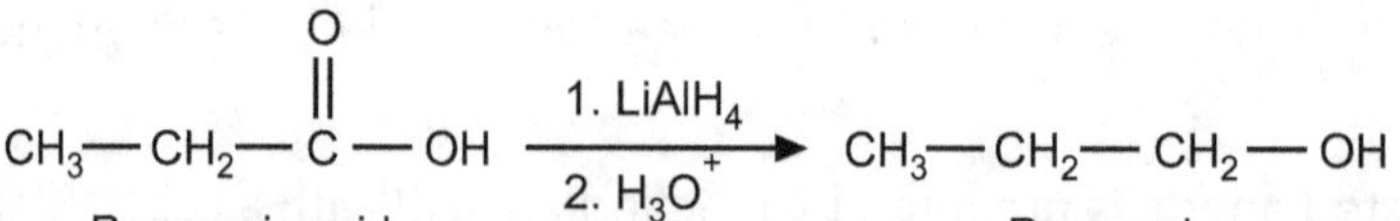

$$CH_3-CH_2-\overset{O}{\overset{\|}{C}}-OH \xrightarrow[\text{2. }H_3O^+]{\text{1. }LiAlH_4} CH_3-CH_2-CH_2-OH$$

Propanoic acid   Propanol

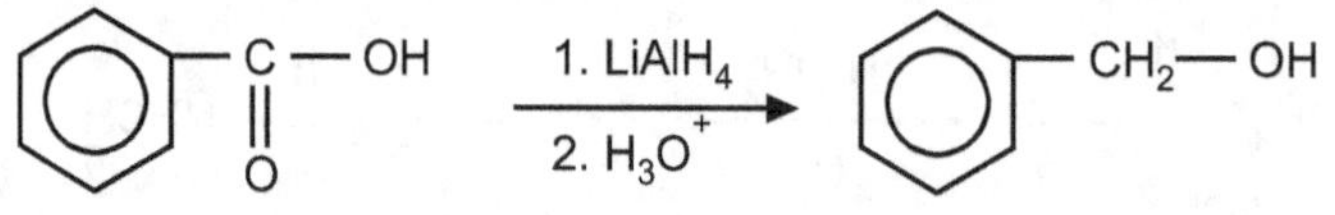

Benzoic acid   Benzyl alcohol

The mechanism involved in this reaction is illustrated below:

<table>
<tr><td>

[Reaction mechanism diagram showing the reduction of acetic acid by $LiAlH_4$ through tetrahedral intermediate, aldehyde intermediate, metal alkoxide complex, to primary alcohol]

</td><td>

1. The first step is probably an acid-base reaction where the hydride of $LiAlH_4$ takes the proton of carboxylic acid and generates hydrogen and a neutral AlH_3.

2. Decomposition of tetrahedral intermediate and displacement of the hydroxyl part of acid as a leaving group produces an aldehyde as an intermediate.

3. The second molecule of the reducing agents transfers a hydride to the polar carbonyl group of the aldehyde and forms an intermediate metal alkoxide complex.

4. Decomposition of the intermediate and protonation of oxygen yields a primary alcohol product.

</td></tr>
</table>

2. Reduction of carboxylic acid to alkanes:

Carboxylic acid is reduced to alkane on reaction with hydrogen iodide (HI) in the presence of red phosphorus at 200°C.

$$RCOOH + 6HI \longrightarrow RCH_3 + 2H_2O + 3I_2$$

(iii) Reactions involving the –COOH group:

1. Decarboxylation reaction :

Decarboxylation is the loss of the acid functional group as carbon dioxide from a carboxylic acid. The reaction product is usually a halocompound or an aliphatic or aromatic hydrocarbon. It can be performed in several ways:

(a) Using sodalime: Soda lime is manufactured by adding sodium hydroxide solution to solid calcium oxide (quicklime). It is essentially a mixture of sodium hydroxide, calcium oxide and calcium hydroxide. The solid sodium salt of carboxylic acid is mixed with solid soda lime, and the mixture is heated. For some acids like benzoic acid, the reaction can be done by taking the acid itself.

$$CH_3COO^-Na^+ \xrightarrow{\text{NaOH, CaO}} CH_3—CH_3$$

Sodium acetate　　　　　Ethane

Benzoic acid　$\xrightarrow[\text{Heat}]{\substack{\text{1. NaOH} \\ \text{2. CaO}}}$　Benzene　$+ Na_2CO_3$

(b) Using copper salts: Aliphatic and aromatic acids can be decarboxylated using simple copper salts.

$$CH_3CH_2C(=O)—OH \xrightarrow[\substack{\text{quinoline} \\ \Delta}]{\text{Cu}} CH_3CH_3 \ + \ CO_2$$

Propionic acid　　　　　Ethane

$$H_2C=CH—C(=O)—OH \xrightarrow[\substack{\text{quinoline} \\ \Delta}]{\text{Copper chromate}} H_2C=CH_2 \ + \ CO_2$$

Propenoic acid　　　　　Ethene

Benzoic acid　$\xrightarrow[\substack{Cu(OH)H_2 \\ \Delta}]{CuCO_3}$　Benzene

(c) Hunsdiecker reaction: In a **Hunsdiecker reaction**, the silver salt of an aromatic carboxylic acid is converted to an aryl halide by reacting it with bromine.

Silver benzoate　$\xrightarrow[CCl_4]{Br_2}$　Bromobenzene　$+ \ CO_2 \ + \ AgBr$

(d) Kolbe electrolysis: In Kolbe electrolysis, electrochemical oxidation occurs in aqueous sodium hydroxide solution, leading to the formation of a hydrocarbon.

$$CH_3CH_2C(=O)—O^-Na^+ \xrightarrow[\text{oxidation}]{\text{Electrochemical}} CH_3CH(CH_3) \ H_2 \ + \ CO_2$$

Sodium propionate　　　　　Propane

(iv) Reactions involving the alkyl moiety, –R:

(a) Hell-Volhard-Zelinsky (H-V-Z) reaction:

Aliphatic carboxylic acids react readily with chlorine or bromine in the presence of a small amount of phosphorous to yield an acid in which the α-hydrogen has been replaced by halogen. This reaction is called the Hell-Volhard-Zelinsky (H-V-Z) reaction. This reaction is especially important in the synthesis due to its regioselectivity. Phosphorous forms PBr_3 on reaction with bromine which converts –COOH to –COBr, which can enolize and add Br_2.

(b) Reaction with hydrogen peroxide:

Carboxylic acids containing a β-hydrogen on reaction with hydrogen peroxide (H_2O_2) get converted to β-hydroxy carboxylic acids as given below:

3-Phenylpropanoic acid   3-Hydroxy-3-phenylpropanoic acid

18.6 DICARBOXYLIC ACIDS

As the name indicates, dicarboxylic acids contain two carboxylic groups in their structure, one on each end of a saturated hydrocarbon chain.

where n = 0, 1, 2, 3, etc.

18.7 NOMENCLATURE OF DICARBOXYLIC ACIDS

While naming the dicarboxylic acids, the location numbers for both carboxyl groups are omitted because both functional groups are expected to occupy the ends of the parent chain. The ending -**dioic acid** is added to the end of the parent chain.

Many dicarboxlic acids are also known by their general names. Some examples of dicarboxylic acids are given below in Table 18.3.

Table 18.3

Structure	Common Name
(structure of phthalic acid)	phthalic acid *o*-phthalic acid
(structure of isophthalic acid)	isophthalic acid *m*-phthalic acid
(structure of terephthalic acid)	terephthalic acid *p*-phthalic acid
HOOC – COOH	oxalic acid
HOOC CH_2 COOH	malonic acid
HOOC $(CH_2)_2$ COOH	succinic acid
HOOC $(CH_2)_3$ COOH	glutaric acid
HOOC $(CH_2)_4$ COOH	adipic acid
HOOC $(CH_2)_5$ COOH	pimelic acid

18.8 METHODS OF PREPARATION OF DICARBOXYLIC ACIDS

The methods of dicarboxylic acids preparation are similar to those for monocarboxylic acids. Following methods are used for preparation:

1. By Cyanide Synthesis:

A very useful method, the starting material used is a α–halogenated acid or polymethylene dibromide.

$$Cl-CH_2-COOH \xrightarrow{\ NaCN\ } NC-CH_2-COOH \xrightarrow{\ H_2O/H^+\ } HOOC-CH_2-COOH$$

Chloroacetic acid   Cyanoacetic acid   Malonic acid

$$\begin{array}{c} CH_2Br \\ | \\ CH_2Br \end{array} \xrightarrow{\ NaCN\ } \begin{array}{c} CH_2CN \\ | \\ CH_2CN \end{array} \xrightarrow{\ H_2O/H^+\ } \begin{array}{c} CH_2COOH \\ | \\ CH_2COOH \end{array}$$

1,2-Dibromoethane   Succinic acid

2. By oxidation of Cyclic Ketones:

Cyclic ketones may be oxidized to dicarboxylic acids. For example, cyclohexanone on treatment with nitric acid (oxidizing agent) gives adipic acid.

Cyclohexanone $\xrightarrow[\ [O]\ ]{\ HNO_3\ }$ Adipic acid

3. By Malonic ester and Acetoacetic ester synthesis:

These methods have been discussed above, in the section concerning synthesis of carboxylic acids.

18.9 PHYSICAL PROPERTIES OF DICARBOXYLIC ACID

Dicarboxylic acids are crystalline solids. Solubility in water and melting point of α, ω-compounds increase in a series as the carbon chains become longer with alternating between odd and even numbers of carbon atoms, so that for even number of carbon atoms the melting point is higher than for the next in the series with an odd number. Lower members dissolve readily in water, solubility decreases with increase in number of carbon atoms.

Effect of heat

1. Acids with 1- or no C-chain: Dicarboxylic acids where the carboxylic groups are separated by none or one carbon atom decompose on heating to give off carbon dioxide and leave behind a monocarboxylic acid. For example:

$$HOOC-COOH \xrightarrow[150°C]{\ \Delta\ } CHOOH + CO_2$$

Oxalic acid   Formic acid

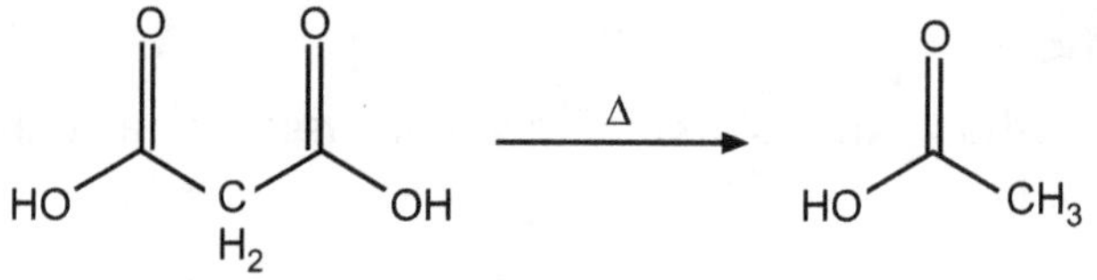

Malonic acid $\xrightarrow{\Delta}$ Acetic acid

2. Acids with 2- and 3-C-chain: When heated, succinic acid and glutaric acid undergo intramolecular dehydration to give cyclic anhydrides having 5- and 6-membered rings respectively. This phenomenon is called **cyclodehydration**.

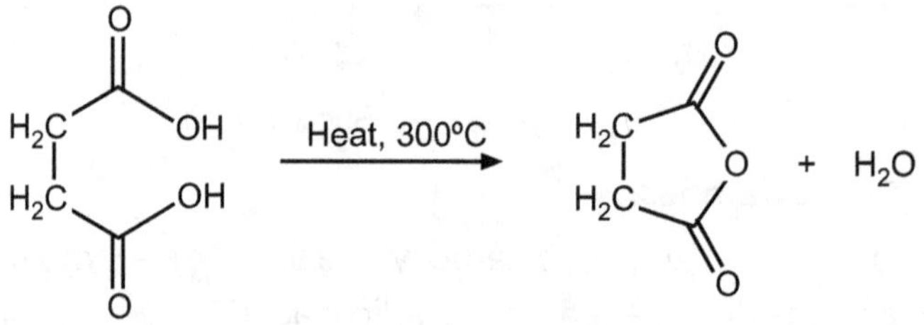

Succinic acid $\xrightarrow{\text{Heat, 300°C}}$ Succinic anhydride $+\ H_2O$

Glutaric acid $\xrightarrow{\text{Heat, 300°C}}$ Glutaric anhydride $+\ H_2O$

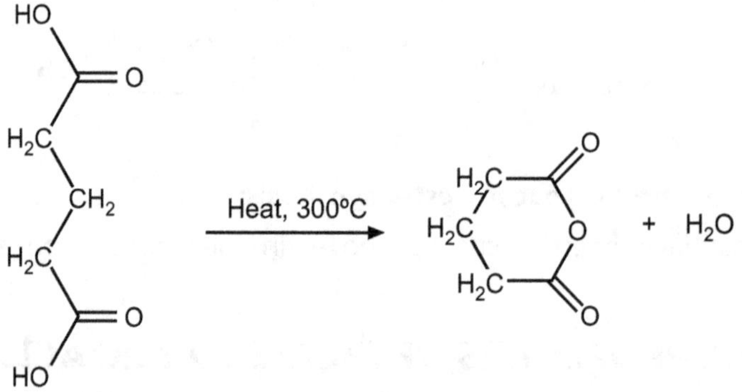

3. Acids with 4- and 5-C-chain: Adipic acid and pimelic acid on heating lose carbon dioxide and water to form cyclic ketones, cyclopentanone and cyclohexanone, respectively.

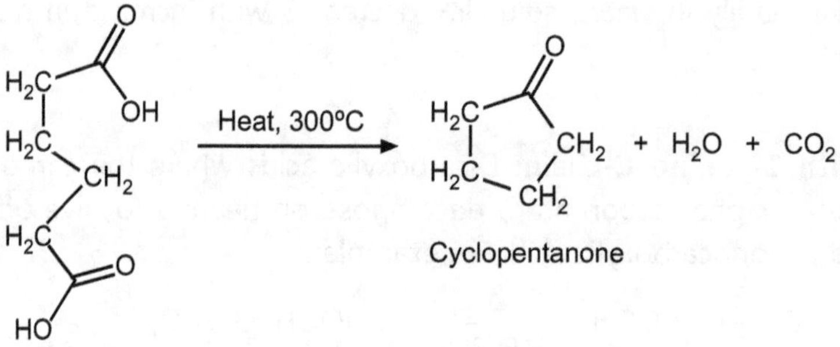

Adipic acid $\xrightarrow{\text{Heat, 300°C}}$ Cyclopentanone $+\ H_2O\ +\ CO_2$

Pimelic acid $\xrightarrow{\text{Heat, 300°C}}$ Cyclohexanone $+ H_2O + CO_2$

4. Acids with 6- or higher chains: An interesting phenomenon of intermolecular dehydration to form a linear polymer occurs when dicarboxylic acids having six-carbon chain are heated.

$$HOOC(CH_2)_6COOH + HOOC(CH_2)_6COOH \longrightarrow HOOC(CH_2)_6COOCO(CH_2)_6COOH$$

Suberic acid   A dimer

The reaction continues with n molecules to yield a linear polymer.

Acidity: Since dicarboxylic acids have two carboxylic groups, they ionize in two steps:

$$HOOC-COOH \underset{K_1}{\rightleftharpoons} HOOC-COO^- + H^+$$

Oxalic acid

$$HOOC-COO^- \underset{K_2}{\rightleftharpoons} {}^-OOC-COO^- + H^+$$

The electron-withdrawing effect of the second carboxylic group enhances the activity of the first COOH. Therefore, the value of the first dissociation constant K_1 is higher than that of acetic acid ($K_{1oxalic\ acid} = 5400 \times 10^{-5}$; $K_{acetic\ acid} = 1.5 \times 10^{-5}$). This inductive effect becomes weaker as the two COOH groups are further separated by CH_2 groups and K_1 decreases as we ascend the series as is depicted in the Table 18.4.

Table 18.4 : Values of melting points and dissociation constants for dicarboxylic acids

Acid	M.P.,°C	$K_1 \times 10^{-5}$	$K_2 \times 10^{-5}$
Oxalic acid	187	5400	5.2
Malonic acid	135	170	0.23
Succinic acid	185	6.8	0.24
Glutaric acid	97.5	4.6	0.28
Adipic acid	151	3.8	0.23
Pimelic acid	105	3.5	0.27

18.10 CHEMICAL PROPERTIES OF DICARBOXYLIC ACID

Dicarboxylic acids undergo the same reactions as shown by carboxylic acids, in duplicate. Thus, they give mono- and di-derivatives such as salts, esters, amides and acid halides. However, in case of lower dicarboxylic acids, where the two carboxylic groups are close together, mutual interaction may influence the reaction.

QUESTIONS

Q.1   What are carboxylic acid derivatives? Give brief account on acidity of carboxylic acids and their two methods of preparation.   **(Dec-2014)**

Q.2   What are carboxylic acid derivatives? Give brief account on acidity of carboxylic acids and their two methods of preparation and reactions.

Q.3   Write a note on preparation methods of carboxylic acids.   **(Dec-2015)**

Q.4   Write a note reactions of carboxylic acid derivatives.   **(May-2014)**

Q.5   Write a note on dicarboxylic acids.

Q.6   Give any two methods of preparation and reactions of esters.

Q.7   Give any two methods of preparation and reactions of amides.

Q.8   Write any two methods of preparation of carboxylic acids.   **(May-2014, May-2015)**

Q.9   Why chloroacetic acid is stronger than acetic acid?   **(May-2015)**

Q.10   Give any two chemical reactions of carboxylic acids.   **(Dec-2014, Dec-2015)**

Q.11   Write any two chemical reactions of acid chloride.   **(May-2015, Dec-2015)**

Q.12   Give any two chemical reactions of anhydrides.   **(May-2014)**

Q.13   Give any two methods of preparation of amides.   **(Dec-2015)**

Q.14   Give any two methods of preparation of ester.

Q.15   Give any two methods of preparation of amides.

Q.16   Write about esterification.   **(Dec-2014)**

Q.17   Explain Hoffmann's degradation of amides.   **(Dec-2014)**